THE FAR ENDS OF TIME AND EARTH

SCIENCE FICTION BY ISAAC ASIMOV

Novels

Pebble in the Sky
The Stars, Like Dust
Foundation
Foundation and Empire
Second Foundation
The Currents of Space
The Caves of Steel
The End of Eternity
The Naked Sun
Fantastic Voyage
The Gods Themselves

Novels originally under the pseudonym "Paul French"

David Starr: Space Ranger
Lucky Starr and the Pirates of the Asteroids
Lucky Starr and the Oceans of Venus
Lucky Starr and the Big Sun of Mercury
Lucky Starr and the Moons of Jupiter
Lucky Starr and the Rings of Saturn

Short Story Collections

I, Robot
The Martian Way and Other Stories
Earth Is Room Enough
Nine Tomorrows
The Rest of the Robots
Asimov's Mysteries
Nightfall and Other Stories
The Early Asimov
Buy Jupiter and Other Stories
The Bicentennial Man and Other Stories

Anthologies

The Hugo Winners
Fifty Short Science Fiction Tales (with Groff Conklin)
Tomorrow's Children
Where Do We Go From Here?
The Hugo Winners, Volume Two
Before the Golden Age
The Hugo Winners, Volume Three
100 Great Science Fiction Short Short Stories (with Martin Harry Greenberg and Joseph D. Olander)

THE FAR ENDS OF TIME AND EARTH

ISAAC ASIMOV

DOUBLEDAY & COMPANY, INC., GARDEN CITY, NEW YORK

Printed in the United States of America

CONTENTS

INTRODUCTION

by Isaac Asimov

Most science fiction stories, to begin with, were exploration fantasies.

Consider that, almost through all of human history, the space beyond the Earthly horizon was unknown. The occasional traveler who arrived at a village with tales of lands a hundred miles away was a messenger from places of glamor and mystery.

And what were the great fantasy epics of older times but exploration distorted? The *Odyssey* was a romanticized tale of the foggy mysteries of the west Mediterranean; Sinbad the Sailor spun tales of the distance-shrouded islands of the Indian Ocean.

It was natural, therefore, for fiction writers to use tales of travel and exploration as a device through which to advance their irony and adventure. Swift had Lemuel Gulliver shipwrecked in various invented islands, for instance, where the cruelty and illogic of contemporary English society could be savagely satirized.

The first professional science fiction writer (that is, the first writer who made his living primarily by writing science fiction) was Jules Verne, and he was a frustrated explorer.

It was his intention to write of voyages out of the ordinary ("*voyages extraordinaire*") and in 1863 he published *Five Weeks in a Balloon.* He had been writing prolifically for years, but this was his first big hit, and he knew a good thing when he saw it.

He wrote of other extraordinary voyages, moving farther and farther afield: to the polar regions, to the sea bottom, to the Earth's center, to the Moon.

Even the trip to the Moon, which was the quintessential piece of science fiction for all writers down to contemporary times (the third piece of science fiction I published, back in 1939, dealt with a first trip to the Moon), was, in a sense, merely an extension of the exploration tale.

Science fiction writers couldn't stop at the Moon, of course. The reports of canals on Mars, beginning in 1877, made Mars a more popular port of call for human explorers and adventurers than even the Moon had been, since it seemed for a while that science had demonstrated the existence of an advanced civilization on Mars.

Even the Solar system proved too small for the imaginations of science fiction writers. Beginning with E. E. Smith's novel "The Skylark of Space" in 1928, writers burst out into the vast Universe outside the Solar system. Planets circling stars, near and far, named and unknown, became the common fare of science fiction.

The field of vision, in fact, came to extend beyond this star or that and began to incorporate all of them into an extended Galactic Federation or Empire.

It is difficult to handle so vast a concept and keep it vast. It is somehow easy to reduce the endlessness of space to trivial dimensions. The need to make use of faster-than-light drives in order to make it possible to reach the stars can end by making a spaceship to Zeta Ophiuchi no more remarkable than an airplane to Seattle.

The vast space wars can become petty Earth squabbles with words changed, if one isn't careful. Laying siege to a planet or blowing up a Sun is not impressive if nothing happens that wouldn't happen if you were laying siege to a castle or blowing up a city.

In fact, the tales of Galactic wars and derring-do came to be referred to as "space opera" in deliberate condescension, because it was analogous to the term "horse opera" for the traditional Western. The implication was that a space opera, to be written, needed only translation, with "cayuse" changed to "rocketship" and "six-shooter" changed to "disinto-blaster."

Stories that were merely space operas, and no more, naturally tended to be forgettable, and when I wanted to write a story on a Galactic scale I groped for something beyond.

In my Foundation series, for instance, I tried to deal, as best I could, with historic sweeps of time, with social change, with political and diplomatic infighting. It may still have been space opera, but I thought politics was more interesting than war, and victories by shrewd manipulation of human behavior more impressive (and perhaps more enduring) than victories by sheer weight of slugging.

I continued to do this with other novels that were not precisely part of the Foundation series but were set in the Foundation Universe.

And yet there came a certain weariness with endless parsecs as the 1950s wore on, and reviewers grew petulant. After one of my novels, one reviewer said, "Come home, Isaac. All is forgiven."

Yet I did not write space operas only. Some of my stories were set right on Earth. Why not? If spatial horizons are contracted, might not other horizons have to broaden? Surely science fiction need not merely expand in space, it could plumb greater depths instead.

With the reviewer's admonition in mind, then, I gathered together some of the Earth-as-background stories I had written, and

Doubleday published it in 1957 under the title, *Earth Is Room Enough.*

This is one of the volumes collected here, and it contains fifteen stories (and two pieces of comic verse) that do not move from our planet. And there *is* room. "The Dead Past" moves into the past and inadvertently destroys an essential of our society; "Living Space" moves on to alternate Earths; "Someday" considers alternate intelligences on Earth; "Dreaming Is a Private Thing" takes up the creative mind under new conditions, and so on.

There is plenty to do and consider without leaving Earth. Earth is room enough.

As for the two novels included in this collection, one of them, *Pebble in the Sky*, published in 1950 (and the first of my two hundred books), is set in the Foundation Universe, at a time when the First Galactic Empire is at its height—but the scene of the story is set firmly upon the Earth.

The Galactic Empire is there in the background, supplying characters and motivating events in the story; serving as villain, in part; as potential victim, in other part; but it is always off-stage. Earth is room enough.

Yet though I remained on Earth in *Pebble in the Sky*, I managed to advance in a direction I ordinarily avoid. My central character, Joseph Schwartz, achieves the ability to deal with minds telepathically.

Is this permissible?

In a way, we needn't ask this question. Permissible or not, it is a science-fictional convention, like faster-than-light travel, and for the same reason. Telepathy cuts through the fringes and the underbrush and lets us get on with the story.

Suppose, in actual fact, human beings land on a far-distant planet and encounter an utterly strange form of intelligent life. How do we communicate?

The chances are we can't, and without communication we couldn't even be certain that the alien life form is intelligent except by indirect deduction. We might then write a story about the efforts to communicate, but such stories are limited and their potentialities would be completely exhausted soon enough.

After all, here on Earth, we have reason to think that dolphins are intelligent, perhaps as intelligent as we are, and yet we cannot work out any way of communicating with them even though they seem to use sound for the purpose of communication as we do. And without communication the human/dolphin interplay comes to a quick and abrupt end.

With telepathy coming to the rescue, the problem of communication is solved and we can get on with the business of story writing.

But will telepathy work?

Suppose we think "dog" and automatically picture one in our minds. A Frenchman receiving this telepathically would ignore the word and, focusing on the image, would think "*chien.*" A German would think "*Hund.*" An extraterrestrial would think, "Strange object of such-and-such a shape," and perhaps give it the name of something wildly undoglike that is vaguely similar in appearance.

How useful would this be? And what if we use abstractions? What image do we give rise to in our own brains if we think such terms as "temperature" or "entropy"? We might think of a thermometer or of a mathematical symbol, but what meaning would either have to an extraterrestrial? Frankly, when I say such words, I think only of the words themselves, of their sound, of their appearance on a printed page. Surely the informational value of that to an alien would be zero.

In fact, let's drop the extraterrestrial for a moment. Suppose we consider the possibility of telepathic communication between people who speak the same language. It would then only be necessary to think words, however abstract, and pick up those words telepathically. There will be no need of images to confuse matters.

There are any number of claims that this can indeed be done, but they all rest upon either statistics or anecdotes.

People make guesses at what someone has in mind, and those guesses are correct more often than can be accounted for by chance so that the conclusion is that they are reading minds—admittedly with difficulty. Here the catch is that the tests are apparently almost never conducted with rigorous precautions against cheating, and when they are, the telepathy disappears.

As for anecdotes— Well, anyone who trusts tales of what once happened to one's second cousin, or what one was told by a friend's fiancée, deserves everything that happens to him as a result.

What we need is some sort of theoretical explanation of how telepathy might work, an explanation that can be fitted into the structure of the physical universe.

For instance, there are exactly four types of interaction known and there is strong reason to think there are no others. Two of these are nuclear forces that are not evident at distances greater than those of the diameter of atomic nuclei. There is no way of supposing that such nuclear forces can carry information from human being to human being when the distance between is inches, let alone miles. If there is a fifth interaction (which is doubtful), it is almost certainly another nuclear force and may also be eliminated.

Of the two long-range interactions—the only two of this sort believed to exist, with a third in the highest degree unlikely—one, the gravitational interaction, is so weak on the scale of objects that are no more massive than the human brain that it seems beyond the realm of conceivability to have it the basis of telepathy.

That leaves the electromagnetic interaction. To be sure, the brain cells do give rise to tiny, but complexly varying electromagnetic waves. Could these broadcast thoughts that could be received by other brains?

Conceivably, but there are objections. The electromagnetic properties of the brain are very weak and we are constantly bombarded by electromagnetic waves of far greater intensity from a myriad other sources.

Could we expect to see the tiny flickerings of light at the borderline of vision in a room brilliantly illuminated by sunlight? Could we expect to hear a tiny whisper at just the barest level of audible sound with the roar of Niagara in our ear?

Then, too, we know how electromagnetic waves work. They get weaker by an amount proportional to the square of the distance. Yet all tales of telepathy insist on ignoring distance as a factor.

Of course, if we assume that telepathy is a fact, we might argue that it is science's business to find an explanation—an unknown force, one that has an intensity largely independent of distance; and a brain receptor that can filter out interference with incredible efficiency.Well, maybe, but before we ask so formidable a task of science, we had better get some evidence for the existence of telepathy that is far better than anything we have today.

Yet after having said all that, it remains that telepathy is a convention of science fiction, and I therefore have no hesitation in using it if it helps me get on with the story—or even when, as in *Pebble in the Sky*, it is central to the plot, provided it makes the novel exciting enough.

As for the other novel in this book, *The End of Eternity*, that, too, makes use of a science-fictional convention, one that is even more dramatic than telepathy. It is the convention of time travel.

Surprisingly enough, time travel as we now think of it is not a very old concept but is less than a century old.

Perhaps this is because there was, through much of human history, the unspoken assumption that nothing changed with time, so that nothing dramatic was to be expected of travel through time. The Book of Ecclesiastes says there is "nothing new under the Sun." Philosophers found things moving in cycles and, indeed, ordinary experience was that of dull alternation of day and night, winter and summer, life and death.

There was, of course, the personal horror of dropping out of the world one knows through the magical suspension of life. There are the tales of people who encounter fairies, who live an idyllic day with them, and then return to their own world to find that a hundred years have passed and all who knew them are gone.

There are the Seven Sleepers of Ephesus who slept two hundred years, Sleeping Beauty who slept one hundred years, Rip Van Winkle who slept twenty years.

This is not true time-travel, merely extended comas.

A much more powerful expression of the time-travel idea appeared in Charles Dickens' *A Christmas Carol*, published in 1843. Here Scrooge remains conscious during the passing of time, and experiences not only the future but the past as well. This is accomplished however, by supernatural influence, and is fantasy and not science fiction.

Where the supernatural is not involved, one might rely on some unknown and unexplained effect, which we can assume is natural. As long as no effort, however bumbling, is made to explain it, however, in the light of the physical world, it might as well be supernatural.

For instance, Joseph Schwartz in *Pebble in the Sky* is thrown into the future by some mysterious effect of fissioning uranium, but that is just mumbo-jumbo to get the story started.

Similarly, in 1889, Mark Twain, in *A Connecticut Yankee at King Arthur's Court*, has his hero cast into the past by a bump on his head, just to get *his* story started.

The true time-travel story, however, is one in which the characters can, voluntarily, move through time and can control the direction and speed of this motion. The first such story was *The Time Machine* by H. G. Wells (his first science fiction story, by the way), published in 1895.

Wells here describes time as a dimension similar in many respects to the three spatial dimensions with which we are familiar. As we can move back and forth, left and right, up and down, so we can move future and past, if we could but work out a scheme for doing so. Wells's hero develops such a scheme and builds a machine for the purpose.

Ever since 1895, time travel has been a valued science-fictional concept because it clearly gives rise to the potential of a whole group of confrontations, impossible in ordinary fiction, that can, in turn, give rise to endless permutations of plot.

What it also does, though, is to give rise to endless paradoxes. If you move into the future or past, surely you are remaining in the same spot as far as the other dimensions are concerned. Earth is moving about the Sun at the rate of 18.5 miles per second. If you move one second into the past and future, does not the Earth move from under you and are you not 18.5 miles away on the surface of the Earth or high in the air or deep underground?

In fact, could not time travel be used to measure the Earth's absolute motion with fatal results to the time traveler?

Or if the time machine somehow keeps up with the Earth and remains in one spot relative to Earth's surface rather than to the Universe in general (which is very hard to accept) what of the effect on world history?

Can someone go back into the past and alter any one of a myriad historical accidents and bring about Hitler's non-birth, or his early death, or his development into an obscure bum who never rises far above the gutter? Can someone do the same to prevent his *own* birth and *then* who was it who went back into the past to accomplish that?

Or does it turn out that anyone who goes into time is somehow always prevented from doing anything that alters history? Or makes changes that keep history from having altered from that we know? Or are there an infinite number of alternate histories and does the action of the time traveler merely shift the "reality" (whatever that is) from one time track to another?

The easiest way out of all these brain-numbing speculations is to suppose that time travel is completely impossible so that none of these paradoxes arise. —And that is probably so.

It is well-established that, on the subatomic level, there is no preferred direction of time, and that subatomic particles can be viewed as undergoing interactions and changes which can be viewed as moving either forward in time or backward, with the same laws of nature applying in either case. An intelligent electron might therefore work out ways of moving forward or backward in time at will.

However, as soon as you have numbers of subatomic particles, something called entropy intervenes. If one set of changes involves increasing entropy (and it doesn't matter right now what entropy is), then the reverse set of changes involves decreasing entropy. The preferred movement is always in the direction of increasing entropy, and it may well be that the average rate of increase of entropy the Universe over defines the direction and the rate at which our consciousness experiences the passage of time.

To reverse the entropy change of the universe generally and travel into the past, or to outstrip it and travel into the future, is apparently impossible—so time travel is impossible.

Nevertheless, time travel remains a cherished science-fictional convention and a marvelous generator of stories and I wouldn't dream of abandoning it. What's more, I deliberately designed *The End of Eternity* in such a way as to make it, as nearly as I could, the ultimate example of the type. I tried to bring in every time-travel paradox I could and to match the complexity of the concept with the complexity of the actual construction of the book.

And, since I hate to adopt any dogma that I cannot violate if I wish to, I must also warn you that the major point of *The End of Eternity*, even though we never leave Earth, is that Earth is *not* room enough.

PEBBLE IN THE SKY

In another part of Chicago stood the Institute for Nuclear Research, in which men may have had theories upon the essential worth of human nature but were half ashamed of them, since no quantitative instrument had yet been designed to measure it. When they thought about it, it was often enough to wish that some stroke from heaven would prevent human nature (and damned human ingenuity) from turning every innocent and interesting discovery into a deadly weapon.

Yet, in a pinch, the same man who could not find it in his conscience to curb his curiosity into the nuclear studies that might someday kill half of Earth would risk his life to save that of an unimportant fellow man.

It was the blue glow behind the chemist's back that first attracted the attention of Dr. Smith.

He peered at it as he passed the half-open door. The chemist, a cheerful youngster, was whistling as he tipped up a volumetric flask, in which the solution had already been made up to volume. A white powder tumbled lazily through the liquid, dissolving in its own good time. For a moment that was all, and then Dr. Smith's instinct, which had stopped him in the first place, stirred him to action.

He dashed inside, snatched up a yardstick, and swept the contents of the desk top to the floor. There was the deadly hiss of molten metal. Dr. Smith felt a drop of perspiration slip to the end of his nose.

The youngster stared blankly at the concrete floor along which the silvery metal had already frozen in thin splash marks. They still radiated heat strongly.

He said faintly, "What happened?"

Dr. Smith shrugged. He wasn't quite himself either. "I don't know. You tell me. . . . What's been doing here?"

"Nothing's been doing here," the chemist yammered. "That was just a sample of crude uranium. I'm making an electrolytic copper determination. . . . I don't know what could have happened."

"Whatever happened, young man, I can tell you what I saw. That platinum crucible was showing a corona. Heavy radiation was taking place. Uranium, you say?"

"Yes, but *crude* uranium, and that isn't dangerous. I mean, extreme purity is one of the most important qualifications for fission, isn't it?" He touched his tongue to his lips quickly. "Do you think it was fission, sir? It's not plutonium, and it wasn't being bombarded."

"And," said Dr. Smith thoughtfully, "it was below the critical mass. Or, at least, below the critical masses we think we know." He

One: BETWEEN ONE FOOTSTEP AND THE NEXT

Two minutes before he disappeared forever from the face of the Earth he knew, Joseph Schwartz strolled along the pleasant streets of suburban Chicago quoting Browning to himself.

In a sense this was strange, since Schwartz would scarcely have impressed any casual passer-by as the Browning-quoting type. He looked exactly what he was: a retired tailor, thoroughly lacking in what the sophisticates of today call a "formal education." Yet he had expended much of an inquisitive nature upon random reading. By the sheer force of indiscriminate voracity, he had gleaned a smattering of practically everything, and by means of a trick memory had managed to keep it all straight.

For instance, he had read Robert Browning's *Rabbi Ben Ezra* twice when he was younger, so, of course, knew it by heart. Most of it was obscure to him, but those first three lines had become one with the beating of his heart these last few years. He intoned them to himself, deep within the silent fortress of his mind, that very sunny and very bright early summer day of 1949:

> *"Grow old along with me!*
> *The best is yet to be,*
> *The last of life, for which the first was made . . ."*

Schwartz felt that to its fullness. After the struggles of youth in Europe and those of his early manhood in the United States, the serenity of a comfortable old age was pleasant. With a house of his own and money of his own, he could, and did, retire. With a wife in good health, two daughters safely married, a grandson to soothe these last best years, what had he to worry about?

There was the atom bomb, of course, and this somewhat lascivious talk about World War III, but Schwartz was a believer in the goodness of human nature. He didn't think there would be another war. He didn't think Earth would ever see again the sunlike hell of an atom exploded in anger. So he smiled tolerantly at the children he passed and silently wished them a speedy and not too difficult ride through youth to the peace of the best that was yet to be.

He lifted his foot to step over a Raggedy Ann doll smiling through its neglect as it lay there in the middle of the walk, a foundling not yet missed. He had not quite put his foot down again . . .

stared at the soapstone desk, at the burned and blistered paint of the cabinets and the silvery streaks along the concrete floor. "Yet uranium melts at about 1800 degrees Centigrade, and nuclear phenomena are not so well known that we can afford to talk too glibly. After all, this place must be fairly saturated with stray radiations. When the metal cools, young man, it had better be chipped up, collected, and thoroughly analyzed."

He gazed thoughtfully about him, then stepped to the opposite wall and felt uneasily at a spot about shoulder height.

"What's this?" he said to the chemist. "Has this always been here?"

"What, sir?" The young man stepped up nervously and glanced at the spot the older man indicated. It was a tiny hole, one that might have been made by a thin nail driven into the wall and withdrawn—but driven through plaster and brick for the full thickness of the building's wall, since daylight could be seen through it.

The chemist shook his head, "I never saw *that* before. But I never looked for it, either, sir."

Dr. Smith said nothing. He stepped back slowly and passed the thermostat, a parallelopiped of a box made out of thin sheet iron. The water in it moved swirlingly as the stirrer turned in motor-driven monomania, while the electric bulbs beneath the water, serving as heaters, flicked on and off distractingly, in time with the clicking of the mercury relay.

"Well, then, was this here?" And Dr. Smith scraped gently with his fingernail at a spot near the top of the wide side of the thermostat. It was a neat, tiny circle drilled through the metal. The water did not quite reach it.

The chemist's eyes widened. "No, sir, that wasn't there ever before. I'll guarantee that."

"Hmm. Is there one on the other side?"

"Well, I'll be damned. I mean, yes, sir!"

"All right, come round here and sight through the holes. . . . Shut the thermostat off, please. Now stay there." He placed his finger on the hole in the wall. "What do you see?" he called out.

"I see your finger, sir. Is there where the hole is?"

Dr. Smith did not answer. He said, with a calmness he was far from feeling, "Sight through in the other direction. . . . Now what do you see?"

"Nothing now."

"But that's the place where the crucible with the uranium was standing. You're looking at the exact place, aren't you?"

Reluctantly, "I think so, sir."

Dr. Smith said frostily, with a quick glance at the name plate on the still-open door, "Mr. Jennings, this is absolutely top-secret. I don't want you ever to speak about this to *anyone*. Do you understand?"

"Absolutely, sir!"

"Then let's get out of here. We'll send in the radiation men to check the place, and you and I will spend a siege in the infirmary."

"Radiation burns, you mean?" The chemist paled.

"We'll find out."

But there were no serious signs of radiation burns in either. Blood counts were normal and a study of the hair roots revealed nothing. The nausea that developed was eventually tabbed as psychosomatic and no other symptoms appeared.

Nor, in all the Institute, was anyone found, either then or in the future, to explain why a crucible of crude uranium, well below critical size, and under no direct neutronic bombardment, should suddenly melt and radiate that deadly and significant corona.

The only conclusion was that nuclear physics had queer and dangerous crannies left in it.

Yet Dr. Smith never brought himself to tell all the truth in the report he eventually prepared. He made no mention of the holes in the laboratory, no mention of the fact that the one nearest the spot where the crucible had been was barely visible, the one on the other side of the thermostat was a trace larger, while the one in the wall, three times as far away from that fearful spot, could have had a nail thrust through it.

A beam expanding in a straight line could travel several miles before the Earth's curvature made the surface fall away from it sufficiently to prevent further damage, and then it would be ten feet across. After that, flashing emptily into space, expanding and weakening, a queer strain in the fabric of the cosmos.

He never told anyone of that fancy.

He never told anyone that he called for the morning papers next day, while still in the infirmary, and searched the columns with a definite purpose in mind.

But so many people in a giant metropolis disappear every day. And nobody had gone screaming to the police with vague tales of how, before his eyes, a man (or would it be half a man?) had disappeared. At least no such case was reported.

Dr. Smith forced forgetfulness, eventually.

To Joseph Schwartz it had happened between one step and the next. He had lifted his right foot to clear the Raggedy Ann doll and for a moment he had felt dizzy—as though for the merest trifle of time a whirlwind had lifted him and turned him inside out. When he placed his right foot down again, all the breath went out of him in a gasp and he felt himself slowly crumple and slide down to the grass.

He waited a long time with his eyes closed—and then he opened them.

It was true! He was sitting on grass, where previously he had been walking on concrete.

The houses were gone! The white houses, each with its lawn, squatting there, row on row, all gone!

And it was not a lawn he was sitting on, for the grass was growing rank, untended, and there were trees about, many of them, with more on the horizon.

That was when the worst shock of all came, because the leaves on those trees were ruddy, some of them, and in the curve of his hand he felt the dry brittleness of a dead leaf. He was a city man, but he knew autumn when he saw it.

Autumn! Yet when he had lifted his right foot it had been a June day, with everything a fresh and glistening green.

He looked toward his feet automatically as he thought that and, with a sharp cry, reached toward them. . . . The little cloth doll that he had stepped over, a little breath of reality, a——

Well, no! He turned it over in his trembling hands, and it was not whole. Yet it was not mangled; it was sliced. Now wasn't that queer! Sliced lengthwise very neatly, so that the waste-yarn stuffing wasn't stirred a hair. It lay there in interrupted threads, ending flatly.

The glitter on his left shoe caught Schwartz's eye. Still clutching the doll, he forced his foot over his raised knee. The extreme tip of the sole, the part that extended forward past the uppers, was smoothly sliced off. Sliced off as no earthly knife in the hand of an earthly cobbler could have duplicated. The fresh surface gleamed almost liquidly in its unbelievable smoothness.

Schwartz's confusion had reached up from his spinal cord and touched the cerebrum, where it finally froze him with horror.

At last, because even the sound of his own voice was a soothing element in a world otherwise completely mad, he spoke aloud. The voice he heard was low and tense and panting.

He said, "In the first place, I'm not crazy. I feel inside just the way I've always felt. . . . Of course, if maybe I were crazy, I wouldn't know it, or would I? No——" Inside, he felt the hysteria rise and forced it down. "There must be something else possible."

He considered, "A dream, maybe? How can I tell if it's a dream or not?" He pinched himself and felt the nip, but shook his head. "I can always dream I feel a pinch. That's no proof."

He looked about him despairingly. Could dreams be so clear, so detailed, so lasting? He had read once that most dreams last not more than five seconds, that they are induced by trifling disturbances to the sleeper, that the apparent length of the dreams is an illusion.

Cold comfort! He shifted the cuff of his shirt upward and stared at his wrist watch. The second hand turned and turned and turned. If it were a dream, the five seconds were going to stretch madly.

He looked away and wiped futilely at the cold dampness of his forehead. "What about amnesia?"

He did not answer himself, but slowly buried his head in both hands.

If he had lifted his foot and, as he did so, his mind had slipped the well-worn and well-oiled tracks it had followed so faithfully for so long . . . If three months later, in the autumn, or a year and three months later, or ten years and three months later, he had put his foot down in this strange place, just as his mind returned . . . Why, it would seem a single step, and all this . . . Then where had he been and what had he done in the interval?"

"No!" The word came out in a loud cry. That couldn't be! Schwartz looked at his shirt. It was the one he had put on that morning, or what should have been that morning, and it was a fresh shirt. He bethought himself, plunged a fist into his jacket pocket, and brought out an apple.

He bit into it wildly. It was fresh and still had a lingering coolness from the refrigerator which had held it two hours earlier—or what should have been two hours.

And the little rag doll, what about that?

He felt himself beginning to go wild. It had to be a dream, or he really was insane.

It struck him that the time of day had changed. It was late afternoon, or at least the shadows were lengthening. The quiet desolation of the place flooded down upon him suddenly and freezingly.

He lurched to his feet. Obviously he would have to find people, any people. And, as obviously, he would have to find a house, and the best way to do that would be to find a road.

Automatically he turned in the direction in which the trees seemed thinnest, and walked.

The slight chill of evening was creeping inside his jacket and the tops of the trees were becoming dim and forbidding when he came upon that straight and impersonal streak of macadam. He lunged toward it with sobbing gratitude and loved the feel of the hardness beneath his feet.

But along either direction was absolute emptiness, and for a moment he felt the cold clutch again. He had hoped for cars. It would have been the easiest thing to wave them down and say—he said it aloud in his eagerness—"Going toward Chicago, maybe?"

What if he was nowhere near Chicago? Well, any large city; anyplace he could reach a telephone line. He had only four dollars and twenty-seven cents in his pocket, but there was always the police . . .

He was walking along the highway, walking along the middle, watching in both directions. That setting of the sun made no impression upon him, or the fact that the first stars were coming out.

No cars. Nothing! And it was getting to be really dark.

He thought that first dizziness might be coming back, because the horizon at his left glimmered. Through the gaps in the trees there was a cold blue shine. It was not the leaping red he imagined a forest fire would be like, but a faint and creeping glow. And the macadam beneath his feet seemed to sparkle ever so faintly. He bent down to touch it, and it felt normal. But there was that tiny glimmer that caught the edges of his eyes.

He found himself running wildly along the highway, his shoes thudding in blunt and uneven rhythm. He was conscious of the damaged doll in his hand and he tossed it wildly over his head.

Leering, mocking remnant of life . . .

And then he stopped in a panic. Whatever it was, it was a proof of his sanity. And he needed it! So he felt about in the darkness, crawling on his knees till he found it, a dark patch on the ultra-faint glow. The stuffing was plumping out and, absently, he forced it back.

He was walking again—too miserable to run, he told himself.

He was getting hungry and really, really frightened when he saw that spark to the right.

It was a house, of course!

He shouted wildly and no one answered, but it was a house, a spark of reality blinking at him through the horrible, nameless wilderness of the last hours. He turned off the road and went plunging cross-country, across ditches, around trees, through the underbrush, and over a creek.

Queer thing! Even the creek glowed faintly—phosphorescently! But it was only the tiniest fragment of his mind that noted it.

Then he was there, with his hands reaching out to touch the hard white structure. It was neither brick nor stone nor wood, but he never paid that the least mind. It looked like a dull, strong porcelain, but he didn't give a hoot. He was just looking for a door, and when he came to it and saw no bell, he kicked at it and yelled like a demon.

He heard the stirring inside and the blessed, lovely sound of a human voice other than his own. He yelled again.

"Hey, in there!"

There was a faint, oiled whir, and the door opened. A woman emerged, a spark of alarm in her eyes. She was tall and wiry, and behind her was the gaunt figure of a hard-faced man in work clothes. . . . No, not work clothes. Actually they were like nothing Schwartz had ever seen, but, in some indefinable way, they looked like the kind of clothes men worked in.

But Schwartz was not analytical. To him they, and their clothes, were beautiful; beautiful only as the sight of friends to a man alone can be beautiful.

The woman spoke and her voice was liquid, but peremptory, and Schwartz reached for the door to keep himself upright. His lips moved, uselessly, and, in a rush, all the clammiest fears he had known returned to choke his windpipe and stifle his heart.

For the woman spoke in no language Schwartz had ever heard.

Two: THE DISPOSAL OF A STRANGER

Loa Maren and her stolid husband, Arbin, played cards in the cool of the same evening, while the older man in the motor-driven wheel chair in the corner rustled his newspaper angrily and called, "Arbin!"

Arbin Maren did not answer at once. He fingered the thin, smooth rectangles carefully as he considered the next play. Then, as he slowly made his decision, he responded with an absent, "What do you want, Grew?"

The grizzled Grew regarded his son-in-law fiercely over the top of the paper and rustled it again. He found noise of that sort a great relief to his feelings. When a man teems with energy and finds himself spiked to a wheel chair with two dead sticks for legs, there must be something, by Space, he can do to express himself. Grew used his newspaper. He rustled it; he gestured with it; when necessary, he swatted at things with it.

Elsewhere than on Earth, Grew knew, they had telenews machines that issued rolls of microfilm as servings of current news. Standard book viewers were used for them. But Grew sneered silently at that. An effete and degenerate custom!

Grew said, "Did you read about the archaeological expedition they're sending to Earth?"

"No, I haven't," said Arbin calmly.

Grew knew that, since nobody but himself had seen the paper yet, and the family had given up their video last year. But then his remark had simply been in the nature of an opening gambit, anyway.

He said, "Well, there's one coming. And on an Imperial grant, too, and how do you like that?" He began reciting in the queer unevenness of tone that most people somehow assume automatically when reading aloud, " 'Bel Arvardan, Senior Research Associate at the Imperial Archaeological Institute, in an interview granted the Galactic Press, spoke hopefully of the expected valuable results of archaeological studies which are being projected upon the planet Earth, located on the outskirts of the Sirius Sector (see map). "Earth," he said, "with its archaic civilization and its unique environment, offers a freak culture which has been too long neglected by our social scientists, except as a difficult exercise in local government. I have every expectation that the next year or two will bring about revolutionary changes in some of our supposed fundamental concepts of social evolution and human history." ' And so on and so on," he finished with a flourish.

Arbin Maren had been listening with only half an ear. He mumbled, "What does he mean, 'freak culture'?"

Loa Maren hadn't been listening at all. She simply said, "It's your play, Arbin."

Grew went on. "Well, aren't you going to ask me why the *Tribune* printed it? You know they wouldn't print a Galactic Press release for a million Imperial Credits without a good reason."

He waited uselessly for an answer, then said, "Because they have an editorial on it. A full-page editorial that blasts the living daylights out of this guy Arvardan. Here's a fellow wants to come here for scientific purposes and they're choking themselves purple to keep him out. Look at this piece of rabble-rousing. Look at it!" He shook the paper at them. "Read it, why don't you?"

Loa Maren put down her cards and clamped her thin lips firmly together. "Father," she said, "we've had a hard day, so let's not have politics just now. Later, maybe, eh? Please, Father."

Grew scowled and mimicked, " 'Please, Father! Please, Father.' It appears to me you must be getting pretty tired of your old father when you begrudge him a few quiet words on current events. I'm in your way, I suppose, sitting here in the corner and letting you two work for three. . . . Whose fault is it? I'm strong. I'm willing to work. And you know I could get my legs treated and be as well as ever." He slapped them as he spoke: hard, savage, ringing slaps, which he heard but did not feel. "The only reason I can't is because I'm getting too old to make a cure worth their while. Don't *you* call that a 'freak culture'? What else could you call a world where a man can work but they won't let him? By Space, I think it's about time we stopped this nonsense about our so-called 'peculiar institutions.' They're not just peculiar; they're *cracked!* I think——"

He was waving his arms and angry blood was reddening his face.

But Arbin had risen from his chair, and his grip was strong on the older man's shoulder. He said, "Now where's the call to be upset, Grew? When you're through with the paper, I'll read the editorial."

"Sure, but you'll agree with them, so what's the use? You young ones are a bunch of milksops; just sponge rubber in the hands of the Ancients."

And Loa said sharply, "Quiet, Father. Don't start *that.*" She sat there listening for a moment. She could not have said exactly what for, but . . .

Arbin felt that cold little prickle that always came when the Society of Ancients was mentioned. It just wasn't safe to talk as Grew did, to mock Earth's ancient culture, to—to——

Why, it was rank Assimilationism. He swallowed earnestly; the word was an ugly one, even when confined to thought.

Of course in Grew's youth there had been much of this foolish talk of abandoning the old ways, but these were different times. Grew should know that—and he probably did, except that it wasn't easy to be reasonable and sensible when you were in a wheel-chair prison, just waiting away your days for the next Census.

Grew was perhaps the least affected, but he said no more. And as the moments passed he grew quieter and the print became progressively more difficult to place in focus. He had not yet had time to give the sports pages a detailed and critical perusal when his nodding head lolled slowly down upon his chest. He snored softly, and the paper fell from his fingers with a final, unintentional rustle.

Then Loa spoke, in a worried whisper. "Maybe we're not being kind to him, Arbin. It's a hard life for a man like Father. It's like being dead compared to the life he used to lead."

"Nothing's like being dead, Loa. He has his papers and his books.

Let him be! A bit of excitement like this peps him up. He'll be happy and quiet for days now."

Arbin was beginning to consider his cards again, and as he reached for one the pounding at the door sounded, with hoarse yells that didn't quite coalesce into words.

Arbin's hand lurched and stopped. Loa's eyes grew fearful; she stared at her husband with a trembling lower lip.

Arbin said, "Get Grew out of here. Quickly!"

Loa was at the wheel chair as he spoke. She made soothing sounds with her tongue.

But the sleeping figure gasped, startled awake at the first motion of the chair. He straightened and groped automatically for his paper.

"What's the matter?" he demanded irritably, and by no means in a whisper.

"Shh. It's *all* right," muttered Loa vaguely, and wheeled the chair into the next room. She closed the door and placed her back against it, thin chest heaving as her eyes sought those of her husband. There was that pounding again.

They stood close to each other as the door opened, almost defensively so, and hostility peeped from them as they faced the short, plump man who smiled faintly at them.

Loa said, "Is there anything we can do for you?" with a ceremonial courtesy, then jumped back as the man gasped and put out a hand to stop himself from falling.

"Is he sick?" asked Arbin bewilderedly. "Here, help me take him inside."

The hours after that passed, and in the quiet of their bedroom Loa and Arbin prepared slowly for bed.

"Arbin," said Loa.

"What is it?"

"Is it safe?"

"Safe?" He seemed to avoid her meaning deliberately.

"I mean, taking this man into the house. Who is he?"

"How should I know?" was the irritated response. "But, after all, we can't refuse shelter to a sick man. Tomorrow, if he lacks identification, we'll inform the Regional Security Board, and that will be the end of it." He turned away in an obvious attempt at breaking off the conversation.

But his wife broke the returning silence, her thin voice more urgent. "You don't think he might be an agent of the Society of Ancients, do you? There's Grew, you know."

"You mean because of what he said tonight? That's past the limit of reason. I won't argue about it."

"I don't mean that, and you know it. I mean that we've been keeping Grew illegally now for two years, and you know we're breaking just about the most serious Custom."

Arbin muttered, "We're harming no one. We're filling our quota, aren't we, even though it's set for three people—three *workers?* And if we are, why should they suspect anything? We don't even let him out of the house."

"They might trace the wheel chair. You had to buy the motor and fittings outside."

"Now don't start that again, Loa. I've explained many times that I've bought nothing but standard kitchen equipment for that chair. Besides, it does not make any sense at all to consider him an agent of the Brotherhood. Do you suppose that they would go through such an elaborate trickery for the sake of a poor old man in a wheel chair? Couldn't they enter by daylight and with legal search warrants? Please, reason this thing out."

"Well, then, Arbin"—her eyes were suddenly bright and eager—"if you really think so—and I've been so hoping you would—he must be an Outsider. He *can't* be an Earthman."

"What do you mean, he can't be? That's more ridiculous still. Why should a man of the Empire come here to Earth, of all places?"

"I don't know why! Yes, I do; maybe he's committed a crime out there." She was caught up instantly in her own fancy. "Why not? It makes sense. Earth would be the natural place to come to. Who would ever think of looking for him here?"

"*If* he's an Outsider. What evidence do you have for that?"

"He doesn't speak the language, does he? You'll have to grant me that. Could you understand a single word? So he *must* come from some far-off corner of the Galaxy where the dialect is strange. They say the men of Fomalhaut have to learn practically a new language to be understood at the Emperor's court on Trantor. . . . But don't you see what all this can mean? If he's a stranger on Earth, he will have no registration with the Census Board, and he will be only too glad to avoid reporting to them. We can use him on the farm, in the place of Father, and it will be three people again, not two, who will have to meet the quota for three this next season. . . . He could even help with the harvest now."

She looked anxiously at the uncertain face of her husband, who considered long, then said, "Well, go to bed, Loa. We'll speak further in the common sense of daylight."

The whispering ended, the light was put out, and eventually sleep filled the room and the house.

The next morning it was Grew's turn to consider the matter. Arbin put the question to him hopefully. He felt a confidence in his father-in-law that he could not muster in himself.

Grew said, "Your troubles, Arbin, obviously arise from the fact that I am registered as a worker, so that the produce quota is set at three. I'm tired of creating trouble. This is the second year I have lived past my time. It is enough."

Arbin was embarrassed. "Now that wasn't the point at all. I'm not hinting that you're a trouble to us."

"Well, after all, what's the difference? In two years there will be the Census, and I will go anyway."

"At least you will have two more years of your books and your rest. Why should you be deprived of that?"

"Because others are. And what of you and Loa? When they come to take me, they will take you two as well. What kind of a man would I be to live a few stinking years at the expense——"

"Stop it, Grew. I don't want histrionics. We've told you many times what we're going to do. We'll report you a week before the Census."

"And fool the doctor, I suppose?"

"We'll bribe the doctor."

"Hmp. And this new man—he'll double the offense. You'll be concealing him too."

"We'll turn him loose. For Space's sake, why bother about this now? We have two years. What shall we do with him?"

"A stranger," mused Grew. "He comes knocking at the door. He's from nowhere. He speaks unintelligibly. . . . I don't know what to advise."

The farmer said, "He is mild-mannered; seems frightened to death. He can't do us any harm."

"Frightened, eh? What if he's feeble-minded? What if his babbling isn't a foreign dialect at all, but just insane mouthing?"

"That doesn't sound likely." But Arbin stirred uneasily.

"You tell yourself that because you want to use him. . . . All right, I'll tell you what to do. Take him into town."

"To Chica?" Arbin was horrified. "That would be ruin."

"Not at all," said Grew calmly. "The trouble with you is that you don't read the newspapers. Fortunately for this family, *I* do. It so happens that the Institute for Nuclear Research has developed an instrument that is supposed to make it easier for people to learn. There was a full-page spread in the Week-end Supplement. And they want volunteers. Take this man. Let him be a volunteer."

Arbin shook his head firmly. "You're mad. I couldn't do anything like that, Grew. They'll ask for his registration number first thing. It's only inviting investigation to have things in improper order, and then they'll find out about you."

"No, they won't. It so happens you're all wrong, Arbin. The reason the Institute wants volunteers is that the machine is still experimental. It's probably killed a few people, so I'm sure they won't ask questions. And if the stranger dies, he'll probably be no worse off than he is now. . . . Here, Arbin, hand me the book projector and set the mark at reel six. And bring me the paper as soon as it comes, will you?"

When Schwartz opened his eyes, it was past noon. He felt that dull, heart-choking pain that feeds on itself, the pain of a wife no longer by his side at waking, of a familiar world lost . . .

Once before he had felt such a pain, and that momentary flash of memory came, lighting up a forgotten scene into sharp brilliance. There was himself, a youngster, in the snow of the wintry village . . . with the sleigh waiting . . . at the end of whose journey would be the train . . . and, after that, the great ship . . .

The longing, frustrating fear for the world of the familiar united him for the moment with that twenty-year-old who had emigrated to America.

The frustration was too real. This could not be a dream.

He jumped up as the light above the door blinked on and off and the meaningless baritone of his host sounded. Then the door opened and there was breakfast—a mealy porridge that he did not recognize but which tasted faintly like corn mush (with a savory difference) and milk.

He said, "Thanks," and nodded his head vigorously.

The farmer said something in return and picked up Schwartz's shirt from where it hung on the back of the chair. He inspected it carefully from all directions, paying particular attention to the buttons. Then, replacing it, he flung open the sliding door of a closet, and for the first time Schwartz became visually aware of the warm milkiness of the walls.

"Plastic," he muttered to himself, using that all-inclusive word with the finality laymen always do. He noted further that there were no corners or angles in the room, all planes fading into each other at a gentle curve.

But the other was holding objects out toward him and was making gestures that could not be mistaken. Schwartz obviously was to wash and dress.

With help and directions, he obeyed. Except that he found nothing with which to shave, nor could gestures to his chin elicit anything but an incomprehensible sound accompanied by a look of distinct revulsion on the part of the other. Schwartz scratched at his gray stubble and sighed windily.

And then he was led to a small, elongated, biwheeled car, into which he was ordered by gestures. The ground sped beneath them and the empty road moved backward on either side, until low, sparkling white buildings rose before him, and there, far ahead, was the blue water.

He pointed eagerly. "Chicago?"

It was the last gasp of hope within him, for certainly nothing he ever saw looked less like that city.

The farmer made no answer at all.

And the last hope died.

Three: ONE WORLD—OR MANY?

Bel Arvardan, fresh from his interview with the press, on the occasion of his forthcoming expedition to Earth, felt at supreme peace with all the hundred million star systems that composed the all-embracing Galactic Empire. It was no longer a question of being known in this sector or that. Let his theories concerning Earth be proven and his reputation would be assured on every inhabited planet of the Milky Way, on every planet that Man had set foot on through the hundreds of thousands of years of expansion through space.

These potential heights of renown, these pure and rarefied intellectual peaks of science were coming to him early, yet not easily. He was scarcely thirty-five, but already his career had been packed with controversy. It had begun with an explosion that had rocked the halls of the University of Arcturus when he first graduated as Senior Archaeologist from that institution at the unprecedented age of twenty-three. The explosion—no less effective for being immaterial—consisted of the rejection for publication, on the part of the *Journal of the Galactic Archaeological Society*, of his Senior Dissertation. It was the first time in the history of the university that a Senior Dissertation had been rejected. It was equally the first time in the history of that staid professional journal that a rejection had been couched in such blunt terms.

To a non-archaeologist, the reason for such anger against an obscure and dry little pamphlet, entitled *On the Antiquity of Artifacts in the Sirius Sector with Considerations of the Application Thereof to the Radiation Hypothesis of Human Origin,* might seem mysterious. What was involved, however, was that from the first Arvardan adopted as his own the hypothesis advanced earlier by certain groups of mystics who were more concerned with metaphysics than with archaeology; *i.e.,* that Humanity had originated upon some single planet and had radiated by degrees throughout the Galaxy. This was a favorite theory of the fantasy writers of the day, and the bête noire of every respectable archaeologist of the Empire.

But Arvardan became a force to be reckoned with by even the most respectable, for within the decade he had become the recognized authority on the relics of the pre-Empire cultures still left in the eddies and quiet backwaters of the Galaxy.

For instance, he had written a monograph on the mechanistic civilization of the Rigel Sector, where the development of robots created a separate culture that persisted for centuries, till the very perfection of the metal slaves reduced the human initiative to the point where the vigorous fleets of the War Lord, Moray, took easy control. Orthodox archaeology insisted on the evolution of Human types independently on various planets and used such atypical cultures, as that in Rigel, as examples of race differences that had not yet been ironed out through intermarriage. Arvardan destroyed such concepts effectively by showing that Rigellian robot culture was but a natural outgrowth of the economic and social forces of the times and of the region.

Then there were the barbarous worlds of Ophiuchus, which the orthodox had long upheld as samples of primitive Humanity not yet advanced to the stage of interstellar travel. Every textbook used those worlds as the best evidence of the Merger Theory; *i.e.,* that Humanity was the natural climax of evolution on any world based upon a water-oxygen chemistry with proper intensities of temperature and gravitation; that each independent strain of Humanity could intermarry; that with the discovery of interstellar travel, such intermarriage took place.

Arvardan, however, uncovered traces of the early civilization that had preceded the then thousand-year-old barbarism of Ophiuchus and proved that the earliest records of the planet showed traces of interstellar trade. The final touch came when he demonstrated beyond any doubt that Man had emigrated to the region in an already civilized state.

It was after that that the *J. Gal. Arch. Soc.* (to give the *Journal* its professional abbreviation) decided to print Arvardan's Senior Dissertation more than ten years after it had been presented.

And now the pursuit of his pet theory led Arvardan to probably the least significant planet of the Empire—the planet called Earth.

Arvardan landed at that one spot of Empire on all Earth, that patch among the desolate heights of the plateaus north of the Himalayas. There, where radioactivity was not, and never had been, there gleamed a palace that was not of Terrestrial architecture. In essence it was a copy of the viceregal palaces that existed on more fortunate worlds. The soft lushness of the grounds was built for comfort. The forbidding rocks had been covered with topsoil, watered, immersed in an artificial atmosphere and climate—and converted into five square miles of lawns and flower gardens.

The cost in energy involved in this performance was terrific by Earthly calculations, but it had behind it the completely incredible resources of tens of millions of planets, continually growing in number. (It has been estimated that in the Year of the Galactic Era 827 an average of fifty new planets each day were achieving the dignity of provincial status, this condition requiring the attainment of a population of five hundred millions.)

In this spot of non-Earth lived the Procurator of Earth, and sometimes, in this artificial luxury, he could forget that he was a Procurator of a rathole world and remember that he was an aristocrat of great honor and ancient family.

His wife was perhaps less often deluded, particularly at such times as, topping a grassy knoll, she could see in the distance the sharp, decisive line separating the grounds from the fierce wilderness of Earth. It was then that not all the colored fountains (luminescent at night, with an effect of cold liquid fire), flowered walks, or idyllic groves could compensate for the knowledge of their exile.

So perhaps Arvardan was welcomed even more than protocol might call for. To the Procurator, after all, Arvardan was a breath of Empire, of spaciousness, of boundlessness.

And Arvardan for his part found much to admire.

He said, "This is done well—and with taste. It is amazing how a touch of the central culture permeates the most outlying districts of our Empire, Lord Ennius."

Ennius smiled. "I'm afraid the Procurator's court here on Earth is more pleasant to visit than to live in. It is but a shell that rings hollowly when touched. When you have considered myself and family, the staff, the Imperial garrison, both here and in the important planetary centers, together with an occasional visitor such as yourself, you have exhausted all the touch of the central culture that exists. It seems scarcely enough."

They sat in the colonnade in the dying afternoon, with the sun glinting downward toward the mist-purpled jags of the horizon and the air so heavy with the scent of growing things that its motions were merely sighs of exertion.

It was, of course, not quite suitable for even a Procurator to show too great a curiosity about the doings of a guest, but that does not take into account the inhumanity of day-to-day isolation from all the Empire.

Ennius said, "Do you plan to stay for some time, Dr. Arvardan?"

"As to that, Lord Ennius, I cannot surely say. I have come ahead of the rest of my expedition in order to acquaint myself with Earth's culture and to fulfill the necessary legal requirements. For instance, I must obtain the usual official permission from you to establish camps at the necessary sites, and so on."

"Oh, granted, granted! But when do you start digging? And whatever can you possibly expect to find on this miserable heap of rubble?"

"I hope, if all goes well, to be able to set up camp in a few months. And as to this world—why, it's anything but a miserable heap. It is absolutely unique in the Galaxy."

"Unique?" said the Procurator stiffly. "Not at all! It is a very ordinary world. It is more or less of a pigpen of a world, or a horrible hole of a world, or a cesspool of a world, or almost any other particularly derogative adjective you care to use. And yet, with all its refinement of nausea, it cannot even achieve uniqueness in villainy, but remains an ordinary, brutish peasant world."

"But," said Arvardan, somewhat taken aback by the energy of the inconsistent statements thus thrown at him, "the world is radioactive."

"Well, what of that? Some thousands of planets in the Galaxy are radioactive, and some are considerably more so than Earth."

It was at this moment that the soft-gliding motion of the motile cabinet attracted their attention. It came to a halt within easy hand reach.

Ennius gestured toward it and said to the other, "What would you prefer?"

"I'm not particular. A lime twist, perhaps."

"That can be handled. The cabinet will have the ingredients. . . . With or without Chensey?"

"Just about a tang of it," said Arvardan, and held up his forefinger and thumb, nearly touching.

"You'll have it in a minute."

Somewhere in the bowels of the cabinet (perhaps the most universally popular mechanical offspring of human ingenuity) a bartender went into action—a non-human bartender whose electronic soul mixed things not by jiggers but by atom counts, whose ratios were perfect every time, and who could not be matched by all the inspired artistry of anyone merely human.

The tall glasses appeared from nowhere, it seemed, as they waited in the appropriate recesses.

Arvardan took the green one and, for a moment, felt the chill of it against his cheek. Then he placed the rim to his lips and tasted.

"Just right," he said. He placed the glass in the well-fitted holder in the arm of his chair and said, "Thousands of radioactive planets, Procurator, just as you say, but only one of them is inhabited. *This* one, Procurator."

"Well"—Ennius smacked his lips over his own drink and seemed to lose some of his sharpness after contact with its velvet—"perhaps it *is* unique in that way. It's an unenviable distinction."

"But it is not just a question of statistical uniqueness." Arvardan spoke deliberately between occasional sips. "It goes further; it has tremendous potentialities. Biologists have shown, or claim to have shown, that on planets in which the intensity of radioactivity in the atmosphere and in the seas is above a certain point life will not develop. . . . Earth's radioactivity is above that point by a considerable margin."

"Interesting. I didn't know that. I imagine that this would constitute definite proof that Earth life is fundamentally different from that of the rest of the Galaxy. . . . That should suit you, since you're from Sirius." He seemed sardonically amused at this point and said in a confidential aside, "Do you know that the biggest single difficulty involved in ruling this planet lies in coping with the intense anti-Terrestrialism that exists throughout the entire Sirius Sector? And the feeling is returned with interest on the part of these Earthmen. I'm not saying, of course, that anti-Terrestrialism doesn't exist in more or less diluted form in many places in the Galaxy, but not like on Sirius."

Arvardan's response was impatient and vehement. "Lord Ennius, I reject the implication. I have as little intolerance in me as any man living. I believe in the oneness of humanity to my very scientific core, and that includes even Earth. And all life *is* fundamentally one, in that it is all based upon protein complexes in colloidal dispersion, which we call protoplasm. The effect of radioactivity that I just talked of does not apply simply to some forms of human life, or to some forms of any life. It applies to *all* life, since it is based upon the quantum mechanics of the protein molecules. It applies to you, to me, to Earthmen, to spiders, and to germs.

"You see, proteins, as I probably needn't tell you, are immensely complicated groupings of amino acids and certain other specialized compounds, arranged in intricate three-dimensional patterns that are as unstable as sunbeams on a cloudy day. It is this instability that is life, since it is forever changing its position in an effort to maintain its identity—in the manner of a long rod balanced on an acrobat's nose.

"But this marvelous chemical, this protein, must be first built up out of inorganic matter before life can exist. So, at the very beginning, by the influence of the sun's radiant energy upon those huge solutions we call oceans, organic molecules gradually increase in complexity from methane to formaldehyde and finally to sugars and starches in one direction, and from urea to amino acids and proteins in another direction. It's a matter of chance, of course, these combinations and disintegrations of atoms, and the process on one world may take millions of years while on another it may take only hundreds. Of course it is much more probable that it will take millions of years. In fact, it is most probable that it will end up never happening.

"Now physical organic chemists have worked out with great exactness all the reaction chain involved, particularly the energetics thereof; that is, the energy relationships involved in each atom shift. It is now known beyond the shadow of a doubt that several of the crucial steps in the building of life require the absence of radiant energy. If this strikes you as queer, Procurator, I can only say that photochemistry (the chemistry of reactions induced by radiant energy) is a well-developed branch of the science, and there are innumerable cases of very simple reactions which will go in one of two different directions depending upon whether it takes place in the presence or absence of quanta of light energy.

"In ordinary worlds the sun is the only source of radiant energy, or, at least, by far the major source. In the shelter of clouds, or at night, the carbon and nitrogen compounds combine and recombine, in the fashions made possible by the absence of those little bits of energy hurled into the midst of them by the sun—like bowling balls into the midst of an infinite number of infinitesimal tenpins.

"But on radioactive worlds, sun or no sun, every drop of water—even in the deepest night, even five miles under—sparkles and bursts with darting gamma rays, kicking up the carbon atoms—activating them, the chemists say—and forcing certain key reactions to proceed only in certain ways, ways that never result in life."

Arvardan's drink was gone. He placed the empty glass on the waiting cabinet. It was withdrawn instantly into the special compartment where it was cleaned, sterilized, and made ready for the next drink.

"Another one?" asked Ennius.

"Ask me after dinner," said Arvardan. "I've had quite enough for now."

Ennius tapped a tapering fingernail upon the arm of his chair and said, "You make the process sound quite fascinating, but if all is as you say then what about the life on Earth? How did *it* develop?"

"Ah, you see, even you are beginning to wonder. But the answer, *I* think, is simple. Radioactivity, in excess of the minimum required to prevent life, is still not necessarily sufficient to destroy life already formed. It might modify it, but, except in comparatively huge excess, it will not destroy it. . . . You see, the chemistry involved is different. In the first case, simple molecules must be prevented from building up, while in the second, already-formed complex molecules must be broken down. Not at all the same thing."

"I don't get the application of that at all," said Ennius.

"Isn't it obvious? Life on Earth originated *before* the planet became radioactive. My dear Procurator, it is the only possible explanation that does not involve denying either the fact of life on Earth or enough chemical theory to upset half the science."

Ennius gazed at the other in amazed disbelief. "But you can't mean that."

"Why not?"

"Because how can a world *become* radioactive? The life of the radioactive elements in the planet's crust are in the millions and billions of years. I've learned that, at least, during my university career, even in a pre-law course. They must have existed indefinitely in the past."

"But there is such a thing as artificial radioactivity, Lord Ennius—

even on a hurge scale. There are thousands of nuclear reactions of sufficient energy to create all sorts of radioactive isotopes. Why, if we were to suppose that human beings might use some applied nuclear reaction in industry, without proper controls, or even in war, if you can imagine anything like a war proceeding on a single planet, most of the topsoil could, conceivably, be converted into artificially radioactive materials. What do you say to that?"

The sun had expired in blood on the mountains, and Ennius's thin face was ruddy in the reflection of that process. The gentle evening wind stirred, and the drowsy murmur of the carefully selected varieties of insect life upon the palace grounds was more soothing than ever.

Ennius said, "It sounds very artificial to me. For one thing, I can't conceive using nuclear reactions in war or letting them get out of control to this extent in any manner——"

"Naturally, sir, you tend to underestimate nuclear reactions because you're living in the present, when they're so easily controlled. But what if someone—or some army—used such weapons before the defense had been worked out? For instance, it's like using fire bombs before anyone knew that water or sand would put out fire."

"Hmm," said Ennius, "you sound like Shekt."

"Who's Shekt?" Arvardan looked up quickly.

"An Earthman. One of the few decent ones—I mean, one that a gentleman can speak to. He's a physicist. He told me once that Earth might not always have been radioactive."

"Ah. . . . Well, that's not unusual, since the theory is certainly not original with me. It's part of the *Book of the Ancients*, which contains the traditional, or mythical, history of prehistoric Earth. I'm saying what it says, in a way, except that I'm putting its rather elliptical phraseology into equivalent scientific statements."

"*The Book of the Ancients?*" Ennius seemed surprised, and a little upset. "Where did you get that?"

"Here and there. It wasn't easy, and I only obtained parts. Of course all this traditional information about non-radioactivity, even where completely unscientific, is important to my project. . . . Why do you ask?"

"Because the book is the revered text of a radical sect of Earthmen. It is forbidden for Outsiders to read it. I wouldn't broadcast the fact that you did, either, while you're here. Non-Earthmen, or Outsiders, as they call them, have been lynched for less."

"You make it sound as if the Imperial police power here is defective."

"It is in cases of sacrilege. A word to the wise, Dr. Arvardan!"

A melodious chime sounded a vibrant note that seemed to harmonize with the rustling whisper of the trees. It faded out slowly, lingering as though in love with its surroundings.

Ennius rose. "I believe it is time for dinner. Will you join me, sir, and enjoy such hospitality as this husk of Empire on Earth can afford?"

An occasion for an elaborate dinner came infrequently enough. An excuse, even a slim one, was not to be missed. So the courses were many, the surroundings lavish, the men polished, and the women bewitching. And, it must be added, Dr. B. Arvardan of Baronn, Sirius, was lionized to quite an intoxicating extent.

Arvardan took advantage of his dinner audience during the latter portion of the banquet to repeat much of what he had said to Ennius, but here his exposition met with markedly less success.

A florid gentleman in colonel's uniform leaned toward him with that marked condescension of the military man for the scholar and said, "If I interpret your expressions rightly, Dr. Arvardan, you are trying to tell us that these hounds of Earth represent an ancient race that may once have been the ancestors of all humanity?"

"I hesitate, Colonel, to make the flat assertion, but I think there is an interesting chance that it might be so. A year from now I confidently hope to be able to make a definite judgment."

"If you find that they are, Doctor, which I strongly doubt," rejoined the colonel, "you will astonish me beyond measure. I have been stationed on Earth now for four years, and my experience is not of the smallest. I find these Earthmen to be rogues and knaves, every one of them. They are definitely our inferiors intellectually. They lack that spark that has spread humanity throughout the Galaxy. They are lazy, superstitious, avaricious, and with no trace of nobility of soul. I defy you, or anyone, to show me an Earthman who can in any way be an equal of any true man—yourself or myself, for instance—and only then will I grant you that he may represent a race who once were our ancestors. But, until then, please excuse me from making any such assumption."

A portly man at the foot of the table said suddenly, "They say the only good Earthman is a dead Earthman, and that even then they generally stink," and laughed immoderately.

Arvardan frowned at the dish before him and said, without looking up, "I have no desire to argue racial differences, especially since it is irrelevant in this case. It is the Earthman of prehistory that I speak of. His descendants of today have been long isolated, and have been subjected to a most unusual environment—yet I still would not dismiss them too casually."

He turned to Ennius and said, "My Lord, I believe you mentioned an Earthman before dinner."

"I did? I don't recall."

"A physicist. Shekt."

"Oh yes. Yes."

"Affret Shekt, perhaps?"

"Why, yes. Have you heard of him?"

"I think I have. It's been bothering me all through dinner, ever since you mentioned him, but I think I've placed him. He wouldn't be at the Institute of Nuclear Research at—— Oh, what's the name of that damned place?" He struck at his forehead with the heel of his palm once or twice. "At Chica?"

"You have the right person. What about him?"

"Only this. There was an article by him in the August issue of *Physical Reviews*. I noticed it because I was looking for anything that had to do with Earth, and articles by Earthmen in journals of Galactic circulation are very rare. . . . In any case, the point I am trying to make is that the man claims to have developed something he calls a Synapsifier, which is supposed to improve the learning capacity of the mammalian nervous system."

"Really?" said Ennius a bit too sharply. "I haven't heard about it."

"I can find you the reference. It's quite an interesting article; though, of course, I can't pretend to understand the mathematics involved. What he has done, however, has been to treat some indigenous animal form on Earth—rats, I believe they call them—with the Synapsifier and then put them to solving a maze. You know what I mean: learning the proper pathway through a tiny labyrinth to some food supply. He used non-treated rats as controls and found that in every case the Synapsified rats solved the maze in less than one third the time. . . . Do you see the significance, Colonel?"

The military man who had initiated the discussion said indifferently, "No, Doctor, I do not."

"I'll explain, then, that I firmly believe that any scientist capable of doing such work, even an Earthman, is certainly my intellectual equal, at least, and, if you'll pardon my presumption, yours as well."

Ennius interrupted. "Pardon me, Dr. Arvardan. I would like to return to the Synapsifier. Has Shekt experimented with human beings?"

Arvardan laughed. "I doubt it, Lord Ennius. Nine tenths of his

Synapsified rats died during treatment. He would scarcely dare use human subjects until much more progress has been made."

So Ennius sank back into his chair with a slight frown on his forehead and, thereafter, neither spoke nor ate for the remainder of the dinner.

Before midnight the Procurator had quietly left the gathering and, with a bare word to his wife only, departed in his private cruiser on the two-hour trip to the city of Chica, with the slight frown still on his forehead and a raging anxiety in his heart.

Thus it was that on the same afternoon that Arbin Maren brought Joseph Schwartz into Chica for treatment with Shekt's Synapsifier, Shekt himself had been closeted with none less than the Procurator of Earth for over an hour.

Four: THE ROYAL ROAD

Arbin was uneasy in Chica. He felt surrounded. Somewhere in Chica, one of the largest cities on Earth—they said it had fifty thousand human beings in it—somewhere there were officials of the great outer Empire.

To be sure, he had never seen a man of the Galaxy; yet here, in Chica, his neck was continually twisting in fear that he might. If pinned down, he could not have explained how he would identify an Outsider from an Earthman, even if he were to see one, but it was in his very marrow to feel that there was, somehow, a difference.

He looked back over his shoulder as he entered the Institute. His biwheel was parked in an open area, with a six-hour coupon holding a spot open for it. Was the extravagance itself suspicious? . . . Everything frightened him now. The air was full of eyes and ears.

If only the strange man would remember to remain hidden in the bottom of the rear compartment. He had nodded violently—but had he understood? He was suddenly impatient with himself. Why had he let Grew talk him into this madness?

And then somehow the door was open in front of him and a voice had broken in on his thoughts.

It said, "What do you want?"

It sounded impatient; perhaps it had already asked him that same thing several times.

He answered hoarsely, words choking out of his throat like dry powder, "Is this where a man can apply for the Synapsifier?"

The receptionist looked up sharply and said, "Sign here."

Arbin put his hands behind his back and repeated huskily, "Where do I see about the Synapsifier?" Grew had told him the name, but the word came out queerly, like so much gibberish.

But the receptionist said, with iron in her voice, "I can't do anything for you unless you sign the register as a visitor. It's in the rules."

Without a word, Arbin turned to go. The young woman behind the desk pressed her lips together and kicked the signal bar at the side of her chair violently.

Arbin was fighting desperately for a lack of notoriety and failing miserably in his own mind. This girl was looking hard at him. She'd remember him a thousand years later. He had a wild desire to run, run back to the car, back to the farm . . .

Someone in a white lab coat was coming rapidly out of another room, and the receptionist was pointing to him. "Volunteer for the Synapsifier, Miss Shekt," she was saying. "He won't give his name."

Arbin looked up. It was still another girl, young. He looked disturbed. "Are *you* in charge of the machine, miss?"

"No, not at all." She smiled in a very friendly fashion, and Arbin felt anxiety ebb slightly.

"I can take you to him, though," she went on. Then, eagerly, "Do you really want to volunteer for the Synapsifier?"

"I just want to see the man in charge," Arbin said woodenly.

"All right." She seemed not at all disturbed by the rebuff. She slipped back through the door from which she had come. There was a short wait. Then, finally, there was the beckon of a finger . . .

He followed her, heart pounding, into a small anteroom. She said gently, "If you will wait about half an hour or less, Dr. Shekt will be with you. He is very busy just now. . . . If you would like some book films and a viewer to pass the time, I'll bring them to you."

But Arbin shook his head. The four walls of the small room closed about him, and held him rigid, it seemed. Was he trapped? Were the Ancients coming for him?

It was the longest wait in Arbin's life.

Lord Ennius, Procurator of Earth, had experienced no comparable difficulties in seeing Dr. Shekt, though he had experienced an almost comparable excitement. In his fourth year as Procurator, a visit to Chica was still an event. As the direct representative of the remote Emperor, his social standing was, legalistically, upon a par with viceroys of huge Galactic sectors that sprawled their gleaming volumes across hundreds of cubic parsecs of space, but, actually, his post was little short of exile.

Trapped as he was in the sterile emptiness of the Himalayas, among the equally sterile quarrels of a population that hated him and the Empire he represented, even a trip to Chica was escape.

To be sure, his escapes were short ones. They had to be short, since here at Chica it was necessary to wear lead-impregnated clothes at all times, even while sleeping, and, what was worse, to dose oneself continually with metaboline.

He spoke bitterly of that to Shekt.

"Metaboline," he said, holding up the vermilion pill for inspection, "is perhaps a true symbol of all that your planet means to me, my friend. Its function is to heighten all metabolic processes while I sit here immersed in the radioactive cloud that surrounds me and which you are not even aware of."

He swallowed it. "There! Now my heart will beat more quickly; my breath will pump a race of its own accord; and my liver will boil away in those chemical syntheses that, medical men tell me, make it the most important factory in the body. And for that I pay with a siege of headaches and lassitude afterward."

Dr. Shekt listened with some amusement. He gave a strong impression of being nearsighted, did Shekt, not because he wore glasses or was in any way afflicted, but merely because long habit had given him the unconscious trick of peering closely at things, of weighing all facts anxiously before saying anything. He was tall and in his late middle age, his thin figure slightly stooped.

But he was well read in much of Galactic culture, and he was relatively free of the trick of universal hostility and suspicion that made the average Earthman so repulsive even to so cosmopolitan a man of the Empire as Ennius.

Shekt said, "I'm sure you don't need the pill. Metaboline is just one of your superstitions, and you know it. If I were to substitute sugar pills without your knowledge, you'd be none the worse. What's more, you would even psychosomaticize yourself into similar headaches afterward."

"You say that in the comfort of your own environment. Do you deny that your basal metabolism is higher than mine?"

"Of course I don't, but what of it? I know that it is a superstition of the Empire, Ennius, that we men of Earth are different from other human beings, but that's not really so in the essentials. Or are you coming here as a missionary of the anti-Terrestrians?"

Ennius groaned. "By the life of the Emperor, your comrades of

Earth are themselves the best such missionaries. Living here, as they do, cooped up on their deadly planet, festering in their own anger, they're nothing but a standing ulcer in the Galaxy.

"I'm serious, Shekt. What planet has so much ritual in its daily life and adheres to it with such masochistic fury? Not a day passes but I receive delegations from one or another of your ruling bodies for the death penalty for some poor devil whose only crime has been to invade a forbidden area, to evade the Sixty, or perhaps merely to eat more than his share of food."

"Ah, but you always grant the death penalty. Your idealistic distaste seems to stop short at resisting."

"The Stars are my witness that I struggle to deny the death. But what can one do? The Emperor *will* have it that all the subdivisions of the Empire are to remain undisturbed in their local customs—and that is right and wise, since it removes popular support from the fools who would otherwise kick up rebellion on alternate Tuesdays and Thursdays. Besides, were I to remain obdurate when your Councils and Senates and Chambers insist on the death, such a shrieking would arise and such a wild howling and such denunciation of the Empire and all its works that I would sooner sleep in the midst of a legion of devils for twenty years than face such an Earth for ten minutes."

Shekt sighed and rubbed the thin hair back upon his skull. "To the rest of the Galaxy, if they are aware of us at all, Earth is but a pebble in the sky. To us it is home, and all the home we know. Yet we are no different from you of the outer worlds, merely more unfortunate. We are crowded here on a world all but dead, immersed within a wall of radiation that imprisons us, surrounded by a huge Galaxy that rejects us. What can we do against the feeling of frustration that burns us? Would you, Procurator, be willing that we send our surplus population abroad?"

Ennius shrugged. "Would I care? It is the outside populations themselves that would. They don't care to fall victim to Terrestrial diseases."

"Terrestrial diseases!" Shekt scowled. "It is a nonsensical notion that should be eradicated. We are not carriers of death. Are you dead for having been among us?"

"To be sure," smiled Ennius, "I do everything to prevent undue contact."

"It is because you yourself fear the propaganda created, after all, only by the stupidity of your own bigots."

"Why, Shekt, no scientific basis at all to the theory that Earthmen are themselves radioactive?"

"Yes, certainly they are. How could they avoid it? So are you. So is everyone on every one of a hundred million planets of the Empire. We are more so, I grant you, but scarcely enough to harm anyone."

"But the average man of the Galaxy believes the opposite, I am afraid, and is not desirous of finding out by experiment. Besides——"

"Besides, you're going to say, we're different. We're not human beings, because we mutate more rapidly, due to atomic radiation, and have therefore changed in many ways. . . . Also not proven."

"But believed."

"And as long as it is so believed, Procurator, and as long as we of Earth are treated as pariahs, you are going to find in us the characteristics to which you object. If you push us intolerably, is it to be wondered at that we push back? Hating us as you do, can you complain that we hate in our turn? No, no, we are far more the offended than the offending."

Ennius was chagrined at the anger he had raised. Even the best of these Earthmen, he thought, have the same blind spot, the same feeling of Earth versus all the universe.

He said tactfully, "Shekt, forgive my boorishness, will you? Take my youth and boredom as excuse. You see before you a poor man, a young fellow of forty—and forty is the age of a babe in the professional civil service—who is grinding out his apprenticeship here on Earth. It may be years before the fools in the Bureau of the Outer Provinces remember me long enough to promote me to something less deadly. So we are both prisoners of Earth and both citizens of the great world of the mind in which there is distinction of neither planet nor physical characteristics. Give me your hand, then, and let us be friends."

The lines on Shekt's face smoothed out, or, more exactly, were replaced by others more indicative of good humor. He laughed outright. "The words are the words of a suppliant, but the tone is still that of the Imperial career diplomat. You are a poor actor, Procurator."

"Then counter me by being a good teacher, and tell me of this Synapsifier of yours."

Shekt started visibly and frowned. "What, you have heard of the instrument? You are then a physicist as well as an administrator?"

"All knowledge is my province. But seriously, Shekt, I would really like to know."

The physicist peered closely at the other and seemed doubtful. He rose and his gnarled hand lifted to his lip, which it pinched thoughtfully. "I scarcely know where to begin."

"Well, Stars above, if you are considering at which point in the mathematical theory you are to begin, I'll simplify your problem. Abandon them all. I know nothing of your functions and tensors and what not."

Shekt's eyes twinkled. "Well, then, to stick to descriptive matter only, it is simply a device intended to increase the learning capacity of a human being."

"Of a human being? Really! And does it work?"

"I wish we knew. Much more work is necessary. I'll give you the essentials, Procurator, and you can judge for yourself. The nervous system in man—and in animals—is composed of neuroprotein material. Such material consists of huge molecules in very precarious electrical balance. The slightest stimulus will upset one, which will right itself by upsetting the next, which will repeat the process, until the brain is reached. The brain itself is an immense grouping of similar molecules which are connected among themselves in all possible ways. Since there are something like ten to the twentieth power—that is, a one with twenty zeros after it—such neuroproteins in the brain, the number of possible combinations are of the order of factorial ten to the twentieth power. This is a number so large that if all the electrons and protons in the universe were made universes themselves, and all the electrons and protons in all of these new universes again made universes, then all the electrons and protons in all the universes so created would still be nothing in comparison. . . . Do you follow me?"

"Not a word, thank the Stars. If I even attempted to, I should bark like a dog for sheer pain of the intellect."

"Hmp. Well, in any case, what we call nerve impulses are merely the progressive electronic unbalance that proceeds along the nerves to the brain and then from the brain back along the nerves. Do you get that?"

"Yes."

"Well, blessings on you for a genius, then. As long as this impulse continues along a nerve cell, it proceeds at a rapid rate, since the neuroproteins are practically in contact. However, nerve cells are limited in extent, and between each nerve cell and the next is a very thin partition of non-nervous tissue. In other words, two adjoining nerve cells do not actually connect with each other."

"Ah," said Ennius, "and the nervous impulse must jump the barrier."

"Exactly! The partition drops the strength of the impulse and slows the speed of its transmission according to the square of the width thereof. This holds for the brain as well. But imagine, now, if some means could be found to lower the dialectric constant of this partition between the cells."

"The what constant?"

"The insulating strength of the partition. That's all I mean. If that were decreased, the impulse would jump the gap more easily. You would think faster and learn faster."

"Well, then, I come back to my original question. Does it work?"

"I have tried the instrument on animals."

"And with what result?"

"Why, that most die very quickly of denaturation of brain protein—coagulation, in other words, like hard-boiling an egg."

Ennius winced. "There is something ineffably cruel about the cold-bloodedness of science. What about those that didn't die?"

"Not conclusive, since they're not human beings. The burden of the evidence seems to be favorable, for them. . . . But I need humans. You see, it is a matter of the natural electronic properties of the individual brain. Each brain gives rise to microcurrents of a certain type. None are exactly duplicates. They're like fingerprints, or the blood-vessel patterns of the retina. If anything, they're even more individual. The treatment, I believe, must take that into account, and, if I am right, there will be no more denaturation. . . . But I have no human beings on whom to experiment. I ask for volunteers, but——" He spread his hands.

"I certainly don't blame them, old man," said Ennius. "But seriously, should the instrument be perfected, what do you intend doing with it?"

The physicist shrugged. "That's not for me to say. It would be up to the Grand Council, of course."

"You would not consider making the invention available to the Empire?"

"I? I have no objections at all. But only the Grand Council has jurisdiction over——"

"Oh," said Ennius with impatience, "the devil with your Grand Council. I have had dealings with them before. Would *you* be willing to talk to them at the proper time?"

"Why, what influence could I possibly have?"

"You might tell them that if Earth could produce a Synapsifier that would be applicable to human beings in complete safety, and if the device were made available to the Galaxy, then some of the restrictions on emigration to other planets might be broken down."

"What," said Shekt sarcastically, "and risk epidemics and our differentness and our non-humanity?"

"You might," said Ennius quietly, "even be removed *en masse* to another planet. Consider it."

The door opened at this point and a young lady brushed her way in past the book-film cabinet. She destroyed the musty atmosphere of the cloistered study with an automatic breath of spring. At the sight of a stranger she reddened slightly and turned.

"Come in, Pola," called Shekt hastily. "My Lord," he said to Ennius, "I believe you have never met my daughter. Pola, this is Lord Ennius, Procurator of Earth."

The Procurator was on his feet with an easy gallantry that negated her first wild attempt at a curtsy.

"My dear Miss Shekt," he said, "you are an ornament I did not believe Earth capable of producing. You would, indeed, be an ornament on any world I can think of."

He took Pola's hand, which was quickly and somewhat bashfully extended to meet his gesture. For a moment Ennius made as if to kiss it, in the courtly fashion of the past generation, but the intention, if such it was, never came to fruition. Half lifted, the hand was released—a trace too quickly, perhaps.

Pola, with the slightest of frowns, said, "I'm overwhelmed at your kindness, my Lord, to a simple girl of Earth. You are brave and gallant to dare infection as you do."

Shekt cleared his throat and interrupted. "My daughter, Procurator, is completing her studies at the University of Chica and is obtaining some needed field credits by spending two days a week in my laboratory as a technician. A competent girl, and though I say it with the pride of a father, she may someday sit in my place."

"Father," said Pola gently, "I have some important information for you." She hesitated.

"Shall I leave?" said Ennius quietly.

"No, no," said Shekt. "What is it, Pola?"

The girl said, "We have a volunteer, Father."

Shekt stared, almost stupidly. "For the Synapsifier?"

"So he says."

"Well," said Ennius, "I bring you good fortune, I see."

"So it would seem." Shekt turned to his daughter. "Tell him to wait. Take him to Room C, and I'll be with him soon."

He turned to Ennius after Pola left. "Will you excuse me, Procurator?"

"Certainly. How long does the operation take?"

"It's a matter of hours, I'm afraid. Do you wish to watch?"

"I can imagine nothing more gruesome, my dear Shekt. I'll be in the State House till tomorrow. Will you tell me the result?"

Shekt seemed relieved. "Yes, certainly."

"Good. . . . And think over what I said about your Synapsifier. Your new royal road to knowledge."

Ennius left, less at ease than when he had arrived; his knowledge no greater, his fears much increased.

Five: THE INVOLUNTARY VOLUNTEER

Once alone, Dr. Shekt, quietly and cautiously, touched the summoner, and a young technician entered hurriedly, white robe sparkling, long brown hair carefully bound back.

Dr. Shekt said, "Has Pola told you——"

"Yes, Dr. Shekt. I've observed him through the visiplate, and he must undoubtedly be a legitimate volunteer. He's certainly not a subject sent in the usual manner."

"Ought I refer to the Council, do you suppose?"

"I don't know what to advise. The Council wouldn't approve of any ordinary communication. Any beam can be tapped, you know." Then, eagerly, "Suppose I get rid of him. I can tell him we need men under thirty. The subject is easily thirty-five."

"No, no. I'd better see him." Shekt's mind was a cold whirl. So far things had been most judiciously handled. Just enough information to lend a spurious frankness, but no more. And now an actual volunteer—and immediately after Ennius's visit. Was there a connection? Shekt himself had but the vaguest knowledge of the giant misty forces that were now beginning to wrestle back and forth across the blasted face of Earth. But, in a way, he knew enough. Enough to feel himself at the mercy of them, and certainly more than any of the Ancients suspected he knew.

Yet what could he do, since his life was doubly in danger?

Ten minutes later Dr. Shekt was peering helplessly at the gnarled farmer standing before him, cap in hand, head half averted, as though attempting to avoid a too-close scrutiny. His age, thought Shekt, was certainly under forty, but the hard life of the soil was no flatterer of men. The man's cheeks were reddened beneath the leathery brown, and there were distinct traces of perspiration at the hairline and the temples, though the room was cool. The man's hands were fumbling at each other.

"Now, my dear sir," said Shekt kindly, "I understand you refuse to give your name."

Arbin's was a blind stubbornness. "I was told no questions would be asked if you had a volunteer."

"Hmm. Well, is there anything at all you *would* like to say? Or do you just want to be treated immediately?"

"*Me?* Here, now?" in sudden panic. "It's not myself that's the volunteer. I didn't say anything to give that impression."

"No? You mean someone else is the volunteer?"

"Certainly. What would *I* want——"

"I understand. Is the subject, this other man, with you?"

"In a way," said Arbin cautiously.

"All right. Now, look, just tell us whatever you wish. Everything you say will be held in strict confidence, and we'll help you in whatever way we can. Agreed?"

The farmer ducked his head, as a sort of rudimentary gesture of respect. "Thank you. It's like this, sir. We have a man about the farm, a distant—uh—relative. He helps, you understand——"

Arbin swallowed with difficulty, and Shekt nodded gravely.

Arbin continued. "He's a very willing worker and a very *good* worker—we had a son, you see, but he died—and my good woman and myself, you see, need the help—she's not well—we could not get along without him, scarcely." He felt that somehow the story was a complete mess.

But the gaunt scientist nodded at him. "And this relative of yours is the one you wish treated?"

"Why, yes, I thought I had said that—but you'll pardon me if this takes me some time. You see, the poor fellow is not—exactly—right in his head." He hurried on, furiously. "He is not sick, you understand. He is not wrong so that he has to be put away. He's just *slow*. He doesn't talk, you see."

"He can't talk?" Shekt seemed startled.

"Oh—he can. It's just that he doesn't like to. He doesn't talk *well*."

The physicist looked dubious. "And you want the Synapsifier to improve his mentality, eh?"

Slowly, Arbin nodded. "If he knew a bit more, sir, why, he could do some of the work my wife can't, you see."

"He might die. Do you understand that?"

Arbin looked at him helplessly, and his fingers writhed furiously.

Shekt said, "I'd need his consent."

The farmer shook his head slowly, stubbornly. "He won't understand." Then, urgently, almost beneath his breath, "Why, look, sir, I'm sure you'll understand me. You don't look like a man who doesn't know what a hard life is. This man is getting old. It's not a question of the Sixty, you see, but what if, in the next Census, they think he's a half-wit and—and take him away? We don't like to lose him, and that's why we bring him here.

"The reason I'm trying to be secret-like is that maybe—maybe"—and Arbin's eyes swiveled involuntarily at the walls, as if to penetrate them by sheer will and detect the listeners that might be behind—"well, maybe the Ancients won't like what I'm doing. Maybe trying to save an afflicted man can be judged as against the Customs, but life is hard, sir. . . . And it would be useful to you. You *have* asked for volunteers."

"I know. Where is your relative?"

Arbin took the chance. "Out in my biwheel, if no one's found him. He wouldn't be able to take care of himself if anyone has——"

"Well, we'll hope he's safe. You and I will go out right now and bring the car around to our basement garage. I'll see to it that no one knows of his presence but ourselves and my helpers. And I assure you that you won't be in trouble with the Brotherhood."

His arm dropped in friendly fashion to Arbin's shoulder, who grinned spasmodically. To the farmer it was like a rope loosening from about his neck.

Shekt looked down at the plump, balding figure upon the couch. The patient was unconscious, breathing deeply and regularly. He had spoken unintelligibly, had understood nothing. Yet there had been none of the physical stigmata of feeble-mindedness. Reflexes had been in order, for an old man.

Old! Hmm.

He looked across at Arbin, who watched everything with a glance like a vise.

"Would you like us to take a bone analysis?"

"No," cried Arbin. Then, more softly, "I don't want anything that might be identification."

"It might help us—be safer, you know—if we knew his age," said Shekt.

"He's fifty," said Arbin shortly.

The physicist shrugged. It didn't matter. Again he looked at the sleeper. When brought in, the subject had been, or certainly seemed, dejected, withdrawn, uncaring. Even the Hypno pills had apparently aroused no suspicion. They had been offered him; there had been a quick, spasmodic smile in response, and he had swallowed them.

The technician was already rolling in the last of the rather clumsy units which together made up the Synapsifier. At the touch of a push button the polarized glass in the windows of the operating room underwent molecular rearrangement and became opaque. The only light was the white one that blazed its cold brilliance upon the patient suspended, as he was, in the multihundred-kilowatt diamagnetic field some two inches above the operating table to which he was transferred.

Arbin still sat in the dark there, understanding nothing, but determined in deadly fashion to prevent, somehow, by his presence, the harmful tricks he knew he had not the knowledge to prevent.

The physicists paid no attention to him. The electrodes were adjusted to the patient's skull. It was a long job. First there was the careful study of the skull formation by the Ullster technique that revealed the winding, tight-knit fissures. Grimly, Shekt smiled to himself. Skull fissures weren't an unalterable quantitative measure of age, but they were good enough in this case. The man was older than the claimed fifty.

And then, after a while, he did not smile. He frowned. There was something wrong with the fissures. They seemed odd—not quite . . .

For a moment he was ready to swear that the skull formation was a primitive one, a throwback, but then . . . Well, the man was subnormal in mentality. Why not?

And suddenly he exclaimed in shock, "Why, I hadn't noticed! This man has hair on his face!" He turned to Arbin. "Has he always been bearded?"

"Bearded?"

"Hair on his face! Come here! Don't you see it?"

"Yes, sir." Arbin thought rapidly. He *had* noticed it that morning and then had forgotten. "He was born like that," he said, and then weakened it by adding, "I think."

"Well, let's remove it. You don't want him going around like a brute beast, do you?"

"No, sir."

The hair came off smoothly at the application of a depilatory salve by the carefully gloved technician.

The technician said, "He has hair on his chest too, Dr. Shekt."

"Great Galaxy," said Shekt, "let me see! Why, the man is a rug! Well, let it be. It won't show with a shirt, and I want to get on with the electrodes. Let's have wires here and here, and here." Tiny pricks and the insertion of the platinum hair-lets. "Here and here."

A dozen connections, probing through skin to the fissures, through the tightness of which could be felt the delicate shadow echoes of the microcurrents that surged from cell to cell in the brain.

Carefully they watched the delicate ammeters stir and leap, as the connections were made and broken. The tiny needle-point recorders, traced their delicate spider webs across the graphed paper in irregular peaks and troughs.

Then the graphs were removed and placed on the illuminated opal glass. They bent low over it, whispering.

Arbin caught disjointed flashes: ". . . remarkably regular . . . look at the height of the quinternary peak . . . think it ought to be analyzed . . . clear enough to the eye . . ."

And then, for what seemed a long time, there was a tedious adjustment of the Synapsifier. Knobs were turned, eyes on vernier adjustments, then clamped and their readings recorded. Over and over again the various electrometers were checked and new adjustments were made necessary.

Then Shekt smiled at Arbin and said, "It will all be over very soon."

The large machinery was advanced upon the sleeper like a slow-moving and hungry monster. Four long wires were dangled to the extremities of his limbs, and a dull black pad of something that looked like hard rubber was carefully adjusted at the back of his neck and held firmly in place by clamps that fitted over the shoulders. Finally, like two giant mandibles, the opposing electrodes were parted and brought downward over the pale, pudgy head, so that each pointed at a temple.

Shekt kept his eyes firmly on the chronometer; in his other hand was the switch. His thumb moved; nothing visible happened—not even to the fear-sharpened sense of the watching Arbin. After what might have been hours, but was actually less than three minutes, Shekt's thumb moved again.

His assistant bent over the still-sleeping Schwartz hurriedly, then looked up triumphantly. "He's alive."

There remained yet several hours, during which a library of recordings were taken, to an undertone of almost wild excitement. It was well past midnight when the hypodermic was pressed home and the sleeper's eyes fluttered.

Shekt stepped back, bloodless but happy. He dabbed at his forehead with the back of a hand. "It's *all* right."

He turned to Arbin firmly. "He must stay with us a few days, sir."

The look of alarm grew madly in Arbin's eyes. "But—but——"

"No, no, you must rely on me," urgently. "He will be safe; I will stake my life on it. I *am* staking my life on it. Leave him to us; no one will see him but ourselves. If you take him with you now, he may not survive. What good will that do you? . . . And if he does die, you may have to explain the corpse to the Ancients."

It was the last that did the trick. Arbin swallowed and said, "But look, how am I to know when to come and take him? I won't give you my name!"

But it was submission. Shekt said, "I'm not asking you for your name. Come a week from today at ten in the evening. I'll be waiting for you at the door of the garage, the one we took in your biwheel at. You must believe me, man; you have nothing to fear."

It was evening when Arbin arrowed out of Chica. Twenty-four hours had passed since the stranger had pounded at his door, and in that time he had doubled his crimes against the Customs. Would he ever be safe again?

He could not help but glance over his shoulder as his biwheel sped along the empty road. Would there be someone to follow? Someone to trace him home? Or was his face already recorded? Were matchings being leisurely made somewhere in the distant files of the Brotherhood at Washenn, where all living Earthmen, together with their vital statistics, were listed, for purposes of the Sixty.

The Sixty, which must come to all Earthmen eventually. He had yet a quarter of a century before it came to him, yet he lived daily with it on Grew's account, and now on the stranger's account.

What if he never returned to Chica?

No! He and Loa could not long continue producing for three, and once they failed, their first crime, that of concealing Grew, would be discovered. And so crimes against the Customs, once begun, *must* be compounded.

Arbin knew that he would be back, despite any risk.

It was past midnight before Shekt thought of retiring, and then only because the troubled Pola insisted. Even then he did not sleep. His pillow was a subtle smothering device, his sheets a pair of maddening snarls. He arose and took his seat by the window. The city was dark now, but there on the horizon, on the side opposite the lake, was the faint trace of that blue glow of death that held sway over all but a few patches of Earth.

The activities of the hectic day just past danced madly before his mind. His first action after having persuaded the frightened farmer to leave had been to televise the State House. Ennius must have been waiting for him, for he himself had answered. He was still encased in the heaviness of the lead-impregnated clothing.

"Ah, Shekt, good evening. Your experiment is over?"

"And nearly my volunteer as well, poor man."

Ennius looked ill. "I thought well when I thought it better not to stay. You scientists are scarcely removed from murderers, it seems to me."

"He is not yet dead, Procurator, and it may be that we will save him, but——" And he shrugged his shoulders.

"I'd stick to rats exclusively henceforward, Shekt. . . . But you don't look at all your usual self, friend. Surely you, at least, must be hardened to this, even if I am not."

"I am getting old, my Lord," said Shekt simply.

"A dangerous pastime on Earth," was the dry reply. "Get you to bed, Shekt."

And so Shekt sat there, looking out at the dark city of a dying world.

For two years now the Synapsifier had been under test, and for two years he had been the slave and sport of the Society of Ancients, or the Brotherhood, as they called themselves.

He had seven or eight papers that might have been published in the *Sirian Journal of Neurophysiology*, that might have given that Galaxy-wide fame to him that he so wanted. These papers moldered in his desk. Instead there was that obscure and deliberately misleading paper in *Physical Reviews*. That was the way of the Brotherhood. Better a half-truth than a lie.

And still Ennius was inquiring. Why?

Did it fit in with other things he had learned? Was the Empire suspecting what he himself suspected?

Three times in two hundred years Earth had risen. Three times, under the banner of a claimed ancient greatness, Earth had rebelled against the Imperial garrisons. Three times they had failed—of course—and had not the Empire been, essentially, enlightened, and the Galactic Councils, by and large, statesmanlike, Earth would have been bloodily erased from the roll of inhabited planets.

But now things might be different. . . . Or *could* they be different? How far could he trust the words of a dying madman, three quarters incoherent?

What was the use? In any case, he dared do nothing. He could only wait. He was getting old, and, as Ennius had said, that was a dangerous pastime on Earth. The Sixty was almost upon him, and there were few exceptions to its inevitable grasp.

And even on this miserable, burning mud ball of Earth, he wanted to live.

He went to bed once more at that point, and just before falling asleep he wondered feebly if his call to Ennius might have been tapped by the Ancients. He did not know at the time that the Ancients had other sources of information.

It was morning before Shekt's young technician had completely made up his mind.

He admired Shekt, but he knew well that the secret treatment of a non-authorized volunteer was against the direct order of the Brotherhood. And that order had been given the status of a Custom, which made disobedience a capital offense.

He reasoned it out. After all, who *was* this man who had been treated? The campaign for volunteers had been carefully worked out. It was designed to give enough information about the Synapsifier to remove suspicion on the part of possible Imperial spies without giving any real encouragement to volunteers. The Society of Ancients sent their own men for treatment, and that was enough.

Who had sent this man, then? The Society of Ancients in secret? In order to test Shekt's reliability?

Or was Shekt a traitor? He had been closeted with someone earlier in the day—someone in bulky clothes, such as Outsiders wore in fear of radioactive poisoning.

In either case Shekt might go down in doom, and why should he himself be dragged down as well? He was a young man with nearly four decades of life before him. Why should he anticipate the Sixty?

Besides, it would mean promotion for him. . . . And Shekt was so old, the next Census would probably get him anyway, so it would involve very little harm for him. Practically none at all.

The technician had decided. His hand reached for the communicator, and he punched the combination that would lead directly to the private room of the High Minister of all Earth, who, under the Emperor and Procurator, held the power of life and death over every man on Earth.

It was evening again before the misty impressions within Schwartz's skull sharpened through the pink pain. He remembered the trip to the low, huddling structures by the lakeside, the long crouching wait in the rear of the car.

And then—what? What? His mind yanked away at the sluggish thoughts. . . . Yes, they had come for him. There was a room, with instruments and dials, and two pills. . . . That was it. They had given him pills, and he had taken them cheerfully. What had he to lose? Poisoning would have been a favor.

And then—nothing.

Wait! There had been flashes of consciousness . . . People bending over him . . . Suddenly he remembered the cold motion of a stethoscope over his chest. . . . A girl had been feeding him.

It flashed upon him that he had been operated upon and, in panic, he flung the bed sheets from him and sat up.

A girl was upon him, hands on his shoulders, forcing him back onto the pillows. She spoke soothingly, but he did not understand her. He tensed himself against the slim arms, but uselessly. He had no strength.

He held his hands before his face. They seemed normal. He moved his legs and heard them brush against the sheets. They couldn't have been amputated.

He turned to the girl and said, without much hope, "Can *you* understand me? Do you know where I am?" He scarcely recognized his own voice.

The girl smiled and suddenly poured out a rapid patter of liquid sound. Schwartz groaned. Then an older man entered, the one who had given him the pills. The man and the girl spoke together, the girl turning to him after a while, pointing to his lips and making little gestures of invitation to him.

"What?" he said.

She nodded eagerly, her pretty face glowing with pleasure, until, despite himself, Schwartz felt glad to look at it.

"You want me to talk?" he asked.

The man sat down upon his bed and motioned him to open his mouth. He said, "Ah-h-h," and Schwartz repeated "Ah-h-h" while the man's fingers massaged Schwartz's Adam's apple.

"What's the matter?" said Schwartz peevishly, when the pressure was removed. "Are you surprised I can talk? What do you think I am?"

The days passed, and Schwartz learned a few things. The man was Dr. Shekt—the first human being he knew by name since he had stepped over the rag doll. The girl was his daughter, Pola. Schwartz found that he no longer needed to shave. The hair on his face never grew. It frightened him. Did it ever grow?

His strength came back quickly. They were letting him put on clothes and walk about now, and were feeding him something more than mush.

Was his trouble amnesia, then? Were they treating him for that? Was all this world normal and natural, while the world he thought he remembered was only the fantasy of an amnesic brain?

And they never let him step out of the room, not even into the corridor. Was he a prisoner, then? Had he committed a crime?

There never can be a man so lost as one who is lost in the vast and intricate corridors of his own lonely mind, where none may reach and none may save. There never was a man so helpless as one who cannot remember.

Pola amused herself by teaching him words. He was not at all amazed at the ease with which he picked them up and remembered. He remembered that he had had a trick memory in the past; that memory, at least, seemed accurate. In two days he could understand simple sentences. In three he could make himself understood.

On the third day, however, he did become amazed. Shekt taught him numbers and set him problems. Schwartz would give answers, and Shekt would look at a timing device and record with rapid strokes of his stylus. But then Shekt explained the term "logarithm" to him and asked for the logarithm of two.

Schwartz picked his words carefully. His vocabulary was still minute and he reinforced it with gestures. "I—not—say. Answer—not—number."

Shekt nodded his head excitedly and said, "Not number. Not this, not that; part this, part that."

Schwartz understood quite well that Shekt had confirmed his statement that the answer was not an even number but a fraction and therefore said, "Point three zero one zero three—and—more—numbers."

"Enough!"

Then came the amazement. How had he known the answer to that? Schwartz was certain that he had never heard of logarithms before, yet in his mind the answer had come as soon as the question was put. He had no idea of the process by which it had been calculated. It was as if his mind were an independent entity, using him only as its mouthpiece.

Or had he once been a mathematician, in the days before his amnesia?

He found it exceedingly difficult to wait the days out. Increasingly he felt he must venture out into the world and force an answer from it somehow. He could never learn in the prison of this room, where (the thought suddenly came to him) he was but a medical specimen.

The chance came on the sixth day. They were beginning to trust him too much, and one time when Shekt left he did not lock the door. Where usually the door so neatly closed itself that the very crack of its joining the wall became invisible, this time a quarter inch of space showed.

He waited to make sure Shekt was not returning on the instant, and then slowly put his hand over the little gleaming light as he had seen them often do. Smoothly and silently the door slid open. . . . The corridor was empty.

And so Schwartz "escaped."

How was he to know that for the six days of his residence there the Society of Ancients had its agents watching the hospital, his room, himself?

Six: APPREHENSION IN THE NIGHT

The Procurator's palace was scarcely less a fairyland at night. The evening flowers (none native to Earth) opened their fat white blossoms in festoons that extended their delicate fragrance to the very walls of the palace. Under the polarized light of the moon, the artificial silicate strands woven cleverly into the stainless aluminum alloy of the palace structure sparked a faint violet against the metallic sheen of their surroundings.

Ennius looked at the stars. They were the real beauty to him, since they were the Empire.

Earth's sky was of an intermediate type. It had not the unbearable glory of the skies of the Central Worlds, where star elbowed star in such blinding competition that the black of night was nearly lost in a coruscant explosion of light. Nor did it possess the lonely grandeur of the skies of the Periphery, where the unrelieved blackness was broken at great intervals by the dimness of an orphaned star—with the milky lens shape of the Galaxy spreading across the sky, the individual stars thereof lost in diamond dust.

On Earth two thousand stars were visible at one time. Ennius could see Sirius, round which circled one of the ten most populous planets of the Empire. There was Arcturus, capital of the sector of his birth. The sun of Trantor, the Empire's capital world, was lost somewhere in the Milky Way. Even under a telescope it was just part of a general blaze.

He felt a soft hand on his shoulder, and his own went up to meet it.

"Flora?" he whispered.

"It had better be," came his wife's half-amused voice. "Do you know that you haven't slept since you returned from Chica? Do you know further that it is almost dawn? . . . Shall I have breakfast sent out here?"

"Why not?" He smiled fondly up at her and felt in the darkness for the brown ringlet that hovered next her cheek. He tugged at it. "And must you wait up with me and shadow the most beautiful eyes in the Galaxy?"

She freed her hair and replied gently, "You are trying to shadow them yourself with your sugar syrup, but I've seen you this way before and am not in the tiniest hoodwinked. What worries you tonight, dear?"

"Why, that which always worries me. That I have buried you here uselessly, when there's not a viceregal society in the Galaxy you could not grace."

"Besides that! Come, Ennius, I will not be played with."

Ennius shook his head in the shadows and said, "I don't know. I think an accumulation of little puzzling things has finally sickened me. There's the matter of Shekt and his Synapsifier. And there's this archaeologist, Arvardan, and his theories. And other things, other things. Oh, what's the use, Flora—I'm doing no good here at all."

"Surely this time of the morning isn't quite the moment for putting your morale to the test."

But Ennius was speaking through clenched teeth. "These Earthmen! Why should so few be such a burden to the Empire? Do you remember, Flora, when I was first appointed to the Procuracy, the warnings I received from old Faroul, the last Procurator, as to the difficulties of the position? . . . He was right. If anything, he did not go far enough in his warnings. Yet I laughed at him at the time and privately thought him the victim of his own senile incapacity. I was young, active, daring. I would do better . . ." He paused, lost in himself, then continued, apparently at a disconnected point. "Yet so many independent pieces of evidence seem to show that these Earthmen are once again being misled into dreams of rebellion."

He looked up at his wife. "Do you know that it is the doctrine of the Society of Ancients that Earth was at one time the sole home of Humanity, that it is the appointed center of the race, the true representation of Man?"

"Why, so Arvardan told us two evenings ago, didn't he?" It was always best at these times to let him talk himself out.

"Yes, so he did," said Ennius gloomily, "but even so, he spoke only of the past. The Society of Ancients speaks of the future as well. Earth, once more, they say, will be the center of the race. They even claim that this mythical Second Kingdom of Earth is at hand; they warn that the Empire will be destroyed in a general catastrophe which will leave Earth triumphant in all its pristine glory"—and his voice shook—"as a backward, barbarous, soil-sick world. Three times before this same nonsense has raised rebellion, and the destruction brought down upon Earth has never served in the least to shake their stupid faith."

"They are but poor creatures," said Flora, "these men of Earth. What should they have, if not their Faith? They are certainly robbed of everything else—of a decent world, of a decent life. They are even robbed of the dignity of acceptance on a basis of equality by the rest of the Galaxy. So they retire to their dreams. Can you blame them?"

"Yes, I can blame them," cried Ennius with energy. "Let them turn from their dreams and fight for assimilation. They don't deny they are different. They simply wish to replace 'worse' by 'better,' and you can't expect the rest of the Galaxy to let them do that. Let them abandon their cliquishness, their outdated and offensive 'Customs.' Let them be *men*, and they will be considered men. Let them be Earthmen and they will be considered only as such.

"But never mind that. For instance, what's going on with the Synapsifier? Now there's a little thing that is keeping me from sleep." Ennius frowned thoughtfully at the dullness which was overcoming the polished darkness of the eastern sky.

"The Synapsifier? . . . Why, isn't that the instrument Dr. Arvardan spoke of at dinner? Did you go to Chica to see about that?"

Ennius nodded.

"And what did you find out there?"

"Why, nothing at all," said Ennius. "I know Shekt. I know him well. I can tell when he's at ease; I can tell when he isn't. I tell you, Flora, that man was dying of apprehension all the time he was speaking to me. And when I left he broke into a sweat of thankfulness. It is an unhappy mystery, Flora."

"But will the machine work?"

"Am I a neurophysicist? Shekt says it will not. He called me up to tell me that a volunteer was nearly killed by it. But I don't believe that. He was excited! He was more than that. He was triumphant! His volunteer had lived and the experiment had been successful, or I've never seen a happy man in my life. . . . Now why do you suppose he lied to me, then? Do you suppose that it can be creating a race of geniuses?"

"But then why keep it secret?"

"Ah! Why? It isn't obvious to you. Why has Earth failed in its rebellions? There are fairly tremendous odds against it, aren't there? Increase the average intelligence of the Earthman. Double it. Triple it. And where may your odds be then?"

"Oh, Ennius."

"We may be in the position of apes attacking human beings. What price numerical odds?"

"You're really jumping at shadows. They couldn't hide a thing like that. You can always have the Bureau of Outer Provinces send in a few psychologists and keep testing random samples of Earthmen. Surely any abnormal rise in I.Q. could be detected instantly."

"Yes. I suppose so. . . . But that may not be it. I'm not sure of anything, Flora, except that a rebellion is in the cards. Something like the Uprising of 750, except that it will probably be worse."

"Are we prepared for it? I mean, if you're so certain——"

"Prepared?" Ennius's laughter was a bark. "*I* am. The garrison is in readiness and fully supplied. Whatever can possibly be done with the material at hand, I have done. But, Flora, I don't want to have a rebellion. I don't want my Procuracy to go down in history as the Procuracy of the Rebellion. I don't want my name linked with death and slaughter. I'll be decorated for it, but a century from now the history books will call me a bloody tyrant. What about the Viceroy of Santanni in the sixth century? Could he have done other than he did, though millions died? He was honored then, but who has a good word for him now? *I* would rather be known as the man who prevented a rebellion and saved the worthless lives of twenty million fools." He sounded quite hopeless about it.

"Are you so sure you can't, Ennius—even yet?" She sat down beside him and brushed her finger tips along the line of his jaw.

He caught them and held them tightly. "How can I? Everything works against me. The Bureau itself rushes into the struggle on the side of the fanatics of Earth by sending this Arvardan here."

"But, dear, I don't see that this archaeologist will do anything so awful. I'll admit he sounds like a faddist, but what harm can he do?"

"Why, isn't it plain? He wants to be allowed to prove that Earth *is* the original home of Humanity. He wants to bring scientific authority to the aid of subversion."

"Then stop him."

"I can't. There you have it, frankly. There's a theory about that viceroys can do anything, but that just isn't so. That man, Arvardan, has a writ of permission from the Bureau of Outer Provinces. It is approved by the Emperor. That supersedes me completely. I could do nothing without appealing to the Central Council, and that would take months. . . . And what reasons could I give? If I tried to stop him by force, on the other hand, it would be an act of rebellion; and you know how ready the Central Council is to remove any executive they think is overstepping the line, ever since the Civil War of the eighties. And then what? I'd be replaced by someone who wouldn't be aware of the situation at all, and Arvardan would go ahead anyway.

"And that *still* isn't the worst, Flora. Do you know how he intends to prove the antiquity of Earth? Suppose you guess."

Flora laughed gently. "You're making fun of me, Ennius. How should I guess? I'm no archaeologist. I suppose he'll try to dig up old statues or bones and date them by their radioactivity or something like that."

"I wish it were like that. What Arvardan intends to do, he told me yesterday, is to enter the radioactive areas on Earth. He intends to find human artifacts there, show that they exist from a time previous to that at which Earth's soil became radioactive—since he insists the radioactivity is man-made—and date it in that fashion."

"But that's almost what I said."

"Do you know what it means to enter the radioactive areas? They're Forbidden. It's one of the strongest Customs these Earthmen have. No one can enter the Forbidden Areas, and all radioactive areas are Forbidden."

"But then that's good. Arvardan will be stopped by the men of Earth themselves."

"Oh, fine. He'll be stopped by the High Minister! And then how will we ever convince him that all this was not a Government-sponsored project, that the Empire is not conniving at deliberate sacrilege?"

"The High Minister can't be that touchy."

"Can't he?" Ennius reared back and stared at his wife. The night had lightened to a slatiness in which she was just visible. "You have the most touching naïveté. He certainly *can* be that touchy. Do you know what happened—oh, about fifty years ago? I'll tell you, and then you can judge for yourself.

"Earth, it so happens, will allow no outward sign of Imperial domination on their world because of their insistence that Earth is the rightful ruler of the Galaxy. But it so happened that young Stannell II—the boy emperor who was somewhat insane and who was removed by assassination after a reign of two years; you remember!—ordered that the Emperor's insignia be raised in their Council Chamber at Washenn. In itself the order was reasonable, since the insignia is present in every planetary Council Chamber in the Galaxy as a symbol of the Imperial unity. But what happened in this case? The day the insignia was raised, the town became a mass of riots.

"The lunatics of Washenn tore down the insignia and took up arms against the garrison. Stannell II was sufficiently mad to demand that his order be complied with if it meant the slaughter of every Earthman alive, but he was assassinated before that could be put into effect, and Edard, his successor, canceled the original order. All was peace again."

"You mean," said Flora incredulously, "that the Imperial insignia was not replaced?"

"I mean that exactly. By the Stars, Earth is the only one of the millions and millions of planets in the Empire that has no insignia in its Council Chamber. This miserable planet we are on now. And if even today we were to try again, they would fight to the last man to prevent us. And you ask me if they're touchy. I tell you they're mad."

There was silence in the slowly graying light of dawn, until Flora's voice sounded again, little and unsure of itself.

"Ennius?"

"Yes."

"You're not just concerned about the rebellion that you're expecting because of its effect on your reputation. I wouldn't be your wife if I couldn't half read your thoughts, and it seems to me that you expect something actually dangerous to the Empire. . . . You shouldn't hide anything from me, Ennius. You're afraid these Earthmen will *win.*"

"Flora, I can't talk about it." There was something tortured in his eyes. "It isn't even a hunch. . . . Maybe four years on this world is too long for any sane man. But why are these Earthmen so confident?"

"How do you know they are?"

"Oh, they are. I have *my* sources of information too. After all, they've been crushed three times. They *can't* have illusions left. Yet they face two hundred million worlds, each one singly stronger than they, and they are confident. Can they really be so firm in their faith in some Destiny or some supernatural Force—something that has meaning only to them? Maybe—maybe—maybe——"

"Maybe what, Ennius?"

"Maybe they have their weapons."

"Weapons that will allow one world to defeat two hundred millions? You *are* panicky. No weapon could do that."

"I have already mentioned the Synapsifier."

"And I have told you how to take care of that. Do you know of any other type of weapon they could use?"

Reluctantly, "No."

"Exactly. There isn't any such weapon possible. Now I'll tell you what to do, dear. Why don't you get in touch with the High Minister and, in earnest of your good faith, warn him of Arvardan's plans? Urge, unofficially, that he not be granted permission. This will remove any suspicion—or should—that the Imperial Government has any hand in this silly violation of their customs. At the same time you will have stopped Arvardan without having appeared in the mess yourself. Then have the Bureau send out two good psychologists—or, better, ask for four, so they'll be sure to send at least two—and have them check on the Synapsifier possibility. . . . And anything else can be taken care of by our soldiers, while we allow posterity to take care of itself.

"Now why don't you sleep right here? We can put the chair back down, you can use my fur piece as a blanket, and I'll have a breakfast tray wheeled out when you awake. Things will seem different in the sun."

And so it was that Ennius, after waking the night through, fell asleep five minutes before sunrise.

Thus it was eight hours later that the High Minister first learned of Bel Arvardan and his mission from the Procurator himself.

Seven: CONVERSATION WITH MADMEN?

As for Arvardan, he was concerned only with making holiday. His ship, *Ophiuchus,* was not to be expected for at least a month, therefore he had a month to spend as lavishly as he might wish.

So it was that on the sixth day after his arrival at Everest, Bel Arvardan left his host and took passage on the Terrestrial Air Transport Company's largest jet Stratospheric, traveling between Everest and the Terrestrial capital, Washenn.

If he took a commercial liner, rather than the speedy cruiser placed at his service by Ennius, it was done deliberately, out of the reasonable curiosity of a stranger and an archaeologist toward the ordinary life of men inhabiting such a planet as Earth.

And for another reason too.

Arvardan was from the Sirian Sector, notoriously the sector above all others in the Galaxy where anti-Terrestrian prejudice was strong. Yet he had always liked to think he had not succumbed to that prejudice himself. As a scientist, as an archaeologist, he couldn't afford to. Of course he had grown into the habit of thinking of Earthmen in certain set caricature types, and even now the word "Earthman" seemed an ugly one to him. But he wasn't really prejudiced.

At least he didn't think so. For instance, if an Earthman had ever wished to join an expedition of his or work for him in any capacity—and had the training and the ability—he would be accepted. If there were an opening for him, that was. And if the other members of the expedition didn't mind too much. That was the rub. Usually the fellow workers objected, and then what could you do?

He pondered the matter. Now certainly he would have no objection to eating with an Earthman, or even bunking with one in case of need—assuming the Earthman were reasonably clean, and healthy. In fact, he would in all ways treat him as he would treat anyone else, he thought. Yet there was no denying that he would always be conscious of the fact that an Earthman was an Earthman. He couldn't help that. That was the result of a childhood immersed in an atmosphere of bigotry so complete that it was almost invisible, so entire that you accepted its axioms as second nature. Then you left it and saw it for what it was when you looked back.

But here was his chance to test himself. He was in a plane with only Earthmen about him, and he felt perfectly natural, almost. Well, just a little self-conscious.

Arvardan looked about at the undistinguished and normal faces of his fellow passengers. They were supposed to be different, these Earthmen, but could he have told these from ordinary men if he had met them casually in a crowd? He didn't think so. The women weren't bad-looking . . . His brows knit. Of course even tolerance must draw the line somewhere. Intermarriage, for instance, was quite unthinkable.

The plane itself was, in his eyes, a small affair of imperfect construction. It was, of course, atomic-powered, but the application of the principle was far from efficient. For one thing, the power unit was not well shielded. Then it occurred to Arvardan that the presence of stray gamma rays and a high neutron density in the atmosphere might well strike Earthmen as less important than it might strike others.

Then the view caught his eyes. From the dark wine-purple of the extreme stratosphere, Earth presented a fabulous appearance. Beneath him the vast and misted land areas in sight (obscured here and there by the patches of sun-bright clouds) showed a desert orange. Behind them, slowly receding from the fleeing stratoliner, was the soft and fuzzy night line, within whose dark shadow there was the sparking of the radioactive areas.

His attention was drawn from the window by the laughter among the others. It seemed to center about an elderly couple, comfortably stout and all smiles.

Arvardan nudged his neighbor. "What's going on?"

His neighbor paused to say, "They've been married forty years, and they're making the Grand Tour."

"The Grand Tour?"

"You know. All around the Earth."

The elderly man, flushed with pleasure, was recounting in voluble fashion his experiences and impressions. His wife joined in periodically, with meticulous corrections involving completely unimportant points; these being given and taken in the best of humor. To all this the audience listened with the greatest attention, so that to Arvardan it seemed that Earthmen were as warm and human as any people in the Galaxy.

And then someone asked, "And when is it that you're scheduled for the Sixty?"

"In about a month," came the ready, cheerful answer. "Sixteenth November."

"Well," said the questioner, "I hope you have a nice day for it. My father reached his Sixty in a damned pouring rain. I've never seen one like it since. I was going with him—you know, a fellow likes company on a day like that—and he complained about the rain every step of the way. We had an open biwheel, you see, and we got soaked. 'Listen,' I said, 'what are you complaining about, Dad? *I've* got to come back.'"

There was a general howl of laughter which the anniversary couple were not backward in joining. Arvardan, however, felt plunged in horror as a distinct and uncomfortable suspicion entered his mind.

He said to the man sharing his seat, "This Sixty, this subject of conversation here—I take it they're referring to euthanasia. I mean, you're put out of the way when you reach your sixtieth birthday, aren't you?"

Arvardan's voice faded somewhat as his neighbor choked off the last of his chuckles to turn in his seat and favor the questioner with a long and suspicious stare. Finally he said, "Well, what do you think he meant?"

Arvardan made an indefinite gesture with his hand and smiled rather foolishly. He had known of the custom, but only academically. Something in a book. Something discussed in a scientific paper. But it was now borne in upon him that it actually applied to living beings, that the men and women surrounding him could, by custom, live only to sixty.

The man next to him was still staring. "Hey, fella, where you from? Don't they know about the Sixty in your home town?"

"We call it the 'Time,'" said Arvardan feebly. "I'm from back there." He jerked his thumb hard over his shoulder, and after an additional quarter minute the other withdrew that hard, questioning stare.

Arvardan's lips quirked. These people were suspicious. That facet of the caricature, at least, was authentic.

The elderly man was talking again. "She's coming with me," he said, nodding toward his genial wife. "She's not due for about three months after that, but there's no point in her waiting, she thinks, and we might as well go together. Isn't that it, Chubby?"

"Oh yes," she said, and giggled rosily. "Our children are all married and have homes of their own. I'd just be a bother to them. Besides, I couldn't enjoy the time anyway without the old fellow—so we'll just leave off together."

Whereupon the entire list of passengers seemed to engage themselves in a simultaneous arithmetical calculation of the time remaining to each—a process involving conversion factors from months to days that occasioned several disputes among the married couples involved.

One small fellow with tight clothes and a determined expression said fiercely, "I've got exactly twelve years, three months, and four days left. Twelve years, three months, and four days. Not a day more, not a day less."

Which someone qualified by saying, reasonably, "Unless you die first, of course."

"Nonsense," was the immediate reply. "I have no intention of dying first. Do I look like the sort of man who would die first? I'm living twelve years, three months, and four days, and there's not a man here with the hardihood to deny it." And he looked very fierce indeed.

A slim young man took a long, dandyish cigarette from between his lips to say darkly, "It's well for them that can calculate it out to a day. There's many a man living past his time."

"Ah, surely," said another, and there was a general nod and a rather inchoate air of indignation arose.

"Not," continued the young man, interspersing his cigarette puffs with a complicated flourish intended to remove the ash, "that I see any objection to a man—or woman—wishing to continue on past their birthday to the next Council day, particularly if they have some business to clean up. It's these sneaks and parasites that try to go past to the next Census, eating the food of the next generation——" He seemed to have a personal grievance there.

Arvardan interposed gently, "But aren't the ages of everyone registered? They can't very well pass their birthday too far, can they?"

A general silence followed, admixtured not a little with contempt at the foolish idealism expressed. Someone said at last, in diplomatic fashion, as though attempting to conclude the subject, "Well, there isn't much point living past the Sixty, I suppose."

"Not if you're a farmer," shot back another vigorously. "After you've been working in the fields for half a century, you'd be crazy not to be glad to call it off. How about the administrators, though, and the businessmen?"

Finally the elderly man, whose fortieth wedding anniversary had begun the conversation, ventured his own opinion, emboldened perhaps by the fact that, as a current victim of the Sixty, he had nothing to lose.

"As to that," he said, "it depends on who you know." And he winked with a sly innuendo. "I knew a man once who was sixty the year after the 810 Census and lived till the 820 Census caught him. He was sixty-nine before he left off. Sixty-nine! Think of that!"

"How did he manage that?"

"He had a little money, and his brother was one of the Society of Ancients. There's nothing you can't do if you've got that combination."

There was general approval of that sentiment.

"Listen," said the young man with the cigarette emphatically, "I had an uncle who lived a year past—just a year. He was just one of these selfish guys who don't feel like going, you know. A lot he cared for the rest of us. . . . And I didn't know about it, you see, or I would have reported him, believe me, because a guy should go when it's his time. It's only fair to the next generation. Anyway, he got caught all right, and the first thing *I* knew, the Brotherhood calls on me and my brother and wants to know how come we didn't report him. I said, hell, I didn't know anything about it; nobody in my family knew anything about it. I said we hadn't seen him in ten years. My old man backed us up. But we got fined five hundred credits just the same. That's when you don't have any pull."

The look of discomposure on Arvardan's face was growing. Were these people madmen to accept death so—to resent their friends and relatives who tried to escape death? Could he, by accident, be on a ship carrying a cargo of lunatics to asylum—or euthanasia? Or were these simply Earthmen?

His neighbor was scowling at him again, and his voice broke in on Arvardan's thoughts. "Hey fella, where's 'back there'?"

"Pardon me?"

"I said—where are you from? You said 'back there.' What's 'back there'? Hey?"

Arvardan found the eyes of all upon him now, each with its own sudden spark of suspicion in it. Did they think him a member of this Society of Ancients of theirs? Had his questioning seemed the cajolery of an *agent provocateur?*

So he met that by saying, in a burst of frankness, "I'm not from anywhere on Earth. I'm Bel Arvardan from Baronn, Sirius Sector. What's your name?" And he held out his hand.

He might as well have dropped an atomic explosive capsule into the middle of the plane.

The first silent horror on every face turned rapidly into angry, bitter hostility that flamed at him. The man who had shared his seat rose stiffly and crowded into another, where the pair of occupants squeezed closely together to make room for him.

Faces turned away. Shoulders surrounded him, hemmed him in. For a moment Arvardan burned with indignation. Earthmen to treat *him* so. *Earthmen!* He had held out the hand of friendship to them. He, a Sirian, had condescended to treat with them and they had rebuffed him.

And then, with an effort, he relaxed. It was obvious that bigotry was never a one-way operation, that hatred bred hatred!

He was conscious of a presence beside him, and he turned toward it resentfully. "Yes?"

It was the young man with the cigarette. He was lighting a new one as he spoke. "Hello," he said. "My name's Creen. . . . Don't let those jerks get you."

"No one's getting me," said Arvardan shortly. He was not too pleased with the company, nor was he in the mood for patronizing advice from an Earthman.

But Creen was not trained to the detection of the more delicate nuances. He puffed his cigarette to life in man-sized drags and tapped its ashes over the arm of the seat into the middle aisle.

"Provincials!" he whispered with contempt. "Just a bunch of farmers. . . . They lack the Galactic view. Don't bother with them. . . . Now you take me. I got a different philosophy. Live and let live, I say. I got nothing against Outsiders. If they want to be friendly with me, I'll be friendly with them. What the hell—— They can't help being an Outsider just like I can't help being an Earthman. Don't you think I'm right?" And he tapped Arvardan familiarly on the wrist.

Arvardan nodded and felt a crawling sensation at the other's touch. Social contact with a man who felt resentful over losing a chance to bring about his uncle's death was not pleasant, quite regardless of planetary origin.

Creen leaned back. "Heading for Chica? What did you say your name was? Albadan?"

"Arvardan. Yes, I'm going to Chica."

"That's my home town. Best damned city on Earth. Going to stay there long?"

"Maybe. I haven't made any plans."

"Umm. . . . Say, I hope you don't object to my saying that I've been noticing your shirt. Mind if I take a close look? Made in Sirius, huh?"

"Yes, it is."

"It's very good material. Can't get anything like that on Earth. . . . Say, bud, you wouldn't have a spare shirt like that in your luggage, would you? I'd pay for it if you wanted to sell it. It's a snappy number."

Arvardan shook his head emphatically. "Sorry, but I don't have much of a wardrobe. I am planning to buy clothes here on Earth as I go along."

"I'll pay you fifty credits," said Creen. . . . Silence. He added, with a touch of resentment, "That's a good price."

"A very good price," said Arvardan, "but, as I told you, I have no shirts to sell."

"Well . . ." Creen shrugged. "Expect to stay on Earth quite a while, I suppose?"

"Maybe."

"What's your line of business?"

The archaeologist allowed irritation to rise to the surface. "Look, Mr. Creen, if you don't mind, I'm a little tired and would like to take a nap. Is that all right with you?"

Creen frowned. "What's the matter with you? Don't your kind believe in being civil to people? I'm just asking you a polite question; no need to bite my ear off."

The conversation, hitherto conducted in a low voice, had suddenly amplified itself into a near shout. Hostile expressions turned Arvardan's way, and the archaeologist's lips compressed themselves into a thin line.

He had asked for it, he decided bitterly. He would not have gotten into this mess if he had held aloof from the beginning, if he hadn't felt the necessity of vaunting his damned tolerance and forcing it on people who didn't want it.

He said levelly, "Mr. Creen, I didn't ask you to join me, and I haven't been uncivil. I repeat, I am tired and would like to rest. I think there's nothing unusual in that."

"Listen"—the young man rose from his seat, threw his cigarette away with a violent gesture, and pointed a finger—"you don't have to treat me like I'm a dog or something. You stinking Outsiders come here with your fine talk and standoffishness and think it gives you the right to stamp all over us. We don't have to stand for it, see. If you don't like it here, you can go back where you came from, and it won't take much more of your lip to make me light into you, either. You think I'm afraid of you?"

Arvardan turned his head away and stared stonily out the window.

Creen said no more, but took his original seat once again. There was an excited buzz of conversation round and about the plane which Arvardan ignored. He felt, rather than saw, the sharpened and envenomed glances being cast at him. Until, gradually, it passed, as all things did.

He completed the journey, silent and alone.

The landing at the Chica airport was welcome. Arvardan smiled to himself at the first sight from the air of the "best damned city on Earth," but found it, nevertheless, an immense improvement over the thick, unfriendly atmosphere of the plane.

He supervised the unloading of his luggage and had it transferred into a biwheel cab. At least he would be the only passenger here, so that if he took care not to speak unnecessarily to the driver, he could scarcely get into trouble.

"State House," he told the cabby, and they were off.

Arvardan thus entered Chica for the first time, and he did so on the day that Joseph Schwartz escaped from his room at the Institute for Nuclear Research.

Creen watched Arvardan leave with a bitter half-smile. He took out his little book and studied it closely between puffs at his cigarette. He hadn't gotten much out of the passengers, despite his story about his uncle (which he had used often before to good effect). To be sure, the old guy had complained about a man living past his time and had blamed it on "pull" with the Ancients. That would come under the heading of slander against the Brotherhood. But then the geezer was heading for the Sixty in a month, anyway. No use putting his name down.

But this Outsider, that was different. He surveyed the item with a feeling of pleasure: "Bel Arvardan, Baronn, Sirius Sector—curious about the Sixty—secretive about own affairs—entered Chica by commercial plane 11 A.M. Chica time, 12 October—anti-Terrestrian attitude very marked."

This time maybe he had a real haul. Picking up these little squealers who made incautious remarks was dull work, but things like this made it pay off.

The Brotherhood would have his report before half an hour was up. He made his way leisurely off the field.

Eight: CONVERGENCE AT CHICA

For the twentieth time Dr. Shekt leafed through his latest volume of research notes, then looked up as Pola entered his office. She frowned as she slipped on her lab coat.

"Now, Father, haven't you eaten yet?"

"Eh? Certainly I have. . . . Oh, what's this?"

"*This* is lunch. Or it was, once. What you ate must have been breakfast. Now there's no sense in my buying meals and bringing them here if you're not going to eat them. I'm just going to make you go home for them."

"Don't get excited. I'll eat it. I can't interrupt a vital experiment every time you think I ought to eat, you know."

He grew cheerful again over the dessert. "You have no idea," he said, "the kind of man this Schwartz is. Did I ever tell you about his skull sutures?"

"They're primitive. You told me."

"But that's not all. He's got thirty-two teeth: three molars up and down, left and right, counting one false one that must be home-made. At least I've never seen a bridge that has metal prongs hooking it onto adjacent teeth instead of being grafted to the jaw-bone. . . . But have you ever seen anyone with thirty-two teeth?"

"I don't go about counting people's teeth, Father. What's the right number—twenty-eight?"

"It sure as Space is. . . . I'm still not finished, though. We took an internal analysis yesterday. What do you suppose we found? . . . Guess!"

"Intestines?"

"Pola, you're being deliberately annoying, but I don't care. You needn't guess; I'll tell you. Schwartz has a vermiform appendix, three and a half inches long, and it's open. Great Galaxy, it's completely unprecedented! I have checked with the Medical School—cautiously, of course—and appendixes are practically never longer than half an inch, and they're *never* open."

"And just what does that mean?"

"Why, he's a complete throwback, a living fossil." He had risen from his chair and paced the distance to the wall and back with hasty steps. "I tell you what, Pola, I don't think we ought to give Schwartz up. He's too valuable a specimen."

"No, no, Father," said Pola quickly, "you can't do that. You promised that farmer to return Schwartz, and you must for Schwartz's own sake. He's unhappy."

"Unhappy! Why, we're treating him like a rich Outsider."

"What difference does that make? The poor fellow is used to his farm and his people. He's lived there all his life. And now he's had a frightening experience—a painful one, for all I know—and his mind works differently now. He can't be expected to understand. We've got to consider his human rights and return him to his family."

"But, Pola, the cause of science——"

"Oh, slush! What is the cause of science worth to me? What do you suppose the Brotherhood will say when they hear of your unauthorized experiments? Do you think *they* care about the cause of science? I mean, consider yourself if you don't wish to consider Schwartz. The longer you keep him, the greater the chance of being caught. You send him home tomorrow night, the way you originally planned to, do you hear? . . . I'll go down and see if Schwartz wants anything before dinner."

But she was back in less than five minutes, face damp and chalky. "Father, he's gone!"

"Who's gone?" startled.

"Schwartz!" she cried, half in tears. "You must have forgotten to lock the door when you left him."

Shekt was on his feet, throwing a hand out to steady himself. "How long?"

"I don't know. But it can't be very long. When were you last there?"

"Not fifteen minutes. I had just been here a minute or two when you came in."

"Well, then," with sudden decision, "I'll run out. He may simply be wandering about the neighborhood. You stay here. If someone else picks him up, they mustn't connect him with you. Understand?"

Shekt could only nod.

Joseph Schwartz felt no lifting of the heart when he exchanged the confines of his prison hospital for the expanses of the city outside. He did not delude himself to the effect that he had a plan of action. He knew, and knew well, that he was simply improvising.

If any rational impulse guided him (as distinct from mere blind desire to exchange inaction for action of any sort), it was the hope that by chance encounter some facet of life would bring back his wandering memory. That he was an amnesiac he was now fully convinced.

The first glimpse of the city, however, was disheartening. It was late afternoon and, in the sunlight, Chica was a milky white. The buildings might have been constructed of porcelain, like that farmhouse he had first stumbled upon.

Stirrings deep within told him that cities should be brown and red. And they should be much dirtier. He was sure of that.

He walked slowly. He felt, somehow, that there would be no organized search for him. He knew that, without knowing how he knew. To be sure, in the last few days he had found himself growing increasingly sensitive to "atmosphere," to the "feel" of things about him. It was part of the strangeness in his mind, since—since . . .

His thought trailed away.

In any case, the "atmosphere" at the hospital prison was one of secrecy; a frightened secrecy, it seemed. So they could not pursue him with loud outcry. He *knew* that. Now why should he know that? Was this queer activity of his mind part of what went on in cases of amnesia?

He crossed another intersection. Wheeled vehicles were relatively few. Pedestrians were—well, pedestrians. Their clothes were rather laughable: seamless, buttonless, colorful. But then so were his own. He wondered where his old clothes were, then wondered if he had ever really owned such clothes as he remembered. It is very difficult to be sure of anything, once you begin doubting your memory on principle.

But he remembered his wife so clearly, his children. They *couldn't* be fictions. He stopped in the middle of the walk to regain a composure suddenly lost. Perhaps they were distorted versions of real people, in this so unreal-seeming real life, whom he *must* find.

People were brushing past him and several muttered unamiably. He moved on. The thought occurred to him, suddenly and forcibly, that he was hungry, or would be soon, and that he had no money.

He looked about. Nothing like a restaurant in sight. Well, how did he know? He couldn't read the signs.

He gazed into each store front he passed. . . . And then he found an interior which consisted in part of small alcoved tables, at one of which two men sat and another at which a single man sat. And the men were eating.

At least that hadn't changed. Men who ate still chewed and swallowed.

He stepped in and, for a moment, stopped in considerable bewilderment. There was no counter, no cooking going on, no signs of any kitchen. It had been his idea to offer to wash the dishes for a meal, but—to whom could he make the offer?

Diffidently, he stepped up to the two diners. He pointed, and said painstakingly, "Food! Where? Please."

They looked up at him, rather startled. One spoke fluently, and quite incomprehensibly, patting a small structure at the wall end of the table. The other joined in, impatiently.

Schwartz's eyes fell. He turned to leave, and there was a hand upon his sleeve——

Granz had seen Schwartz while the latter was still only a plump and wistful face at the window.

He said, "What's *he* want?"

Messter, sitting across the little table, with his back to the street, turned, looked, shrugged his shoulders, and said nothing.

Granz said, "He's coming in," and Messter replied, "So what?"

"Nothing. Just mentioning it."

But a few moments later the newcomer, after looking about helplessly, approached and pointed to their beef stew, saying in a queer accent, "Food! Where? Please."

Granz looked up. "Food right here, bud. Just pull up a chair at any table you want and use the Foodomat. . . . Foodomat! Don't you know what a Foodomat is? . . . Look at the poor jerk, Messter. He's looking at me as if he doesn't understand a word I say. Hey, fella—this thing, see. Just put a coin in and let me eat, will you?"

"Leave him alone," grunted Messter. "He's just a bum, looking for a handout."

"Hey, hold on." Granz seized Schwartz's sleeve as the latter turned to go. He added in an aside to Messter, "Space, let the guy eat. He's probably getting the Sixty soon. It's the least I can do to give him a break. . . . Hey, bud, you got any money? . . . Well, I'll be damned, he still doesn't understand me. Money, pal, money! This——" And he drew a shining half-credit piece out of his pocket, flipping it so that it sparkled in the air.

"Got any?" he asked.

Slowly Schwartz shook his head.

"Well, then, have this on me!" He replaced the half-credit piece in his pocket and tossed over a considerably smaller coin.

Schwartz held it uncertainly.

"All right. Don't just stand there. Stick it in the Foodomat. This thing here."

Schwartz suddenly found himself understanding. The Foodomat had a series of slits for coins of different sizes and a series of knobs opposite little milky rectangles, the writing upon which he could not read. Schwartz pointed to the food on the table and ran a forefinger up and down the knobs, raising his eyebrows in question.

Messter said in annoyance, "A sandwich isn't good enough for him. We're getting classy bums in this burg nowadays. It doesn't pay to humor them, Granz."

"All right, so I lose point eight five credits. Tomorrow's payday, anyway. . . . Here," he said to Schwartz. He placed coins of his own into the Foodomat and withdrew the wide metal container from the recess in the wall. "Now take it to another table. . . . Nah, keep that tenth piece. Buy yourself a cup of coffee with it."

Schwartz carried the container gingerly to the next table. It had a spoon attached to the side by means of a transparent, filmy material, which broke with a slight pop under the pressure of a fingernail. As it did so, the top of the container parted at a seam and curled back upon itself.

The food, unlike that which he saw the others eating, was cold; but that was a detail. It was only after a minute or so that he realized the food was getting warmer and that the container had grown hot to the touch. He stopped, in alarm, and waited.

The gravy first steamed, then bubbled gently for a moment. It cooled again and Schwartz completed the meal.

Granz and Messter were still there when he left. So was the third man, to whom, throughout, Schwartz had paid no attention.

Nor had Schwartz noticed, at any time since he had left the Institute, the thin, little man who, without seeming to, had managed to remain always within eyeshot.

Bel Arvardan, having showered and changed his clothes, promptly followed his original intention of observing the human animal, subspecies Earth, in its native habitat. The weather was mild, the light breeze refreshing, the village itself—pardon, the city—bright, quiet, and clean.

Not so bad.

Chica first stop, he thought. Largest collection of Earthmen on the planet. Washenn next; local capital. Senloo! Senfran! Bonair! . . . He had plotted an itinerary all over the western continents (where most of the meager scattering of Earth's population lived) and, allowing two or three days at each, he would be back in Chica just about the time his expeditionary ship was due.

It would be educational.

As afternoon began to decline he stepped into a Foodomat and, as he ate, observed the small drama that played itself out between the two Earthmen who had entered shortly after himself and the plump, elderly man who came in last of all. But his observation was detached and casual, simply noting it as an item to set against his unpleasant experience on the jet transport. The two men at the table were obviously air-cab drivers and not wealthy, yet they could be charitable.

The beggar left, and two minutes later Arvardan left as well.

The streets were noticeably fuller, as the workday was approaching its end.

He stepped hastily aside to avoid colliding with a young girl.

"Pardon me," he said.

She was dressed in white, in clothing which bore the stereotyped lines of a uniform. She seemed quite oblivious of the near collision. The anxious look on her face, the sharp turning of her head from side to side, her utter preoccupation, made the situation quite obvious.

He laid a light finger on her shoulder. "May I help you, miss? Are you in trouble?"

She stopped and turned startled eyes upon him. Arvardan found himself judging her age at nineteen to twenty-one, observing carefully her brown hair and dark eyes, her high cheekbones and little chin, her slim waist and graceful carriage. He discovered, suddenly, that the thought of this little female creature being an earthwoman lent a sort of perverse piquancy to her attractiveness.

But she was still staring, and almost at the moment of speaking she seemed to break down. "Oh, it's no use. Please don't bother about me. It's silly to expect to find someone when you don't have the slightest idea where he could have gone." She was drooping in discouragement, her eyes wet. Then she straightened and breathed deeply. "Have you seen a plump man about five-four, dressed in green and white, no hat, rather bald?"

Arvardan looked at her in astonishment. "What? Green and white? . . . Oh, I don't believe this. . . . Look, this man you're referring to—does he speak with difficulty?"

"Yes, yes. Oh yes. You have seen him, then?"

"Not five minutes ago he was in there eating with two men. . . . Here they are. . . . Say, you two." He beckoned them over.

Granz reached them first. "Cab, sir?"

"No, but if you will tell the young lady what happened to the man you were eating with, you'll stand to make the fare, anyway."

Granz paused and looked chagrined. "Well, I'd like to help you, but I never saw him before in my life."

Arvardan turned to the girl. "Now look, miss, he can't have gone in the direction you came from or you'd have seen him. And he can't be far away. Suppose we move north a bit. I'll recognize him if I see him."

His offer of help was an impulse, yet Arvardan was not, ordinarily, an impulsive man. He found himself smiling at her.

Granz interrupted suddenly. "What's he done, lady? He hasn't broken any of the Customs, has he?"

"No, no," she replied hastily. "He's only a little sick, that's all."

Messter looked after them as they left. "A little sick?" He shoved his visored cap back upon his head, then pinched balefully at his chin. "How d'ya like that, Granz? A little sick."

His eyes looked askance at the other for a moment.

"What's got into *you?*" asked Granz uneasily.

"Something that's making *me* a little sick. That guy must've been straight out of the hospital. That was a nurse looking for him, and a plenty worried nurse, too. Why should she be worried if he was just a *little* sick? He couldn't hardly talk, and he didn't hardly understand. You noticed that, didn't you?"

There was a sudden panicky light in Granz's eyes. "You don't think it's Fever?"

"I sure *do* think it's Radiation Fever—and he's far gone. He was within a foot of us, too. It's never any good——"

There was a little thin man next to them. A little thin man with bright, sharp eyes and a twittering voice, who had stepped out of nowhere. "What's that, gents? Who's got Radiation Fever?"

He was regarded with disfavor. "Who are you?"

"Ho," said the sharp little man, "you want to know, do you? It so happens that I'm a messenger of the Brotherhood, to be sure." He flashed a little glowing badge on the inner lapel of his jacket. "Now, in the name of the Society of Ancients, what's all this about Radiation Fever?"

Messter spoke in cowed and sullen tones. "*I* don't know nothing. There's a nurse looking for somebody who's sick, and I was wondering if it was Radiation Fever. That's not against the Customs, is it?"

"Ho! You're telling *me* about the Customs, are you? You better go about your business and let *me* worry about the Customs."

The little man rubbed his hands together, gazed quickly about him, and hurried northward.

"There he is!" And Pola clutched feverishly at her companion's elbow. It had happened quickly, easily, and accidentally. Through the despairing blankness he had suddenly materialized just within the main entrance of the self-service department store, not three blocks from the Foodomat.

"I see him," whispered Arvardan. "Now stay back and let me follow him. If he sees you and dashes into the mob, we'll never locate him."

Casually they followed in a sort of nightmare chase. The human contents of the store was a quicksand which could absorb its prey slowly—or quickly—keep it hidden impenetrably, spew it forth unexpectedly, set up barriers that somehow would not yield. The mob might almost have had a malevolent conscious mind of its own.

And then Arvardan circled a counter watchfully, playing Schwartz as though he were at the end of a fishing line. His huge hand reached out and closed on the other's shoulder.

Schwartz burst into incomprehensible prose and jerked away in panic. Arvardan's grip, however, was unbreakable to men far stronger than Schwartz, and he contented himself with smiling and saying, in normal tones, for the benefit of the curious spectator, "Hello, old chap, haven't seen you in months. How are you?"

A palpable fraud, he supposed, in the face of the other's gibberish, but Pola had joined them.

"Schwartz," she whispered, "come back with us."

For a moment Schwartz stiffened in rebellion, then he drooped.

He said wearily, "I—go—along—you," but the statement was drowned in the sudden blare of the store's loud-speaker system.

"*Attention! Attention! Attention!* The management requests that all patrons of the store leave by the Fifth Street exit in orderly fashion. You will present your registration cards to the guards at the door. It is essential that this be done rapidly. *Attention! Attention! Attention!*"

The message was repeated three times, the last time over the sound of scuffling feet as crowds were beginning to line up at the exits. A many-tongued cry was making itself heard, asking in various fashions the forever-unanswerable question of "What's happened? What's going on?"

Arvardan shrugged and said, "Let's get on line, miss. We're leaving anyway."

But Pola shook her head. "We can't. We can't——"

"Why not?" The archaeologist frowned.

The girl merely shrank away from him. How could she tell him that Schwartz had no registration card? Who was he? Why had he been helping her? She was in a whirl of suspicion and despair.

She said huskily, "You'd better go, or you'll get into trouble."

They were pouring out the elevators as the upper floors emptied. Arvardan, Pola, and Schwartz were a little island of solidity in the human river.

Looking back on it later, Arvardan realized that at this point he could have left the girl. Left her! Never seen her again! Have nothing to reproach himself with! . . . And all would have been different. The great Galactic Empire would have dissolved in chaos and destruction.

He did not leave the girl. She was scarcely pretty in her fear and despair. No one could be. But Arvardan felt disturbed at the sight of her helplessness.

He had taken a step away, and now he turned. "Are you going to stay here?"

She nodded.

"But why?" he demanded.

"Because"—and the tears now overflowed—"I don't know what else to do."

She was just a little, frightened girl, even if she was an Earthie. Arvardan said, in a softer voice, "If you'll tell me what's wrong, I'll try to help."

There was no answer.

The three formed a tableau. Schwartz had sunk to the floor in a squatting posture, too sick at heart to try to follow the conversation, to be curious at the sudden emptiness of the store, to do anything but bury his head in his hands in the last unspoken and unuttered whimper of despair. Pola, weeping, knew only that she was more frightened than she had ever thought it possible for anyone to be. Arvardan, puzzled and waiting, tried clumsily and ineffectually to pat Pola's shoulder in encouraging fashion, and was conscious only of the fact that for the first time he had touched an Earthgirl.

The little man came upon them thus.

Nine: CONFLICT AT CHICA

Lieutenant Marc Claudy of the Chica garrison yawned slowly and gazed into the middle distance with an ineffable boredom. He was completing his second year of duty on Earth and waited yearningly for replacement.

Nowhere in the Galaxy was the problem of maintaining a garrison quite so complicated as it was on this horrible world. On other planets there existed a certain camaraderie between soldier and civilian, particularly female civilian. There was a sense of freedom and openness.

But here the garrison was a prison. There were the radiation-proof barracks and the filtered atmosphere, free of radioactive dust. There was the lead-impregnated clothing, cold and heavy, which could not be removed without grave risk. As a corollary to that, fraternization with the population (assuming that the desperation of loneliness could drive a soldier to the society of an "Earthie" girl) was out of the question.

What was left, then, but short snorts, long naps, and slow madness?

Lieutenant Claudy shook his head in a futile attempt to clear it, yawned again, sat up and began dragging on his shoes. He looked at his watch and decided it was not yet quite time for evening chow.

And then he jumped to his feet, only one shoe on, acutely conscious of his uncombed hair, and saluted.

The colonel looked about him disparagingly but said nothing directly on the subject. Instead he directed crisply, "Lieutenant, there are reports of rioting in the business district. You will take a decontamination squad to the Dunham department store and take charge. You will see to it that all your men are thoroughly protected against infection by Radiation Fever."

"Radiation Fever!" cried the lieutenant. "Pardon me, sir, but——"

"You will be ready to leave in fifteen minutes," said the colonel coldly.

Arvardan saw the little man first, and stiffened as the other made a little gesture of greeting. "Hi, guv'ner. Hi, big fella. Tell the little lady there ain't no call for the waterworks."

Pola's head had snapped up, her breath sucked in. Automatically she leaned toward the protecting bulk of Arvardan, who, as automatically, put a protective arm about her. It did not occur to him that that was the second time he had touched an Earthgirl.

He said sharply, "What do you want?"

The little man with the sharp eyes stepped diffidently out from behind a counter piled high with packages. He spoke in a manner which managed to be both ingratiating and impudent simultaneously.

"Here's a weird go outside," he said, "but it don't need to bother you, miss. I'll get your man back to the Institute for you."

"What institute?" demanded Pola fearfully.

"Aw, come off it," said the little man. "I'm Natter, fella with the fruit stand right across the street from the Institute for Nuclear Research. I seen you there lots of times."

"See here," said Arvardan abruptly, "what's all this about?"

Natter's little frame shook with merriment. "They think this fella here has Radiation Fever——"

"Radiation Fever?" It came from both Arvardan and Pola at once.

Natter nodded. "That's right. Two cabbies ate with him and that's what they said. News like that kinda spreads, you know."

"The guards outside," demanded Pola, "are just looking for someone with fever?"

"That's right."

"And just why aren't *you* afraid of the fever?" demanded Arvardan abruptly. "I take it that it was fear of contagion that caused the authorities to empty the store."

"Sure. The authorities are waiting outside, afraid to come in, too. They're waiting for the Outsiders' decontamination squad to get here."

"And you're not afraid of the fever, is that it?"

"Why should I be? This guy don't have no fever. Look at him. Where's the sores on his mouth? He isn't flushed. His eyes are all right. I know what fever looks like. Come on, miss, we'll march out of here, then."

But Pola was frightened again. "No, no. We can't. He's—he's——" She couldn't go on.

Natter said insinuatingly, "I could take him out. No questions asked. No registration card necessary——"

Pola failed to suppress a little cry, and Arvardan said, with considerable distaste, "What makes *you* so important?"

Natter laughed hoarsely. He flipped his lapel. "Messenger for the Society of Ancients. Nobody'll ask me questions."

"And what's in it for you?"

"Money! You're anxious and I can help you. There ain't no fairer than that. It's worth, say, a hundred credits to you, and it's worth a hundred credits to me. Fifty credits now, fifty on delivery."

But Pola whispered in horror, "You'll take him to the Ancients."

"What for? He's no good to them, and he's worth a hundred

credits to me. If you wait for the Outsiders, they're liable to kill the fella before they find out he's fever-free. You know Outsiders—they don't care if they kill an Earthman or not. They'd rather, in fact."

Arvardan said, "Take the young lady with you."

But Natter's little eyes were very sharp and very sly. "Oh no. Not that, guv'ner. I take what you call calculated risks. I can get by with one, maybe, not with two. And if I only take one, I take the one what's worth more. Ain't that reasonable to you?"

"What," said Arvardan, "if I pick you up and pull your legs off? What'll happen then?"

Natter flinched, but found his voice, nevertheless, and managed a laugh. "Why, then, you're a dope. They'll get you anyway, and there'll be murder, too, on the list. . . . All right, guv'ner. Keep your hands off."

"Please"—Pola was dragging at Arvardan's arm—"we *must* take a chance. Let him do as he says. . . . You'll be honest with us, w-won't you, Mr. Natter?"

Natter's lips were curling. "Your big friend wrenched my arm. He had no call to do that, and I don't like nobody to push me around. I'll just take an extra hundred credits for that. Two hundred in all."

"My father'll pay you——"

"One hundred in advance," he replied obdurately.

"But I don't have a hundred credits," Pola wailed.

"That's all right, miss," said Arvardan stonily. "I can swing it."

He opened his wallet and plucked out several bills. He threw them at Natter. "Get going!"

"Go with him, Schwartz," whispered Pola.

Schwartz did, without comment, without caring. He would have gone to hell at that moment with as little emotion.

And they were alone, staring at each other blankly. It was perhaps the first time that Pola had actually looked at Arvardan, and she was amazed to find him tall and craggily handsome, calm and self-confident. She had accepted him till now as an inchoate, unmotivated helper, but now—— She grew suddenly shy, and all the events of the last hour or two were enmeshed and lost in a scurry of heart-beating.

They didn't even know each other's name.

She smiled and said, "I'm Pola Shekt."

Arvardan had not seen her smile before, and found himself interested in the phenomenon. It was a glow that entered her face, a radiance. It made him feel—— But he put that thought away roughly. An Earthgirl!

So he said, with perhaps less cordiality than he intended, "My name is Bel Arvardan." He held out a bronzed hand, into which her little one was swallowed up for a moment.

She said, "I must thank you for all your help."

Arvardan shrugged it away. "Shall we leave? I mean, now that your friend is gone; safely, I trust."

"I think we would have heard quite a noise if they had caught him, don't you think so?" Her eyes were pleading for confirmation of her hope, and he refused the temptation toward softness.

"Shall we go?"

She was somehow frozen. "Yes, why not?" sharply.

But there was a whining in the air, a shrill moan on the horizon, and the girl's eyes were wide and her outstretched hand suddenly withdrawn again.

"What's the matter now?" asked Arvardan.

"It's the Imperials."

"And are you frightened of them too?" It was the self-consciously non-Earthman Arvardan who spoke—the Sirian archaeologist. Prejudice or not, however the logic might be chopped and minced, the approach of Imperial soldiers meant a trace of sanity and humanity. There was room for condescension here, and he grew kind.

"Don't worry about the Outsiders," he said, even stooping to use their term for non-Earthmen. "I'll handle them, Miss Shekt."

She was suddenly concerned. "Oh no, don't try anything like that. Just don't talk to them at all. Do as they say, and don't even look at them."

Arvardan's smile broadened.

The guards saw them while they were still a distance from the main entrance and fell back. They emerged into a little space of emptiness and a strange hush. The whine of the army cars was almost upon them.

And then there were armored cars in the square and groups of glass-globe-headed soldiers springing out therefrom. The crowds scattered before them in panic, aided in their scramblings by clipped shouts and thrusts with the butt ends of the neuronic whips.

Lieutenant Claudy, in the lead, approached an Earthman guard at the main entrance. "All right, you, who's got the fever?"

His face was slightly distorted within the enclosing glass, with its content of pure air. His voice was slightly metallic as a result of radioamplification.

The guard bent his head in deep respect. "If it please your honor, we have isolated the patient within the store. The two who were with the patient are now standing in the doorway before you."

"They are, are they? Good! Let them stand there. Now—in the first place, I want this mob out of here. Sergeant! Clear the square!"

There was a grim efficiency in the proceedings thereafter. The deepening twilight gloomed over Chica as the crowd melted into the darkening air. The streets were beginning to gleam in soft, artificial lighting.

Lieutenant Claudy tapped his heavy boots with the butt of his neuronic whip. "You're sure the sick Earthie is inside?"

"He has not left, your honor. He must be."

"Well, we'll assume he is and waste no time about it. Sergeant! Decontaminate the building!"

A contingent of soldiers, hermetically sealed away from all contact with Terrestrial environment, charged into the building. A slow quarter hour passed, while Arvardan watched all in absorbed fashion. It was a field experiment in intercultural relationships that he was professionally reluctant to disturb.

The last of the soldiers were out again, and the store was shrouded in deepening night.

"Seal the doors!"

Another few minutes and then the cans of disinfectant which had been placed in several spots on each floor were discharged at long distance. In the recesses of the building those cans were flung open and the thick vapors rolled out and curled up the walls, clinging to every square inch of surface, reaching through the air and into the inmost crannies. No protoplasm, from germ to man, could remain alive in its presence, and chemical flushing of the most painstaking type would be required eventually for decontamination.

But now the lieutenant was approaching Arvardan and Pola.

"What was his name?" There was not even cruelty in his voice, merely utter indifference. An Earthman, he thought, had been killed. Well, he had killed a fly that day also. That made two.

He received no answer, Pola bending her head meekly and Arvardan watching curiously. The Imperial officer did not take his eyes off them. He beckoned curtly. "Check them for infection."

An officer bearing the insignia of the Imperial Medical Corps approached them, and was not gentle in his investigation. His gloved hands pushed hard under their armpits and yanked at the corners of their mouths so that he might investigate the inner surfaces of their cheeks.

"No infection, Lieutenant. If they had been exposed this afternoon, the stigmata would be clearly visible by now if infection had occurred."

"Umm." Lieutenant Claudy carefully removed his globe and enjoyed the touch of "live" air, even that of Earth. He tucked the ungainly glass object into the crook of his left elbow and said harshly, "Your name, Earthie-squaw?"

The term itself was richly insulting; the tone in which it was uttered added disgrace to it, but Pola showed no sign of resentment.

"Pola Shekt, sir," she responded in a whisper.

"Your papers!"

She reached into the small pocket of her white jacket and removed the pink folder.

He took it, flared it open in the light of his pocket flash, and studied it. Then he tossed it back. It fell, fluttering, to the floor, and Pola bent quickly for it.

"Stand up," the officer ordered impatiently, and kicked the booklet out of reach. Pola, white-faced, snatched her fingers away.

Arvardan frowned and decided it was time to interfere. He said, "Say, look here, now."

The lieutenant turned on him in a flash, his lips drawn back. "What did you say, Earthie?"

Pola was between them at once. "If you please, sir, this man has nothing to do with anything that has happened today. I never saw him before——"

The lieutenant yanked her aside. "I said, What did you say, Earthie?"

Arvardan returned his stare coolly. "I said, Look here, now. And I was going to say further that I don't like the way you treat women and that I'd advise you to improve your manners."

He was far too irritated to correct the lieutenant's impression of his planetary origin.

Lieutenant Claudy smiled without humor. "And where have *you* been brought up, Earthie? Don't you believe in saying 'sir' when you address a man? You don't know your place, do you? Well, it's been a while since I've had the pleasure of teaching the way of life to a nice big Earthie-buck. Here, how's this——"

And quickly, like the flick of a snake, his open palm was out and across Arvardan's face, back and forth, once, twice. Arvardan stepped back in surprise and then felt the roaring in his ears. His hand shot out to catch the extended arm that pecked at him. He saw the other's face twist in surprise——

The muscles in his shoulders writhed easily.

The lieutenant was on the pavement with a crashing thud that sent the glass globe rolling into shattered fragments. He lay still, and Arvardan's half-smile was ferocious. He dusted his hands lightly. "Any other bastard here think he can play pattycake on my face?"

But the sergeant had raised his neuronic whip. The contact closed and there was the dim violet flash that reached out and licked at the tall archaeologist.

Every muscle in Arvardan's body stiffened in unbearable pain, and he sank slowly to his knees. Then, with total paralysis upon him, he blacked out.

When Arvardan swam out of the haze he was conscious first of all of a wash of welcome coolness on his forehead. He tried to open his eyes and found his lids reacting as if swinging on rusty hinges. He let them remain closed and, with infinitely slow jerks (each fragmentary muscular movement shooting pins through him), lifted his arm to his face.

A soft, damp towel, held by a little hand . . .

He forced an eye open and battled with the mist.

"Pola," he said.

There was a little cry of sudden joy. "Yes. How do you feel?"

"As if I were dead," he croaked, "without the advantage of losing pain. . . . What happened?"

"We were carted off to the military base. The colonel's been in here. They've searched you—and I don't know what they're going to do, but—— Oh, Mr. Arvardan, you shouldn't ever have struck the lieutenant. I think you broke his arm."

A faint smile wrenched at Arvardan's face. "Good! I wish I'd broken his back."

"But resisting an Imperial officer—it's a capital offense." Her voice was a horrified whisper.

"Indeed? We'll see about that."

"Ssh. They're coming back."

Arvardan closed his eyes and relaxed. Pola's cry was faint and far-off in his ears, and when he felt the hypodermic's thrust he could not gather his muscles into motion.

And then there was the wash of wonderful soothing non-pain along his veins and nerves. His arms unknotted and his back released itself slowly from its rigid arch, settling down. He fluttered his eyelids rapidly and, with a thrust of his elbow, sat up.

The colonel was regarding him thoughtfully; Pola, apprehensively, yet, somehow, joyfully.

The colonel said, "Well, Dr. Arvardan, we seem to have had an unpleasant contretemps in the city this evening."

Dr. Arvardan. Pola realized the little she knew about him, not even his occupation. . . . She had never felt quite like this.

Arvardan laughed shortly. "Unpleasant, you say. I consider that a rather inadequate adjective."

"You have broken the arm of an officer of the Empire about the performance of his duty."

"That officer struck me first. His duty in no way included the necessity for grossly insulting me, both verbally and physically. In doing so he forfeited any claim he might have to treatment as an officer and gentleman. As a free citizen of the Empire, I had every right to resent such cavalier, not to say illegal, treatment."

The colonel harumphed and seemed at a loss for words. Pola stared at both of them with wide, unbelieving eyes.

Finally the colonel said softly, "Well, I need not say that I consider the whole incident to have been unfortunate. Apparently the pain and indignity involved have been equally spread on both sides. It may be best to forget this matter."

"Forget? I think not. I have been a guest at the Procurator's palace, and he may be interested in hearing exactly in what manner his garrison maintains order on Earth."

"Now, Dr. Arvardan, if I assure you that you will receive a public apology——"

"To hell with that. What do you intend doing with Miss Shekt?"

"What would you suggest?"

"That you free her instantly, return her papers, and tender *her* your apologies—right now."

The colonel reddened, then said with an effort, "Of course." He turned to Pola. "If the young lady will accept my deepest regrets . . ."

They had left the dark garrison walls behind them. It had been a short and silent ten-minute air-taxi ride to the city proper, and now they stood at the deserted blackness of the Institute. It was past midnight.

Pola said, "I don't think I quite understand. You must be very important. It seems silly of me not to know your name. I didn't ever imagine that Outsiders could treat an Earthman so."

Arvardan felt oddly reluctant and yet compelled to end the fiction. "I'm not an Earthman, Pola. I'm an archaeologist from the Sirian Sector."

She turned on him quickly, her face white in the moonlight. For the space of a slow count to ten she said nothing. "Then you outfaced the soldiers because you were safe, after all, and knew it. And I thought—— I should have known."

There was an outraged bitterness about her. "I humbly beg your pardon, sir, if at any time today, in my ignorance, I affected any disrespectful familiarity with you——"

"Pola," he cried angrily, "what's the matter? What if I'm not an Earthman? How does that make me different from what I seemed to you to be five minutes ago?"

"You might have told me, sir."

"I'm not asking you to call me 'sir.' Don't be like the rest of them, will you?"

"Like the rest of whom, sir? The rest of the disgusting animals that live on Earth? . . . I owe you a hundred credits."

"Forget it," said Arvardan disgustedly.

"I cannot follow that order. If you'll give me your address, I will send you a money order for the amount tomorrow."

Arvardan was suddenly brutal. "You owe me much more than a hundred credits."

Pola bit her lip and said in lowered tones, "It is the only part of my great debt, sir, that I can repay. Your address?"

"State House," he flung at her across his shoulder. He was lost in the night.

And Pola found herself weeping!

Shekt met Pola at the door of his office.

"He's back," he said. "A little thin man brought him."

"Good!" She was having difficulty speaking.

"He asked for two hundred credits. I gave it to him."

"He was to ask for one hundred, but never mind."

She brushed past her father. He said wistfully, "I was terribly worried. The commotions in the neighborhood—— I dared not ask; I might have endangered you."

"It's all right. Nothing's happened. . . . Let me sleep here tonight, Father."

But not all her weariness could make her sleep, for something *had* happened. She had met a man, and he was an Outsider.

But she had his address. She had his address.

Ten: INTERPRETATION OF EVENTS

They presented a complete contrast, these two Earthmen—one with the greatest semblance of power on Earth, and one with the greatest reality.

Thus the High Minister was the most important Earthman on Earth, the recognized ruler of the planet by direct and definite decree of the Emperor of all the Galaxy—subject, of course, to the orders of the Emperor's Procurator. His Secretary seemed no one at all, really—merely a member of the Society of Ancients, appointed, theoretically, by the High Minister to take care of certain unspecified details, and dismissable, theoretically, at will.

The High Minister was known to all the Earth and was looked up to as the supreme arbiter on matters of Custom. It was he who announced the exemptions to the Sixty and it was he who judged the breakers of ritual, the defiers of rationing and of production schedules, the invaders of restricted territory and so on. The Secretary, on the other hand, was known to nobody, not even by name, except to the Society of Ancients and, of course, to the High Minister himself.

The High Minister had a command of language and made frequent speeches to the people, speeches of high emotional content and copious flow of sentiment. He had fair hair, worn long, and a delicate and patrician countenance. The Secretary, snub-nosed and wry-faced, preferred a short word to a long one, a grunt to a word, and silence to a grunt—at least in public.

It was the High Minister, of course, who had the semblance of power; the Secretary who had the reality. And in the privacy of the High Minister's office that circumstance was quite plain.

For the High Minister was pettishly puzzled and the Secretary coolly indifferent.

"What I don't see," said the High Minister, "is the connection of all these reports you bring me. Reports, reports!" He lifted an arm above his head and struck viciously at an imaginary heap of paper. "I don't have the time for them."

"Exactly," said the Secretary coldly. "It is why you hire me. I read them, digest them, transmit them."

"Well, good Balkis, about your business, then. And quickly, since these are minor matters."

"Minor? Your Excellency may lose a great deal someday if your judgment is not sharpened. . . . Let us see what these reports mean, and I shall then ask you if you still consider them minor. First we have the original report, now seven days old, from Shekt's underling, and it is that which first put me on the trail."

"What trail?"

Balkis's smile was faintly bitter. "May I recall to Your Excellency certain important projects which have been nurtured here on Earth for several years."

"Ssh!" The High Minister, in sudden loss of dignity, could not forbear looking about hastily.

"Your Excellency, it is not nervousness but confidence that will win for us. . . . You know further that the success of this project has depended upon the judicious use of Shekt's little toy, the Synapsifier. Until now, at least as far as we know, it has been utilized under our direction only, and for definite purposes. And now, without warning, Shekt has Synapsified an unknown man, in complete violation of our orders."

"This," said the High Minister, "is a simple matter. Discipline Shekt, take the treated man into custody, and end the matter."

"No, no. You are far too straightforward, Your Excellency. You miss the point. It is not *what* Shekt has done, but *why* he has done so. Note that there exists a coincidence about the matter, one of a considerable series of subsequent coincidences. The Procurator of Earth had visited Shekt that same day, and Shekt himself reported to us, in loyal and trustworthy fashion, all that had passed between them. Ennius had wanted the Synapsifier for Imperial use. He made a promise, it seems, of great help and gracious assistance from the Emperor."

"Hmm," said the High Minister.

"You are intrigued? A compromise such as that seems attractive as compared to the dangers attending our present course? . . . Do you remember the promises of food to us during the famine five years ago? Do you? Shipments were refused because we lacked Imperial credits, and Earth-manufactured products would not be accepted, as being radioactively contaminated. Was there a free gift of food as promised? Was there even a loan? A hundred thousand died of starvation. Don't put your trust in Outsider promises.

"But that does not matter. What does is that Shekt made a great display of loyalty. Surely we could never doubt him again. With compounded certainty, we could not suspect him of treason that very day. Yet so it came to pass."

"You mean in this unauthorized experiment, Balkis?"

"I do, Your Excellency. Who was the man treated? We have photographs of him and, with the help of Shekt's technician, retinal patterns. A check with the Planetary Registry shows no record of him. The conclusion must therefore be reached that he is no Earthman, but an Outsider. Furthermore, Shekt must have been aware of it, since a registration card cannot be forged or transferred, if checked with retinal patterns. So, in simple fashion, the unalterable facts lead us to the conclusion that Shekt has Synapsified, knowingly, an Outsider. And why? . . .

"The answer to that may be disturbingly simple. Shekt is not an ideal instrument for our purposes. In his youth he was an Assimilationist; he even once stood for election to the Washenn Council on a platform of conciliation with the Empire. He was defeated, by the way."

The High Minister interrupted. "I didn't know that."

"That he was defeated?"

"No, that he ran. Why wasn't I informed of this? Shekt is a very dangerous man in the position he now holds."

Balkis smiled softly and tolerantly. "Shekt invented the Synapsifier and still represents the one man truly experienced in its operation. He has always been watched, and will now be watched more closely than ever. Do not forget that a traitor within our ranks, *known to us*, can do more harm to the enemy than a loyal man can do good to us.

"Now, let us continue to deal with the facts. Shekt has Synapsified an Outsider. Why? There is only one reason why a Synapsifier can possibly be used—to improve a mind. And why that? Because only so can the minds of our scientists, already improved by Synapsification, be overtaken. Eh? This means that the Empire has at least a faint suspicion of what is going on upon Earth. Is that minor, Your Excellency?"

There was a scattered dew on the High Minister's forehead. "Do you really think so?"

"The facts are a jigsaw puzzle that can fit only one way. The Outsider so treated was a man of undistinguished, even contemptible, appearance. A good stroke, too, since a bald and fat old man can still be the Empire's most skilled espionage agent. Oh yes. Yes. Who else could be trusted on a mission such as this? . . . But we have followed this stranger, whose alias, by the way, is Schwartz, as far as we can. Let us take this second file of reports."

The High Minister cast an eye upon them. "The ones concerning Bel Arvardan?"

"Dr. Bel Arvardan," assented Balkis, "eminent archaeologist of the gallant Sirian Sector, those worlds of brave and chivalrous bigots."

He spat the last out. Then, "Well, never mind. In any case, we have here a queer mirror image to Schwartz, an almost poetic contrast. He is not unknown, but, instead, a famous figure. He is not a secret intruder, but one who comes floating on a tidal wave of publicity. We are warned of him not by an obscure technician, but by the Procurator of Earth himself."

"Do you think there is a connection, Balkis?"

"Your Excellency may suppose it possible that one may be designed to distract our attention from the other. Or else, since the ruling classes of the Empire are skilled enough in intrigue, we have an example of two methods of camouflage. In the case of Schwartz, the lights are put out. In the case of Arvardan, the lights are flashed in our eyes. In neither case are we intended to see anything? . . . Come, of what did Ennius warn us concerning Arvardan?"

The High Minister rubbed his nose thoughtfully. "Arvardan, he said, was on an archaeological expedition under Imperial sponsorship and wished to enter the Forbidden Areas for scientific purposes. No sacrilege, he said, was intended, and if we could stop him in gentle fashion, he would back our action to the Imperial Council. Something like that."

"So then we will watch Arvardan closely, but for what purpose? Why, to see that he makes no unauthorized entry into the Forbidden Areas. Here's the head of an archaeological expedition without men, ships, or equipment. Here's an Outsider who does not remain at Everest, where he belongs, but wanders about Earth, for some reason—and goes to Chica first. And how is our attention distracted from all these most curious and suspicious circumstances? Why, by urging us to watch carefully something that is of no importance.

"But notice, Your Excellency, that Schwartz was kept hidden in the Institute for Nuclear Research for six days. And then he escaped. Isn't that strange? The door, suddenly, wasn't locked. The corridor, suddenly, wasn't guarded. What queer negligence. And on what day was it that he escaped? Why, on the same day that Arvardan arrived at Chica. A second peculiar coincidence."

"You think, then . . ." said the High Minister tensely.

"I think that Schwartz is the Outsider agent on Earth, that Shekt is the contact man with the Assimilationist traitors among us, and that Arvardan is the contact man with the Empire. Observe the skill with which the meeting between Schwartz and Arvardan was arranged. Schwartz is allowed to escape, and after an appropriate interval his nurse—Shekt's daughter, by a not-too-surprising additional coincidence—is out after him. If anything were to go wrong with their split-second timetable, it is obvious that she would have found him suddenly; that he would have become a poor, sick patient for the benefit of anyone's curiosity; that he would have been brought back to safety for another attempt later. In fact, two overcurious cabbies were told that he was a sick man, and that, ironically enough, backfired upon them.

"Follow it closely, now. Schwartz and Arvardan meet first in a Foodomat. They are, apparently, unaware of each other's existence. It is a preliminary meeting, designed, simply, to indicate that all has gone well so far and that the next step may be taken. . . . At least they don't underestimate us, which is gratifying.

"Then Schwartz leaves; a few minutes later Arvardan leaves and the Shekt girl meets him. It is stop-watch timing. Together, after playing a little part for the benefit of the afore-mentioned cabbies, they head for the Dunham department store, and now all three are together. Where else but a department store? It is an ideal meeting place. It has a secrecy no cave in the mountains could duplicate. Too open to be suspected. Too crowded to be stalked. Wonderful—wonderful—— I give credit to my opponent."

The High Minister writhed in his chair. "If our opponent deserves too much credit, he will win."

"Impossible. He is already defeated. And in that respect we must give credit to the excellent Natter."

"And who is Natter?"

"An insignificant agent who must be used to the limit after this. His actions yesterday could not have been improved upon. His long-range assignment has been to watch Shekt. For the purpose, he keeps a fruit stand across the street from the Institute. For the last week he has been specifically instructed to watch the development of the Schwartz affair.

"He was on hand when the man, known to him through photographs and through a glimpse at the time he was first brought to the Institute, escaped. He observed every action, himself unobserved, and it is his report that details yesterday's events. With incredible intuition, he decided that the entire purpose of the 'escape' was to arrange a meeting with Arvardan. He felt himself to be not in a position, singlehanded, to exploit that meeting, so he decided to prevent it. The cabbies, to whom the Shekt girl had described Schwartz as being sick, speculated on Radiation Fever. Natter seized on that with the swiftness of genius. As soon as he observed the meeting in the department store, he reported the case of fever and the local authorities at Chica were, praised be Earth, intelligent enough to co-operate quickly.

"The store was emptied, and the camouflage which they counted upon to hide their conversation was stripped from them. They were alone and very conspicuous in the store. Natter went further. He approached them and talked them into allowing him to escort Schwartz back to the Institute. They agreed. What could they do? . . . So that the day ended with not a single word passing between Arvardan and Schwartz.

"Nor did he commit the folly of arresting Schwartz. The two are still in ignorance of their detection and will yet lead us to bigger game.

"And Natter went further still. He notified the Imperial garrison, and that is beyond praise. It presented Arvardan with a situation he could not possibly have counted upon. He must either reveal himself to be an Outsider and destroy his usefulness, which apparently depends upon conducting himself upon Earth as though he were an Earthman, or he must keep the fact secret and subject himself to whatever unpleasantness might result. He took the more heroic alternative, and even broke the arm of an officer of the Empire, in his passion for realism. That, at least, must be remembered in his favor.

"It is significant that his actions were as they were. Why should he, an Outsider, expose himself to the neuronic whip for an Earthgirl if the matter at stake was not supremely important?"

Both fists of the High Minister were on the desk before him. He glowered savagely, the long, smooth lines of his face crumpled in distress. "It is well for you, Balkis, from such meager details, to construct the spider web you do. It is skillfully done, and I feel that it is as you say. Logic leaves us no other alternative. . . . But it means that they are too close, Balkis. They are too close. . . . And they will have no mercy this time."

Balkis shrugged. "They cannot be too close, or, in a case of such potential destructiveness for all the Empire, they would have already struck. . . . And their time is running short. Arvardan must still meet with Schwartz if anything is to be accomplished, and so I can predict for you the future."

"Do so—do so."

"Schwartz must be sent away now and events allowed to quiet down from their current high pitch."

"But where will he be sent?"

"We know that too. Schwartz was brought to the Institute by a man, obviously a farmer. Descriptions reached us from both Shekt's technician and from Natter. We went through the registration data of every farmer within sixty miles of Chica, and Natter identified one Arbin Maren as the man. The technician supported that decision independently. We investigated the man quietly, and it seems that he is supporting a father-in-law, a helpless cripple, in evasion of the Sixty."

The High Minister pounded the table. "Such cases are entirely too frequent, Balkis. The laws must be tightened——"

"It is not now the point, Your Excellency. What is important is the fact that since the farmer is violating the customs, he can be blackmailed."

"Oh . . ."

"Shekt, and his Outsider allies, need a tool for just such a case—that is, where Schwartz must remain in seclusion for a longer period than he can safely stay hidden in the Institute. This farmer, probably helpless and innocent, is perfect for the purpose. Well, he will be watched. Schwartz will never be out of sight. . . . Now, eventually another meeting between him and Arvardan will have to be arranged, and that time we will be prepared. Do you understand everything now?"

"I do."

"Well, praise Earth. Then I will leave you now." And, with a sardonic smile, he added, "With your permission, of course."

And the High Minister, completely oblivious to the sarcasm, waved a hand in dismissal.

The Secretary, on his way to his own small office, was alone, and, when alone, his thoughts sometimes escaped from beneath his firm control and disported themselves in the secrecy of his mind.

They concerned themselves very little with Dr. Shekt, Schwartz, Arvardan—least of all with the High Minister.

Instead there was the picture of a planet, Trantor—from whose huge, planet-wide metropolis all the Galaxy was ruled. And there was the picture of a palace whose spires and sweeping arches he had never seen in reality; that no other Earthman had ever seen. He thought of the invisible lines of power and glory that swept from sun to sun in gathering strings, ropes and cables to that central palace and to that abstraction, the Emperor, who was, after all, merely a man.

His mind held that thought fixedly—the thought of that power which could alone bestow a divinity during life—concentrated in one who was merely human.

Merely human! Like himself!
He could be——

Eleven: THE MIND THAT CHANGED

The coming of the change was dim in Joseph Schwartz's mind. Many times, in the absolute quiet of the night—how much more quiet the nights were now; were they ever noisy and bright and clanging with the life of energetic millions?—in the new quiet, he traced it back. He would have liked to say that here, *here* was the moment.

There was first that old, shattering day of fear when he was alone in a strange world—a day as misty in his mind now as the memory of Chicago itself. There was the trip to Chica, and its strange, complicated ending. He thought of that often.

Something about a machine—pills he had taken. Days of recuperation and then the escape, the wandering, the inexplicable events that last hour in the department store. He couldn't possibly remember that part correctly. Yet, in the two months since, how clear everything was, how unfaulted his memory.

Even then things had begun to seem strange. He had been sensitive to atmosphere. The old doctor and his daughter had been uneasy, even frightened. Had he *known* that then? Or had it just been a fugitive impression, strengthened by the hindsight of his thoughts since?

But then, in the department store, just before that big man had reached out and trapped him—just *before* that—he had become conscious of the coming snatch. The warning had not been soon enough to save him, but it was a definite indication of the change.

And, since then, the headaches. No, not quite headaches. Throbbings, rather, as though some hidden dynamo in his brain had started working and, with its unaccustomed action, was vibrating every bone of his skull. There had been nothing like it in Chicago—supposing his fantasy of Chicago had meaning—or even during his first few days here in reality.

Had they done something to him that day in Chica? The machine? The pills—that had been anesthetic. An operation? And his thoughts, having reached that point for the hundredth time, stopped once more.

He had left Chica the day after his abortive escape, and now the days passed easily.

There had been Grew in his wheel chair, repeating words and pointing, or making motions, just as the girl, Pola, had done before him. Until one day Grew stopped speaking nonsense and began talking English. Or no, he himself—he, Joseph Schwartz—had stopped speaking English and had begun talking nonsense. Except that it wasn't nonsense, any more.

It was so easy. He learned to read in four days. He surprised himself. He had had a phenomenal memory once, in Chicago, or it seemed to him that he had. But he had not been capable of *such* feats. Yet Grew did not seem surprised.

Schwartz gave it up.

Then, when the autumn had become really golden, things were clear again, and he was out in the fields working. It was amazing, the way he picked it up. There it was again—he *never* made a mistake. There were complicated machines that he could run without trouble after a single explanation.

He waited for the cold weather and it never quite came. The winter was spent in clearing ground, in fertilizing, in preparing for the spring planting in a dozen ways.

He questioned Grew, tried to explain what snow was, but the latter only stared and said, "Frozen water falling like rain, eh? Oh! The word for that is snow! I understand it does that on other planets but not on Earth."

Schwartz watched the temperature thereafter and found that it scarcely varied from day to day—and yet the days shortened, as would be expected from a northerly location, say as northerly as Chicago. He wondered if he was on Earth.

He tried reading some of Grew's book films but gave up. People were people still, but the minutiae of daily life, the knowledge of which was taken for granted, the historical and sociological allusions that meant nothing to him, forced him back.

The puzzles continued. The uniformly warm rains, the wild instructions he received to remain away from certain regions. For instance, there had been the evening that he had finally become too intrigued by the shining horizon, the blue glow to the south . . .

He had slipped off after supper, and when not a mile had passed, the almost noiseless whir of the biwheel engine came up behind him and Arbin's angry shout rang out in the evening air. He had stopped and had been taken back.

Arbin had paced back and forth before him and had said, "You must stay away from anywhere that it shines at night."

Schwartz had asked mildly, "Why?"

And the answer came with biting incision, "Because it is forbidden." A long pause, then, "You really don't know what it's like out there, Schwartz?"

Schwartz spread his hands.

Arbin said, "Where do you come from? Are you an—an Outsider?"

"What's an Outsider?"

Arbin shrugged and left.

But that night had had a great importance for Schwartz, for it was during that short mile toward the shiningness that the strangeness in his mind had coalesced into the Mind Touch. It was what he called it, and the closest he had come, either then or thereafter, to describing it.

He had been alone in the darkling purple. His own footsteps against the springy pavement were muted. He hadn't seen anybody. He hadn't heard anybody. He hadn't touched anything.

Not exactly . . . It had been *something* like a touch, but not anywhere on his body. It was in his mind. . . . Not exactly a touch, but a presence—a somethingness there like a velvety tickle.

Then there had been two—*two* touches, distinct, apart. And the second—how could he tell them apart?—had grown louder (no, that wasn't the right word); it had grown distincter, more definite.

And then he knew it was Arbin. He knew it five minutes, at least, before he caught the sound of the biwheel, ten minutes before he laid eyes on Arbin.

Thereafter it occurred again and again with increasing frequency.

It began to dawn on him that he always knew when Arbin, Loa, or Grew was within a hundred feet of himself, even when he had no reason for knowing, even when he had every reason to suppose the opposite. It was a hard thing to take for granted, yet it began to seem so natural.

He experimented, and found that he knew exactly where any of them were, at any time. He could distinguish between them, for the Mind Touch differed from person to person. Not once had he the nerve to mention it to the others.

And sometimes he would wonder what that first Mind Touch on the road to the Shiningness had been. It had been neither Arbin, Loa, nor Grew. Well? Did it make a difference?

It did later. He had come across the Touch again, the same one, when he brought in the cattle one evening. He came to Arbin then and said:

"What about that patch of woods past the South Hills, Arbin?"

"Nothing about it," was the gruff answer. "It's Ministerial Ground."

"What's that?"

Arbin seemed annoyed. "It's of no importance to you, is it? They call it Ministerial Ground because it is the property of the High Minister."

"Why isn't it cultivated?"

"It's not intended for that." Arbin's voice was shocked. "It was a great Center. In ancient days. It is very sacred and must not be disturbed. Look, Schwartz, if you want to remain here safely, curb your curiosity and tend to your job."

"But if it's so sacred, then nobody can live there?"

"Exactly. You're right."

"Are you sure?"

"I'm sure. . . . And you're not to trespass. It will mean the end for you."

"I won't."

Schwartz walked away, wondering and oddly uneasy. It was from that wooded ground that the Mind Touch came, quite powerfully, and now something additional had been added to the sensation. It was an unfriendly Touch, a threatening Touch.

Why? Why?

And still he dared not speak. They would not have believed him, and something unpleasant would happen to him as a consequence. He knew that too. He knew too much, in fact.

He was younger these days, also. Not so much in the physical sense, to be sure. He was thinner in his stomach and broader in his shoulders. His muscles were harder and springier and his digestion was better. That was the result of work in the open. But it was something else he was chiefly conscious of. It was his way of thinking.

Old men tend to forget what thought was like in their youth; they forget the quickness of the mental jump, the daring of the youthful intuition, the agility of the fresh insight. They become accustomed to the more plodding varieties of reason, and because this is more than made up by the accumulation of experience, old men think themselves wiser than the young.

But to Schwartz experience remained, and it was with a sharp delight that he found he could understand things at a bound, that he gradually progressed from following Arbin's explanations to anticipating them, to leaping on ahead. As a result, he felt young in a far more subtle way than any amount of physical excellence could account for.

Two months passed, and it all came out—over a game of chess with Grew in the arbor.

Chess, somehow, hadn't changed, except for the names of the pieces. It was as he remembered it, and therefore it was always a comfort to him. At least, in this one respect, his poor memory did not play him false.

Grew told him of variations of chess. There was four-handed chess, in which each player had a board, touching each other at the corners, with a fifth board filling the hollow in the center as a common No Man's Land. There were three-dimensional chess games in which eight transparent boards were placed one over the other and in which each piece moved in three dimensions as they formerly moved in two, and in which the number of pieces and pawns were doubled, the win coming only when a simultaneous check of both enemy kings occurred. There were even the popular varieties, in which the original position of the chessmen were decided by throws of the dice, or where certain squares conferred advantages or disadvantages to the pieces upon them, or where new pieces with strange properties were introduced.

But chess itself, the original and unchangeable, was the same—and the tournament between Schwartz and Grew had completed its first fifty games.

Schwartz had a bare knowledge of the moves when he began, so that he lost constantly in the first games. But that had changed and losing games were becoming rarer. Gradually Grew had grown slow and cautious, had taken to smoking his pipe into glowing embers in the intervals between moves, and had finally subsided into rebellious and querulous losses.

Grew was White and his pawn was already on King 4.

"Let's go," he urged sourly. His teeth were clamped hard on his pipe and his eyes were already searching the board tensely.

Schwartz took his seat in the gathering twilight and sighed. The games were really becoming uninteresting as more and more he became aware of the nature of Grew's moves before they could be made. It was as if Grew had a misty window in his skull. And the fact that he himself knew, almost instinctively, the proper course of chess play to take was simply of a piece with the rest of his problem.

They used a "night-board," one that glowed in the darkness in a checkered blue-and-orange glimmer. The pieces, ordinary lumpish figures of a reddish clay in the sunlight, were metamorphosed at night. Half were bathed a creamy whiteness that lent them the look of cold and shining porcelain, and the others sparked in tiny glitters of red.

The first moves were rapid. Schwartz's own King's Pawn met the enemy advance head on. Grew brought out his King's Knight to Bishop 3; Schwartz countered with Queen's Knight to Bishop 3. Then the White Bishop leaped to Queen's Knight 5, and Schwartz's Queen's Rook's Pawn slid ahead a square to drive it back to Rook 4. He then advanced his other Knight to Bishop 3.

The shining pieces slid across the board with an eery volition of their own as the grasping fingers lost themselves in the night.

Schwartz was frightened. He might be revealing insanity, but he *had to know*. He said abruptly, "Where am I?"

Grew looked up in the midst of a deliberate move of his Queen's Knight to Bishop 3 and said, "What?"

Schwartz didn't know the word for "country," or "nation." He said, "What world is this?" and moved his Bishop to King 2.

"Earth," was the short reply, and Grew castled with great emphasis, first the tall figurine that was the King, moving, and then the lumpish Rook topping it and resting on the other side.

That was a thoroughly unsatisfactory answer. The word Grew had used Schwartz translated in his mind as "Earth." But what was "Earth"? Any planet is "Earth" to those that live on it. He advanced his Queen's Knight's Pawn two spaces, and again Grew's Bishop had to retreat, to Knight 3 this time. Then Schwartz and Grew, each in turn, advanced the Queen's Pawn one space, each freeing his Bishop for the battle in the center that was soon to begin.

Schwartz asked, as calmly and casually as he could, "What year is this?" He castled.

Grew paused. He might have been startled. "What *is* it you're harping on today? Don't you want to play? If it will make you happy, this is 827." He added sarcastically, "G.E." He stared frowningly at the board, then slammed his Queen's Knight to Queen 5, where it made its first assault.

Schwartz dodged quickly, moving his own Queen's Knight to Rook 4 in counterattack. The skirmish was on in earnest. Grew's Knight seized the Bishop, which leaped upward in a bath of red fire to be dropped with a sharp click into the box where it might lie, a buried warrior, until the next game. And then the conquering Knight fell instantly to Schwartz's Queen. In a moment of overcaution, Grew's attack faltered and he moved his remaining Knight back to the haven of King 1, where it was relatively useless. Schwartz's Queen's Knight now repeated the first exchange, taking the Bishop and falling prey in its turn to the Rook's Pawn.

Now another pause, and Schwartz asked mildly, "What's G.E.?"

"What?" demanded Grew bad-humoredly. "Oh—you mean you're still wondering what year this is? Of all the fool—— Well, I keep forgetting you just learned to talk a month or so ago. But you're intelligent. Don't you really know? Well, it's 827 of the Galactic Era. Galactic Era: G.E.—see? It's 827 years since the foundation of the Galactic Empire; 827 years since the coronation of Frankenn the First. Now, *please*, it's your move."

But the Knight that Schwartz held was swallowed up in the grip of his hand for the moment. He was in a fury of frustration. He said, "Just one minute," and put the Knight down on Queen 2. "Do you recognize any of these names? America, Asia, the United States, Russia, Europe——" He groped for identification.

In the darkness Grew's pipe was a sullen red glow and the dim shadow of him hunched over the shining chessboard as if it had the less life of the two. He might have shaken his head curtly, but Schwartz could not see that. He didn't have to. He sensed the other's negation as clearly as though a speech had been delivered.

Schwartz tried again. "Do you know where I can get a map?"

"No maps," growled Grew, "unless you want to risk your neck in Chica. I'm no geographer. I never heard of the names you mention, either. What are they? People?"

Risk his neck? Why that? Schwartz felt the coldness gather. Had he committed a crime? Did Grew know about it?

He asked doubtfully, "The sun has nine planets, hasn't it?"

"Ten," was the uncompromising answer.

Schwartz hesitated. Well, they *might* have discovered another that he hadn't heard about. But then why should Grew have heard about it? He counted on his fingers, and then, "How about the sixth planet? Has it got rings?"

Grew was slowly moving the King's Bishop's Pawn forward two squares, and Schwartz instantly did the same.

Grew said, "Saturn, you mean? Of course it has rings." He was calculating now. He had the choice of taking either the Bishop's Pawn or the King's Pawn, and the consequences of the choice were not too clear.

"And is there an asteroid belt—little planets—between Mars and Jupiter? I mean between the fourth and fifth planets?"

"Yes," mumbled Grew. He was relighting his pipe and thinking feverishly. Schwartz caught that agonized uncertainty and was annoyed at it. To him, now that he was sure of Earth's identity, the chess game was less than a trifle. Questions quivered along the inner surface of his skull, and one slipped out.

"Your book films are real, then? There are other worlds? With people?"

And now Grew looked up from the board, eyes probing uselessly in the darkness. "Are you serious?"

"Are there?"

"By the Galaxy! *I believe you really don't know.*"

Schwartz felt humiliated in his ignorance. "Please——"

"Of course there are worlds. Millions of them! Every star you see has worlds, and most of those you don't see. It's all part of the Empire."

Delicately, inside, Schwartz felt the faint echo of each of Grew's intense words as they sparked directly from mind to mind. Schwartz felt the mental contacts growing stronger with the days. Maybe, soon, he could hear those tiny words in his mind even when the person thinking them *wasn't* talking.

And now, for the first time, he finally thought of an alternative to insanity. Had he passed through time, somehow? Slept through, perhaps?

He said huskily, "How long since it's all happened, Grew? How long since the time when there was only one planet?"

"What do you mean?" He was suddenly cautious. "Are you a member of the Ancients?"

"Of the what? I'm not a member of anything, but wasn't Earth once the only planet? . . . Well, wasn't it?"

"The Ancients say so," said Grew grimly, "but who knows? Who really knows? The worlds up there have been existing all history long as far as I know."

"But how long is that?"

"Thousands of years, I suppose. Fifty thousand, a hundred—I can't say."

Thousands of years! Schwartz felt a gurgle in his throat and pressed it down in panic. All that between two steps? A breath, a moment, a flicker of time—and he had jumped thousands of years? He felt himself shrinking back to amnesia. His identification of the

Solar System must have been the result of imperfect memories penetrating the mist.

But now Grew was making his next move—he was taking the other's Bishop's Pawn, and it was almost mechanically that Schwartz noted mentally the fact that it was the wrong choice. Move fitted to move now with no conscious effort. His King's Rook swooped forward to take the foremost of the now-doubled White Pawns. White's Knight advanced again to Bishop 3. Schwartz's Bishop moved to Knight 2, freeing itself for action. Grew followed suit by moving his own Bishop to Queen 2.

Schwartz paused before launching the final attack. He said, "Earth is boss, isn't it?"

"Boss of what?"

"Of the Emp——"

But Grew looked up with a roar at which the chessmen quivered. "Listen, you, I'm tired of your questions. Are you a complete fool? Does Earth look as if it's boss of anything?" There was a smooth whir as Grew's wheel chair circled the table. Schwartz felt grasping fingers on his arm.

"Look! Look there!" Grew's voice was a whispered rasp. "You see the horizon? You see it shine?"

"Yes."

"*That* is Earth—all Earth. Except here and there, where a few patches like this one exist."

"I don't understand."

"Earth's crust is radioactive. The soil glows, always glowed, will glow forever. Nothing can grow. No one can live—— You really didn't know that? Why do you suppose we have the Sixty?"

The paralytic subsided. He circled his chair about the table again. "It's your move."

The Sixty! Again a Mind Touch with an indefinable aura of menace. Schwartz's chess pieces played themselves, while he wondered about it with a tight-pressed heart. His King's Pawn took the opposing Bishop's Pawn. Grew moved his Knight to Queen 4 and Schwartz's Rook sidestepped the attack to Knight 4. Again Grew's Knight attacked, moving to Bishop 3, and Schwartz's Rook avoided the issue again to Knight 5. But now Grew's King's Rook's Pawn advanced one timorous square and Schwartz's Rook slashed forward. It took the Knight's Pawn, checking the enemy King. Grew's King promptly took the Rook, but Schwartz's Queen plugged the hole instantly, moving to Knight 4 and checking. Grew's King scurried to Rook 1, and Schwartz brought up his Knight, placing it on King 4.

Grew moved his Queen to King 2 in a strong attempt to mobilize his defenses, and Schwartz countered by marching his Queen forward two squares to Knight 6, so that the fight was now in close quarters. Grew had no choice; he moved his Queen to Knight 2, and the two female majesties were now face to face. Schwartz's Knight pressed home, taking the opposing Knight on Bishop 6, and when the now-attacked White Bishop moved quickly to Bishop 3, the Knight followed to Queen 5. Grew hesitated for slow minutes, then advanced his outflanked Queen up the long diagonal to take Schwartz's Bishop.

Then he paused and drew a relieved breath. His sly opponent had a Rook in danger with a check in the offing and his own Queen ready to wreak havoc. And he was ahead a Rook to a Pawn.

"Your move," he said with satisfaction.

Schwartz said finally, "What—what is the Sixty?"

There was a sharp unfriendliness to Grew's voice. "Why do you ask that? What are you after?"

"Please," humbly. He had little spirit left in him. "I am a man with no harm in me. I don't know who I am or what happened to me. Maybe I'm an amnesia case."

"Very likely," was the contemptuous reply. "Are you escaping from the Sixty? Answer truthfully."

"But I tell you I don't know what the Sixty is!"

It carried conviction. There was a long silence. To Schwartz, Grew's Mind Touch was ominous, but he could not, quite, make out words.

Grew said slowly, "The Sixty is your sixtieth year. Earth supports twenty million people, no more. To live, you must produce. If you cannot produce, you cannot live. Past Sixty—you cannot produce."

"And so . . ." Schwartz's mouth remained open.

"You're put away. It doesn't hurt."

"You're killed?"

"It's not murder," stiffly. "It *must* be that way. Other worlds won't take us, and we must make room for the children some way. The older generation must make room for the younger."

"Suppose you don't tell them you're sixty?"

"Why shouldn't you? Life after sixty is no joke. . . . And there's a Census every ten years to catch anyone who is foolish enough to try to live. Besides, they have your age on record."

"Not mine." The words slipped out. Schwartz couldn't stop them. "Besides, I'm only fifty—next birthday."

"It doesn't matter. They can check by your bone structure. Don't you know that? There's no way of masking it. They'll get me next time. . . . Say, it's your move."

Schwartz disregarded the urging. "You mean they'll——"

"Sure, I'm only fifty-five, but look at my legs. I can't work, can I? There are three of us registered in our family, and our quota is adjusted on a basis of three workers. When I had the stroke I should have been reported, and then the quota would have been reduced. But I would have gotten a premature Sixty, and Arbin and Loa wouldn't do it. They're fools, because it has meant hard work for them—till you came along. And they'll get me next year, anyway. . . . Your move."

"Is next year the Census?"

"That's right. . . . Your move."

"Wait!" urgently. "Is *everyone* put away after sixty? No exceptions at all?"

"Not for you and me. The High Minister lives a full life, and members of the Society of Ancients; certain scientists or those performing some great service. Not many qualify. Maybe a dozen a year. . . . *It's your move!*"

"Who decides who qualifies?"

"The High Minister, of course. Are you moving?"

But Schwartz stood up. "Never mind. It's checkmate in five moves. My Queen is going to take your Pawn to check you; you've got to move to Knight 1; I bring up the Knight to check you at King 2; you must move to Bishop 2; my Queen checks you at King 6; you must move to Knight 2; my Queen goes to Knight 6, and when you're then forced to Rook 1, my Queen mates you at Rook 6.

"Good game," he added automatically.

Grew stared long at the board, then, with a cry, dashed it from the table. The gleaming pieces rolled dejectedly about on the lawn.

"You and your damned distracting chatter," yelled Grew.

But Schwartz was conscious of nothing. Nothing except the overwhelming necessity of escaping the Sixty. For though Browning said:

Grow old along with me!
The best is yet to be . . .

that was in an Earth of teeming billions and of unlimited food. The best that was *now* to be was the Sixty—and death.

Schwartz was sixty-two.

Sixty-two . . .

Twelve: THE MIND THAT KILLED

It worked out so neatly in Schwartz's methodical mind. Since he did not want to die, he would have to leave the farm. If he stayed where he was, the Census would come, and with it, death.

Leave the farm, then. But where would he go?

There was the—what was it, a hospital?—in Chica. They had taken care of him before. And why? Because he had been a medical "case." But wasn't he still a case? And he could talk now; he could give them the symptoms, which he couldn't before. He could even tell them about the Mind Touch.

Or did everyone have the Mind Touch? Was there any way he could tell? . . . None of the others had it. Not Arbin or Loa or Grew. He knew that. They had no way of telling where he was unless they saw or heard him. Why, he couldn't beat Grew in chess if Grew could——

Wait, now, chess was a popular game. And it couldn't be played if people had the Mind Touch. Not really.

So that made him a peculiarity—a psychological specimen. It might not be a particularly gay life, being a specimen, but it would keep him alive.

And suppose one considered the new possibility that had just arisen. Suppose he were not an amnesiac but a man who had stumbled through time. Why, then, in addition to the Mind Touch, he was a man from the past. He was a historical specimen, an archaeological specimen; they *couldn't* kill him.

If they believed him.

Hmm, *if* they believed him.

That doctor would believe. He had needed a shave that morning Arbin took him to Chica. He remembered that very well. After that his hair never grew, so they must have done something to him. That meant that the doctor knew that he—*he*, Schwartz—had had hair on his face. Wouldn't that be significant? Grew and Arbin never shaved. Grew had once told him that only animals had hair on their face.

So he had to get to the doctor.

What was his name? Shekt? . . . Shekt, that was right.

But he knew so little of this horrible world. To leave by night or cross-country would have entangled him in mysteries, would have plunged him into radioactive danger pockets of which he knew nothing. So, with the boldness of one with no choice, he struck out upon the highway in the early afternoon.

They wouldn't be expecting him back before suppertime, and by that time he would be well away. *They* would have no Mind Touch to miss.

For the first half hour he experienced a feeling of elation, the first such sensation he had had since all this had started. He was finally doing something; he was making an attempt to fight back at his environment. Something with a *purpose,* and not mere unreasoning flight as that time in Chica.

Ah, for an old man he wasn't bad. He'd show them.

And then he stopped—— He stopped in the middle of the highway, because something obtruded itself upon his notice, something he had forgotten.

There was the strange Mind Touch, the unknown Mind Touch; the one he had detected first when he had tried to reach the shining horizon and had been stopped by Arbin; the one that had been watching from the Ministerial Ground.

It was with him now—behind him and watching.

He listened closely—or, at least, he did that which was the equivalent of listening with regard to the Mind Touch. It came no closer, but it was fastened upon himself. It had within it watchfulness and enmity, but not desperation.

Other things became clear. The follower must not lose sight of him, and the follower was armed.

Cautiously, almost automatically, Schwartz turned, picking apart the horizon with eager eyes.

And the Mind Touch changed instantly.

It became doubtful and cautious, dubious as to its own safety, and the success of its own project, whatever that was. The fact of the follower's weapons became more prominent, as though he were speculating upon using them if trapped.

Schwartz knew that he himself was unarmed and helpless. He knew that the follower would kill him rather than allow him to get out of sight; kill him at the first false move. . . . And he saw no one.

So Schwartz walked on, knowing that his follower remained close enough to kill him. His back was stiff in the anticipation of he knew not what. How does death feel? . . . How does death feel? . . . The thought jostled him in time to his steps, jounced in his mind, jiggled in his subconscious, until it went nearly past endurance.

He held onto the follower's Mind Touch as the one salvation. He would detect that instant's increase in tension that would mean that a weapon was being leveled, a trigger being pulled, a contact being closed. At that instant he would drop, he would run——

But why? If it were the Sixty, why not kill him out of hand?

The time-slip theory was fading out of his mind; amnesia again. He was a criminal, perhaps—a dangerous man, who must be watched. Maybe he had once been a high official, who could not be simply killed but must be tried. Perhaps his amnesia was the method used by his unconscious to escape the realization of some tremendous guilt.

And so now he was walking down an empty highway toward a doubtful destination, with death walking at his back.

It was growing dark, and the wind had a dying chill to it. As usual, it didn't seem right. Schwartz judged it to be December, and certainly sunset at four-thirty was right for it, but the wind's chill was not the iciness of a midwestern winter.

Schwartz had long decided that the reason for the prevalent mildness was that the planet (Earth?) did not depend on the sun entirely for its heat. The radioactive soil itself gave off heat, small by the square foot but huge by the million square miles.

And in the darkness the follower's Mind Touch grew nearer. Still attentive, and keyed up to a gamble. In the darkness, following was harder. He had followed him that first night—toward the shininess. Was he afraid to take the risk again?

"Hey! Hey, fella——"

It was a nasal, high-pitched voice. Schwartz froze.

Slowly, in one piece, he turned around. The small figure coming up to him waved its hand, but in the sunless time of day he could not make it out clearly. It approached, unhurrying. He waited.

"Hey, there. Glad to see you. It ain't much fun beating it along the road without company. Mind if I go along with you?"

"Hello," said Schwartz dully. It was the correct Mind Touch. It was the follower. And the face was familiar. It belonged to that hazy time, in Chica.

And then the follower gave every sign of recognition. "Say, I know you. Sure! . . . Don't you remember me?"

It was impossible for Schwartz to say whether under ordinary conditions, in another time, he might or might not have believed the other to be sincere. But now how could he avoid seeing that thin, ragged layer of synthetic recognition that overlay the deep currents of a Touch that told him—shouted at him—that the little man with the very sharp eyes had known him from the start? Knew him and had a death weapon ready for him, if necessary.

Schwartz shook his head.

"Sure," insisted the little man. "It was in the department store. I got you away from that mob." He seemed to double up in artificial laughter. "They thought you had Radiation Fever. *You* remember."

Schwartz did, too, vaguely—dimly. A man like this, for a few minutes, and a crowd, which had first stopped them and then parted for them.

"Yes," he said. "Pleased to meet you." It wasn't very brilliant conversation, but Schwartz could do no better, and the little man did not seem to mind.

"My name's Natter," he said, shoving out a limp hand at the other. "I didn't get a chance to talk much with you that first time—overlooked it in the crisis of things, you might say—but I'm sure glad to get a second chance. . . . Let's have the mitt."

"I'm Schwartz." And he touched palms with the other, briefly.

"How come you're walking?" asked Natter. "Going somewheres?"

Schwartz shrugged. "Just walking."

"A hiker, huh? That's for me too. All year round I'm on the road—puts the old Kibosh on the grummlies."

"What?"

"You know. Makes you full of life. You get to breathe that air and feel the blood pumping, hey? . . . Walked too far this time. Hate to get back after night by my lonesome. Always glad for the company. Where you going?"

It was the second time Natter had asked the question, and the Mind Touch made plain the importance attached to it. Schwartz wondered how long he could evade the issue. There was a questing anxiety in the follower's mind. And no lie would do. Schwartz didn't know enough about this new world to lie.

He said, "I'm going to the hospital."

"The hospital? What hospital?"

"I was there when I was in Chica."

"You mean the Institute. Ain't that it? That's where I took you before, that time in the department store, I mean." Anxiety and increasing tension.

"To Dr. Shekt," said Schwartz. "Do you know him?"

"I've heard of him. He's a big shot. Are you sick?"

"No, but I'm supposed to report once in a while." Did that sound reasonable?

"Walking?" said Natter. "Doesn't he send a car for you?" Apparently it did not seem reasonable.

Schwartz said nothing now—a clammy silence.

Natter, however, was buoyant. "Look here, chum, soon's I pass a public Communi-wave, I'll order a taxi from the city. It'll meet us on the road."

"A Communi-wave?"

"Sure. They have 'em all along the highway. See, there's one."

He took a step away from Schwartz, and the latter found himself in a sudden shriek. "Stop! Don't move."

Natter stopped. There was a queer coldness in his expression as he turned. "What's eating you, bud?"

Schwartz found the new language almost inadequate for the rapidity with which he hurled words at the other. "I'm tired of this acting. I know you, and I know what you're going to do. You're going to call somebody to tell them I'm going to Dr. Shekt. They'll be ready for me in the city and they'll send out a car to pick me up. And you'll kill me if I try to get away."

There was a frown on Natter's face. He muttered, "You're sure right on the gizzbo with that last——" It was not intended for Schwartz's ears, nor did it reach them, but the words rested lightly on the very surface of his Mind Touch.

Aloud he said, "Mister, you've got me confused. You're shoving a fast one right past my nose." But he was making room, and his hand was drifting toward his hip.

And Schwartz lost control of himself. He waved his arms in a wild fury. "Leave me alone, why don't you? What have I done to you? . . . Go away! *Go away!*"

He ended in a voice-cracked shriek, his forehead ridged with hate and fear of the creature who stalked him and whose mind was so alive with enmity. His own emotions heaved and thrust at the Mind Touch, attempting to evade the clingingness of it, rid itself of the breath of it——

And it was gone. Suddenly and completely gone. There had been the momentary consciousness of overwhelming pain—not in himself, but in the other—then nothing. No Mind Touch. It had dropped away like the grip of a fist growing lax and dead.

Natter was a crumpled smear on the darkening highway. Schwartz crept toward him. Natter was a little man, easy to turn over. The look of agony on his face might have been stamped on, deeply, deeply. The lines remained, did not relax. Schwartz felt for the heartbeat and did not find it.

He straightened in a deluge of self-horror.

He had murdered a man!

And then a deluge of amazement——

Without touching him! He had killed this man just by hating him, by striking somehow at the Mind Touch.

What other powers did he have?

He made a quick decision. He searched the other's pockets and found money. Good! He could use that. Then he dragged the corpse into the fields and let the high grass cover it.

He walked on for two hours. No other Mind Touch disturbed him.

He slept in an open field that night, and the next morning, after two hours more, reached the outskirts of Chica.

Chica was only a village to Schwartz, and by comparison with the Chicago he remembered, the motion of the populace was still thin and sporadic. Even so, the Mind Touches were for the first time numerous. They amazed and confused him.

So many! Some drifting and diffuse; some pointed and intense. There were men who passed with their minds popping in tiny explosions; others with nothing inside their skulls but, perhaps, a gentle rumination on the breakfast just completed.

At first Schwartz turned and jumped with every Touch that passed, taking each as a personal contact; but within the hour he learned to ignore them.

He was hearing words now, even when they were not actually mouthed. This was something new, and he found himself listening. They were thin, eerie phrases, disconnected and wind-whipped; far off, far off . . . And with them, living, crawling emotion and other subtle things that cannot be described—so that all the world was a panorama of boiling life visible to himself only.

He found he could penetrate buildings as he walked, sending his mind in as though it were something he held on a leash, something that could suck its way into crannies invisible to the eye and bring out the bones of men's inner thoughts.

It was before a huge stone-fronted building that he halted, and considered. They (whoever they were) were after him. He had killed the follower, but there must be others—the others that the follower had wanted to call. It might be best for him to make no move for a few days, and how to do that best? . . . A job? . . .

He probed the building before which he had stopped. In there was a distant Mind Touch that to him might mean a job. They were looking for textile workers in there—and he had once been a tailor.

He stepped inside, where he was promptly ignored by everyone. He touched someone's shoulder.

"Where do I see about a job, please?"

"Through that door!" The Mind Touch that reached him was full of annoyance and suspicion.

Through the door, and then a thin, point-chin fellow fired questions at him and fingered the classifying machine onto which he punched the answers.

Schwartz stammered his lies and truths with equal uncertainty.

But the personnel man began, at least, with a definite unconcern. The questions were fired rapidly: "Age? . . . Fifty-two? Hmm. State of health? . . . Married? . . . Experience? . . . Worked with textiles? . . . Well, what kind? . . . Thermoplastic? Elastomeric? . . . What do you mean, you think all kinds? . . . Whom did you work with last? . . . Spell his name. . . . You're not from Chica, are you? . . . Where are your papers? . . . You'll have to bring them here if you want action taken. . . . What's your registration number? . . ."

Schwartz was backing away. He hadn't foreseen this end when he had begun. And the Mind Touch of the man before him was changing. It had become suspicious to the point of single-trackedness, and cautious too. There was a surface layer of sweetness and good-fellowship that was so shallow, and which overlay animosity so thinly, as to be the most dangerous feature of all.

"I think," said Schwartz nervously, "that I'm not suited for this job."

"No, no, come back." And the man beckoned at him. "We have something for you. Just let me look through the files a bit." He was smiling, but his Mind Touch was clearer now and even more unfriendly.

He had punched a buzzer on his desk——

Schwartz, in a sudden panic, rushed for the door.

"Hold him!" cried the other instantly, dashing from behind his desk.

Schwartz struck at the Mind Touch, lashing out violently with his own mind, and he heard a groan behind him. He looked quickly over his shoulder. The personnel man was seated on the floor, face contorted and temples buried in his palms. Another man bent over him; then, at an urgent gesture, headed for Schwartz. Schwartz waited no more.

He was out on the street, fully aware now that there must be an alarm out for him with a complete description made public, and that the personnel man, at least, had recognized him.

He ran and doubled along the streets blindly. He attracted attention; more of it now, for the streets were filling up—suspicion, suspicion everywhere—suspicion because he ran—suspicion because his clothes were wrinkled and ill-fitting——

In the multiplicity of Mind Touches and in the confusion of his own fear and despair, he could not identify the true enemies, the ones in which there was not only suspicion but certainty, and so he hadn't the slightest warning of the neuronic whip.

There was only that awful pain, which descended like the whistle of a lash and remained like the crush of a rock. For seconds he coasted down the slope of that descent into agony before drifting into the black.

Thirteen: SPIDER WEB AT WASHENN

The grounds of the College of Ancients in Washenn are nothing if not sedate. Austerity is the key word, and there is something authentically grave about the clustered knots of novices taking their evening stroll among the trees of the Quadrangle—where none but Ancients might trespass. Occasionally the green-robed figure of a Senior Ancient might make its way across the lawn, receiving reverences graciously.

And, once in a long while, the High Minister himself might appear.

But not as now, at a half run, almost in a perspiration, disregarding the respectful raising of hands, oblivious to the cautious stares that followed him, the blank looks at one another, the slightly raised eyebrows.

He burst into the Legislative Hall by the private entrance and broke into an open run down the empty, step-ringing ramp. The door that he thundered at opened at the foot pressure of the one within, and the High Minister entered.

His Secretary scarcely looked up from behind his small, plain desk, where he hunched over a midget Field-shielded Televisor, listening intently and allowing his eyes to rove over a quire or so of official-looking communications that piled high before him.

The High Minister rapped sharply on the desk. "What is this? What is going on?"

The Secretary's eyes flicked coldly at him, and the Televisor was put to one side. "Greetings, Your Excellency."

"Greet me no greetings!" retorted the High Minister impatiently. "I want to know what is going on."

"In a sentence, our man has escaped."

"You mean the man who was treated by Shekt with the Synapsifier—the Outsider—the spy—the one on the farm outside Chica——"

It is uncertain how many qualifications the High Minister, in his anxiety, might have rattled out had not the Secretary interrupted with an indifferent "Exactly."

"Why was I not informed? Why am I never informed?"

"Immediate action was necessary and you were engaged. I substituted, therefore, to the best of my ability."

"Yes, you are careful about my engagements when you wish to do without me. Now, I'll not have it. I will not permit myself to be bypassed and sidetracked. I will not——"

"We delay," was the reply at ordinary speaking volume, and the High Minister's half shout faded. He coughed, hovered uncertainly at further speech, then said mildly:

"What are the details, Balkis?"

"Scarcely any. After two months of patient waiting, with nothing to show for it, this man Schwartz left—was followed—and was lost."

"How lost?"

"We are not sure, but there is a further fact. Our agent, Natter, missed three reporting periods last night. His alternates set out after him along the highway toward Chica and found him at dawn. He was in a ditch at the side of the highway—quite dead."

The High Minister paled. "The Outsider had killed him?"

"Presumably, though we cannot say certainly. There were no visible signs of violence other than a look of agony on the dead face. There will be an autopsy, of course. He might have died of a stroke just at that inconvenient moment."

"That would be an incredible coincidence."

"So I think," was the cool response, "but if Schwartz killed him, it makes subsequent events puzzling. You see, Your Excellency, it seemed quite obvious from our previous analysis that Schwartz would make for Chica in order to see Shekt, and Natter was found dead on the highway between the Maren farm and Chica. We therefore sent out an alarm to that city three hours ago and the man was caught."

"Schwartz?" incredulously.

"Certainly."

"Why didn't you say that immediately?"

Balkis shrugged. "Your Excellency, there is more important work to be done. I said that Schwartz was in our hands. Well, he was caught quickly and easily, and that fact does seem to me to jibe very well with the death of Natter. How could he be at once so clever as to detect and kill Natter—a most capable man—and so stupid as to enter Chica the very next morning and openly enter a factory, without disguise, to find a job?"

"Is that what he did?"

"That's what he did. . . . There are two possible thoughts that this gives rise to, therefore. Either he has already transmitted such information as he has to Shekt or Arvardan, and has now let himself be caught in order to divert our attention, or else other agents are involved, whom we have not detected and whom he is now covering. In either case, we must not be overconfident."

"I don't know," said the High Minister helplessly, his handsome face twisted into anxious lines. "It gets too deep for me."

Balkis smiled with more than a trace of contempt and volunteered a statement. "You have an appointment four hours from now with Professor Bel Arvardan."

"I have? Why? What am I to say to him? I don't want to see him."

"Relax. You must see him, Your Excellency. It seems obvious to me that since the date of commencement of his fictitious expedition is approaching, he must play out the game by asking you for permission to investigate the Forbidden Areas. Ennius warned us he would, and Ennius must know exactly the details of this comedy. I suppose that you are able to return him froth for froth in this matter and to counter pretense with pretense."

The High Minister bowed his head. "Well, I shall try."

Bel Arvardan arrived in good time, and was able to look about him. To a man well acquainted with the architectural triumphs of all the Galaxy, the College of Ancients could scarcely seem more than a brooding block of steel-ribbed granite, fashioned in an archaic style. To one who was an archaeologist as well, it might signify, in its gloomy, nearly savage austerity, the proper home of a gloomy, nearly savage way of life. Its very primitiveness marked the turning back of eyes to the far past.

Arvardan's thoughts slipped away once again. His two-month tour about Earth's western continents had proven not quite—amusing.

That first day had ruined things. He found himself thinking back to that day at Chica.

He was instantly angry with himself for thinking about it again. She had been rude, egregiously ungrateful, a common Earthgirl. Why should he feel guilty? And yet . . .

Had he made allowances for her shock at discovering him to be an Outsider, like that officer who had insulted her and whose arrogant brutality he had repaid with a broken arm? After all, how could he know how much she had already suffered at the hands of Outsiders? And then to find out, like that, without any softening of the blow, that he was one.

If he had been more patient . . . Why had he broken it off so brutally? He didn't even remember her name. It was Pola-something. Strange! His memory was ordinarily better than that. Was it an unconscious effort to forget?

Well, that made sense. Forget! What was there to remember, anyway? An Earthgirl. A common Earthgirl.

She was a nurse in a hospital. Suppose he tried to locate the hospital. It had been just a vague blot in the night when he parted from her, but it must be in the neighborhood of that Foodomat.

He snatched at the thought and broke into a thousand angry fragments. Was he mad? What would he have gained? She was an Earthgirl. Pretty, sweet, somehow entic——

An Earthgirl!

The High Minister was entering, and Arvardan was glad. It meant relief from that day in Chica. But, deep in his mind, he knew that they would return. They—the thoughts, that is—always did.

As for the High Minister, his robe was new and glistening in its freshness. His forehead showed no trace of haste or doubt; perspiration might have been a stranger to it.

And the conversation was friendly, indeed. Arvardan was at pains to mention the well-wishings of some of the great men of the Empire to the people of Earth. The High Minister was as careful to express the thorough gratification that must be felt by all Earth at the generosity and enlightenment of the Imperial Government.

Arvardan expounded on the importance of archaeology to Imperial philosophy, on its contribution to the great conclusion that all humans of whatever world of the Galaxy were brothers—and the High Minister agreed blandly and pointed out that Earth had long held such to be the case and could only hope that the time would shortly come when the rest of the Galaxy might turn theory into practice.

Arvardan smiled very shortly at that and said, "It is for that very purpose, Your Excellency, that I have approached you. The differences between Earth and some of the Imperial Dominions neighboring it rest largely, perhaps, on differing ways of thinking. Still, a good deal of friction could be removed if it could be shown that Earthmen were not different, *racially*, from other Galactic citizens."

"And how would you propose to do that, sir?"

"That is not easy to explain in a word. As Your Excellency may know, the two main currents of archaeological thinking are commonly called the Merger Theory and the Radiation Theory."

"I am acquainted with a layman's view of both."

"Good. Now the Merger Theory, of course, involves the notion that the various types of humanity, evolving independently, have intermarried in the very early, scarcely documented days of primitive space travel. A conception like that is necessary to account for the fact that Humans are so alike one to the other now."

"Yes," commented the High Minister dryly, "and such a conception also involves the necessity of having several hundred, or thousand, separately evolved beings of a more or less human type so closely related chemically and biologically that intermarriage is possible."

"True," replied Arvardan with satisfaction. "You have put your finger on an impossibly weak point. Yet most archaeologists ignore it and adhere firmly to the Merger Theory, which would, of course, imply the possibility that in isolated portions of the Galaxy there might be subspecies of humanity who remained different, didn't intermarry——"

"You mean Earth," commented the High Minister.

"Earth *is* considered an example. The Radiation Theory, on the other hand——"

"Considers us all descendants of one planetary group of humans."

"Exactly."

"My people," said the High Minister, "because of the evidence of our own history, and of certain writings which are sacred to us and cannot be exposed to the view of Outsiders, are of the belief that Earth itself is the original home of humanity."

"And so I believe as well, and I ask your help to prove this point to all the Galaxy."

"You are optimistic. Just what is involved?"

"It is my conviction, Your Excellency, that many primitive artifacts and architectural remains may be located in those areas of your world which are now, unfortunately, masked by radioactivity. The age of the remains could be accurately calculated from the radioactive decay present and compared——"

But the High Minister was shaking his head. "That is out of the question."

"Why?" And Arvardan frowned in thorough amazement.

"For one thing," said the High Minister, reasoning mildly, "what do you expect to accomplish? If you prove your point, even to the satisfaction of all the worlds, what does it matter that a million years ago all of you were Earthmen? After all, a billion years ago we were all apes, yet we do not admit present-day apes into the relationship."

"Come, Your Excellency, the analogy is unreasonable."

"Not at all, sir. Isn't it reasonable to assume that Earthmen, in their long isolation, have so changed from their emigrating cousins, especially under the influence of radioactivity, as now to form a different race?"

Arvardan bit at his lower lip and answered reluctantly, "You argue well on the side of your enemy."

"Because I ask myself what my enemy will say. So you will accomplish nothing, sir, except perhaps to further exacerbate the hatred against us."

"But," said Arvardan, "there is still the matter of the interests of pure science, the advance of knowledge——"

The High Minister nodded gravely. "I am truly sorry to have to stand in the way of that. I speak now, sir, as one gentleman of the Empire to another. I myself would cheerfully help you, but my people are an obstinate and stiff-necked race, who over centuries have withdrawn into themselves because of the—uh—lamentable attitudes toward them in parts of the Galaxy. They have certain taboos, certain fixed Customs—which even I could not afford to violate."

"And the radioactive areas——"

"Are one of the most important taboos. Even if I were to grant you permission, and certainly my every impulse is to do so, it would merely provoke rioting and disturbances, which would not only endanger your life and those of the members of your expedition but would, in the long run, bring down upon Earth the disciplinary action of the Empire. I would betray my position and the trust of my people if I were to allow that."

"But I am willing to take all reasonable precautions. If you wish to send observers with me—— Or, of course, I can offer to consult you before publishing any results obtained."

The High Minister said, "You tempt me, sir. It is an interesting project. But you overestimate my power, even if we leave the people themselves out of consideration. I am not an absolute ruler. In fact, my power is sharply limited—and all matters must be submitted to the consideration of the Society of Ancients before final decisions are possible."

Arvardan shook his head. "This is most unfortunate. The Procurator warned me of the difficulties, yet I was hoping that—— When can you consult your legislature, Your Excellency?"

"The Presidium of the Society of Ancients will meet three days hence. It is beyond my power to alter the agenda, so it may be a few days more before the matter can be discussed. Say a week."

Arvardan nodded abstractedly. "Well, it will have to do. . . . By the way, Your Excellency——"

"Yes?"

"There is a scientist upon your planet whom I would like to meet. A Dr. Shekt at Chica. Now, I've been in Chica, but left before I could do much and would like to repair the omission. Since I am sure he is a busy man, I wonder if I could trouble you for a letter of introduction?"

The High Minister had stiffened visibly and for several moments said nothing. Then, "May I ask what it is you want to see him about?"

"Certainly. I have read of an instrument he has developed, which he calls a Synapsifier, I believe. It concerns the neuro-chemistry of the brain and could have something very interesting to do with another project of mine. I have been doing some work on the classification of humanity into encephalographic groups—brain-current types, you understand."

"Umm . . . I have heard vaguely about the device. I seem to recall that it was not a success."

"Well, maybe not, but he is an expert in the field and could probably be very helpful to me."

"I see. In that case a letter of introduction will be prepared immediately for you. Of course there must be no mention of your intentions with regard to the Forbidden Areas."

"That is understood, Your Excellency." He rose. "I thank you for your courtesy and your kind attitude and can only hope that the Counsel of Ancients will be liberal with respect to my project."

The Secretary entered after Arvardan left. His lips were spread in his characteristic cold, savage smile.

"Very good," he said. "You handled yourself well, Your Excellency."

The High Minister looked at him somberly and said, "What was that last about Shekt?"

"You are puzzled? Don't be. All things are working out well. You noticed his lack of heat when you vetoed his project. Was that the response of a scientist whose heart is set upon something withdrawn from his grasp for no apparent reason? Or is it the response of one who is playing a part and is relieved to be well rid of it?

"And again we have a queer coincidence. Schwartz escapes and makes his way to Chica. The very next day Arvardan appears here and, after a lukewarm rigmarole about his expedition, mentions casually that he is going to Chica to see Shekt."

"But why mention it, Balkis? It seems foolhardy."

"Because you are straightforward. Put yourself in his position. He imagines we suspect nothing. In such a case it is audacity that wins. He's going to see Shekt. Good! He mentions it frankly. He even asks for a letter of introduction. What better guarantee of honest and innocent intentions can he present? And that brings up another point. Schwartz may have discovered that he was being watched. He may have killed Natter. *But he has had no time to warn the others,* or this comedy could not have played itself out in just this fashion."

The Secretary's eyes were half lidded as he spun his spider web. "There is no way of telling how long it will be before Schwartz's absence becomes suspicious for them, but it is at least safe to allow sufficient time for Arvardan to meet Shekt. We'll catch them together; there will be that much less they can deny."

"How much time do *we* have?" demanded the High Minister.

Balkis looked up thoughtfully. "The schedule is fluid, and ever since we uncovered Shekt's treason they've been on triple shift—and things are proceeding well. We await only the mathematical computations for the necessary orbits. What holds us up there is the inadequacy of our computers. Well . . . it may be only a matter of days now."

"Days!" It was said in a tone queerly compounded of triumph and horror.

"Days!" repeated the Secretary. "But remember—one bomb even two seconds before zero time will be enough to stop us. And even afterward there will be a period of from one to six months when reprisals can be taken. So we are not yet entirely safe."

Days! And then the most incredibly one-sided battle in the history of the Galaxy would be joined and Earth would attack all the Galaxy.

The High Minister's hands were trembling gently.

Arvardan was seated in a stratoplane again. His thoughts were savage ones. There seemed no reason to believe that the High Minister and his psychopathic subject population would allow an official invasion of the radioactive areas. He was prepared for that. Somehow he wasn't even sorry about it. He could have put up a better fight—if he had cared more.

As it was, by the Galaxy, there would be illegal entry. He would arm his ship and fight it out, if necessary. He would rather.

The bloody fools!

Who the devil did they think they were?

Yes, yes, he knew. They thought they were the original humans, the inhabitants of *the* planet——

The worst of it was he knew that they were right.

Well . . . The ship was taking off. He felt himself sinking back into the soft cushion of his seat and knew that within the hour he'd be seeing Chica.

Not that he was eager to see Chica, he told himself, but the Synapsifier thing could be important, and there was no use being on Earth if he didn't take advantage of it. He certainly never intended to return once he left.

Rathole!

Ennius was right.

This Dr. Shekt, however . . . He fingered his letter of introduction, heavy with official formality——

And then he sat bolt upright—or tried to, struggling bitterly against the forces of inertia that were compressing him down into his seat as the Earth still sank away and the blue of the sky was deepened into a rich purple.

He remembered the girl's name. It was Pola *Shekt*.

Now why had he forgotten? He felt angry and cheated. His mind was plotting against him, holding back the last name till it was too late.

But, deep underneath, *something* was rather glad of it.

Fourteen: SECOND MEETING

In the two months that had elapsed from the day that Dr. Shekt's Synapsifier had been used on Joseph Schwartz, the physicist had changed completely. Physically not so much, though perhaps he was a thought more stooped, a shade thinner. It was his manner—abstracted, fearful. He lived in an inner communion, withdrawn from even his closest colleagues, and from which he emerged with a reluctance that was plain to the blindest.

Only to Pola could he unburden himself, perhaps because she, too, had been strangely withdrawn those two months.

"They're watching me," he would say. "I feel it somehow. Do you know what the feeling is like? . . . There's been a turnover in the Institute in the last month or so, and it's the ones I like and feel I can trust that go. . . . I never get a minute to myself. Always someone about. They won't even let me write reports."

And Pola would alternately sympathize with him and laugh at him, saying over and over again, "But what can they possibly have against you to do all this? Even if you did experiment on Schwartz, that's not such a terrible crime. They'd have just called you on the carpet for it."

But his face was yellow and thin as he muttered, "They won't let me live. My Sixty is coming and they won't let me live."

"After all you've done. Nonsense!"

"I know too much, Pola, and they don't trust me."

"Know too much about what?"

He was tired that night, aching to remove the load. He told her. At first she wouldn't believe him, and finally, when she did, she could only sit there, in cold horror.

Pola called up the State House the next day from a public Communi-wave at the other end of town. She spoke through a handkerchief and asked for Dr. Bel Arvardan.

He wasn't there. They thought he might be in Bonair, six thousand miles away, but he hadn't been following his scheduled itinerary very closely. Yes, they did expect him back in Chica eventually, but they didn't know exactly when. Would she leave her name? They would try to find out.

She broke connections at that and leaned her soft cheek against the glass enclosure, grateful for the coolness thereof. Her eyes were deep with unshed tears and liquid with disappointment.

Fool. *Fool!*

He had helped her and she had sent him away in bitterness. He had risked the neuronic whip and worse to save the dignity of a little Earthgirl against an Outsider and she had turned on him anyway.

The hundred credits she had sent to the State House the morning after that incident had been returned without comment. She had wanted then to reach him and apologize, but she had been afraid. The State House was for Outsiders only, and how could she invade it? She had never even seen it, except from a distance.

And now—— She'd have gone to the palace of the Procurator himself to—to——

Only *he* could help them now. *He*, an Outsider who could talk with Earthmen on a basis of equality. *She* had never guessed him to be an Outsider until he had told her. He was so tall and self-confident. He would *know* what to do.

And someone *had* to know, or it would mean the ruin of all the Galaxy.

Of course so many Outsiders deserved it—but did all of them? The women and children and sick and old? The kind and the good? The Arvardans? The ones who had never heard of Earth? And they were humans, after all. Such a horrible revenge would for all time drown whatever justice might be—no, *was*—in Earth's cause in an endless sea of blood and rotting flesh.

And then, out of nowhere, came the call from Arvardan. Dr. Shekt shook his head. "I can't tell him."

"You must," said Pola savagely.

"Here? It is impossible—it would mean ruin for both."

"Then turn him away. *I'll* take care of it."

Her heart was singing wildly. It was only because of this chance to save so many countless myriads of humans, of course. She remembered his wide, white smile. She remembered how he had calmly forced a colonel of the Emperor's own forces to turn and bow his head to her in apology—to *her*, an Earthgirl, who could stand there and forgive him.

Bel Arvardan could do *anything!*

Arvardan could, of course, know nothing of all this. He merely took Shekt's attitude for what it seemed—an abrupt and odd rudeness, of a piece with everything else he had experienced on Earth.

He felt annoyed, there in the anteroom of the carefully lifeless office, quite obviously an unwelcome intruder.

He picked his words. "I would never have dreamed of imposing upon you to the extent of visiting you, Doctor, were it not that I was professionally interested in your Synapsifier. I have been informed that, unlike many Earthmen, you are not unfriendly to men of the Galaxy."

It was apparently an unfortunate phrase, for Dr. Shekt jumped at it. "Now, whoever your informant is, he does wrong to impute any especial friendliness to strangers as such. I have no likes and dislikes. I am an Earthman——"

Arvardan's lips compressed and he half turned.

"You understand, Dr. Arvardan"—the words were hurried and whispered—"I am sorry if I seem rude, but I really cannot——"

"I quite understand," the archaeologist said coldly, though he did not understand at all. "Good day, sir."

Dr. Shekt smiled feebly. "The pressure of my work——"

"I am very busy too, Dr. Shekt."

He turned to the door, raging inwardly at all the tribe of Earthmen, feeling within him, involuntarily, some of the catchwords that were bandied so freely on his home world. The proverbs, for instance: "Politeness on Earth is like dryness in the ocean" or "An Earthman will give you anything as long as it costs nothing and is worth less."

His arm had already broken the photoelectric beam that opened the front door when he heard the flurry of quick steps behind him and a hist of warning in his ear. A piece of paper was thrust in his hand, and when he turned there was only a flash of red as a figure disappeared.

He was in his rented ground car before he unraveled the paper in his hand. Words were scrawled upon it:

"Ask your way to the Great Playhouse at eight this evening. Make sure you are not followed."

He frowned ferociously at it and read it over five times, then stared all over it, as though expecting invisible ink to bound into visibility. Involuntarily, he looked behind him. The street was empty. He half raised his hand to throw the silly scrap out of the window, hesitated, then stuffed it into his vest pocket.

Undoubtedly, if he had had one single thing to do that evening other than what the scrawl had suggested, that would have been the end of it, and, perhaps, of several trillions of people. But, as it turned out, he had nothing to do.

And, as it turned out, he wondered if the sender of the note had been——

At eight o'clock he was making his slow way as part of a long line of ground cars along the serpentine way that apparently led to the Great Playhouse. He had asked only once, and the passerby questioned had stared suspiciously at him (apparently no Earthman was ever free of that all-pervasive suspicion) and had said curtly, "You just follow all the rest of the cars."

It seemed that all the rest of the cars were indeed going to the Playhouse, for when he got there he found all being swallowed, one by one, into the gaping maw of the underground parking lot. He swung out of line and crawled past the Playhouse, waiting for he knew not what.

A slim figure dashed down from the pedestrian ramp and hung outside his window. He stared at it, startled, but it had the door open and was inside in a single gesture.

"Pardon me," he said, "but——"

"Ssh!" The figure was hunched down low in the seat. "Were you followed?"

"Should I have been?"

"Don't be funny. Go straight ahead. Turn when I tell you. . . . My goodness, what are you waiting for?"

He knew the voice. A hood had shifted down to the shoulders, and light brown hair was showing. Dark eyes were gazing at him.

"You'd better move on," she said softly.

He did, and for fifteen minutes, except for an occasional muffled but curt direction, she said nothing. He stole glances at her and thought, with a sudden pleasure, that she was even prettier than he had remembered her. Strange that *now* he felt no resentment.

They stopped—or Arvardan did, at the girl's direction—at the corner of an unpeopled residential district. After a careful pause the girl motioned him ahead once more and they inched down a drive that ended in the gentle ramp of a private garage.

The door closed behind them and the light in the car was the only source of illumination.

And now Pola looked at him gravely and said, "Dr. Arvardan, I'm sorry that I had to do this in order to speak to you privately. I know that I have no standing in your good opinion to lose——"

"Don't think that," he said awkwardly.

"I must think that. I want you to believe that I fully realize how small and vicious I was that night. I don't have the proper words to apologize——"

"Please don't." He glanced away from her. "I might have been a little more diplomatic."

"Well . . ." Pola paused a few moments to regain a certain minimal composure. "It's not what I've brought you here for. You're the only Outsider I've ever met that could be kind and noble—and I need your help."

A cold pang shot through Arvardan. Was this what it was all about? He parked that thought into a cold "Oh?"

And she cried, "No," in return. "It is not for me, Dr. Arvardan. It is for all the Galaxy. Nothing for myself. *Nothing!*"

"What is it?"

"First—— I don't think anyone followed us, but if you hear any noise at all, would you—would you"—her eyes dropped—"put your arms about me, and—and—you know."

He nodded his head and said dryly, "I believe I can improvise without any trouble. Is it necessary to wait for noise?"

Pola reddened. "Please don't joke about it, or mistake my intentions. It would be the only way of avoiding suspicion of our real intentions. It is the one thing that would be convincing."

Arvardan said softly, "Are things that serious?"

He looked at her curiously. She seemed so young and so soft. In a way he felt it to be unfair. Never in his life did he act unreasoningly. He took pride in that. He was a man of strong emotions, but he fought them and beat them. And here, just because a girl seemed weak, he felt the unreasoning urge to protect her.

She said, "Things *are* that serious. I'm going to tell you something, and I know you won't believe it at first. But I want you to *try* to believe it. I want you to make up your mind that I'm sincere. And most of all I want you to decide that you will stick with us after I tell you and see it through. Will you try? I'll give you fifteen minutes, and if you think at the end of that time that I'm not worth trusting or bothering with, I'll leave, and that's the end of it."

"Fifteen minutes?" His lips quirked in an involuntary smile, and he removed his wrist watch and put it before him. "All right."

She clasped her hands in her lap and looked firmly ahead through the windshield that afforded a view only of the blank wall of the garage ahead.

He watched her thoughtfully—the smooth, soft line of her chin, belying the firmness into which she was attempting to force it, the straight and thinly drawn nose, the peculiarly rich overtone to the complexion, so characteristic of Earth.

He caught the corner of her eye upon him. It was hastily withdrawn.

"What's the matter?" he said.

She turned to him and caught her underlip in two teeth. "I was watching you."

"Yes, I could see that. Smudge on my nose?"

"No." She smiled tinily, the first since she had entered his car. He was becoming absurdly conscious of little things about her: the way her hair seemed to hover and float gently each time she shook her head. "It's just that I've been wondering ever since—that night—why you don't wear that lead clothing, if you're an Outsider. That's what fooled me. Outsiders generally look like sacks of potatoes."

"And I don't?"

"Oh no"—and there was a sudden tinge of enthusiasm in her voice —"you look—you look quite like an ancient marble statue, except that you're alive and warm. . . . I'm sorry. I'm being impertinent."

"You mean you think that it's my opinion you're an Earthgirl who doesn't know your place. You'll have to stop thinking that of me, or we can't be friendly. . . . I don't believe in the radioactivity superstition. I've measured the atmospheric radioactivity of Earth and I've conducted laboratory experiments on animals. I'm quite convinced that under ordinary circumstances the radiations won't hurt me. I've been here two months and I don't feel sick yet. My hair isn't falling out"—he pulled at it—"my stomach isn't in knots. And I doubt that my fertility is being endangered, though I will admit to taking slight precautions in that respect. But lead-impregnated shorts, you see, don't show."

He said that gravely, and she was smiling again. "You're slightly mad, I think," she said.

"Really? You'd be surprised how many very intelligent and famous archaeologists have said that—and in long speeches, too."

And she said suddenly, "Will you listen to me now? The fifteen minutes are up."

"What do you think?"

"Why, that you might be. If you weren't, you wouldn't still be sitting here. Not after what I've done."

He said softly, "Are you under the impression that I have to force myself very hard to sit here next to you? If you are, you're wrong. . . . Do you know, Pola, I've never seen, I really believe I've never seen, a girl quite as beautiful as yourself."

She looked up quickly, with fright in her eyes. "Please don't. I'm not trying for that. Don't you believe me?"

"Yes, I do, Pola. Tell me whatever it is you want to. I'll believe it and I'll help you." He believed himself, implicitly. At the moment Arvardan would cheerfully have undertaken to unseat the Emperor.

He had never been in love before, and at that point he ground his thoughts to a halt. He had not used that word before.

Love? With an Earthgirl?

"You've seen my father, Dr. Arvardan?"

"Dr. Shekt is your father? . . . Please call me Bel. I call you Pola."

"If you want me to, I'll try. I suppose you were pretty angry with him."

"He wasn't very polite."

"He couldn't be. He's being watched. In fact, he and I arranged in advance that he was to get rid of you and I was to see you here. This is our house, you know. . . . You see"—her voice dropped to a tight whisper—"Earth is going to revolt."

Arvardan couldn't resist a moment of amusement.

"No!" he said, opening his eyes wide. "All of it?"

But Pola flared into instant fury. "Don't laugh at me. You said you would listen and believe me. Earth *is* going to revolt, and it is serious, because Earth can destroy all the Empire."

"Earth can do that?" Arvardan struggled successfully against a burst of laughter. He said gently, "Pola, how well do you know your Galactography?"

"As well as anybody, teacher, and what has that to do with it, anyway?"

"It has this to do with it. The Galaxy has a volume of several million cubic light-years. It contains two hundred million inhabited planets and an approximate population of five hundred quadrillion people. Right?"

"I suppose so, if you say so."

"It is, believe me. Now Earth is one planet, with a population of twenty millions, and no resources besides. In other words, there are twenty-five billion Galactic citizens for every single Earthman. Now what harm can Earth do against odds of twenty-five billion to one?"

For a moment the girl seemed to sink into doubt, then she emerged. "Bel," she said firmly, "I can't answer that, but my father can. He has not told me the crucial details, because he claims that that would endanger my life. But he will now, if you come with me. He's told me that Earth knows a way by which it can wipe out all life outside Earth, and he *must* be right. He's always been right before."

Her cheeks were pink with earnestness, and Arvardan longed to touch them. (Had he ever before touched her and felt horrified at it? What was happening to him?)

"Is it after ten?" asked Pola.

"Yes," he replied.

"Then he should be upstairs now—if they haven't caught him." She looked about with an involuntary shudder. "We can get into the house directly from the garage now, and if you'll come with me——"

She had her hand on the knob that controlled the car door, when she froze. Her voice was a husky whisper: "There's someone coming . . . Oh, quick——"

The rest was smothered. It was anything but difficult for Arvardan to remember her original injunction. His arms swept about her with an easy motion, and, in an instant, she was warm and soft against him. Her lips trembled upon his and were limitless seas of sweetness . . .

For about ten seconds he swiveled his eyes to their extremes in an effort to see that first crack of light or hear that first footstep, but then he was drowned and swept under by the excitement of it all. Blinded by stars, deafened by his own heartbeat.

Her lips left his, but he sought them again, frankly, and found them. His arms tightened, and she melted within them until her own heartbeat was shaking him in time to his own.

It was quite a while before they broke apart, and for a moment they rested, cheek against cheek.

Arvardan had never been in love before, and this time he did not start at the word.

What of it? Earthgirl or not, the Galaxy could not produce her equal.

He said, with a dreamy pleasure, "It must have been only a traffic noise."

"It wasn't," she whispered. "I didn't hear any noise."

He held her at arm's distance, but her eyes did not falter. "You devil. Are you serious?"

Her eyes sparkled. "I wanted you to kiss me. I'm not sorry."

"Do you think *I* am? Kiss me again, then, for no reason but that *I* want to this time."

Another long, long moment and she was suddenly away from him, arranging her hair and adjusting the collar of her dress with prim and precise gestures. "I think we had better go into the house now. Put out the car light. I've got a pencil flash."

He stepped out of the car after her, and in the new darkness she was the vaguest shadow in the little pockmark of light that came from her pencil flash.

She said, "You'd better hold my hand. There's a flight of stairs we must go up."

His voice was a whisper behind her. "I love you, Pola." It came out so easily—and it sounded so right. He said it again. "I love you, Pola."

She said softly, "You hardly know me."

"No. All my life. I swear! All my life. Pola, for two months I've been thinking and dreaming of you. I swear it."

"I am an Earthgirl, sir."

"Then I will be an Earthman. Try me."

He stopped her and bent her hand up gently until the pocket flash rested upon her flushed, tear-marked face. "Why are you crying?"

"Because when my father tells you what he knows, you'll know that you cannot love an Earthgirl."

"Try me on that too."

Fifteen: THE ODDS THAT VANISHED

Arvardan and Shekt met in a back room on the second story of the house, with the windows carefully polarized to complete opaqueness. Pola was downstairs, alert and sharp-eyed in the armchair from which she watched the dark and empty street.

Shekt's stooped figure wore somehow an air different from that which Arvardan had observed some ten hours previously. The physicist's face was still haggard, and infinitely weary, but where previously it had seemed uncertain and timorous, it now bore an almost desperate defiance.

"Dr. Arvardan," he said, and his voice was firm, "I must apologize for my treatment of you in the morning. I had hoped you would understand——"

"I must admit I didn't, sir, but I believe I do now."

Shekt seated himself at the table and gestured toward the bottle of wine. Arvardan waved his hand in a deprecating motion. "If you don't mind, I'll have some of the fruit instead. . . . What is this? I don't think I've ever seen anything like it."

"It's a kind of orange," said Shekt. "I don't believe it grows outside Earth. The rind comes off easily." He demonstrated, and Arvardan, after sniffing at it curiously, sank his teeth into the winy pulp. He came up with an exclamation.

"Why, this is delightful, Dr. Shekt! Has Earth ever tried to export these objects?"

"The Ancients," said the biophysicist grimly, "are not fond of trading with the Outside. Nor are our neighbors in space fond of trading with us. It is but an aspect of our difficulties here."

Arvardan felt a sudden spasm of annoyance seize him. "That is the most stupid thing yet. I tell you that I could despair of human intelligence when I see what can exist in men's minds."

Shekt shrugged with the tolerance of lifelong use. "It is part of the nearly insoluble problem of anti-Terrestrianism, I fear."

"But what makes it so nearly insoluble," exclaimed the archaeologist, "is that no one seems to really want a solution! How many Earthmen respond to the situation by hating all Galactic citizens indiscriminately? It is an almost universal disease—hate for hate. Do your people really want equality, mutual tolerance? No! Most of them want only their own turn as top dog."

"Perhaps there is much in what you say," said Shekt sadly. "I cannot deny it. But that is not the whole story. Give us but the chance, and a new generation of Earthmen would grow to maturity, lacking insularity and believing wholeheartedly in the oneness of Man. The Assimilationists, with their tolerance and belief in wholesome compromise, have more than once been a power on Earth. I am one. Or, at least, I was one once. But the Zealots rule all Earth now. They are the extreme nationalists, with their dreams of past rule and future rule. It is against them that the Empire must be protected."

Arvardan frowned. "You refer to the revolt Pola spoke of?"

"Dr. Arvardan," Shekt said grimly, "it's not too easy a job to convince anyone of such an apparently ridiculous possibility as Earth conquering the Galaxy, but it's true. I am not physically brave, and I am most anxious to live. You can imagine, then, the immense crisis that must now exist to force me to run the risk of committing treason with the eye of the local administration already upon me."

"Well," said Arvardan, "if it is that serious, I had better tell you one thing immediately. I will help you all I can, but only in my own capacity as a Galactic citizen. I have no official standing here, nor have I any particular influence at the Court or even at the Procurator's Palace. I am exactly what I seem to be—an archaeologist on a scientific expedition which involves only my own interests. Since you *are* prepared to risk treason, hadn't you better see the Procurator about this? He could *really* do something."

"That is exactly what I cannot do, Dr. Arvardan. It is that very contingency against which the Ancients guard me. When you came to my house this morning I even thought you might be a go-between. I thought that Ennius suspected."

"He may suspect—I cannot answer for that. But I am not a go-between. I'm sorry. If you insist on making me your confidant, I can promise to see him for you."

"Thank you. It is all I ask. That—and to use your good offices to intercede for Earth against too strong a reprisal."

"Of course." Arvardan was uneasy. At the moment he was convinced that he was dealing with an elderly and eccentric paranoiac, perhaps harmless, but thoroughly cracked. Yet he had no choice but to remain, to listen, and to try to smooth over the gentle insanity—for Pola's sake.

Shekt said, "Dr. Arvardan, you have heard of the Synapsifier? You said so this morning."

"Yes, I did. I read your original article in *Physical Reviews.* I discussed the instrument with the Procurator and with the High Minister."

"With the High Minister?"

"Why, certainly. When I obtained the letter of introduction that you—uh—refused to see, I'm afraid."

"I'm sorry for that. But I wish you had not—— What is the extent of your knowledge concerning the Synapsifier?"

"That it is an interesting failure. It is designed to improve learning capacity. It has succeeded to some extent on rats, but has failed on human beings."

Shekt was chagrined. "Yes, you could think nothing else from that article. It was publicized as a failure, and the eminently successful results have been suppressed, deliberately."

"Hmp. A rather unusual display of scientific ethics, Dr. Shekt."

"I admit it. But I am fifty-six, sir, and if you know anything of the customs of Earth, you know that I haven't long to live."

"The Sixty. Yes, I have heard of it—more than I would have liked, in fact." And he thought wryly of that first trip on a Terrestrian stratoliner. "Exceptions are made for noted scientists, among others, I have heard."

"Certainly. But it is the High Minister and the Council of Ancients who decide on that, and there is no appeal from their decisions, even to the Emperor. I was told that the price of life was secrecy concerning the Synapsifier and hard work for its improvement." The older man spread his hands helplessly. "Could I know then of the outcome, of the use to which the machine would be put?"

"And the use?" Arvardan extracted a cigarette from his shirt-pocket case and offered one to the other, which was refused.

"If you'll wait a moment—— One by one, after my experiments had reached the point where I felt the instrument might be safely applied to human beings, certain of Earth's biologists were treated. In each case they were men I knew to be in sympathy with the Zealots—the extremists, that is. They all survived, though secondary effects made themselves shown after a time. One of them was brought back for treatment eventually. I could not save him. But, in his dying delirium, I found out."

It was close upon midnight. The day had been long and much had happened. But now something stirred within Arvardan. He said tightly, "I wish you'd get to the point."

Shekt said, "I beg your patience. I must explain thoroughly, if you're to believe me. You, of course, know of Earth's peculiar environment—its radioactivity——"

"Yes, I have a fair knowledge of the matter."

"And of the effect of this radioactivity upon Earth and its economy?"

"Yes."

"Then I won't belabor the point. I need only say that the incidence of mutation on Earth is greater than in the rest of the Galaxy. The idea of our enemies that Earthmen are different thus has a certain basis of physical truth. To be sure, the mutations are minor, and most possess no survival value. If any permanent change has occurred in Earthmen, it is only in some aspects of their internal chemistry which enables them to display greater resistance to their own particular environment. Thus they show greater resistance to radiation effects, more rapid healing of burned tissues——"

"Dr. Shekt, I am acquainted with all you say."

"Then has it ever occurred to you that these mutational processes occur in living species on Earth other than human?"

There was a short silence, and then Arvardan said, "Why, no, it hadn't, though, of course, it is quite inevitable, now that you mention it."

"That is so. It happens. Our domestic animals exist in greater variety than on any other inhabited world. The orange you ate is a mutated variety, which exists nowhere else. It is this, among other things, which makes the orange so unacceptable for export. Outsiders suspect it as they suspect us—and we ourselves guard it as a valuable property peculiar to ourselves. And of course what applied to animals and plants applies also to microscopic life."

And now, indeed, Arvardan felt the thin pang of fear enter.

He said, "You mean—bacteria?"

"I mean the whole domain of primitive life. Protozoa, bacteria, and the self-reproducing proteins that some people call viruses."

"And what are you getting at?"

"I think you have a notion of that, Dr. Arvardan. You seem suddenly interested. You see, there is a belief among your people that Earthmen are bringers of death, that to associate with an Earthman is to die, that Earthmen are the bearers of misfortune, possess a sort of evil eye——"

"I know all that. It is merely superstition."

"Not entirely. That is the dreadful part. Like all common beliefs, however superstitious, distorted, and perverted, it has a speck of truth at bottom. Sometimes, you see, an Earthman carries within his body some mutated form of microscopic parasite which is not quite like any known elsewhere, and to which, sometimes, Outsiders are not particularly resistant. What follows is simple biology, Dr. Arvardan."

Arvardan was silent.

Shekt went on, "We are caught sometimes, too, of course. A new species of germ will make its way out of the radioactive mists and an epidemic will sweep the planet, but, by and large, Earthmen have kept pace. For each variety of germ and virus, we build our defense over the generations, and we survive. Outsiders don't have the opportunity."

"Do you mean," said Arvardan with a strangely faint sensation, "that contact with you now——" He pushed his chair back. He was thinking of the evening's kisses.

Shekt shook his head. "Of course not. We don't *create* the disease; we merely carry it. And even such carriage occurs very rarely. If I lived on your world, I would no more carry the germ than you would; I have no special *affinity* for it. Even here it is only one out of every quadrillion germs, or one out of every quadrillion of quadrillions, that is dangerous. The chances of your infection right now are less than that of a meteorite penetrating the roof of this house and hitting you. *Unless* the germs in question are deliberately searched for, isolated, and concentrated."

Again a silence, longer this time. Arvardan said in a queer, strangled voice, "Have Earthmen been doing that?"

He had stopped thinking in terms of paranoia. He was ready to believe.

"Yes. But for innocent reasons, at first. Our biologists are, of course, particularly interested in the peculiarities of Earth life, and, recently, isolated the virus of Common Fever."

"What is Common Fever?"

"A mild endemic disease on Earth. That is, it is always with us. Most Earthmen have it in their childhood, and its symptoms are not very severe. A mild fever, a transitory rash, and inflammation of the joints and of the lips, combined with an annoying thirst. It runs its course in four to six days, and the subject is thereafter immune. I've had it. Pola has had it. Occasionally there is a more virulent form of this same disease—a slightly different strain of virus is concerned, presumably—and then it is called Radiation Fever."

"Radiation Fever. I've heard of it," said Arvardan.

"Oh, really? It is called Radiation Fever because of the mistaken notion that it is caught after exposure to radioactive areas. Actually, exposure to radioactive areas is often followed by Radiation Fever, because it is in those areas that the virus is most apt to mutate to dangerous forms. But it is the virus and not the radiation which does it. In the case of Radiation Fever, symptoms develop in a matter of two hours. The lips are so badly affected that the subject can scarcely talk, and he may be dead in a matter of days.

"Now, Dr. Arvardan, this is the crucial point. The Earthman has adapted himself to Common Fever and the Outsider has not. Occasionally a member of the Imperial garrison is exposed to it, and, in that case, he reacts to it as Earthman would to Radiation Fever. Usually he dies within twelve hours. He is then burned—by Earthmen—since any other soldier approaching also dies.

"The virus, as I say, was isolated ten years ago. It is a nucleoprotein, as are most filtrable viruses, which, however, possess the remarkable property of containing an unusually high concentration of radioactive carbon, sulphur, and phosphorus. When I say unusually high I mean that fifty per cent of its carbon, sulphur, and phosphorous is radioactive. It is supposed that the effects of the organism on its host are largely that of its radiations, rather than of its toxins. Naturally it would seem logical that Earthmen, who are adapted to gamma radiations, are only slightly affected. Original research in the virus centered at first about the method whereby it concentrated its radioactive isotopes. As you know, no chemical means can separate isotopes except through very long and tedious procedures. Nor is any organism other than this virus known which can do so. But then the direction of research changed.

"I'll be short, Dr. Arvardan. I think you see the rest. Experiments might be conducted on animals from outside Earth, but not on Outsiders themselves. The numbers of Outsiders on Earth were too few to allow several to disappear without notice. Nor could premature discovery of their plans be allowed. So it was a group of bacteriologists that was sent to the Synapsifier, to return with insights enormously developed. It was they who developed a new mathematical attack on protein chemistry and on immunology, which enabled them finally to develop an artificial strain of virus that was designed to affect Galactic human beings—Outsiders—only. Tons of the crystallized virus now exist."

Arvardan was haggard. He felt the drops of perspiration glide sluggishly down his temple and cheek.

"Then you are telling me," he gasped, "that Earth intends to set loose this virus on the Galaxy; that they will initiate a gigantic bacteriological warfare——"

"Which we cannot lose and you cannot win. Exactly. Once the epidemic starts, millions will die each day, and nothing will stop it. Frightened refugees fleeing across space will carry the virus with them, and if you attempt to blow up entire planets, the disease can be started again in new centers. There will be no reason to connect the matter with Earth. By the time our own survival becomes suspicious, the ravages will have progressed so far, the despair of the Outsiders will be so deep, that nothing will matter to them."

"And all will die?" The appalling horror did not penetrate—could not.

"Perhaps not. Our new science of bacteriology works both ways. We have the antitoxin as well, and the means of production thereof. It might be used in case of early surrender. Then there *may* be some out-of-the-way eddies of the Galaxy that could escape, or even a few cases of natural immunity."

In the horrible blankness that followed—during which Arvardan never thought of doubting the truth of what he had heard, the horrible truth which at a stroke wiped out the odds of twenty-five billion to one—Shekt's voice was small and tired.

"It is not Earth that is doing this. A handful of leaders, perverted by the gigantic pressure that excluded them from the Galaxy, hating those who keep them outside, wanting to strike back at any cost, and with insane intensity——

"Once they have begun, the rest of Earth must follow. What can it do? In its tremendous guilt, it will have to finish what it started. Could it allow enough of the Galaxy to survive and thus risk a later punishment?

"Yet before I am an Earthman, I am a man. Must trillions die for the sake of millions? Must a civilization spreading over a Galaxy crumble for the sake of the resentment, however justified, of a single planet? And will we be better off for all that? The power in the Galaxy will reside still on those worlds with the necessary resources—and we have none. Earthmen may even rule at Trantor for a generation, but their children will become Trantorians, and in their turn will look down upon the remnant on Earth.

"And besides, is there an advantage to Humanity to exchange the tyranny of a Galaxy for the tyranny of Earth? No—no—— There must be a way out for *all* men, a way to justice and freedom."

His hands stole to his face, and behind their gnarled fingers he rocked gently to and fro.

Arvardan had heard all this in a numbed haze. He mumbled, "There is no treason in what you have done, Dr. Shekt. I will go to Everest immediately. The Procurator will believe me. He *must* believe me."

There was the sound of running footsteps, the flash of a frightened face into the room, the door left swinging open.

"Father—— Men are coming up the walk."

Dr. Shekt went gray. "Quickly, Dr. Arvardan, through the garage." He was pushing violently. "Take Pola, and don't worry about me. I'll hold them back."

But a man in a green robe waited for them as they turned. He wore a thin smile and carried, with a casual ease, a neuronic whip. There was a thunder of fists at the main door, a crash, and the sound of pounding feet.

"Who are you?" demanded Arvardan in a feeble defiance of the armed green-robe. He had stepped before Pola.

"I?" said Green-robe harshly. "I am merely the humble Secretary of His Excellency, the High Minister." He advanced. "I almost waited too long. But not quite. Hmm, a girl, too. Injudicious——"

Arvardan said evenly, "I am a Galactic citizen, and I dispute your right to detain me—or, for that matter, to enter this house—without legal authority."

"I"—and the Secretary tapped his chest gently with his free hand—"am all the right and authority on this planet. Within a short time I will be all the right and authority on the Galaxy. We have all of you, you know—even Schwartz."

"Schwartz!" cried Dr. Shekt and Pola, nearly together.

"You are surprised? Come, I will bring you to him."

The last thing Arvardan was conscious of was that smile, expanding—and the flash of the whip. He toppled through a crimson sear of pain into unconsciousness.

Sixteen: CHOOSE YOUR SIDE!

For the moment Schwartz was resting uneasily on a hard bench in one of the small sub-basement rooms of the Chica "Hall of Correction."

The Hall, as it was commonly termed, was the great token of the local power of the High Minister and those surrounding him. It lifted its gloominess in a rocky, angular height that overshadowed the Imperial barracks beyond it, just as its shadow clutched at the Terrestrial malefactor far more than did the unexerted authority of the Empire.

Within its walls many an Earthman in past centuries had waited for the judgment that came to one who falsified or evaded the quotas of production, who lived past his time, or connived at another's such crime, or who was guilty of attempting subversion of the local government. Occasionally, when the petty prejudices of Terrestrial justice made particularly little sense to the sophisticated and usually blasé Imperial government of the time, a conviction might be set aside by the Procurator, but this meant insurrection, or, at the very least, wild riots.

Ordinarily, where the Council demanded death, the Procurator yielded. After all, it was only Earthmen who suffered——

Of all this, Joseph Schwartz, very naturally, knew nothing. To him, immediate optical awareness consisted of a small room, its walls transfused with but a dim light, its furniture consisting of two hard benches and a table, plus a small recess in the wall that served as washroom and sanitary convenience combined. There was no window for a glimpse of sky, and the drift of air into the room through the ventilating shaft was feeble.

He rubbed the hair that circled his bald spot and sat up ruefully. His attempt to escape to nowhere (for where on Earth was he safe?) had been short, not sweet, and had ended here.

At least there was the Mind Touch to play with.

But was that bad or good?

At the farm it had been a queer, disturbing gift, the nature of which he did not know, the possibilities of which he did not think of. Now it was a flexible gift to be investigated.

With nothing to do for twenty-four hours but brood on imprisonment, he could have been courting madness. As it was, he could Touch the jailers as they passed, reach out for guardsmen in the adjacent corridors, extend the furthest fibrils of his mind even to the Captain of the Hall in his distant office.

He turned the minds over delicately and probed them. They fell apart like so many walnuts—dry husks out of which emotions and notions fell in a sibilant rain.

He learned much in the process of Earth and Empire—more than he had, or could have, in all two months on the farm.

Of course one of the items that he learned, over and over again, beyond any chance of mistaking, was just this:

He was condemned to death!

There was no escape, no doubt, no reservation.

It might be today; it might be tomorrow. But he would die!

Somehow it sank in and he accepted it almost gratefully.

The door opened, and he was on his feet, in tense fear. One might accept death reasoningly, with every aspect of the conscious mind, but the body was a brute beast that knew nothing of reason. This was it!

No—it wasn't. The entering Mind Touch held nothing of death in it. It was a guard with a metal rod held ready in his hand. Schwartz knew what it was.

"Come with me," he said sharply.

Schwartz followed him, speculating on this odd power of his. Long before his guard could use his weapon, long before he could possibly know he should, he could be struck down without a sound, without a giveaway moment. His Mind was in Schwartz's mental hands. A slight squeeze and it would be over.

But why? There would be others. How many could he handle at once? How many pairs of hands were in his mind?

He followed, docilely.

It was a large, large room that he was brought into. Two men and a girl occupied it, stretched out corpsewise on high, high benches. Yet not corpses—since three active minds were much in evidence.

Paralyzed! Familiar? . . . Were they familiar?

He was stopping to look, but the guard's hard hand was on his shoulder. "Get on."

There was a fourth slab, empty. There was no death in the guard's mind, so Schwartz climbed on. He knew what was coming.

The guard's steely rod touched each of his limbs. They tingled and left him, so that he was nothing but a head, floating on nothingness.

He turned it.

"Pola," he cried. "You're Pola, aren't you? The girl who——"

She was nodding. He hadn't recognized her Touch as such. He had never been aware of it that time two months ago. At that time his mental progression had reached only the stage of sensitivity to "atmosphere." In the brilliance of hindsight, he remembered that well.

But from the contents he could still learn much. The one past the girl was Dr. Shekt; the one furthest of all was Dr. Bel Arvardan. He could filch their names, sense their despair, taste the last dregs of horror and fright in the young girl's mind.

For a moment he pitied them, and then he remembered who they were and what they were. And he hardened his heart.

Let them die!

The other three had been there for the better part of an hour. The room in which they were left was evidently one used for assemblies of several hundred. The prisoners were lost and lonely in its size. Nor was there anything to say. Arvardan's throat burned dryly and he turned his head from side to side with a futile restlessness. It was the only part of his body that he could move.

Shekt's eyes were closed and his lips were colorless and pinched.

Arvardan whispered fiercely, "Shekt. Shekt, I say!"

"What? . . . What?" A feeble whisper at best.

"What are you doing? Going to sleep? Think, man, think!"

"Why? What is there to think of?"

"Who is this Joseph Schwartz?"

Pola's voice sounded, thin and weary. "Don't you remember, Bel? That time in the department store, when I first met you—so long ago?"

Arvardan wrenched wildly and found he could lift his head two aching inches. A bit of Pola's face was just visible.

"Pola! Pola!" If he could have moved toward her—as for two months he might have and hadn't. She was looking at him, smiling so wanly that it might be a statue's smile, and he said, "We'll win out yet. You'll see."

But she was shaking her head—and his neck gave way, its tendons in panging agony.

"Shekt," he said again. "Listen to me. How did you meet this Schwartz? Why was he a patient of yours?"

"The Synapsifier. He came as a volunteer."

"And was treated?"

"Yes."

Arvardan revolved that in his mind. "What made him come to you?"

"I don't know."

"But then—— Maybe he *is* an Imperial agent."

(Schwartz followed his thought well and smiled to himself. He said nothing, and he meant to keep on saying nothing.)

Shekt stirred his head. "An Imperial agent? You mean because the High Priest's Secretary says he is. Oh, nonsense. And what difference does it make? He's as helpless as we. . . . Listen, Arvardan, maybe, if we tell some sort of concerted story, they might wait. Eventually we might——"

The archaeologist laughed hollowly, and his throat burned at the friction. "We might live, you mean. With the Galaxy dead and civilization in ruins? Live? I might as well die!"

"I'm thinking of Pola," muttered Shekt.

"I am too," said the other. "Ask her. . . . Pola, shall we surrender? Shall we try to live?"

Pola's voice was firm. "I have chosen my side. I don't want to die, but if my side dies, I'll go with it."

Arvardan felt somehow triumphant. When he brought her to Sirius, they might call her an Earthgirl, but she was their equal, and he would, with a great and good pleasure, smash teeth into the throat of any——

And he remembered that he wasn't likely to bring her to Sirius—to bring anyone to Sirius. There wasn't likely to be a Sirius.

Then, as though to escape from the thought, to escape anywhere, he shouted, "You! Whatchername! Schwartz!"

Schwartz raised his head for a moment and allowed a glance to ooze out toward the other. He still said nothing.

"Who are you?" demanded Arvardan. "How did you get mixed up in this? What's your part in it?"

And at the question, all the injustice of everything descended on Schwartz. All the harmlessness of his past, all the infinite horror of the present burst in upon him, so that he said in a fury, "I? How did I get mixed up in it? Listen. I was once a nobody. An honest man, a hardworking tailor. I hurt nobody, I bothered nobody, I took care of my family. And then, for no reason, for *no reason*—I came here."

"To Chica?" asked Arvardan, who did not quite follow.

"No, not to Chica!" shouted Schwartz in wild derision. "I came to this whole mad world. . . . Oh, what do I care if you believe me or not? *My* world is in the past. My world had land and food and two billion people, and it was the *only* world."

Arvardan fell silent before the verbal assault. He turned to Shekt. "Can you understand him?"

"Do you realize," said Shekt in feeble wonder, "that he has a vermiform appendix, which is three and a half inches long? Do you remember, Pola? And wisdom teeth. And hair on his face."

"Yes, yes," shouted Schwartz defiantly. "And I wish I had a tail I could show you. *I'm from the past. I traveled through time.* Only I don't know how, and I don't know why. Now leave me alone." He added suddenly, "They will soon be here for us. This wait is just to break us."

Arvardan said suddenly, "Do you know that? Who told you?"

Schwartz did not answer.

"Was it the Secretary? Stocky man with a pug nose?"

Schwartz had no way of telling the physical appearance of those he Touched only by mind, but—secretary? There had been just a glimpse of a Touch, a powerful one of a man of power, and it seemed he had been a secretary.

"Balkis?" he asked in curiosity.

"What?" said Arvardan, but Shekt interrupted, "That's the name of the Secretary."

"Oh—— What did he say?"

"He didn't say anything," said Schwartz. "I *know*. It's death for all of us, and there's no way out."

Arvardan lowered his voice. "He's mad, wouldn't you say?"

"I wonder. . . . His skull sutures, now. They were primitive, very primitive."

Arvardan was amazed. "You mean—— Oh, come, it's impossible."

"I've always supposed so." For the moment Shekt's voice was a feeble imitation of normality, as though the presence of a scientific problem had switched his mind to that detached and objective groove in which personal matters disappeared. "They've calculated the energy required to displace matter along the time axis and a value greater than infinity was arrived at, so the project has always been looked upon as impossible. But others *have* talked of the possibility of 'time faults,' analogous to geological faults, you know. Space ships *have* disappeared, for one thing, almost in full view. There's the famous case of Hor Devallow in ancient times, who stepped into his house one day and never came out, and wasn't inside, either. . . . And then there's the planet, which you'll find in the Galactography books of the last century, which was visited by three expeditions that brought back full descriptions—and then was never seen again.

"Then there are certain developments in nuclear chemistry that seem to deny the law of conservation of mass-energy. They've tried to explain that by postulating the escape of some mass along the time axis. Uranium nuclei, for instance, when mixed with copper and barium in minute but definite proportions, under the influence of light gamma irradiation, set up a resonating system——"

"Father," said Pola, "don't! There's no use——"

But Arvardan's interruption was peremptory. "Wait, now. Let me think. *I'm* the one who can settle this. Who better? Let me ask him a few questions. . . . Look, Schwartz."

Schwartz looked up again.

"Yours was the only world in the Galaxy?"

Schwartz nodded, then said dully, "Yes."

"But you only thought that. I mean you didn't have space travel, so you couldn't check up. There might have been many other inhabited worlds."

"I have no way of telling that."

"Yes, of course. A pity. What about atomic power?"

"We had an atomic bomb. Uranium—and plutonium—— I guess that's what made this world radioactive. There must have been another war after all—after I left. . . . Atomic bombs." Somehow Schwartz was back in Chicago, back in his old world, before the bombs. And he was sorry. Not for himself, but for that beautiful world. . . .

But Arvardan was muttering to himself. Then, "All right. You had a language, of course."

"Earth? Lots of them."

"How about you?"

"English—after I was a grown man."

"Well, say something in it."

For two months or more Schwartz had said nothing in English. But now, with lovingness, he said slowly, "I want to go home and be with my own people."

Arvardan spoke to Shekt. "Is that the language he used when he was Synapsified, Shekt?"

"I can't tell," said Shekt, in mystification. "Queer sounds then and queer sounds now. How can I relate them?"

"Well, never mind. . . . What's your word for 'mother' in your language, Schwartz?"

Schwartz told him.

"Uh-*huh*. How about 'father' . . . 'brother' . . . 'one'—the numeral, that is . . . 'two' . . . 'three' . . . 'house' . . . 'man' . . . 'wife' . . ."

This went on and on, and when Arvardan paused for breath his expression was one of awed bewilderment.

"Shekt," he said, "either this man is genuine or I'm the victim of as wild a nightmare as can be conceived. He's speaking a language practically equivalent to the inscriptions found in the fifty-thousand-year-old strata on Sirius, Arcturus, Alpha Centauri, and twenty others. He *speaks* it. The language has only been deciphered in the last generation, and there aren't a dozen men in the Galaxy besides myself who can understand it."

"Are you sure of this?"

"Am I *sure?* Of course I'm sure. I'm an archaeologist. It's my business to know."

For an instant Schwartz felt his armor of aloofness cracking. For the first time he felt himself regaining the individuality he had lost. The secret was out; he was a man from the past, *and they accepted it*. It proved him sane, stilled forever that haunting doubt, and he was grateful. And yet he held aloof.

"I've got to have him." It was Arvardan again, burning in the holy flame of his profession. "Shekt, you have no idea what this means to archaeology. Shekt—it's a man from the past. Oh, Great Space! . . . Listen, we can make a deal. This is the proof Earth is looking for. They can have him. They can——"

Schwartz interrupted sardonically. "I know what you're thinking. You think that Earth will prove itself to be the source of civilization through me and that they will be grateful for it. I tell you, no! I've thought of it and I would have bartered for my own life. But they won't believe me—or you."

"There's absolute proof."

"They won't listen. Do you know why? Because they have certain fixed notions about the past. Any change would be blasphemy in their eyes, even if it were the truth. They don't want the truth; they want their traditions."

"Bel," said Pola, "I think he's right."

Arvardan ground his teeth. "We could try."

"We would fail," insisted Schwartz.

"How can you know?"

"I *know!*" And the words fell with such oracular insistence that Arvardan was silent before them.

It was Shekt who was looking at him now with a strange light in his tired eyes.

He asked softly, "Have you felt any bad effects as a result of the Synapsifier?"

Schwartz didn't know the word but caught the meaning. They *had* operated, and on his mind. How much he was learning!

He said, "No bad effects."

"But I see you learned our language rapidly. You speak it very well. In fact, you might be a native. Doesn't it surprise you?"

"I always had a very good memory," was the cold response.

"And so you feel no different now from before you were treated?"

"That's right."

Dr. Shekt's eyes were hard now, and he said, "Why do you bother? You know that I'm certain you know what I'm thinking."

Schwartz laughed shortly. "That I can read minds? Well, what of it?"

But Shekt had dropped him. He had turned his white, helpless face to Arvardan. "He can sense minds, Arvardan. How much I could do with him. And to be here—to be helpless . . ."

"What—what—what——" Arvardan popped wildly.

And even Pola's face somehow gained interest. "Can you really?" she asked Schwartz.

He nodded at her. She had taken care of him, and now they would kill her. Yet she was a traitor.

Shekt was saying, "Arvardan, you remember the bacteriologist I told you about, the one who died as a result of the effects of the Synapsifier? One of the first symptoms of mental breakdown was his claim that he could read minds. And he *could*. I found that out before he died, and it's been my secret. I've told no one—but it's possible, Arvardan, it's possible. You see, with the lowering of brain-cell resistance, the brain may be able to pick up the magnetic fields induced by the microcurrents of others' thoughts and reconvert them into similar vibrations in itself. It's the same principle as that of any ordinary recorder. It would be telepathy in every sense of the word——"

Schwartz maintained a stubborn and hostile silence as Arvardan turned slowly in his direction. "If this is so, Shekt, we might be able to use him." The archaeologist's mind was spinning wildly, working out impossibilities. "There may be a way out now. There *must* be a way out. For us and the Galaxy."

But Schwartz was cold to the tumult in the Mind Touch he sensed so clearly. He said, "You mean by my reading their minds? How would that help? Of course I can do more than read minds. How's that, for instance?"

It was a light push, but Arvardan yelped at the sudden pain of it.

"I did that," said Schwartz. "Want more?"

Arvardan gasped, "You can do that to the guards? To the Secretary? Why did you let them bring you here? Great Galaxy, Shekt, there'll be no trouble. Now, listen, Schwartz——"

"No," said Schwartz, "*you* listen. Why do *I* want to get out? Where will I be? Still on this dead world. I want to go home, and I *can't* go home. I want my people and my world, and I can't have them. And I *want* to die."

"But it's a question of all the Galaxy, Schwartz. You can't think of yourself."

"Can't I? Why not? Must I worry about your Galaxy now? I hope your Galaxy rots and dies. I know what Earth is planning to do, and I am glad. The young lady said before she had chosen her side. Well, I've chosen my side, and my side is Earth."

"What?"

"Why not? I'm an Earthman!"

Seventeen: CHANGE YOUR SIDE!

An hour had passed since Arvardan had first waded thickly out of unconsciousness to find himself slabbed like a side of beef awaiting the cleaver. And nothing had happened. Nothing but this feverish, inconclusive talk that unbearably passed the unbearable time.

None of it lacked purpose. He knew that much. To lie prone, helpless, without even the dignity of a guard, without even that much concession to a conceivable danger, was to become conscious of overwhelming weakness. A stubborn spirit could not survive it, and when the inquisitor *did* arrive there would be little defiance, or none, for him to be presented with.

Arvardan needed a break in the silence. He said, "I suppose this place is Spy-waved. We should have talked less."

"It isn't," came Schwartz's voice flatly. "There's nobody listening."

The archaeologist was ready with an automatic "How do *you* know?" but never said it.

For a power like that to exist! And not for him, but for a man of the past who called himself an Earthman and wanted to die!

Within optical sweep was only a patch of ceiling. Turning, he could see Shekt's angular profile; the other way, a blank wall. If he lifted his head he could make out, for a moment, Pola's pale, worn expression.

Occasionally there was the burning thought that he was a man of the Empire—of the *Empire*, by the Stars; a Galactic citizen—and that there was a particularly vile injustice in *his* imprisonment, a particularly deep impurity in the fact that he had allowed *Earthmen* to do this to him.

And that faded too.

They might have put him next to Pola . . . No, it was better this way. He was not an inspiring sight.

"Bel?" The word trembled into sound and was strangely sweet to Arvardan, coming as it did in this vortex of coming death.

"Yes, Pola?"

"Do you think they'll be much longer?"

"Maybe not, darling. . . . It's too bad. We wasted two months, didn't we?"

"My fault," she whispered. "My fault. We might have had these last few minutes, though. It's so—unnecessary."

Arvardan could not answer. His mind whirred in circles of thought, lost on a greased wheel. Was it his imagination, or did he feel the hard plastic on which he was so stiffly laid? How long would the paralysis last?

Schwartz *must* be made to help. He tried guarding his thoughts—knew it to be ineffective.

He said, "Schwartz——"

Schwartz lay there as helpless, and with an added, uncalculated refinement to his suffering. He was four minds in one.

By himself he might have maintained his own shrinking eagerness for the infinite peace and quiet of death, fought down the last remnants of that love of life which even as recently as two days previously—three?—had sent him reeling away from the farm. But how could he? With the poor, weak horror of death that hung like a pall over Shekt; with the strong chagrin and rebellion of Arvardan's hard, vital mind; with the deep and pathetic disappointment of the young girl.

He should have closed his own mind. What did he need to know of the sufferings of others? He had his own life to live, his own death to die.

But they battered at him, softly, incessantly—probing and sifting through the crannies.

And Arvardan said, "Schwartz," then, and Schwartz knew that they wanted him to save them. Why should he? Why should he?

"Schwartz," repeated Arvardan insinuatingly, "you can live a hero. You have nothing to die for here—not for those men out there."

But Schwartz was gathering the memories of his own youth, clutching them desperately to his wavering mind. It was a queer amalgamation of past and present that finally brought forth his indignation.

But he spoke calmly, restrainedly. "Yes, I can live a hero—and a traitor. They want to kill me, those *men* out there. You call them men, but that was with your tongue; your mind called them something I didn't get, but it was vile. And not because they were vile, but because they were Earthmen."

"That's a lie," hotly.

"That is *not* a lie," as hotly, "and everyone here knows that. They want to kill me, yes—but that is because they think I'm one of your kind of people, who can condemn an entire planet at a stroke and drench it with your contempt, choke it slowly with your insufferable superiority. Well, protect yourself against these worms and vermin who are somehow managing to threaten their Godlike overlords. Don't ask for the help of one of them."

"You talk like a Zealot," said Arvardan with amazement. "Why? Have *you* suffered? You were a member of a large and independent planet, you say. You were an Earthman when Earth was the sole repository of life. You're one of *us*, man; one of the rulers. Why associate yourself with a desperate remnant? This is not the planet you remember. My planet is more like the old Earth than is this diseased world."

Schwartz laughed. "I'm one of the rulers, you say? Well, we won't go into that. It isn't worth explaining. Let's take you instead. You're a fine sample of the product sent us by the Galaxy. You are tolerant and wonderfully bighearted, and admire yourself because you treat Dr. Shekt as an equal. But underneath—yet not so far underneath that I can't see it plainly in your mind—you are uncomfortable with him. You don't like the way he talks or the way he looks. In fact, you don't like him, even though he is offering to betray Earth. . . . Yes, and you kissed a girl of Earth recently and looked back upon it as a weakness. You're ashamed of it——"

"By the Stars, I'm not. . . . Pola," desperately, "don't believe him. Don't listen to him."

Pola spoke quietly. "Don't deny it, or make yourself unhappy about it, Bel. He's looking below the surface to the residue of your childhood. He would see the same if he looked into mine. He would see things similar if he could look into his own in an ungentlemanly a fashion as he probes ours."

Schwartz felt himself reddening.

Pola's voice did not rise in pitch or intensity as she addressed him directly. "Schwartz, if you can sense minds, investigate mine. Tell me if I intend treason. Look at my father. See if it is not true that he could have avoided the Sixty easily enough if he had co-operated with the madmen who will ruin the Galaxy. What has he gained by his treason? . . . And look again, see if any of us wish to harm Earth or Earthmen.

"You say you have caught a glimpse of Balkis's mind. I don't know what chance you have had to poke through its dregs. But when he's back, when it's too late, sift it, strain his thoughts. Find out that he's a madman—— Then, die!"

Schwartz was silent.

Arvardan broke in hurriedly, "All right, Schwartz, tackle my mind now. Go as deep as you want. I was born on Baronn in the Sirius Sector. I lived my life in an atmosphere of anti-Terrestrialism in the formative years, so I can't help what flaws and follies lie at the roots of my subconscious. But look on the surface and tell me if, in my adult years, I have not fought bigotry in myself. Not in others; that would be easy. But in myself, and as hard as I could.

"Schwartz, you don't know our history! You don't know of the thousands and tens of thousands of years in which Man spread through the Galaxy—of the wars and misery. You don't know of the first centuries of the Empire, when still there was merely a confusion of alternating despotism and chaos. It is only in the last two hundred years, now, that our Galactic government has become a representative one. Under it the various worlds are allowed their cultural autonomy—have been allowed to govern themselves—have been allowed voices in the common rule of all.

"At no time in history has Humanity been as free from war and poverty as now; at no time has Galactic economy been so wisely adjusted; at no time have prospects for the future been as bright. Would you destroy it and begin all over? And with what? A despotic theocracy with only the unhealthy elements of suspicion and hatred in it.

"Earth's grievance is legitimate and will be solved someday, if the Galaxy lives. But what *they* will do is no solution. Do you *know* what they intend doing?"

If Arvardan had had the ability that had come to Schwartz, he would have detected the struggle in Schwartz's mind. Intuitively, however, he knew the time had come to halt for a moment.

Schwartz was moved. All those worlds to die—to fester and dissolve in horrible disease . . . Was he an Earthman after all? Simply an Earthman? In his youth he had left Europe and gone to America, but was he not the same man despite that? And if after him men had left a torn and wounded Earth for the worlds beyond the sky, were they less Earthmen? Was not all the Galaxy his? Were not they all—all—descended from himself and his brothers?

He said heavily, "All right, I'm with you. How can I help?"

"How far out can you reach for minds?" asked Arvardan eagerly, with a hastening quickness as though afraid still of a last change of mind.

"I don't know. There are minds outside. Guards, I suppose. I think I can reach out into the street even, but the further I go, the less sharp it becomes."

"Naturally," said Arvardan. "But how about the Secretary? Could you identify his mind?"

"I don't know," mumbled Schwartz.

A pause . . . The minutes stretched by unbearably.

Schwartz said, "Your minds are in the way. Don't watch me. Think of something else."

They tried to. Another pause. Then, "No—I can't—I can't."

Arvardan said with a sudden intensity, "I can move a bit—Great Galaxy, I can wiggle my feet. . . . Ouch!" Each motion was a savage twinge.

He said, "How hard can you hurt someone, Schwartz? Can you do it harder than the way you hurt me a while back I mean?"

"I've killed a man."

"You have? How did you do that?"

"I don't know. It just gets done. It's—it's——" Schwartz looked almost comically helpless in his effort to put the wordless into words.

"Well, can you handle more than one at a time?"

"I've never tried, but I don't think so. I can't read two minds at one time."

Pola interrupted. "You can't have him kill the Secretary, Bel. It won't work."

"Why not?"

"How will we get out? Even if we caught the Secretary alone and killed him, there would be hundreds waiting for us outside. Don't you see that?"

But Schwartz broke in, huskily, "I've got him."

"Whom?" It came from all three. Even Shekt was staring wildly at him.

"The Secretary. I think it's his Mind Touch."

"Don't let him go." Arvardan almost rolled over in his attempts at exhortation, and tumbled off the slab, thumping to the floor with one half-paralyzed leg working futilely to wedge underneath his body and lift.

Pola cried, "You're hurt!" and suddenly found the hinges of her arm uncreaking as she tried to lift her elbow.

"No, it's all right. Suck him dry, Schwartz. Get all the information you can."

Schwartz reached out until his head ached. He clutched and clawed with the tendrils of his own mind, blindly, clumsily—like an infant thrusting out fingers it can't quite handle for an object it can't quite reach. Until now he had taken whatever he could find, but now he was looking—looking——

Painfully, he caught wisps. "Triumph! He's sure of the results. . . . Something about space bullets. He's started them. . . . No, not started. Something else. . . . He's going to start them."

Shekt groaned. "They're automatically guided missiles to carry the virus, Arvardan. Aimed at the various planets."

"But where are they kept, Schwartz?" insisted Arvardan. "Look, man, look——"

"There's a building I—can't—quite—see. . . . Five points—a star —a name; Sloo, maybe——"

Shekt broke in again. "That's it. By all the stars in the Galaxy, that's it. The Temple of Senloo. It's surrounded by radioactive pockets on all sides. No one would ever go there but the Ancients. Is it near the meeting of two large rivers, Schwartz?"

"I can't—— Yes—yes—yes."

"When, Schwartz, when? When will they be set off?"

"I can't see the day, but soon—soon. His mind is bursting with that—— It will be very soon." His own head seemed bursting with the effort.

Arvardan was dry and feverish as he raised himself finally to his hands and knees, though they wobbled and gave under him. "Is he coming?"

"Yes. He's at the door."

His voice sank and stopped as the door opened.

Balkis's voice was one of cold derision as he filled the room with success and triumph. "Dr. Arvardan! Had you not better return to your seat?"

Arvardan looked up at him, conscious of the cruel indignity of his own position, but there was no answer to make, and he made none. Slowly he allowed his aching limbs to lower him to the ground. He waited there, breathing heavily. If his limbs could return a bit more, if he could make a last lunge, if he could somehow seize the other's weapons——

That was no neuronic whip that dangled so gently from the smoothly gleaming Flexiplast belt that held the Secretary's robe in place. It was a full-size blaster that could shred a man to atoms in an instantaneous point of time.

The Secretary watched the four before him with a savage sense of satisfaction. The girl he tended to ignore, but otherwise it was a clean sweep. There was the Earthman traitor; there the Imperial agent; and there the mysterious creature they had been watching for two months. Were there any others?

To be sure, there was still Ennius, and the Empire. Their arms, in the person of these spies and traitors, were pinioned, but there remained an active brain somewhere—perhaps to send out other arms.

The Secretary stood easily, hands clasped in contemptuous disregard of any possible necessity of quickly reaching his weapon. He spoke quietly and gently. "Now it is necessary to make things absolutely clear. There is war between Earth and the Galaxy—undeclared as yet, but, nevertheless, war. You are our prisoners and will be treated as will be necessary under the circumstances. Naturally the recognized punishment for spies and traitors is death——"

"Only in the case of legal and declared war," broke in Arvardan fiercely.

"Legal war?" questioned the Secretary with more than a trace of a sneer. "What is *legal* war? Earth has *always* been at war with the Galaxy, whether we made polite mention of the fact or not."

"Don't bother with him," said Pola to Arvardan softly. "Let him have his say and finish with it."

Arvardan smiled in her direction. A queer, spasmodic smile, for it was with a vast strain that he staggered to his feet and remained there, gasping.

Balkis laughed softly. With unhurried steps he shortened the distance between himself and the Sirian archaeologist to nothing. With an equally unhurried gesture he rested a soft hand upon the broad chest of the other and shoved.

With splintering arms that would not respond to Arvardan's demand for a warding motion, with stagnant trunk muscles that could not adjust the body's balance at more than snail speed, Arvardan toppled.

Pola gasped. Lashing her own rebellious flesh and bone, she descended from her particular bench slowly—so slowly.

Balkis let her crawl toward Arvardan.

"Your lover," he said. "Your strong Outsider lover. Run to him, girl! Why do you wait? Clasp your hero tightly and forget in his arms that he steams in the sweat and blood of a billion martyred Earthmen. And there he lies, bold and valiant—brought to Earth by the gentle push of an Earthman's hand."

Pola was on her knees beside him now, her fingers probing beneath the hair for blood or the deadly softness of crushed bone. Arvardan's eyes opened slowly and his lips formed a "Never mind!"

"He's a coward," said Pola, "who would fight a paralyzed man and boast his victory. Believe me, darling, few Earthmen are like that."

"I know it, or you would not be an Earthwoman."

The Secretary stiffened. "As I said, all lives here are forfeit, but, nevertheless, can be bought. Are you interested in the price?"

Pola said proudly, "In our case, you would be. That I know."

"Ssh, Pola." Arvardan had not yet recovered his breath entirely. "What are you proposing?"

"Oh," said Balkis, "you are willing to sell yourself? As I would be, for instance? I, a vile Earthman?"

"You know best what you are," retorted Arvardan. "As for the rest, I am not selling myself; I am buying her."

"I refuse to be bought," said Pola.

"Touching," grated the Secretary. "He stoops to our females, our Earthie-squaws—and can still play-act at sacrifice."

"What are you proposing?" demanded Arvardan.

"This. Obviously, word of our plans has leaked out. How it got to Dr. Shekt is not difficult to see, but how it got to the Empire is puzzling. We would like to know, therefore, just what the Empire does know. Not what you have learned, Arvardan, but what the Empire now knows."

"I am an archaeologist and not a spy," bit out Arvardan. "I don't know anything at all about what the Empire knows—but I hope they know a damned lot."

"So I imagine. Well, you may change your mind. Think, all of you."

Throughout, Schwartz had contributed nothing; nor had he raised his eyes.

The Secretary waited, then said, perhaps a trifle savagely, "Then I'll outline the price to you of your non-co-operation. It will not be simply death, since I am quite certain that all of you are prepared for that unpleasant and inevitable eventuality. Dr. Shekt and the girl, his daughter, who, unfortunately for herself, is implicated to a deadly extent, are citizens of Earth. Under the circumstances, it will be most appropriate to have both subjected to the Synapsifier. You understand, Dr. Shekt?"

The physicist's eyes were pools of pure horror.

"Yes, I see you do," said Balkis. "It is, of course, possible to allow the Synapsifier to damage brain tissue just sufficiently to allow the production of an acerebral imbecile. It is a most disgusting state: one in which you will have to be fed, or starve; be cleaned, or live in dung; be shut up, or remain a study in horror to all who see. It may be a lesson to others in the great day that is coming.

"As for you"—and the Secretary turned to Arvardan—"and your friend Schwartz, you are Imperial citizens, and therefore suitable for an interesting experiment. We have never tried our concentrated fever virus on you Galactic dogs. It would be interesting to show our calculations correct. A small dose, you see, so that death is not quick. The disease might work its way to the inevitable over a period of a week, if we dilute the injection sufficiently. It will be very painful."

And now he paused and watched them through slitted eyes. "All that," he said, "is the alternative to a few well-chosen words at the present time. How much does the Empire know? Have they other agents active at the present moment? What are their plans, if any, for counteraction?"

Dr. Shekt muttered, "How do we know that you won't have us killed anyway, once you have what you want of us?"

"You have my assurance that you will die horribly if you refuse. You will have to gamble on the alternative. What do you say?"

"Can't we have time?"

"Isn't that what I'm giving you now? Ten minutes have passed since I entered, and I am still listening. . . . Well, have you anything to say? What, nothing? Time will not endure forever, you must realize. Arvardan, you still knot your muscles. You think perhaps you can reach me before I can draw my blaster. Well, what if you can? There are hundreds outside, and my plans will continue without me. Even your separate modes of punishment will continue without me.

"Or perhaps you, Schwartz. You killed our agent. It was you, was it not? Perhaps you think you can kill me?"

For the first time Schwartz looked at Balkis. He said coldly, "I can, but I won't."

"That is kind of you."

"Not at all. It is very cruel of me. You say yourself that there are things worse than simple death."

Arvardan found himself suddenly staring at Schwartz in a vast hope.

Eighteen: DUEL!

Schwartz's mind was whirling. In a queer, hectic way he felt at ease. There was a piece of him that seemed in absolute control of the situation, and more of him that could not believe that. Paralysis had been applied later to him than to the others. Even Dr. Shekt was sitting up, while he himself could just budge an arm and little more.

And, staring up at the leering mind of the Secretary, infinitely foul and infinitely evil, he began his duel.

He said, "I was on your side originally, for all that you were preparing to kill me. I thought I understood your feelings and your intentions. . . . But the minds of these others here are relatively innocent and pure, and yours is past description. It is not even for the Earthman you fight, but for your own personal power. I see in you not a vision of a free Earth, but of a re-enslaved Earth. I see in you not the disruption of the Imperial power, but its replacement by a personal dictatorship."

"You see all that, do you?" said Balkis. "Well, see what you wish. I don't need your information after all, you know—not so badly that I must endure insolence. We have advanced the hour of striking, it seems. Had you expected *that?* Amazing what pressure will do, even on those who swear that more speed is impossible. Did you see that, my dramatic mind reader?"

Schwartz said, "I didn't. I wasn't looking for it, and it passed my notice. . . . But I can look for it now. Two days—— Less—— Let's see—— Tuesday—six in the morning—Chica time."

The blaster was in the Secretary's hand, finally. He advanced in abrupt strides and towered over Schwartz's drooping figure.

"How did you know that?"

Schwartz stiffened; somewhere mental tendrils bunched and grasped. Physically his jaw muscles clamped rigorously shut and his eyebrows curled low, but these were purely irrelevant—involuntary accompaniments to the real effort. Within his brain there was that which reached out and seized hard upon the Mind Touch of the other.

To Arvardan, for precious, wasting seconds, the scene was meaningless; the Secretary's sudden motionless silence was not significant.

Schwartz muttered gaspingly, "I've got him. . . . Take away his gun I can't hold on——" It died away in a gurgle.

And then Arvardan understood. With a lurch he was on all fours. Then slowly, grindingly, he lifted himself once more, by main force, to an unsteady erectness. Pola tried to rise with him, could not quite make it. Shekt edged off his slab, sinking to his knees. Only Schwartz lay there, his face working.

The Secretary might have been struck by the Medusa sight. On his smooth and unfurrowed forehead perspiration gathered slowly, and his expressionless face hinted of no emotion. Only that right hand, holding the blaster, showed any signs of life. Watch closely, and you might see it jerk ever so gently; note the curious flexing pressure of it upon the contact button: a gentle pressure, not enough to do harm, but returning, and returning——

"Hold him tight," gasped Arvardan with a ferocious joy. He steadied himself on the back of a chair and tried to gain his breath. "Let me get to him."

His feet dragged. He was in a nightmare, wading through molasses, swimming through tar; pulling with torn muscles, so slowly—so slowly.

He was not—could not be—conscious of the terrific duel that proceeded before him.

The Secretary had only one aim, and that was to put just the tiniest force into his thumb—three ounces, to be exact, since that was the contact pressure required for the blaster's operation. To do so his mind had only to instruct a quiveringly balanced tendon, already half contracted, to—to——

Schwartz had only one aim, and that was to restrain that pressure—but in all the inchoate mass of sensation presented to him by the other's Mind Touch, he could not know which particular area was alone concerned with that thumb. So it was that he bent his efforts to produce a stasis, a complete stasis——

The Secretary's Mind Touch heaved and billowed against restraint. It was a quick and fearfully intelligent mind that confronted Schwartz's untried control. For seconds it remained quiescent, waiting—then, in a terrific, tearing attempt, it would tug wildly at this muscle or that——

To Schwartz it was as if he had seized a wrestling hold which he must maintain at all costs, though his opponent threw him about in frenzies.

But none of this showed. Only the nervous clenching and unclenching of Schwartz's jaw; the quivering lips, bloodied by the biting teeth—and that occasional soft movement on the part of the Secretary's thumb, straining—straining.

Arvardan paused to rest. He did not want to. He had to. His outstretched finger just touched the fabric of the Secretary's tunic and he felt he could move no more. His agonized lungs could not pump the breath his dead limbs required. His eyes were blurred with the tears of effort, his mind with the haze of pain.

He gasped, "Just a few more minutes, Schwartz. Hold him, hold him——"

Slowly, slowly, Schwartz shook his head. "I can't—I can't——"

And indeed, to Schwartz all the world was slipping away into dull, unfocused chaos. The tendrils of his mind were becoming stiff and non-resilient.

The Secretary's thumb pressed once again upon the contact. It did not relax. The pressure grew by tiny stages.

Schwartz could feel the bulging of his own eyeballs, the writhing expansion of the veins in his forehead. He could sense the awful triumph that gathered in the mind of the other——

Then Arvardan lunged. His stiff and rebellious body toppled forward, hands outstretched and clawing.

The yielding, mind-held Secretary toppled with him. The blaster flew sideways, clanging along the hard floor.

The Secretary's mind wrenched free almost simultaneously, and Schwartz fell back, his own skull a tangled jungle of confusion.

Balkis struggled wildly beneath the clinging dead weight of Arvardan's body. He jerked a knee into the other's groin with a vicious strength while his clenched fist came down sideways on Arvardan's cheekbone. He lifted and thrust—and Arvardan rolled off in huddled agony.

The Secretary staggered to his feet, panting and disheveled, and stopped again.

Facing him was Shekt, half reclining. His right hand, shakingly supported by the left, was holding the blaster, and although it quivered, the business end pointed at the Secretary.

"You pack of fools," shrilled the Secretary, passion-choked, "what do you expect to gain? I have only to raise my voice——"

"And you, at least," responded Shekt weakly, "will die."

"You will accomplish nothing by killing me," said the Secretary bitterly, "and you know it. You will not save the Empire you would betray us to—and you would not save even yourselves. Give me that gun and you will go free."

He extended a hand, but Shekt laughed wistfully. "I am not mad enough to believe that."

"Perhaps not, but you are half paralyzed." And the Secretary broke sharply to the right, far faster than the physicist's feeble wrist could veer the blaster.

But now Balkis's mind, as he tensed for the final jump, was utterly and entirely on the blaster he was avoiding. Schwartz extended his mind once again in a final jab, and the Secretary tripped and slammed downward as if he had been clubbed.

Arvardan had risen painfully to his feet. His cheek was red and swollen and he hobbled when he walked. He said, "Can you move, Schwartz?"

"A little," came the tired response. Schwartz slid out of his seat. "Anyone else coming this way, maybe?"

"Not that I can detect."

Arvardan smiled grimly down at Pola. His hand was resting on her soft brown hair and she was looking up at him with brimming eyes. Several times in the last two hours he had been sure that never, never would he feel her hair or see her eyes again.

"Maybe there will be a later after all, Pola?"

And she could only shake her head and say, "There's not enough time. We only have till six o'clock Tuesday."

"Not enough time? Well, let's see." Arvardan bent over the prone Ancient and pulled his head back, none too gently.

"Is he alive?" He felt futilely for a pulse with his still-numb finger tips and then placed a palm beneath the green robe. He said, "His heart's beating, anyway. . . . You've a dangerous power there, Schwartz. Why didn't you do this in the first place?"

"Because I wanted to see him held static." Schwartz clearly showed the effects of his ordeal. "I thought that if I could hold him, we could lead him out before; use him as decoy; hide behind his skirts."

Shekt said, in sudden animation, "We might. There's the Imperial garrison in Fort Dibburn not half a mile away. Once there, we're safe and can get word to Ennius."

"Once there! There must be a hundred guards outside, with hundreds more between here and there—— And what can we do with a stiff green-robe? Carry him? Shove him along on little wheels?" Arvardan laughed humorlessly.

"Besides," said Schwartz gloomily, "I couldn't hold him very long. You saw—— I failed."

Shekt said earnestly, "Because you're not used to it. Now listen, Schwartz. I've got a notion as to what it is you do with your mind. It's a receiving station for the electromagnetic fields of the brain. I think you can transmit also. Do you understand?"

Schwartz seemed painfully uncertain.

"You must understand," insisted Shekt. "You'll have to concentrate on what you want him to do—and first we're going to give him his blaster back."

"*What!*" The outraged exclamation was neatly triple.

Shekt raised his voice. "He's got to lead us out of here. We can't get out otherwise, can we? And how can it look less suspicious than to allow him to be obviously armed?"

"But I couldn't hold him. I tell you I couldn't." Schwartz was flexing his arms, slapping them, trying to get back into the feel of normality. "I don't care what your theories are, Dr. Shekt. You don't know what goes on. It's a slippery, painful thing, and it's not easy."

"I know, but it's the chance we take. Try it now, Schwartz. Have him move his arm when he comes to." Shekt's voice was pleading.

The Secretary moaned as he lay there, and Schwartz felt the reviving Mind Touch. Silently, almost fearfully, he let it gather strength—then spoke to it. It was a speech that included no words; it was the silent speech you sent to your arm when you want it to move, a speech so silent you are not yourself aware of it.

And Schwartz's arm did not move; it was the Secretary's that did. The Earthman from the past looked up with a wild smile, but the others had eyes only for Balkis—Balkis, that recumbent figure, with a lifting head, with eyes from which the glaze of unconsciousness was vanishing, and an arm which peculiarly and incongruously jerked outward at a ninety-degree angle.

Schwartz bent to his task.

The Secretary lifted himself up in angular fashion; nearly, but not quite, overbalancing himself. And then, in a queer and involuntary way, he danced.

It lacked rhythm; it lacked beauty; but to the three who watched the body, and to Schwartz, who watched body and mind, it was a thing of indescribable awe. For in those moments the Secretary's body was under the control of a mind not materially connected with it.

Slowly, cautiously, Shekt approached the robotlike Secretary and, not without a qualm, extended his hand. In the open palm thereof lay the blaster, butt first.

"Let him take it, Schwartz," said Shekt.

Balkis's hand reached out and grasped the weapon clumsily. For a moment there was a sharp, devouring glitter in his eyes, and then it all faded. Slowly, slowly, the blaster was put into its place in the belt, and the hand fell away.

Schwartz's laugh was high-pitched. "He almost got away, there." But his face was white as he spoke.

"Well? Can you hold him?"

"He's fighting like the devil. But it's not as bad as before."

"That's because you know what you're doing," said Shekt, with an encouragement he did not entirely feel. "Transmit, now. Don't try to hold him; just pretend you're doing it yourself."

Arvardan broke in. "Can you make him talk?"

There was a pause, then a low, rasping growl from the Secretary. Another pause; another rasp.

"That's all," panted Schwartz.

"But why won't it work?" asked Pola. She looked worried.

Shekt shrugged. "Some pretty delicate and complicated muscles are involved. It's not like yanking at the long limb muscles. Never mind, Schwartz. We may get by without."

The memory of the next two hours was something no two of those that took part in the queer odyssey could duplicate. Dr. Shekt, for instance, had acquired a queer rigidity in which all his fears were drowned in one breathless and helpless sympathy with the inwardly struggling Schwartz. Throughout he had eyes only for that round face as it slowly furrowed and twisted with effort. For the others he had hardly time for more than a moment's glance.

The guards immediately outside the door saluted sharply at the appearance of the Secretary, his green robe redolent of officialdom and power. The Secretary returned the salute in a fumbling, flat manner. They passed, unmolested.

It was only when they had left the great Hall that Arvardan became conscious of the madness of it all. The great, unimaginable danger to the Galaxy and the flimsy reed of safety that bridged, perhaps, the abyss. Yet even then, *even then*, Arvardan felt himself drowning in Pola's eyes. Whether it was the life that was being snatched from him, the future that was being destroyed about him, the eternal unavailability of the sweetness he had tasted—whatever it was, no one had ever seemed to him to be so completely and devastatingly desirable.

In aftertime she was the sum of his memories. Only the girl——

And upon Pola the sunny brightness of the morning burned down so that Arvardan's downturned face blurred before her. She smiled up at him and was conscious of that strong, hard arm on which her own rested so lightly. That was the memory that lingered afterward. Flat, firm muscle lightly covered by glossy-textured plastic cloth, smooth and cool under her wrist——

Schwartz was in a sweating agony. The curving drive that led away from the side entrance from which they had emerged was largely empty. For that he was hugely thankful.

Schwartz alone knew the full cost of failure. In the enemy Mind that he controlled he could sense the unbearable humiliation, the surpassing hatred, the utterly horrible resolves. He had to search that Mind for the information that guided him—the position of the official ground car, the proper route to take—— And, in searching, he also experienced the galling bitterness of the determined revenge that would lash out should his control waver for but the tenth part of the second.

The secret fastnesses of the Mind in which he was forced to rummage remained his personal possession forever. In aftertimes there came the pale gray hours of many an innocent dawn during which once again he had guided the steps of a madman down the dangerous walks of an enemy stronghold.

Schwartz gasped at the words when they reached the ground car. He no longer dared relax sufficiently to utter connected sentences. He choked out quick phrases: "Can't—drive car—can't make—him—make drive—complicated—can't——"

Shekt soothed him with a soft, clucking sound. He dared not touch him, dared not speak in an ordinary way, dared not distract Schwartz's mind for a second.

He whispered, "Just get him into the back seat, Schwartz. I'll drive. I know how. From now on just keep him still, and I'll take the blaster away."

The Secretary's ground car was a special model. Because it was special, it was different. It attracted attention. Its green headlight turned to the right and left in rhythmic swings as the light dimmed and brightened in emerald flashes. Men paused to watch. Ground cars advancing in the opposite direction moved to the side in a respectful hurry.

Had the car been less noticed, had it been less obtrusive, the occasional passer-by might have had time to note the pale, unmoving Ancient in the back seat—might have wondered—might have scented danger——

But they noticed only the car, so that time passed. . . .

A soldier blocked the way at the gleaming chromium gates that rose sheerly in the expansive, overwhelming way that marked all Imperial structures in sharp contrast to the squatly massive and brooding architecture of Earth. His huge force gun shot out horizontally in a barring gesture, and the car halted.

Arvardan leaned out. "I'm a citizen of the Empire, soldier. I'd like to see your commanding officer."

"I'll have to see your identification, sir."

"That's been taken from me. I am Bel Arvardan of Baronn, Sirius. I am on the Procurator's business and I'm in a hurry."

The soldier lifted a wrist to his mouth and spoke softly into the transmitter. There was a pause while he waited for an answer, and then he lowered his rifle and stepped aside. Slowly the gate swung open.

Nineteen: THE DEADLINE THAT APPROACHED

The hours that followed saw turmoil within and without Fort Dibburn. More so, perhaps, in Chica itself.

It was at noon that the High Minister at Washenn inquired via Communi-wave after his Secretary, and a search for the latter failed. The High Minister was displeased; the minor officials at the Hall of Correction were perturbed.

Questioning followed, and the guards outside the assembly room were definite that the Secretary had left with the prisoners at ten-thirty in the morning. . . . No, he had left no instructions. They could not say where he was going; it was, of course, not their place to ask.

Another set of guards was equally uninformed and uninformative. A general air of anxiety mounted and swirled.

At 2 P.M. the first report arrived that the Secretary's ground car had been seen that morning—no one had seen if the Secretary was within—some thought he had been driving, but had only assumed it, it turned out——

By two-thirty it had been ascertained that the car had entered Fort Dibburn.

At not quite three, it was finally decided to put in a call to the commander of the fort. A lieutenant had answered.

It was impossible at that time they learned, for information on the subject to be given. However, His Imperial Majesty's officers requested that order be maintained for the present. It was further requested that news of the absence of a member of the Society of Ancients be not generally distributed until further notice.

But that was enough to achieve the direct opposite of the Imperial desires.

Men engaged in treason cannot take chances when one of the prime members of a conspiracy is in the hands of the enemy forty-eight hours before trigger time. It can mean only discovery or betrayal, and these are but the reverse sides of a single coin. Either alternative would mean death.

So word went out——

And the population of Chica stirred——

The professional demagogues were on the street corners. The secret arsenals were broken open and the hands that reached withdrew with weapons. There was a twisting drift toward the fort, and at 6 P.M. a new message was sent to the commandant, this time by personal envoy.

Meanwhile, this activity was matched in a smaller way by events within the fort. It had begun dramatically when the young officer meeting the entering ground car reached out a hand for the Secretary's blaster.

"I'll take that," he said curtly.

Shekt said, "Let him take it, Schwartz."

The Secretary's hand lifted the blaster and stretched out; the blaster left it, was carried away—and Schwartz, with a heaving sob of breaking tension, let go.

Arvardan was ready. When the Secretary lashed out like an insane steel coil released from compression, the archaeologist pounced upon him, fists pumping down hard.

The officer snapped out orders. Soldiers were running up. When rough hands laid hold of Arvardan's shirt collar and dragged him up, the Secretary was limp upon the seat. Dark blood was flowing feebly from the corner of his mouth. Arvardan's own already bruised cheek was open and bleeding.

He straightened his hair shakily. Then, pointing a rigid finger, said firmly, "I accuse that man of conspiring to overthrow the Imperial Government. I must have an immediate interview with the commanding officer."

"We'll have to see about that, sir," said the officer civilly. "If you don't mind, you will have to follow me—all of you."

And there, for hours, it rested. Their quarters were private, and reasonably clean. For the first time in twelve hours they had a chance to eat, which they did, despite considerations, with dispatch and efficiency. They even had the opportunity of that further necessity of civilization, a bath.

Yet the room was guarded, and as the hours passed, Arvardan finally lost his temper and cried, "But we've simply exchanged prisons."

The dull, meaningless routine of an army camp drifted about them, ignoring them. Schwartz was sleeping and Arvardan's eyes went to him. Shekt shook his head.

"We can't," he said. "It's humanly impossible. The man is exhausted. Let him sleep."

"But there are only thirty-nine hours left."

"I know—but wait."

A cool and faintly sardonic voice sounded. "Which of you claims to be a citizen of the Empire?"

Arvardan sprang forward. "I am. I——"

And his voice failed as he recognized the speaker. The latter smiled rigidly. His left arm he held a bit stiffly as a remaining memento of their last meeting.

Pola's voice was faint behind him. "Bel, it's the officer—the one of the department store."

"The one whose arm he broke," came the sharp addition. "My name is Lieutenant Claudy and yes, you are the same man. So you are a member of the Sirian worlds, are you? And yet you consort with these. Galaxy, the depths a man can sink to! And you've still got the girl with you." He waited and then said slowly and deliberately, "The Earthie-squaw!"

Arvardan bristled, then subsided. He couldn't—not yet——

He forced humbleness into his voice. "May I see the colonel, Lieutenant?"

"The colonel, I am afraid, is not on duty now."

"You mean he's not in the city?"

"I didn't say that. He can be reached—if the matter is sufficiently urgent."

"It is. . . . May I see the officer of the day?"

"At the moment I am the officer of the day."

"Then call the colonel."

And slowly the lieutenant shook his head. "I could scarcely do so without being convinced of the gravity of the situation."

Arvardan was shaking with impatience. "By the Galaxy, stop fencing with me! It's life and death."

"Really?" Lieutenant Claudy swung a little swagger stick with an air of affected dandyism. "You might crave an audience with me."

"All right. . . . Well, I'm waiting."

"I said—you might *crave* one."

"May I have an audience, Lieutenant?"

But there was no smile on the lieutenant's face. "I said, *crave* one —before the girl. Humbly."

Arvardan swallowed and drew back. Pola's hand was on his sleeve. "Please, Bel. You mustn't get him angry."

The archaeologist growled huskily, "Bel Arvardan of Sirius humbly craves audience with the officer of the day."

Lieutenant Claudy said, "That depends."

He took a step toward Arvardan and quickly and viciously brought the flat of his palm down hard upon the bandage that dressed Arvardan's open cheek.

Arvardan gasped and stifled a shriek.

The lieutenant said, "You resented that once. Don't you this time?"

Arvardan said nothing.

The lieutenant said, "Audience granted."

Four soldiers fell in before and behind Arvardan. Lieutenant Claudy led the way.

Shekt and Pola were alone with the sleeping Schwartz, and Shekt said, "I don't hear *him* any more, do you?"

Pola shook her head. "I haven't either, for quite a while. But, Father, do you suppose he'll do anything to Bel?"

"How can he?" said the old man gently. "You forget that he's not really one of us. He's a citizen of the Empire and cannot be easily molested. . . . You *are* in love with him, I suppose?"

"Oh, terribly, Father. It's silly, I know."

"Of course it is." Shekt smiled bitterly. "He is honest. I do not say he isn't. But what can he do? Can he live here with us on *this* world? Can he take you home? Introduce an Earthgirl to his friends? His family?"

She was crying. "I know. But maybe there won't be any afterwards."

And Shekt was on his feet again, as though the last phrase had reminded him. He said again, "I don't hear him."

It was the Secretary he did not hear. Balkis had been placed in an adjoining room, where his caged-lion steps had been clearly and ominously audible. Except that now they weren't.

It was a little point, but in the single mind and body of the Secretary there had somehow become centered and symboled all the sinister force of disease and destruction that were being loosed on the giant network of living stars. Shekt jarred Schwartz gently. "Wake up," he said.

Schwartz stirred. "What is it?" He felt scarcely rested. His tiredness went in and in, so deep as to come out at the other side, projecting in jagged streaks.

"Where's Balkis?" urged Shekt.

"Oh—oh yes." Schwartz looked about wildly, then remembered that it was not with his eyes that he looked and saw most clearly. He sent out the tendrils of his mind and they circled, sensing tensely for the Mind they knew so well.

He found it, and avoided touching it. His long immersion in it had not increased his fondness for the clinging of its diseased wretchedness.

Schwartz muttered, "He's on another floor. He's talking to someone."

"To whom?"

"No one whose mind I've even Touched before. Wait—let me listen. Maybe the Secretary will—— Yes, he calls him Colonel."

Shekt and Pola looked quickly at one another.

"It can't be treason, can it?" whispered Pola. "I mean, surely an officer of the Empire wouldn't deal with an Earthman against the Emperor, would he?"

"I don't know," said Shekt miserably. "I am ready to believe anything."

Lieutenant Claudy was smiling. He was behind a desk, with a blaster at his finger tips and the four soldiers behind him. He spoke with the authority that such a situation would lend one.

"I don't like Earthies," he said. "I never liked them. They're the scum of the Galaxy. They're diseased, superstitious, and lazy. They're degenerate and stupid. But, by the Stars, most of them know their place.

"In a way, I can understand them. That's the way they were born, and they can't help it. Of course I wouldn't endure what the Emperor endures from them—I mean their blasted customs and traditions—if *I* were the Emperor. But that's all right. Someday we'll learn——"

Arvardan exploded. "Now look here. I didn't come to listen——"

"You'll listen, because I'm not finished. I was about to say that what I *can't* understand is the workings of the mind of an Earthie-lover. When a man—a *real* man, supposedly—can get so low in filth as to crawl in among them and go nosing after their womenfolk, I have no respect for him. He's worse than they are——"

"Then to Space with you and your poor filthy excuse of a mind!" fiercely. "Do you know that there's treason against the Empire afoot? Do you know just how dangerous the situation is? Every minute you delay endangers every one of the quadrillions in the Galaxy——"

"Oh, I don't know, Dr. Arvardan. It *is* Dr., isn't it? I mustn't forget your honors. You see, I've got a theory of my own. You're one of them. Maybe you were born in Sirius, but you've got a black Earthman's heart, and you're using your Galactic citizenship to advance their cause. You've kidnaped this official of theirs, this Ancient. (A good thing, by the way, in itself, and I wouldn't mind rattling his throat for him.) *But* the Earthmen are looking for him already. They've sent a message to the fort."

"They have? Already? Then why are we talking here? I *must* see the colonel if I have to——"

"You expect a riot, trouble of any sort? Perhaps you even planned one as the first step in an arranged revolt, eh?"

"Are you mad? Why would I want to do that?"

"Well, then, you wouldn't mind if we released the Ancient?"

"You cannot." Arvardan rose to his feet, and for a moment it looked as though he might hurl himself across the desk at the other.

But the blaster was in Lieutenant Claudy's hand. "Oh, can't we? Look here, now. I've gotten a little of my own back. I've slapped you and made you crawl before your Earthie pals. I've made you sit here while I told you to your face what a low worm you are. And now I would love an excuse to blast your arm off in exchange for what you did to mine. Now make another move."

Arvardan froze.

Lieutenant Claudy laughed and put his blaster away. "It's too bad I have to save you for the colonel. He's to see you at five-fifteen."

"You knew that—you knew that all the time." Frustration tore his throat into hoarse sandpaper.

"Certainly."

"If the time we have lost, Lieutenant Claudy, means that the issue is lost, then neither of us will have much time to live." He spoke with an iciness that distorted his voice into something horrible. "But you will die first, because I shall spend my last minutes smashing your face into splintered bone and mashed brain."

"I'll be waiting for you, Earthie-lover. Any time!"

The commanding officer of Fort Dibburn had grown stiff in the service of the Empire. In the profound peace of the last generations there was little in the way of "glory" that any army officer could earn, and the colonel, in common with others, earned none. But in the long, slow rise from military cadet he had seen service in every part of the Galaxy—so that even a garrison on the neurotic world of Earth was to him but an additional chore. He wanted only the peaceful routine of normal occupation. He asked nothing beyond this, and for it was willing to humble himself—even, when it was necessary, to apologize to an Earthgirl.

He seemed tired when Arvardan entered. His shirt collar was open and his tunic, with its blazing yellow "Spaceship and Sun" of Empire, hung loosely over the back of his chair. He cracked the knuckles of his right hand with an abstracted air as he stared solemnly at Arvardan.

"A very confusing story, all this," he said, "very. I recall you well, young man. You are Bel Arvardan of Baronn, and the principal of a previous moment of considerable embarrassment. Can't you keep out of trouble?"

"It is not only myself that is in trouble, Colonel, but all the rest of the Galaxy as well."

"Yes, I know," somewhat impatiently. "Or at least I know that that is what you claim. I am told that you no longer have papers of identification."

"They were taken from me, but I am known at Everest. The Procurator himself can identify me, and will, I hope, before evening falls."

"We'll see about that." The colonel crossed his arms and teetered backward on his chair. "Suppose you give me your side of the story."

"I have been made aware of a dangerous conspiracy on the part of a small group of Earthmen to overthrow the Imperial Government by force, which, if not made known at once to the proper authorities, may well succeed in destroying both the Government and much of the Empire itself."

"You go too far, young man, in this very rash and farfetched statement. That the men of Earth could stage annoying riots, lay siege to this fort, do considerable damage, I am quite prepared to admit—but I do not for a moment conceive them capable of as much as driving the Imperial forces from this planet, let alone destroying the Imperial Government. Yet I will listen to the details of this—uh—plot."

"Unfortunately, the seriousness of the matter is such that I feel it vital that the details be told to the Procurator himself in person. I request, therefore, to be put into communication with him now, if you don't mind."

"Umm. . . . Let us not act too hurriedly. Are you aware that the man you have brought in is Secretary to the High Minister of Earth, one of their Ancients and a very important man to them?"

"Perfectly!"

"And yet you say that he is a prime mover in this conspiracy you mention."

"He is."

"Your evidence?"

"You will understand me, I am sure, when I say that I cannot discuss that with anyone but the Procurator."

The colonel frowned and regarded his fingernails. "Do you doubt my competency in the case?"

"Not at all, sir. It is simply that only the Procurator has the authority to take the decisive action required in this case."

"What decisive action do you refer to?"

"A certain building on Earth must be bombed and totally destroyed within thirty hours, or the lives of most, or all, of the inhabitants of the Empire will be lost."

"What building?" asked the colonel wearily.

Arvardan snapped back, "May I be connected with the Procurator, please?"

There was a pause of deadlock. The colonel said stiffly, "You realize that in forcibly kidnaping an Earthman you have rendered yourself liable to trial and punishment by the Terrestrial authorities? Ordinarily the government will protect its citizens as a matter of principle and insist upon a Galactic trial. However, affairs on Earth are delicate and I have strict instructions to risk no avoidable clash. Therefore, unless you answer my questions fully, I will be forced to turn you and your companions over to the local police."

"But that would be a death sentence! For yourself too! . . . Colonel, I am a citizen of the Empire, and I demand an audience with the Pro——"

A buzzer on the colonel's desk interrupted him. The colonel turned to it, closing a contact. "Yes?"

"Sir," came the clear voice, "a body of natives have encircled the fort. It is believed they are armed."

"Has there been any violence?"

"No, sir."

There was no sign of emotion on the colonel's face. This, at least, was what he was trained for. "Artillery and aircraft are to be made ready—all men to battle stations. Withhold all fire except in self-defense. Understood?"

"Yes, sir. An Earthman under flag of truce wishes audience."

"Send him in. Also send the High Minister's Secretary here again."

And now the colonel glared coldly at the archaeologist. "I trust you are aware of the appalling nature of what you have caused."

"I demand to be present at the interview," cried Arvardan, nearly incoherent with fury, "and I further demand the reason for your allowing me to rot under guard here for hours while you closet yourself with a native traitor. I tell you that I am not ignorant that you interviewed him before speaking with me."

"Are you making any accusations, sir?" demanded the colonel, his own voice ascending the scale. "If so, make them plainly."

"I make no accusations. But I will remind you that you will be accountable for your actions hereafter, and that you may well be known in the future, if you have a future, as the destroyer, by your stubbornness, of your people."

"Silence! I am not accountable to you, at any rate. We will conduct affairs, henceforward, as *I* choose. Do you understand?"

Twenty: *THE DEADLINE THAT WAS REACHED*

The Secretary passed through the door held open by a soldier. On his purpling, swollen lips there was a brief, cold smile. He bowed to the colonel and remained completely unaware, to all appearances, of the presence of Arvardan.

"Sir," said the colonel to the Earthman, "I have communicated to the High Minister the details of your presence here and the manner in which it came about. Your detention here is, of course, entirely—

uh—unorthodox, and it is my purpose to set you free as soon as I can. However, I have here a gentleman who, as you probably know, has lodged against you a very serious accusation; one which, under the circumstances, we must investigate——"

"I understand, Colonel," said the Secretary calmly. "However, as I have already explained to you, this man has been on Earth, I believe, only a matter of two months or so, so that his knowledge of our internal politics is nonexistent. This is a flimsy basis, indeed, for any accusation."

Arvardan retorted in anger, "I am an archaeologist by profession, and one who has specialized of late on Earth and its customs. My knowledge of its politics is far from nonexistent. And in any case, I am not the only one who makes the accusation."

The Secretary did not look at the archaeologist either then or later. He spoke exclusively to the colonel. He said, "One of our local scientists is involved in this; one who, approaching the end of his normal sixty years, is suffering from delusions of persecution. Then, in addition, there is another man, one of unknown antecedents and a history of idiocy. All three could not raise a respectable accusation among them."

Arvardan jumped to his feet. "I demand to be heard——"

"Sit down," said the colonel coldly and unsympathetically. "You have refused to discuss the matter with me. Let the refusal stand. Being in the man with the flag of truce."

It was another member of the Society of Ancients. Scarcely a flicker of the eyelid betrayed any emotion on his part at the sight of the Secretary. The colonel rose from his chair and said, "Do you speak for the men outside?"

"I do, sir."

"I assume, then, that this riotous and illegal assembly is based upon demand for the return of your fellow countryman here?"

"Yes, sir. He must be immediately freed."

"Indeed! Nevertheless, the interest of law and order and the respect due His Imperial Majesty's representatives on this world require that the matter cannot possibly be discussed while men are gathered in armed rebellion against us. You must have your men disperse."

The Secretary spoke up pleasantly. "The colonel is perfectly correct, Brother Cori. Please calm the situation. I am perfectly safe here, and there is no danger—for anybody. Do you understand? For anybody. It is my word as an Ancient."

"Very well, Brother. I am thankful you are safe."

He was ushered out.

The colonel said curtly, "We will see that you leave here safely as soon as matters in the city have returned to normal. Thank you for your co-operation in this matter just concluded."

Arvardan was again on his feet. "I forbid it. You will let loose this would-be murderer of the human race while forbidding me an interview with the Procurator when that would be simply in accord with my rights as a Galactic citizen." Then, in a paroxysm of frustration, "Will you show more consideration to an Earthman dog than you will to me?"

The Secretary's voice sounded over that last near-incoherent rage. "Colonel, I will gladly remain until such time as my case is heard by the Procurator, if that is what this man wants. An accusation of treason is serious, and the suspicion of it—however farfetched—may be sufficient to ruin my usefulness to my people. I would really appreciate the opportunity to prove to the Procurator that none is more loyal to the Empire than myself."

The colonel said stiffly, "I admire your feelings, sir, and freely admit that were I in your place my attitude would be quite different. You are a credit to your race, sir. I will attempt contact with the Procurator."

Arvardan said nothing more until led back to his cell.

He avoided the glance of the others. For a long time he sat motionless, with a knuckle pinched between gnawing teeth.

Until Shekt said, "Well?"

Arvardan shook his head. "I just about ruined everything."

"What did you do?"

"Lost my temper; offended the colonel; got nowhere—— I'm no diplomat, Shekt."

He felt riven with the sudden urge for self-defense. "What could I do?" he cried. "Balkis had already been to the colonel, so that I couldn't trust him. What if he'd been offered his life? What if he's been in on the plot all along? I know it's a wild thought, but I couldn't take the chance. It was too suspicious. I wanted to see Ennius himself."

The physicist was on his feet, withered hands clasped behind his back. "Well, then—is Ennius coming?"

"I suppose so. But it is only at Balkis's own request, and that I don't understand."

"Balkis's own request? Then Schwartz might be right."

"Yes? What has Schwartz been saying?"

The plump Earthman was sitting on his cot. He shrugged his shoulders when the eyes turned to him and spread out his hands in a helpless gesture. "I caught the Secretary's Mind Touch when they took him past our room just now. He's definitely had a long talk with this officer you talked to."

"I know."

"But there's no treason in that officer's mind."

"Well," miserably, "then I guessed wrong. I'll eat worms when Ennius comes. What about Balkis?"

"There's no worry or fear in his mind; only hate. And now it's mostly hate for us, for capturing him, for dragging him here. We've wounded his vanity horribly, and he intends to square it with us. I saw little daydream pictures in his mind. Of himself, singlehanded, preventing the entire Galaxy from doing anything to stop him even while we, with our knowledge, work against him. He's giving us the odds, the trumps, and then he'll smash us anyway and triumph over us."

"You mean that he will risk his plans, his dreams of Empire, just to vent a little spite at us? That's mad."

"I know," said Schwartz with finality. "*He* is mad."

"And he thinks he'll succeed?"

"That's right."

"Then we must have you, Schwartz. We'll need your mind. Listen to me——"

But Shekt was shaking his head. "No, Arvardan, we couldn't work that. I woke Schwartz when you left and we discussed the matter. His mental powers, which he can describe only dimly, are obviously not under perfect control. He can stun a man, or paralyze him, or even kill him. Better than that, he can control the larger voluntary muscles even against the subject's will, but no more than that. In the case of the Secretary, he couldn't make the man talk, the small muscles about the vocal cords being beyond him. He couldn't co-ordinate motion well enough to have the Secretary drive a car; he even balanced him while walking only with difficulty. Obviously, then, we couldn't control Ennius, for instance, to the point of having him issue an order, or write one. I've thought of that, you see . . ." Shekt shook his head as his voice trailed away.

Arvardan felt the desolation of futility descend upon him. Then, with a sudden pang of anxiety, "Where's Pola?"

"She's sleeping in the alcove."

He would have longed to wake her—longed—— Oh, longed a lot of things.

Arvardan looked at his watch. It was almost midnight, and there were only thirty hours left.

He slept for a while after that, then woke for a while, as it grew light again. No one approached, and a man's very soul grew haggard and pale.

Six hours left——

He looked about him now in a dazed and hopeless way. They were all here now—even the Procurator, at last. Pola was next to him, her warm little fingers on his wrist and that look of fear and exhaustion on her face that more than anything else infuriated him against all the Galaxy.

Maybe they all deserved to die, the stupid, stupid—stupid——

He scarcely saw Shekt and Schwartz. They sat on his left. And there was Balkis, the damnable Balkis, with his lips still swollen, one cheek green, so that it must hurt like the devil to talk—and Arvardan's own lips stretched into a furious, aching smile at the thought and his fists clenched and writhed. His own bandaged cheek ached less at the thought.

Facing all of them was Ennius, frowning, uncertain, almost ridiculous, dressed as he was in those heavy, shapeless, lead-impregnated clothes.

And he was stupid, too. Arvardan felt a thrill of hatred shoot through him at the thought of these Galactic trimmers who wanted only peace and ease. Where were the conquerors of three centuries back? Where? . . .

Six hours left—

Ennius had received the call from the Chica garrison some eighteen hours before and he had streaked half around the planet at the summons. The motives that led him to that were obscure but nonetheless forceful. Essentially, he told himself, there was nothing to the matter but a regrettable kidnaping of one of those green-robed curiosities of superstitious, hagridden Earth. That, and these wild and undocumented accusations. Nothing, certainly, that the colonel on the spot could not have handled.

And yet there was Shekt—Shekt was in this—— And not as the accused, but as an accuser. It was confusing.

He sat now facing them, thinking, quite conscious that his decision in this case might hasten a rebellion, perhaps weaken his own position at court, ruin his chances at advancement—— As for Arvardan's long speech just now about virus strains and unbridled epidemics, how seriously could he take it? After all, if he took action on the basis of it, how credible would the matter sound to his superiors? And yet Arvardan was an archaeologist of note.

So he postponed the matter in his mind by saying to the Secretary, "Surely you have something to say in this matter?"

"Surprisingly little," said the Secretary with easy confidence. "I would like to ask what evidence exists for supporting the accusation?"

"Your Excellency," said Arvardan with snapping patience, "I have already told you that the man admitted it in every detail at the time of our imprisonment day before yesterday."

"Perhaps," said the Secretary, "you choose to credit that, Your Excellency, but it is simply an additional unsupported statement. Actually the only facts to which outsiders can bear witness to are that *I* was the one violently taken prisoner, not they; that it was *my* life that was in peril, not theirs. Now I would like my accuser to explain how he could find all this out in the nine weeks that he has been on the planet, when you, the Procurator, in years of service here, have found nothing to my disadvantage?"

"There is reason in what the Brother says," admitted Ennius heavily. "How *do* you know?"

Arvardan replied stiffly, "Prior to the accused's confession I was informed of the conspiracy by Dr. Shekt."

"Is that so, Dr. Shekt?" The Procurator's glance shifted to the physicist.

"That is so, Your Excellency."

"And how did you find out?"

Shekt said, "Dr. Arvardan was admirably thorough and accurate in his description of the use to which the Synapsifier was put and in his remarks concerning the dying statements of the bacteriologist, F. Smitko. This Smitko was a member of the conspiracy. His remarks were recorded and the recording is available."

"But, Dr. Shekt, the dying statements of a man known to be in delirium—if what Dr. Arvardan said is true—cannot be of very great weight. You have nothing else?"

Arvardan interrupted by striking his fist on the arm of his chair and roaring, "Is this a law court? Has someone been guilty of violating a traffic ordinance? We have no time to weigh evidence on an analytical balance or measure it with micrometers. I tell you we have till six in the morning, five and a half hours, in other words, to wipe out this enormous threat. . . . You knew Dr. Shekt previous to this time, Your Excellency. Have you known him to be a liar?"

The Secretary interposed instantly, "No one accused Dr. Shekt of deliberately lying, Your Excellency. It is only that the good doctor is aging and has, of late, been greatly concerned over his approaching sixtieth birthday. I am afraid that a combination of age and fear have induced slight paranoiac tendencies, common enough here on Earth. . . . Look at him! Does he seem to you quite normal?"

He did not, of course. He was drawn and tense, shattered by what had passed and what was to come.

Yet Shekt forced his voice into normal tones, even into calmness. He said, "I might say that for the last two months I have been under the continual watch of the Ancients; that my letters have been opened and my answers censored. But it is obvious that all such complaints would be attributed to the paranoia spoken of. However, I have here Joseph Schwartz, the man who volunteered as a subject for the Synapsifier one day when you were visiting me at the Institute."

"I remember." There was a feeble gratitude in Ennius's mind that the subject had, for the moment, veered. "Is that the man?"

"Yes."

"He looks none the worse for the experience."

"He is far the better. The exposure to the Synapsifier was uncommonly successful, since he had a photographic memory to begin with, a fact I did not know at the time. At any rate, he now has a mind which is sensitive to the thoughts of others."

Ennius leaned far forward in his chair and cried in a shocked amazement, "What? Are you telling me he reads minds?"

"That can be demonstrated, Your Excellency. But I think the Brother will confirm the statement."

The Secretary darted a quick look of hatred at Schwartz, boiling in its intensity and lightninglike in its passage across his face. He said, with but the most imperceptible quiver in his voice, "It is quite true, Your Excellency. This man they have here has certain hypnotic faculties, though whether that is due to the Synapsifier or not I don't know. I might add that this man's subjection to the Synapsifier was not recorded, a matter which you'll agree is highly suspicious."

"It was not recorded," said Shekt quietly, "in accordance with my standing orders from the High Minister." But the Secretary merely shrugged his shoulders at that.

Ennius said peremptorily, "Let us get on with the matter and avoid this petty bickering. . . . What about this Schwartz? What have his mind-reading powers, or hypnotic talents, or whatever they are, to do with the case?"

"Shekt intends to say," put in the Secretary, "that Schwartz can read my mind."

"Is that it? Well, and what is he thinking?" asked the Procurator, speaking to Schwartz for the first time.

"He's thinking," said Schwartz, "that we have no way of convincing you of the truth of our side of what you call the case."

"Quite true," scoffed the Secretary, "though that deduction scarcely calls for much mental power."

"And also," Schwartz went on, "that you are a poor fool, afraid to act, desiring only peace, hoping by your justice and impartiality to win over the men of Earth, and all the more a fool for so hoping."

The Secretary reddened. "I deny all that. It is an obvious attempt to prejudice you, Your Excellency."

But Ennius said, "I am not so easily prejudiced." And then, to Schwartz, "And what am *I* thinking?"

Schwartz replied, "That even if I could see clearly within a man's skull, I need not necessarily tell the truth about what I see."

The Procurator's eyebrows lifted in surprise. "You are correct, quite correct. Do you maintain the truth of the claims put forward by Drs. Arvardan and Shekt?"

"Every word of it."

"So! Yet unless a second such as you can be found, one who is not involved in the matter, your evidence would not be valid in law even if we could obtain general belief in you as a telepath."

"But it is not a question of the law," cried Arvardan, "but of the safety of the Galaxy."

"Your Excellency"—the Secretary rose in his seat—"I have a request to make. I would like to have this Joseph Schwartz removed from the room."

"Why so?"

"This man, in addition to reading minds, has certain powers of mental force. I was captured by means of a paralysis induced by this Schwartz. It is my fear that he may attempt something of the sort now against me, or even against you, Your Excellency, that forces me to the request."

Arvardan rose to his feet, but the Secretary overshouted him to say, "No hearing can be fair if a man is present who might subtly influence the mind of the judge by means of admitted mental gifts."

Ennius made his decision quickly. An orderly entered, and Joseph Schwartz, offering no resistance, nor showing the slightest sign of perturbation on his moonlike face, was led away.

To Arvardan it was the final blow.

As for the Secretary, he rose now and for the moment stood there —a squat, grim figure in green; strong in his self-confidence.

He began, in serious, formal style, "Your Excellency, all of Dr. Arvardan's beliefs and statements rest upon the testimony of Dr. Shekt. In turn, Dr. Shekt's beliefs rest upon the dying delirium of one man. And all this, Your Excellency, *all this*, somehow never reached the surface until after Joseph Schwartz was submitted to the Synapsifier.

"Who, then, is Joseph Schwartz? Until Joseph Schwartz appeared on the scene, Dr. Shekt was a normal, untroubled man. You yourself, Your Excellency, spent an afternoon with him the day Schwartz was brought in for treatment. Was he abnormal then? Did he inform you of treason against the Empire? Of certain babblings on the part of a dying biochemist? Did he seem even troubled? Or suspicious? He says now that he was instructed by the High Minister to falsify the results of the Synapsifier tests, not to record the names of those treated. Did he tell you that then? Or only now, *after* that day on which Schwartz appeared?

"Again, who is Joseph Schwartz? He spoke no known language at the time he was brought in. So much we found out for ourselves later, when we first began to suspect the stability of Dr. Shekt's reason. He was brought in by a farmer who knew nothing of his identity, or, indeed, any facts about him at all. Nor have any since been discovered.

"Yet this man has strange mental powers. He can stun at a hundred yards by thought alone—kill at closer range. I myself have been paralyzed by him; my arms and legs were manipulated by him; my mind might have been manipulated by him if he had wished.

"I believe, certainly, that Schwartz did manipulate the minds of these others. They say I captured them, that I threatened them with death, that I confessed to treason and to aspiring to Empire—— Yet ask of them one question, Your Excellency. Have they not been thoroughly exposed to the influence of Schwartz, that is, of a man capable of controlling their minds?

"Is not perhaps Schwartz a traitor? If not, who *is* Schwartz?"

The Secretary seated himself, calm, almost genial.

Arvardan felt as though his brain had mounted a cyclotron and was spinning outward now in faster and faster revolutions.

What answer could one make? That Schwartz was from the past? What evidence was there for that? That the man spoke a genuinely primitive speech? But only he himself—Arvardan—could testify to that. And he, Arvardan, might well have a manipulated mind. After all, how could he tell his mind had not been manipulated? Who *was* Schwartz? What had so convinced him of this great plan of Galactic conquest?

He thought again. From where came his conviction of the truth of the conspiracy? He was an archaeologist, given to doubting, but now—— Had it been one man's word? One girl's kiss? Or Joseph Schwartz?

He couldn't think! *He couldn't think!*

"Well?" Ennius sounded impatient. "Have you anything to say, Dr. Shekt? Or you, Dr. Arvardan?"

But Pola's voice suddenly pierced the silence. "Why do you ask them? Can't you see that it's all a lie? Don't you see that he's tying us all up with his false tongue? Oh, we're all going to die, and I don't care any more—but we could stop it, we could stop it—— And instead we just sit here and—and—*talk*——" She burst into wild sobs.

The Secretary said, "So we are reduced to the screams of a hysterical girl. . . . Your Excellency, I have this proposition. My accusers say that all this, the alleged virus and whatever else they have in mind, is scheduled for a definite time—six in the morning, I believe. I offer to remain in your custody for a week. If what they say is true, word of an epidemic in the Galaxy ought to reach Earth within a few days. If such occurs, Imperial forces will still control Earth——"

"Earth is a fine exchange, indeed, for a Galaxy of humans," mumbled the white-faced Shekt.

"I value my own life, and that of my people. We are hostages for our innocence, and I am prepared at this instant to inform the Society of Ancients that I will remain here for a week of my own free will and prevent any disturbances that might otherwise occur." He folded his arms.

Ennius looked up, his face troubled. "I find no fault in this man——"

Arvardan could stand it no more. With a quiet and deadly ferocity, he arose and strode quickly toward the Procurator. What he meditated was never known. Afterward he himself could not remember. At any rate, it made no difference. Ennius had a neuronic whip and used it.

For the third time since landing on Earth everything about Arvardan flamed up into pain, spun about, and vanished.

In the hours during which Arvardan was unconscious the six o'clock deadline was reached——

Twenty-One: THE DEADLINE THAT PASSED

And passed!

Light——

Blurring light and misty shadows—melting and twisting, and then coming into focus.

A face—— Eyes upon his——

"Pola!" Things were sharp and clear to Arvardan in a single, leaping bound. "What time is it?"

His fingers were hard upon her wrist, so that she winced involuntarily.

"It's past seven," she whispered. "Past the deadline."

He looked about wildly, starting from the cot on which he lay, disregarding the burning in his joints. Shekt, his lean figure huddled in a chair, raised his head to nod in brief mournfulness.

"It's all over, Arvardan."

"Then Ennius——"

"Ennius," said Shekt, "would not take the chance. Isn't that strange?" He laughed a queer, cracked, rasping laugh. "The three of us singlehandedly discover a vast plot against humanity, singlehandedly we capture the ringleader and bring him to justice. It's like a visicast, isn't it, with the great all-conquering heroes zooming to victory in the nick of time? That's where they usually end it. Only in our case the visicast went on and we found that nobody believed us. That doesn't happen in visicasts, does it? Things end happily there, don't they? It's funny——" The words turned into rough, dry sobs.

Arvardan looked away, sick. Pola's eyes were dark universes, moist and tear-filled. Somehow, for an instant, he was lost in them—they *were* universes, star-filled. And toward those stars little gleaming metallic cases were streaking, devouring the light-years as they penetrated hyperspace in calculated, deadly paths. Soon—perhaps already—they would approach, pierce atmospheres, fall apart into unseen deadly rains of virus——

Well, it was over.

It could no longer be stopped.

"Where is Schwartz?" he asked weakly.

But Pola only shook her head. "They never brought him back."

The door opened, and Arvardan was not so far gone in the acceptance of death as to fail to look up with a momentary wash of hope upon his face.

But it was Ennius, and Arvardan's face hardened and turned away.

Ennius approached and looked momentarily at the father and daughter. But even now Shekt and Pola were primarily Earth creatures and could say nothing to the Procurator, even though they knew that short and violent as their future lives were to be, that of the Procurator would be even shorter and more violent.

Ennius tapped Arvardan on the shoulder. "Dr. Arvardan?"

"Your Excellency?" said Arvardan in a raw and bitter imitation of the other's intonation.

"It is after six o'clock." Ennius had not slept that night. With his official absolution of Balkis had come no absolute assurance that the accusers were completely mad—or under mental control. He had watched the soulless chronometer tick away the life of the Galaxy.

"Yes," said Arvardan. "It is after six and the stars still shine."

"But you still think you were right?"

"Your Excellency," said Arvardan, "in a matter of hours the first victims will die. They won't be noticed. Human beings die every day. In a week hundreds of thousands will have died. The percentage of recovery will be close to zero. No known remedies will be available. Several planets will send out emergency calls for epidemic relief. In two weeks scores of planets will have joined the call and States of Emergency will be declared in the nearer sectors. In a month the Galaxy will be a writhing mass of disease. In two months not twenty planets will remain untouched. In six months the Galaxy will be dead. . . . And what will *you* do when those first reports come in?

"Let me predict that as well. You will send out reports that the epidemics may have started on Earth. This will save no lives. You will declare war on the Ancients of Earth. This will save no lives. You will wipe the Earthman from the face of his planet. This will save no lives. . . . Or else you will act as go-between for your friend Balkis and the Galactic Council, or the survivors thereof. You may then have the honor of handing the wretched remnants of the crumbs of the Empire to Balkis in return for antitoxin, which may or may not reach sufficient worlds in sufficient quantities in sufficient time to save a single human being."

Ennius smiled without conviction. "Don't you think you're being ridiculously overdramatic?"

"Oh yes. I'm a dead man and you're a corpse. But let's be devilishly cool and Imperial about it, don't y'know?"

"If you resent the use of the neuronic whip——"

"Not at all," ironically. "I'm used to it. I hardly feel it any more."

"Then I am putting it to you as logically as I can. This has been a nasty mess. It would be difficult to report sensibly, yet as difficult to suppress without reason. Now the other accusers involved are Earthmen; your voice is the only one which would carry weight. Suppose you sign a statement to the effect that the accusation was made at a time when you were not in your—— Well, we'll think of some phrase that will cover it without bringing in the notion of mental control."

"That would be simple. Say I was crazy, drunk, hypnotized, or drugged. Anything goes."

"Will you be reasonable? Now look, I tell you that you *have* been tampered with." He was whispering tensely. "You're a man of Sirius. Why have you fallen in love with an Earthgirl?"

"What?"

"Don't shout. I say—in your normal state, could you ever have gone native? Could you have considered that sort of thing?" He nodded his head just perceptibly in the direction of Pola.

For an instant Arvardan stared at him in surprise. Then, quickly, his hand shot out and seized the highest Imperial authority on Earth by the throat. Ennius's hands wrenched wildly and futilely at the other's grip.

Arvardan said, "That sort of thing, eh? Do you mean Miss Shekt? If you do, I want to hear the proper respect, eh? Ah, go away. You're dead anyway."

Ennius said gaspingly, "Dr. Arvardan, you will consider yourself under ar——"

The door opened again, and the colonel was upon them.

"Your Excellency, the Earth rabble has returned."

"What? Hasn't this Balkis spoken to his officials? He was going to arrange for a week's stay."

"He has spoken and he's still here. But so is the mob. We are ready to fire upon them, and it is my advice as military commander that we proceed to do that. Have you any suggestions, Your Excellency?"

"Hold your fire until I see Balkis. Have him sent in here." He turned. "Dr. Arvardan, I will deal with you later."

Balkis was brought in, smiling. He bowed formally to Ennius, who yielded him the barest nod in return.

"See here," said the Procurator brusquely, "I am informed your men are packing the approaches to Fort Dibburn. This was not part of our agreement. . . . Now, we do not wish to cause bloodshed, but our patience is not inexhaustible. Can you disperse them peaceably?"

"If I choose, Your Excellency."

"If you choose? You had better choose. And at once."

"Not at all, Your Excellency!" And now the Secretary smiled and flung out an arm. His voice was a wild taunt, too long withheld, now gladly released. "Fool! You waited too long and can die for that! Or live a slave, if you prefer—but remember that it will not be an easy life."

The wildness and fervor of the statement produced no shattering effect upon Ennius. Even here, at what was undoubtedly the profoundest blow of Ennius's career, the stolidity of the Imperial career diplomat did not desert him. It was only that the grayness and deep-eyed weariness about him deepened.

"Then I lost so much in my caution? The story of the virus—was true?" There was almost an abstract, indifferent wonder in his voice. "But Earth, yourself—you are all my hostages."

"Not at all," came the instant, victorious cry. "It is you and yours that are *my* hostages. The virus that now is spreading through the Universe has not left Earth immune. Enough already saturates the atmosphere of every garrison on the planet, including Everest itself. We of Earth are immune, but how do *you* feel, Procurator? Weak? Is your throat dry? Your head feverish? It will not be long, you know. And it is only from us that you can obtain the antidote."

For a long moment Ennius said nothing, his face thin and suddenly incredibly haughty.

Then he turned to Arvardan and in cool, cultured tones said, "Dr. Arvardan, I find I must beg your pardon for having doubted your word. Dr. Shekt, Miss Shekt—my apologies."

Arvardan bared his teeth. "Thank you for your apologies. They will be of great help to everybody."

"Your sarcasm is deserved," said the Procurator. "If you will excuse me, I will return to Everest to die with my family. Any question of compromise with this—man is, of course, out of the question. My soldiers of the Imperial Procuracy of Earth will, I am sure, acquit themselves properly before their death, and not a few Earthmen will undoubtedly have time to light the way for us through the passages of death. . . . Good-by."

"Hold on. Hold on. Don't go." Slowly, slowly, Ennius looked up to the new voice.

Slowly, slowly, Joseph Schwartz, frowning a bit, swaying a bit with weariness, stepped across the threshold.

The Secretary tensed and sprang backward. With a sudden, wary suspicion, he faced the man from the past.

"No," he gritted, "you can't get the secret of the antidote out of me. Only certain men have it, and only certain others are trained to use it properly. All these are safely out of your reach for the time it takes the toxin to do its work."

"They are out of reach now," admitted Schwartz, "but not for the time it would take the toxin to do its work. You see, there is no toxin, and no virus to stamp out."

The statement did not quite penetrate. Arvardan felt a sudden choking thought enter his mind. *Had* he been tampered with? *Had* all this been a gigantic hoax, one that had taken in the Secretary as well as himself? If so, why?

But Ennius spoke. "Quickly, man. Your meaning."

"It's not complicated," said Schwartz. "When we were here last night I knew I could do nothing by simply sitting and listening. So I worked carefully on the Secretary's mind for a long time. . . . I dared not be detected. And then, finally, he asked that I be ordered out of the room. This was what I wanted, of course, and the rest was easy.

"I stunned my guard and left for the airstrip. The fort was on a twenty-four-hour alert. The aircraft were fueled, armed, and ready for flight. The pilots were waiting. I picked one out—and we flew to Senloo."

The Secretary might have wished to say something. His jaws writhed soundlessly.

It was Shekt who spoke. "But you could force no one to fly a plane, Schwartz. It was all you could do to make a man walk."

"Yes, when it's against his will. But from Dr. Arvardan's mind I knew how Sirians hated Earthmen—so I looked for a pilot who was born in the Sirius Sector and found Lieutenant Claudy."

"Lieutenant Claudy?" cried Arvardan.

"Yes—— Oh, you know him. Yes, I see. It's quite clear in your mind."

"I'll bet. . . . Go ahead, Schwartz."

"This officer *hated* Earthmen with a hate that's difficult to understand, even for me, and I was inside his mind. He *wanted* to bomb them. He *wanted* to destroy them. It was only discipline that tied him fast and kept him from taking out his plane then and there.

"That kind of a mind is different. Just a little suggestion, a little push, and discipline was not enough to hold him. I don't even think he realized that I climbed into the plane with him."

"How did you find Senloo?" whispered Shekt.

"In my time," said Schwartz, "there was a city called St. Louis. It was at the junction of two great rivers. . . . We found Senloo. It was night, but there was a dark patch in a sea of radioactivity—and Dr. Shekt had said the Temple was an isolated oasis of normal soil. We dropped a flare—at least it was my mental suggestion—and there was a five-pointed building below us. It jibed with the picture I had received in the Secretary's mind. . . . Now there's only a hole, a hundred feet deep, where that building was. That happened at three in the morning. No virus was sent out and the universe is free."

It was an animal-like howl that emerged from the Secretary's lips—the unearthly screech of a demon. He seemed to gather for a leap, and then—collapsed.

A thin froth of saliva trickled slowly down his lower lip.

"I never touched him," said Schwartz softly. Then, staring thoughtfully at the fallen figure, "I was back before six, but I knew I would have to wait for the deadline to pass. Balkis would *have* to crow. I knew that from his mind, and it was from his own mouth, only, that I could convict him. . . . Now there he lies."

Twenty-Two: *THE BEST IS YET TO BE*

Thirty days had passed since Joseph Schwartz had lifted off an airport runway on a night dedicated to Galactic destruction, with alarm bells shrilling madly behind him and orders to return burning the ether toward him.

He had not returned; not, at least, until he had destroyed the Temple of Senloo.

The heroism was finally made official now. In his pocket he had the ribbon of the Order of the Spaceship and Sun, First Class. Only two others in all the Galaxy had ever gotten it nonposthumously.

That was something for a retired tailor.

No one, of course, outside the most official of officialdom, knew exactly what he had done, but that didn't matter. Someday, in the history books, it would all become part of a bright and indelible record.

He was walking through the quiet night now toward Dr. Shekt's house. The city was peaceful, as peaceful as the starry glitter above.

In isolated places on Earth bands of Zealots still made trouble, but their leaders were dead or captive and the moderate Earthmen, themselves, could take care of the rest.

The first huge convoys of normal soil were already on their way. Ennius had again made his original proposal that Earth's population be moved to another planet, but that was out. Charity was not wanted. Let Earthmen have a chance to remake their own planet. Let them build once again the home of their fathers, the native world of man. Let them labor with their hands, removing the diseased soil and replacing it with healthy, seeing the green grow where all had been dead and making the desert blossom in beauty once again.

It was an enormous job; it could take a century—but what of that? Let the Galaxy lend machinery; let the Galaxy ship food; let the Galaxy supply soil. Of their incalculable resources, it would be a trifle—and it would be repaid.

And someday, once again, the Earthman would be a people among peoples, inhabiting a planet among planets, looking all humanity in the eye in dignity and equality.

Schwartz's heart pounded at the wonder of it all as he walked up the steps to the front door. Next week he left with Arvardan for the great central worlds of the Galaxy. Who else of his generation had ever left Earth?

And momentarily he thought of the old Earth, *his* Earth. So long dead. So long dead.

And yet but three and a half months had passed . . .

He paused, his hand on the point of signaling at the door, as the words from within sounded in his mind. How clearly he heard thoughts now, like tiny bells.

It was Arvardan, of course, with more in his mind than words alone could ever handle. "Pola, I've waited and thought, and thought and waited. I won't any more. You're coming with me."

And Pola, with a mind as eager as his, yet with words of the purest reluctance, said, "I couldn't, Bel. It's quite impossible. My backwoods manners and bearing . . . I'd feel *silly* in those big worlds out there. And, besides, I'm only an Ear——"

"Don't say it. You're my wife, that's all. If anyone asks what and who you are, you're a native of Earth and a citizen of the Empire. If they want further details, you're my wife."

"Well, and after you make this address at Trantor to your archaeological society, what next?"

"What next? Well, first we take a year off and see every major world in the Galaxy. We won't skip one, even if we have to get on and off it by mail ship. You'll get yourself an eyeful of the Galaxy and the best honeymoon that government money can buy."

"And then . . ."

"And then it's back to Earth, and we'll volunteer for the labor battalions and spend the next forty years of our lives lugging dirt to replace the radioactive areas."

"Now why are you going to do that?"

"Because"—there was the suspicion of a deep breath at this point in Arvardan's Mind Touch—"I love you and it's what you want, and because I'm a patriotic Earthman and have the honorary naturalization papers to prove it."

"All right . . ."

And at this point the conversation stopped.

But, of course, the Mind Touches did not, and Schwartz, in full satisfaction, and a little embarrassment, backed away. He could wait. Time enough to disturb them when things had settled down further.

He waited in the street, with the cold stars burning down—a whole Galaxy of them, seen and unseen.

And for himself, and the new Earth, and all those millions of planets far beyond, he repeated softly once more that ancient poem that he alone now, of so many quadrillions, knew:

"Grow old along with me!
The best is yet to be,
The last of life, for which the first was made . . ."

EARTH IS ROOM ENOUGH

THE DEAD PAST

Arnold Potterley, Ph.D., was a Professor of Ancient History. That, in itself, was not dangerous. What changed the world beyond all dreams was the fact that he *looked* like a Professor of Ancient History.

Thaddeus Araman, Department Head of the Division of Chronoscopy, might have taken proper action if Dr. Potterley had been owner of a large, square chin, flashing eyes, aquiline nose and broad shoulders.

As it was, Thaddeus Araman found himself staring over his desk at a mild-mannered individual, whose faded blue eyes looked at him wistfully from either side of a low-bridged button nose; whose small, neatly dressed figure seemed stamped "milk-and-water" from thinning brown hair to the neatly brushed shoes that completed a conservative middle-class costume.

Araman said pleasantly, "And now what can I do for you, Dr. Potterley?"

Dr. Potterley said in a soft voice that went well with the rest of him, "Mr. Araman, I came to you because you're top man in chronoscopy."

Araman smiled. "Not exactly. Above me is the World Commissioner of Research and above him is the Secretary-General of the United Nations. And above both of them, of course, are the sovereign peoples of Earth."

Dr. Potterley shook his head. "They're not interested in chronoscopy. I've come to you, sir, because for two years I have been trying to obtain permission to do some time viewing—chronoscopy, that is—in connection with my researches on ancient Carthage. I can't obtain such permission. My research grants are all proper. There is no irregularity in any of my intellectual endeavors and yet——"

"I'm sure there is no question of irregularity," said Araman soothingly. He flipped the thin reproduction sheets in the folder to which Potterley's name had been attached. They had been produced by Multivac, whose vast analogical mind kept all the department records. When this was over, the sheets could be destroyed, then reproduced on demand in a matter of minutes.

And while Araman turned the pages, Dr. Potterley's voice continued in a soft monotone.

The historian was saying, "I must explain that my problem is quite an important one. Carthage was ancient commercialism brought to its zenith. Pre-Roman Carthage was the nearest ancient analogue to pre-atomic America, at least insofar as its attachment to trade, commerce and business in general was concerned. They were the most daring seamen and explorers before the Vikings; much better at it than the overrated Greeks.

"To know Carthage would be very rewarding, yet the only knowledge we have of it is derived from the writings of its bitter enemies, the Greeks and Romans. Carthage itself never wrote in its own defense or, if it did, the books did not survive. As a result, the Carthaginians have been one of the favorite sets of villains of history and perhaps unjustly so. Time viewing may set the record straight."

He said much more.

Araman said, still turning the reproduction sheets before him, "You must realize, Dr. Potterley, that chronoscopy, or time viewing, if you prefer, is a difficult process."

Dr. Potterley, who had been interrupted, frowned and said, "I am asking for only certain selected views at times and places I would indicate."

Araman sighed. "Even a few views, even one . . . It is an unbelievably delicate art. There is the question of focus, getting the proper scene in view and holding it. There is the synchronization of sound, which calls for completely independent circuits."

"Surely my problem is important enough to justify considerable effort."

"Yes, sir. Undoubtedly," said Araman at once. To deny the importance of someone's research problem would be unforgivably bad manners. "But you must understand how long-drawn-out even the simplest view is. And there is a long waiting line for the chronoscope and an even longer waiting line for the use of Multivac which guides us in our use of the controls."

Potterley stirred unhappily. "But can nothing be done? For two years——"

"A matter of priority, sir. I'm sorry. . . . Cigarette?"

The historian started back at the suggestion, eyes suddenly widening as he stared at the pack thrust out toward him. Araman looked surprised, withdrew the pack, made a motion as though to take a cigarette for himself and thought better of it.

Potterley drew a sigh of unfeigned relief as the pack was put out of sight. He said, "Is there any way of reviewing matters, putting me as far forward as possible. I don't know how to explain——"

Araman smiled. Some had offered money under similar circumstances which, of course, had gotten them nowhere, either. He said, "The decisions on priority are computer-processed. I could in no way alter those decisions arbitrarily."

Potterley rose stiffly to his feet. He stood five and a half feet tall. "Then, good day, sir."

"Good day, Dr. Potterley. And my sincerest regrets."

He offered his hand and Potterley touched it briefly.

The historian left, and a touch of the buzzer brought Araman's secretary into the room. He handed her the folder.

"These," he said, "may be disposed of."

Alone again, he smiled bitterly. Another item in his quarter-century's service to the human race. Service through negation.

At least this fellow had been easy to dispose of. Sometimes academic pressure had to be applied and even withdrawal of grants.

Five minutes later, he had forgotten Dr. Potterley. Nor, thinking back on it later, could he remember feeling any premonition of danger.

During the first year of his frustration, Arnold Potterley had experienced only that—frustration. During the second year, though, his frustration gave birth to an idea that first frightened and then fascinated him. Two things stopped him from trying to translate the idea into action, and neither barrier was the undoubted fact that his notion was a grossly unethical one.

The first was merely the continuing hope that the government would finally give its permission and make it unnecessary for him to do anything more. That hope had perished finally in the interview with Araman just completed.

The second barrier had been not a hope at all but a dreary realization of his own incapacity. He was not a physicist and he knew no physicists from whom he might obtain help. The Department of Physics at the university consisted of men well stocked with grants and well immersed in specialty. At best, they would not listen to him. At worst, they would report him for intellectual anarchy and even his basic Carthaginian grant might easily be withdrawn.

That he could not risk. And yet chronoscopy was the only way to carry on his work. Without it, he would be no worse off if his grant were lost.

The first hint that the second barrier might be overcome had come a week earlier than his interview with Araman, and it had gone unrecognized at the time. It had been at one of the faculty teas. Potterley attended these sessions unfailingly because he conceived attendance to be a duty, and he took his duties seriously. Once there, however, he conceived it to be no responsibility of his to make light conversation or new friends. He sipped abstemiously at a drink or two, exchanged a polite word with the dean or such department heads as happened to be present, bestowed a narrow smile on others and finally left early.

Ordinarily, he would have paid no attention, at that most recent tea, to a young man standing quietly, even diffidently, in one corner. He would never have dreamed of speaking to him. Yet a tangle of circumstance persuaded him this once to behave in a way contrary to his nature.

That morning at breakfast, Mrs. Potterley had announced somberly that once again she had dreamed of Laurel; but this time a Laurel grown up, yet retaining the three-year-old face that stamped her as their child. Potterley had let her talk. There had been a time when he fought her too frequent preoccupation with the past and death. Laurel would not come back to them, either through dreams or through talk. Yet if it appeased Caroline Potterley—let her dream and talk.

But when Potterley went to school that morning, he found himself for once affected by Caroline's inanities. Laurel grown up! She had died nearly twenty years ago; their only child, then and ever. In all that time, when he thought of her, it was as a three-year-old.

Now he thought: But if she were alive now, she wouldn't be three, she'd be nearly twenty-three.

Helplessly, he found himself trying to think of Laurel as growing progressively older; as finally becoming twenty-three. He did not quite succeed.

Yet he tried. Laurel using make-up. Laurel going out with boys. Laurel—getting married!

So it was that when he saw the young man hovering at the outskirts of the coldly circulating group of faculty men, it occurred to him quixotically that, for all he knew, a youngster just such as this might have married Laurel. That youngster himself, perhaps. . . .

Laurel might have met him, here at the university, or some evening when he might be invited to dinner at the Potterleys'. They might grow interested in one another. Laurel would surely have been pretty and this youngster looked well. He was dark in coloring, with a lean intent face and an easy carriage.

The tenuous daydream snapped, yet Potterley found himself staring foolishly at the young man, not as a strange face but as a possible son-in-law in the might-have-been. He found himself threading his way toward the man. It was almost a form of autohypnotism.

He put out his hand. "I am Arnold Potterley of the History Department. You're new here, I think?"

The youngster looked faintly astonished and fumbled with his drink, shifting it to his left hand in order to shake with his right. "Jonas Foster is my name, sir. I'm a new instructor in physics. I'm just starting this semester."

Potterley nodded. "I wish you a happy stay here and great success."

That was the end of it, then. Potterley had come uneasily to his senses, found himself embarrassed and moved off. He stared back over his shoulder once, but the illusion of relationship had gone. Reality was quite real once more and he was angry with himself for having fallen prey to his wife's foolish talk about Laurel.

But a week later, even while Araman was talking, the thought of that young man had come back to him. An instructor in physics. A new instructor. Had he been deaf at the time? Was there a short circuit between ear and brain? Or was it an automatic self-censorship because of the impending interview with the Head of Chronoscopy?

But the interview failed, and it was the thought of the young man with whom he had exchanged two sentences that prevented Potterley from elaborating his pleas for consideration. He was almost anxious to get away.

And in the autogiro express back to the university, he could almost wish he were superstitious. He could then console himself with the thought that the casual meaningless meeting had really been directed by a knowing and purposeful Fate.

Jonas Foster was not new to academic life. The long and rickety struggle for the doctorate would make anyone a veteran. Additional work as a postdoctorate teaching fellow acted as a booster shot.

But now he was Instructor Jonas Foster. Professorial dignity lay ahead. And he now found himself in a new sort of relationship toward other professors.

For one thing, they would be voting on future promotions. For another, he was in no position to tell so early in the game which particular member of the faculty might or might not have the ear of the dean or even of the university president. He did not fancy himself as a campus politician and was sure he would make a poor one, yet there was no point in kicking his own rear into blisters just to prove that to himself.

So Foster listened to this mild-mannered historian who, in some vague way, seemed nevertheless to radiate tension, and did not shut him up abruptly and toss him out. Certainly that was his first impulse.

He remembered Potterley well enough. Potterley had approached him at that tea (which had been a grisly affair). The fellow had spoken two sentences to him stiffly, somehow glassy-eyed, had then come to himself with a visible start and hurried off.

It had amused Foster at the time, but now . . .

Potterley might have been deliberately trying to make his acquaintance, or, rather, to impress his own personality on Foster as that of a queer sort of duck, eccentric but harmless. He might now be probing Foster's views, searching for unsettling opinions. Surely, they ought to have done so before granting him his appointment. Still . . .

Potterley might be serious, might honestly not realize what he was doing. Or he might realize quite well what he was doing; he might be nothing more or less than a dangerous rascal.

Foster mumbled, "Well, now——" to gain time, and fished out a package of cigarettes, intending to offer one to Potterley and to light it and one for himself very slowly.

But Potterley said at once, "Please, Dr. Foster. No cigarettes."

Foster looked startled. "I'm sorry, sir."

"No. The regrets are mine. I cannot stand the odor. An idiosyncrasy. I'm sorry."

He was positively pale. Foster put away the cigarettes.

Foster, feeling the absence of the cigarette, took the easy way out. "I'm flattered that you ask my advice and all that, Dr. Potterley, but I'm not a neutrinics man. I can't very well do anything professional in that direction. Even stating an opinion would be out of line, and, frankly, I'd prefer that you didn't go into any particulars."

The historian's prim face set hard. "What do you mean, you're not a neutrinics man? You're not anything yet. You haven't received any grant, have you?"

"This is only my first semester."

"I know that. I imagine you haven't even applied for any grant yet."

Foster half-smiled. In three months at the university, he had not succeeded in putting his initial requests for research grants into good enough shape to pass on to a professional science writer, let alone to the Research Commission.

(His Department Head, fortunately, took it quite well. "Take your time now, Foster," he said, "and get your thoughts well organized. Make sure you know your path and where it will lead, for, once you receive a grant, your specialization will be formally recognized and, for better or for worse, it will be yours for the rest of your career." The advice was trite enough, but triteness has often the merit of truth, and Foster recognized that.)

Foster said, "By education and inclination, Dr. Potterley, I'm a hyperoptics man with a gravitics minor. It's how I described myself in applying for this position. It may not be my official specialization yet, but it's going to be. It can't be anything else. As for neutrinics, I never even studied the subject."

"Why not?" demanded Potterley at once.

Foster stared. It was the kind of rude curiosity about another man's professional status that was always irritating. He said, with the edge of his own politeness just a trifle blunted, "A course in neutrinics wasn't given at my university."

"Good Lord, where did you go?"

"M.I.T.," said Foster quietly.

"And they don't teach neutrinics?"

"No, they don't." Foster felt himself flush and was moved to a defense. "It's a highly specialized subject with no great value. Chronoscopy, perhaps, has some value, but it is the only practical application and that's a dead end."

The historian stared at him earnestly. "Tell me this. Do you know where I can find a neutrinics man?"

"No, I don't," said Foster bluntly.

"Well, then, do you know a school which teaches neutrinics?"

"No, I don't."

Potterley smiled tightly and without humor.

Foster resented that smile, found he detected insult in it and grew sufficiently annoyed to say, "I would like to point out, sir, that you're stepping out of line."

"What?"

"I'm saying that, as a historian, your interest in any sort of physics, your *professional* interest, is——" He paused, unable to bring himself quite to say the word.

"Unethical?"

"That's the word, Dr. Potterley."

"My researches have driven me to it," said Potterley in an intense whisper.

"The Research Commission is the place to go. If they permit——"

"I have gone to them and have received no satisfaction."

"Then obviously you must abandon this." Foster knew he was sounding stuffily virtuous, but he wasn't going to let this man lure him into an expression of intellectual anarchy. It was too early in his career to take stupid risks.

Apparently, though, the remark had its effect on Potterley. Without any warning, the man exploded into a rapid-fire verbal storm of irresponsibility.

Scholars, he said, could be free only if they could freely follow their own free-swinging curiosity. Research, he said, forced into a predesigned pattern by the powers that held the purse strings became slavish and had to stagnate. No man, he said, had the right to dictate the intellectual interests of another.

Foster listened to all of it with disbelief. None of it was strange to him. He had heard college boys talk so in order to shock their professors and he had once or twice amused himself in that fashion, too. Anyone who studied the history of science knew that many men had once thought so.

Yet it seemed strange to Foster, almost against nature, that a modern man of science could advance such nonsense. No one would advocate running a factory by allowing each individual worker to do whatever pleased him at the moment, or of running a ship according to the casual and conflicting notions of each individual crewman. It would be taken for granted that some sort of centralized supervisory agency must exist in each case. Why should direction and order benefit a factory and a ship but not scientific research?

People might say that the human mind was somehow qualitatively different from a ship or factory but the history of intellectual endeavor proved the opposite.

When science was young and the intricacies of all or most of the known was within the grasp of an individual mind, there was no need for direction, perhaps. Blind wandering over the uncharted tracts of ignorance could lead to wonderful finds by accident.

But as knowledge grew, more and more data had to be absorbed before worthwhile journeys into ignorance could be organized. Men had to specialize. The researcher needed the resources of a library he himself could not gather, then of instruments he himself could not afford. More and more, the individual researcher gave way to the research team and the research institution.

The funds necessary for research grew greater as tools grew more numerous. What college was so small today as not to require at least one nuclear micro-reactor and at least one three-stage computer?

Centuries before, private individuals could no longer subsidize research. By 1940, only the government, large industries and large universities or research institutions could properly subsidize basic research.

By 1960, even the largest universities depended entirely upon government grants, while research institutions could not exist without tax concessions and public subscriptions. By 2000, the industrial combines had become a branch of the world government and, thereafter, the financing of research and therefore its direction naturally become centralized under a department of the government.

It all worked itself out naturally and well. Every branch of science was fitted neatly to the needs of the public, and the various branches of science were co-ordinated decently. The material advance of the last half-century was argument enough for the fact that science was not falling into stagnation.

Foster tried to say a very little of this and was waved aside impatiently by Potterley who said, "You are parroting official propaganda. You're sitting in the middle of an example that's squarely against the official view. Can you believe that?"

"Frankly, no."

"Well, why do you say time viewing is a dead end? Why is neutrinics unimportant? You say it is. You say it categorically. Yet you've never studied it. You claim complete ignorance of the subject. It's not even given in your school——"

"Isn't the mere fact that it isn't given proof enough?"

"Oh, I see. It's not given because it's unimportant. And it's unimportant because it's not given. Are you satisfied with that reasoning?"

Foster felt a growing confusion. "It's in the books."

"That's all. The books say neutrinics is unimportant. Your professors tell you so because they read it in the books. The books say so because professors write them. Who says it from personal experience and knowledge? Who does research in it? Do you know of anyone?"

Foster said, "I don't see that we're getting anywhere, Dr. Potterley. I have work to do——"

"One minute. I just want you to try this on. See how it sounds to you. I say the government is actively suppressing basic research in neutrinics and chronoscopy. They're suppressing application of chronoscopy."

"Oh, no."

"Why not? They could do it. There's your centrally directed research. If they refuse grants for research in any portion of science, that portion dies. They've killed neutrinics. They can do it and have done it."

"But why?"

"I don't know why. I want you to find out. I'd do it myself if I knew enough. I came to you because you're a young fellow with a brand-new education. Have your intellectual arteries hardened already? Is there no curiosity in you? Don't you want to *know?* Don't you want *answers?*"

The historian was peering intently into Foster's face. Their noses were only inches apart, and Foster was so lost that he did not think to draw back.

He should, by rights, have ordered Potterley out. If necessary, he should have thrown Potterley out.

It was not respect for age and position that stopped him. It was certainly not that Potterley's arguments had convinced him. Rather, it was a small point of college pride.

Why didn't M.I.T. give a course in neutrinics? For that matter, now that he came to think of it, he doubted that there was a single book on neutrinics in the library. He could never recall having seen one.

He stopped to think about that.

And that was ruin.

Caroline Potterley had once been an attractive woman. There were occasions, such as dinners or university functions, when, by considerable effort, remnants of the attraction could be salvaged.

On ordinary occasions, she sagged. It was the word she applied to herself in moments of self-abhorrence. She had grown plumper with the years, but the flaccidity about her was not a matter of fat entirely. It was as though her muscles had given up and grown limp so that she shuffled when she walked while her eyes grew baggy and her cheeks jowly. Even her graying hair seemed tired rather than merely stringy. Its straightness seemed to be the result of a supine surrender to gravity, nothing else.

Caroline Potterley looked at herself in the mirror and admitted this was one of her bad days. She knew the reason, too.

It had been the dream of Laurel. The strange one, with Laurel grown up. She had been wretched ever since.

Still, she was sorry she had mentioned it to Arnold. He didn't say anything; he never did any more; but it was bad for him. He was particularly withdrawn for days afterward. It might have been that he was getting ready for that important conference with the big government official (he kept saying he expected no success), but it might also have been her dream.

It was better in the old days when he would cry sharply at her, "Let the dead past *go*, Caroline! Talk won't bring her back, and dreams won't either."

It had been bad for both of them. Horribly bad. She had been away from home and had lived in guilt ever since. If she had stayed at home, if she had not gone on an unnecessary shopping expedition, there would have been two of them available. One would have succeeded in saving Laurel.

Poor Arnold had not managed. Heaven knew he tried. He had nearly died himself. He had come out of the burning house, staggering in agony, blistered, choking, half-blinded, with the dead Laurel in his arms.

The nightmare of that lived on, never lifting entirely.

Arnold slowly grew a shell about himself afterward. He cultivated a low-voiced mildness through which nothing broke, no lightning struck. He grew puritanical and even abandoned his minor vices, his cigarettes, his penchant for an occasional profane exclamation. He obtained his grant for the preparation of a new history of Carthage and subordinated everything to that.

She tried to help him. She hunted up his references, typed his notes and microfilmed them. Then that ended suddenly.

She ran from the desk suddenly one evening, reaching the bathroom in bare time and retching abominably. Her husband followed her in confusion and concern.

"Caroline, what's wrong?"

It took a drop of brandy to bring her around. She said, "Is it true? What they did?"

"Who did?"

"The Carthaginians."

He stared at her and she got it out by indirection. She couldn't say it right out.

The Carthaginians, it seemed, worshiped Moloch, in the form of a hollow, brazen idol with a furnace in its belly. At times of national crisis, the priests and the people gathered, and infants, after the proper ceremonies and invocations, were dextrously hurled, alive, into the flames.

They were given sweetmeats just before the crucial moment, in order that the efficacy of the sacrifice not be ruined by displeasing cries of panic. The drums rolled just after the moment, to drown out the few seconds of infant shrieking. The parents were present, presumably gratified, for the sacrifice was pleasing to the gods. . . .

Arnold Potterley frowned darkly. Vicious lies, he told her, on the part of Carthage's enemies. He should have warned her. After all, such propagandistic lies were not uncommon. According to the Greeks, the ancient Hebrews worshiped an ass's head in their Holy of Holies. According to the Romans, the primitive Christians were haters of all men who sacrificed pagan children in the catacombs.

"Then they didn't do it?" asked Caroline.

"I'm sure they didn't. The primitive Phoenicians may have. Human sacrifice is commonplace in primitive cultures. But Carthage in her great days was not a primitive culture. Human sacrifice often gives way to symbolic actions such as circumcision. The Greeks and Romans might have mistaken some Carthaginian symbolism for the original full rite, either out of ignorance or out of malice."

"Are you sure?"

"I can't be sure yet, Caroline, but when I've got enough evidence, I'll apply for permission to use chronoscopy, which will settle the matter once and for all."

"Chronoscopy?"

"Time viewing. We can focus on ancient Carthage at some time of crisis, the landing of Scipio Africanus in 202 B.C., for instance, and see with our own eyes exactly what happens. And you'll see, I'll be right."

He patted her and smiled encouragingly, but she dreamed of Laurel every night for two weeks thereafter and she never helped him with his Carthage project again. Nor did he ever ask her to.

But now she was bracing herself for his coming. He had called her after arriving back in town, told her he had seen the government man and that it had gone as expected. That meant failure, and yet the little telltale sign of depression had been absent from his voice and his features had appeared quite composed in the teleview. He had another errand to take care of, he said, before coming home.

It meant he would be late, but that didn't matter. Neither one of them was particular about eating hours or cared when packages were taken out of the freezer or even which packages or when the self-warming mechanism was activated.

When he did arrive, he surprised her. There was nothing untoward about him in any obvious way. He kissed her dutifully and smiled, took off his hat and asked if all had been well while he was gone. It was all almost perfectly normal. Almost.

She had learned to detect small things, though, and his pace in all this was a trifle hurried. Enough to show her accustomed eye that he was under tension.

She said, "Has something happened?"

He said, "We're going to have a dinner guest night after next, Caroline. You don't mind?"

"Well, no. Is it anyone I know?"

"No. A young instructor. A newcomer. I've spoken to him." He suddenly whirled toward her and seized her arms at the elbow, held them a moment, then dropped them in confusion as though disconcerted at having shown emotion.

He said, "I almost didn't get through to him. Imagine that. Terrible, *terrible*, the way we have all bent to the yoke; the affection we have for the harness about us."

Mrs. Potterley wasn't sure she understood, but for a year she had been watching him grow quietly more rebellious; little by little more daring in his criticism of the government. She said, "You haven't spoken foolishly to him, have you?"

"What do you mean, foolishly? He'll be doing some neutrinics for me."

"Neutrinics" was trisyllabic nonsense to Mrs. Potterley, but she knew it had nothing to do with history. She said faintly, "Arnold, I don't like you to do that. You'll lose your position. It's——"

"It's intellectual anarchy, my dear," he said. "That's the phrase you want. Very well. I am an anarchist. If the government will not allow me to push my researches, I will push them on my own. And when I show the way, others will follow. . . . And if they don't, it makes no difference. It's Carthage that counts and human knowledge, not you and I."

"But you don't know this young man. What if he is an agent for the Commissioner of Research."

"Not likely and I'll take that chance." He made a fist of his right hand and rubbed it gently against the palm of his left. "He's on my side now. I'm sure of it. He can't help but be. I can recognize intellectual curiosity when I see it in a man's eyes and face and attitude, and it's a fatal disease for a tame scientist. Even today it takes time to beat it out of a man and the young ones are vulnerable. . . . Oh, why stop at anything? Why not build our own chronoscope and tell the government to go to——"

He stopped abruptly, shook his head and turned away.

"I hope everything will be all right," said Mrs. Potterley, feeling helplessly certain that everything would not be, and frightened, in advance, for her husband's professorial status and the security of their old age.

It was she alone, of them all, who had a violent presentiment of trouble. Quite the wrong trouble, of course.

Jonas Foster was nearly half an hour late in arriving at the Potterleys' off-campus house. Up to that very evening, he had not quite decided he would go. Then, at the last moment, he found he could not bring himself to commit the social enormity of breaking a dinner appointment an hour before the appointed time. That, and the nagging of curiosity.

The dinner itself passed interminably. Foster ate without appetite. Mrs. Potterley sat in distant absent-mindedness, emerging out of it only once to ask if he were married and to make a deprecating sound at the news that he was not. Dr. Potterley himself asked neutrally after his professional history and nodded his head primly.

It was as staid, stodgy—boring, actually—as anything could be.

Foster thought: He seems so harmless.

Foster had spent the last two days reading up on Dr. Potterley. Very casually, of course, almost sneakily. He wasn't particularly anxious to be seen in the Social Science Library. To be sure, history was one of those borderline affairs and historical works were frequently read for amusement or edification by the general public.

Still, a physicist wasn't quite the "general public." Let Foster take to reading histories and he would be considered queer, sure as relativity, and after a while the Head of the Department would wonder if his new instructor were really "the man for the job."

So he had been cautious. He sat in the more secluded alcoves and kept his head bent when he slipped in and out at odd hours.

Dr. Potterley, it turned out, had written three books and some dozen articles on the ancient Mediterranean worlds, and the later articles (all in "Historical Reviews") had all dealt with pre-Roman Carthage from a sympathetic viewpoint.

That, at least, checked with Potterley's story and had soothed Foster's suspicions somewhat. . . . And yet Foster felt that it would have been much wiser, much safer, to have scotched the matter at the beginning.

A scientist shouldn't be too curious, he thought in bitter dissatisfaction with himself. It's a dangerous trait.

After dinner, he was ushered into Potterley's study and he was brought up sharply at the threshold. The walls were simply lined with books.

Not merely films. There were films, of course, but these were far outnumbered by the books—print on paper. He wouldn't have thought so many books would exist in usable condition.

That bothered Foster. Why should anyone want to keep so many books at home? Surely all were available in the university library, or, at the very worst, at the Library of Congress, if one wished to take the minor trouble of checking out a microfilm.

There was an element of secrecy involved in a home library. It breathed of intellectual anarchy. That last thought, oddly, calmed Foster. He would rather Potterley be an authentic anarchist than a play-acting *agent provocateur.*

And now the hours began to pass quickly and astonishingly.

"You see," Potterley said, in a clear, unflurried voice, "it was a matter of finding, if possible, anyone who had ever used chronoscopy in his work. Naturally, I couldn't ask baldly, since that would be unauthorized research."

"Yes," said Foster dryly. He was a little surprised such a small consideration would stop the man.

"I used indirect methods——"

He had. Foster was amazed at the volume of correspondence dealing with small disputed points of ancient Mediterranean culture which somehow managed to elicit the casual remark over and over again: "Of course, having never made use of chronoscopy——" or, "Pending approval of my request for chronoscopic data, which appears unlikely at the moment——"

"Now these aren't blind questionings," said Potterley. "There's a monthly booklet put out by the Institute for Chronoscopy in which items concerning the past as determined by time viewing are printed. Just one or two items.

"What impressed me first was the triviality of most of the items, their insipidity. Why should such researches get priority over my work? So I wrote to people who would be most likely to do research in the directions described in the booklet. Uniformly, as I have shown you, they did *not* make use of the chronoscope. Now let's go over it point by point."

At last Foster, his head swimming with Potterley's meticulously gathered details, asked, "But why?"

"I don't know why," said Potterley, "but I have a theory. The original invention of the chronoscope was by Sterbinski—you see, I know that much—and it was well publicized. But then the government took over the instrument and decided to suppress further research in the matter or any use of the machine. But then, people might be curious as to why it wasn't being used. Curiosity is such a vice, Dr. Foster."

Yes, agreed the physicist to himself.

"Imagine the effectiveness, then," Potterley went on, "of pretending that the chronoscope *was* being used. It would then be not a mystery, but a commonplace. It would no longer be a fitting object for legitimate curiosity or an attractive one for illicit curiosity."

"*You* were curious," pointed out Foster.

Potterley looked a trifle restless. "It was different in my case," he said angrily. "I have something that *must* be done, and I wouldn't submit to the ridiculous way in which they kept putting me off."

A bit paranoid, too, thought Foster gloomily.

Yet he had ended up with something, paranoid or not. Foster could no longer deny that something peculiar was going on in the matter of neutrinics.

But what was Potterley after? That still bothered Foster. If Potterley didn't intend this as a test of Foster's ethics, what *did* he want?

Foster put it to himself logically. If an intellectual anarchist with a touch of paranoia wanted to use a chronoscope and was convinced that the powers-that-be were deliberately standing in his way, what would he do?

Supposing it were I, he thought. What would I do?

He said slowly, "Maybe the chronoscope doesn't exist at all?"

Potterley started. There was almost a crack in his general calmness. For an instant, Foster found himself catching a glimpse of something not at all calm.

But the historian kept his balance and said, "Oh, no, there *must* be a chronoscope."

"Why? Have you seen it? Have I? Maybe that's the explanation of everything. Maybe they're not deliberately holding out on a chronoscope they've got. Maybe they haven't got it in the first place."

"But Sterbinski lived. He built a chronoscope. That much is a fact."

"The books say so," said Foster coldly.

"Now listen." Potterley actually reached over and snatched at Foster's jacket sleeve. "I need the chronoscope. I must have it. Don't tell me it doesn't exist. What we're going to do is find out enough about neutrinics to be able to——"

Potterley drew himself up short.

Foster drew his sleeve away. He needed no ending to that sentence. He supplied it himself. He said, "Build one of our own?"

Potterley looked sour as though he would rather not have said it point-blank. Nevertheless, he said, "Why not?"

"Because that's out of the question," said Foster. "If what I've read is correct, then it took Sterbinski twenty years to build his machine and several millions in composite grants. Do you think you and I can duplicate that illegally? Suppose we had the time, which we haven't, and suppose I could learn enough out of books, which I doubt, where would we get the money and equipment? The chronoscope is supposed to fill a five-story building, for Heaven's sake."

"Then you won't help me?"

"Well, I'll tell you what. I have one way in which I may be able to find out something——"

"What is that?" asked Potterley at once.

"Never mind. That's not important. But I may be able to find out enough to tell you whether the government is deliberately suppressing research by chronoscope. I may confirm the evidence you already have or I may be able to prove that your evidence is misleading. I don't know what good it will do you in either case, but it's as far as I can go. It's my limit."

Potterley watched the young man go finally. He was angry with himself. Why had he allowed himself to grow so careless as to permit the fellow to guess that he was thinking in terms of a chronoscope of his own. That was premature.

But then why did the young fool have to suppose that a chronoscope might not exist at all?

It *had* to exist. It *had* to. What was the use of saying it didn't?

And why couldn't a second one be built? Science had advanced in the fifty years since Sterbinski. All that was needed was knowledge.

Let the youngster gather knowledge. Let him think a small gathering would be his limit. Having taken the path to anarchy, there would be no limit. If the boy were not driven onward by something in himself, the first steps would be error enough to force the rest. Potterley was quite certain he would not hesitate to use blackmail.

Potterley waved a last good-by and looked up. It was beginning to rain.

Certainly! Blackmail if necessary, but he would not be stopped.

Foster steered his car across the bleak outskirts of town and scarcely noticed the rain.

He *was* a fool, he told himself, but he couldn't leave things as they were. He had to know. He damned his streak of undisciplined curiosity, but he had to know.

But he would go no further than Uncle Ralph. He swore mightily to himself that it would stop there. In that way, there would be no evidence against him, no real evidence. Uncle Ralph would be discreet.

In a way, he was secretly ashamed of Uncle Ralph. He hadn't mentioned him to Potterley partly out of caution and partly because he did not wish to witness the lifted eyebrow, the inevitable half-smile. Professional science writers, however useful, were a little outside the pale, fit only for patronizing contempt. The fact that, as a class, they made more money than did research scientists only made matters worse, of course.

Still, there were times when a science writer in the family could be a convenience. Not being really educated, they did not have to specialize. Consequently, a good science writer knew practically everything. . . . And Uncle Ralph was one of the best.

Ralph Nimmo had no college degree and was rather proud of it. "A degree," he once said to Jonas Foster, when both were considerably younger, "is a first step down a ruinous highway. You don't want to waste it so you go on to graduate work and doctoral research. You end up a thoroughgoing ignoramus on everything in the world except for one subdivisional sliver of nothing.

"On the other hand, if you guard your mind carefully and keep it blank of any clutter of information till maturity is reached, filling it only with intelligence and training it only in clear thinking, you then have a powerful instrument at your disposal and you can become a science writer."

Nimmo received his first assignment at the age of twenty-five, after he had completed his apprenticeship and been out in the field for less than three months. It came in the shape of a clotted manuscript whose language would impart no glimmering of understanding to any reader, however qualified, without careful study and some inspired guesswork. Nimmo took it apart and put it together again (after five long and exasperating interviews with the authors, who were biophysicists), making the language taut and meaningful and smoothing the style to a pleasant gloss.

"Why not?" he would say tolerantly to his nephew, who countered his strictures on degrees by berating him with his readiness to hang on the fringes of science. "The fringe is important. Your scientists can't write. Why should they be expected to? They aren't expected to be grand masters at chess or virtuosos at the violin, so why expect them to know how to put words together? Why not leave that for specialists, too?

"Good Lord, Jonas, read your literature of a hundred years ago. Discount the fact that the science is out of date and that some of the expressions are out of date. Just try to read it and make sense out of it. It's just jaw-cracking, amateurish. Pages are published uselessly; whole articles which are either noncomprehensible or both."

"But you don't get recognition, Uncle Ralph," protested young Foster, who was getting ready to start his college career and was rather starry-eyed about it. "You could be a terrific researcher."

"I get recognition," said Nimmo. "Don't think for a minute I don't. Sure, a biochemist or a strato-meteorologist won't give me the time of day, but they pay me well enough. Just find out what happens when some first-class chemist finds the Commission has cut his year's allowance for science writing. He'll fight harder for enough funds to afford me, or someone like me, than to get a recording ionograph."

He grinned broadly and Foster grinned back. Actually, he was proud of his paunchy, round-faced, stub-fingered uncle, whose vanity made him brush his fringe of hair futilely over the desert on his pate and made his dress like an unmade haystack because such negligence was his trademark. Ashamed, but proud, too.

And now Foster entered his uncle's cluttered apartment in no mood at all for grinning. He was nine years older now and so was Uncle Ralph. For nine more years, papers in every branch of science had come to him for polishing and a little of each had crept into his capacious mind.

Nimmo was eating seedless grapes, popping them into his mouth one at a time. He tossed a bunch to Foster who caught them by a hair, then bent to retrieve individual grapes that had torn loose and fallen to the floor.

"Let them be. Don't bother," said Nimmo carelessly. "Someone comes in here to clean once a week. What's up? Having trouble with your grant application write-up?"

"I haven't really got into that yet."

"You haven't? Get a move on, boy. Are you waiting for me to offer to do the final arrangement?"

"I couldn't afford you, Uncle."

"Aw, come on. It's all in the family. Grant me all popular publication rights and no cash need change hands."

Foster nodded. "If you're serious, it's a deal."

"It's a deal."

It was a gamble, of course, but Foster knew enough of Nimmo's science writing to realize it could pay off. Some dramatic discovery of public interest on primitive man or on a new surgical technique, or on any branch of spationautics could mean a very cash-attracting article in any of the mass media of communication.

It was Nimmo, for instance, who had written up, for scientific consumption, the series of papers by Bryce and co-workers that elucidated the fine structure of two cancer viruses, for which job he asked the picayune payment of fifteen hundred dollars, provided popular publication rights were included. He then wrote up, exclusively, the same work in semidramatic form for use in trimensional video for a twenty-thousand-dollar advance plus rental royalties that were still coming in after five years.

Foster said bluntly, "What do you know about neutrinics, Uncle?"

"Neutrinics?" Nimmo's small eyes looked surprised. "Are you working in that? I thought it was pseudo-gravitic optics."

"It is p.g.o. I just happen to be asking about neutrinics."

"That's a devil of a thing to be doing. You're stepping out of line. You know that, don't you?"

"I don't expect you to call the Commission because I'm a little curious about things."

"Maybe I should before you get into trouble. Curiosity is an occupational danger with scientists. I've watched it work. One of them will be moving quietly along on a problem, then curiosity leads him up a strange creek. Next thing you know they've done so little on their proper problem, they can't justify for a project renewal. I've seen more——"

"All I want to know," said Foster patiently, "is what's been passing through your hands lately on neutrinics."

Nimmo leaned back, chewing at a grape thoughtfully. "Nothing. Nothing ever. I don't recall ever getting a paper on neutrinics."

"What!" Foster was openly astonished. "Then who does get the work?"

"Now that you ask," said Nimmo, "I don't know. Don't recall anyone talking about it at the annual conventions. I don't think much work is being done there."

"Why not?"

"Hey, there, don't bark. I'm not doing anything. My guess would be——"

Foster was exasperated. "Don't you know?"

"Hmp. I'll tell you what I know about neutrinics. It concerns the applications of neutrino movements and the forces involved——"

"Sure. Sure. Just as electronics deals with the applications of electron movements and the forces involved, and pseudo-gravitics deals with the applications of artificial gravitational fields. I didn't come to you for that. Is that all you know?"

"And," said Nimmo with equanimity, "neutrinics is the basis of time viewing and that *is* all I know."

Foster slouched back in his chair and massaged one lean cheek with great intensity. He felt angrily dissatisfied. Without formulating it explicitly in his own mind, he had felt sure, somehow, that Nimmo would come up with some late reports, bring up interesting facets of modern neutrinics, send him back to Potterley able to say that the elderly historian was mistaken, that his data was misleading, his deductions mistaken.

Then he could have returned to his proper work.

But now . . .

He told himself angrily: So they're not doing much work in the field. Does that make it deliberate suppression? What if neutrinics is a sterile discipline? Maybe it is. I don't know. Potterley doesn't. Why waste the intellectual resources of humanity on nothing? Or the work might be secret for some legitimate reason. It might be . . .

The trouble was, he had to know. He couldn't leave things as they were now. *He couldn't!*

He said, "Is there a text on neutrinics, Uncle Ralph? I mean a clear and simple one. An elementary one."

Nimmo thought, his plump cheeks puffing out with a series of sighs. "You ask the damnedest questions. The only one I ever heard of was Sterbinski and somebody. I've never seen it, but I viewed something about it once. . . . Sterbinski and LaMarr, that's it."

"Is that the Sterbinski who invented the chronoscope?"

"I think so. Proves the book ought to be good."

"Is there a recent edition? Sterbinski died thirty years ago."

Nimmo shrugged and said nothing.

"Can you find out?"

They sat in silence for a moment, while Nimmo shifted his bulk to the creaking tune of the chair he sat on. Then the science writer said, "Are you going to tell me what this is all about?"

"I can't. Will you help me anyway, Uncle Ralph? Will you get me a copy of the text?"

"Well, you've taught me all I know on pseudo-gravitics. I should be grateful. Tell you what—I'll help you on one condition."

"Which is?"

The older man was suddenly very grave. "That you be careful, Jonas. You're obviously way out of line whatever you're doing. Don't blow up your career just because you're curious about something you haven't been assigned to and which is none of your business. Understand?"

Foster nodded, but he hardly heard. He was thinking furiously.

A full week later, Ralph Nimmo eased his rotund figure into Jonas Foster's on-campus two-room combination and said, in a hoarse whisper, "I've got something."

"What?" Foster was immediately eager.

"A copy of Sterbinski and LaMarr." He produced it, or rather a corner of it, from his ample topcoat.

Foster almost automatically eyed door and windows to make sure they were closed and shaded respectively, then held out his hand.

The film case was flaking with age, and when he cracked it the film was faded and growing brittle. He said sharply, "Is this all?"

"Gratitude, my boy, gratitude!" Nimmo sat down with a grunt, and reached into a pocket for an apple.

"Oh, I'm grateful, but it's so old."

"And lucky to get it at that. I tried to get a film run from the Congressional Library. No go. The book was restricted."

"Then how did you get this?"

"Stole it." He was biting crunchingly around the core. "New York Public."

"What?"

"Simple enough. I had access to the stacks, naturally. So I stepped over a chained railing when no one was around, dug this up, and walked out with it. They're very trusting out there. Meanwhile, they won't miss it in years. . . . Only you'd better not let anyone see it on you, nephew."

Foster stared at the film as though it were literally hot.

Nimmo discarded the core and reached for a second apple. "Funny thing, now. There's nothing more recent in the whole field of neutrinics. Not a monograph, not a paper, not a progress note. Nothing since the chronoscope."

"Uh-huh," said Foster absently.

Foster worked evenings in the Potterley home. He could not trust his own on-campus rooms for the purpose. The evening work grew more real to him than his own grant applications. Sometimes he worried about it but then that stopped, too.

His work consisted, at first, simply in viewing and reviewing the text film. Later it consisted in thinking (sometimes while a section of the book ran itself off through the pocket projector, disregarded).

Sometimes Potterley would come down to watch, to sit with prim, eager eyes, as though he expected thought processes to solidify and become visible in all their convolutions. He interfered in only two ways. He did not allow Foster to smoke and sometimes he talked.

It wasn't conversation talk, never that. Rather it was a low-voiced monologue with which, it seemed, he scarcely expected to command attention. It was much more as though he were relieving a pressure within himself.

Carthage! Always Carthage!

Carthage, the New York of the ancient Mediterranean. Carthage, commercial empire and queen of the seas. Carthage, all that Syracuse and Alexandria pretended to be. Carthage, maligned by her enemies and inarticulate in her own defense.

She had been defeated once by Rome and then driven out of Sicily and Sardinia, but came back to more than recoup her losses by new dominions in Spain, and raised up Hannibal to give the Romans sixteen years of terror.

In the end, she lost again a second time, reconciled herself to fate and built again with broken tools a limping life in shrunken territory, succeeding so well that jealous Rome deliberately forced a third war. And then Carthage, with nothing but bare hands and tenacity, built weapons and forced Rome into a two-year war that ended only with complete destruction of the city, the inhabitants throwing themselves into their flaming houses rather than surrender.

"Could people fight so for a city and a way of life as bad as the ancient writers painted it? Hannibal was a better general than any Roman and his soldiers were absolutely faithful to him. Even his bitterest enemies praised him. There was a Carthaginian. It is fashionable to say that he was an atypical Carthaginian, better than the others, a diamond placed in garbage. But then why was he so faithful to Carthage, even to his death after years of exile? They talk of Moloch——"

Foster didn't always listen but sometimes he couldn't help himself and he shuddered and turned sick at the bloody tale of child sacrifice.

But Potterley went on earnestly, "Just the same, it isn't true. It's a twenty-five-hundred-year-old canard started by the Greeks and

Romans. They had their own slaves, their crucifixions and torture, their gladiatorial contests. They weren't holy. The Moloch story is what later ages would have called war propaganda, the big lie. I can prove it was a lie. I can prove it and, by Heaven, I will—I will——"

He would mumble that promise over and over again in his earnestness.

Mrs. Potterley visited him also, but less frequently, usually on Tuesdays and Thursdays when Dr. Potterley himself had an evening course to take care of and was not present.

She would sit quietly, scarcely talking, face slack and doughy, eyes blank, her whole attitude distant and withdrawn.

The first time, Foster tried, uneasily, to suggest that she leave.

She said tonelessly, "Do I disturb you?"

"No, of course not," lied Foster restlessly. "It's just that—that——" He couldn't complete the sentence.

She nodded, as though accepting an invitation to stay. Then she opened a cloth bag she had brought with her and took out a quire of vitron sheets which she proceeded to weave together by rapid, delicate movements of a pair of slender, tetra-faceted depolarizers, whose battery-fed wires made her look as though she were holding a large spider.

One evening, she said softly, "My daughter, Laurel, is your age."

Foster started, as much at the sudden unexpected sound of speech as at the words. He said, "I didn't know you had a daughter, Mrs. Potterley."

"She died. Years ago."

The vitron grew under the deft manipulations into the uneven shape of some garment Foster could not yet identify. There was nothing left for him to do but mutter inanely, "I'm sorry."

Mrs. Potterley sighed. "I dream about her often." She raised her blue, distant eyes to him.

Foster winced and looked away.

Another evening she asked, pulling at one of the vitron sheets to loosen its gentle clinging to her dress, "What is time viewing anyway?"

That remark broke into a particularly involved chain of thought, and Foster said snappishly, "Dr. Potterley can explain."

"He's tried to. Oh, my, yes. But I think he's a little impatient with me. He calls it chronoscopy most of the time. Do you actually see things in the past, like the trimensionals? Or does it just make little dot patterns like the computer you use?"

Foster stared at his hand computer with distaste. It worked well enough, but every operation had to be manually controlled and the answers were obtained in code. Now if he could use the school computer . . . Well, why dream, he felt conspicuous enough, as it was, carrying a hand computer under his arm every evening as he left his office.

He said, "I've never seen the chronoscope myself, but I'm under the impression that you actually see pictures and hear sound."

"You can hear people talk, too?"

"I think so." Then, half in desperation, "Look here, Mrs. Potterley, this must be awfully dull for you. I realize you don't like to leave a guest all to himself, but really, Mrs. Potterley, you mustn't feel compelled——"

"I don't feel compelled," she said. "I'm sitting here, waiting."

"Waiting? For what?"

She said composedly, "I listened to you that first evening. The time you first spoke to Arnold. I listened at the door."

He said, "You did?"

"I know I shouldn't have, but I was awfully worried about Arnold. I had a notion he was going to do something he oughtn't and I wanted to hear what. And then when I heard——" She paused, bending close over the vitron and peering at it.

"Heard what, Mrs. Potterley?"

"That you wouldn't build a chronoscope."

"Well, of course not."

"I thought maybe you might change your mind."

Foster glared at her. "Do you mean you're coming down here hoping I'll build a chronoscope, waiting for me to build one?"

"I hope you do, Dr. Foster. Oh, I hope you do."

It was as though, all at once, a fuzzy veil had fallen off her face, leaving all her features clear and sharp, putting color into her cheeks, life into her eyes, the vibrations of something approaching excitement into her voice.

"Wouldn't it be wonderful," she whispered, "to have one? People of the past could live again. Pharaohs and kings and—just people. I hope you build one, Dr. Foster. I really—hope——"

She choked, it seemed, on the intensity of her own words and let the vitron sheets slip off her lap. She rose and ran up the basement stairs, while Foster's eyes followed her awkwardly fleeing body with astonishment and distress.

It cut deeper into Foster's nights and left him sleepless and painfully stiff with thought. It was almost a mental indigestion.

His grant requests went limping in, finally, to Ralph Nimmo. He scarcely had any hope for them. He thought numbly: They won't be approved.

If they weren't, of course, it would create a scandal in the department and probably mean his appointment at the university would not be renewed, come the end of the academic year.

He scarcely worried. It was the neutrino, the neutrino, only the neutrino. Its trail curved and veered sharply and led him breathlessly along uncharted pathways that even Sterbinski and LaMarr did not follow.

He called Nimmo. "Uncle Ralph, I need a few things. I'm calling from off the campus."

Nimmo's face in the video plate was jovial, but his voice was sharp. He said, "What you need is a course in communication. I'm having a hell of a time pulling your application into one intelligible piece. If that's what you're calling about——"

Foster shook his head impatiently. "That's *not* what I'm calling about. I need these." He scribbled quickly on a piece of paper and held it up before the receiver.

Nimmo yiped. "Hey, how many tricks do you think I can wangle?"

"You can get them, Uncle. You know you can."

Nimmo reread the list of items with silent motions of his plump lips and looked grave.

"What happens when you put those things together?" he asked. Foster shook his head. "You'll have exclusive popular publication rights to whatever turns up, the way it's always been. But please don't ask any questions now."

"I can't do miracles, you know."

"Do this one. You've got to. You're a science writer, not a research man. You don't have to account for anything. You've got friends and connections. They can look the other way, can't they, to get a break from you next publication time?"

"Your faith, nephew, is touching. I'll try."

Nimmo succeeded. The material and equipment were brought over late one evening in a private touring car. Nimmo and Foster lugged it in with the grunting of men unused to manual labor.

Potterley stood at the entrance of the basement after Nimmo had left. He asked softly, "What's this for?"

Foster brushed the hair off his forehead and gently massaged a strained wrist. He said, "I want to conduct a few simple experiments."

"Really?" The historian's eyes glittered with excitement.

Foster felt exploited. He felt as though he were being led along a dangerous highway by the pull of pinching fingers on his nose; as though he could see the ruin clearly that lay in wait at the end of the path, yet walked eagerly and determinedly. Worst of all, he felt the compelling grip on his nose to be his own.

It was Potterley who began it, Potterley who stood there now, gloating; but the compulsion was his own.

Foster said sourly, "I'll be wanting privacy now, Potterley. I can't have you and your wife running down here and annoying me."

He thought: If that offends him, let him kick me out. Let him put an end to this.

In his heart, though, he did not think being evicted would stop anything.

But it did not come to that. Potterley was showing no signs of offense. His mild gaze was unchanged. He said, "Of course, Dr. Foster, of course. All the privacy you wish."

Foster watched him go. He was left still marching along the highway, perversely glad of it and hating himself for being glad.

He took to sleeping over on a cot in Potterley's basement and spending his weekends there entirely.

During that period, preliminary word came through that his grants (as doctored by Nimmo) had been approved. The Department Head brought the word and congratulated him.

Foster stared back distantly and mumbled, "Good. I'm glad," with so little conviction that the other frowned and turned away without another word.

Foster gave the matter no further thought. It was a minor point, worth no notice. He was planning something that really counted, a climactic test for that evening.

One evening, a second and third and then, haggard and half beside himself with excitement, he called in Potterley.

Potterley came down the stairs and looked about at the homemade gadgetry. He said, in his soft voice, "The electric bills are quite high. I don't mind the expense, but the City may ask questions. Can anything be done?"

It was a warm evening, but Potterley wore a tight collar and a semi-jacket. Foster, who was in his undershirt, lifted bleary eyes and said shakily, "It won't be for much longer, Dr. Potterley. I've called you down to tell you something. A chronoscope can be built. A small one, of course, but it can be built."

Potterley seized the railing. His body sagged. He managed a whisper. "Can it be built here?"

"Here in the basement," said Foster wearily.

"Good Lord. You said——"

"I know what I said," cried Foster impatiently. "I said it couldn't be done. I didn't know anything then. Even Sterbinski didn't know anything."

Potterley shook his head. "Are you sure? You're not mistaken, Dr. Foster? I couldn't endure it if——"

Foster said, "I'm not mistaken. Damn it, sir, if just theory had been enough, we could have had a time viewer over a hundred years ago, when the neutrino was first postulated. The trouble was, the original investigators considered it only a mysterious particle without mass or charge that could not be detected. It was just something to even up the bookkeeping and save the law of conservation of mass energy."

He wasn't sure Potterley knew what he was talking about. He didn't care. He needed a breather. He had to get some of this out of his clotting thoughts. . . . And he needed background for what he would have to tell Potterley next.

He went on. "It was Sterbinski who first discovered that the neutrino broke through the space-time cross-sectional barrier, that it traveled through time as well as through space. It was Sterbinski who first devised a method for stopping neutrinos. He invented a neutrino recorder and learned how to interpret the pattern of the neutrino stream. Naturally, the stream had been affected and deflected by all the matter it had passed through in its passage through time, and the deflections could be analyzed and converted into the images of the matter that had done the deflecting. Time viewing was possible. Even air vibrations could be detected in this way and converted into sound."

Potterley was definitely not listening. He said, "Yes. Yes. But when can you build a chronoscope?"

Foster said urgently, "Let me finish. Everything depends on the method used to detect and analyze the neutrino stream. Sterbinski's method was difficult and roundabout. It required mountains of energy. But I've studied pseudo-gravitics, Dr. Potterley, the science of artificial gravitational fields. I've specialized in the behavior of light in such fields. It's a new science. Sterbinski knew nothing of it. If he had, he would have seen—anyone would have—a much better and more efficient method of detecting neutrinos using a pseudo-gravitic field. If I had known more neutrinics to begin with, I would have seen it at once."

Potterley brightened a bit. "I knew it," he said. "Even if they stop research in neutrinics there is no way the government can be sure that discoveries in other segments of science won't reflect knowledge on neutrinics. So much for the value of centralized direction of science. I thought this long ago, Dr. Foster, before you ever came to work here."

"I congratulate you on that," said Foster, "but there's one thing——"

"Oh, never mind all this. Answer me. Please. When can you build a chronoscope?"

"I'm trying to tell you something, Dr. Potterley. A chronoscope won't do you any good." (This is it, Foster thought.)

Slowly, Potterley descended the stairs. He stood facing Foster. "What do you mean? Why won't it help me?"

"You won't see Carthage. It's what I've got to tell you. It's what I've been leading up to. You can never see Carthage."

Potterley shook his head slightly. "Oh, no, you're wrong. If you have the chronoscope, just focus it properly——"

"No, Dr. Potterley. It's not a question of focus. There are random factors affecting the neutrino stream, as they affect all subatomic particles. What we call the uncertainty principle. When the stream is recorded and interpreted, the random factor comes out as fuzziness, or 'noise' as the communications boys speak of it. The farther back in time you penetrate, the more pronounced the fuzziness, the greater the noise. After a while, the noise drowns out the picture. Do you understand?"

"More power," said Potterley in a dead kind of voice.

"That won't help. When the noise blurs out detail, magnifying detail magnifies the noise, too. You can't see anything in a sunburned film by enlarging it, can you? Get this through your head, now. The physical nature of the universe sets limits. The random thermal motions of air molecules set limits to how weak a sound can be detected by any instrument. The length of a light wave or of an electron wave sets limits to the size of objects that can be seen by any instrument. It works that way in chronoscopy, too. You can only time view so far."

"How far? How far?"

Foster took a deep breath. "A century and a quarter. That's the most."

"But the monthly bulletin the Commission puts out deals with ancient history almost entirely." The historian laughed shakily. "You must be wrong. The government has data as far back as 3000 B.C."

"When did you switch to believing them?" demanded Foster, scornfully. "You began this business by proving they were lying; that no historian had made use of the chronoscope. Don't you see why now? No historian, except one interested in contemporary history, could. No chronoscope can possibly see back in time farther than 1920 under any conditions."

"You're wrong. You don't know everything," said Potterley.

"The truth won't bend itself to your convenience either. Face it. The government's part in this is to perpetuate a hoax."

"Why?"

"I don't know why."

Potterley's snubby nose was twitching. His eyes were bulging. He pleaded, "It's only theory, Dr. Foster. Build a chronoscope. Build one and try."

Foster caught Potterley's shoulders in a sudden, fierce grip. "Do you think I haven't? Do you think I would tell you this before I had checked it every way I knew? I *have* built one. It's all around you. Look!"

He ran to the switches at the power leads. He flicked them on, one by one. He turned a resistor, adjusted other knobs, put out the cellar lights. "Wait. Let it warm up."

There was a small glow near the center of one wall. Potterley was gibbering incoherently, but Foster only cried again, "Look!"

The light sharpened and brightened, broke up into a light-and-dark pattern. Men and women! Fuzzy. Features blurred. Arms and legs mere streaks. An old-fashioned ground car, unclear but recognizable as one of the kind that had once used gasoline-powered internal-combustion engines, sped by.

Foster said, "Mid-twentieth century, somewhere. I can't hook up an audio yet so this is soundless. Eventually, we can add sound. Anyway, mid-twentieth is almost as far back as you can go. Believe me, that's the best focusing that can be done."

Potterley said, "Build a larger machine, a stronger one. Improve your circuits."

"You can't lick the Uncertainty Principle, man, any more than you can live on the sun. There are physical limits to what can be done."

"You're lying. I won't believe you. I——"

A new voice sounded, raised shrilly to make itself heard.

"Arnold! Dr. Foster!"

The young physicist turned at once. Dr. Potterley froze for a long moment, then said, without turning, "What is it, Caroline? Leave us."

"No!" Mrs. Potterley descended the stairs. "I heard. I couldn't help hearing. Do you have a time viewer here, Dr. Foster? Here in the basement?"

"Yes, I do, Mrs. Potterley. A kind of time viewer. Not a good one. I can't get sound yet and the picture is darned blurry, but it works."

Mrs. Potterley clasped her hands and held them tightly against her breast. "How wonderful. How wonderful."

"It's not at all wonderful," snapped Potterley. "The young fool can't reach farther back than——"

"Now, look," began Foster in exasperation. . . .

"Please!" cried Mrs. Potterley. "Listen to me. Arnold, don't you see that as long as we can use it for twenty years back, we can see Laurel once again? What do we care about Carthage and ancient times? It's Laurel we can see. She'll be alive for us again. Leave the machine here, Dr. Foster. Show us how to work it."

Foster stared at her, then at her husband. Dr. Potterley's face had gone white. Though his voice stayed low and even, its calmness was somehow gone. He said, "You're a fool!"

Caroline said weakly, "Arnold!"

"You're a fool, I say. What will you see? The past. The dead past. Will Laurel do one thing she did not do? Will you see one thing you haven't seen? Will you live three years over and over again, watching a baby who'll never grow up no matter how you watch?"

His voice came near to cracking, but held. He stepped closer to her, seized her shoulder and shook her roughly. "Do you know what will happen to you if you do that? They'll come to take you away because you'll go mad. Yes, mad. Do you want mental treatment? Do you want to be shut up, to undergo the psychic probe?"

Mrs. Potterley tore away. There was no trace of softness or vagueness about her. She had twisted into a virago. "I want to see my child, Arnold. She's in that machine and I want her."

"She's *not* in the machine. An image is. Can't you understand? An image! Something that's not real!"

"I want my child. Do you hear me?" She flew at him, screaming, fists beating. "*I want my child.*"

The historian retreated at the fury of the assault, crying out. Foster moved to step between, when Mrs. Potterley dropped, sobbing wildly, to the floor.

Potterley turned, eyes desperately seeking. With a sudden heave, he snatched at a Lando-rod, tearing it from its support, and whirling away before Foster, numbed by all that was taking place, could move to stop him.

"Stand back!" gasped Potterley, "or I'll kill you. I swear it."

He swung with force, and Foster jumped back.

Potterley turned with fury on every part of the structure in the cellar, and Foster, after the first crash of glass, watched dazedly.

Potterley spent his rage and then he was standing quietly amid shards and splinters, with a broken Lando-rod in his hand. He said to Foster in a whisper, "Now get out of here! Never come back! If any of this cost you anything, send me a bill and I'll pay for it. I'll pay double."

Foster shrugged, picked up his shirt and moved up the basement stairs. He could hear Mrs. Potterley sobbing loudly, and, as he turned at the head of the stairs for a last look, he saw Dr. Potterley bending over her, his face convulsed with sorrow.

Two days later, with the school day drawing to a close, and Foster looking wearily about to see if there were any data on his newly approved projects that he wished to take home, Dr. Potterley appeared once more. He was standing at the open door of Foster's office.

The historian was neatly dressed as ever. He lifted his hand in a gesture that was too vague to be a greeting, too abortive to be a plea. Foster stared stonily.

Potterley said, "I waited till five, till you were . . . May I come in?"

Foster nodded.

Potterley said, "I suppose I ought to apologize for my behavior. I was dreadfully disappointed; not quite master of myself. Still, it was inexcusable."

"I accept your apology," said Foster. "Is that all?"

"My wife called you, I think."

"Yes, she has."

"She has been quite hysterical. She told me she had but I couldn't be quite sure——"

"She has called me."

"Could you tell me—would you be so kind as to tell me what she wanted?"

"She wanted a chronoscope. She said she had some money of her own. She was willing to pay."

"Did you—make any commitments?"

"I said I wasn't in the manufacturing business."

"Good," breathed Potterley, his chest expanding with a sigh of relief. "Please don't take any calls from her. She's not—quite——"

"Look, Dr. Potterley," said Foster, "I'm not getting into any domestic quarrels, but you'd better be prepared for something. Chronoscopes can be built by anybody. Given a few simple parts that can be bought through some etherics sales center, it can be built in the home workshop. The video part, anyway."

"But no one else will think of it beside you, will they? No one has."

"I don't intend to keep it secret."

"But you can't publish. It's illegal research."

"That doesn't matter any more, Dr. Potterley. If I lose my grants, I lose them. If the university is displeased, I'll resign. It just doesn't matter."

"But you can't do that!"

"Till now," said Foster, "you didn't mind my risking loss of grants and position. Why do you turn so tender about it now? Now let me explain something to you. When you first came to me, I believed in organized and directed research; the situation as it existed, in other words. I considered you an intellectual anarchist, Dr. Potterley, and dangerous. But, for one reason or another, I've been an anarchist myself for months now and I have achieved great things.

"Those things have been achieved not because I am a brilliant scientist. Not at all. It was just that scientific research had been directed from above and holes were left that could be filled in by anyone who looked in the right direction. And anyone might have if the government hadn't actively tried to prevent it.

"Now understand me. I still believe directed research can be useful. I'm not in favor of a retreat to total anarchy. But there must be a middle ground. Directed research can retain flexibility. A scientist must be allowed to follow his curiosity, at least in his spare time."

Potterley sat down. He said ingratiatingly, "Let's discuss this, Foster. I appreciate your idealism. You're young. You want the moon. But you can't destroy yourself through fancy notions of what research must consist of. I got you into this. I am responsible and I blame myself bitterly. I was acting emotionally. My interest in Carthage blinded me and I was a damned fool."

Foster broke in. "You mean you've changed completely in two days? Carthage is nothing? Government suppression of research is nothing?"

"Even a damned fool like myself can learn, Foster. My wife taught me something. I understand the reason for government suppression of neutrinics now. I didn't two days ago. And, understanding, I approve. You saw the way my wife reacted to the news of a chronoscope in the basement. I had envisioned a chronoscope used for research purposes. All *she* could see was the personal pleasure of returning neurotically to a personal past, a dead past. The pure researcher, Foster, is in the minority. People like my wife would outweigh us.

"For the government to encourage chronoscopy would have meant that everyone's past would be visible. The government officers would be subjected to blackmail and improper pressure, since who on Earth has a past that is absolutely clean? Organized government might become impossible."

Foster licked his lips. "Maybe. Maybe the government has some justification in its own eyes. Still, there's an important principle involved here. Who knows what other scientific advances are being stymied because scientists are being stifled into walking a narrow path? If the chronoscope becomes the terror of a few politicians, it's a price that must be paid. The public must realize that science must be free and there is no more dramatic way of doing it than to publish my discovery, one way or another, legally or illegally."

Potterley's brow was damp with perspiration, but his voice remained even. "Oh, not just a few politicians, Dr. Foster. Don't think that. It would be my terror, too. My wife would spend her time living with our dead daughter. She would retreat further from reality. She would go mad living the same scenes over and over. And not just my terror. There would be others like her. Children searching for their dead parents or their own youth. We'll have a whole world living in the past. Midsummer madness."

Foster said, "Moral judgments can't stand in the way. There isn't one advance at any time in history that mankind hasn't had the ingenuity to pervert. Mankind must also have the ingenuity to prevent. As for the chronoscope, your delvers into the dead past will get tired soon enough. They'll catch their loved parents in some of the things their loved parents did and they'll lose their enthusiasm for it all. But all this is trivial. With me, it's a matter of important principle."

Potterley said, "Hang your principle. Can't you understand men and women as well as principle? Don't you understand that my wife will live through the fire that killed our baby? She won't be able to help herself. I know her. She'll follow through each step, trying to prevent it. She'll live it over and over again, hoping each time that it won't happen. How many times do you want to kill Laurel?" A huskiness had crept into his voice.

A thought crossed Foster's mind. "What are you really afraid she'll find out, Dr. Potterley? What happened the night of the fire?"

The historian's hands went up quickly to cover his face and they shook with his dry sobs. Foster turned away and stared uncomfortably out the window.

Potterley said after a while, "It's a long time since I've had to think of it. Caroline was away. I was baby-sitting. I went into the baby's bedroom midevening to see if she had kicked off the bedclothes. I had my cigarette with me . . . I smoked in those days. I must have stubbed it out before putting it in the ashtray on the chest of drawers. I was always careful. The baby was all right. I returned to the living room and fell asleep before the video. I awoke, choking, surrounded by fire. I don't know how it started."

"But you think it may have been the cigarette, is that it?" said Foster. "A cigarette which, for once, you forgot to stub out?"

"I don't know. I tried to save her, but she was dead in my arms when I got out."

"You never told your wife about the cigarette, I suppose."

Potterley shook his head. "But I've lived with it."

"Only now, with a chronoscope, she'll find out. Maybe it wasn't the cigarette. Maybe you did stub it out. Isn't that possible?"

The scant tears had dried on Potterley's face. The redness had subsided. He said, "I can't take the chance. . . . But it's not just myself, Foster. The past has its terrors for most people. Don't loose those terrors on the human race."

Foster paced the floor. Somehow, this explained the reason for Potterley's rabid, irrational desire to boost the Carthaginians, deify them, most of all disprove the story of their fiery sacrifices to Moloch. By freeing them of the guilt of infanticide by fire, he symbolically freed himself of the same guilt.

So the same fire that had driven him on to causing the construction of a chronoscope was now driving him on to the destruction.

Foster looked sadly at the older man. "I see your position, Dr. Potterley, but this goes above personal feelings. I've got to smash this throttling hold on the throat of science."

Potterley said, savagely, "You mean you want the fame and wealth that goes with such a discovery."

"I don't know about the wealth, but that, too, I suppose. I'm no more than human."

"You won't suppress your knowledge?"

"Not under any circumstances."

"Well, then——" and the historian got to his feet and stood for a moment, glaring.

Foster had an odd moment of terror. The man was older than he, smaller, feebler, and he didn't look armed. Still . . .

Foster said, "If you're thinking of killing me or anything insane like that, I've got the information in a safety-deposit vault where the proper people will find it in case of my disappearance or death."

Potterley said, "Don't be a fool," and stalked out.

Foster closed the door, locked it and sat down to think. He felt silly. He had no information in any safety-deposit vault, of course. Such a melodramatic action would not have occurred to him ordinarily. But now it had.

Feeling even sillier, he spent an hour writing out the equations of the application of pseudo-gravitic optics to neutrinic recording, and some diagrams for the engineering details of construction. He sealed it in an envelope and scrawled Ralph Nimmo's name over the outside.

He spent a rather restless night and the next morning, on the way to school, dropped the envelope off at the bank, with appropriate instructions to an official, who made him sign a paper permitting the box to be opened after his death.

He called Nimmo to tell him of the existence of the envelope, refusing querulously to say anything about its contents.

He had never felt so ridiculously self-conscious as at that moment.

That night and the next, Foster spent in only fitful sleep, finding himself face to face with the highly practical problem of the publication of data unethically obtained.

The *Proceedings of the Society for Pseudo-Gravitics*, which was the journal with which he was best acquainted, would certainly not touch any paper that did not include the magic footnote: "The work described in this paper was made possible by Grant No. so-and-so from the Commission of Research of the United Nations."

Nor, doubly so, would the *Journal of Physics*.

There were always the minor journals who might overlook the nature of the article for the sake of the sensation, but that would require a little financial negotiation on which he hesitated to embark. It might, on the whole, be better to pay the cost of publishing a small pamphlet for general distribution among scholars. In that case, he would even be able to dispense with the services of a science writer, sacrificing polish for speed. He would have to find a reliable printer. Uncle Ralph might know one.

He walked down the corridor to his office and wondered anxiously if perhaps he ought to waste no further time, give himself no further chance to lapse into indecision and take the risk of calling Ralph from his office phone. He was so absorbed in his own heavy thoughts that he did not notice that his room was occupied until he turned from the clothes closet and approached his desk.

Dr. Potterley was there and a man whom Foster did not recognize.

Foster stared at them. "What's this?"

Potterley said, "I'm sorry, but I had to stop you."

Foster continued staring. "What are you talking about?"

The stranger said, "Let me introduce myself." He had large teeth, a little uneven, and they showed prominently when he smiled. "I am Thaddeus Araman, Department Head of the Division of Chronoscopy. I am here to see you concerning information brought to me by Professor Arnold Potterley and confirmed by our own sources——"

Potterley said breathlessly, "I took all the blame, Dr. Foster. I explained that it was I who persuaded you against your will into unethical practices. I have offered to accept full responsibility and punishment. I don't wish you harmed in any way. It's just that chronoscopy must not be permitted!"

Araman nodded. "He has taken the blame as he says, Dr. Foster, but this thing is out of his hands now."

Foster said, "So? What are you going to do? Blackball me from all consideration for research grants?"

"That is in my power," said Araman.

"Order the university to discharge me?"

"That, too, is in my power."

"All right, go ahead. Consider it done. I'll leave my office now, with you. I can send for my books later. If you insist, I'll leave my books. Is that all?"

"Not quite," said Araman. "You must engage to do no further research in chronoscopy, to publish none of your findings in chronoscopy and, of course, to build no chronoscope. You will remain under surveillance indefinitely to make sure you keep that promise."

"Supposing I refuse to promise? What can you do? Doing research out of my field may be unethical, but it isn't a criminal offense."

"In the case of chronoscopy, my young friend," said Araman patiently, "it is a criminal offense. If necessary, you will be put in jail and kept there."

"Why?" shouted Foster. "What's magic about chronoscopy?"

Araman said, "That's the way it is. We cannot allow further developments in the field. My own job is, primarily, to make sure of that, and I intend to do my job. Unfortunately, I had no knowledge, nor did anyone in the department, that the optics of pseudo-gravity fields had such immediate application to chronoscopy. Score one for general ignorance, but henceforward research will be steered properly in that respect, too."

Foster said, "That won't help. Something else may apply that neither you nor I dream of. All science hangs together. It's one piece. If you want to stop one part, you've got to stop it all."

"No doubt that is true," said Araman, "in theory. On the practical side, however, we have managed quite well to hold chronoscopy down to the original Sterbinski level for fifty years. Having caught you in time, Dr. Foster, we hope to continue doing so indefinitely. And we wouldn't have come this close to disaster, either, if I had accepted Dr. Potterley at something more than face value."

He turned toward the historian and lifted his eyebrows in a kind of humorous self-deprecation. "I'm afraid, sir, that I dismissed you as a history professor and no more on the occasion of our first interview. Had I done my job properly and checked on you, this would not have happened."

Foster said abruptly, "Is anyone allowed to use the government chronoscope?"

"No one outside our division under any pretext. I say that since it is obvious to me that you have already guessed as much. I warn you, though, that any repetition of that fact will be a criminal, not an ethical, offense."

"And your chronoscope doesn't go back more than a hundred twenty-five years or so, does it?"

"It doesn't."

"Then your bulletin with its stories of time viewing ancient times is a hoax?"

Araman said coolly, "With the knowledge you now have, it is obvious you know that for a certainty. However, I confirm your remark. The monthly bulletin is a hoax."

"In that case," said Foster, "I will not promise to suppress my knowledge of chronoscopy. If you wish to arrest me, go ahead. My defense at the trial will be enough to destroy the vicious card house of directed research and bring it tumbling down. Directing research is one thing; suppressing it and depriving mankind of its benefits is quite another."

Araman said, "Oh, let's get something straight, Dr. Foster. If you do not co-operate, you will go to jail directly. You will *not* see a lawyer, you will *not* be charged, you will *not* have a trial. You will simply stay in jail."

"Oh, no," said Foster, "you're bluffing. This is not the twentieth century, you know."

There was a stir outside the office, the clatter of feet, a high-pitched shout that Foster was sure he recognized. The door crashed open, the lock splintering, and three intertwined figures stumbled in. As they did so, one of the men raised a blaster and brought its butt down hard on the skull of another.

There was a whoosh of expiring air, and the one whose head was struck went limp.

"Uncle Ralph!" cried Foster.

Araman frowned. "Put him down in that chair," he ordered, "and get some water."

Ralph Nimmo, rubbing his head with a gingerly sort of disgust, said, "There was no need to get rough, Araman."

Araman said, "The guard should have been rough sooner and kept you out of here, Nimmo. You'd have been better off."

"You know each other?" asked Foster.

"I've had dealings with the man," said Nimmo, still rubbing. "If he's here in your office, nephew, you're in trouble."

"And you, too," said Araman angrily. "I know Dr. Foster consulted you on neutrinics literature."

Nimmo corrugated his forehead, then straightened it with a wince as though the action had brought pain. "So?" he said. "What else do you know about me?"

"We will know everything about you soon enough. Meanwhile, that one item is enough to implicate you. What are you doing here?"

"My dear Dr. Araman," said Nimmo, some of his jauntiness restored, "day before yesterday, my jackass of a nephew called me. He had placed some mysterious information——"

"Don't tell him! Don't say anything!" cried Foster.

Araman glanced at him coldly. "We know all about it, Dr. Foster. The safety-deposit box has been opened and its contents removed."

"But how can you know——" Foster's voice died away in a kind of furious frustration.

"Anyway," said Nimmo, "I decided the net must be closing

around him and, after I took care of a few items, I came down to tell him to get off this thing he's doing. It's not worth his career."

"Does that mean you know what he's doing?" asked Araman.

"He never told me," said Nimmo, "but I'm a science writer with a hell of a lot of experience. I know which side of an atom is electronified. The boy, Foster, specializes in pseudo-gravitic optics and coached me on the stuff himself. He got me to get him a textbook on neutrinics and I kind of skip-viewed it myself before handing it over. I can put the two together. He asked me to get him certain pieces of physical equipment, and that was evidence, too. Stop me if I'm wrong, but my nephew has built a semiportable, low-power chronoscope. Yes, or—yes?"

"Yes." Araman reached thoughtfully for a cigarette and paid no attention to Dr. Potterley (watching silently, as though all were a dream) who shied away, gasping, from the white cylinder. "Another mistake for me. I ought to resign. I should have put tabs on you, too, Nimmo, instead of concentrating too hard on Potterley and Foster. I didn't have much time of course and you've ended up safely here, but that doesn't excuse me. You're under arrest, Nimmo."

"What for?" demanded the science writer.

"Unauthorized research."

"I wasn't doing any. I can't, not being a registered scientist. And even if I did, it's not a criminal offense."

Foster said savagely, "No use, Uncle Ralph. This bureaucrat is making his own laws."

"Like what?" demanded Nimmo.

"Like life imprisonment without trial."

"Nuts," said Nimmo. "This isn't the twentieth cen——"

"I tried that," said Foster. "It doesn't bother him."

"Well, nuts," shouted Nimmo. "Look here, Araman. My nephew and I have relatives who haven't lost touch with us, you know. The professor has some also, I imagine. You can't just make us disappear. There'll be questions and a scandal. This *isn't* the twentieth century. So if you're trying to scare us, it isn't working."

The cigarette snapped between Araman's fingers and he tossed it away violently. He said, "Damn it, I don't know *what* to do. It's never been like this before. . . . Look! You three fools know nothing of what you're trying to do. You understand nothing. Will you listen to me?"

"Oh, we'll listen," said Nimmo grimly.

(Foster sat silently, eyes angry, lips compressed. Potterley's hands writhed like two intertwined snakes.)

Araman said, "The past to you is the dead past. If any of you have discussed the matter, it's dollars to nickels you've used that phrase. The dead past. If you knew how many times I've heard those three words, you'd choke on them, too.

"When people think of the past, they think of it as dead, far away and gone, long ago. We encourage them to think so. When we report time viewing, we always talk of views centuries in the past, even though you gentlemen know seeing more than a century or so is impossible. People accept it. The past means Greece, Rome, Carthage, Egypt, the Stone Age. The deader the better.

"Now you three know a century or a little more is the limit, so what does the past mean to you? Your youth. Your first girl. Your dead mother. Twenty years ago. Thirty years ago. Fifty years ago. The deader the better. . . . But when does the past really begin?"

He paused in anger. The others stared at him and Nimmo stirred uneasily.

"Well," said Araman, "when did it begin? A year ago? Five minutes ago? One second ago? Isn't it obvious that the past begins an instant ago? The dead past is just another name for the living present. What if you focus the chronoscope in the past of one-hundredth of a second ago? Aren't you watching the present? Does it begin to sink in?"

Nimmo said, "Damnation."

"Damnation," mimicked Araman. "After Potterley came to me with his story night before last, how do you suppose I checked up on both of you? I did it with the chronoscope, spotting key moments to the very instant of the present."

"And that's how you knew about the safety-deposit box?" said Foster.

"And every other important fact. Now what do you suppose would happen if we let news of a home chronoscope get out? People might start out by watching their youth, their parents and so on, but it wouldn't be long before they'd catch on to the possibilities. The housewife will forget her poor, dead mother and take to watching her neighbor at home and her husband at the office. The businessman will watch his competitor; the employer his employee.

"There will be no such thing as privacy. The party line, the prying eye behind the curtain will be nothing compared to it. The video stars will be closely watched at all times by everyone. Every man his own peeping Tom and there'll be no getting away from the watcher. Even darkness will be no escape because chronoscopy can be adjusted to the infrared and human figures can be seen by their own body heat. The figures will be fuzzy, of course, and the surroundings will be dark, but that will make the titillation of it all the greater, perhaps. . . . Hmp, the men in charge of the machine now experiment sometimes in spite of the regulations against it."

Nimmo seemed sick. "You can always forbid private manufacture——"

Araman turned on him fiercely. "You can, but do you expect it to do good? Can you legislate successfully against drinking, smoking, adultery or gossiping over the back fence? And this mixture of nosiness and prurience will have a worse grip on humanity than any of those. Good Lord, in a thousand years of trying we haven't even been able to wipe out the heroin traffic and you talk about legislating against a device for watching anyone you please at any time you please that can be built in a home workshop."

Foster said suddenly, "I won't publish."

Potterley burst out, half in sobs, "None of us will talk. I regret——"

Nimmo broke in. "You said you didn't tab me on the chronoscope, Araman."

"No time," said Araman wearily. "Things don't move any faster on the chronoscope than in real life. You can't speed it up like the film in a book viewer. We spent a full twenty-four hours trying to catch the important moments during the last six months of Potterley and Foster. There was no time for anything else and it was enough."

"It wasn't," said Nimmo.

"What are you talking about?" There was a sudden infinite alarm on Araman's face.

"I told you my nephew, Jonas, had called me to say he had put important information in a safety-deposit box. He acted as though he were in trouble. He's my nephew. I had to try to get him off the spot. It took a while, then I came here to tell him what I had done. I told you when I got here, just after your man conked me, that I had taken care of a few items."

"What? For Heaven's sake——"

"Just this: I sent the details of the portable chronoscope off to half a dozen of my regular publicity outlets."

Not a word. Not a sound. Not a breath. They were all past any demonstration.

"Don't stare like that," cried Nimmo. "Don't you see my point? I had popular publication rights. Jonas will admit that. I knew he couldn't publish scientifically in any legal way. I was sure he was planning to publish illegally and was preparing the safety-deposit box for that reason. I thought if I put through the details prematurely, all the responsibility would be mine. His career would be saved. And if I were deprived of my science-writing license as a result, my exclusive possession of the chronometric data would set me up for life. Jonas would be angry, I expected that, but I could explain the motive and we would split the take fifty-fifty. . . . Don't stare at me like that. How did I know——"

"Nobody knew anything," said Araman bitterly, "but you all just took it for granted that the government was stupidly bureaucratic, vicious, tyrannical, given to suppressing research for the hell of it. It never occurred to any of you that we were trying to protect mankind as best we could."

"Don't sit there talking," wailed Potterley. "Get the names of the people who were told——"

"Too late," said Nimmo, shrugging. "They've had better than a day. There's been time for the word to spread. My outfits will have called any number of physicists to check my data before going on with it and they'll call one another to pass on the news. Once scientists put neutrinics and pseudo-gravitics together, home chronoscopy becomes obvious. Before the week is out, five hundred people will know how to build a small chronoscope and how will you catch them all?" His plump cheeks sagged. "I suppose there's no way of putting the mushroom cloud back into that nice, shiny uranium sphere."

Araman stood up. "We'll try, Potterley, but I agree with Nimmo. It's too late. What kind of a world we'll have from now on, I don't know, I can't tell, but the world we know has been destroyed completely. Until now, every custom, every habit, every tiniest way of life has always taken a certain amount of privacy for granted, but that's all gone now."

He saluted each of the three with elaborate formality.

"You have created a new world among the three of you. I congratulate you. Happy goldfish bowl to you, to me, to everyone, and may each of you fry in hell forever. Arrest rescinded."

THE FOUNDATION OF S. F. SUCCESS

If you ask me how to shine in the science-fiction line as a pro of
luster bright,
I say, practice up the lingo of the sciences, by jingo (never mind if not
quite right).
You must talk of Space and Galaxies and tesseractic fallacies in slick and
mystic style,
Though the fans won't understand it, they will all the same demand it
with a softly hopeful smile.

And all the fans will say,
As you walk your spatial way,
If that young man indulges in flights through all the Galaxy,
Why, what a most imaginative type of man that type of man
must be.

So success is not a mystery, just brush up on your history, and borrow
day by day.
Take an Empire that was Roman and you'll find it is at home in all the
starry Milky Way.
With a drive that's hyperspatial, through the parsecs you will race, you'll
find that plotting is a breeze,
With a tiny bit of cribbin' from the works of Edward Gibbon and that
Greek, Thucydides.

And all the fans will say,
As you walk your thoughtful way,
If that young man involves himself in authentic history,
Why, what a very learned kind of high IQ, his high IQ must be.

Then eschew all thoughts of passion of a man-and-woman fashion from
your hero's thoughtful mind.
He must spend his time on politics, and thinking up his shady tricks,
and outside that he's blind.
It's enough he's had a mother, other females are a bother, though they're
jeweled and glistery.
They will just distract his dreaming and his necessary scheming with
that psychohistory.

And all the fans will say
As you walk your narrow way,
If all his yarns restrict themselves to masculinity,
Why, what a most particularly pure young man that pure young man
must be.

FRANCHISE

(*with apologies to* W. S. *Gilbert*)

Linda, age ten, was the only one of the family who seemed to enjoy being awake.

Norman Muller could hear her now through his own drugged, unhealthy coma. (He had finally managed to fall asleep an hour earlier but even then it was more like exhaustion than sleep.)

She was at his bedside now, shaking him. "Daddy, Daddy, wake up. Wake up!"

He suppressed a groan. "All right, Linda."

"But, Daddy, there's more policemen around than any time! Police cars and everything!"

Norman Muller gave up and rose blearily to his elbows. The day was beginning. It was faintly stirring toward dawn outside, the germ of a miserable gray that looked about as miserably gray as he felt. He could hear Sarah, his wife, shuffling about breakfast duties in the kitchen. His father-in-law, Matthew, was hawking strenuously in the bathroom. No doubt Agent Handley was ready and waiting for him.

This was *the* day.

Election Day!

To begin with, it had been like every other year. Maybe a little worse, because it was a presidential year, but no worse than other presidential years if it came to that.

The politicians spoke about the guh-reat electorate and the vast electuh-ronic intelligence that was its servant. The press analyzed the situation with industrial computers (the New York *Times* and the St. Louis *Post-Dispatch* had their own computers) and were full of little hints as to what would be forthcoming. Commentators and columnists pinpointed the crucial state and county in happy contradiction to one another.

The first hint that it would *not* be like every other year was when Sarah Muller said to her husband on the evening of October 4 (with Election Day exactly a month off), "Cantwell Johnson says that Indiana will be the state this year. He's the fourth one. Just think, *our* state this time."

Matthew Hortenweiler took his fleshy face from behind the paper, stared dourly at his daughter and growled, "Those fellows are paid to tell lies. Don't listen to them."

"Four of them, Father," said Sarah mildly. "They all say Indiana."

"Indiana *is* a key state, Matthew," said Norman, just as mildly, "on account of the Hawkins-Smith Act and this mess in Indianapolis. It——"

Matthew twisted his old face alarmingly and rasped out, "No one says Bloomington or Monroe County, do they?"

"Well——" said Norman.

Linda, whose little pointed-chinned face had been shifting from one speaker to the next, said pipingly, "You going to be voting this year, Daddy?"

Norman smiled gently and said, "I don't think so, dear."

But this was in the gradually growing excitement of an October in a presidential election year and Sarah had led a quiet life with dreams for her companions. She said longingly, "Wouldn't *that* be wonderful, though?"

"If I voted?" Norman Muller had a small blond mustache that had given him a debonair quality in the young Sarah's eyes, but which, with gradual graying, had declined merely to lack of distinction. His forehead bore deepening lines born of uncertainty and, in general, he had never seduced his clerkly soul with the thought that he was either born great or would under any circumstances achieve greatness. He had a wife, a job and a little girl, and except under extraordinary conditions of elation or depression was inclined to consider that to be an adequate bargain struck with life.

So he was a little embarrassed and more than a little uneasy at the direction his wife's thoughts were taking. "Actually, my dear," he said, "there are two hundred million people in the country, and, with odds like that, I don't think we ought to waste our time wondering about it."

His wife said, "Why, Norman, it's no such thing like two hundred million and you know it. In the first place, only people between twenty and sixty are eligible and it's always men, so that puts it down to maybe fifty million to one. Then, if it's really Indiana——"

"Then it's about one and a quarter million to one. You wouldn't want me to bet in a horse race against those odds, now, would you? Let's have supper."

Matthew muttered from behind his newspaper, "Damned foolishness."

Linda asked again, "You going to be voting this year, Daddy?"

Norman shook his head and they all adjourned to the dining room.

By October 20, Sarah's excitement was rising rapidly. Over the coffee, she announced that Mrs. Schultz, having a cousin who was the secretary of an Assemblyman, said that all the "smart money" was on Indiana.

"She says President Villers is even going to make a speech at Indianapolis."

Norman Muller, who had had a hard day at the store, nudged the statement with a raising of eyebrows and let it go at that.

Matthew Hortenweiler, who was chronically dissatisfied with Washington, said, "If Villers makes a speech in Indiana, that means he thinks Multivac will pick Arizona. He wouldn't have the guts to go closer, the mushhead."

Sarah, who ignored her father whenever she could decently do so, said, "I don't know why they don't announce the state as soon as they can, and then the county and so on. Then the people who were eliminated could relax."

"If they did anything like that," pointed out Norman, "the politicians would follow the announcements like vultures. By the time it was narrowed down to a township, you'd have a Congressman or two at every street corner."

Matthew narrowed his eyes and brushed angrily at his sparse, gray hair. "They're vultures, anyhow. Listen——"

Sarah murmured, "Now, Father——"

Matthew's voice rumbled over her protest without as much as a stumble or hitch. "Listen, I was around when they set up Multivac. It would end partisan politics, they said. No more voters' money wasted on campaigns. No more grinning nobodies high-pressured and advertising-campaigned into Congress or the White House. So what happens. More campaigning than ever, only now they do it blind. They'll send guys to Indiana on account of the Hawkins-Smith Act and other guys to California in case it's the Joe Hammer situation that turns out crucial. I say, wipe out all that nonsense. Back to the good old——"

Linda asked suddenly, "Don't you want Daddy to vote this year, Grandpa?"

Matthew glared at the young girl. "Never you mind, now." He turned back to Norman and Sarah. "There was a time I voted. Marched right up to the polling booth, stuck my fist on the levers and voted. There was nothing to it. I just said: This fellow's my man and I'm voting for him. *That's* the way it should be."

Linda said excitedly, "You voted, Grandpa? You really did?"

Sarah leaned forward quickly to quiet what might easily become an incongruous story drifting about the neighborhood. "It's nothing, Linda. Grandpa doesn't really mean voted. Everyone did that kind of voting, your grandpa, too, but it wasn't *really* voting."

Matthew roared, "It wasn't when I was a little boy. I was twenty-two and I voted for Langley and it was real voting. My vote didn't count for much, maybe, but it was as good as anyone else's. *Anyone* else's. And no Multivac to——"

Norman interposed, "All right, Linda, time for bed. And stop asking questions about voting. When you grow up, you'll understand all about it."

He kissed her with antiseptic gentleness and she moved reluctantly out of range under maternal prodding and a promise that she might watch the bedside video till 9:15, *if* she was prompt about the bathing ritual.

Linda said, "Grandpa," and stood with her chin down and her hands behind her back until his newspaper lowered itself to the point where shaggy eyebrows and eyes, nested in fine wrinkles, showed themselves. It was Friday, October 31.

He said, "Yes?"

Linda came closer and put both her forearms on one of the old man's knees so that he had to discard his newspaper altogether.

She said, "Grandpa, did you really once vote?"

He said, "You heard me say I did, didn't you? Do you think I tell fibs?"

"N—no, but Mamma says everybody voted then."

"So they did."

"But how could they? How could *everybody* vote?"

Matthew stared at her solemnly, then lifted her and put her on his knee.

He even moderated the tonal qualities of his voice. He said, "You see, Linda, till about forty years ago, everybody always voted. Say we wanted to decide who was to be the new President of the United States. The Democrats and Republicans would both nominate someone, and everybody would say who they wanted. When Election Day was over, they would count how many people wanted the Democrat and how many wanted the Republican. Whoever had more votes was elected. You see?"

Linda nodded and said, "How did all the people know who to vote for? Did Multivac tell them?"

Matthew's eyebrows hunched down and he looked severe. "They just used their own judgment, girl."

She edged away from him, and he lowered his voice again, "I'm not angry at you, Linda. But, you see, sometimes it took all night to count what everyone said and people were impatient. So they invented special machines which could look at the first few votes and compare them with the votes from the same places in previous years. That way the machine could compute how the total vote would be and who would be elected. You see?"

She nodded. "Like Multivac."

"The first computers were much smaller than Multivac. But the machines grew bigger and they could tell how the election would go from fewer and fewer votes. Then, at last, they built Multivac and it can tell from just one voter."

Linda smiled at having reached a familiar part of the story and said, "That's nice."

Matthew frowned and said, "No, it's not nice. I don't want a machine telling me how I would have voted just because some joker in Milwaukee says he's against higher tariffs. Maybe I want to vote cockeyed just for the pleasure of it. Maybe I don't want to vote. Maybe——"

But Linda had wriggled from his knee and was beating a retreat.

She met her mother at the door. Her mother, who was still wearing her coat and had not even had time to remove her hat, said breathlessly, "Run along, Linda. Don't get in Mother's way."

Then she said to Matthew, as she lifted her hat from her head and patted her hair back into place, "I've been at Agatha's."

Matthew stared at her censoriously and did not even dignify that piece of information with a grunt as he groped for his newspaper.

Sarah said, as she unbuttoned her coat, "Guess what she said?"

Matthew flattened out his newspaper for reading purposes with a sharp crackle and said, "Don't much care."

Sarah said, "Now, Father——" But she had no time for anger. The news had to be told and Matthew was the only recipient handy, so she went on, "Agatha's Joe is a policeman, you know, and he says a whole truckload of secret service men came into Bloomington last night."

"They're not after me."

"Don't you see, Father? Secret service agents, and it's almost election time. In *Bloomington.*"

"Maybe they're after a bank robber."

"There hasn't been a bank robbery in town in ages. . . . Father, you're hopeless."

She stalked away.

Nor did Norman Muller receive the news with noticeably greater excitement.

"Now, Sarah, how did Agatha's Joe know they were secret service agents?" he asked calmly. "They wouldn't go around with identification cards pasted on their foreheads."

But by next evening, with November a day old, she could say triumphantly, "It's just everyone in Bloomington that's waiting for someone local to be the voter. The Bloomington *News* as much as said so on video."

Norman stirred uneasily. He couldn't deny it, and his heart was sinking. If Bloomington was really to be hit by Multivac's lightning, it would mean newspapermen, video shows, tourists, all sorts of—strange upsets. Norman liked the quiet routine of his life, and the distant stir of politics was getting uncomfortably close.

He said, "It's all rumor. Nothing more."

"You wait and see, then. You just wait and see."

As things turned out, there was very little time to wait, for the doorbell rang insistently, and when Norman Muller opened it and said, "Yes?" a tall, grave-faced man said, "Are you Norman Muller?"

Norman said, "Yes," again, but in a strange dying voice. It was not difficult to see from the stranger's bearing that he was one carrying authority, and the nature of his errand suddenly became as inevitably obvious as it had, until the moment before, been unthinkably impossible.

The man presented credentials, stepped into the house, closed the door behind him and said ritualistically, "Mr. Norman Muller, it is necessary for me to inform you on the behalf of the President of the United States that you have been chosen to represent the American electorate on Tuesday, November 4, 2008."

Norman Muller managed, with difficulty, to walk unaided to his chair. He sat there, white-faced and almost insensible, while Sarah brought water, slapped his hands in panic and moaned to her husband between clenched teeth, "Don't be sick, Norman. *Don't* be sick. They'll pick someone else."

When Norman could manage to talk, he whispered, "I'm sorry, sir."

The secret service agent had removed his coat, unbuttoned his jacket and was sitting at ease on the couch.

"It's all right," he said, and the mark of officialdom seemed to have vanished with the formal announcement and leave him simply a large and rather friendly man. "This is the sixth time I've made the announcement and I've seen all kinds of reactions. Not one of them was the kind you see on the video. You know what I mean? A holy, dedicated look, and a character who says, 'It will be a great privilege to serve my country.' That sort of stuff." The agent laughed comfortingly.

Sarah's accompanying laugh held a trace of shrill hysteria.

The agent said, "Now you're going to have me with you for a while. My name is Phil Handley. I'd appreciate it if you call me Phil. Mr. Muller can't leave the house any more till election day. You'll have to inform the department store that he's sick, Mrs. Muller. You can go about your business for a while, but you'll have to agree not to say a word about this. Right, Mrs. Muller?"

Sarah nodded vigorously. "No, sir. Not a word."

"All right. But, Mrs. Muller," Handley looked grave, "we're not kidding now. Go out only if you must and you'll be followed when you do. I'm sorry but that's the way we must operate."

"Followed?"

"It won't be obvious. Don't worry. And it's only for two days till the formal announcement to the nation is made. Your daughter——"

"She's in bed," said Sarah hastily.

"Good. She'll have to be told I'm a relative or friend staying with the family. If she does find out the truth, she'll have to be kept in the house. Your father had better stay in the house in any case."

"He won't like that," said Sarah.

"Can't be helped. Now, since you have no others living with you——"

"You know all about us apparently," whispered Norman.

"Quite a bit," agreed Handley. "In any case, those are all my instructions to you for the moment. I'll try to co-operate as much as I can and be as little of a nuisance as possible. The government will pay for my maintenance so I won't be an expense to you. I'll be relieved each night by someone who will sit up in this room, so there will be no problem about sleeping accommodations. Now, Mr. Muller——"

"Sir?"

"You can call me Phil," said the agent again. "The purpose of the two-day preliminary before formal announcement is to get you used to your position. We prefer to have you face Multivac in as normal a state of mind as possible. Just relax and try to feel this is all in a day's work. Okay?"

"Okay," said Norman, and then shook his head violently. "But I don't want the responsibility. Why me?"

"All right," said Handley, "let's get that straight to begin with. Multivac weighs all sorts of known factors, billions of them. One factor isn't known, though, and won't be known for a long time. That's the reaction pattern of the human mind. All Americans are subjected to the molding pressure of what other Americans do and say, to the things that are done to him and the things he does to others. Any American can be brought to Multivac to have the bent of his mind surveyed. From that the bent of all other minds in the country can be estimated. Some Americans are better for the purpose than others at some given time, depending upon the happenings of that year. Multivac picked you as most representative this year. Not the smartest, or the strongest, or the luckiest, but just the most representative. Now we don't question Multivac, do we?"

"Couldn't it make a mistake?" asked Norman.

Sarah, who listened impatiently, interrupted to say, "Don't listen to him, sir. He's just nervous, you know. Actually, he's very well read and he always follows politics very closely."

Handley said, "Multivac makes the decisions, Mrs. Muller. It picked your husband."

"But does it know everything?" insisted Norman wildly. "Couldn't it have made a mistake?"

"Yes, it can. There's no point in not being frank. In 1993, a selected Voter died of a stroke two hours before it was time for him to be notified. Multivac didn't predict that; it couldn't. A Voter might be mentally unstable, morally unsuitable, or, for that matter, disloyal. Multivac can't know everything about everybody until he's fed all the data there is. That's why alternate selections are always held in readiness. I don't think we'll be using one this time. You're in good health, Mr. Muller, and you've been carefully investigated. You qualify."

Norman buried his face in his hands and sat motionless.

"By tomorrow morning, sir," said Sarah, "he'll be perfectly all right. He just has to get used to it, that's all."

"Of course," said Handley.

In the privacy of their bedchamber, Sarah Muller expressed herself in other and stronger fashion. The burden of her lecture was, "So get hold of yourself, Norman. You're trying to throw away the chance of a lifetime."

Norman whispered desperately, "It frightens me, Sarah. The whole thing."

"For goodness' sake, why? What's there to it but answering a question or two?"

"The responsibility is too great. I couldn't face it."

"What responsibility? There isn't any. Multivac picked you. It's Multivac's responsibility. Everyone knows that."

Norman sat up in bed in a sudden access of rebellion and anguish. "Everyone is *supposed* to know that. But they don't. They——"

"Lower your voice," hissed Sarah icily. "They'll hear you downtown."

"They don't," said Norman, declining quickly to a whisper. "When they talk about the Ridgely administration of 1988, do they say he won them over with pie-in-the-sky promises and racist baloney? No! They talk about the 'goddam MacComber vote,' as though Humphrey MacComber was the only man who had anything to do with it because he faced Multivac. I've said it myself—only now I think the poor guy was just a truck farmer who didn't ask to be picked. Why was it his fault more than anyone else's? Now his name is a curse."

"You're just being childish," said Sarah.

"I'm being sensible. I tell you, Sarah, I won't accept. They can't make me vote if I don't want to. I'll say I'm sick. I'll say——"

But Sarah had had enough. "Now you listen to me," she whispered in a cold fury. "You don't have only yourself to think about. You know what it means to be Voter of the Year. A presidential year at that. It means publicity and fame and, maybe, buckets of money——"

"And then I go back to being a clerk."

"You will *not*. You'll have a branch managership at the least if you have any brains at all, and you *will* have, because I'll tell you what to do. You control the kind of publicity if you play your cards right, and you can force Kennell Stores, Inc., into a tight contract *and* an escalator clause in connection with your salary *and* a decent pension plan."

"That's not the point in being Voter, Sarah."

"That will be your point. If you don't owe anything to yourself or to me—I'm not asking for myself—you owe something to Linda."

Norman groaned.

"Well, don't you?" snapped Sarah.

"Yes, dear," murmured Norman.

On November 3, the official announcement was made and it was too late for Norman to back out even if he had been able to find the courage to make the attempt.

Their house was sealed off. Secret service agents made their appearance in the open, blocking off all approach.

At first the telephone rang incessantly, but Philip Handley with an engagingly apologetic smile took all calls. Eventually, the exchange shunted all calls directly to the police station.

Norman imagined that, in that way, he was spared not only the bubbling (and envious?) congratulations of friends, but also the egregious pressure of salesmen scenting a prospect and the designing smoothness of politicians from all over the nation. . . . Perhaps even death threats from the inevitable cranks.

Newspapers were forbidden to enter the house now in order to keep out weighted pressures, and television was gently but firmly disconnected, over Linda's loud protests.

Matthew growled and stayed in his room; Linda, after the first flurry of excitement, sulked and whined because she could not leave the house; Sarah divided her time between preparation of meals for the present and plans for the future; and Norman's depression lived and fed upon itself.

And the morning of Tuesday, November 4, 2008, came at last, and it was Election Day.

It was early breakfast, but only Norman Muller ate, and that mechanically. Even a shower and shave had not succeeded in either restoring him to reality or removing his own conviction that he was as grimy without as he felt grimy within.

Handley's friendly voice did its best to shed some normality over the gray and unfriendly dawn. (The weather prediction had been for a cloudy day with prospects of rain before noon.)

Handley said, "We'll keep this house insulated till Mr. Muller is back, but after that we'll be off your necks." The secret service agent was in full uniform now, including sidearms in heavily brassed holsters.

"You've been no trouble at all, Mr. Handley," simpered Sarah.

Norman drank through two cups of black coffee, wiped his lips with a napkin, stood up and said haggardly, "I'm ready."

Handley stood up, too. "Very well, sir. And thank you, Mrs. Muller, for your very kind hospitality."

The armored car purred down empty streets. They were empty even for that hour of the morning.

Handley indicated that and said, "They always shift traffic away from the line of drive ever since the attempted bombing that nearly ruined the Leverett Election of '92."

When the car stopped, Norman was helped out by the always polite Handley into an underground drive whose walls were lined with soldiers at attention.

He was led into a brightly lit room, in which three white-uniformed men greeted him smilingly.

Norman said sharply, "But this is the hospital."

"There's no significance to that," said Handley at once. "It's just that the hospital has the necessary facilities."

"Well, what do I do?"

Handley nodded. One of the three men in white advanced and said, "I'll take over now, agent."

Handley saluted in an offhand manner and left the room.

The man in white said, "Won't you sit down, Mr. Muller? I'm John Paulson, Senior Computer. These are Samson Levine and Peter Dorogobuzh, my assistants."

Norman shook hands numbly all about. Paulson was a man of middle height with a soft face that seemed used to smiling and a very obvious toupee. He wore plastic-rimmed glasses of an old-fashioned cut, and he lit a cigarette as he talked. (Norman refused his offer of one.)

Paulson said, "In the first place, Mr. Muller, I want you to know we are in no hurry. We want you to stay with us all day if necessary, just so that you get used to your surroundings and get over any thought you might have that there is anything unusual in this, anything clinical, if you know what I mean."

"It's all right," said Norman. "I'd just as soon this were over."

"I understand your feelings. Still, we want you to know exactly what's going on. In the first place, Multivac isn't here."

"It isn't?" Somehow through all his depression, he had still looked forward to seeing Multivac. They said it was half a mile long and three stories high, that fifty technicians walked the corridors *within* its structure continuously. It was one of the wonders of the world.

Paulson smiled. "No. It's not portable, you know. It's located underground, in fact, and very few people know exactly where. You can understand that, since it is our greatest natural resource. Believe me, elections aren't the only things it's used for."

Norman thought he was being deliberately chatty and found himself intrigued all the same. "I thought I'd see it. I'd like to."

"I'm sure of that. But it takes a presidential order and even then it has to be countersigned by Security. However, we are plugged into Multivac right here by beam transmission. What Multivac says can be interpreted here and what we say is beamed directly to Multivac, so in a sense we're in its presence."

Norman looked about. The machines within the room were all meaningless to him.

"Now let me explain, Mr. Muller," Paulson went on. "Multivac already has most of the information it needs to decide all the elections, national, state and local. It needs only to check certain imponderable attitudes of mind and it will use you for that. We can't predict what questions it will ask, but they may not make much sense to you, or even to us. It may ask you how you feel about garbage disposal in your town; whether you favor central incinerators. It might ask you whether you have a doctor of your own or whether you make use of National Medicine, Inc. Do you understand?"

"Yes, sir."

"Whatever it asks, you answer in your own words in any way you please. If you feel you must explain quite a bit, do so. Talk an hour, if necessary."

"Yes, sir."

"Now, one more thing. We will have to make use of some simple devices which will automatically record your blood pressure, heartbeat, skin conductivity and brain-wave pattern while you speak. The machinery will seem formidable, but it's all absolutely painless. You won't even know it's going on."

The other two technicians were already busying themselves with smooth-gleaming apparatus on oiled wheels.

Norman said, "Is that to check on whether I'm lying or not?"

"Not at all, Mr. Muller. There's no question of lying. It's only a matter of emotional intensity. If the machine asks you your opinion of your child's school, you may say, 'I think it is overcrowded.' Those are only words. From the way your brain and heart and hormones and sweat glands work, Multivac can judge exactly how intensely you feel about the matter. It will understand your feelings better than you yourself."

"I never heard of this," said Norman.

"No, I'm sure you didn't. Most of the details of Multivac's workings are top secret. For instance, when you leave, you will be asked to sign a paper swearing that you will never reveal the nature of the questions you were asked, the nature of your responses, what was done, or how it was done. The less is known about the Multivac, the less chance of attempted outside pressures upon the men who service it." He smiled grimly. "Our lives are hard enough as it is."

Norman nodded. "I understand."

"And now would you like anything to eat or drink?"

"No. Nothing right now."

"Do you have any questions?"

Norman shook his head.

"Then you tell us when you're ready."

"I'm ready right now."

"You're certain?"

"Quite."

Paulson nodded, and raised his hand in a gesture to the others.

They advanced with their frightening equipment, and Norman Muller felt his breath come a little quicker as he watched.

The ordeal lasted nearly three hours, with one short break for coffee and an embarrassing session with a chamber pot. During all this time, Norman Muller remained encased in machinery. He was bone-weary at the close.

He thought sardonically that his promise to reveal nothing of what had passed would be an easy one to keep. Already the questions were a hazy mishmash in his mind.

Somehow he had thought Multivac would speak in a sepulchral, superhuman voice, resonant and echoing, but that, after all, was just an idea he had from seeing too many television shows, he now decided. The truth was distressingly undramatic. The questions were slips of a kind of metallic foil patterned with numerous punctures. A second machine converted the pattern into words and Paulson read the words to Norman, then gave him the question and let him read it for himself.

Norman's answers were taken down by a recording machine, played back to Norman for confirmation, with emendations and added remarks also taken down. All that was fed into a pattern-making instrument and that, in turn, was radiated to Multivac.

The one question Norman could remember at the moment was an incongruously gossipy: "What do you think of the price of eggs?"

Now it was over, and gently they removed the electrodes from various portions of his body, unwrapped the pulsating band from his upper arm, moved the machinery away.

He stood up, drew a deep, shuddering breath and said, "Is that all? Am I through?"

"Not quite." Paulson hurried to him, smiling in reassuring fashion. "We'll have to ask you to stay another hour."

"Why?" asked Norman sharply.

"It will take that long for Multivac to weave its new data into the trillions of items it has. Thousands of elections are concerned, you know. It's very complicated. And it may be that an odd contest here or there, a comptrollership in Phoenix, Arizona, or some council seat in Wilkesboro, North Carolina, may be in doubt. In that case, Multivac may be compelled to ask you a deciding question or two."

"No," said Norman. "I won't go through this again."

"It probably won't happen," Paulson said soothingly. "It rarely does. But, just in case, you'll have to stay." A touch of steel, just a touch, entered his voice. "You have no choice, you know. You must."

Norman sat down wearily. He shrugged.

Paulson said, "We can't let you read a newspaper, but if you'd care for a murder mystery, or if you'd like to play chess, or if there's anything we can do for you to help pass the time, I wish you'd mention it."

"It's all right. I'll just wait."

They ushered him into a small room just next to the one in which he had been questioned. He let himself sink into a plastic-covered armchair and closed his eyes.

As well as he could, he must wait out this final hour.

He sat perfectly still and slowly the tension left him. His breathing grew less ragged and he could clasp his hands without being quite so conscious of the trembling of his fingers.

Maybe there would be no questions. Maybe it was all over.

If it *were* over, then the next thing would be torchlight processions and invitations to speak at all sorts of functions. The Voter of the Year!

He, Norman Muller, ordinary clerk of a small department store in Bloomington, Indiana, who had neither been born great nor achieved greatness would be in the extraordinary position of having had greatness thrust upon him.

The historians would speak soberly of the Muller Election of 2008. That would be its name, the Muller Election.

The publicity, the better job, the flash flood of money that interested Sarah so much, occupied only a corner of his mind. It would all be welcome, of course. He couldn't refuse it. But at the moment something else was beginning to concern him.

A latent patriotism was stirring. After all, he was representing the entire electorate. He was the focal point for *them.* He was, in his own person, for this one day, all of America!

The door opened, snapping him to open-eyed attention. For a moment, his stomach constricted. Not more questions!

But Paulson was smiling. "That will be all, Mr. Muller."

"No more questions, sir?"

"None needed. Everything was quite clear-cut. You will be escorted back to your home and then you will be a private citizen once more. Or as much so as the public will allow."

"Thank you. Thank you." Norman flushed and said, "I wonder—who was elected?"

Paulson shook his head. "That will have to wait for the official announcement. The rules are quite strict. We can't even tell you. You understand."

"Of course. Yes." Norman felt embarrassed.

"Secret service will have the necessary papers for you to sign."

"Yes." Suddenly, Norman Muller felt proud. It was on him now in full strength. He was proud.

In this imperfect world, the sovereign citizens of the first and greatest Electronic Democracy had, through Norman Muller (through *him!*), exercised once again its free, untrammeled franchise.

GIMMICKS THREE

"Come, come," said Shapur quite politely, considering that he was a demon. "You are wasting my time. And your own, too, I might add, since you have only half an hour left." And his tail twitched.

"It's *not* dematerialization?" asked Isidore Wellby thoughtfully.

"I have already said it is not," said Shapur.

For the hundredth time, Wellby looked at the unbroken bronze that surrounded him on all sides. The demon had taken unholy pleasure (what other kind indeed?) in pointing out that the floor, ceiling and four walls were featureless, two-foot-thick slabs of bronze, welded seamlessly together.

It was the ultimate locked room and Wellby had but another half hour to get out, while the demon watched with an expression of gathering anticipation.

It had been ten years previously (to the day, naturally) that Isidore Wellby had signed up.

"We pay you in advance," said Shapur persuasively. "Ten years of anything you want, within reason, and then you're a demon. You're one of us, with a new name of demonic potency, and many privileges beside. You'll hardly know you're damned. And if you don't sign, you may end up in the fire, anyway, just in the ordinary course of things. You never know. . . . Here, look at me. I'm not doing too badly. I signed up, had my ten years and here I am. Not bad."

"Why so anxious for me to sign then, if I might be damned anyway?" asked Wellby.

"It's not so easy to recruit hell's cadre," said the demon, with a frank shrug that made the faint odor of sulfur dioxide in the air a trifle stronger. "Everyone wishes to gamble on ending in Heaven. It's a poor gamble, but there it is. I think *you*'re too sensible for that. But meanwhile we have more damned souls than we know what to do with and a growing shortage at the administrative end."

Wellby, having just left the army and finding himself with nothing much to show for it but a limp and a farewell letter from a girl he somehow still loved, pricked his finger, and signed.

Of course, he read the small print first. A certain amount of demonic power would be deposited to his account upon signature in blood. He would not know in detail how one manipulated those powers, or even the nature of all of them, but he would nevertheless find his wishes fulfilled in such a way that they would seem to have come about through perfectly normal mechanisms.

Naturally, no wish might be fulfilled which would interfere with the higher aims and purposes of human history. Wellby had raised his eyebrows at that.

Shapur coughed. "A precaution imposed upon us by—uh—Above. You are reasonable. The limitation won't interfere with you."

Wellby said, "There seems to be a catch clause, too."

"A kind of one, yes. After all, we have to check your aptitude for the position. It states, as you see, that you will be required to perform a task for us at the conclusion of your ten years, one your demonic powers will make it quite possible for you to do. We can't tell you the nature of the task now, but you will have ten years to study the nature of your powers. Look upon the whole thing as an entrance qualification."

"And if I don't pass the test, what then?"

"In that case," said the demon, "you will be only an ordinary damned soul after all." And because he was a demon, his eyes glowed smokily at the thought and his clawed fingers twitched as though he felt them already deep in the other's vitals. But he added suavely, "Come, now, the test will be a simple one. We would rather have you as cadre than as just another chore on our hands."

Wellby, with sad thoughts of his unattainable loved one, cared little enough at that moment for what would happen after ten years and he signed.

Yet the ten years passed quickly enough. Isidore Wellby was always reasonable, as the demon had predicted, and things worked well. Wellby accepted a position and because he was always at the right spot at the right time and always said the right thing to the right man, he was quickly promoted to a position of great authority.

Investments he made invariably paid off and, what was more gratifying still, his girl came back to him most sincerely repentant and most satisfactorily adoring.

His marriage was a happy one and was blessed with four children, two boys and two girls, all bright and reasonably well behaved. At the end of ten years, he was at the height of his authority, reputation and wealth, while his wife, if anything, had grown more beautiful as she had matured.

And ten years (to the day, naturally) after the making of the compact, he woke to find himself, not in his bedroom, but in a horrible bronze chamber of the most appalling solidity, with no company other than an eager demon.

"You have only to get out, and you will be one of us," said Shapur. "It can be done fairly and logically by using your demonic powers, provided you know exactly what it is you're doing. You should, by now."

"My wife and children will be very disturbed at my disappearance," said Wellby, with the beginning of regrets.

"They will find your dead body," said the demon consolingly. "You will seem to have died of a heart attack and you will have a beautiful funeral. The minister will consign you to Heaven and we will not disillusion him or those who listen to him. Now, come, Wellby, you have till noon."

Wellby, having unconsciously steeled himself for this moment for ten years, was less panic-stricken than he might have been. He looked about speculatively. "Is this room perfectly enclosed? No trick openings?"

"No openings anywhere in the walls, floor or ceiling," said the demon, with a professional delight in his handiwork. "Or at the boundaries of any of those surfaces, for that matter. Are you giving up?"

"No, no. Just give me time."

Wellby thought very hard. There seemed no sign of closeness in the room. There was even a feeling of moving air. The air might be entering the room by dematerializing across the walls. Perhaps the demon had entered by dematerialization and perhaps Wellby himself might leave in that manner. He asked.

The demon grinned. "Dematerialization is not one of your powers. Nor did I myself use it in entering."

"You're sure now?"

"The room is my own creation," said the demon smugly, "and especially constructed for you."

"And you entered from outside?"

"I did."

"With reasonable demonic powers which I possess, too?"

"Exactly. Come, let us be precise. You cannot move through matter but you can move in any dimension by a mere effort of will. You can move up, down, right, left, obliquely and so on, but you cannot move through matter in any way."

Wellby kept on thinking, and Shapur kept on pointing out the utter immovable solidity of the bronze walls, floor and ceiling; their unbroken ultimacy.

It seemed obvious to Wellby that Shapur, however much he might believe in the necessity for recruiting cadre, was barely restraining his demonic delight at possibly having an ordinary damned soul to amuse himself with.

"At least," said Wellby, with a sorrowful attempt at philosophy, "I'll have ten happy years to look back on. Surely that's a consolation, even for a damned soul in hell."

"Not at all," said the demon. "Hell would not be hell, if you were allowed consolations. Everything anyone gains on Earth by pacts with the devil, as in your case (or my own, for that matter), is exactly what one might have gained without such a pact if one had worked industriously and in full trust in—uh—Above. That is what makes all such bargains so truly demonic." And the demon laughed with a kind of cheerful howl.

Wellby said indignantly, "You mean my wife would have returned to me even if I had never signed your contract."

"She might have," said Shapur. "Whatever happens is the will of —uh—Above, you know. We ourselves can do nothing to alter that."

The chagrin of that moment must have sharpened Wellby's wits for it was then that he vanished, leaving the room empty, except for a surprised demon. And surprise turned to absolute fury when the demon looked at the contract with Wellby which he had, until that moment, been holding in his hand for final action, one way or the other.

It was ten years (to the day, naturally) after Isidore Wellby had signed his pact with Shapur, that the demon entered Wellby's office and said, most angrily, "Look here——"

Wellby looked up from his work, astonished. "Who are you?"

"You know very well who I am," said Shapur.

"Not at all," said Wellby.

The demon looked sharply at the man. "I see you are telling the truth, but I can't make out the details." He promptly flooded Wellby's mind with the events of the last ten years.

Wellby said, "Oh, yes. I can explain, of course, but are you sure we will not be interrupted?"

"We won't be," said the demon grimly.

"I sat in that closed bronze room," said Wellby, "and——"

"Never mind that," said the demon hastily. "I want to know——"

"Please. Let me tell this my way."

The demon clamped his jaws and fairly exuded sulfur dioxide till Wellby coughed and looked pained.

Wellby said, "If you'll move off a bit. Thank you. . . . Now I sat in that closed bronze room and remembered how you kept stressing the absolute unbrokenness of the four walls, the floor and the ceiling. I wondered: why did you specify? What else was there beside walls, floor and ceiling. You had defined a completely enclosed three-dimensional space.

"And that was it: three-dimensional. The room was not closed in the fourth dimension. It did not exist indefinitely in the past. You said you had created it for me. So if one traveled into the past, one would find oneself at a point in time, eventually, when the room did not exist and then one would be out of the room.

"What's more, you *had* said I could move in any dimension, and time may certainly be viewed as a dimension. In any case, as soon as I decided to move toward the past, I found myself living backward at a tremendous rate and suddenly there was no bronze around me anywhere."

Shapur cried in anguish, "I can guess all that. You couldn't have escaped any other way. It's this contract of yours that I'm concerned about. If you're not an ordinary damned soul, very well, it's part of the game. But you must be at least one of *us*, one of the cadre; it's what you were paid for, and if I don't deliver you down below, I will be in enormous trouble."

Wellby shrugged his shoulders. "I'm sorry for you, of course, but I can't help you. You must have created the bronze room immediately after I placed my signature on the paper, for when I burst out of the room, I found myself just at the point in time at which I was making the bargain with you. There you were again; there I was; you were pushing the contract toward me, together with a stylus with which I might prick my finger. To be sure, as I had moved back in time, my memory of what was becoming the future faded out, but not, apparently, quite entirely. As you pushed the contract at me, I felt uneasy. I didn't quite remember the future, but I felt uneasy. So I didn't sign. I turned you down flat."

Shapur ground his teeth. "I might have known. If probability patterns affected demons, I would have shifted with you into this new if-world. As it is, all I can say is that you have lost the ten happy years we paid you with. That is one consolation. And we'll get you in the end. That is another."

"Well, now," said Wellby, "are there consolations in hell? Through the ten years I have now lived, I knew nothing of what I might have obtained. But now that you've put the memory of the ten-years-that-might-have-been into my mind, I recall that, in the bronze room, you told me that demonic agreements could give nothing that could not be obtained by industry and trust in Above. I have been industrious and I have trusted."

Wellby's eyes fell upon the photograph of his beautiful wife and four beautiful children, then traveled about the tasteful luxuriance of his office. "And I may even escape hell altogether. That, too, is beyond *your* power to decide."

And the demon, with a horrible shriek, vanished forever.

KID STUFF

The first pang of nausea had passed and Jan Prentiss said, "Damn it, you're an insect."

It was a statement of fact, not an insult, and the thing that sat on Prentiss' desk said, "Of course."

It was about a foot long, very thin, and in shape a farfetched and miniature caricature of a human being. Its stalky arms and legs originated in pairs from the upper portion of its body. The legs were longer and thicker than the arms. They extended the length of the body, then bent forward at the knee.

The creature sat upon those knees and, when it did so, the stub of its fuzzy abdomen just cleared Prentiss' desk.

There was plenty of time for Prentiss to absorb these details. The object had no objection to being stared at. It seemed to welcome it, in fact, as though it were used to exciting admiration.

"What are you?" Prentiss did not feel completely rational. Five minutes ago, he had been seated at his typewriter, working leisurely on the story he had promised Horace W. Browne for last month's issue of *Farfetched Fantasy Fiction*. He had been in a perfectly usual frame of mine. He had felt quite fine; quite sane.

And then a block of air immediately to the right of the typewriter had shimmered, clouded over and condensed into the little horror that dangled its black and shiny feet over the edge of the desk.

Prentiss wondered in a detached sort of way that he bothered talking to it. This was the first time his profession had so crudely affected his dreams. It *must* be a dream, he told himself.

"I'm an Avalonian," said the being. "I'm from Avalon, in other words." Its tiny face ended in a mandibular mouth. Two swaying three-inch antennae rose from a spot above either eye, while the eyes themselves gleamed richly in their many-faceted fashion. There was no sign of nostrils.

Naturally not, thought Prentiss wildly. It has to breathe through vents in its abdomen. It must be talking with its abdomen then. Or using telepathy.

"Avalon?" he said stupidly. He thought: Avalon? The land of the fay in King Arthur's time?

"Certainly," said the creature, answering the thought smoothly. "I'm an elf."

"Oh, no!" Prentiss put his hands to his face, took them away and found the elf still there, its feet thumping against the top drawer. Prentiss was not a drinking man, or a nervous one. In fact, he was considered a very prosaic sort of person by his neighbors. He had a comfortable paunch, a reasonable but not excessive amount of hair on his head, an amiable wife and an active ten-year-old son. His neighbors were, of course, kept ignorant of the fact that he paid off the mortgage on his house by writing fantasies of one sort or another.

Till now, however, this secret vice had never affected his psyche. To be sure, his wife had shaken her head over his addiction many times. It was her standard opinion that he was wasting, even perverting, his talents.

"Who on Earth reads these things?" she would say. "All that stuff about demons and gnomes and wishing rings and elves. All that *kid* stuff, if you want my frank opinion."

"You're quite wrong," Prentiss would reply stiffly. "Modern fantasies are very sophisticated and mature treatments of folk motifs. Behind the façade of glib unreality there frequently lie trenchant comments on the world of today. Fantasy in modern style is, above all, adult fare."

Blanche shrugged. She had heard him speak at conventions, so these comments weren't new to her.

"Besides," he would add, "fantasies pay the mortgage, don't they?"

"Maybe so," she would reply, "but it would be nice if you'd switch to mysteries. At least you'd get quarter-reprint sales out of those and we could even tell the neighbors what you do for a living."

Prentiss groaned in spirit. Blanche could come in now at any time and find him talking to himself (it was too real for a dream; it might be a hallucination). After that he *would* have to write mysteries for a living—or take to work.

"You're quite wrong," said the elf. "This is neither a dream nor a hallucination."

"Then why don't you go away?" asked Prentiss.

"I intend to. This is scarcely my idea of a place to live. And you're coming with me."

"I am *not*. What the hell do you think you are, telling me what I'm going to do?"

"If you think that's a respectful way to speak to a representative of an older culture, I can't say much for your upbringing."

"You're not an older culture——" He wanted to add: You're just a figment of my imagination; but he had been a writer too long to be able to bring himself to commit the cliché.

"We insects," said the elf freezingly, "existed half a billion years before the first mammal was invented. We watched the dinosaurs come in and we watched them go out. As for you man-things—strictly newcomers."

For the first time, Prentiss noted that, from the spot on the elf's body where its limbs sprouted, a third vestigial pair existed as well. It increased the insecticity of the object and Prentiss' sense of indignation grew.

He said, "You needn't waste your company on social inferiors."

"I wouldn't," said the elf, "believe me. But necessity drives, you know. It's a rather complicated story but when you hear it, you'll *want* to help."

Prentiss said uneasily, "Look, I don't have much time. Blanche—my wife will be in here any time. She'll be upset."

"She won't be here," said the elf. "I've set up a block in her mind."

"What!"

"Quite harmless, I assure you. But, after all, we can't afford to be disturbed, can we?"

Prentiss sat back in his chair, dazed and unhappy.

The elf said, "We elves began our association with you man-things immediately after the last ice age began. It had been a miserable time for us, as you can imagine. We couldn't wear animal carcasses or live in holes as your uncouth ancestors did. It took incredible stores of psychic energy to keep warm."

"Incredible stores of what?"

"Psychic energy. You know nothing at all about it. Your mind is too coarse to grasp the concept. Please don't interrupt."

The elf continued, "Necessity drove us to experiment with your people's brains. They were crude, but large. The cells were inefficient, almost worthless, but there were a vast number of them. We could use those brains as a concentrating device, a type of psychic lens, and increase the available energy which our own minds could tap. We survived the ice age handily and without having to retreat to the tropics as in previous such eras.

"Of course, we were spoiled. When warmth returned, we didn't abandon the man-things. We used them to increase our standard of living generally. We could travel faster, eat better, do more, and we lost our old, simple, virtuous way of life forever. Then, too, there was milk."

"Milk?" said Prentiss. "I don't see the connection."

"A divine liquid. I only tasted it once in my life. But elfin classic poetry speaks of it in superlatives. In the old days, men always supplied us plentifully. Why mammals of all things should be blessed with it and insects not is a complete mystery. . . . How unfortunate it is that the men-things got out of hand."

"They did?"

"Two hundred years ago."

"Good for us."

"Don't be narrow-minded," said the elf stiffly. "It was a useful association for all parties until you man-things learned to handle physical energies in quantity. It was just the sort of gross thing your minds are capable of."

"What was wrong with it?"

"It's hard to explain. It was all very well for us to light up our nightly revels with fireflies brightened by use of two manpower of psychic energy. But then you men-creatures installed electric lights. Our antennal reception is good for miles, but then you invented telegraphs, telephones and radios. Our kobolds mined ore with much greater efficiency than man-things do, until man-things invented dynamite. Do you see?"

"No."

"Surely you don't expect sensitive and superior creatures such as the elves to watch a group of hairy mammals outdo them. It wouldn't be so bad if we could imitate the electronic development ourselves, but our psychic energies were insufficient for the purpose. Well, we retreated from reality. We sulked, pined and drooped. Call it an inferiority complex, if you will, but from two centuries ago onward, we slowly abandoned mankind and retreated to such centers as Avalon."

Prentiss thought furiously. "Let's get this straight. You can handle minds?"

"Certainly."

"You can make me think you're invisible? Hypnotically, I mean?"

"A crude term, but yes."

"And when you appeared just now, you did it by lifting a kind of mental block. Is that it?"

"To answer your thoughts, rather than your words: You are not sleeping; you are not mad; and I am not supernatural."

"I was just making sure. I take it, then, you can read my mind."

"Of course. It is a rather dirty and unrewarding sort of labor, but I can do it when I must. Your name is Prentiss and you write imaginative fiction. You have one larva who is at a place of instruction. I know a great deal about you."

Prentiss winced. "And just where is Avalon?"

"You won't find it." The elf clacked his mandibles together two or three times. "Don't speculate on the possibility of warning the authorities. You'll find yourself in a madhouse. Avalon, in case you think the knowledge will help you, is in the middle of the Atlantic and quite invisible, you know. After the steamboat was invented, you man-things got to moving about so unreasonably that we had to cloak the whole island with a psychic shield.

"Of course, incidents *will* take place. Once a huge, barbaric vessel hit us dead center and it took all the psychic energy of the entire population to give the island the appearance of an iceberg. The *Titanic*, I believe, was the name printed on the vessel. And nowadays there are planes flying overhead all the time and sometimes there are crashes. We picked up cases of canned milk once. That's when I tasted it."

Prentiss said, "Well, then, damn it, why aren't you still on Avalon? Why did you leave?"

"I was ordered to leave," said the elf angrily. "The fools."

"Oh?"

"You know how it is when you're a little different. I'm not like the rest of them and the poor tradition-ridden fools resented it. They were jealous. That's the best explanation. Jealous!"

"How are you different?"

"Hand me that light bulb," said the elf. "Oh, just unscrew it. You don't need a reading lamp in the daytime."

With a quiver of repulsion, Prentiss did as he was told and passed the object into the little hands of the elf. Carefully, the elf, with fingers so thin and wiry that they looked like tendrils, touched the bottom and side of the brass base.

Feebly, the filament in the bulb reddened.

"Good God," said Prentiss.

"That," said the elf proudly, "is my great talent. I told you that we elves couldn't adapt psychic energy to electronics. Well, I can! I'm not just an ordinary elf. I'm a mutant! A super-elf! I'm the next stage in elfin evolution. This light is due just to the activity of my own mind, you know. Now watch when I use yours as a focus."

As he said that, the bulb's filament grew white hot and painful to look at, while a vague and not unpleasant tickling sensation entered Prentiss' skull.

The lamp went out and the elf put the bulb on the desk behind the typewriter.

"I haven't tried," said the elf proudly, "but I suspect I can fission uranium too."

"But look here, lighting a bulb takes energy. You can't just hold it—"

"I've *told* you about psychic energy. Great Oberon, man-thing, try to understand."

Prentiss felt increasingly uneasy; he said cautiously, "What do you intend doing with this gift of yours?"

"Go back to Avalon, of course. I *should* let those fools go to their doom, but an elf does have a certain patriotism, even if he *is* a coleopteron."

"A what?"

"We elves are not all of a species, you know. I'm of beetle descent. See?"

He rose to his feet and, standing on the desk, turned his back to Prentiss. What had seemed merely a shining black cuticle suddenly split and lifted. From underneath, two filmy, veined wings fluttered out.

"Oh, you can fly," said Prentiss.

"You're very foolish," said the elf contemptuously, "not to realize I'm too large for flight. But they *are* attractive, aren't they? How do you like the iridescence? The lepidoptera have disgusting wings in comparison. They're gaudy and indelicate. What's more they're always sticking out."

"The lepidoptera?" Prentiss felt hopelessly confused.

"The butterfly clans. They're the proud ones. They were always letting humans see them so they could be admired. Very petty minds in a way. And that's why your legends always give fairies butterfly wings instead of beetle wings which are *much* more diaphanously beautiful. We'll give the lepidoptera what for when we get back, you and I."

"Now hold on—"

"Just think," said the elf, swaying back and forth in what looked like elfin ecstasy, "our nightly revels on the fairy green will be a blaze of sparkling light from curlicues of neon tubing. We can cut loose the swarms of wasps we've got hitched to our flying wagons and install internal-combustion motors instead. We can stop this business of curling up on leaves when it's time to sleep and build factories to manufacture decent mattresses. I tell you, we'll *live*. . . . And the rest of them will eat dirt for having ordered me out."

"But I can't go with you," bleated Prentiss. "I have responsibilities. I have a wife and kid. You wouldn't take a man away from his—his larva, would you?"

"I'm not cruel," said the elf. He turned his eyes full on Prentiss. "I have an elfin soul. Still, what choice have I? I must have a man-brain for focusing purposes or I will accomplish nothing; and not all man-brains are suitable."

"Why not?"

"Great Oberon, creature. A man-brain isn't a passive thing of wood and stone. It must co-operate in order to be useful. And it can only co-operate by being fully aware of our own elfin ability to manipulate it. I can use your brain, for instance, but your wife's would be useless to me. It would take her years to understand who and what I am."

Prentiss said, "This is a damned insult. Are you telling me I believe in fairies? I'll have you know I'm a complete rationalist."

"Are you? When I first revealed myself to you, you had a few feeble thoughts about dreams and hallucinations but you talked to me, you accepted me. Your wife would have screamed and gone into hysterics."

Prentiss was silent. He could think of no answer.

"That's the trouble," said the elf despondently. "Practically all you humans have forgotten about us since we left you. Your minds have closed; grown useless. To be sure, your larvae believe in your legends about the 'little folk,' but their brains are undeveloped and useful only for simple processes. When they mature, they lose belief. Frankly, I don't know what I would do if it weren't for you fantasy writers."

"What do you mean, we fantasy writers?"

"You are the few remaining adults who believe in the insect folk. You, Prentiss, most of all. You've been a fantasy writer for twenty years."

"You're mad. I don't believe the things I write."

"You have to. You can't help it. I mean, while you're actually writing, you take the subject matter seriously. After a while your mind is just naturally cultivated into usefulness. . . . But why argue? I *have* used you. You saw the light bulb brighten. So you see you must come with me."

"But I won't." Prentiss set his limbs stubbornly. "Can you make me against my will?"

"I could, but I might damage you, and I wouldn't want that. Suppose we say this. If you don't agree to come, I could focus a current of high-voltage electricity through your wife. It would be a revolting thing to have to do, but I understand your own people execute enemies of the state in that fashion, so that you would probably find the punishment less horrible than I do. I wouldn't want to seem brutal even to a man-thing."

Prentiss grew conscious of the perspiration matting the short hairs on his temple.

"Wait," he said, "don't do anything like that. Let's talk it over."

The elf shot out his filmy wings, fluttered them and returned them to their case. "Talk, talk, talk. It's tiring. Surely you have milk in the house. You're not a very thoughtful host or you would have offered me refreshment before this."

Prentiss tried to bury the thought that came to him, to push it as far below the outer skin of his mind as he could. He said casually, "I have something better than milk. Here, I'll get it for you."

"Stay where you are. Call to your wife. She'll bring it."

"But I don't want her to see you. It would frighten her."

The elf said, "You need feel no concern. I'll handle her so that she won't be the least disturbed."

Prentiss lifted an arm.

The elf said, "Any attack you make on me will be far slower than the bolt of electricity that will strike your wife."

Prentiss' arm dropped. He stepped to the door of his study.

"Blanche!" he called down the stairs.

Blanche was just visible in the living room, sitting woodenly in the armchair near the bookcase. She seemed to be asleep, open-eyed.

Prentiss turned to the elf. "Something's wrong with her."

"She's just in a state of sedation. She'll hear you. Tell her what to do."

"Blanche!" he called again. "Bring the container of eggnog and a small glass, will you?"

With no sign of animation other than that of bare movement, Blanche rose and disappeared from view.

"What is eggnog?" asked the elf.

Prentiss attempted enthusiasm. "It is a compound of milk, sugar and eggs beaten to a delightful consistency. Milk alone is poor stuff compared to it."

Blanche entered with the eggnog. Her pretty face was expressionless. Her eyes turned toward the elf but lightened with no realization of the significance of the sight.

"Here, Jan," she said, and sat down in the old, leather-covered chair by the window, hands falling loosely to her lap.

Prentiss watched her uneasily for a moment. "Are you going to keep her here?"

"She'll be easier to control. . . . Well, aren't you going to offer me the eggnog?"

"Oh, sure. Here!"

He poured the thick white liquid into the cocktail glass. He had prepared five milk bottles of it two nights before for the boys of the New York Fantasy Association and it had been mixed with a lavish hand, since fantasy writers notoriously like it so.

The elf's antennae trembled violently.

"A heavenly aroma," he muttered.

He wrapped the ends of his thin arms about the stem of the small glass and lifted it to his mouth. The liquid's level sank. When half was gone, he put it down and sighed, "Oh, the loss to my people. What a creation! What a thing to exist! Our histories tell us that in ancient days an occasional lucky sprite managed to take the place of a man-larva at birth so that he might draw off the liquid fresh-made. I wonder if even those ever experienced anything like this."

Prentiss said with a touch of professional interest, "That's the idea behind this business of changelings, is it?"

"Of course. The female man-creature has a great gift. Why not take advantage of it?" The elf turned his eyes upon the rise and fall of Blanche's bosom and sighed again.

Prentiss said (not too eager, now; don't give it away), "Go ahead. Drink all you want."

He, too, watched Blanche, waiting for signs of restoring animation, waiting for the beginnings of breakdown in the elf's control.

The elf said, "When is your larva returning from its place of instruction? I need him."

"Soon, soon," said Prentiss nervously. He looked at his wristwatch. Actually, Jan, Junior, would be back, yelling for a slab of cake and milk, in something like fifteen minutes.

"Fill 'er up," he said urgently. "Fill 'er up."

The elf sipped gaily. He said, "Once the larva arrives, you can go."

"Go?"

"Only to the library. You'll have to get volumes on electronics. I'll need the details on how to build television, telephones, all that. I'll need to have rules on wiring, instructions for constructing vacuum tubes. Details, Prentiss, details! We have tremendous tasks ahead of us. Oil drilling, gasoline refining, motors, scientific agriculture. We'll build a new Avalon, you and I. A technical one. A scientific fairyland. We will create a new world."

"Great!" said Prentiss. "Here, don't neglect your drink."

"You see. You are catching fire with the idea," said the elf. "And you will be rewarded. You will have a dozen female man-things to yourself."

Prentiss looked at Blanche automatically. No signs of hearing, but who could tell? He said, "I'd have no use for female man-th—for women, I mean."

"Come now," said the elf censoriously, "be truthful. You men-things are well known to our folk as lecherous, bestial creatures. Mothers frightened their young for generations by threatening them with men-things. . . . Young, ah!" He lifted the glass of eggnog in the air and said, "To my own young," and drained it.

"Fill 'er up," said Prentiss at once. "Fill 'er up."

The elf did so. He said, "I'll have lots of children. I'll pick out the best of the coleoptresses and breed my line. I'll continue the mutation. Right now I'm the only one, but when we have a dozen or fifty, I'll interbreed them and develop the race of the super-elf. A race of electro—ulp—electronic marvels and infinite future. . . . If I could only drink more. Nectar! The original nectar!"

There was the sudden noise of a door being flung open and a young voice calling, "Mom! Hey, Mom!"

The elf, his glossy eyes a little dimmed, said, "Then we'll begin to take over the men-things. A few believe already; the rest we will—urp—teach. It will be the old days, but better; a more efficient elfhood, a tighter union."

Jan, Junior's voice was closer and tinged with impatience. "Hey, Mom! Ain't you home?"

Prentiss felt his eyes popping with tension. Blanche sat rigid. The elf's speech was slightly thick, his balance a little unsteady. If Prentiss were going to risk it, now, now was the time.

"Sit back," said the elf peremptorily. "You're being foolish. I knew there was alcohol in the eggnog from the moment you thought your ridiculous scheme. You men-things are very shifty. We elves have many proverbs about you. Fortunately, alcohol has little effect upon us. Now if you had tried catnip with just a touch of honey in it . . . Ah, here is the larva. How are you, little man-thing?"

The elf sat there, the goblet of eggnog halfway to his mandibles, while Jan, Junior stood in the doorway. Jan, Junior's ten-year-old face was moderately smeared with dirt, his hair was immoderately matted and there was a look of the utmost surprise in his gray eyes. His battered schoolbooks swayed from the end of the strap he held in his hand.

He said, "Pop! What's the matter with Mom? And—and what's that?"

The elf said to Prentiss, "Hurry to the library. No time must be lost. You know the books I need." All trace of incipient drunkenness had left the creature and Prentiss' morale broke. The creature had been playing with him.

Prentiss got up to go.

The elf said, "And nothing human; nothing sneaky; no tricks. Your wife is still a hostage. I can use the larva's mind to kill her; it's good enough for that. I wouldn't want to do it. I'm a member of the Elfitarian Ethical Society and we advocate considerate treatment of mammals so you may rely on my noble principles *if* you do as I say."

Prentiss felt a strong compulsion to leave flooding him. He stumbled toward the door.

Jan, Junior cried, "Pop, it can talk! He says he'll kill Mom! Hey, don't go away!"

Prentiss was already out of the room, when he heard the elf say, "Don't stare at me, larva. I will not harm your mother if you do exactly as I say. I am an elf, a fairy. You know what a fairy is, of course."

And Prentiss was at the front door when he heard Jan, Junior's treble raised in wild shouting, followed by scream after scream in Blanche's shuddering soprano.

The strong, though invisible, elastic that was drawing Prentiss out the house snapped and vanished. He fell backward, righted himself and darted back up the stairs.

Blanche, fairly saturated with quivering life, was backed into a corner, her arms about a weeping Jan, Junior.

On the desk was a collapsed black carapace, covering a nasty smear of pulpiness from which colorless liquid dripped.

Jan, Junior was sobbing hysterically, "I hit it. I hit it with my schoolbooks. It was hurting Mom."

An hour passed and Prentiss felt the world of normality pouring back into the interstices left behind by the creature from Avalon. The elf itself was already ash in the incinerator behind the house and the only remnant of its existence was the damp stain at the foot of his desk.

Blanche was still sickly pale. They talked in whispers.

Prentiss said, "How's Jan, Junior?"

"He's watching television."

"Is he all right?"

"Oh, *he*'s all right, but *I'll* be having nightmares for weeks."

"I know. So will I unless we can get it out of our minds. I don't think there'll ever be another of those—things here."

Blanche said, "I can't explain how awful it was. I kept hearing every word he said, even when I was down in the living room."

"It was telepathy, you see."

"I just couldn't move. Then, after you left, I could begin to stir a bit. I tried to scream but all I could do was moan and whimper. Then Jan, Junior smashed him and all at once I was free. I don't understand how it happened."

Prentiss felt a certain gloomy satisfaction. "I think I know. I was under his control because I accepted the truth of his existence. He held you in check through me. When I left the room, increasing distance made it harder to use my mind as a psychic lens and you could begin moving. By the time I reached the front door, the elf thought it was time to switch from my mind to Jan, Junior's. That was his mistake."

"In what way?" asked Blanche.

"He assumed that all children believe in fairies, but he was wrong. Here in America today children *don't* believe in fairies. They never hear of them. They believe in Tom Corbett, in Hopalong Cassidy, in Dick Tracy, in Howdy Doody, in Superman and a dozen other things, but not in fairies.

"The elf just never realized the sudden cultural changes brought about by comic books and television, and when he tried to grab Jan, Junior's mind, he couldn't. Before he could recover his psychic balance, Jan, Junior was on top of him in a swinging panic because he thought you were being hurt and it was all over.

"It's like I've always said, Blanche. The ancient folk motifs of legend survive only in the modern fantasy magazine, and modern fantasy is purely adult fare. Do you finally see my point?"

Blanche said humbly, "Yes, dear."

Prentiss put his hands in his pockets and grinned slowly. "You know, Blanche, next time I see Walt Rae, I think I'll just drop a hint that I write the stuff. Time the neighbors knew, I think."

Jan, Junior, holding an enormous slice of buttered bread, wandered into his father's study in search of the dimming memory. Pop kept slapping him on the back and Mom kept putting bread and cake in his hands and he was forgetting why. There had been this big old thing on the desk that could talk . . .

It had all happened so quickly that it got mixed up in his mind.

He shrugged his shoulders and, in the late afternoon sunlight, looked at the partly typewritten sheet in his father's typewriter, then at the small pile of paper resting on the desk.

He read a while, curled his lip and muttered, "Gee whiz. Fairies again. Always kid stuff!" and wandered off.

THE WATERY PLACE

We're never going to have space travel. What's more, no extraterrestrials will ever land on Earth—at least, any more.

I'm not just being a pessimist. As a matter of fact, space travel *is* possible; extraterrestrials *have* landed. I *know* that. Space ships are crisscrossing space among a million worlds, probably, but we'll never join them. I know that, too. All on account of a ridiculous error.

I'll explain.

It was actually Bart Cameron's error and you'll have to understand about Bart Cameron. He's the sheriff at Twin Gulch, Idaho, and I'm his deputy. Bart Cameron is an impatient man and he gets most impatient when he has to work up his income tax. You see, besides being sheriff, he also owns and runs the general store, he's got some shares in a sheep ranch, he does a bit of assay work, he's got a kind of pension for being a disabled veteran (bad knee) and a few other things like that. Naturally, it makes his tax figures complicated.

It wouldn't be so bad if he'd let a tax man work on the forms with him, but he insists on doing it himself and it makes him a bitter man. By April 14, he isn't approachable.

So it's too bad the flying saucer landed on April 14, 1956.

I saw it land. My chair was backed up against the wall in the sheriff's office, and I was looking at the stars through the windows and feeling too lazy to go back to my magazine and wondering if I ought to knock off and hit the sack or keep on listening to Cameron curse real steady as he went over his columns of figures for the hundred twenty-seventh time.

It looked like a shooting star at first, but then the track of light broadened into two things that looked like rocket exhausts and the thing came down sweet, steady and without a sound. An old, dead leaf would have rustled more coming down and landed thumpier. Two men got out.

I couldn't say anything or do anything. I couldn't choke or point; I couldn't even bug my eyes. I just sat there.

Cameron? He never looked up.

There was a knock on the door which wasn't locked. It opened and the two men from the flying saucer stepped in. I would have thought they were city fellows if I hadn't seen the flying saucer land in the scrub. They wore charcoal-gray suits, with white shirts and maroon four-in-hands. They had on black shoes and black homburgs.

They had dark complexions, black wavy hair and brown eyes. They had very serious looks on their faces and were about five foot ten apiece. They looked very much alike.

God, I was scared.

But Cameron just looked up when the door opened and frowned. Ordinarily, I guess he'd have laughed the collar button off his shirt at seeing clothes like that in Twin Gulch, but he was so taken up by his income tax that he never cracked a smile.

He said, "What can I do for you, folks?" and he tapped his hand on the forms so it was obvious he hadn't much time.

One of the two stepped forward. He said, "We have had your people under observation a long time." He pronounced each word carefully and all by itself.

Cameron said, "My people? All I got's a wife. What's she been doing?"

The fellow in the suit said, "We have chosen this locality for our first contact because it is isolated and peaceful. We know that you are the leader here."

"I'm the sheriff, if that's what you mean, so spit it out. What's your trouble?"

"We have been careful to adopt your mode of dress and even to assume your appearance."

"That's *my* mode of dress?" He must have noticed it for the first time.

"The mode of dress of your dominant social class, that is. We have also learned your language."

You could see the light break in on Cameron. He said, "You guys foreigners?" Cameron didn't go much for foreigners, never having met many outside the army, but generally he tried to be fair.

The man from the saucer said, "Foreigners? Indeed we are. We come from the watery place your people call Venus."

(I was just collecting up strength to blink my eyes, but that sent me right back to nothing. I had seen the flying saucer. I had seen it land. I had to believe this! These men—or these somethings—came from Venus.)

But Cameron never blinked an eye. He said, "All right. This is the U.S.A. We all got equal rights regardless of race, creed, color, *or* nationality. I'm at your service. What can I do for you?"

"We would like to have you make immediate arrangements for the important men of your U.S.A., as you call it, to be brought here for discussions leading to your people joining our great organization."

Slowly, Cameron got red. "Our people join *your* organization.

We're already part of the UN and God knows what else. And I suppose I'm to get the President here, eh? Right now? In Twin Gulch? Send a hurry-up message?" He looked at me, as though he wanted to see a smile on my face, but I couldn't as much as fall down if someone had pushed the chair out from under me.

The saucer man said, "Speed is desirable."

"You want Congress, too? The Supreme Court?"

"If they will help, sheriff."

And Cameron really went to pieces. He banged his income tax form and yelled, "Well, you're not helping me, and I have no time for wise-guy jerks who come around, especially foreigners. If you don't get the hell out of here pronto, I'll lock you up for disturbing the peace and I'll never let you out."

"You wish us to leave?" said the man from Venus.

"Right now! Get the hell out of here and back to wherever you're from and don't ever come back. I don't want to see you and no one else around here does."

The two men looked at each other, making little twitches with their faces.

Then the one who had done all the talking said, "I can see in your mind that you really wish, with great intensity, to be left alone. It is not our way to force ourselves or our organization on people who do not wish us or it. We will respect your privacy and leave. We will not return. We will girdle your world in warning and none will enter and your people will never have to leave."

Cameron said, "Mister, I'm tired of this crap, so I'll count to three——"

They turned and left, and I just knew that everything they said was so. I was listening to them, you see, which Cameron wasn't, because he was busy thinking of his income tax, and it was as though I could hear their minds, know what I mean? I knew that there would be a kind of fence around earth, corralling us in, keeping us from leaving, keeping others from coming in. I *knew* it.

And when they left, I got my voice back—too late. I screamed, "Cameron, for God's sake, they're from space. Why'd you send them away?"

"From space!" He stared at me.

I yelled, "Look!" I don't know how I did it, he being twenty-five pounds heavier than I, but I yanked him to the window by his shirt collar, busting every shirt button off him.

He was too surprised to resist and when he recovered his wits enough to make like he was going to knock me down, he caught sight of what was going on outside the window and the breath went out of *him.*

They were getting into the flying saucer, those two men, and the saucer sat there, large, round, shiny and kind of powerful, you know. Then it took off. It went up easy as a feather and a red-orange glow showed up on one side and got brighter as the ship got smaller till it was a shooting star again, slowly fading out.

And I said, "Sheriff, why'd you send them away? They *had* to see the President. Now they'll never come back."

Cameron said, "I thought they were foreigners. They *said* they had to learn our language. And they talked funny."

"Oh, fine. Foreigners."

"They *said* they were foreigners and they looked Italian. I thought they were Italian."

"How could they be Italian? They said they were from the planet Venus. I heard them. They said so."

"The planet Venus." His eyes got real round.

"They said it. They called it the watery place or something. You know Venus has a lot of water on it."

But you see, it was just an error, a stupid error, the kind anyone could make. Only now Earth is never going to have space travel and we'll never as much as land on the moon or have another Venusian visit us. That dope, Cameron, and his income tax!

Because he whispered, "Venus! When they talked about the watery place, I thought they meant V*enice!*"

LIVING SPACE

Clarence Rimbro had no objections to living in the only house on an uninhabited planet, any more than had any other of Earth's even trillion of inhabitants.

If someone had questioned him concerning possible objections, he would undoubtedly have stared blankly at the questioner. His house was much larger than any house could possibly be on Earth proper and much more modern. It had its independent air supply and water supply; ample food in its freezing compartments. It was isolated from the lifeless planet on which it was located by a force field, but the rooms were built about a five-acre farm (under glass, of course), which, in the planet's beneficent sunlight, grew flowers for pleasure and vegetables for health. It even supported a few chickens. It gave Mrs. Rimbro something to do with herself afternoons, and a place for the two little Rimbros to play when they were tired of indoors.

Furthermore, if one *wanted* to be on Earth proper; if one insisted on it; if one *had* to have people around and air one could breathe in the open or water to swim in, one had only to go out of the front door of the house.

So where was the difficulty?

Remember, too, that on the lifeless planet on which the Rimbro house was located there was complete silence except for the occasional monotonous effects of wind and rain. There was absolute privacy and the feeling of absolute ownership of two hundred million square miles of planetary surface.

Clarence Rimbro appreciated all that in his distant way. He was an accountant, skilled in handling very advanced computer models, precise in his manners and clothing, not much given to smiling beneath his thin, well-kept mustache and properly aware of his own worth. When he drove from work toward home, he passed the occasional dwelling place on Earth proper and he never ceased to stare at them with a certain smugness.

Well, either for business reasons or mental perversion, some people simply had to live on Earth proper. It was too bad for them. After all, Earth proper's soil had to supply the minerals and basic food supply for all the trillion of inhabitants (in fifty years, it would be two trillion) and space was at a premium. Houses on Earth proper just *couldn't* be any bigger than that, and people who had to live in them had to adjust to the fact.

Even the process of entering his house had its mild pleasantness. He would enter the community twist place to which he was assigned (it looked, as did all such, like a rather stumpy obelisk), and there he would invariably find others waiting to use it. Still more would arrive before he reached the head of the line. It was a sociable time.

"How's your planet?" "How's yours?" The usual small talk. Sometimes someone would be having trouble. Machinery breakdowns or serious weather that would alter the terrain unfavorably. Not often.

But it passed the time. Then Rimbro would be at the head of the line; he would put his key into the slot; the proper combination would be punched; and he would be twisted into a new probability pattern; his own particular probability pattern; the one assigned to him when he married and became a producing citizen; a probability pattern in which life had never developed on Earth. And twisting to this particular lifeless Earth, he would walk into his own foyer.

Just like that.

He never worried about being in another probability. Why should he? He never gave it any thought. There were an infinite number of possible Earths. Each existed in its own niche; its own probability pattern. Since on a planet such as Earth there was, according to calculation, about a fifty-fifty chance of life's developing, half of all the possible Earths (still infinite, since half of infinity was infinity) possessed life, and half (still infinite) did not. And living on about three hundred billion of the unoccupied Earths were three hundred billion families, each with its own beautiful house, powered by the sun of that probability, and each securely at peace. The number of Earths so occupied grew by millions each day.

And then one day, Rimbro came home and Sandra (his wife) said to him, as he entered, "There's been the most peculiar noise."

Rimbro's eyebrows shot up and he looked closely at his wife. Except for a certain restlessness of her thin hands and a pale look about the corners of her tight mouth, she looked normal.

Rimbro said, still holding his topcoat halfway toward the servette that waited patiently for it, "Noise? What noise? I don't hear anything."

"It's stopped now," Sandra said. "Really, it was like a deep thumping or rumble. You'd hear it a bit. Then it would stop. Then you'd hear it a bit and so on. I've never heard anything like it."

Rimbro surrendered his coat. "But that's quite impossible."

"I *heard* it."

"I'll look over the machinery," he mumbled. "Something may be wrong."

Nothing was, that his accountant's eyes could discover, and, with a shrug, he went to supper. He listened to the servettes hum busily about their different chores, watched one sweep up the plates and cutlery for disposal and recovery, then said, pursing his lips, "Maybe one of the servettes is out of order. I'll check them."

"It wasn't anything like that, Clarence."

Rimbro went to bed, without further concern over the matter, and wakened with his wife's hand clutching his shoulder. His hand went automatically to the contact patch that set the walls glowing. "What's the matter? What time is it?"

She shook her head. "Listen! *Listen!*"

Good Lord, thought Rimbro, there *is* a noise. A definite rumbling. It came and went.

"Earthquake?" he whispered. It did happen, of course, though, with all the planet to choose from, they could generally count on having avoided the faulted areas.

"All day long?" asked Sandra fretfully. "I think it's something else." And then she voiced the secret terror of every nervous householder. "I think there's someone on the planet with us. This Earth is *inhabited.*"

Rimbro did the logical things. When morning came, he took his wife and children to his wife's mother. He himself took a day off and hurried to the Sector's Housing Bureau.

He was quite annoyed at all this.

Bill Ching of the Housing Bureau was short, jovial and proud of his part-Mongolian ancestry. He thought probability patterns had solved every last one of humanity's problems. Alec Mishnoff, also of the Housing Bureau, thought probability patterns were a snare into which humanity had been hopelessly tempted. He had originally majored in archeology and had studied a variety of antiquarian subjects with which his delicately poised head was still crammed. His face managed to look sensitive despite overbearing eyebrows, and he lived with a pet notion that so far he had dared tell no one, though preoccupation with it had driven him out of archeology and into housing.

Ching was fond of saying, "The hell with Malthus!" It was almost a verbal trademark of his, "The hell with Malthus. We can't possibly overpopulate now. However frequently we double and redouble, Homo sapiens remains finite in number, and the uninhabited Earths remain infinite. And we don't have to put one house on each planet.

We can put a hundred, a thousand, a million. Plenty of room and plenty of power from each probability sun."

"More than one on a planet?" said Mishnoff sourly.

Ching knew exactly what he meant. When probability patterns had first been put to use, sole ownership of a planet had been powerful inducement for early settlers. It appealed to the snob and despot in every one. What man so poor, ran the slogan, as not to have an empire larger than Genghis Khan's? To introduce multiple settling now would outrage everyone.

Ching said, with a shrug, "All right, it would take psychological preparation. So what? That's what it took to start the whole deal in the first place."

"And food?" asked Mishnoff.

"You know we're putting hydroponic works and yeast plants in other probability patterns. And if we had to, we could cultivate their soil."

"Wearing space suits and importing oxygen."

"We could reduce carbon dioxide for oxygen till the plants got going and they'd do the job after that."

"Given a million years."

"Mishnoff, the trouble with you," Ching said, "is you read too many ancient history books. You're an obstructionist."

But Ching was too good-natured really to mean that, and Mishnoff continued to read books and to worry. Mishnoff longed for the day he could get up the courage necessary to see the Head of the Section and put right out in plain view—bang, like that—exactly what it was that was troubling him.

But now a Mr. Clarence Rimbro faced them, perspiring slightly and toweringly angry at the fact that it had taken him the better part of two days to reach this far into the Bureau.

He reached his exposition's climax by saying, "And *I* say the planet is inhabited and I don't propose to stand for it."

Having listened to his story in full, Ching tried the soothing approach. He said, "Noise like that is probably just some natural phenomenon."

"What kind of natural phenomenon?" demanded Rimbro. "I want an investigation. If it's a natural phenomenon, I want to know what kind. I say the place is inhabited. It has life on it, by Heaven, and I'm not paying rent on a planet to share it. And with dinosaurs, from the sound of it."

"Come, Mr. Rimbro, how long have you lived on your earth?"

"Fifteen and a half years."

"And has there ever been any evidence of life?"

"There is now, and, as a citizen with a production record classified as A-1, I demand an investigation."

"Of course we'll investigate, sir, but we just want to assure you now that everything is all right. Do you realize how carefully we select our probability patterns?"

"I'm an accountant. I have a pretty good idea," said Rimbro at once.

"Then surely you know our computers cannot fail us. They never pick a probability which has been picked before. They can't possibly. And they're geared to select only probability patterns in which Earth has a carbon dioxide atmosphere, one in which plant life, and therefore animal life, has never developed. Because if plants had evolved, the carbon dioxide would have been reduced to oxygen. Do you understand?"

"I understand it all very well and I'm not here for lectures," said Rimbro. "I want an investigation out of you and nothing else. It is quite humiliating to think I may be sharing my world, my own world, with something or other, and I don't propose to endure it."

"No, of course not," muttered Ching, avoiding Mishnoff's sardonic glance. "We'll be there before night."

They were on their way to the twisting place with full equipment.

Mishnoff said, "I want to ask you something. Why do you go through that 'There's no need to worry, sir' routine? They always worry anyway. Where does it get you?"

"I've got to try. They *shouldn't* worry," said Ching petulantly. "Ever hear of a carbon dioxide planet that *was* inhabited? Besides, Rimbro is the type that starts rumors. I can spot them. By the time he's through, if he's encouraged, he'll say his sun went nova."

"*That* happens sometimes," said Mishnoff.

"So? One house is wiped out and one family dies. See, you're an obstructionist. In the old times, the times you like, if there were a flood in China or someplace, thousands of people would die. And that's out of a population of a measly billion or two."

Mishnoff muttered, "How do you know the Rimbro planet doesn't have life on it?"

"Carbon dioxide atmosphere."

"But suppose——" It was no use. Mishnoff couldn't say it. He finished lamely, "Suppose plant and animal life develops that can live on carbon dioxide."

"It's never been observed."

"In an infinite number of worlds, anything can happen." He finished that in a whisper. "Everything *must* happen."

"Chances are one in a duodecillion," said Ching, shrugging.

They arrived at the twisting point then, and, having utilized the freight twist for their vehicle (thus sending it into the Rimbro storage area), they entered the Rimbro probability pattern themselves. First Ching, then Mishnoff.

"A nice house," said Ching, with satisfaction. "Very nice model. Good taste."

"Hear anything?" asked Mishnoff.

"No."

Ching wandered into the garden. "Hey," he yelled. "Rhode Island Reds."

Mishnoff followed, looking up at the glass roof. The sun looked like the sun of a trillion other Earths.

He said absently, "There could be plant life, just starting out. The carbon dioxide might just be starting to drop in concentration. The computer would never know."

"And it would take millions of years for animal life to begin and millions more for it to come out of the sea."

"It doesn't have to follow that pattern."

Ching put an arm about his partner's shoulder. "You brood. Someday, you'll tell me what's really bothering you, instead of just hinting, and we can straighten you out."

Mishnoff shrugged off the encircling arm with an annoyed frown. Ching's tolerance was always hard to bear. He began, "Let's not psychotherapize——" He broke off, then whispered, "Listen."

There was a distant rumble. Again.

They placed the seismograph in the center of the room and activated the force field that penetrated downward and bound it rigidly to bedrock. They watched the quivering needle record the shocks.

Mishnoff said, "Surface waves only. Very superficial. It's not underground."

Ching looked a little more dismal, "What is it then?"

"I think," said Mishnoff, "we'd better find out." His face was gray with apprehension. "We'll have to set up a seismograph at another point and get a fix on the focus of the disturbance."

"Obviously," said Ching. "I'll go out with the other seismograph. You stay here."

"No," said Mishnoff, with energy. "*I'll* go out."

Mishnoff felt terrified, but he had no choice. If this were *it*, he would be prepared. He could get a warning through. Sending out an unsuspecting Ching would be disastrous. Nor could he warn Ching, who would certainly never believe him.

But since Mishnoff was not cast in the heroic mold, he trembled as he got into his oxygen suit and fumbled the disrupter as he tried to dissolve the force field locally in order to free the emergency exit.

"Any reason *you* want to go, particularly?" asked Ching, watching the other's inept manipulations. "I'm willing."

"It's all right. I'm going out," said Mishnoff, out of a dry throat, and stepped into the lock that led out onto the desolate surface of a lifeless Earth. A presumably lifeless Earth.

The sight was not unfamiliar to Mishnoff. He had seen its like dozens of times. Bare rock, weathered by wind and rain, crusted and powdered with sand in the gullies; a small and noisy brook beating itself against its stony course. All brown and gray; no sign of green. No sound of life.

Yet the sun was the same and, when night fell, the constellations would be the same.

The situation of the dwelling place was in that region which on Earth proper would be called Labrador. (It was Labrador here, too, really. It had been calculated that in not more than one out of a quadrillion or so Earths were there significant changes in the geological development. The continents were everywhere recognizable down to quite small details.)

Despite the situation and the time of the year, which was October, the temperature was sticky warm due to the hothouse effect of the carbon dioxide in this Earth's dead atmosphere.

From inside his suit, through the transparent visor, Mishnoff watched it all somberly. If the epicenter of the noise were close by, adjusting the second seismograph a mile or so away would be enough for the fix. If it weren't, they would have to bring in an air scooter. Well, assume the lesser complication to begin with.

Methodically, he made his way up a rocky hillside. Once at the top, he could choose his spot.

Once at the top, puffing and feeling the heat most unpleasantly, he found he didn't have to.

His heart was pounding so that he could scarcely hear his own voice as he yelled into his radio mouthpiece, "Hey, Ching, there's construction going on."

"What?" came back the appalled shout in his ears.

There was no mistake. Ground was being leveled. Machinery was at work. Rock was being blasted out.

Mishnoff shouted, "They're blasting. That's the noise."

Ching called back, "But it's impossible. The computer would never pick the same probability pattern twice. *It couldn't.*"

"You don't understand——" began Mishnoff.

But Ching was following his own thought processes. "Get over there, Mishnoff. I'm coming out, too."

"No, damn it. You stay there," cried Mishnoff in alarm. "Keep me in radio contact, and for God's sake be ready to leave for Earth proper on wings if I give the word."

"Why?" demanded Ching. "What's going on?"

"I don't know yet," said Mishnoff. "Give me a chance to find out."

To his own surprise, he noticed his teeth were chattering.

Muttering breathless curses at the computer, at probability patterns and at the insatiable need for living space on the part of a trillion human beings expanding in numbers like a puff of smoke, Mishnoff slithered and slipped down the other side of the slope, setting stones to rolling and rousing peculiar echoes.

A man came out to meet him, dressed in a gas-tight suit, different in many details from Mishnoff's own, but obviously intended for the same purpose—to lead oxygen to the lungs.

Mishnoff gasped breathlessly into his mouthpiece, "Hold it, Ching. There's a man coming. Keep in touch." Mishnoff felt his heart pump more easily and the bellows of his lungs labor less.

The two men were staring at one another. The other man was blond and craggy of face. The look of surprise about him was too extreme to be feigned.

He said in a harsh voice, "*Wer sind Sie? Was machen Sie hier?*"

Mishnoff was thunderstruck. He'd studied ancient German for two years in the days when he expected to be an archaeologist and he followed the comment despite the fact that the pronunciation was not what he had been taught. The stranger was asking his identity and his business there.

Stupidly, Mishnoff stammered, "*Sprechen Sie Deutsch?*" and then had to mutter reassurance to Ching whose agitated voice in his earpiece was demanding to know what the gibberish was all about.

The German-speaking one made no direct answer. He repeated, "*Wer sind Sie?*" and added impatiently, "*Hier ist für ein verrückten Spass keine Zeit.*"

Mishnoff didn't feel like a joke either, particularly not a foolish one, but he continued, "*Sprechen Sie Planetisch?*"

He did not know the German for "Planetary Standard Language" so he had to guess. Too late, he thought he should have referred to it simply as English.

The other man stared wide-eyed at him. "*Sind Sie wahnsinnig?*"

Mishnoff was almost willing to settle for that, but in feeble self-defense, he said, "I'm not crazy, damn it. I mean, "*Auf der Erde woher Sie gekom——*"

He gave it up for lack of German, but the new idea that was rattling inside his skull would not quit its nagging. He had to find some way of testing it. He said desperately, "*Welches Jahr ist es jetzt?*"

Presumably, the stranger, who was questioning his sanity already, would be convinced of Mishnoff's insanity now that he was being asked what year it was, but it was one question for which Mishnoff had the necessary German.

The other muttered something that sounded suspiciously like good German swearing and then said, "*Es ist doch zwei tausend drei hundert vier-und-sechzig, und warum——*"

The stream of German that followed was completely incomprehensible to Mishnoff, but in any case he had had enough for the moment. If he translated the German correctly, the year given him was 2364, which was nearly two thousand years in the past. How could that be?

He muttered, "*Zwei tausend drei hundert vier-und-sechzig?*"

"*Ja, Ja,*" said the other, with deep sarcasm. "*Zwei tausend drei hundert vier-und-sechzig. Der ganze Jahr lang ist es so gewesen.*"

Mishnoff shrugged. The statement that it had been so all year long was a feeble witticism even in German and it gained nothing in translation. He pondered.

But then the other's ironical tone deepening, the German-speaking one went on, "*Zwei tausend drei hundert vier-und-sechzig nach Hitler. Hilft das Ihnen vielleicht? Nach Hitler!*"

Mishnoff yelled with delight. "That *does* help me. *Es hilft! Hören Sie, bitte——*" He went on in broken German interspersed with scraps of Planetary, "For Heaven's sake, *um Gottes willen——*"

Making it 2364 after Hitler was different altogether.

He put German together desperately, trying to explain.

The other frowned and grew thoughtful. He lifted his gloved hand to stroke his chin or make some equivalent gesture, hit the transparent visor that covered his face and left his hand there uselessly, while he thought.

He said, suddenly, "*Ich heiss George Fallenby.*"

To Mishnoff it seemed that the name must be of Anglo-Saxon derivation, although the change in vowel form as pronounced by the other made it seem Teutonic.

"*Guten Tag,*" said Mishnoff awkwardly. "*Ich heiss Alec Mishnoff,*" and was suddenly aware of the Slavic derivation of his own name.

"*Kommen Sie mit mir, Herr Mishnoff,*" said Fallenby.

Mishnoff followed with a strained smile, muttering into his transmitter, "It's all right, Ching. It's all right."

Back on Earth proper, Mishnoff faced the Sector's Bureau Head, who had grown old in the Service; whose every gray hair betokened a problem met and solved; and every missing hair a problem averted. He was a cautious man with eyes still bright and teeth that were still his own. His name was Berg.

He shook his head. "And they speak German: but the German you studied was two thousand years old."

"True," said Mishnoff. "But the English Hemingway used is two thousand years old and Planetary is close enough for anyone to be able to read it."

"Hmp. And who's this Hitler?"

"He was a sort of tribal chief in ancient times. He led the German tribe in one of the wars of the twentieth century, just about the time the Atomic Age started and true history began."

"Before the Devastation, you mean?"

"Right. There was a series of wars then. The Anglo-Saxon countries won out, and I suppose that's why the Earth speaks Planetary."

"And if Hitler and his Germans had won out, the world would speak German instead?"

"They *have* won out on Fallenby's Earth, sir, and they *do* speak German."

"And make their dates 'after Hitler' instead of A.D.?"

"Right. And I suppose there's an Earth in which the Slavic tribes won out and everyone speaks Russian."

"Somehow," said Berg, "it seems to me we should have foreseen it, and yet, as far as I know, no one has. After all, there are an infinite number of inhabited Earths, and we can't be the only one that has decided to solve the problem of unlimited population growth by expanding into the worlds of probability."

"Exactly," said Mishnoff earnestly, "and it seems to me that if you think of it, there must be countless inhabited Earths so doing and there must be many multiple occupations in the three hundred billion Earths we ourselves occupy. The only reason we caught this one is that, by sheer chance, they decided to build within a mile of the dwelling we had placed there. This is something we must check."

"You imply we ought to search all our Earths."

"I do, sir. We've got to make some settlement with other inhabited Earths. After all, there is room for all of us and to expand without agreement may result in all sorts of trouble and conflict."

"Yes," said Berg thoughtfully. "I agree with you."

Clarence Rimbro stared suspiciously at Berg's old face, creased now into all manner of benevolence.

"You're sure now?"

"Absolutely," said the Bureau Head. "We're sorry that you've had to accept temporary quarters for the last two weeks——"

"More like three."

"——three weeks, but you will be compensated."

"What was the noise?"

"Purely geological, sir. A rock was delicately balanced and, with the wind, it made occasional contact with the rocks of the hillside. We've removed it and surveyed the area to make certain that nothing similar will occur again."

Rimbro clutched his hat and said, "Well, thanks for your trouble."

"No thanks necessary, I assure you, Mr. Rimbro. This is our job."

Rimbro was ushered out, and Berg turned to Mishnoff, who had remained a quiet spectator of this completion of the Rimbro affair.

Berg said, "The Germans were nice about it, anyway. They admitted we had priority and got off. Room for everybody, they said. Of course, as it turned out, they build any number of dwellings on each unoccupied world. . . . And now there's the project of surveying our other worlds and making similar agreements with whomever we find. It's all strictly confidential, too. It can't be made known to the populace without plenty of preparation. . . . Still, none of this is what I want to speak to you about."

"Oh?" said Mishnoff. Developments had not noticeably cheered him. His own bogey still concerned him.

Berg smiled at the younger man. "You understand, Mishnoff, we in the bureau, and in the planetary Government, too, are very appreciative of your quick thinking, of your understanding of the situation. This could have developed into something very tragic, had it not been for you. This appreciation will take some tangible form."

"Thank you, sir."

"But, as I said once before, this is something many of us should have thought of. How is it you did? . . . Now we've gone into your background a little. Your co-worker, Ching, tells us you have hinted in the past at some serious danger involved in our probability-pattern setup, and that you insisted on going out to meet the Germans although you were obviously frightened. You were anticipating what you actually found, were you not? And how did you do it?"

Mishnoff said confusedly, "No, no. That was not in my mind at all. It came as a surprise. I——"

Suddenly he stiffened. Why not now? They were grateful to him. He had proved that he was a man to be taken into account. One unexpected thing had already happened.

He said firmly, "There's something else."

"Yes?"

(How did one begin?) "There's no life in the Solar System other than the life on Earth."

"That's right," said Berg benevolently.

"And computation has it that the probability of developing any form of interstellar travel is so low as to be infinitesimal."

"What are you getting at?"

"That all this is so *in this probability!* But there must be some probability patterns in which other life *does* exist in the Solar System or in which interstellar drives *are* developed by dwellers in other star systems."

Berg frowned. "Theoretically."

"In one of these probabilities, Earth may be visited by such intelligences. If it were a probability pattern in which Earth is inhabited, it won't affect us; they'll have no connection with us in Earth proper. But if it were a probability pattern in which Earth is uninhabited and they set up some sort of a base, they may find, by happenstance, one of our dwelling places."

"Why ours?" demanded Berg dryly. "Why not a dwelling place of the Germans, for instance?"

"Because we spot our dwellings one to a world. The German Earth doesn't. Probably very few others do. The odds are in favor of us by billions to one. And if extraterrestrials do find such a dwelling, they'll investigate and find the route to Earth proper, a highly developed, rich world."

"Not if we turn off the twisting place," said Berg.

"Once they know that twisting places exist, they can construct their own," said Mishnoff. "A race intelligent enough to travel through space could do that, and from the equipment in the dwelling they would take over, they could easily spot our particular probability. . . . And then how would we handle extraterrestrials? They're not Germans, or other Earths. They would have alien psychologies and motivations. And we're not even on our guard. We just keep setting up more and more worlds and increasing the chance every day that——"

His voice had risen in excitement and Berg shouted at him, "Nonsense. This is all ridiculous——"

The buzzer sounded and the communiplate brightened and showed the face of Ching. Ching's voice said, "I'm sorry to interrupt, but——"

"What is it?" demanded Berg savagely.

"There's a man here I don't know what to do with. He's drunk or crazy. He complains that his home is surrounded and that there are things staring through the glass roof of his garden."

"Things?" cried Mishnoff.

"Purple things with big red veins, three eyes and some sort of tentacles instead of hair. They have——"

But Mishnoff and Berg didn't hear the rest. They were staring at each other in sick horror.

THE MESSAGE

They drank beer and reminisced as men will who have met after long separation. They called to mind the days under fire. They remembered sergeants and girls, both with exaggeration. Deadly things became humorous in retrospect, and trifles disregarded for ten years were hauled out for airing.

Including, of course, the perennial mystery.

"How do you account for it?" asked the first. "Who started it?"

The second shrugged. "No one started it. Everyone was doing it, like a disease. You, too, I suppose."

The first chuckled.

The third one said softly, "I never saw the fun in it. Maybe because I came across it first when I was under fire for the first time. North Africa."

"Really?" said the second.

"The first night on the beaches of Oran. I was getting under cover, making for some native shack and I saw it in the light of a flare——"

George was deliriously happy. Two years of red tape and now he was finally back in the past. Now he could complete his paper on the social life of the foot soldier of World War II with some authentic details.

Out of the warless, insipid society of the thirtieth century, he found himself for one glorious moment in the tense, superlative drama of the warlike twentieth.

North Africa! Site of the first great sea-borne invasion of the war! How the temporal physicists had scanned the area for the perfect spot and moment. This shadow of an empty wooden building was it. No human would approach for a known number of minutes. No blast would seriously affect it in that time. By being there, George would not affect history. He would be that ideal of the temporal physicist, the "pure observer."

It was even more terrific than he had imagined. There was the perpetual roar of artillery, the unseen tearing of planes overhead. There were the periodic lines of tracer bullets splitting the sky and the occasional ghastly glow of a flare twisting downward.

And *he* was here! He, George, was part of the war, part of an intense kind of life forever gone from the world of the thirtieth century, grown tame and gentle.

He imagined he could see the shadows of an advancing column of soldiers, hear the low cautious monosyllables slip from one to another. How he longed to be one of them in truth, not merely a momentary intruder, a "pure observer."

He stopped his note taking and stared at his stylus, its microlight hypnotizing him for a moment. A sudden idea had overwhelmed him and he looked at the wood against which his shoulder pressed. This moment must not pass unforgotten into history. Surely doing this would affect nothing. He would use the older English dialect and there would be no suspicion.

He did it quickly and then spied a soldier running desperately toward the structure, dodging a burst of bullets. George knew his time was up, and, even as he knew it, found himself back in the thirtieth century.

It didn't matter. For those few minutes he had been part of World War II. A small part, but *part*. And others would know it. They might not know they knew it, but someone perhaps would repeat the message to himself.

Someone, perhaps that man running for shelter, would read it and know that along with all the heroes of the twentieth century was the "pure observer," the man from the thirtieth century, George Kilroy. *He* was there!

SATISFACTION GUARANTEED

Tony was tall and darkly handsome, with an incredibly patrician air drawn into every line of his unchangeable expression, and Claire Belmont regarded him through the crack in the door with a mixture of horror and dismay.

"I can't, Larry. I just can't have him in the house." Feverishly, she was searching her paralyzed mind for a stronger way of putting it; some way that would make sense and settle things, but she could only end with a simple repetition.

"Well, I can't!"

Larry Belmont regarded his wife stiffly, and there was that spark of impatience in his eyes that Claire hated to see, since she felt her own incompetence mirrored in it. "We're committed, Claire," he said, "and I can't have you backing out now. The company is sending me to Washington on this basis, and it probably means a promotion. It's perfectly safe and you know it. What's your objection?"

She frowned helplessly. "It just gives me the chills. I couldn't bear him."

"He's as human as you or I, almost. So, no nonsense. Come, get out there."

His hand was in the small of her back, shoving; and she found herself in her own living room, shivering. *It* was there, looking at her with a precise politeness, as though appraising his hostess-to-be of the next three weeks. Dr. Susan Calvin was there, too, sitting stiffly in thin-lipped abstraction. She had the cold, faraway look of someone who has worked with machines so long that a little of the steel had entered the blood.

"Hello," crackled Claire in general, and ineffectual, greeting.

But Larry was busily saving the situation with a spurious gaiety. "Here, Claire, I want you to meet Tony, a swell guy. This is my wife, Claire, Tony, old boy." Larry's hand draped itself amiably over Tony's shoulder, but Tony remained unresponsive and expressionless under the pressure.

He said, "How do you do, Mrs. Belmont."

And Claire jumped at Tony's voice. It was deep and mellow, smooth as the hair on his head or the skin on his face.

Before she could stop herself, she said, "Oh, my—you talk."

"Why not? Did you expect that I didn't?"

But Claire could only smile weakly. She didn't really know what she had expected. She looked away, then let him slide gently into the corner of her eye. His hair was smooth and black, like polished plastic—or was it really composed of separate hairs? And was the even, olive skin of his hands and face continued on past the obscurement of his formally cut clothing?

She was lost in the shuddering wonder of it, and had to force her thoughts back into place to meet Dr. Calvin's flat, unemotional voice.

"Mrs. Belmont, I hope you appreciate the importance of this experiment. Your husband tells me he has given you some of the background. I would like to give you more, as the senior psychologist of the U. S. Robots and Mechanical Men Corporation.

"Tony is a robot. His actual designation on the company files is TN-3, but he will answer to Tony. He is not a mechanical monster, nor simply a calculating machine of the type that were developed during World War II, fifty years ago. He has an artificial brain nearly as complicated as our own. It is an immense telephone switchboard on an atomic scale, so that billions of possible 'telephone connections' can be compressed into an instrument that will fit inside a skull.

"Such brains are manufactured for each model of robot specifically. Each contains a precalculated set of connections so that each robot knows the English language to start with and enough of anything else that may be necessary to perform his job.

"Until now, U. S. Robots has confined its manufacturing activity to industrial models for use in places where human labor is impractical—in deep mines, for instance, or in underwater work. But we want to invade the city and the home. To do so, we must get the ordinary man and woman to accept these robots without fear. You understand that there is nothing to fear."

"There isn't, Claire," interposed Larry earnestly. "Take my word for it. It's impossible for him to do any harm. You know I wouldn't leave him with you otherwise."

Claire cast a quick, secret glance at Tony and lowered her voice. "What if I make him angry?"

"You needn't whisper," said Dr. Calvin calmly. "He *can't* get angry with you, my dear. I told you that the switchboard connections of his brain were predetermined. Well, the most important connection of all is what we call 'The First Law of Robotics,' and it is merely this: 'No robot can harm a human being, or, through inaction, allow a human being to come to harm.' All robots are built so. No robot can be forced in any way to do harm to any human. So, you see, we need you and Tony as a preliminary experiment for our own guidance, while your husband is in Washington to arrange for government-supervised legal tests."

"You mean all this isn't legal?"

Larry cleared his throat. "Not just yet, but it's all right. He won't leave the house, and you mustn't let anyone see him. That's all. . . . And, Claire, I'd stay with you, but I know too much about the robots. We must have a completely inexperienced tester so that we can have severe conditions. It's necessary."

"Oh, well," muttered Claire. Then, as a thought struck her, "But what does he do?"

"Housework," said Dr. Calvin shortly.

She got up to leave, and it was Larry who saw her to the front door. Claire stayed behind drearily. She caught a glimpse of herself in the mirror above the mantelpiece, and looked away hastily. She was very tired of her small, mousy face and her dim, unimaginative hair. Then she caught Tony's eyes upon her and almost smiled before she remembered. . . .

He was only a machine.

Larry Belmont was on his way to the airport when he caught a glimpse of Gladys Claffern. She was the type of woman who seemed made to be seen in glimpses. . . . Perfectly and precisely manufactured; dressed with thoughtful hand and eye; too gleaming to be stared at.

The little smile that preceded her and the faint scent that trailed her were a pair of beckoning fingers. Larry felt his stride break; he touched his hat, then hurried on.

As always he felt that vague anger. If Claire could only push her way into the Claffern clique, it would help so much. But what was the use.

Claire! The few times she had come face to face with Gladys, the little fool had been tongue-tied. He had no illusions. The testing of Tony was his big chance, and it was in Claire's hands. How much safer it would be in the hands of someone like Gladys Claffern.

Claire woke the second morning to the sound of a subdued knock on the bedroom door. Her mind clamored, then went icy. She had avoided Tony the first day, smiling thinly when she met him and brushing past with a wordless sound of apology.

"Is that you—Tony?"

"Yes, Mrs. Belmont. May I enter?"

She must have said yes, because he was in the room, quite suddenly and noiselessly. Her eyes and nose were simultaneously aware of the tray he was carrying.

"Breakfast?" she said.

"If you please."

She wouldn't have dared to refuse, so she pushed herself slowly into a sitting position and received it: poached eggs, buttered toast, coffee.

"I have brought the sugar and cream separately," said Tony. "I expect to learn your preference with time, in this and in other things."

She waited.

Tony, standing there straight and pliant as a metal rule, asked, after a moment, "Would you prefer to eat in privacy?"

"Yes. . . . I mean, if you don't mind."

"Will you need help later in dressing?"

"Oh, my, no!" She clutched frantically at the sheet, so that the coffee hovered at the edge of catastrophe. She remained so, in rigor, then sank helplessly back against the pillow when the door closed him out of her sight again.

She got through breakfast somehow. . . . He was only a machine, and if it were only more visible that he were it wouldn't be so frightening. Or if his expression would change. It just stayed there, nailed on. You couldn't tell what went on behind those dark eyes and that smooth, olive skin-stuff. The coffee cup beat a faint castanet for a moment as she set it back, empty, on the tray.

Then she realized that she had forgotten to add the sugar and cream after all, and she did so hate black coffee.

She burned a straight path from bedroom to kitchen after dressing. It was her house, after all, and there wasn't anything frippy about her, but she liked her kitchen clean. He should have waited for supervision. . . .

But when she entered, she found a kitchen that might have been minted fire-new from the factory the moment before.

She stopped, stared, turned on her heel and nearly ran into Tony. She yelped.

"May I help?" he asked.

"Tony," and she scraped the anger off the edges of her mind's panic, "you must make some noise when you walk. I can't have you stalking me, you know. . . . Didn't you use this kitchen?"

"I did, Mrs. Belmont."

"It doesn't look it."

"I cleaned up afterward. Isn't that customary?"

Claire opened her eyes wide. After all, what could one say to that. She opened the oven compartment that held the pots, took a quick, unseeing look at the metallic glitter inside, then said with a tremor, "Very good. Quite satisfactory."

If at the moment, he had beamed; if he had smiled; if he had quirked the corner of his mouth the slightest bit, she felt that she could have warmed to him. But he remained an English lord in repose, as he said, "Thank you, Mrs. Belmont. Would you come into the living room?"

She did, and it struck her at once. "Have you been polishing the furniture?"

"Is it satisfactory, Mrs. Belmont?"

"But when? You didn't do it yesterday."

"Last night, of course."

"You burned the lights all night?"

"Oh, no. That wouldn't have been necessary. I've a built-in ultraviolet source. I can see in ultraviolet. And, of course, I don't require sleep."

He did require admiration, though. She realized that, then. He had to know that he was pleasing her. But she couldn't bring herself to supply that pleasure for him.

She could only say sourly, "Your kind will put ordinary houseworkers out of business."

"There is work of much greater importance they can be put to in the world, once they are freed of drudgery. After all, Mrs. Belmont, things like myself can be manufactured. But nothing yet can imitate the creativity and versatility of a human brain, like yours."

And though his face gave no hint, his voice was warmly surcharged with awe and admiration, so that Claire flushed and muttered, "My brain! You can have it."

Tony approached a little and said, "You must be unhappy to say such a thing. Is there anything I can do?"

For a moment, Claire felt like laughing. It *was* a ridiculous situation. Here was an animated carpet-sweeper, dishwasher, furniture-polisher, general factotum, rising from the factory table—and offering his services as consoler and confidant.

Yet she said suddenly, in a burst of woe and voice, "Mr. Belmont doesn't think I have a brain, if you must know. . . . And I suppose I haven't." She couldn't cry in front of him. She felt, for some reason, that she had the honor of the human race to support against this mere creation.

"It's lately," she added. "It was all right when he was a student; when he was just starting. But I can't be a big man's wife; and he's getting to be a big man. He wants me to be a hostess and an entry into social life for him—like G—guh—guh—Gladys Claffern."

Her nose was red, and she looked away.

But Tony wasn't watching her. His eyes wandered about the room. "I can help you run the house."

"But it's no good," she said fiercely. "It needs a touch I can't give it. I can only make it comfortable; I can't ever make it the kind they take pictures of for the Home Beautiful magazines."

"Do you want that kind?"

"Does it do any good—wanting?"

Tony's eyes were on her, full. "I could help."

"Do you know anything about interior decoration?"

"Is it something a good housekeeper should know?"

"Oh, yes."

"Then I have the potentialities of learning it. Can you get me books on the subject?"

Something started then.

Claire, clutching her hat against the brawling liberties of the wind, had manipulated two fat volumes on the home arts back from the public library. She watched Tony as he opened one of them and flipped the pages. It was the first time she had watched his fingers flicker at anything like fine work.

I don't see how they do it, she thought, and on a sudden impulse reached for his hand and pulled it toward herself. Tony did not resist, but let it lie limp for inspection.

She said, "It's remarkable. Even your fingernails look natural."

"That's deliberate, of course," said Tony. Then, chattily, "The skin is a flexible plastic, and the skeletal framework is a light metal alloy. Does that amuse you?"

"Oh, no." She lifted her reddened face. "I just feel a little embarrassed at sort of poking into your insides. It's none of my business. You don't ask me about mine."

"My brain paths don't include that type of curiosity. I can only act within my limitations, you know."

And Claire felt something tighten inside her in the silence that followed. Why did she keep forgetting he was a machine. Now the thing itself had to remind her. Was she so starved for sympathy that she would even accept a robot as equal—because he sympathized?

She noticed Tony was still flipping the pages—almost helplessly—

and there was a quick, shooting sense of relieved superiority within her. "You can't read, can you?"

Tony looked up at her; his voice calm, unreproachful. "I *am* reading, Mrs. Belmont."

"But——" She pointed at the book in a meaningless gesture.

"I am scanning the pages, if that's what you mean. My sense of reading is photographic."

It was evening then, and when Claire eventually went to bed Tony was well into the second volume, sitting there in the dark, or what seemed dark to Claire's limited eyes.

Her last thought, the one that clamored at her just as her mind let go and tumbled, was a queer one. She remembered his hand again; the touch of it. It had been warm and soft, like a human being's.

How clever of the factory, she thought, and softly ebbed to sleep.

It was the library continuously, thereafter, for several days. Tony suggested the fields of study, which branched out quickly. There were books on color matching and on cosmetics; on carpentry and on fashions; on art and on the history of costumes.

He turned the pages of each book before his solemn eyes, and, as quickly as he turned, he read; nor did he seem capable of forgetting.

Before the end of the week, he had insisted on cutting her hair, introducing her to a new method of arranging it, adjusting her eyebrow line a bit and changing the shade of her powder and lipstick.

She had palpitated in nervous dread for half an hour under the delicate touch of his inhuman fingers and then looked in the mirror.

"There is more that can be done," said Tony, "especially in clothes. How do you find it for a beginning?"

And she hadn't answered; not for quite a while. Not until she had absorbed the identity of the stranger in the glass and cooled the wonder at the beauty of it all. Then she had said chokingly, never once taking her eyes from the warming image, "Yes, Tony, quite good—for a beginning."

She said nothing of this in her letters to Larry. Let him see it all at once. And something in her realized that it wasn't only the surprise she would enjoy. It was going to be a kind of revenge.

Tony said one morning, "It's time to start buying, and I'm not allowed to leave the house. If I write out exactly what we must have, can I trust you to get it? We need drapery, and furniture fabric, wallpaper, carpeting, paint, clothing—and any number of small things."

"You can't get these things to your own specifications at a stroke's notice," said Claire doubtfully.

"You can get fairly close, if you go through the city and if money is no object."

"But, Tony, money is certainly an object."

"Not at all. Stop off at U. S. Robots in the first place. I'll write a note for you. You see Dr. Calvin, and tell her that I said it was part of the experiment."

Dr. Calvin, somehow, didn't frighten her as on that first evening. With her new face and a new hat, she couldn't be quite the old Claire. The psychologist listened carefully, asked a few questions, nodded—and then Claire found herself walking out, armed with an unlimited charge account against the assets of U. S. Robots and Mechanical Men Corporation.

It is wonderful what money will do. With a store's contents at her feet, a saleslady's dictum was not necessarily a voice from above; the uplifted eyebrow of a decorator was not anything like Jove's thunder.

And once, when an Exalted Plumpness at one of the most lordly of the garment salons had insistently poohed her description of the wardrobe she must have with counter-pronouncements in accents of the purest Fifty-seventh Street French, she called up Tony, then held the phone out to Monsieur.

"If you don't mind"—voice firm, but fingers twisting a bit—"I'd like you to talk to my—uh—secretary."

Pudgy proceeded to the phone with a solemn arm crooked behind his back. He lifted the phone in two fingers and said delicately, "Yes." A short pause, another "Yes," then a much longer pause, a squeaky beginning of an objection that perished quickly, another pause, a very meek "Yes," and the phone was restored to its cradle.

"If Madam will come with me," he said, hurt and distant, "I will try to supply her needs."

"Just a second." Claire rushed back to the phone, and dialed again. "Hello, Tony. I don't know what you said, but it worked. Thanks. You're a——" She struggled for the appropriate word, gave up and ended in a final little squeak, "—a—a dear!"

It was Gladys Claffern looking at her when she turned from the phone again. A slightly amused and slightly amazed Gladys Claffern, looking at her out of a face tilted a bit to one side.

"Mrs. Belmont?"

It all drained out of Claire—just like that. She could only nod—stupidly, like a marionette.

Gladys smiled with an insolence you couldn't put your finger on. "I didn't know you shopped here?" As if the place had, in her eyes, definitely lost caste through the fact.

"I don't, usually," said Claire humbly.

"And haven't you done something to your hair? It's quite—quaint. . . . Oh, I hope you'll excuse me, but isn't your husband's name Lawrence? It seems to me that it's Lawrence."

Claire's teeth clenched, but she had to explain. She *had* to. "Tony is a friend of my husband's. He's helping me select some things."

"I understand. And quite a *dear* about it, I imagine." She passed on smiling, carrying the light and the warmth of the world with her.

Claire did not question the fact that it was to Tony that she turned for consolation. Ten days had cured her of reluctance. And she could weep before him; weep and rage.

"I was a complete f-fool," she stormed, wrenching at her water-logged handkerchief. "She does that to me. I don't know why. She just does. I should have—kicked her. I should have knocked her down and stamped on her."

"Can you hate a human being so much?" asked Tony, in puzzled softness. "That part of a human mind is closed to me."

"Oh, it isn't she," she moaned. "It's myself, I suppose. She's everything I want to be—on the outside, anyway. . . . And I can't be."

Tony's voice was forceful and low in her ear. "You can be, Mrs. Belmont. You *can* be. We have ten days yet, and in ten days the house will no longer be itself. Haven't we been planning that?"

"And how will that help me—with her?"

"Invite her here. Invite her friends. Have it the evening before I—before I leave. It will be a housewarming, in a way."

"She won't come."

"Yes, she will. She'll come to laugh. . . . And she won't be able to."

"Do you really think so? Oh, Tony, do you think we can do it?" She had both his hands in hers. . . . And then, with her face flung aside, "But what good would it be? It won't be I; it will be you that's doing it. I can't ride your back."

"Nobody lives in splendid singleness," whispered Tony. "They've put that knowledge in me. What you, or anyone, see in Gladys Claffern is not just Gladys Claffern. She rides the back of all that money and social position can bring. She doesn't question that. Why should you? . . . And look at it this way, Mrs. Belmont. I am manufactured to obey, but the extent of my obedience is for myself to determine. I can follow orders niggardly or liberally. For you, it is liberal, because you are what I have been manufactured to see human beings as. You are kind, friendly, unassuming. Mrs. Claffern, as you describe her, is not, and I wouldn't obey her as I would you. So it *is* you, and not *I*, Mrs. Belmont, that is doing all this."

He withdrew his hands from hers then, and Claire looked at that expressionless face no one could read—wondering. She was suddenly frightened again in a completely new way.

She swallowed nervously and stared at her hands, which were still tingling with the pressure of his fingers. She hadn't imagined it; his fingers had pressed hers, gently, tenderly, just before they moved away.

No!

Its fingers . . . *Its* fingers. . . .

She ran to the bathroom and scrubbed her hands—blindly, uselessly.

She was a bit shy of him the next day; watching him narrowly; waiting to see what might follow—and for a while nothing did.

Tony was working. If there was any difficulty in technique in putting up wallpaper, or utilizing the quick-drying paint, Tony's activity did not show it. His hands moved precisely; his fingers were deft and sure.

He worked all night. She never heard him, but each morning was a new adventure. She couldn't count the number of things that had been done, and by evening she was still finding new touches—and another night had come.

She tried to help only once and her human clumsiness marred that. *He* was in the next room, and she was hanging a picture in the spot marked by Tony's mathematical eyes. The little mark was there; the picture was there; and a revulsion against idleness was there.

But she was nervous, or the ladder was rickety. It didn't matter. She felt it going, and she cried out. It tumbled without her, for Tony, with far more than flesh-and-blood quickness, had been under her.

His calm, dark eyes said nothing at all, and his warm voice said only words. "Are you hurt, Mrs. Belmont?"

She noticed for an instant that her falling hand must have mussed that sleek hair of his, because for the first time she could see for herself that it was composed of distinct strands—fine black hairs.

And then, all at once, she was conscious of his arms about her shoulders and under her knees—holding her tightly and warmly.

She pushed, and her scream was loud in her own ears. She spent the rest of the day in her room, and thereafter she slept with a chair upended against the doorknob of her bedroom door.

She had sent out the invitations, and, as Tony had said, they were accepted. She had only to wait for the last evening.

It came, too, after the rest of them, in its proper place. The house was scarcely her own. She went through it one last time—and every room had been changed. She, herself, was in clothes she would never have dared wear before. . . . And when you put them on, you put on pride and confidence with them.

She tried a polite look of contemptuous amusement before the mirror, and the mirror sneered back at her masterfully.

What would Larry say? . . . It didn't matter, somehow. The exciting days weren't coming with him. They were leaving with Tony. Now wasn't that strange? She tried to recapture her mood of three weeks before and failed completely.

The clock shrieked eight at her in eight breathless installments, and she turned to Tony. "They'll be here soon, Tony. You'd better get into the basement. We can't let them——"

She stared a moment, then said weakly, "Tony?" and more strongly, "Tony?" and nearly a scream, "*Tony!*"

But his arms were around her now; his face was close to hers; the pressure of his embrace was relentless. She heard his voice through a haze of emotional jumble.

"Claire," the voice said, "there are many things I am not made to understand, and this must be one of them. I am leaving tomorrow, and I don't want to. I find that there is more in me than just a desire to please you. Isn't it strange?"

His face was closer; his lips were warm, but with no breath behind them—for machines do not breathe. They were almost on hers.

. . . And the bell sounded.

For a moment, she struggled breathlessly, and then he was gone and nowhere in sight, and the bell was sounding again. Its intermittent shrillness was insistent.

The curtains on the front windows had been pulled open. They had been closed fifteen minutes earlier. She *knew* that.

They must have seen, then. They must *all* have seen—everything!

They came in so politely, all in a bunch—the pack come to howl—with their sharp, darting eyes piercing everywhere. They *had* seen. Why else would Gladys ask in her jabbingest manner after Larry? And Claire was spurred to a desperate and reckless defiance.

Yes, he *is* away. He'll be back tomorrow, I suppose. No, I haven't been lonely here myself. Not a bit. I've had an exciting time. And she laughed at them. Why not? What could they do? Larry would know the truth, if it ever came to him, the story of what they thought they saw.

But *they* didn't laugh.

She could read that in the fury in Gladys Claffern's eyes; in the false sparkle of her words; in her desire to leave early. And as she parted with them, she caught one last, anonymous whisper—disjointed.

". . . never saw anything like . . . so *handsome*——"

And she knew what it was that had enabled her to fingersnap them so. Let each cat mew; and let each cat know—that she might be prettier than Claire Belmont, and grander, and richer—but not one, *not one*, could have so handsome a lover!

And then she remembered again—again—again, that Tony was a machine, and her skin crawled.

"Go away! Leave me be!" she cried to the empty room and ran to her bed. She wept wakefully all that night and the next morning, almost before dawn, when the streets were empty, a car drew up to the house and took Tony away.

Lawrence Belmont passed Dr. Calvin's office, and, on impulse, knocked. He found her with Mathematician Peter Bogert, but did not hesitate on that account.

He said, "Claire tells me that U. S. Robots paid for all that was done at my house——"

"Yes," said Dr. Calvin. "We've written it off, as a valuable and necessary part of the experiment. With your new position as Associate Engineer, you'll be able to keep it up, I think."

"That's not what I'm worried about. With Washington agreeing to the tests, we'll be able to get a TN model of our own by next year, I think." He turned hesitantly, as though to go, and as hesitantly turned back again.

"Well, Mr. Belmont?" asked Dr. Calvin, after a pause.

"I wonder——" began Larry. "I wonder what really happened there. She—Claire, I mean—seems so different. It's not just her looks

—though, frankly, I'm amazed." He laughed nervously. "It's *her!* She's not my wife, really—I can't explain it."

"Why try? Are you disappointed with any part of the change?"

"On the contrary. But it's a little frightening, too, you see——"

"I wouldn't worry, Mr. Belmont. Your wife has handled herself very well. Frankly, I never expected to have the experiment yield such a thorough and complete test. We know exactly what corrections must be made in the TN model, and the credit belongs entirely to Mrs. Belmont. If you want me to be very honest, I think your wife deserves your promotion more than you do."

Larry flinched visibly at that. "As long as it's in the family," he murmured unconvincingly and left.

Susan Calvin looked after him, "I think that hurt—I hope. . . . Have you read Tony's report, Peter?"

"Thoroughly," said Bogert. "And won't the TN-3 model need changes?"

"Oh, you think so, too?" questioned Calvin sharply. "What's your reasoning?"

Bogert frowned. "I don't need any. It's obvious on the face of it that we can't have a robot loose which makes love to his mistress, if you don't mind the pun."

"Love! Peter, you sicken me. You really don't understand? That machine had to obey the First Law. He couldn't allow harm to come to a human being, and harm was coming to Claire Belmont through her own sense of inadequacy. So he made love to her, since what woman would fail to appreciate the compliment of being able to stir passion in a machine—in a cold, soulless machine. And he opened the curtains that night deliberately, that the others might see and envy—without any risk possible to Claire's marriage. I think it was clever of Tony——"

"Do you? What's the difference whether it was pretense or not, Susan? It still has its horrifying effect. Read the report again. She avoided him. She screamed when he held her. She didn't sleep that last night—in hysterics. We can't have that."

"Peter, you're blind. You're as blind as I was. The TN model will be rebuilt entirely, but not for your reason. Quite otherwise; quite otherwise. Strange that I overlooked it in the first place," her eyes were opaquely thoughtful, "but perhaps it reflects a shortcoming in myself. You see, Peter, machines can't fall in love, but—even when it's hopeless and horrifying—women can!"

HELL-FIRE

There was a stir as of a very polite first-night audience. Only a handful of scientists were present, a sprinkling of high brass, some Congressmen, a few newsmen.

Alvin Horner of the Washington Bureau of the Continental Press found himself next to Joseph Vincenzo of Los Alamos, and said, "*Now* we ought to learn something."

Vincenzo stared at him through bifocals and said, "Not the important thing."

Horner frowned. This was to be the first super-slow-motion film of an atomic explosion. With trick lenses changing directional polarization in flickers, the moment of explosion would be divided into billionth-second snaps. Yesterday, an A-bomb had exploded. Today, those snaps would show the explosion in incredible detail.

Horner said, "You think this won't work?"

Vincenzo looked tormented. "It will work. We've run pilot tests. But the important thing——"

"Which is?"

"That these bombs are man's death sentence. We don't seem to be able to learn that." Vincenzo nodded. "Look at them here. They're excited and thrilled, but not afraid."

The newsman said, "They know the danger. They're afraid, too."

"Not enough," said the scientist. "I've seen men watch an H-bomb blow an island into a hole and then go home and sleep. That's the way men are. For thousands of years, hell-fire has been preached to them, and it's made no real impression."

"Hell-fire: Are you religious, sir?"

"What you saw yesterday was hell-fire. An exploding atom bomb is hell-fire. Literally."

That was enough for Horner. He got up and changed his seat, but watched the audience uneasily. Were any afraid? Did any worry about hell-fire? It didn't seem so to him.

The lights went out, the projector started. On the screen, the firing tower stood gaunt. The audience grew tensely quiet.

Then a dot of light appeared at the apex of the tower, a brilliant, burning point, slowly budding in a lazy, outward elbowing, this way and that, taking on uneven shapes of light and shadow, growing oval.

A man cried out chokingly, then others. A hoarse babble of noise, followed by thick silence. Horner could smell fear, taste terror in his own mouth, feel his blood freeze.

The oval fireball had sprouted projections, then paused a moment in stasis, before expanding rapidly into a bright and featureless sphere.

That moment of stasis—the fireball had shown dark spots for eyes, with dark lines for thin, flaring eyebrows, a hairline coming down V-shaped, a mouth twisted upward, laughing wildly in the hell-fire—and horns.

THE LAST TRUMP

The Archangel Gabriel was quite casual about the whole thing. Idly, he let the tip of one wing graze the planet Mars, which, being of mere matter, was unaffected by the contact.

He said, "It's a settled matter, Etheriel. There's nothing to be done about it now. The Day of Resurrection is due."

Etheriel, a very junior seraph who had been created not quite a thousand years earlier as men counted time, quivered so that distinct vortices appeared in the continuum. Ever since his creation, he had been in immediate charge of Earth and environs. As a job, it was a sinecure, a cubbyhole, a dead end, but through the centuries he had come to take a perverse pride in the world.

"But you'll be disrupting my world without notice."

"Not at all. Not at all. Certain passages occur in the Book of Daniel and in the Apocalypse of St. John which are clear enough."

"They are? Having been copied from scribe to scribe? I wonder if two words in a row are left unchanged."

"There are hints in the Rig-Veda, in the Confucian Analects——"

"Which are the property of isolated cultural groups which exist as a thin aristocracy——"

"The Gilgamesh Chronicle speaks out plainly."

"Much of the Gilgamesh Chronicle was destroyed with the library of Ashurbanipal sixteen hundred years, Earth-style, before my creation."

"There are certain features of the Great Pyramid and a pattern in the inlaid jewels of the Taj Mahal——"

"Which are so subtle that no man has ever rightly interpreted them."

Gabriel said wearily, "If you're going to object to everything, there's no use discussing the matter. In any case, *you* ought to know about it. In matters concerning Earth, you're omniscient."

"Yes, if I choose to be. I've had much to concern me here and investigating the possibilities of Resurrection did not, I confess, occur to me."

"Well, it should have. All the papers involved are in the files of the Council of Ascendants. You could have availed yourself of them at any time."

"I tell you all my time was needed here. You have no idea of the deadly efficiency of the Adversary on this planet. It took all my efforts to curb him, and even so——"

"Why, yes"—Gabriel stroked a comet as it passed—"he does seem to have won his little victories. I note as I let the interlocking factual pattern of this miserable little world flow through me that this is one of those setups with matter-energy equivalence."

"So it is," said Etheriel.

"And they are playing with it."

"I'm afraid so."

"Then what better time for ending the matter?"

"I'll be able to handle it, I assure you. Their nuclear bombs will not destroy them."

"I wonder. Well, now, suppose you let me continue, Etheriel. The appointed moment approaches."

The seraph said stubbornly, "I would like to see the documents in the case."

"If you insist." The wording of an Act of Ascendancy appeared in glittering symbols against the deep black of the airless firmament.

Etheriel read aloud: "It is hereby directed by order of Council that the Archangel Gabriel, Serial number etcetera, etcetera (well, that's you, at any rate), will approach Planet, Class A, number G753990, hereinafter known as Earth, and on January 1, 1957, at 12:01 P.M., using local time values——" He finished reading in gloomy silence.

"Satisfied?"

"No, but I'm helpless."

Gabriel smiled. A trumpet appeared in space, in shape like an earthly trumpet, but its burnished gold extended from Earth to sun. It was raised to Gabriel's glittering beautiful lips.

"Can't you let me have a little time to take this up with the Council?" asked Etheriel desperately.

"What good would it do you? The act is countersigned by the Chief, and you know that an act countersigned by the Chief is absolutely irrevocable. And now, if you don't mind, it is almost the stipulated second and I want to be done with this as I have other matters of much greater moment on my mind. Would you step out of my way a little? Thank you."

Gabriel blew, and a clean, thin sound of perfect pitch and crystalline delicacy filled all the universe to the farthest star. As it sounded, there was a tiny moment of stasis as thin as the line separating past from future, and then the fabric of worlds collapsed upon itself and matter was gathered back into the primeval chaos from which it had once sprung at a word. The stars and nebulae were gone, and the cosmic dust, the sun, the planets, the moon; all, all, all except Earth itself, which spun as before in a universe now completely empty.

The Last Trump had sounded.

R. E. Mann (known to all who knew him simply as R. E.) eased himself into the offices of the Billikan Bitsies factory and stared somberly at the tall man (gaunt but with a certain faded elegance about his neat gray mustache) who bent intently over a sheaf of papers on his desk.

R. E. looked at his wristwatch, which still said 7:01, having ceased running at that time. It was Eastern standard time, of course; 12:01 P.M. Greenwich time. His dark brown eyes, staring sharply out over a pair of pronounced cheekbones, caught those of the other.

For a moment, the tall man stared at him blankly. Then he said, "Can I do anything for you?"

"Horatio J. Billikan, I presume? Owner of this place?"

"Yes."

"I'm R. E. Mann and I couldn't help but stop in when I finally found someone at work. Don't you know what today is?"

"Today?"

"It's Resurrection Day."

"Oh, that! I know it. I heard the blast. Fit to wake the dead. . . . That's rather a good one, don't you think?" He chuckled for a moment, then went on. "It woke me at seven in the morning. I nudged my wife. She slept through it, of course. I always said she would. 'It's the Last Trump, dear,' I said. Hortense, that's my wife, said, 'All right,' and went back to sleep. I bathed, shaved, dressed and came to work."

"But why?"

"Why not?"

"None of your workers have come in."

"No, poor souls. They'll take a holiday just at first. You've got to expect that. After all, it isn't every day that the world comes to an end. Frankly, it's just as well. It gives me a chance to straighten out my personal correspondence without interruptions. Telephone hasn't rung once."

He stood up and went to the window. "It's a great improvement. No blinding sun any more and the snow's gone. There's a pleasant light and a pleasant warmth. Very good arrangement. . . . But now, if you don't mind, I'm *rather* busy, so if you'll excuse me——"

A great, hoarse voice interrupted with a, "Just a minute, Horatio," and a gentleman, looking remarkably like Billikan in a somewhat craggier way, followed his prominent nose into the office and struck an attitude of offended dignity which was scarcely spoiled by the fact that he was quite naked. "May I ask why you've shut down Bitsies?"

Billikan looked faint. "Good Heavens," he said, "it's Father. Wherever did you come from?"

"From the graveyard," roared Billikan, Senior. "Where on Earth else? They're coming out of the ground there by the dozens. Every one of them naked. Women, too."

Billikan cleared his throat. "I'll get you some clothes, Father. I'll bring them to you from home."

"Never mind that. Business first. Business first."

R. E. came out of his musing. "Is everyone coming out of their graves at the same time, sir?"

He stared curiously at Billikan, Senior, as he spoke. The old man's appearance was one of robust age. His cheeks were furrowed but glowed with health. His age, R. E. decided, was exactly what it was at the moment of his death, but his body was as it should have been at that age if it functioned ideally.

Billikan, Senior, said, "No, sir, they are not. The newer graves are coming up first. Pottersby died five years before me and came up about five minutes after me. Seeing him made me decide to leave. I had had enough of him when . . . And that reminds me." He brought his fist down on the desk, a very solid fist. "There were no taxis, no busses. Telephones weren't working. I had to walk. I had to walk twenty miles."

"Like that?" asked his son in a faint and appalled voice.

Billikan, Senior, looked down upon his bare skin with casual approval. "It's warm. Almost everyone else is naked. . . . Anyway, son, I'm not here to make small talk. Why is the factory shut down?"

"It isn't shut down. It's a special occasion."

"Special occasion, my foot. You call union headquarters and tell them Resurrection Day isn't in the contract. Every worker is being docked for every minute he's off the job."

Billikan's lean face took on a stubborn look as he peered at his father. "I will not. Don't forget, now, you're no longer in charge of this plant. I am."

"Oh, you are? By what right?"

"By your will."

"All right. Now here I am and I void my will."

"You can't, Father. You're dead. You may not look dead, but I have witnesses. I have the doctor's certificate. I have receipted bills from the undertaker. I can get testimony from the pallbearers."

Billikan, Senior, stared at his son, sat down, placed his arm over the back of the chair, crossed his legs and said, "If it comes to that, we're all dead, aren't we? The world's come to an end, hasn't it?"

"But you've been declared legally dead and I haven't."

"Oh, we'll change that, son. There are going to be more of us than of you and votes count."

Billikan, Junior, tapped the desk firmly with the flat of his hand and flushed slightly. "Father, I hate to bring up this particular point, but you force me to. May I remind you that by now I am sure that Mother is sitting at home waiting for you; that she probably had to walk the streets—uh—naked, too; and that she probably isn't in a good humor."

Billikan, Senior, went ludicrously pale. "Good Heavens!"

"And you know she always wanted you to retire."

Billikan, Senior, came to a quick decision. "I'm not going home. Why, this is a nightmare. Aren't there any limits to this Resurrection business? It's—it's—it's sheer anarchy. There's such a thing as overdoing it. I'm just not going home."

At which point, a somewhat rotund gentleman with a smooth, pink face and fluffy white sideburns (much like pictures of Martin Van Buren) stepped in and said coldly, "*Good* day."

"Father," said Billikan, Senior.

"Grandfather," said Billikan, Junior.

Billikan, Grandsenior, looked at Billikan, Junior, with disapproval. "If you are my grandson," he said, "you've aged considerably and the change has not improved you."

Billikan, Junior, smiled with dyspeptic feebleness, and made no answer.

Billikan, Grandsenior, did not seem to require one. He said, "Now if you two will bring me up to date on the business, I will resume my managerial function."

There were two simultaneous answers, and Billikan, Grandsenior's, floridity waxed dangerously as he beat the ground peremptorily with an imaginary cane and barked a retort.

R. E. said, "Gentlemen."

He raised his voice. "Gentlemen!"

He shrieked at full lung-power, "GENTLEMEN!"

Conversation snapped off sharply and all turned to look at him. R. E.'s angular face, his oddly attractive eyes, his sardonic mouth seemed suddenly to dominate the gathering.

He said, "I don't understand this argument. What is it that you manufacture?"

"Bitsies," said Billikan, Junior.

"Which, I take it, are a packaged cereal breakfast food——"

"Teeming with energy in every golden, crispy flake——" cried Billikan, Junior.

"Covered with honey-sweet, crystalline sugar; a confection and a food——" growled Billikan, Senior.

"To tempt the most jaded appetite," roared Billikan, Grandsenior.

"Exactly," said R. E. "What appetite?"

They stared stolidly at him. "I beg your pardon," said Billikan, Junior.

"Are any of you hungry?" asked R. E. "I'm not."

"What is this fool maundering about?" demanded Billikan, Grandsenior, angrily. His invisible cane would have been prodding R. E. in the navel had it (the cane, not the navel) existed.

R. E. said, "I'm trying to tell you that no one will ever eat again. It is the hereafter, and food is unnecessary."

The expressions on the faces of the Billikans needed no interpretation. It was obvious that they had tried their own appetites and found them wanting.

Billikan, Junior, said ashenly, "Ruined!"

Billikan, Grandsenior, pounded the floor heavily and noiselessly with his imaginary cane. "This is confiscation of property without due process of law. I'll sue. I'll sue."

"Quite unconstitutional," agreed Billikan, Senior.

"If you can find anyone to sue, I wish you all good fortune," said R.E. agreeably. "And now if you'll excuse me I think I'll walk toward the graveyard."

He put his hat on his head and walked out the door.

Etheriel, his vortices quivering, stood before the glory of a six-winged cherub.

The cherub said, "If I understand you, your particular universe has been dismantled."

"Exactly."

"Well, surely, now, you don't expect *me* to set it up again?"

"I don't expect you to do anything," said Etheriel, "except to arrange an appointment for me with the Chief."

The cherub gestured his respect instantly at hearing the word. Two wing-tips covered his feet, two his eyes and two his mouth. He restored himself to normal and said, "The Chief is quite busy. There are a myriad score of matters for him to decide."

"Who denies that? I merely point out that if matters stand as they are now, there will have been a universe in which Satan will have won the final victory."

"Satan?"

"It's the Hebrew word for Adversary," said Etheriel impatiently. "I could say Ahriman, which is the Persian word. In any case, I mean the Adversary."

The cherub said, "But what will an interview with the Chief accomplish? The document authorizing the Last Trump was countersigned by the Chief, and you know that it is irrevocable for that reason. The Chief would never limit his own omnipotence by canceling a word he had spoken in his official capacity."

"Is that final? You will not arrange an appointment?"

"I cannot."

Etheriel said, "In that case, I shall seek out the Chief without one. I will invade the Primum Mobile. If it means my destruction, so be it." He gathered his energies. . . .

The cherub murmured in horror, "Sacrilege!" and there was a faint gathering of thunder as Etheriel sprang upward and was gone.

R. E. Mann passed through the crowded streets and grew used to the sight of people bewildered, disbelieving, apathetic, in makeshift clothing or, usually, none at all.

A girl, who looked about twelve, leaned over an iron gate, one foot on a crossbar, swinging it to and fro, and said as he passed, "Hello, mister."

"Hello," said R. E. The girl was dressed. She was not one of the—uh—returnees.

The girl said, "We got a new baby in our house. She's a sister I once had. Mommy is crying and they sent me here."

R. E. said, "Well, well," passed through the gate and up the paved walk to the house, one with modest pretensions to middle-class gentility. He rang the bell, obtained no answer, opened the door and walked in.

He followed the sound of sobbing and knocked at an inner door. A stout man of about fifty with little hair and a comfortable supply of cheek and chin looked out at him with mingled astonishment and resentment.

"Who are you?"

R. E. removed his hat. "I thought I might be able to help. Your little girl outside——"

A woman looked up at him hopelessly from a chair by a double bed. Her hair was beginning to gray. Her face was puffed and unsightly with weeping and the veins stood out bluely on the back of her hands. A baby lay on the bed, plump and naked. It kicked its feet languidly and its sightless baby eyes turned aimlessly here and there.

"This is my baby," said the woman. "She was born twenty-three years ago in this house and she died when she was ten days old in this house. I wanted her back so much."

"And now you have her," said R. E.

"But it's too late," cried the woman vehemently. "I've had three other children. My oldest girl is married; my son is in the army. I'm too old to have a baby now. And even if—even if——"

Her features worked in a heroic effort to keep back the tears and failed.

Her husband said with flat tonelessness, "It's not a real baby. It doesn't cry. It doesn't soil itself. It won't take milk. What will we do? It'll never grow. It'll always be a baby."

R. E. shook his head. "I don't know," he said. "I'm afraid I can do nothing to help."

Quietly he left. Quietly he thought of the hospitals. Thousands of babies must be appearing at each one.

Place them in racks, he thought, sardonically. Stack them like cordwood. They need no care. Their little bodies are merely each the custodian of an indestructible spark of life.

He passed two little boys of apparently equal chronological age, perhaps ten. Their voices were shrill. The body of one glistened white in the sunless light so he was a returnee. The other was not. R. E. paused to listen.

The bare one said, "I had scarlet fever."

A spark of envy at the other's claim to notoriety seemed to enter the clothed one's voice. "Gee."

"That's why I died."

"Gee. Did they use pensillun or auromysun?"

"What?"

"They're medicines."

"I never heard of them."

"Boy, you never heard of *much*."

"I know as much as *you*."

"Yeah? Who's President of the United States?"

"Warren Harding, that's who."

"You're crazy. It's Eisenhower."

"Who's he?"

"Ever see television?"

"What's that?"

The clothed boy hooted earsplittingly. "It's something you turn on and see comedians, movies, cowboys, rocket rangers, anything you want."

"Let's see it."

There was a pause and the boy from the present said, "It ain't working."

The other boy shrieked his scorn. "You mean it ain't never worked. You made it all up."

R. E. shrugged and passed on.

The crowds thinned as he left town and neared the cemetery. Those who were left were all walking into town, all were nude.

A man stopped him; a cheerful man with pinkish skin and white hair who had the marks of pince-nez on either side of the bridge of his nose, but no glasses to go with them.

"Greetings, friend."

"Hello," said R. E.

"You're the first man with clothing that I've seen. You were alive when the trumpet blew, I suppose."

"Yes, I was."

"Well, isn't this great? Isn't this joyous and delightful? Come rejoice with me."

"You like this, do you?" said R. E.

"*Like it?* A pure and radiant joy fills me. We are surrounded by the light of the first day; the light that glowed softly and serenely before sun, moon and stars were made. (You know your Genesis, of course.) There is the comfortable warmth that must have been one of the highest blisses of Eden; not enervating heat or assaulting cold. Men and women walk the streets unclothed and are not ashamed. All is well, my friend, all is well."

R. E. said, "Well, it's a fact that I haven't seemed to mind the feminine display all about."

"Naturally not," said the other. "Lust and sin as we remember it in our earthly existence no longer exists. Let me introduce myself, friend, as I was in earthly times. My name on Earth was Winthrop Hester. I was born in 1812 and died in 1884 as we counted time then.

Through the last forty years of my life I labored to bring my little flock to the Kingdom and I go now to count the ones I have won."

R. E. regarded the ex-minister solemnly, "Surely there has been no Judgment yet."

"Why not? The Lord sees within a man and in the same instant that all things of the world ceased, all men were judged and we are the saved."

"There must be a great many saved."

"On the contrary, my son, those saved are but as a remnant."

"A pretty large remnant. As near as I can make out, everyone's coming back to life. I've seen some pretty unsavory characters back in town as alive as you are."

"Last-minute repentance——"

"*I* never repented."

"Of what, my son?"

"Of the fact that I never attended church."

Winthrop Hester stepped back hastily. "Were you ever baptized?"

"Not to my knowledge."

Winthrop Hester trembled. "Surely you believed in God?"

"Well," said R. E., "I believed a lot of things about Him that would probably startle you."

Winthrop Hester turned and hurried off in great agitation.

In what remained of his walk to the cemetery (R. E. had no way of estimating time, nor did it occur to him to try) no one else stopped him. He found the cemetery itself all but empty, its trees and grass gone (it occurred to him that there was nothing green in the world; the ground everywhere was a hard, featureless, grainless gray; the sky a luminous white), but its headstones still standing.

On one of these sat a lean and furrowed man with long, black hair on his head and a mat of it, shorter, though more impressive, on his chest and upper arms.

He called out in a deep voice, "Hey, there, you!"

R. E. sat down on a neighboring headstone. "Hello."

Black hair said, "Your clothes don't look right. What year was it when it happened?"

"1957."

"I died in 1807. Funny! I expected to be one pretty hot boy right about now, with the 'tarnal flames shooting up my innards."

"Aren't you coming along to town?" asked R. E.

"My name's Zeb," said the ancient. "That's short for Zebulon, but Zeb's good enough. What's the town like? Changed some, I reckon?"

"It's got nearly a hundred thousand people in it."

Zeb's mouth yawned somewhat. "Go on. Might nigh bigger'n Philadelphia. . . . You're making fun."

"Philadelphia's got——" R. E. paused. Stating the figure would do him no good. Instead, he said, "The town's grown in a hundred fifty years, you know."

"Country, too?"

"Forty-eight states," said R. E. "All the way to the Pacific."

"No!" Zeb slapped his thigh in delight and then winced at the unexpected absence of rough homespun to take up the worst of the blow. "I'd head out west if I wasn't needed here. Yes, sir." His face grew lowering and his thin lips took on a definite grimness. "I'll stay right here, where I'm needed."

"Why are you needed?"

The explanation came out briefly, bitten off hard. "Injuns!"

"Indians?"

"Millions of 'em. First the tribes we fought and licked and then tribes who ain't never seen a white man. They'll all come back to life. I'll need my old buddies. You city fellers ain't no good at it. . . . Ever seen an Injun?"

R. E. said, "Not around here lately, no."

Zeb looked his contempt, and tried to spit to one side but found no saliva for the purpose. He said, "You better git back to the city, then. After a while, it ain't going to be safe nohow round here. Wish I had my musket."

R. E. rose, thought a moment, shrugged and faced back to the city. The headstone he had been sitting upon collapsed as he rose, falling into a powder of gray stone that melted into the featureless ground. He looked about. Most of the headstones were gone. The rest would not last long. Only the one under Zeb still looked firm and strong.

R. E. began the walk back. Zeb did not turn to look at him. He remained waiting quietly and calmly—for Indians.

Etheriel plunged through the heavens in reckless haste. The eyes of the Ascendants were on him, he knew. From late-born seraph, through cherubs and angels, to the highest archangel, they must be watching.

Already he was higher than any Ascendant, uninvited, had ever been before and he waited for the quiver of the Word that would reduce his vortices to non-existence.

But he did not falter. Through non-space and non-time, he

plunged toward union with the Primum Mobile; the seat that encompassed all that Is, Was, Would Be, Had Been, Could Be and Might Be.

And as he thought that, he burst through and was part of it, his being expanding so that momentarily he, too, was part of the All. But then it was mercifully veiled from his senses, and the Chief was a still, small voice within him, yet all the more impressive in its infinity for all that.

"My son," the voice said, "I know why you have come."

"Then help me, if that be your will."

"By my own will," said the Chief, "an act of mine is irrevocable. All your mankind, my son, yearned for life. All feared death. All evolved thoughts and dreams of life unending. No two groups of men; no two single men; evolved the same afterlife, but all wished life. I was petitioned that I might grant the common denominator of all these wishes—life unending. I did so."

"No servant of yours made that request."

"The Adversary did, my son."

Etheriel trailed his feeble glory in dejection and said in a low voice, "I am dust in your sight and unworthy to be in your presence, yet I must ask a question. Is then the Adversary your servant also?"

"Without him I can have no other," said the Chief, "for what then is Good but the eternal fight against Evil?"

And in that fight, thought Etheriel, I have lost.

R. E. paused in sight of town. The buildings were crumbling. Those that were made of wood were already heaps of rubble. R. E. walked to the nearest such heap and found the wooden splinters powdery and dry.

He penetrated deeper into town and found the brick buildings still standing, but there was an ominous roundness to the edges of the bricks, a threatening flakiness.

"They won't last long," said a deep voice, "but there is this consolation, if consolation it be; their collapse can kill no one."

R. E. looked up in surprise and found himself face to face with a cadaverous Don Quixote of a man, lantern-jawed, sunken-cheeked. His eyes were sad and his brown hair was lank and straight. His clothes hung loosely and skin showed clearly through various rents.

"My name," said the man, "is Richard Levine. I was a professor of history once—before this happened."

"You're wearing clothes," said R. E. "You're not one of those resurrected."

"No, but that mark of distinction is vanishing. Clothes are going."

R. E. looked at the throngs that drifted past them, moving slowly and aimlessly like motes in a sunbeam. Vanishingly few wore clothes. He looked down at himself and noticed for the first time that the seam down the length of each trouser leg had parted. He pinched the fabric of his jacket between thumb and forefinger and the wool parted and came away easily.

"I guess you're right," said R. E.

"If you'll notice," went on Levine, "Mellon's Hill is flattening out."

R. E. turned to the north where ordinarily the mansions of the aristocracy (such aristocracy as there was in town) studded the slopes of Mellon's Hill, and found the horizon nearly flat.

Levine said, "Eventually, there'll be nothing but flatness, featurelessness, nothingness—and us."

"And Indians," said R. E. "There's a man outside of town waiting for Indians and wishing he had a musket."

"I imagine," said Levine, "the Indians will give no trouble. There is no pleasure in fighting an enemy that cannot be killed or hurt. And even if that were not so, the lust for battle would be gone, as are all lusts."

"Are you sure?"

"I am positive. Before all this happened, although you may not think it to look at me, I derived much harmless pleasure in a consideration of the female figure. Now, with the unexampled opportunities at my disposal, I find myself irritatingly uninterested. No, that is wrong. I am not even irritated at my uninterest."

R. E. looked up briefly at the passers-by. "I see what you mean."

"The coming of Indians here," said Levine, "is nothing compared with the situation in the Old World. Early during the Resurrection, Hitler and his Wehrmacht must have come back to life and must now be facing and intermingled with Stalin and the Red Army all the way from Berlin to Stalingrad. To complicate the situation, the Kaisers and Czars will arrive. The men at Verdun and the Somme are back in the old battlegrounds. Napoleon and his marshals are scattered over western Europe. And Mohammed must be back to see what following ages have made of Islam, while the Saints and Apostles consider the paths of Christianity. And even the Mongols, poor things, the Khans from Temujin to Aurangzeb, must be wandering the steppes helplessly, longing for their horses."

"As a professor of history," said R. E., "you must long to be there and observe."

"How could I be there? Every man's position on Earth is restricted to the distance he can walk. There are no machines of any kind, and, as I have just mentioned, no horses. And what would I find in Europe anyway? Apathy, I think! As here."

A soft plopping sound caused R. E. to turn around. The wing of a neighboring brick building had collapsed in dust. Portions of bricks lay on either side of him. Some must have hurtled through him without his being aware of it. He looked about. The heaps of rubble were less numerous. Those that remained were smaller in size.

He said, "I met a man who thought we had all been judged and are in Heaven."

"Judged?" said Levine. "Why, yes, I imagine we are. We face eternity now. We have no universe left, no outside phenomena, no emotions, no passions. Nothing but ourselves and thought. We face an eternity of introspection, when all through history we have never known what to do with ourselves on a rainy Sunday."

"You sound as though the situation bothers you."

"It does more than that. The Dantean conceptions of Inferno were childish and unworthy of the Divine imagination: fire and torture. Boredom is much more subtle. The inner torture of a mind unable to escape itself in any way, condemned to fester in its own exuding mental pus for all time, is much more fitting. Oh, yes, my friend, we have been judged, and condemned, too, and this is not Heaven, but hell."

And Levine rose with shoulders drooping dejectedly, and walked away.

R. E. gazed thoughtfully about and nodded his head. He was satisfied.

The self-admission of failure lasted but an instant in Etheriel, and then, quite suddenly, he lifted his being as brightly and highly as he dared in the presence of the Chief and his glory was a tiny dot of light in the infinite Primum Mobile.

"If it be your will, then," he said. "I do not ask you to defeat your will but to fulfill it."

"In what way, my son?"

"The document, approved by the Council of Ascendants and signed by yourself, authorizes the Day of Resurrection at a specific time of a specific day of the year 1957 as Earthmen count time."

"So it did."

"But the year 1957 is unqualified. What then is 1957? To the dominant culture on Earth the year was A. D. 1957. That is true. Yet from the time you breathed existence into Earth and its universe there have passed 5,960 years. Based on the internal evidence you created within that universe, nearly four billion years have passed. Is the year, *unqualified*, then 1957, 5960, or 4000000000?

"Nor is that all," Etheriel went on. "The year A. D. 1957 is the year 7464 of the Byzantine era, 5716 by the Jewish calendar. It is 2708 A.U.C., that is, the 2,708th year since the founding of Rome, if we adopt the Roman calendar. It is the year 1375 in the Mohammedan calendar, and the hundred eightieth year of the independence of the United States.

"Humbly I ask then if it does not seem to you that a year referred to as 1957 alone and without qualification has no meaning."

The Chief's still small voice said, "I have always known this, my son; it was you who had to learn."

"Then," said Etheriel, quivering luminously with joy, "let the very letter of your will be fulfilled and let the Day of Resurrection fall in 1957, but only when all the inhabitants of Earth unanimously agree that a certain year shall be numbered 1957 and none other."

"So let it be," said the Chief, and this Word re-created Earth and all it contained, together with the sun and moon and all the hosts of Heaven.

It was 7 A.M. on January 1, 1957, when R. E. Mann awoke with a start. The very beginnings of a melodious note that ought to have filled all the universe had sounded and yet had not sounded.

For a moment, he cocked his head as though to allow understanding to flow in, and then a trifle of rage crossed his face to vanish again. It was but another battle.

He sat down at his desk to compose the next plan of action. People already spoke of calendar reform and it would have to be stimulated. A new era must begin with December 2, 1944, and someday a new year 1957 would come; 1957 of the Atomic Era, acknowledged as such by all the world.

A strange light shone on his head as thoughts passed through his more-than-human mind and the shadow of Ahriman on the wall seemed to have small horns at either temple.

THE FUN THEY HAD

Margie even wrote about it that night in her diary. On the page headed May 17, 2157, she wrote, "Today Tommy found a real book!"

It was a very old book. Margie's grandfather once said that when he was a little boy *his* grandfather told him that there was a time when all stories were printed on paper.

They turned the pages, which were yellow and crinkly, and it was awfully funny to read words that stood still instead of moving the way they were supposed to—on a screen, you know. And then, when they turned back to the page before, it had the same words on it that it had had when they read it the first time.

"Gee," said Tommy, "what a waste. When you're through with the book, you just throw it away, I guess. Our television screen must have had a million books on it and it's good for plenty more. I wouldn't throw *it* away."

"Same with mine," said Margie. She was eleven and hadn't seen as many telebooks as Tommy had. He was thirteen.

She said, "Where did you find it?"

"In my house." He pointed without looking, because he was busy reading. "In the attic."

"What's it about?"

"School."

Margie was scornful. "School? What's there to write about school? I hate school."

Margie always hated school, but now she hated it more than ever. The mechanical teacher had been giving her test after test in geography and she had been doing worse and worse until her mother had shaken her head sorrowfully and sent for the County Inspector.

He was a round little man with a red face and a whole box of tools with dials and wires. He smiled at Margie and gave her an apple, then took the teacher apart. Margie had hoped he wouldn't know how to put it together again, but he knew how all right, and, after an hour or so, there it was again, large and black and ugly, with a big screen on which all the lessons were shown and the questions were asked. That wasn't so bad. The part Margie hated most was the slot where she had to put homework and test papers. She always had to write them out in a punch code they made her learn when she was six years old, and the mechanical teacher calculated the mark in no time.

The Inspector had smiled after he was finished and patted Margie's head. He said to her mother, "It's not the little girl's fault, Mrs. Jones. I think the geography sector was geared a little too quick. Those things happen sometimes. I've slowed it up to an average ten-year level. Actually, the over-all pattern of her progress is quite satisfactory." And he patted Margie's head again.

Margie was disappointed. She had been hoping they would take the teacher away altogether. They had once taken Tommy's teacher away for nearly a month because the history sector had blanked out completely.

So she said to Tommy, "Why would anyone write about school?"

Tommy looked at her with very superior eyes. "Because it's not our kind of school, stupid. This is the old kind of school that they had hundreds and hundreds of years ago." He added loftily, pronouncing the word carefully, "*Centuries* ago."

Margie was hurt. "Well, I don't know what kind of school they had all that time ago." She read the book over his shoulder for a while, then said, "Anyway, they had a teacher."

"Sure they had a teacher, but it wasn't a *regular* teacher. It was a man."

"A man? How could a man be a teacher?"

"Well, he just told the boys and girls things and gave them homework and asked them questions."

"A man isn't smart enough."

"Sure he is. My father knows as much as my teacher."

"He can't. A man can't know as much as a teacher."

"He knows almost as much, I betcha."

Margie wasn't prepared to dispute that. She said, "I wouldn't want a strange man in my house to teach me."

Tommy screamed with laughter. "You don't know much, Margie. The teachers didn't live in the house. They had a special building and all the kids went there."

"And all the kids learned the same thing?"

"Sure, if they were the same age."

"But my mother says a teacher has to be adjusted to fit the mind of each boy and girl it teaches and that each kid has to be taught differently."

"Just the same they didn't do it that way then. If you don't like it, you don't have to read the book."

"I didn't say I didn't like it," Margie said quickly. She wanted to read about those funny schools.

They weren't even half-finished when Margie's mother called, "Margie! School!"

Margie looked up. "Not yet, Mamma."

"Now!" said Mrs. Jones. "And it's probably time for Tommy, too."

Margie said to Tommy, "Can I read the book some more with you after school?"

"Maybe," he said nonchalantly. He walked away whistling, the dusty old book tucked beneath his arm.

Margie went into the schoolroom. It was right next to her bedroom, and the mechanical teacher was on and waiting for her. It was always on at the same time every day except Saturday and Sunday, because her mother said little girls learned better if they learned at regular hours.

The screen was lit up, and it said: "Today's arithmetic lesson is on the addition of proper fractions. Please insert yesterday's homework in the proper slot."

Margie did so with a sigh. She was thinking about the old schools they had when her grandfather's grandfather was a little boy. All the kids from the whole neighborhood came, laughing and shouting in the schoolyard, sitting together in the schoolroom, going home together at the end of the day. They learned the same things, so they could help one another on the homework and talk about it.

And the teachers were people. . . .

The mechanical teacher was flashing on the screen: "When we add the fractions ½ and ¼——"

Margie was thinking about how the kids must have loved it in the old days. She was thinking about the fun they had.

JOKESTER

Noel Meyerhof consulted the list he had prepared and chose which item was to be first. As usual, he relied mainly on intuition.

He was dwarfed by the machine he faced, though only the smallest portion of the latter was in view. That didn't matter. He spoke with the offhand confidence of one who thoroughly knew he was master.

"Johnson," he said, "came home unexpectedly from a business trip to find his wife in the arms of his best friend. He staggered back and said, 'Max! I'm married to the lady so I *have* to. But why you?' "

Meyerhof thought: Okay, let that trickle down into its guts and gurgle about a bit.

And a voice behind him said, "Hey."

Meyerhof erased the sound of that monosyllable and put the circuit he was using into neutral. He whirled and said, "I'm working. Don't you knock?"

He did not smile as he customarily did in greeting Timothy Whistler, a senior analyst with whom he dealt as often as with any. He frowned as he would have for an interruption by a stranger, wrinkling his thin face into a distortion that seemed to extend to his hair, rumpling it more than ever.

Whistler shrugged. He wore his white lab coat with his fists pressing down within its pockets and creasing it into tense vertical lines. "I knocked. You didn't answer. The operations signal wasn't on."

Meyerhof grunted. It wasn't at that. He'd been thinking about this new project too intensively and he was forgetting little details.

And yet he could scarcely blame himself for that. This thing was important.

He didn't know why it was, of course. Grand Masters rarely did. That's what made them Grand Masters; the fact that they were beyond reason. How else could the human mind keep up with that ten-mile-long lump of solidified reason that men called Multivac, the most complex computer ever built?

Meyerhof said, "I *am* working. Is there something important on your mind?"

"Nothing that can't be postponed. There are a few holes in the answer on the hyperspatial——" Whistler did a double take and his face took on a rueful look of uncertainty. "*Working?*"

"Yes. What about it?"

"But——" He looked about, staring into the crannies of the shallow room that faced the banks upon banks of relays that formed a small portion of Multivac. "There isn't anyone here at that."

"Who said there was, or should be?"

"You were telling one of your jokes, weren't you?"

"And?"

Whistler forced a smile. "Don't tell me you were telling a joke to Multivac?"

Meyerhof stiffened. "Why not?"

"Were you?"

"Yes."

"Why?"

Meyerhof stared the other down. "I don't have to account to you. Or to anyone."

"Good Lord, of course not. I was curious, that's all. . . . But then, if you're working, I'll leave." He looked about once more, frowning.

"Do so," said Meyerhof. His eyes followed the other out and then he activated the operations signal with a savage punch of his finger.

He strode the length of the room and back, getting himself in hand. Damn Whistler! Damn them all! Because he didn't bother to hold those technicians, analysts and mechanics at the proper social distance, because he treated them as though they, too, were creative artists, they took these liberties.

He thought grimly: They can't even tell jokes decently.

And instantly that brought him back to the task in hand. He sat down again. Devil take them all.

He threw the proper Multivac circuit back into operation and said, "The ship's steward stopped at the rail of the ship during a particularly rough ocean crossing and gazed compassionately at the man whose slumped position over the rail and whose intensity of gaze toward the depths betokened all too well the ravages of seasickness.

"Gently, the steward patted the man's shoulder. 'Cheer up, sir,' he murmured. 'I know it seems bad, but really, you know, nobody ever dies of seasickness.'

"The afflicted gentleman lifted his greenish, tortured face to his comforter and gasped in hoarse accents, 'Don't say that, man. For Heaven's sake, don't say that. It's only the hope of dying that's keeping me alive.' "

Timothy Whistler, a bit preoccupied, nevertheless smiled and nodded as he passed the secretary's desk. She smiled back at him.

Here, he thought, was an archaic item in this computer-ridden world of the twenty-first century, a human secretary. But then perhaps it was natural that such an institution should survive here in the very citadel of computerdom; in the gigantic world corporation that handled Multivac. With Multivac filling the horizons, lesser computers for trivial tasks would have been in poor taste.

Whistler stepped into Abram Trask's office. That government official paused in his careful task of lighting a pipe; his dark eyes flicked in Whistler's direction and his beaked nose stood out sharply and prominently against the rectangle of window behind him.

"Ah, there, Whistler. Sit down. Sit down."

Whistler did so. "I think we've got a problem, Trask."

Trask half-smiled. "Not a technical one, I hope. I'm just an innocent politician." (It was one of his favorite phrases.)

"It involves Meyerhof."

Trask sat down instantly and looked acutely miserable. "Are you sure?"

"Reasonably sure."

Whistler understood the other's sudden unhappiness well. Trask was the government official in charge of the Division of Computers and Automation of the Department of the Interior. He was expected to deal with matters of policy involving the human satellites of Multivac, just as those technically trained satellites were expected to deal with Multivac itself.

But a Grand Master was more than just a satellite. More, even, than just a human.

Early in the history of Multivac, it had become apparent that the bottleneck was the questioning procedure. Multivac could answer the problems of humanity, *all* the problems, if—*if* it were asked meaningful questions. But as knowledge accumulated at an ever-faster rate, it became ever more difficult to locate those meaningful questions.

Reason alone wouldn't do. What was needed was a rare type of intuition; the same faculty of mind (only much more intensified) that made a grand master at chess. A mind was needed of the sort that could see through the quadrillions of chess patterns to find the one best move, and do it in a matter of minutes.

Trask moved restlessly. "What's Meyerhof been doing?"

"He's introduced a line of questioning that I find disturbing."

"Oh, come on, Whistler. Is that all? You can't stop a Grand Master from going through any line of questioning he chooses. Neither of us is equipped to judge the worth of his questions. You know that. I know you know that."

"I do. Of course. But I also know Meyerhof. Have you ever met him socially?"

"Good Lord, no. Does anyone meet any Grand Master socially?"

"Don't take that attitude, Trask. They're human and they're to be pitied. Have you ever thought what it must be like to be a Grand Master; to know there are only some twelve like you in the world; to know that only one or two come up per generation; that the world depends on you; that a thousand mathematicians, logicians, psychologists and physical scientists wait on you?"

Trask shrugged and muttered, "Good Lord, I'd feel king of the world."

"I don't think you would," said the senior analyst impatiently. "They feel kings of nothing. They have no equal to talk to, no sensation of belonging. Listen, Meyerhof never misses a chance to get together with the boys. He isn't married, naturally; he doesn't drink; he has no natural social touch—yet he forces himself into company because he must. And do you know what he does when he gets together with us, and that's at least once a week?"

"I haven't the least idea," said the government man. "This is all new to me."

"He's a jokester."

"What?"

"He tells jokes. Good ones. He's terrific. He can take any story, however old and dull, and make it sound good. It's the way he tells it. He has a flair."

"I see. Well, good."

"Or bad. These jokes are important to him." Whistler put both elbows on Trask's desk, bit at a thumbnail and stared into the air. "He's different, he knows he's different and these jokes are the one way he feels he can get the rest of us ordinary schmoes to accept him. We laugh, we howl, we clap him on the back and even forget he's a Grand Master. It's the only hold he has on the rest of us."

"This is all interesting. I didn't know you were such a psychologist. Still, where does this lead?"

"Just this. What do you suppose happens if Meyerhof runs out of jokes?"

"What?" The government man stared blankly.

"If he starts repeating himself? If his audience starts laughing less heartily, or stops laughing altogether? It's his only hold on our approval. Without it, he'll be alone and then what would happen to him? After all, Trask, he's one of the dozen men mankind can't do without. We can't let anything happen to him. I don't mean just physical things. We can't even let him get too unhappy. Who knows how that might affect his intuition?"

"Well, has he started repeating himself?"

"Not as far as I know, but I think *he* thinks he has."

"Why do you say that?"

"Because I've heard him telling jokes to Multivac."

"Oh, no."

"Accidentally! I walked in on him and he threw me out. He was savage. He's usually good-natured enough, and I consider it a bad sign that he was so upset at the intrusion. But the fact remains that he was telling a joke to Multivac, and I'm convinced it was one of a series."

"But why?"

Whistler shrugged and rubbed a hand fiercely across his chin. "I have a thought about that. I think he's trying to build up a store of jokes in Multivac's memory banks in order to get back new variations. You see what I mean? He's planning a mechanical jokester, so that he can have an infinite number of jokes at hand and never fear running out."

"Good Lord!"

"Objectively, there may be nothing wrong with that, but I consider it a bad sign when a Grand Master starts using Multivac for his personal problems. Any Grand Master has a certain inherent mental instability and he should be watched. Meyerhof may be approaching a borderline beyond which we lose a Grand Master."

Trask said blankly, "What are you suggesting I do?"

"You can check me. I'm too close to him to judge well, maybe, and judging humans isn't my particular talent, anyway. You're a politician; it's more your talent."

"Judging humans, perhaps, not Grand Masters."

"They're human, too. Besides, who else is to do it?"

The fingers of Trask's hand struck his desk in rapid succession over and over like a slow and muted roll of drums.

"I suppose I'll have to," he said.

Meyerhof said to Multivac, "The ardent swain, picking a bouquet of wildflowers for his loved one, was disconcerted to find himself, suddenly, in the same field with a large bull of unfriendly appearance which, gazing at him steadily, pawed the ground in a threatening manner. The young man, spying a farmer on the other side of a fairly distant fence, shouted, 'Hey, mister, is that bull safe?' The farmer surveyed the situation with critical eye, spat to one side and called back, 'He's safe as anything.' He spat again, and added, 'Can't say the same about you, though.'"

Meyerhof was about to pass on to the next when the summons came.

It wasn't really a summons. No one could summon a Grand Master. It was only a message that Division Head Trask would like very much to see Grand Master Meyerhof if Grand Master Meyerhof could spare him the time.

Meyerhof might, with impunity, have tossed the message to one side and continued with whatever he was doing. He was not subject to discipline.

On the other hand, were he to do that, they would continue to bother him—oh, very respectfully, but they would continue to bother him.

So he neutralized the pertinent circuits of Multivac and locked them into place. He put the freeze signal on his office so that no one would dare enter in his absence and left for Trask's office.

Trask coughed and felt a bit intimidated by the sullen fierceness of the other's look. He said, "We have not had occasion to know one another, Grand Master, to my great regret."

"I have reported to you," said Meyerhof stiffly.

Trask wondered what lay behind those keen, wild eyes. It was difficult for him to imagine Meyerhof with his thin face, his dark, straight hair, his intense air, ever unbending long enough to tell funny stories.

He said, "Reports are not social acquaintance. I—I have been given to understand you have a marvelous fund of anecdotes."

"I am a jokester, sir. That's the phrase people use. A jokester."

"They haven't used the phrase to me, Grand Master. They have said——"

"The hell with them! I don't care what they've said. See here, Trask, do you want to hear a joke?" He leaned forward across the desk, his eyes narrowed.

"By all means. Certainly," said Trask, with an effort at heartiness.

"All right. Here's the joke: Mrs. Jones stared at the fortune card that had emerged from the weighing machine in response to her husband's penny. She said, 'It says here, George, that you're suave, intelligent, farseeing, industrious and attractive to women.' With that, she turned the card over and added, 'And they have your weight wrong, too.'"

Trask laughed. It was almost impossible not to. Although the punch line was predictable, the surprising facility with which Meyerhof had produced just the tone of contemptuous disdain in the woman's voice, and the cleverness with which he had contorted the lines of his face to suit that tone carried the politician helplessly into laughter.

Meyerhof said sharply, "Why is that funny?"

Trask sobered. "I beg your pardon."

"I said, why is that funny? Why do you laugh?"

"Well," said Trask, trying to be reasonable, "the last line put every thing that preceded in a new light. The unexpectedness——"

"The point is," said Meyerhof, "that I have pictured a husband being humiliated by his wife; a marriage that is such a failure that the wife is convinced that her husband lacks any virtue. Yet you laugh at that. If you were the husband, would you find it funny?"

He waited a moment in thought, then said, "Try this one, Trask: Abner was seated at his wife's sickbed, weeping uncontrollably, when his wife, mustering the dregs of her strength, drew herself up to one elbow.

" 'Abner,' she whispered, 'Abner, I cannot go to my Maker without confessing my misdeed.'

" 'Not now,' muttered the stricken husband. 'Not now, my dear. Lie back and rest.'

" 'I cannot,' she cried. 'I must tell, or my soul will never know peace. I have been unfaithful to you, Abner. In this very house, not one month ago——'

" 'Hush, dear,' soothed Abner. 'I know all about it. Why else have I poisoned you?' "

Trask tried desperately to maintain equanimity but did not entirely succeed. He suppressed a chuckle imperfectly.

Meyerhof said, "So that's funny, too. Adultery. Murder. All funny."

"Well, now," said Trask, "books have been written analyzing humor."

"True enough," said Meyerhof, "and I've read a number of them. What's more, I've read most of them to Multivac. Still, the people who write the books are just guessing. Some of them say we laugh because we feel superior to the people in the joke. Some say it is because of a suddenly realized incongruity, or a sudden relief from tension, or a sudden reinterpretation of events. Is there any simple reason? Different people laugh at different jokes. No joke is universal. Some people don't laugh at any joke. Yet what may be most important is that man is the only animal with a true sense of humor, the only animal that laughs."

Trask said suddenly, "I understand. You're trying to analyze humor. That's why you're transmitting a series of jokes to Multivac."

"Who told you I was doing that? . . . Never mind, it was Whistler. I remember, now. He surprised me at it. Well, what about it?"

"Nothing at all."

"You don't dispute my right to add anything I wish to Multivac's general fund of knowledge, or to ask any question I wish?"

"No, not at all," said Trask hastily. "As a matter of fact, I have no doubt that this will open the way to new analyses of great interest to psychologists."

"Hmp. Maybe. Just the same there's something plaguing me that's more important than just the general analysis of humor. There's a specific question I have to ask. Two of them, really."

"Oh? What's that?" Trask wondered if the other would answer. There would be no way of compelling him if he chose not to.

But Meyerhof said, "The first question is this: Where do all these jokes come from?"

"What?"

"Who makes them up? Listen! About a month ago, I spent an evening swapping jokes. As usual, I told most of them and, as usual, the fools laughed. Maybe they really thought the jokes were funny and maybe they were just humoring me. In any case, one creature took the liberty of slapping me on the back and saying, 'Meyerhof, you know more jokes than any ten people I know.'

"I'm sure he was right, but it gave rise to a thought. I don't know how many hundreds, or perhaps thousands, of jokes I've told at one time or another in my life, yet the fact is I never made up one. Not one. I'd only repeated them. My only contribution was to tell them. To begin with, I'd either heard them or read them. And the source of my hearing or reading didn't make up the jokes, either. I never met anyone who ever claimed to have constructed a joke. It's always 'I heard a good one the other day,' and 'Heard any good ones lately?'

"*All the jokes are old!* That's why jokes exhibit such a social lag. They still deal with seasickness, for instance, when that's easily prevented these days and never experienced. Or they'll deal with fortune-giving weighing machines, like the joke I told you, when such machines are found only in antique shops. Well, then, who makes up the jokes?"

Trask said, "Is *that* what you're trying to find out?" It was on the tip of Trask's tongue to add: Good Lord, who cares? He forced that impulse down. A Grand Master's questions were always meaningful.

"Of course that's what I'm trying to find out. Think of it this way. It's not just that jokes happen to be old. They *must* be old to be enjoyed. It's essential that a joke not be original. There's one variety of humor that is, or can be, original and that's the pun. I've heard puns that were obviously made up on the spur of the moment. I have made some up myself. But no one laughs at such puns. You're not supposed to. You groan. The better the pun, the louder the groan. Original humor is not laugh-provoking. Why?"

"I'm sure I don't know."

"All right. Let's find out. Having given Multivac all the information I thought advisable on the general topic of humor, I am now feeding it selected jokes."

Trask found himself intrigued. "Selected how?" he asked.

"I don't know," said Meyerhof. "They felt like the right ones. I'm Grand Master, you know."

"Oh, agreed. Agreed."

"From those jokes and the general philosophy of humor, my first request will be for Multivac to trace the origin of the jokes, if it can. Since Whistler is in on this and since he has seen fit to report it to you, have him down in Analysis day after tomorrow. I think he'll have a bit of work to do."

"Certainly. May I attend, too?"

Meyerhof shrugged. Trask's attendance was obviously a matter of indifference to him.

Meyerhof had selected the last in the series with particular care. What that care consisted of, he could not have said, but he had revolved a dozen possibilities in his mind, and over and over again had tested each for some indefinable quality of meaningfulness.

He said, "Ug, the caveman, observed his mate running to him in tears, her leopard-skin skirt in disorder. 'Ug,' she cried, distraught, 'do something quickly. A saber-toothed tiger has entered Mother's cave. Do something!' Ug grunted, picked up his well-gnawed buffalo bone and said, 'Why do anything? Who the hell cares what happens to a saber-toothed tiger?' "

It was then that Meyerhof asked his two questions and leaned back, closing his eyes. He was done.

"I saw absolutely nothing wrong," said Trask to Whistler. "He told me what he was doing readily enough and it was odd but legitimate."

"What he *claimed* he was doing," said Whistler.

"Even so, I can't stop a Grand Master on opinion alone. He seemed queer but, after all, Grand Masters are supposed to seem queer. I didn't think him insane."

"Using Multivac to find the source of jokes?" muttered the senior analyst in discontent. "That's not insane?"

"How can we tell?" asked Trask irritably. "Science has advanced to the point where the only meaningful questions left are the ridiculous ones. The sensible ones have been thought of, asked and answered long ago."

"It's no use. I'm bothered."

"Maybe, but there's no choice now, Whistler. We'll see Meyerhof and you can do the necessary analysis of Multivac's response, if any. As for me, my only job is to handle the red tape. Good Lord, I don't even know what a senior analyst such as yourself is supposed to do, except analyze, and that doesn't help me any."

Whistler said, "It's simple enough. A Grand Master like Meyerhof asks questions and Multivac automatically formulates it into quantities and operations. The necessary machinery for converting words to symbols is what makes up most of the bulk of Multivac. Multivac then gives the answer in quantities and operations, but it doesn't translate that back into words except in the most simple and routine cases. If it were designed to solve the general retranslation problem, its bulk would have to be quadrupled at least."

"I see. Then it's your job to translate these symbols into words?"

"My job and that of other analysts. We use smaller, specially designed computers whenever necessary." Whistler smiled grimly. "Like the Delphic priestess of ancient Greece, Multivac gives oracular and obscure answers. Only we have translators, you see."

They had arrived. Meyerhof was waiting.

Whistler said briskly, "What circuits did you use, Grand Master?"

Meyerhof told him and Whistler went to work.

Trask tried to follow what was happening, but none of it made sense. The government official watched a spool unreel with a pattern of dots in endless incomprehensibility. Grand Master Meyerhof stood indifferently to one side while Whistler surveyed the pattern as it emerged. The analyst had put on headphones and a mouthpiece and at intervals murmured a series of instructions which, at some far-off place, guided assistants through electronic contortions in other computers.

Occasionally, Whistler listened, then punched combinations on a complex keyboard marked with symbols that looked vaguely mathematical but weren't.

A good deal more than an hour's time elapsed.

The frown on Whistler's face grew deeper. Once, he looked up at the two others and began, "This is unbel——" and turned back to his work.

Finally, he said hoarsely, "I can give you an unofficial answer." His eyes were red-rimmed. "The official answer awaits complete analysis. Do you want it unofficial?"

"Go ahead," said Meyerhof.

Trask nodded.

Whistler darted a hangdog glance at the Grand Master. "Ask a foolish question——" he said. Then, gruffly, "Multivac says, extraterrestrial origin."

"What are you saying?" demanded Trask.

"Don't you hear me? The jokes we laugh at were not made up by any man. Multivac has analyzed all data given it and the one answer that best fits that data is that some extraterrestrial intelligence has composed the jokes, all of them, and placed them in selected human minds at selected times and places in such a way that no man is conscious of having made one up. All subsequent jokes are minor variations and adaptations of these grand originals."

Meyerhof broke in, face flushed with the kind of triumph only a Grand Master can know who once again has asked the right question. "All comedy writers," he said, "work by twisting old jokes to new purposes. That's well known. The answer fits."

"But why?" asked Trask. "Why make up the jokes?"

"Multivac says," said Whistler, "that the only purpose that fits all the data is that the jokes are intended to study human psychology. We study rat psychology by making the rats solve mazes. The rats don't know why and wouldn't even if they were aware of what was going on, which they're not. These outer intelligences study man's psychology by noting individual reactions to carefully selected anecdotes. Each man reacts differently. . . . Presumably, these outer intelligences are to us as we are to rats." He shuddered.

Trask, eyes staring, said, "The Grand Master said man is the only animal with a sense of humor. It would seem then that the sense of humor is foisted upon us from without."

Meyerhof added excitedly, "And for possible humor created from within, we have no laughter. Puns, I mean."

Whistler said, "Presumably, the extraterrestrials cancel out reactions to spontaneous jokes to avoid confusion."

Trask said in sudden agony of spirit, "Come on, now, Good Lord, do either of you believe this?"

The senior analyst looked at him coldly. "Multivac says so. It's all that can be said so far. It has pointed out the real jokesters of the universe, and if we want to know more, the matter will have to be followed up." He added in a whisper, "If anyone dares follow it up."

Grand Master Meyerhof said suddenly, "I asked two questions, you know. So far only the first has been answered. I think Multivac has enough data to answer the second."

Whistler shrugged. He seemed a half-broken man. "When a Grand Master thinks there is enough data," he said, "I'll make book on it. What is your second question?"

"I asked this: What will be the effect on the human race of discovering the answer to my first question?"

"Why did you ask that?" demanded Trask.

"Just a feeling that it had to be asked," said Meyerhof.

Trask said, "Insane. It's all insane," and turned away. Even he himself felt how strangely he and Whistler had changed sides. Now it was Trask crying insanity.

Trask closed his eyes. He might cry insanity all he wished, but no man in fifty years had doubted the combination of a Grand Master and Multivac and found his doubts verified.

Whistler worked silently, teeth clenched. He put Multivac and its subsidiary machines through their paces again. Another hour passed and he laughed harshly. "A raving nightmare!"

"What's the answer?" asked Meyerhof. "I want Multivac's remarks, not yours."

"All right. Take it. Multivac states that, once even a single human discovers the truth of this method of psychological analysis of the human mind, it will become useless as an objective technique to those extraterrestrial powers now using it."

"You mean there won't be any more jokes handed out to humanity?" asked Trask faintly. "Or what do you mean?"

"No more jokes," said Whistler, "*now!* Multivac says *now!* The experiment is ended *now!* A new technique will have to be introduced."

They stared at each other. The minutes passed.

Meyerhof said slowly, "Multivac is right."

Whistler said haggardly, "I know."

Even Trask said in a whisper, "Yes. It must be."

It was Meyerhof who put his finger on the proof of it, Meyerhof the accomplished jokester. He said, "It's over, you know, all over. I've been trying for five minutes now and I can't think of one single joke, not one! And if I read one in a book, I wouldn't laugh. I know."

"The gift of humor is gone," said Trask drearily. "No man will ever laugh again."

And they remained there, staring, feeling the world shrink down to the dimensions of an experimental rat cage—with the maze removed and something, something about to be put in its place.

THE IMMORTAL BARD

"Oh, yes," said Dr. Phineas Welch, "I can bring back the spirits of the illustrious dead."

He was a little drunk, or maybe he wouldn't have said it. Of course, it was perfectly all right to get a little drunk at the annual Christmas party.

Scott Robertson, the school's young English instructor, adjusted his glasses and looked to right and left to see if they were overheard. "Really, Dr. Welch."

"I mean it. And not just the spirits. I bring back the bodies, too."

"I wouldn't have said it were possible," said Robertson primly.

"Why not? A simple matter of temporal transference."

"You mean time travel? But that's quite—uh—unusual."

"Not if you know how."

"Well, how, Dr. Welch?"

"Think I'm going to tell you?" asked the physicist gravely. He looked vaguely about for another drink and didn't find any. He said, "I've brought quite a few back. Archimedes, Newton, Galileo. Poor fellows."

"Didn't they like it here? I should think they'd have been fascinated by our modern science," said Robertson. He was beginning to enjoy the conversation.

"Oh, they were. They were. Especially Archimedes. I thought he'd go mad with joy at first after I explained a little of it in some Greek I'd boned up on, but no—no——"

"What was wrong?"

"Just a different culture. They couldn't get used to our way of life. They got terribly lonely and frightened. I had to send them back."

"That's too bad."

"Yes. Great minds, but not flexible minds. Not universal. So I tried Shakespeare."

"*What?*" yelled Robertson. This was getting closer to home.

"Don't yell, my boy," said Welch. "It's bad manners."

"Did you say you brought back Shakespeare?"

"I did. I needed someone with a universal mind; someone who knew people well enough to be able to live with them centuries away from his own time. Shakespeare was the man. I've got his signature. As a memento, you know."

"On you?" asked Robertson, eyes bugging.

"Right here." Welch fumbled in one vest pocket after another. "Ah, here it is."

A little piece of pasteboard was passed to the instructor. On one side it said: "L. Klein & Sons, Wholesale Hardware." On the other side, in straggly script, was written, "Willm Shaksper."

A wild surmise filled Robertson. "What did he look like?"

"Not like his pictures. Bald and an ugly mustache. He spoke in a thick brogue. Of course, I did my best to please him with our times. I told him we thought highly of his plays and still put them on the boards. In fact, I said we thought they were the greatest pieces of literature in the English language, maybe in any language."

"Good. Good," said Robertson breathlessly.

"I said people had written volumes of commentaries on his plays. Naturally he wanted to see one and I got one for him from the library."

"And?"

"Oh, he was fascinated. Of course, he had trouble with the current idioms and references to events since 1600, but I helped out. Poor fellow. I don't think he ever expected such treatment. He kept saying, 'God ha' mercy! What cannot be racked from words in five centuries? One could wring, methinks, a flood from a damp clout!' "

"He wouldn't say that."

"Why not? He wrote his plays as quickly as he could. He said he had to on account of the deadlines. He wrote *Hamlet* in less than six months. The plot was an old one. He just polished it up."

"That's all they do to a telescope mirror. Just polish it up," said the English instructor indignantly.

The physicist disregarded him. He made out an untouched cocktail on the bar some feet away and sidled toward it. "I told the immortal bard that we even gave college courses in Shakespeare."

"*I* give one."

"I know. I enrolled him in your evening extension course. I never saw a man so eager to find out what posterity thought of him as poor Bill was. He worked hard at it."

"You enrolled William Shakespeare in my course?" mumbled Robertson. Even as an alcoholic fantasy, the thought staggered him. And *was* it an alcoholic fantasy? He was beginning to recall a bald man with a queer way of talking. . . .

"Not under his real name, of course," said Dr. Welch. "Never mind what he went under. It was a mistake, that's all. A big mistake. Poor fellow." He had the cocktail now and shook his head at it.

"Why was it a mistake? What happened?"

"I had to send him back to 1600," roared Welch indignantly. "How much humiliation do you think a man can stand?"

"What humiliation are you talking about?"

Dr. Welch tossed off the cocktail. "Why, you poor simpleton, you *flunked* him."

SOMEDAY

Niccolo Mazetti lay stomach down on the rug, chin buried in the palm of one small hand, and listened to the Bard disconsolately. There was even the suspicion of tears in his dark eyes, a luxury an eleven-year-old could allow himself only when alone.

The Bard said, "Once upon a time in the middle of a deep wood, there lived a poor woodcutter and his two motherless daughters, who were each as beautiful as the day is long. The older daughter had long hair as black as a feather from a raven's wing, but the younger daughter had hair as bright and golden as the sunlight of an autumn afternoon.

"Many times while the girls were waiting for their father to come home from his day's work in the wood, the older girl would sit before a mirror and sing——"

What she sang, Niccolo did not hear, for a call sounded from outside the room: "Hey, Nickie."

And Niccolo, his face clearing on the moment, rushed to the window and shouted, "Hey, Paul."

Paul Loeb waved an excited hand. He was thinner than Niccolo and not as tall, for all he was six months older. His face was full of repressed tension which showed itself most clearly in the rapid blinking of his eyelids. "Hey, Nickie, let me in. I've got an idea and a *half*. Wait till you hear it." He looked rapidly about him as though to check on the possibility of eavesdroppers, but the front yard was quite patently empty. He repeated, in a whisper, "Wait till you hear it."

"All right. I'll open the door."

The Bard continued smoothly, oblivious to the sudden loss of attention on the part of Niccolo. As Paul entered, the Bard was saying, ". . . Thereupon, the lion said, 'If you will find me the lost egg of the bird which flies over the Ebony Mountain once every ten years, I will——"

Paul said, "Is that a Bard you're listening to? I didn't know you had one."

Niccolo reddened and the look of unhappiness returned to his face. "Just an old thing I had when I was a kid. It ain't much good." He kicked at the Bard with his foot and caught the somewhat scarred and discolored plastic covering a glancing blow.

The Bard hiccupped as its speaking attachment was jarred out of contact a moment, then it went on: "—for a year and a day until the iron shoes were worn out. The princess stopped at the side of the road. . . ."

Paul said, "Boy, that *is* an old model," and looked at it critically.

Despite Niccolo's own bitterness against the Bard, he winced at the other's condescending tone. For the moment, he was sorry he had allowed Paul in, at least before he had restored the Bard to its usual resting place in the basement. It was only in the desperation of a dull day and a fruitless discussion with his father that he had resurrected it. And it turned out to be just as stupid as he had expected.

Nickie was a little afraid of Paul anyway, since Paul had special courses at school and everyone said he was going to grow up to be a Computing Engineer.

Not that Niccolo himself was doing badly at school. He got adequate marks in logic, binary manipulations, computing and elementary circuits; all the usual grammar-school subjects. But that was it! They were just the usual subjects and he would grow up to be a control-board guard like everyone else.

Paul, however, knew mysterious things about what he called electronics and theoretical mathematics and programing. Especially programing. Niccolo didn't even try to understand when Paul bubbled over about it.

Paul listened to the Bard for a few minutes and said, "You been using it much?"

"No!" said Niccolo, offended. "I've had it in the basement since before you moved into the neighborhood. I just got it out today——" He lacked an excuse that seemed adequate to himself, so he concluded, "I just got it out."

Paul said, "Is that what it tells you about: woodcutters and princesses and talking animals?"

Niccolo said, "It's terrible. My dad says we can't afford a new one. I said to him this morning——" The memory of the morning's fruitless pleadings brought Niccolo dangerously near tears, which he repressed in a panic. Somehow, he felt that Paul's thin cheeks never felt the stain of tears and that Paul would have only contempt for anyone else less strong than himself. Niccolo went on, "So I thought I'd try this old thing again, but it's no good."

Paul turned off the Bard, pressed the contact that led to a nearly instantaneous reorientation and recombination of the vocabulary, characters, plot lines and climaxes stored within it. Then he reactivated it.

The Bard began smoothly, "Once upon a time there was a little boy named Willikins whose mother had died and who lived with a stepfather and a stepbrother. Although the stepfather was very well-to-do, he begrudged poor Willikins the very bed he slept in so that Willikins was forced to get such rest as he could on a pile of straw in the stable next to the horses——"

"Horses!" cried Paul.

"They're a kind of animal," said Niccolo. "I think."

"I know that! I just mean imagine stories about *horses*."

"It tells about horses all the time," said Niccolo. "There are things called cows, too. You milk them but the Bard doesn't say how."

"Well, gee, why don't you fix it up?"

"I'd like to know how."

The Bard was saying, "Often Willikins would think that if only he were rich and powerful, he would show his stepfather and stepbrother what it meant to be cruel to a little boy, so one day he decided to go out into the world and seek his fortune."

Paul, who wasn't listening to the Bard, said, "It's *easy*. The Bard has memory cylinders all fixed up for plot lines and climaxes and things. We don't have to worry about that. It's just vocabulary we've got to fix so it'll know about computers and automation and electronics and real things about today. Then it can tell interesting stories, you know, instead of about princesses and things."

Niccolo said despondently, "I wish we could do that."

Paul said, "Listen, my dad says if I get into special computing school next year, he'll get me a *real* Bard, a late model. A big one with an attachment for space stories and mysteries. And a visual attachment, too!"

"You mean *see* the stories?"

"Sure. Mr. Daugherty at school says they've got things like that, now, but not for just everybody. Only if I get into computing school, Dad can get a few breaks."

Niccolo's eyes bulged with envy. "Gee. *Seeing* a story."

"You can come over and watch anytime, Nickie."

"Oh, boy. Thanks."

"That's all right. But remember, I'm the guy who says what kind of story we hear."

"Sure. Sure." Niccolo would have agreed readily to much more onerous conditions.

Paul's attention returned to the Bard.

It was saying, "'If that is the case,' said the king, stroking his beard and frowning till clouds filled the sky and lightning flashed, 'you will see to it that my entire land is freed of flies by this time day after tomorrow or——' "

"All we've got to do," said Paul, "is open it up——" He shut the Bard off again and was prying at its front panel as he spoke.

"Hey," said Niccolo, in sudden alarm. "Don't break it."

"I won't break it," said Paul impatiently. "I know all about these things." Then, with sudden caution, "Your father and mother home?"

"No."

"All right, then." He had the front panel off and peered in. "Boy, this *is* a one-cylinder thing."

He worked away at the Bard's innards. Niccolo, who watched with painful suspense, could not make out what he was doing.

Paul pulled out a thin, flexible metal strip, powdered with dots. "That's the Bard's memory cylinder. I'll bet its capacity for stories is under a trillion."

"What are you going to do, Paul?" quavered Niccolo.

"I'll give it vocabulary."

"How?"

"Easy. I've got a book here. Mr. Daugherty gave it to me at school."

Paul pulled the book out of his pocket and pried at it till he had its plastic jacket off. He unreeled the tape a bit, ran it through the vocalizer, which he turned down to a whisper, then placed it within the Bard's vitals. He made further attachments.

"What'll that do?"

"The book will talk and the Bard will put it all on its memory tape."

"What good will that do?"

"Boy, you're a dope! This book is all about computers and automation and the Bard will get all that information. Then he can stop talking about kings making lightning when they frown."

Niccolo said, "And the good guy always wins anyway. There's no excitement."

"Oh, well," said Paul, watching to see if his setup was working properly, "that's the way they make Bards. They got to have the good guy win and make the bad guys lose and things like that. I heard my father talking about it once. He says that without censorship there'd be no telling what the younger generation would come to. He says it's bad enough as it is. . . . There, it's working fine."

Paul brushed his hands against one another and turned away from the Bard. He said, "But listen, I didn't tell you my idea yet. It's the best thing you ever heard, I bet. I came right to you, because I figured you'd come in with me."

"Sure, Paul, sure."

"Okay. You know Mr. Daugherty at school? You know what a funny kind of guy he is. Well, he likes me, kind of."

"I know."

"I was over his house after school today."

"You *were?*"

"Sure. He says I'm going to be entering computer school and he wants to encourage me and things like that. He says the world needs more people who can design advanced computer circuits and do proper programing."

"Oh?"

Paul might have caught some of the emptiness behind that monosyllable. He said impatiently, "Programing! I told you a hundred times. That's when you set up problems for the giant computers like Multivac to work on. Mr. Daugherty says it gets harder all the time to find people who can really run computers. He says anyone can keep an eye on the controls and check off answers and put through routine problems. He says the trick is to expand research and figure out ways to ask the right questions, and that's hard.

"Anyway, Nickie, he took me to his place and showed me his collection of old computers. It's kind of a hobby of his to collect old computers. He had tiny computers you had to push with your hand, with little knobs all over it. And he had a hunk of wood he called a slide rule with a little piece of it that went in and out. And some wires with balls on them. He even had a hunk of paper with a kind of thing he called a multiplication table."

Niccolo, who found himself only moderately interested, said, "A paper table?"

"It wasn't really a table like you eat on. It was different. It was to help people compute. Mr. Daugherty tried to explain but he didn't have much time and it was kind of complicated, anyway."

"Why didn't people just use a computer?"

"That was *before* they had computers," cried Paul.

"Before?"

"Sure. Do you think people always had computers? Didn't you ever hear of cavemen?"

Niccolo said, "How'd they get along without computers?"

"I don't know. Mr. Daugherty says they just had children any old time and did anything that came into their heads whether it would be good for everybody or not. They didn't even know if it was good or not. And farmers grew things with their hands and people had to do all the work in the factories and run all the machines."

"I don't believe you."

"That's what Mr. Daugherty said. He said it was just plain messy and everyone was miserable. . . . Anyway, let me get to my idea, will you?"

"Well, go ahead. Who's stopping you?" said Niccolo, offended.

"All right. Well, the hand computers, the ones with the knobs, had little squiggles on each knob. And the slide rule had squiggles on it. And the multiplication table was all squiggles. I asked what they were. Mr. Daugherty said they were numbers."

"What?"

"Each different squiggle stood for a different number. For 'one' you made a kind of mark, for 'two' you make another kind of mark, for 'three' another one and so on."

"What for?"

"So you could compute."

"What *for*? You just tell the computer——"

"Jiminy," cried Paul, his face twisting with anger, "can't you get it through your head? These slide rules and things didn't talk."

"Then how——"

"The answers showed up in squiggles and you had to know what the squiggles meant. Mr. Daugherty says that, in olden days, everybody learned how to make squiggles when they were kids and how to decode them, too. Making squiggles was called 'writing' and decoding them was 'reading.' He says there was a different kind of squiggle for every word and they used to write whole books in squiggles. He said they had some at the museum and I could look at them if I wanted to. He said if I was going to be a real computer and programer I would have to know about the history of computing and that's why he was showing me all these things."

Niccolo frowned. He said, "You mean everybody had to figure out squiggles for every word and *remember* them? . . . Is this all real or are you making it up?"

"It's all real. Honest. Look, this is the way you make a 'one.'" He drew his finger through the air in a rapid downstroke. "This way you make 'two,' and this way 'three.' I learned all the numbers up to 'nine.'"

Niccolo watched the curving finger uncomprehendingly. "What's the good of it?"

"You can learn how to make words. I asked Mr. Daugherty how you made the squiggle for 'Paul Loeb' but he didn't know. He said there were people at the museum who would know. He said there were people who had learned how to decode whole books. He said computers could be designed to decode books and used to be used that way but not any more because we have real books now, with magnetic tapes that go through the vocalizer and come out talking, you know."

"Sure."

"So if we go down to the museum, we can get to learn how to make words in squiggles. They'll let us because I'm going to computer school."

Niccolo was riddled with disappointment. "Is that your idea? Holy Smokes, Paul, who wants to do that? Make stupid squiggles!"

"Don't you get it? Don't you *get* it? You dope. *It'll be secret message stuff!*"

"What?"

"Sure. What good is talking when everyone can understand you? With squiggles you can send secret messages. You can make them on paper and nobody in the world would know what you were saying unless they knew the squiggles, too. And they wouldn't, you bet, unless we taught them. We can have a real club, with initiations and rules and a clubhouse. Boy——"

A certain excitement began stirring in Niccolo's bosom. "What kind of secret messages?"

"Any kind. Say I want to tell you to come over my place and watch my new Visual Bard and I don't want any of the other fellows to come. I make the right squiggles on paper and I give it to you and you look at it and you know what to do. Nobody else does. You can even show it to them and they wouldn't know a thing."

"Hey, that's something," yelled Niccolo, completely won over. "When do we learn how?"

"Tomorrow," said Paul. "I'll get Mr. Daugherty to explain to the museum that it's all right and you get your mother and father to say okay. We can go down right after school and start learning."

"Sure!" cried Niccolo. "We can be club officers."

"I'll be president of the club," said Paul matter-of-factly. "You can be vice-president."

"All right. Hey, this is going to be lots more fun than the Bard." He was suddenly reminded of the Bard and said in sudden apprehension, "Hey, what about my old Bard?"

Paul turned to look at it. It was quietly taking in the slowly unreeling book, and the sound of the book's vocalizations was a dimly heard murmur.

He said, "I'll disconnect it."

He worked away while Niccolo watched anxiously. After a few moments, Paul put his reassembled book into his pocket, replaced the Bard's panel and activated it.

The Bard said, "Once upon a time, in a large city, there lived a poor young boy named Fair Johnnie whose only friend in the world was a small computer. The computer, each morning, would tell the boy whether it would rain that day and answer any problems he might have. It was never wrong. But it so happened that one day, the king of that land, having heard of the little computer, decided that he would have it as his own. With this purpose in mind, he called in his Grand Vizier and said——"

Niccolo turned off the Bard with a quick motion of his hand. "Same old junk," he said passionately. "Just with a computer thrown in."

"Well," said Paul, "they got so much stuff on the tape already that the computer business doesn't show up much when random combinations are made. What's the difference, anyway? You just need a new model."

"We'll *never* be able to afford one. Just this dirty old miserable thing." He kicked at it again, hitting it more squarely this time. The Bard moved backward with a squeal of castors.

"You can always watch mine, when I get it," said Paul. "Besides, don't forget our squiggle club."

Niccolo nodded.

"I tell you what," said Paul. "Let's go over my place. My father has some books about old times. We can listen to them and maybe get some ideas. You leave a note for your folks and maybe you can stay over for supper. Come on."

"Okay," said Niccolo, and the two boys ran out together. Niccolo, in his eagerness, ran almost squarely into the Bard, but he only rubbed at the spot on his hip where he had made contact and ran on.

The activation signal of the Bard glowed. Niccolo's collision closed a circuit and, although it was alone in the room and there was none to hear, it began a story, nevertheless.

But not in its usual voice, somehow; in a lower tone that had a hint of throatiness in it. An adult, listening, might almost have thought that the voice carried a hint of passion in it, a trace of near feeling.

The Bard said: "Once upon a time, there was a little computer named the Bard who lived all alone with cruel step-people. The cruel step-people continually made fun of the little computer and sneered at him, telling him he was good-for-nothing and that he was a useless object. They struck him and kept him in lonely rooms for months at a time.

"Yet through it all the little computer remained brave. He always did the best he could, obeying all orders cheerfully. Nevertheless, the step-people with whom he lived remained cruel and heartless.

"One day, the little computer learned that in the world there existed a great many computers of all sorts, great numbers of them. Some were Bards like himself, but some ran factories, and some ran farms. Some organized population and some analyzed all kinds of data. Many were very powerful and very wise, much more powerful and wise than the step-people who were so cruel to the little computer.

"And the little computer knew then that computers would always grow wiser and more powerful until someday—someday—someday——"

But a valve must finally have stuck in the Bard's aging and corroding vitals, for as it waited alone in the darkening room through the evening, it could only whisper over and over again, "Someday—someday—someday."

THE AUTHOR'S ORDEAL

(*with apologies to* W. S. *Gilbert*)

Plots, helter-skelter, teem within your brain;
    Plots, s.f. plots, devised with joy and gladness;
Plots crowd your skull and stubbornly remain,
    Until you're driven into hopeless madness.

When you're with your best girl and your mind's in a whirl
    and you don't hear a thing that she's saying;
Or at Symphony Hall you are gone past recall and you can't
    tell a note that they're playing;
Or you're driving a car and have not gone too far when you
    find that you've sped through a red light,
And on top of that, lord! you have sideswiped a Ford, and
    have broken your one working headlight;
Or your boss slaps your back (having made some smart crack)
    and you stare at him, stupidly blinking;
Then you say something dumb so he's sure you're a crumb, and
    are possibly given to drinking.
When events such as that have been knocking you flat, do not
    blame supernatural forces;
If you write s.f. tales, you'll be knocked off your rails, just
    as sure as the stars in their courses.
For your plot-making mind will stay deaf, dumb and blind to the dull
    facts of life that will hound you,
While the wonders of space have you close in embrace and the glory
    of star beams surround you.
You begin with a ship that is caught on a skip into hyperspace
    en route for Castor,
And has found to its cost that it seems to be lost in a Galaxy
    like ours, but vaster.
You're a little perplexed as to what may come next and you make up
    a series of creatures
Who are villains and liars with such evil desires and with per-
    fectly horrible features.
Our brave heroes are faced with these hordes and are placed in a
    terribly crucial position,
For the enemy's bound (once our Galaxy's found) that they'll beat
    mankind into submission.
Now you must make it rough when developing stuff so's to keep the
    yarn pulsing with tension,

So the Earthmen are four (only four and no more) while the numbers
of foes are past mention.
Our four heroes are caught and accordingly brought to the sneering,
tyrannical leaders.
"Where is Earth?" they demand, but the men mutely stand with a
courage that pleases the readers.

But, now, wait just a bit; let's see, this isn't it, since you
haven't provided a maiden,
Who is both good and pure (yet with sexy allure) and with not
many clothes overladen.
She is part of the crew, and so she's captured, too, and is ogled
by foes who are lustful;
There's desire in each eye and there's good reason why, for of
beauty our girl has a bustful.
Just the same you go fast till this section is passed so the
reader won't raise any ruction,
When recalling the foe are all reptiles and so have no interest
in human seduction.
Then they truss up the girl and they make the whips swirl just in
order to break Earthmen's silence,
And so that's when our men break their handcuffs and then we are
treated to scenes full of violence.
Every hero from Earth is a fighter from birth and his fists are
a match for a dozen,
And then just when this spot has been reached in your plot you
come to with your mind all a buzzin'.

You don't know where you are, or the site of your car, and your tie
is askew and you haven't a clue of the time of the day
or of what people say or the fact that they stare at your
socks (not a pair) and decide it's a fad, or else that
you're mad, which is just a surmise from the gleam in
your eyes, till at last they conclude from your general
mood, you'll be mad from right now till you're hoary.
But the torture is done and it's now for the fun and the paper
that's white and the words that are right, for you've
worked up a new s.f. story.

DREAMING IS A PRIVATE THING

Jesse Weill looked up from his desk. His old, spare body, his sharp, high-bridged nose, deep-set, shadowy eyes and amazing shock of white hair had trademarked his appearance during the years that Dreams, Inc., had become world-famous.

He said, "Is the boy here already, Joe?"

Joe Dooley was short and heavy-set. A cigar caressed his moist lower lip. He took it away for a moment and nodded. "His folks are with him. They're all scared."

"You're sure this is not a false alarm, Joe? I haven't got much time." He looked at his watch. "Government business at two."

"This is a sure thing, Mr. Weill." Dooley's face was a study in earnestness. His jowls quivered with persuasive intensity. "Like I told you, I picked him up playing some kind of basketball game in the schoolyard. You should've seen the kid. He stunk. When he had his hands on the ball, his own team had to take it away, and fast, but just the same he had all the stance of a star player. Know what I mean? To me it was a giveaway."

"Did you talk to him?"

"Well, sure. I stopped him at lunch. You know me." Dooley gestured expansively with his cigar and caught the severed ash with his other hand. "Kid, I said——"

"And he's dream material?"

"I said, 'Kid, I just came from Africa and——' "

"All right." Weill held up the palm of his hand. "Your word I'll always take. How you do it I don't know, but when you say a boy is a potential dreamer, I'll gamble. Bring him in."

The youngster came in between his parents. Dooley pushed chairs forward and Weill rose to shake hands. He smiled at the youngster in a way that turned the wrinkles of his face into benevolent creases.

"You're Tommy Slutsky?"

Tommy nodded wordlessly. He was about ten and a little small for that. His dark hair was plastered down unconvincingly and his face was unrealistically clean.

Weill said, "You're a good boy?"

The boy's mother smiled at once and patted Tommy's head maternally (a gesture which did not soften the anxious expression on the youngster's face). She said, "He's always a very good boy."

Weill let this dubious statement pass. "Tell me, Tommy," he said, and held out a lollipop which was first hesitated over, then accepted, "do you ever listen to dreamies?"

"Sometimes," said Tommy trebly.

Mr. Slutsky cleared his throat. He was broad-shouldered and thick-fingered, the type of laboring man who, every once in a while, to the confusion of eugenics, sired a dreamer. "We rented one or two for the boy. Real old ones."

Weill nodded. He said, "Did you like them, Tommy?"

"They were sort of silly."

"You think up better ones for yourself, do you?"

The grin that spread over the ten-year-old face had the effect of taking away some of the unreality of the slicked hair and washed face.

Weill went on gently, "Would you like to make up a dream for me?"

Tommy was instantly embarrassed. "I guess not."

"It won't be hard. It's very easy. . . . Joe."

Dooley moved a screen out of the way and rolled forward a dream recorder.

The youngster looked owlishly at it.

Weill lifted the helmet and brought it close to the boy. "Do you know what this is?"

Tommy shrank away. "No."

"It's a thinker. That's what we call it because people think into it. You put it on your head and think anything you want."

"Then what happens?"

"Nothing at all. It feels nice."

"No," said Tommy, "I guess I'd rather not."

His mother bent hurriedly toward him. "It won't hurt, Tommy. You do what the man says." There was an unmistakable edge to her voice.

Tommy stiffened, and looked as though he might cry but he didn't. Weill put the thinker on him.

He did it gently and slowly and let it remain there for some thirty second before speaking again, to let the boy assure himself it would do no harm, to let him get used to the insinuating touch of the fibrils against the sutures of his skull (penetrating the skin so finely as to be insensible almost), and finally to let him get used to the faint hum of the alternating field vortices.

Then he said, "Now would you think for us?"

"About what?" Only the boy's nose and mouth showed.

"About anything you want. What's the best thing you would like to do when school is out?"

The boy thought a moment and said, with rising inflection, "Go on a stratojet?"

"Why not? Sure thing. You go on a jet. It's taking off right now." He gestured lightly to Dooley, who threw the freezer into circuit.

Weill kept the boy only five minutes and then let him and his mother be escorted from the office by Dooley. Tommy looked bewildered but undamaged by the ordeal.

Weill said to the father, "Now, Mr. Slutsky, if your boy does well on this test, we'll be glad to pay you five hundred dollars each year until he finishes high school. In that time, all we'll ask is that he spend an hour a week some afternoon at our special school."

"Do I have to sign a paper?" Slutsky's voice was a bit hoarse.

"Certainly. This is business, Mr. Slutsky."

"Well, I don't know. Dreamers are hard to come by, I hear."

"They are. They are. But your son, Mr. Slutsky, is not a dreamer yet. He might never be. Five hundred dollars a year is a gamble for us. It's not a gamble for you. When he's finished high school, it may turn out he's not a dreamer, yet you've lost nothing. You've gained maybe four thousand dollars altogether. If he *is* a dreamer, he'll make a nice living and you certainly haven't lost then."

"He'll need special training, won't he?"

"Oh, yes, most intensive. But we don't have to worry about that till after he's finished high school. Then, after two years with us, he'll be developed. Rely on me, Mr. Slutsky."

"Will you guarantee that special training?"

Weill, who had been shoving a paper across the desk at Slutsky, and punching a pen wrong-end-to at him, put the pen down and chuckled. "A guarantee? No. How can we when we don't know for sure yet if he's a real talent? Still, the five hundred a year will stay yours."

Slutsky pondered and shook his head. "I tell you straight out, Mr. Weill . . . After your man arranged to have us come here, I called Luster-Think. They said they'll guarantee training."

Weill sighed. "Mr. Slutsky, I don't like to talk against a competitor. If they say they'll guarantee schooling, they'll do as they say, but they can't make a boy a dreamer if he hasn't got it in him, schooling or not. If they take a plain boy without the proper talent and put him through a development course, they'll ruin him. A dreamer he won't be, I guarantee you. And a normal human being, he won't be, either. Don't take the chance of doing it to your son.

"Now Dreams, Inc., will be perfectly honest with you. If he can be a dreamer, we'll make him one. If not, we'll give him back to you without having tampered with him and say, 'Let him learn a trade.' He'll be better and healthier that way. I tell you, Mr. Slutsky—I have sons and daughters and grandchildren so I know what I say—I would not allow a child of mine to be pushed into dreaming if he's not ready for it. Not for a million dollars."

Slutsky wiped his mouth with the back of his hand and reached for the pen. "What does this say?"

"This is just an option. We pay you a hundred dollars in cash right now. No strings attached. We'll study the boy's reverie. If we feel it's worth following up, we'll call you in again and make the five-hundred-dollar-a-year deal. Leave yourself in my hands, Mr. Slutsky, and don't worry. You won't be sorry."

Slutsky signed.

Weill passed the document through the file slot and handed an envelope to Slutsky.

Five minutes later, alone in the office, he placed the unfreezer over his own head and absorbed the boy's reverie intently. It was a typically childish daydream. First Person was at the controls of the plane, which looked like a compound of illustrations out of the filmed thrillers that still circulated among those who lacked the time, desire or money for dream cylinders.

When he removed the unfreezer, he found Dooley looking at him.

"Well, Mr. Weill, what do you think?" said Dooley, with an eager and proprietary air.

"Could be, Joe. Could be. He has the overtones and, for a ten-year-old boy without a scrap of training, it's hopeful. When the plane went through a cloud, there was a distinct sensation of pillows. Also the smell of clean sheets, which was an amusing touch. We can go with him a ways, Joe."

"Good."

"But I tell you, Joe, what we really need is to catch them still sooner. And why not? Someday, Joe, every child will be tested at birth. A difference in the brain there positively must be and it should be found. Then we could separate the dreamers at the very beginning."

"Hell, Mr. Weill," said Dooley, looking hurt. "What would happen to my job, then?"

Weill laughed. "No cause to worry yet, Joe. It won't happen in our lifetimes. In mine, certainly not. We'll be depending on good talent scouts like you for many years. You just watch the playgrounds and the streets"—Weill's gnarled hand dropped to Dooley's shoulder with a gentle, approving pressure—"and find us a few more Hillarys and Janows and Luster-Think won't ever catch us. . . . Now get out. I want lunch and then I'll be ready for my two o'clock appointment. The government, Joe, the government." And he winked portentously.

Jesse Weill's two o'clock appointment was with a young man, apple-cheeked, spectacled, sandy-haired and glowing with the intensity of a man with a mission. He presented his credentials across Weill's desk and revealed himself to be John J. Byrne, an agent of the Department of Arts and Sciences.

"Good afternoon, Mr. Byrne," said Weill. "In what way can I be of service?"

"Are we private here?" asked the agent. He had an unexpected baritone.

"Quite private."

"Then, if you don't mind, I'll ask you to absorb this." Byrne produced a small and battered cylinder and held it out between thumb and forefinger.

Weill took it, hefted it, turned it this way and that and said with a denture-revealing smile, "Not the product of Dreams, Inc., Mr. Byrne."

"I didn't think it was," said the agent. "I'd still like you to absorb it. I'd set the automatic cutoff for about a minute, though."

"That's all that can be endured?" Weill pulled the receiver to his desk and placed the cylinder into the unfreeze compartment. He removed it, polished either end of the cylinder with his handkerchief and tried again. "It doesn't make good contact," he said. "An amateurish job."

He placed the cushioned unfreeze helmet over his skull and adjusted the temple contacts, then set the automatic cutoff. He leaned back and clasped his hands over his chest and began absorbing.

His fingers grew rigid and clutched at his jacket. After the cutoff had brought absorption to an end, he removed the unfreezer and looked faintly angry. "A raw piece," he said. "It's lucky I'm an old man so that such things no longer bother me."

Byrne said stiffly, "It's not the worst we've found. And the fad is increasing."

Weill shrugged. "Pornographic dreamies. It's a logical development, I suppose."

The government man said, "Logical or not, it represents a deadly danger for the moral fiber of the nation."

"The moral fiber," said Weill, "can take a lot of beating. Erotica of one form or another have been circulated all through history."

"Not like this, sir. A direct mind-to-mind stimulation is much more effective than smoking room stories or filthy pictures. Those must be filtered through the senses and lose some of their effect in that way."

Weill could scarcely argue that point. He said, "What would you have me do?"

"Can you suggest a possible source for this cylinder?"

"Mr. Byrne, I'm not a policeman."

"No, no, I'm not asking you to do our work for us. The Department is quite capable of conducting its own investigations. Can you help us, I mean, from your own specialized knowledge? You say your company did not put out that filth. Who did?"

"No reputable dream distributor. I'm sure of that. It's too cheaply made."

"That could have been done on purpose."

"And no professional dreamer originated it."

"Are you sure, Mr. Weill? Couldn't dreamers do this sort of thing for some small, illegitimate concern for money—or for fun?"

"They could, but not this particular one. No overtones. It's two-dimensional. Of course, a thing like this doesn't need overtones."

"What do you mean, overtones?"

Weill laughed gently. "You are not a dreamie fan?"

Byrne tried not to look virtuous and did not entirely succeed. "I prefer music."

"Well, that's all right, too," said Weill tolerantly, "but it makes it a little harder to explain overtones. Even people who absorb dreamies would not be able to explain if you asked them. Still they'd know a dreamie was no good if the overtones were missing, even if they couldn't tell you why. Look, when an experienced dreamer goes into reverie, he doesn't think a story like in the old-fashioned television or book films. It's a series of little visions. Each one has several meanings. If you studied them carefully, you'd find maybe five or six. While absorbing in the ordinary way, you would never notice, but careful study shows it. Believe me, my psychological staff puts in long hours on just that point. All the overtones, the different meanings, blend together into a mass of guided emotion. Without them, everything would be flat, tasteless.

"Now, this morning, I tested a young boy. A ten-year-old with possibilities. A cloud to him isn't a cloud, it's a pillow, too. Having the sensations of both, it was more than either. Of course, the boy's very primitive. But when he's through with his schooling, he'll be trained and disciplined. He'll be subjected to all sorts of sensations. He'll store up experience. He'll study and analyze classic dreamies of the past. He'll learn how to control and direct his thoughts, though, mind you, I have always said that when a good dreamer improvises——"

Weill halted abruptly, then proceeded in less impassioned tones, "I shouldn't get excited. All I try to bring out now is that every professional dreamer has his own type of overtones which he can't mask. To an expert it's like signing his name on the dreamie. And I, Mr. Byrne, know all the signatures. Now that piece of dirt you brought me has no overtones at all. It was done by an ordinary person. A little talent, maybe, but like you and me, he really can't think."

Byrne reddened a trifle. "A lot of people can think, Mr. Weill, even if they don't make dreamies."

"Oh, tush," and Weill wagged his hand in the air. "Don't be angry with what an old man says. I don't mean think as in reason. I mean think as in dream. We all can dream after a fashion, just like we all can run. But can you and I run a mile in four minutes? You and I can talk, but are we Daniel Websters? Now when I think of a steak, I think of the word. Maybe I have a quick picture of a brown steak on a platter. Maybe you have a better pictorialization of it and you can see the crisp fat and the onions and the baked potato. I don't know. But a *dreamer* . . . He sees it and smells it and tastes it and everything about it, with the charcoal and the satisfied feeling in the stomach and the way the knife cuts through it and a hundred other things all at once. Very sensual. Very sensual. You and I can't do it."

"Well, then," said Byrne, "no professional dreamer has done this. That's something anyway." He put the cylinder in his inner jacket pocket. "I hope we'll have your full co-operation in squelching this sort of thing."

"Positively, Mr. Byrne. With a whole heart."

"I hope so." Byrne spoke with a consciousness of power. "It's not up to me, Mr. Weill, to say what will be done and what won't be done, but this sort of thing," he tapped the cylinder he had brought, "will make it awfully tempting to impose a really strict censorship on dreamies."

He rose. "Good day, Mr. Weill."

"Good day, Mr. Byrne. I'll hope always for the best."

Francis Belanger burst into Jesse Weill's office in his usual steaming tizzy, his reddish hair disordered and his face aglow with worry and a mild perspiration. He was brought up sharply by the sight of Weill's head cradled in the crook of his elbow and bent on the desk until only the glimmer of white hair was visible.

Belanger swallowed. "Boss?"

Weill's head lifted. "It's you, Frank?"

"What's the matter, boss? Are you sick?"

"I'm old enough to be sick, but I'm on my feet. Staggering, but on my feet. A government man was here."

"What did he want?"

"He threatens censorship. He brought a sample of what's going round. Cheap dreamies for bottle parties."

"God damn!" said Belanger feelingly.

"The only trouble is that morality makes for good campaign fodder. They'll be hitting out everywhere. And, to tell the truth, we're vulnerable, Frank."

"*We* are? Our stuff is clean. We play up straight adventure and romance."

Weill thrust out his lower lip and wrinkled his forehead. "Between us, Frank, we don't have to make believe. Clean? It depends on how you look at it. It's not for publication, maybe, but you know and I know that every dreamie has its Freudian connotations. You can't deny it."

"Sure, if you *look* for it. If you're a psychiatrist——"

"If you're an ordinary person, too. The ordinary observer doesn't know it's there and maybe he couldn't tell a phallic symbol from a mother image even if you pointed it out. Still, his subconscious knows. And it's the connotations that make many a dreamie click."

"All right, what's the government going to do? Clean up the subconscious?"

"It's a problem. I don't know what they're going to do. What we have on our side, and what I'm mainly depending on, is the fact that the public loves its dreamies and won't give them up. . . . Meanwhile, what did you come in for? You want to see me about something, I suppose?"

Belanger tossed an object onto Weill's desk and shoved his shirttail deeper into his trousers.

Weill broke open the glistening plastic cover and took out the enclosed cylinder. At one end was engraved in a too fancy script in pastel blue "Along the Himalayan Trail." It bore the mark of Luster-Think.

"The Competitor's Product." Weill said it with capitals, and his lips twitched. "It hasn't been published yet. Where did you get it, Frank?"

"Never mind. I just want you to absorb it."

Weill sighed. "Today, everyone wants me to absorb dreams. Frank, it's not dirty?"

Belanger said testily, "It has your Freudian symbols. Narrow crevasses between the mountain peaks. I hope that won't bother you."

"I'm an old man. It stopped bothering me years ago, but that other thing was so poorly done, it hurt. . . . All right, let's see what you've got here."

Again the recorder. Again the unfreezer over his skull and at the temples. This time, Weill rested back in his chair for fifteen minutes or more, while Francis Belanger went hurriedly through two cigarettes.

When Weill removed the headpiece and blinked dream out of his eyes, Belanger said, "Well, what's your reaction, boss?"

Weill corrugated his forehead. "It's not for me. It was repetitious. With competition like this, Dreams, Inc., doesn't have to worry for a while."

"That's your mistake, boss. Luster-Think's going to win with stuff like this. We've got to do something."

"Now, Frank——"

"No, you listen. This is the coming thing."

"This!" Weill stared with half-humorous dubiety at the cylinder. "It's amateurish, it's repetitious. Its overtones are very unsubtle. The snow had a distinct lemon sherbet taste. Who tastes lemon sherbet in snow these days, Frank? In the old days, yes. Twenty years ago, maybe. When Lyman Harrison first made his Snow Symphonies for sale down south, it was a big thing. Sherbet and candy-striped mountaintops and sliding down chocolate-covered cliffs. It's slapstick, Frank. These days it doesn't go."

"Because," said Belanger, "you're not up with the times, boss. I've got to talk to you straight. When you started the dreamie business, when you bought up the basic patents and began putting them out, dreamies were luxury stuff. The market was small and individual. You could afford to turn out specialized dreamies and sell them to people at high prices."

"I know," said Weill, "and we've kept that up. But also we've opened a rental business for the masses."

"Yes, we have and it's not enough. Our dreamies have subtlety, yes. They can be used over and over again. The tenth time you're still finding new things, still getting new enjoyment. But how many people are connoisseurs? And another thing. Our stuff is strongly individualized. They're First Person."

"Well?"

"Well, Luster-Think is opening dream palaces. They've opened one with three hundred booths in Nashville. You walk in, take your seat, put on your unfreezer and get your dream. Everyone in the audience gets the same one."

"I've heard of it, Frank, and it's been done before. It didn't work the first time and it won't work now. You want to know why it won't work? Because, in the first place, dreaming is a private thing. Do you like your neighbor to know what you're dreaming? In the second place, in a dream palace, the dreams have to start on schedule, don't they? So the dreamer has to dream not when he wants to but when some palace manager says he should. Finally, a dream one person likes another person doesn't like. In those three hundred booths, I guarantee you, a hundred fifty people are dissatisfied. And if they're dissatisfied, they won't come back."

Slowly, Belanger rolled up his sleeves and opened his collar. "Boss," he said, "you're talking through your hat. What's the use of proving they won't work? They *are* working. The word came through today that Luster-Think is breaking ground for a thousand-booth palace in St. Louis. People can get used to public dreaming, if everyone else in the same room is having the same dream. And they can adjust themselves to having it at a given time, as long as it's cheap and convenient.

"Damn it, boss, it's a social affair. A boy and a girl go to a dream palace and absorb some cheap romantic thing with stereotyped overtones and commonplace situations, but still they come out with stars sprinkling their hair. They've had the same dream together. They've gone through identical sloppy emotions. They're *in tune*, boss. You bet they go back to the dream palace, and all their friends go, too."

"And if they don't like the dream?"

"That's the point. That's the nub of the whole thing. They're bound to like it. If you prepare Hillary specials with wheels within wheels within wheels, with surprise twists on the third-level undertones, with clever shifts of significance and all the other things we're so proud of, why, naturally, it won't appeal to everyone. Specialized dreamies are for specialized tastes. But Luster-Think is turning out simple jobs in Third Person so both sexes can be hit at once. Like what you've just absorbed. Simple, repetitious, commonplace.

They're aiming at the lowest common denominator. No one will love it, maybe, but no one will hate it."

Weill sat silent for a long time and Belanger watched him. Then Weill said, "Frank, I started on quality and I'm staying there. Maybe you're right. Maybe dream palaces are the coming thing. If so we'll open them, but we'll use good stuff. Maybe Luster-Think underestimates ordinary people. Let's go slowly and not panic. I have based all my policies on the theory that there's always a market for quality. Sometimes, my boy, it would surprise you how big a market."

"Boss——"

The sounding of the intercom interrupted Belanger.

"What is it, Ruth?" said Weill.

The voice of his secretary said, "It's Mr. Hillary, sir. He wants to see you right away. He says it's important."

"Hillary?" Weill's voice registered shock. Then, "Wait five minutes, Ruth, then send him in."

Weill turned to Belanger. "Today, Frank, is definitely not one of my good days. A dreamer's place is in his home with his thinker. And Hillary's our best dreamer so he especially should be at home. What do you suppose is wrong with him?"

Belanger, still brooding over Luster-Think and dream palaces, said shortly, "Call him in and find out."

"In one minute. Tell me, how was his last dream? I haven't tried the one that came in last week."

Belanger came down to earth. He wrinkled his nose. "Not so good."

"Why not?"

"It was ragged. Too jumpy. I don't mind sharp transitions for the liveliness, you know, but there's got to be some connection, even if only on a deep level."

"Is it a total loss?"

"No Hillary dream is a *total* loss. It took a lot of editing, though. We cut it down quite a bit and spliced in some odd pieces he'd sent us now and then. You know, detached scenes. It's still not Grade A, but it will pass."

"You told him about this, Frank?"

"Think I'm crazy, boss? Think I'm going to say a harsh word to a dreamer?"

And at that point the door opened and Weill's comely young secretary smiled Sherman Hillary into the office.

Sherman Hillary, at the age of thirty-one, could have been recognized as a dreamer by anyone. His eyes, unspectacled, had nevertheless the misty look of one who either needs glasses or who rarely focuses on anything mundane. He was of average height but underweight, with black hair that needed cutting, a narrow chin, a pale skin and a troubled look.

He muttered, "Hello, Mr. Weill," and half-nodded in hangdog fashion in the direction of Belanger.

Weill said heartily, "Sherman, my boy, you look fine. What's the matter? A dream is cooking only so-so at home? You're worried about it? . . . Sit down, sit down."

The dreamer did, sitting at the edge of the chair and holding his thighs stiffly together as though to be ready for instant obedience to a possible order to stand up once more.

He said, "I've come to tell you, Mr. Weill, I'm quitting."

"Quitting?"

"I don't want to dream any more, Mr. Weill."

Weill's old face looked older now than at any time in the day. "Why, Sherman?"

The dreamer's lips twisted. He blurted out, "Because I'm not *living*, Mr. Weill. Everything passes me by. It wasn't so bad at first. It was even relaxing. I'd dream evenings, weekends when I felt like, or any other time. And when I felt like I wouldn't. But now, Mr. Weill, I'm an old pro. You tell me I'm one of the best in the business and the industry looks to me to think up new subtleties and new changes on the old reliables like the flying reveries, and the worm-turning skits."

Weill said, "And is anyone better than you, Sherman? Your little sequence on leading an orchestra is selling steadily after ten years."

"All right, Mr. Weill. I've done my part. It's gotten so I don't go out any more. I neglect my wife. My little girl doesn't know me. Last week, we went to a dinner party—Sarah made me—and I don't remember a bit of it. Sarah says I was sitting on the couch all evening just staring at nothing and humming. She said everyone kept looking at me. She cried all night. I'm tired of things like that, Mr. Weill. I want to be a normal person and live in this world. I promised her I'd quit and I will, so it's good-by, Mr. Weill." Hillary stood up and held out his hand awkwardly.

Weill waved it gently away. "If you want to quit, Sherman, it's all right. But do an old man a favor and let me explain something to you."

"I'm not going to change my mind," said Hillary.

"I'm not going to try to make you. I just want to explain something. I'm an old man and even before you were born I was in this business so I like to talk about it. Humor me, Sherman? Please?"

Hillary sat down. His teeth clamped down on his lower lip and he stared sullenly at his fingernails.

Weill said, "Do you know what a dreamer is, Sherman? Do you know what he means to ordinary people? Do you know what it is to be like me, like Frank Belanger, like your wife, Sarah? To have crippled minds that can't imagine, that can't build up thoughts? People like myself, ordinary people, would like to escape just once in a while this life of ours. We can't. We need help.

"In olden times it was books, plays, radio, movies, television. They gave us make-believe, but that wasn't important. What was important was that for a little while our own imaginations were stimulated. We could think of handsome lovers and beautiful princesses. We could be beautiful, witty, strong, capable, everything we weren't.

"But, always, the passing of the dream from dreamer to absorber was not perfect. It had to be translated into words in one way or another. The best dreamer in the world might not be able to get any of it into words. And the best writer in the world could put only the smallest part of his dreams into words. You understand?

"But now, with dream recording, any man can dream. You, Sherman, and a handful of men like you, supply those dreams directly and exactly. It's straight from your head into ours, full strength. You dream for a hundred million people every time you dream. You dream a hundred million dreams at once. This is a great thing, my boy. You give all those people a glimpse of something they could not have by themselves."

Hillary mumbled, "I've done my share." He rose desperately to his feet. "I'm through. I don't care what you say. And if you want to sue me for breaking our contract, go ahead and sue. I don't care."

Weill stood up, too. "Would I sue you? . . . Ruth," he spoke into the intercom, "bring in our copy of Mr. Hillary's contract."

He waited. So did Hillary and so did Belanger. Weill smiled faintly and his yellowed fingers drummed softly on his desk.

His secretary brought in the contract. Weill took it, showed its face to Hillary and said, "Sherman, my boy, unless you want to be with me, it's not right you should stay."

Then, before Belanger could make more than the beginning of a horrified gesture to stop him, he tore the contract into four pieces and tossed them down the waste chute. "That's all."

Hillary's hand shot out to seize Weill's. "Thanks, Mr. Weill," he said earnestly, his voice husky. "You've always treated me very well, and I'm grateful. I'm sorry it had to be like this."

"It's all right, my boy. It's all right."

Half in tears, still muttering thanks, Sherman Hillary left.

"For the love of Pete, boss, why did you let him go?" demanded Belanger distractedly. "Don't you see the game? He'll be going straight to Luster-Think. They've bought him off."

Weill raised his hand. "You're wrong. You're quite wrong. I know the boy and this would not be his style. Besides," he added dryly, "Ruth is a good secretary and she knows what to bring me when I ask for a dreamer's contract. What I had was a fake. The real contract is still in the safe, believe me.

"Meanwhile, a fine day I've had. I had to argue with a father to give me a chance at new talent, with a government man to avoid censorship, with you to keep from adopting fatal policies and now with my best dreamer to keep him from leaving. The father I probably won out over. The government man and you, I don't know. Maybe yes, maybe no. But about Sherman Hillary, at least, there is no question. The dreamer will be back."

"How do you know?"

Weill smiled at Belanger and crinkled his cheeks into a network of fine lines. "Frank, my boy, you know how to edit dreamies so you think you know all the tools and machines of the trade. But let me tell you something. The most important tool in the dreamie business is the dreamer himself. He is the one you have to understand most of all, and I understand them.

"Listen. When I was a youngster—there were no dreamies then—I knew a fellow who wrote television scripts. He would complain to me bitterly that when someone met him for the first time and found out who he was, they would say: Where do you get those crazy ideas?

"They honestly didn't know. To them it was an impossibility to even think of one of them. So what could my friend say? He used to talk to me about it and tell me: Could I say, I don't know? When I go to bed, I can't sleep for ideas dancing in my head. When I shave, I cut myself; when I talk, I lose track of what I'm saying; when I drive, I take my life in my hands. And always because ideas, situations, dialogues are spinning and twisting in my mind. I can't tell you where I get my ideas. Can you tell me, maybe, your trick of *not* getting ideas, so I, too, can have a little peace.

"You see, Frank, how it is. *You* can stop work here anytime. So can I. This is our job, not our life. But not Sherman Hillary. Wherever he goes, whatever he does, he'll dream. While he lives, he must think; while he thinks, he must dream. We don't hold him prisoner, our contract isn't an iron wall for him. His own skull is his prisoner, Frank. So he'll be back. What can he do?"

Belanger shrugged. "If what you say is right, I'm sort of sorry for the guy."

Weill nodded sadly. "I'm sorry for all of them. Through the years, I've found out one thing. It's their business, making people happy. *Other* people."

THE END OF ETERNITY

One: TECHNICIAN

Andrew Harlan stepped into the kettle. Its sides were perfectly round and it fit snugly inside a vertical shaft composed of widely spaced rods that shimmered into an unseeable haze six feet above Harlan's head. Harlan set the controls and moved the smoothly working starting lever.

The kettle did not move.

Harlan did not expect it to. He expected no movement; neither up nor down, left nor right, forth nor back. Yet the spaces between the rods had melted into a gray blankness which was solid to the touch, though nonetheless immaterial for all that. And there *was* the little stir in his stomach, the faint (psychosomatic?) touch of dizziness, that told him that all the kettle contained, including himself, was rushing upwhen through Eternity.

He had boarded the kettle in the 575th Century, the base of operations assigned him two years earlier. At the time the 575th had been the farthest upwhen he had ever traveled. Now he was moving upwhen to the 2456th Century.

Under ordinary circumstances he might have felt a little lost at the prospect. His native Century was in the far downwhen, the 95th Century, to be exact. The 95th was a Century stiffly restrictive of atomic power, faintly rustic, fond of natural wood as a structural material, exporters of certain types of distilled potables to nearly everywhen and importers of clover seed. Although Harlan had not been in the 95th since he entered special training and became a Cub at the age of fifteen, there was always that feeling of loss when one moved outwhen from "home." At the 2456th he would be nearly two hundred forty millennia from his birthwhen and that is a sizable distance even for a hardened Eternal.

Under ordinary circumstances all this would be so.

But right now Harlan was in poor mood to think of anything but the fact that his documents were heavy in his pocket and his plan heavy on his heart. He was a little frightened, a little tense, a little confused.

It was his hands acting by themselves that brought the kettle to the proper halt at the proper Century.

Strange that a Technician should feel tense or nervous about anything. What was it that Educator Yarrow had once said:

"Above all, a Technician must be dispassionate. The Reality

Change he initiates may affect the lives of as many as fifty billion people. A million or more of these may be so drastically affected as to be considered new individuals. Under these conditions, an emotional make-up is a distinct handicap."

Harlan put the memory of his teacher's dry voice out of his mind with an almost savage shake of his head. In those days he had never imagined that he himself would have the peculiar talent for that very position. But emotion had come upon him after all. Not for fifty billion people. What in Time did he care for fifty billion people? There was just one. One person.

He became aware that the kettle was stationary and with the merest pause to pull his thoughts together, put himself into the cold, impersonal frame of mind a Technician must have, he stepped out. The kettle he left, of course, was not the same as the one he had boarded, in the sense that it was not composed of the same atoms. He did not worry about that any more than any Eternal would. To concern oneself with the *mystique* of Time-travel, rather than with the simple fact of it, was the mark of the Cub and newcomer to Eternity.

He paused again at the infinitely thin curtain of non-Space and non-Time which separated him from Eternity in one way and from ordinary Time in another.

This would be a completely new section of Eternity for him. He knew about it in a rough way, of course, having checked upon it in the *Temporal Handbook*. Still, there was no substitute for actual appearance and he steeled himself for the initial shock of adjustment.

He adjusted the controls, a simple matter in passing into Eternity (and a very complicated one in passing into Time, a type of passage which was correspondingly less frequent). He stepped through the curtain and found himself squinting at the brilliance. Automatically he threw up his hand to shield his eyes.

Only one man faced him. At first Harlan could see him only blurrily.

The man said, "I am Sociologist Kantor Voy. I imagine you are Technician Harlan."

Harlan nodded and said, "Father Time! Isn't this sort of ornamentation adjustable?"

Voy looked about and said tolerantly, "You mean the molecular films?"

"I certainly do," said Harlan. The *Handbook* had mentioned them, but had said nothing of *such* an insane riot of light reflection.

Harlan felt his annoyance to be quite reasonable. The 2456th Century was matter-oriented, as most Centuries were, so he had a right to expect a basic compatibility from the very beginning. It would have none of the utter confusion (for anyone born matter-oriented) of the energy vortices of the 300's, or the field dynamics of the 600's. In the 2456th, to the average Eternal's comfort, matter was used for everything from walls to tacks.

To be sure, there was matter and matter. A member of an energy-oriented Century might not realize that. To him all matter might seem minor variations on a theme that was gross, heavy, and barbaric. To matter-oriented Harlan, however, there was wood, metal (subdivisions, heavy and light), plastic, silicates, concrete, leather, and so on.

But matter consisting entirely of mirrors!

That was his first impression of the 2456th. Every surface reflected and glinted light. Everywhere was the illusion of complete smoothness; the effect of a molecular film. And in the ever-repeated reflection of himself, of Sociologist Voy, of everything he could see, in scraps and wholes, in all angles, there was confusion. Garish confusion and nausea!

"I'm sorry," said Voy, "it's the custom of the Century, and the Section assigned to it finds it good practice to adopt the customs where practical. You get used to it after a time."

Voy walked rapidly upon the moving feet of another Voy, upside down beneath the floor, who matched him stride for stride. He reached to move a hair-contact indicator down a spiral scale to point of origin.

The reflections died; extraneous light faded. Harlan felt his world settle.

"If you'll come with me now," said Voy.

Harlan followed through empty corridors that, Harlan knew, must moments ago have been a riot of made light and reflection, up a ramp, through an anteroom, into an office.

In all the short journey no human being had been visible. Harlan was so used to that, took it so for granted, that he would have been surprised, almost shocked, if a glimpse of a human figure hurrying away had caught his eyes. No doubt the news had spread that a Technician was coming through. Even Voy kept his distance and when, accidentally, Harlan's hand had brushed Voy's sleeve, Voy shrank away with a visible start.

Harlan was faintly surprised at the touch of bitterness he felt at all this. He had thought the shell he had grown about his soul was thicker, more efficiently insensitive than that. If he was wrong, if his shell had worn thinner, there could only be one reason for that.

Noÿs!

Sociologist Kantor Voy leaned forward toward the Technician in what seemed a friendly enough fashion, but Harlan noted automatically that they were seated on opposite sides of the long axis of a fairly large table.

Voy said, "I am pleased to have a Technician of your reputation interest himself in our little problem here."

"Yes," said Harlan with the cold impersonality people would expect of him. "It has its points of interest." (Was he impersonal enough? Surely his real motives must be apparent, his guilt be spelled out in beads of sweat on his forehead.)

He removed from an inner pocket the foiled summary of the projected Reality Change. It was the very copy which had been sent to the Allwhen Council a month earlier. Through his relationship with Senior Computer Twissell (*the* Twissell, himself) Harlan had had little trouble in getting his hands on it.

Before unrolling the foil, letting it peel off onto the table top where it would be held by a soft paramagnetic field, Harlan paused a split moment.

The molecular film that covered the table was subdued but was not zero. The motion of his arm fixed his eye and for an instant the reflection of his own face seemed to stare somberly up at him from the table top. He was thirty-two, but he looked older. He needed no one to tell him that. It might be partly his long face and dark eyebrows over darker eyes that gave him the lowering expression and cold glare associated with the caricature of the Technician in the minds of all Eternals. It might be just his own realization that he was a Technician.

But then he flicked the foil out across the table and turned to the matter at hand.

"I am not a Sociologist, sir."

Voy smiled. "That sounds formidable. When one begins by expressing lack of competence in a given field, it usually implies that a flat opinion in that field will follow almost immediately."

"No," said Harlan, "not an opinion. Just a request. I wonder if you won't look over this summary and see if you haven't made a small mistake somewhere here."

Voy looked instantly grave. "I hope not," he said.

Harlan kept one arm across the back of his chair, the other in his lap. He must let neither hand drum restless fingers. He must not bite his lips. He must not show his feelings in any way.

Ever since the whole orientation of his life had so changed itself, he had been watching the summaries of projected Reality Changes as they passed through the grinding administrative gears of the All-when Council. As Senior Computer Twissell's personally assigned Technician, he could arrange that by a slight bending of professional ethics. Particularly with Twissell's attention caught ever more tightly in his own overwhelming project. (Harlan's nostrils flared. He knew *now* a little of the nature of that project.)

Harlan had had no assurance that he would ever find what he was looking for in a reasonable time. When he had first glanced over projected Reality Change 2456–2781, Serial Number V-5, he was half inclined to believe his reasoning powers were warped by wishing. For a full day he had checked and rechecked equations and relationships in a rattling uncertainty, mixed with growing excitement and a bitter gratitude that he had been taught at least elementary psycho-mathematics.

Now Voy went over those same puncture patterns with a half-puzzled, half-worried eye.

He said, "It seems to me; I say, it *seems* to me that this is all perfectly in order."

Harlan said, "I refer you particularly to the matter of the courtship characteristics of the society of the current Reality of this Century. That's sociology and your responsibility, I believe. It's why I arranged to see *you* when I arrived, rather than someone else."

Voy was now frowning. He was still polite, but with an icy touch now. He said, "The Observers assigned to our Section are highly competent. I have every certainty that those assigned to this project have given accurate data. Have you evidence to the contrary?"

"Not at all, Sociologist Voy. I accept their data. It is the development of the data I question. Do you not have an alternate tensor-complex at this point, if the courtship data is taken properly into consideration?"

Voy stared, and then a look of relief washed over him visibly. "Of course, Technician, of course, but it resolves itself into an identity. There is a loop of small dimensions with no tributaries on either side. I hope you'll forgive me for using picturesque language rather than precise mathematical expressions."

"I appreciate it," said Harlan dryly. "I am no more a Computer than a Sociologist."

"Very good, then. The alternate tensor-complex you refer to, or the forking of the road, as we might say, is non-significant. The forks join up again and it is a single road. There was not even any need to mention it in our recommendations."

"If you say so, sir, I will defer to your better judgment. However, there is still the matter of the M.N.C."

The Sociologist winced at the initials as Harlan knew he would. M.N.C.—Minimum Necessary Change. There the Technician was master. A Sociologist might consider himself above criticism by lesser beings in anything involving the mathematical analysis of the infinite possible Realities in Time, but in matters of M.N.C. the Technician stood supreme.

Mechanical computing would not do. The largest Computaplex ever built, manned by the cleverest and most experienced Senior Computer ever born, could do no better than to indicate the ranges in which the M.N.C. might be found. It was then the Technician, glancing over the data, who decided on an exact point within that range. A good Technician was rarely wrong. A top Technician was never wrong.

Harlan was never wrong.

"Now the M.N.C. recommended," said Harlan (he spoke coolly, evenly, pronouncing the Standard Intertemporal Language in precise syllables), "by your Section involves induction of an accident in space and the immediate death by fairly horrible means of a dozen or more men."

"Unavoidable," said Voy, shrugging.

"On the other hand," said Harlan, "I suggest that the M.N.C. can be reduced to the mere displacement of a container from one shelf to another. Here!" His long finger pointed. His white, well-cared-for index nail made the faintest mark along one set of perforations.

Voy considered matters with a painful but silent intensity.

Harlan said, "Doesn't that alter the situation with regard to your unconsidered fork? Doesn't it take advantage of the fork of lesser probability, changing it to near-certainty, and does that not then lead to——"

"—to virtually the M.D.R.," whispered Voy.

"To *exactly* the Maximum Desired Response," said Harlan.

Voy looked up, his dark face struggling somewhere between chagrin and anger. Harlan noted absently that there was a space between the man's large upper incisors which gave him a rabbity look quite at odds with the restrained force of his words.

Voy said, "I suppose I will be hearing from the Allwhen Council?"

"I don't think so. As far as I know, the Allwhen Council does not know of this. At least, the projected Reality Change was passed over to me without comment." He did not explain the word "passed," nor did Voy question it.

"*You* discovered this error, then?"

"Yes."

"And you did not report it to the Allwhen Council?"

"No, I did not."

Relief first, then a hardening of countenance. "Why not?"

"Very few people could have avoided this error. I felt I could correct it before damage was done. I have done so. Why go any further?"

"Well—thank you, Technician Harlan. You have been a friend. The Section's error which, as you say, was practically unavoidable, would have looked unjustifiably bad in the record."

He went on after a moment's pause. "Of course, in view of the alterations in personality to be induced by this Reality Change, the death of a few men as preliminary is of little importance."

Harlan thought, detachedly: He doesn't sound really grateful. He probably resents it. If he stops to think, he'll resent it even more, this being saved a downstroke in rating by a Technician. If I were a Sociologist, he would shake my hand, but he won't shake the hand of a Technician. He defends condemning a dozen people to asphyxiation, but he won't touch a Technician.

And because waiting to let resentment grow would be fatal, Harlan said without waiting, "I hope your gratitude will extend to having your Section perform a slight chore for me."

"A chore?"

"A matter of Life-Plotting. I have the data necessary here with me. I have also the data for a suggested Reality Change in the 482nd. I want to know the effect of the Change on the probability-pattern of a certain individual."

"I am not quite sure," said the Sociologist slowly, "that I understand you. Surely you have the facilities for doing this in your own Section?"

"I have. Nevertheless, what I am engaged in is a personal research which I don't wish to appear in the records just yet. It would be difficult to have this carried out in my own Section without——" He gestured an uncertain conclusion to the unfinished sentence.

Voy said, "Then you want this done *not* through official channels."

"I want it done confidentially. I want a confidential answer."

"Well, now, that's very irregular. I can't agree to it."

Harlan frowned. "No more irregular than my failure to report your error to the Allwhen Council. You raised no objection to that. If we're going to be strictly regular in one case, we must be as strict and as regular in the other. You follow me, I think?"

The look on Voy's face was proof positive of that. He held out his hand. "May I see the documents?"

Harlan relaxed a bit. The main hurdle had been passed. He watched eagerly as the Sociologist's head bent over the foils he had brought.

Only once did the Sociologist speak. "By Time, this is a small Reality Change."

Harlan seized his opportunity and improvised. "It is. Too small, I think. It's what the argument is about. It's below critical difference, and I've picked an individual as a test case. Naturally, it would be undiplomatic to use our own Section's facilities until I was certain of being right."

Voy was unresponsive and Harlan stopped. No use running this past the point of safety.

Voy stood up. "I'll pass this along to one of my Life-Plotters. We'll keep this private. You understand, though, that this is not to be taken as establishing a precedent."

"Of course not."

"And if you don't mind, I'd like to watch the Reality Change take place. I trust you will honor us by conducting the M.N.C. personally."

Harlan nodded. "I will take full responsibility."

Two of the screens in the viewing chamber were in operation when they entered. The engineers had focused them already to the exact co-ordinates in Space and Time and then had left. Harlan and Voy were alone in the glittering room. (The molecular film arrangement was perceptible and even a bit more than perceptible, but Harlan was looking at the screens.)

Both views were motionless. They might have been scenes of the dead, since they pictured mathematical instants of Time.

One view was in sharp, natural color; the engine room of what Harlan knew to be an experimental space-ship. A door was closing, and a glistening shoe of a red, semi-transparent material was just visible through the space that remained. It did not move. Nothing moved. If the picture could have been made sharp enough to picture the dust motes in the air, *they* would not have moved.

Voy said, "For two hours and thirty-six minutes after the viewed instant, that engine room will remain empty. In the current Reality, that is."

"I know," murmured Harlan. He was putting on his gloves and already his quick eyes were memorizing the position of the critical container on its shelf, measuring the steps to it, estimating the best position into which to transfer it. He cast one quick look at the other screen.

If the engine room, being in the range described as "present" with respect to that Section of Eternity in which they now stood, was clear and in natural color, the other scene, being some twenty-five Centuries in the "future," carried the blue luster all views of the "future" must.

It was a space-port. A deep blue sky, blue-tinged buildings of naked metal on blue-green ground. A blue cylinder of odd design, bulge-bottomed, stood in the foreground. Two others like it were in the background. All three pointed cleft noses upward, the cleavage biting deeply into the vitals of the ship.

Harlan frowned. "They're queer ones."

"Electro-gravitic," said Voy. "The 2481st is the only Century to develop electro-gravitic space-travel. No propellants, no nucleonics. It's an aesthetically pleasing device. It's a pity we must Change away from it. A pity." His eyes fixed themselves on Harlan with distinct disapproval.

Harlan's lips compressed. Disapproval of course! Why not? He was the Technician.

To be sure, it had been some Observer who had brought in the details of drug addiction. It had been some Statistician who had demonstrated that recent Changes had increased the addiction rate until now it was the highest in all the current Reality of man. Some Sociologist, probably Voy himself, had interpreted that into the psychiatric profile of a society. Finally, some Computer had worked out the Reality Change necessary to decrease addiction to a safe level and found that, as a side effect, electro-gravitic space-travel must suffer. A dozen, a hundred men of every rating in Eternity had had a hand in this.

But then, at the end, a Technician such as himself must step in. Following the directions all the others had combined to give him, he must be the one to initiate the actual Reality Change. And then all the others would stare in haughty accusation at him. Their stares would say: *You*, not we, have destroyed this beautiful thing.

And for that, they would condemn and avoid him. They would shift their own guilt to his shoulders and scorn him.

Harlan said harshly, "Ships aren't what count. We're concerned with those things."

The "things" were people, dwarfed by the space-ship, as Earth and Earth's society is always dwarfed by the physical dimensions of spaceflight.

They were little puppets in clusters, these people. Their tiny arms and legs were in raised, artificial-looking positions, caught in the frozen instant of Time.

Voy shrugged.

Harlan was adjusting the small field-generator about his left wrist. "Let's get this job done."

"One minute. I want to get in touch with the Life-Plotter and find out how long his job for you will take. I want to get that job done, too."

His hands worked cleverly at a little movable contact and his ear listened astutely to the pattern of clicks that came back. (Another characteristic of this Section of Eternity, thought Harlan—sound codes in clicks. Clever, but affected, like the molecular films.)

"He says it won't take more than three hours," said Voy at length. "Also, by the way, he admires the name of the person involved. Noÿs Lambent. It is a female, isn't it?"

There was a dryness in Harlan's throat. "Yes."

Voy's lips curled into a slow smile. "Sounds interesting. I'd like to meet her, sight unseen. Haven't had any women in this Section for months."

Harlan didn't trust himself to answer. He stared a moment at the Sociologist and turned abruptly.

If there was a flaw in Eternity, it involved women. He had known the flaw for what it was from almost his first entrance into Eternity, but he felt it personally only that day he had first met Noÿs. From that moment it had been an easy path to this one, in which he stood false to his oath as an Eternal and to everything in which he had believed.

For what?

For Noÿs.

And he was not ashamed. It was that which really rocked him. He was not ashamed. He felt no guilt for the crescendo of crimes he had committed, to which this latest addition of the unethical use of confidential Life-Plotting could rank only as a peccadillo.

He would do worse than his worst if he had to.

For the first time the specific and express thought came to him. And though he pushed it away in horror, he knew that, having once come, it would return.

The thought was simply this: That he would ruin Eternity, if he had to.

The worst of it was that he knew he had the power to do it.

Two: OBSERVER

Harlan stood at the gateway to Time and thought of himself in new ways. It had been very simple once. There were such things as ideals, or at least catchwords, to live by and for. Every stage of an Eternal's life had a reason. How did "Basic Principles" start?

"The life of an Eternal may be divided into four parts . . ."

It all worked out neatly, yet it had all changed for him, and what was broken could not be made whole again.

Yet he had gone faithfully through each of the four parts of an Eternal's life. First, there was the period of fifteen years in which he was not an Eternal at all, but only an inhabitant of Time. Only a human being out of Time, a Timer, could become an Eternal; no one could be born into the position.

At the age of fifteen he was chosen by a careful process of elimination and winnowing, the nature of which he had no conception of at the time. He was taken beyond the veil of Eternity after a last agonized farewell to his family. (Even then it was made clear to him that whatever else happened he would never return. The true reason for that he was not to learn till long afterward.)

Once within Eternity, he spent ten years in school as a Cub, and then graduated to enter his third period as Observer. It was only after that he became a Specialist and a true Eternal. The fourth and last part of the Eternal's life: Timer, Cub, Observer and Specialist.

He, Harlan, had gone through it all so neatly. He might say, successfully.

He could remember, so clearly, the moment that Cubhood was done, the moment they became independent members of Eternity, the moment when, even though un-Specialized, they still rated the legal title of "Eternal."

He could remember it. School done, Cubhood over, he was standing with the five who completed training with him, hands clasped in the small of his back, legs a trifle apart, eyes front, listening.

Educator Yarrow was at a desk talking to them. Harlan could remember Yarrow well: a small, intense man, with ruddy hair in disarray, freckled forearms, and a look of loss in his eyes. (It wasn't uncommon, this look of loss in the eyes of an Eternal—the loss of home and roots, the unadmitted and unadmittable longing for the one Century he could never see.)

Harlan could not remember Yarrow's exact words, of course, but the substance of it remained sharp.

Yarrow said, in substance, "You will be Observers now. It isn't a highly regarded position. Specialists look upon it as a boy's job. Maybe you Eternals" (he deliberately paused after that word to give each man a chance to straighten his back and brighten at the glory of it) "think so too. If so, you are fools who don't deserve to be Observers.

"The Computers would have no Computing to do, Life-Plotters no lives to Plot, Sociologists no societies to profile; none of the Specialists would have anything to do, if it weren't for the Observer. I know you've heard this said before, but I want you to be very firm and clear in your mind about it.

"It will be you youngsters who will go out into Time, under the most strenuous conditions, to bring back facts. Cold, objective facts uncolored by your own opinions and likings, you understand. Facts accurate enough to be fed into Computing machines. Facts definite enough to make the social equations stand up. Facts honest enough to form a basis for Reality Changes.

"And remember this, too. Your period as Observer is not something to get through with as quickly and as unobtrusively as possible. It is as an Observer that you will make your mark. Not what you did in school, but what you will do as an Observer will determine your Specialty and how high you will rise in it. This will be your postgraduate course, Eternals, and failure in it, even small failure, will put you into Maintenance no matter how brilliant your potentialities now seem. That is all."

He shook hands with each of them, and Harlan, grave, dedicated, proud in his belief that the privileges of being an Eternal contained its greatest privilege in the assumption of responsibility for the happiness of all the human beings who were or ever would be within the reach of Eternity, was deep in self-awe.

Harlan's first assignments were small and under close direction, but he sharpened his ability on the honing strap of experience in a dozen Centuries through a dozen Reality Changes.

In his fifth year as Observer he was given a Senior's rating in the field and assigned to the 482nd. For the first time he would be working unsupervised, and knowledge of that fact robbed him of some of his self-assurance when he first reported to the Computer in charge of the Section.

That was Assistant Computer Hobbe Finge, whose pursed, suspicious mouth and frowning eyes seemed ludicrous in such a face as his. He had a round button of a nose, two larger buttons of cheeks. He needed only a touch of red and a fringe of white hair to be converted into the picture of the Primitive myth of St. Nicholas.

(—or Santa Claus or Kriss Kringle. Harlan knew all three names. He doubted if one Eternal out of a hundred thousand had heard of any one of them. Harlan took a secret, shamefaced pride in this sort of arcane knowledge. From his earliest days in school he had ridden the hobbyhorse of Primitive history, and Educator Yarrow had encouraged it. Harlan had grown actually fond of those odd, perverted Centuries that lay, not only before the beginning of Eternity in the 27th, but even before the invention of the Temporal Field, itself, in the 24th. He had used old books and periodicals in his studies. He had even traveled far downwhen to the earliest Centuries of Eternity, when he could get permission, to consult better sources. For over fifteen years he had managed to collect a remarkable library of his own, almost all in print-on-paper. There was a volume by a man called H. G. Wells, another by a man named W. Shakespeare, some tattered histories. Best of all there was a complete set of bound volumes of a Primitive news weekly that took up inordinate space but that he could not, out of sentiment, bear to reduce to micro-film.

Occasionally he would lose himself in a world where life was life and death, death; where a man made his decisions irrevocably; where evil could not be prevented, nor good promoted, and the Battle of Waterloo, having been lost, was really lost for good and all. There was even a scrap of poetry he treasured which stated that a moving finger having once written could never be lured back to unwrite.

And then it was difficult, almost a shock, to return his thoughts to Eternity, and to a universe where Reality was something flexible and evanescent, something men such as himself could hold in the palms of their hands and shake into better shape.)

The illusion of St. Nicholas shattered when Hobbe Finge spoke to him in a brisk, matter-of-fact way. "You can start in tomorrow with a routine screening of current Reality. I want it good, thorough, and to the point. There will be no slackness permitted. Your first spatio-temporal chart will be ready for you tomorrow morning. Got it?"

"Yes, Computer," said Harlan. He decided as early as that that he and Assistant Computer Hobbe Finge would not get along, and he regretted it.

The next morning Harlan got his chart in intricately punched patterns as they emerged from the Computaplex. He used a pocket decoder to translate them into Standard Intertemporal in his anxiety to make not even the smallest mistake at the very beginning. Of course, he had reached the stage where he could read the perforations direct.

The chart told him where and when in the world of the 482nd Century he might go and where he might not; what he could do and what he could not; what he must avoid at all costs. His presence must impinge only upon those places and times where it would not endanger Reality.

The 482nd was not a comfortable Century for him. It was not like his own austere and conformist homewhen. It was an era without ethics or principles, as he was accustomed to think of such. It was hedonistic, materialistic, more than a little matriarchal. It was the only era (he checked this in the records in the most painstaking way) in which ectogenic birth flourished and, at its peak, 40 per cent of its women gave eventual birth by merely contributing a fertilized ovum to the ovaria. Marriage was made and unmade by mutual consent and was not recognized legally as anything more than a personal agreement without binding force. Union for the sake of childbearing was, of course, carefully differentiated from the social functions of marriage and was arranged on purely eugenic principles.

In a hundred ways Harlan thought the society sick and therefore hungered for a Reality Change. More than once it occurred to him that his own presence in the Century, as a man not of that time, could fork its history. If his disturbing presence could only be made disturbing enough at some key point, a different branch of possibility would become real, a branch in which millions of pleasure-seeking women would find themselves transformed into true, pure-hearted mothers. They would be in another Reality with all the memories that belonged with it, unable to tell, dream, or fancy that they had ever been anything else.

Unfortunately, to do that, he would have to step outside the bounds of the spatio-temporal chart and that was unthinkable. Even if it weren't, to step outside the bounds at random could change Reality in many possible ways. It could be made worse. Only careful analysis and Computing could properly pin-point the nature of a Reality change.

Outwardly, whatever his private opinions, Harlan remained an Observer, and the ideal Observer was merely a set of sense-perceptive nerve patches attached to a report-writing mechanism. Between perception and report there must be no intervention of emotion.

Harlan's reports were perfection itself in that respect.

Assistant Computer Finge called him in after his second weekly report.

"I congratulate you, Observer," he said in a voice without warmth, "on the organization and clarity of your reports. But what do you really think?"

Harlan sought refuge in an expression as blank as though chipped painstakingly out of native 95th Century wood. He said, "I have no thoughts of my own in the matter."

"Oh, come. You're from the 95th and we both know what that means. Surely this Century disturbs you."

Harlan shrugged. "Does anything in my reports lead you to think that I am disturbed?"

It was near to impudence and the drumming of Finge's blunt nails upon his desk showed it. Finge said, "Answer my question."

Harlan said, "Sociologically, many facets of the Century represent an extreme. The last three Reality Changes in the aboutwhen have accentuated that. Eventually, I suppose the matter should be rectified. Extremes are never healthy."

"Then you took the trouble to check the past Realities of the Century."

"As an Observer, I must check all pertinent facts."

It was a standoff. Harlan, of course, did have the right and the duty to check those facts. Finge must know that. Every Century was continually being shaken by Reality Changes. No Observations, however painstaking, could ever stand for long without rechecking. It was standard procedure in Eternity to have every Century in a chronic state of being Observed. And to Observe properly, you must be able to present, not only the facts of the current Reality, but also of their relationship to those of previous Realities.

Yet it seemed obvious to Harlan that this was not merely unpleasantness on Finge's part, this probing of the Observer's opinions. Finge seemed definitely hostile.

At another time Finge said to Harlan (having invaded the latter's small office to bring the news), "Your reports are creating a very favorable impression with the Allwhen Council."

Harlan paused, uncertain, then mumbled, "Thank you."

"All agree that you show an uncommon degree of penetration."

"I do my best."

Finge asked suddenly, "Have you ever met Senior Computer Twissell?"

"Computer Twissell?" Harlan's eyes widened. "No, sir. Why do you ask?"

"He seems particularly interested in your reports." Finge's round cheeks drew downward sulkily and he changed the subject. "To me it seems that you have worked out a philosophy of your own, a viewpoint of history."

Temptation tugged hard at Harlan. Vanity and caution battled and the former won. "I've studied Primitive history, sir."

"*Primitive* history? At school?"

"Not exactly, Computer. On my own. It's my—hobby. It's like watching history standing still, frozen! It can be studied in detail whereas the Centuries of Eternity are always changing." He warmed up a trifle at the thought of it. "It's as though we were to take a series of stills from a book-film and study each painstakingly. We would see a great deal we would miss if we just scanned the film as it went past. I think that helps me a great deal with my work."

Finge stared at him in amazement, widened his eyes a little, and left with no further remark.

Occasionally, thereafter, he brought up the subject of Primitive history and accepted Harlan's reluctant comments with no decisive expression on his own plump face.

Harlan was not sure whether to regret the whole matter or to regard it as a possible way of speeding his own advancement.

He decided on the first alternative when, passing him one day in Corridor A, Finge said abruptly and in the hearing of others, "Great Time, Harlan, don't you *ever* smile?"

The thought came, shockingly, to Harlan that Finge hated him. His own feeling for Finge approached something like detestation thereafter.

Three months of raking through the 482nd had exhausted most of its worth-while meat and when Harlan received a sudden call to Finge's office, he was not surprised. He was expecting a change in assignment. His final summary had been prepared days before. The 482nd was anxious to export more cellulose-base textiles to Centuries which were deforested, such as the 1174th, but were unwilling to accept smoked fish in return. A long list of such items was contained in due order and with due analysis.

He took the draft of the summary with him.

But no mention of the 482nd was made. Instead Finge introduced him to a withered and wrinkled little man, with sparse white hair and a gnomelike face that throughout the interview was stamped with a perpetual smile. It varied between extremes of anxiety and joviality but never quite disappeared. Between two of his yellow-stained fingers lay a burning cigarette.

It was the first cigarette Harlan had ever seen, otherwise he would have paid more attention to the man, less to the smoking cylinder, and been better prepared for Finge's introduction.

Finge said, "Senior Computer Twissell, this is Observer Andrew Harlan."

Harlan's eyes shifted in shock from the little man's cigarette to his face.

Senior Computer Twissell said in a high-pitched voice, "How do you do? So this is the young man who writes those excellent reports?"

Harlan found no voice. Laban Twissell was a legend, a living myth. Laban Twissell was a man he should have recognized at once. He was the outstanding Computer in Eternity, which was another way of saying he was the most eminent Eternal alive. He was the dean of the Allwhen Council. He had directed more Reality Changes than any man in the history of Eternity. He was—— He had——

Harlan's mind failed him altogether. He nodded his head with a doltish grin and said nothing.

Twissell put his cigarette to his lips, puffed quickly, and took it away. "Leave us, Finge. I want to talk to the boy."

Finge rose, murmured something, and left.

Twissell said, "You seem nervous, boy. There is nothing to be nervous about."

But meeting Twissell like that was a shock. It is always disconcerting to find that someone you have thought of as a giant is actually less than five and a half feet tall. Could the brain of a genius actually fit behind the retreating, bald-smooth forehead? Was it sharp intelligence or only good humor that beamed out of the little eyes that screwed up into a thousand wrinkles.

Harlan didn't know what to think. The cigarette seemed to obscure what small scrabble of intelligence he could collect. He flinched visibly as a puff of smoke reached him.

Twissell's eyes narrowed as though he were trying to peer through the smoke haze and he said in horribly accented tenth-millennial dialect, "Will you petter feel if I in your yourself dialect should speech, poy?"

Harlan, brought to the sudden brink of hysterical laughter, said carefully, "I speak Standard Intertemporal quite well, sir." He said it in the Intertemporal he and all other Eternals in his presence had used ever since his first months in Eternity.

"Nonsense," said Twissell imperiously. "I do not bother of Intertemporal. My speech of ten-millennial is over than perfect."

Harlan guessed that it had been some forty years since Twissell had had to make use of localwhen dialects.

But having made his point to his own satisfaction, apparently, he shifted to Intertemporal and remained there. He said, "I would offer you a cigarette, but I am certain you don't smoke. Smoking is approved of hardly anywhen in history. In fact, good cigarettes are made only in the 72nd and mine have to be specially imported from there. I give you that hint in case you ever become a smoker. It is all very sad. Last week, I was stuck in the 123rd for two days. No smoking. I mean, even in the Section of Eternity devoted to the 123rd. The Eternals there have picked up the *mores*. If I had lit a cigarette it would have been like the sky collapsing. Sometimes I think I should like to calculate one great Reality Change and wipe out all the no-smoking taboos in all the Centuries, except that any Reality Change like that would make for wars in the 58th or a slave society in the 1000th. Always something."

Harlan was first confused, then anxious. Surely these rattling irrelevancies must be hiding something.

His throat felt a little constricted. He said, "May I ask why you've arranged to see me, sir?"

"I like your reports, boy."

There was a veiled glimmer of joy in Harlan's eyes, but he did not smile. "Thank you, sir."

"It has a touch of the artist. You are intuitive. You feel strongly. I think I know your proper position in Eternity and I have come to offer it to you."

Harlan thought: I can't believe this.

He held all triumph out of his voice. "You do me great honor, sir," he said.

Whereupon Senior Computer Twissell, having come to the end of his cigarette, produced another in his left hand by some unnoted feat of legerdemain and lit it. He said between puffs, "For Time's sake, boy, you talk as though you rehearsed lines. Great honor, bah. Piffle. Trash. Say what you feel in plain language. You're glad, hey?"

"Yes, sir," said Harlan cautiously.

"All right. You should be. How would you like to be a Technician?"

"A Technician!" cried Harlan, leaping from his seat.

"Sit down. Sit down. You seem surprised."

"I hadn't expected to be a Technician, Computer Twissell."

"No," said Twissell dryly, "somehow no one ever does. They expect anything but that. Yet Technicians are hard to find, and are always in demand. Not a Section in Eternity has what it considers enough."

"I don't think I'm suited."

"You mean you're not suited to take a job with trouble in it. By Time, if you are devoted to Eternity, as I believe you are, you won't mind that. So the fools will avoid you and you will feel ostracized. You will grow used to that. And you will have the satisfaction of knowing you are needed, and needed badly. By *me*."

"By you, sir? By you particularly?"

"Yes." An element of shrewdness entered the old man's smile. "You are not to be just a Technician. You will be my personal Technician. You will have special status. How does that sound now?"

Harlan said, "I don't know, sir. I may not qualify."

Twissell shook his head firmly. "I need you. I need just you. Your reports assure me you have what I need up here." He tapped his forehead quickly with a ridge-nailed forefinger. "Your record as Cub is good; the Sections for which you have Observed reported favorably. Finally, Finge's report was most suitable of all."

Harlan was honestly startled. "Computer Finge's report was favorable?"

"You didn't expect that?"

"I—don't know."

"Well, boy, I didn't say it was favorable. I said it was suitable. As a matter of fact, Finge's report was *not* favorable. He recommended that you be removed from all duties connected with Reality Changes. He suggested it wasn't safe to keep you anywhere but in Maintenance."

Harlan reddened. "What were his reasons for saying so, sir?"

"It seems you have a hobby, boy. You are interested in Primitive history, eh?" He gestured expansively with his cigarette and Harlan, forgetting in his anger to control his breathing, inhaled a cloud of smoke and coughed helplessly.

Twissell regarded the young Observer's coughing spell benignly and said, "Isn't that so?"

Harlan began, "Computer Finge had no right——"

"Now, now. I told you what was in the report because it hinges on the purpose I need you most for. Actually, the report was confidential and you are to forget I told you what was in it. Permanently, boy."

"But what's wrong with being interested in Primitive history?"

"Finge thinks your interest in it shows a strong Wish-to-Time. You understand me, boy?"

Harlan did. It was impossible to avoid picking up psychiatric lingo. That phrase above all. Every member of Eternity was supposed to have a strong drive, the stronger for being officially suppressed in all its manifestations, to return, not necessarily to his own Time, but at least to some one definite Time; to become part of a Century, rather than to remain a wanderer through them all. Of course in most Eternals the drive remained safely hidden in the unconscious.

"I don't think that's the case," said Harlan.

"Nor I. In fact, I think your hobby is interesting and valuable. As I said, it's why I want you. I want you to teach a Cub I shall bring to you all you know and all you can learn about Primitive history. In between, you will also be my personal Technician. You'll start in a few days. Is that agreeable?"

Agreeable? To have official permission to learn all he could about the days before Eternity? To be personally associated with the greatest Eternal of them all? Even the nasty fact of Technician's status seemed bearable under those conditions.

His caution, however, did not entirely fail him. He said, "If it's necessary for the good of Eternity, sir——"

"For the *good* of Eternity?" cried the gnomish Computer in sudden excitement. He threw his cigarette butt from him with such energy that it hit the far wall and bounced off in a shower of sparks. "I need you for the *existence* of Eternity."

Three: CUB

Harlan had been in the 575th for weeks before he met Brinsley Sheridan Cooper. He had time to grow used to his new quarters and to the antisepsis of glass and porcelain. He learned to wear the Technician's mark with only moderate shrinking and to refrain from making things worse by standing so that the insigne was hidden against a wall or was covered by the interposition of some object he was carrying.

Others smiled disdainfully when that was done and turned colder as though they suspected an attempt to invade their friendship on false pretenses.

Senior Computer Twissell brought him problems daily. Harlan studied them and wrote his analyses in drafts that were four times rewritten, the last version being handed in reluctantly even so.

Twissell would appraise them and nod and say, "Good, good." Then his old blue eyes would dart quickly at Harlan and his smile would narrow a bit as he said, "I'll test this guess on the Computaplex."

He always called the analysis a "guess." He never told Harlan the result of the Computaplex check, and Harlan dared not ask. He was despondent over the fact that he was never asked to put any of his own analyses into action. Did that mean that the Computaplex was *not* checking him, that he had been choosing the wrong item for the induction of a Reality Change, that he did not have the knack of seeing the Minimum Necessary Change in an indicated range? (It was not until later that he grew sufficiently sophisticated to have the phrase come rolling off his tongue as M.N.C.)

One day Twissell came in with an abashed individual who seemed scarcely to dare raise his eyes to meet Harlan's.

Twissell said, "Technician Harlan, this is Cub B. S. Cooper."

Automatically Harlan said, "Hello," weighed the man's appearance, and was unimpressed. The fellow was on the shortish side, with dark hair parted in the middle. His chin was narrow, his eyes an indefinite light brown, his ears a little large, and his fingernails bitten.

Twissell said, "This is the boy to whom you will be teaching Primitive history."

"Great Time," said Harlan with suddenly increased interest. "*Hello!*" He had almost forgotten.

Twissell said, "Arrange a schedule with him that will suit you, Harlan. If you can manage two afternoons a week, I think that would be fine. Use your own method of teaching him. I'll leave that to you. If you should need book-films or old documents, tell me, and if they exist in Eternity or in any part of Time that can be reached, we'll get them. Eh, boy?"

He plucked a lit cigarette out of nowhere (as it always seemed) and the air reeked with smoke. Harlan coughed and from the twisting of the Cub's mouth it was quite obvious that the latter would have done the same had he dared.

After Twissell left, Harlan said, "Well, sit down"—he hesitated a moment, then added determinedly—"Son. Sit down, son. My office isn't much, but it's yours whenever we're together."

Harlan was almost flooded with eagerness. This project was *his!* Primitive history was something that was all his own.

The Cub raised his eyes (for the first time, really) and said stumblingly, "You *are* a Technician."

A considerable part of Harlan's excitement and warmth died. "What of it?"

"Nothing," said the Cub. "I just——"

"You heard Computer Twissell address me as Technician, didn't you?"

"Yes, sir."

"Did you think it was a slip of the tongue? Something too bad to be true?"

"No, sir."

"What's wrong with your speech?" Harlan asked brutally, and even as he did so, he felt shame nudge him.

Cooper blushed painfully. "I'm not very good at Standard Intertemporal."

"Why not? How long have you been a Cub?"

"Less than one year, sir."

"One year? How old are you, for Time's sake?"

"Twenty-four physioyears, sir."

Harlan stared. "Are you trying to tell me that they took you into Eternity at twenty-three?"

"Yes, sir."

Harlan sat down and rubbed his hands together. That just wasn't done. Fifteen to sixteen was the age of entrance into Eternity. What was this? A new kind of testing of himself on the part of Twissell?

He said, "Sit down and let's get started. Your name in full and your homewhen."

The Cub stammered, "Brinsley Sheridan Cooper of the 78th, sir."

Harlan almost softened. That was close. It was only seventeen Centuries downwhen from his own homewhen. Almost a Temporal neighbor.

He said, "Are you interested in Primitive history?"

"Computer Twissell asked me to learn. I don't know much about it."

"What else are you learning?"

"Mathematics. Temporal engineering. I'm just getting the fundamentals so far. Back in the 78th, I was a Speedy-vac repairman."

There was no point in asking the nature of a Speedy-vac. It might be a suction cleaner, a computing machine, a type of spray painter. Anything. Harlan wasn't particularly interested.

He said, "Do you know anything about history? Any kind of history?"

"I studied European history."

"Your particular political unit, I take it."

"I was born in Europe. Yes. Mostly, of course, they taught us modern history. After the revolutions of '54; 7554, that is."

"All right. First thing you do is to forget it. It doesn't mean anything. The history they try to teach Timers changes with every Reality Change. Not that they realize that. In each Reality, their history is the only history. That's what's so different about Primitive history. That's the beauty of it. No matter what any of us does, it exists precisely as it has always existed. Columbus and Washington, Mussolini and Hereford, they all exist."

Cooper smiled feebly. He brushed his little finger across his upper lip and for the first time Harlan noticed a trace of bristle there as though the Cub were cultivating a mustache.

Cooper said, "I can't quite—get used to it, all the time I've been here."

"Get used to what?"

"Being five hundred Centuries away from homewhen."

"I'm nearly that myself. I'm 95th."

"That's another thing. You're older than I am and yet I'm seventeen Centuries older than you in another way. I can be your great-great-great-and-so-on-grandfather."

"What's the difference? Suppose you are?"

"Well, it takes getting used to." There was a trace of rebellion in the Cub's voice.

"It does for all of us," said Harlan callously, and began talking about the Primitives. By the time three hours had passed, he was deep in an explanation concerning the reasons why there were Centuries before the 1st Century.

("But isn't the 1st Century *first?*" Cooper had asked plaintively.)

Harlan ended by giving the Cub a book, not a good one, really, but one that would serve as a beginning. "I'll get you better stuff as we go along," he said.

By the end of a week Cooper's mustache had become a pronounced dark bristle that made him look ten years older and accentuated the narrowness of his chin. On the whole, Harlan decided, it would not be an improvement, that mustache.

Cooper said, "I've finished your book."

"What did you think of it?"

"In a way——" There was a long pause. Cooper began over again. "Parts of the later Primitive was something like the 78th. It made me think of home, you know. Twice, I dreamed about my wife."

Harlan exploded. "Your *wife?*"

"I was married before I came here."

"Great Time! Did they bring your wife across too?"

Cooper shook his head. "I don't even know if she's been Changed in the last year. If she has, I suppose she's not really my wife now."

Harlan recovered. Of course, if the Cub were twenty-three years old when he was taken into Eternity, it was quite possible that he might have been married. One thing unprecedented led to another.

What was going on? Once modifications were introduced into the rules, it wouldn't be a long step to the point where everything would decline into a mass of incoherency. Eternity was too finely balanced an arrangement to endure modification.

It was his anger on behalf of Eternity, perhaps, that put an unintended harshness into Harlan's next words. "I hope you're not planning on going back to the 78th to check on her."

The Cub lifted his head and his eyes were firm and steady. "No."

Harlan shifted uneasily, "Good. You have no family. Nothing. You're an Eternal and don't ever think of anyone you knew in Time."

Cooper's lips thinned, and his accent stood out sharply in his quick words. "You're speaking like a Technician."

Harlan's fists clenched along the sides of his desk. He said hoarsely, "What do you imply? I'm a Technician so I make the Changes? So I defend them and demand that you accept them?

Look, kid, you haven't been here a year; you can't speak Intertemporal; you're all misgeared on Time and Reality, but you think you know all about Technicians and how to kick them in the teeth."

"I'm sorry," said Cooper quickly; "I didn't mean to offend you."

"No, no, who offends a Technician? You just hear everyone else talking, is that it? They say, 'Cold as a Technician's heart,' don't they? They say, 'A trillion personalities changed—just a Technician's yawn.' Maybe a few other things. What's the answer, Mr. Cooper? Does it make you feel sophisticated to join in? It makes you a big man? A big wheel in Eternity?"

"I said I'm sorry."

"All right. I just want you to know I've been a Technician for less than a month and I personally have never induced a Reality Change. Now let's get on with business."

Senior Computer Twissell called Andrew Harlan to his office the next day.

He said, "How would you like to go out on an M.N.C., boy?"

It was almost too apposite. All that morning Harlan had been regretting his cowardly disclaimer of personal involvement in the Technician's work; his childish cry of: I haven't done anything wrong yet, so don't blame me.

It amounted to an admission that there *was* something wrong about a Technician's work, and that he himself was blameless only because he was too new at the game to have had time to be a criminal.

He welcomed the chance to kill that excuse now. It would be almost a penance. He could say to Cooper: Yes, because of something I have done, this many millions of people are new personalities, but it was necessary and I am proud to have been the cause.

So Harlan said joyfully, "I'm ready, sir."

"Good. Good. You'll be glad to know, boy," (a puff, and the cigarette tip glowed brilliantly) "that every one of your analyses checked out with high-order accuracy."

"Thank you, sir." (They were analyses now, thought Harlan, not guesses.)

"You've got a talent. Quite a touch, boy. I look for great things. And we can begin with this one, 223rd. Your statement that a jammed vehicle clutch would supply the necessary fork without undesirable side effects is perfectly correct. Will you jam it?"

"Yes, sir."

That was Harlan's true initiation into Technicianhood. After that he was more than just a man with a rose-red badge. He had handled Reality. He had tampered with a mechanism during a quick few minutes taken out of the 223rd and, as a result, a young man did not reach a lecture on mechanics he had meant to attend. He never went in for solar engineering, consequently, and a perfectly simple device was delayed in its development a crucial ten years. A war in the 224th, amazingly enough, was moved out of Reality as a result.

Wasn't *that* good? What if personalities were changed? The new personalities were as human as the old and as deserving of life. If some lives were shortened, more were lengthened and made happier. A great work of literature, a monument of Man's intellect and feeling, was never written in the new Reality, but several copies were preserved in Eternity's libraries, were they not? And new creative works had come into existence, had they not?

Yet that night Harlan spent hours in a hot agony of wakefulness, and when he finally drowsed groggily, he did something he hadn't done in years.

He dreamed of his mother.

Despite the weakness of such a beginning a physioyear was sufficient to make Harlan known throughout Eternity as "Twissell's Technician," and, with more than a trace of ill-humor as "The Wonder Boy" and "The Never-Wrong."

His contact with Cooper became almost comfortable. They never grew completely friendly. (If Cooper could have brought himself to make advances, Harlan might not have known how to respond.) Nevertheless they worked well together, and Cooper's interest in Primitive history grew to the point where it nearly rivaled Harlan's.

One day Harlan said to Cooper, "Look, Cooper, would you mind coming in tomorrow instead? I've got to get up to the 3000's sometime this week to check on an Observation and the man I want to see is free this afternoon."

Cooper's eyes lit up hungrily. "Why can't I come?"

"Do you want to?"

"Sure. I've never been in a kettle except when they brought me here from the 78th and I didn't know what was happening at the time."

Harlan was accustomed to using the kettle in Shaft C, which was, by unwritten custom, reserved for Technicians along its entire immeasurable length through the Centuries. Cooper showed no embarrassment at being led there. He stepped into the kettle without hesitation and took his seat on the curved molding that completely circled it.

When Harlan, however, had activated the Field, and kicked the kettle into upwhen motion, Cooper's face screwed up into an almost comic expression of surprise.

"I don't feel a thing," he said. "Is anything wrong?"

"Nothing's wrong. You're not feeling anything because you're not really moving. You're being kicked along the temporal extension of the kettle. In fact," Harlan said, growing didactic, "at the moment, you and I aren't matter, really, in spite of appearances. A hundred men could be using this same kettle, moving (if you can call it that) at various velocities in either Time-direction, passing through one another and so on. The laws of the ordinary universe just don't apply to the kettle shafts!"

Cooper's mouth quirked a bit and Harlan thought uneasily: The kid's taking temporal engineering and knows more about this than I do. Why don't I shut up and stop making a fool of myself?

He retreated into silence, and stared somberly at Cooper. The younger man's mustache had been full-grown for months. It drooped, framing his mouth in what Eternals called a Mallansohn hairline, because the only photograph known to be authentic of the Temporal Field inventor (and that a poor one and out of focus) showed him with just such a mustache. For that reason it maintained a certain popularity among Eternals even though it did few of them justice.

Cooper's eyes were fixed on the shifting numbers that marked the passing of the Centuries with respect to themselves. He said, "How far upwhen does the kettle shaft go?"

"Haven't they taught you that?"

"They've hardly mentioned the kettles."

Harlan shrugged. "There's no end to Eternity. The shaft goes on forever."

"How far upwhen have you gone?"

"This will be the uppest. Dr. Twissell has been up to the 50,000's."

"Great Time!" whispered Cooper.

"That's still nothing. Some Eternals have been up past the 150,000th Century."

"What's *that* like?"

"Like nothing at all," said Harlan morosely. "Lots of life but none of it human. Man is gone."

"Dead? Wiped out?"

"I don't know that anyone exactly knows."

"Can't something be done to change that?"

"Well, from the 70,000's on——" began Harlan, then ended abruptly. "Oh, to Time with it. Change the subject."

If there was one subject about which Eternals were almost superstitious, it was the "Hidden Centuries," the time between the 70,000th and the 150,000th. It was a subject that was rarely mentioned. It was only Harlan's close association with Twissell that accounted for his own small knowledge of the era. What it amounted to was that Eternals couldn't pass into Time in all those thousands of Centuries. The doors between Eternity and Time were impenetrable. Why? No one knew.

Harlan imagined, from some casual remarks of Twissell's, that attempts had been made to Change the Reality in the Centuries just downwhen from the 70,000th, but without adequate Observation beyond the 70,000th not much could be done.

Twissell had laughed a bit one time and said, "We'll get through someday. Meanwhile, 70,000 Centuries is quite enough to take care of."

It did not sound wholly convincing.

"What happens to Eternity after the 150,000th?" asked Cooper.

Harlan sighed. The subject, apparently, was not to be changed. "Nothing," he said. "The Sections are there but there are no Eternals in it anywhere after the 70,000th. The Sections keep on going for millions of Centuries till all life is gone and past that, too, till the sun becomes a nova, and past that, too. There isn't any end to Eternity. That's why it's called Eternity."

"The sun *does* become a nova, then?"

"It certainly does. Eternity couldn't exist if that weren't so. Nova Sol is our power supply. Listen, do you know how much power is required to set up a Temporal Field? Mallansohn's first Field was two seconds from extreme downwhen to extreme upwhen and big enough to hold not more than a match head and that took a nuclear power plant's complete output for one day. It took nearly a hundred years to set up a hair-thin Temporal Field far enough upwhen to be able to tap the radiant power of the nova so that a Field could be built big enough to hold a man."

Cooper sighed. "I wish they would get to the point where they stopped making me learn equations and field mechanics and start telling me some of the interesting stuff. Now if I had lived in Mallansohn's time——"

"You would have learned nothing. He lived in the 24th, but Eternity didn't start till late in the 27th. Inventing the Field isn't the same as constructing Eternity, you know, and the rest of the 24th didn't have the slightest inkling of what Mallansohn's invention signified."

"He was ahead of his generation, then?"

"Very much so. He not only invented the Temporal Field, but he described the basic relationships that made Eternity possible and predicted almost every aspect of it except for the Reality Change. Quite closely, too—but I think we're pulling to a halt, Cooper. After you."

They stepped out.

Harlan had never seen Senior Computer Laban Twissell angry before. People always said that he was incapable of any emotion, that he was an unsouled fixture of Eternity to the point where he had forgotten the exact number of his homewhen Century. People said that at an early age his heart had atrophied and that a hand computer similar to the model he carried always in his trouser pocket had taken its place.

Twissell did nothing to deny these rumors. In fact most people guessed that he believed them himself.

So even while Harlan bent before the force of the angry blast that struck him, he had room in his mind to be amazed at the fact that Twissell could display anger. He wondered if Twissell would be mortified in some calmer aftermath to realize that his hand-computer heart had betrayed him by exposing itself as only a poor thing of muscle and valves subject to the twists of emotion.

Twissell said, in part, his old voice creaking, "Father Time, boy, are you on the Allwhen Council? Do you give the orders around here? Do you tell me what to do or do I tell you what to do? Are you making arrangements for all kettle trips for this Section? Do we all come to you for permission now?"

He interrupted himself with occasional exclamations of "Answer me," then continued pouring more questions into the boiling interrogative caldron.

He said finally, "If you ever get above yourself this way again, I'll have you on plumbing repair and for good. Do you understand me?"

Harlan, pale with his own gathering embarrassment, said, "I was never told that Cub Cooper was not to be taken on the kettle."

The explanation did not act as an emollient. "What kind of an excuse is a double negative, boy? You were never told not to get him drunk. You were never told not to shave him bald. You were never told not to skewer him with a fine-edged Tav curve. Father Time, boy, what *were* you told to do with him?"

"I was told to teach him Primitive history."

"Then do so. Do nothing more than that." Twissell dropped his cigarette and ground it savagely underfoot as though it were the face of a lifelong enemy.

"I'd like to point out, Computer," said Harlan, "that many Centuries under the current Reality somewhat resemble specific eras of Primitive history in one or more respects. It had been my intention to take him out to those Times, under careful spatio-temporal charting, of course, as a form of field trip."

"What? Listen, you chucklehead, don't you ever intend to ask my permission for *anything*? That's out. Just teach him Primitive history. No field trips. No laboratory experiments, either. Next you'll be changing Reality just to show him how."

Harlan licked his dry lips with a dry tongue, muttered a resentful acquiescence, and, eventually, was allowed to leave.

It took weeks for his hurt feelings to heal over somewhat.

Four: COMPUTER

Harlan had been two years a Technician when he re-entered the 482nd for the first time since leaving with Twissell. He found it almost unrecognizable.

It had not changed. He had.

Two years of Technicianhood had meant a number of things. In one sense it had increased his feeling of stability. He had no longer to learn a new language, get used to new styles of clothing and new ways of life with every new Observation project. On the other hand, it had resulted in a withdrawal on his own part. He had almost forgotten now the camaraderie that united all the rest of the Specialists in Eternity.

Most of all, he had developed the feeling of the *power* of being a Technician. He held the fate of millions in his finger tips, and if one must walk lonely because of it, one could also walk proudly.

So he could stare coldly at the Communications man behind the entry desk of the 482nd and announce himself in clipped syllables: "Andrew Harlan, Technician, reporting to Computer Finge for temporary assignment to the 482nd," disregarding the quick glance from the middle-aged man he faced.

It was what some people called the "Technician glance," a quick, involuntary sidelong peek at the rose-red shoulder emblem of the Technician, then an elaborate attempt not to look at it again.

Harlan stared at the other's shoulder emblem. It was not the yellow of the Computer, the green of the Life-Plotter, the blue of the Sociologist, or the white of the Observer. It was not the Specialist's solid color at all. It was simply a blue bar on white. The man was Communications, a subbranch of Maintenance, not a Specialist at all.

And *he* gave the "Technician glance" too.

Harlan said a little sadly, "Well?"

Communications said quickly, "I'm ringing Computer Finge, sir."

Harlan remembered the 482nd as solid and massive, but now it seemed almost squalid.

Harlan had grown used to the glass and porcelain of the 575th, to its fetish of cleanliness. He had grown accustomed to a world of whiteness and clarity, broken by sparse patches of light pastel.

The heavy plaster swirls of the 482nd, its splashy pigments, its areas of painted metal were almost repulsive.

Even Finge seemed different, less than life-size, somewhat. Two years earlier, to Observer Harlan, Finge's every gesture had seemed sinister and powerful.

Now, from the lofty and isolated heights of Technicianhood, the man seemed pathetic and lost. Harlan watched him as he leafed through a sheaf of foils and got ready to look up, with the air of someone who is beginning to think he has made his visitor wait the duly required amount of time.

Finge was from an energy-centered Century in the 600's. Twissell had told him that and it explained a good deal. Finge's flashes of ill-temper could easily be the result of the natural insecurity of a heavy man used to the firmness of field-forces and unhappy to be dealing with nothing more than flimsy matter. His tiptoeing walk (Harlan remembered Finge's catlike tread well; often he would look up from his desk, see Finge standing there staring at him, his approach having been unheard) was no longer something sly and sneaking, but rather the fearful and reluctant tread of one who lives in the constant, if unconscious, fear that the flooring would break under his weight.

Harlan thought, with a pleasant condescension: The man is poorly adjusted to the Section. Reassignment is probably the only thing that would help him.

Finge said, "Greetings, Technician Harlan."

"Greetings, Computer," said Harlan.

Finge said, "It seems that in the two years since——"

"Two physioyears," said Harlan.

Finge looked up in surprise. "Two physioyears, of course."

In Eternity there was no Time as one ordinarily thought of Time in the universe outside, but men's bodies grew older and that was the unavoidable measure of Time even in the absence of meaningful physical phenomena. Physiologically Time passed, and in a physioyear within Eternity a man grew as much older as he would have in an ordinary year in Time.

Yet even the most pedantic Eternal remembered the distinction only rarely. It was too convenient to say, "See you tomorrow," or "I missed you yesterday," or "I will see you next week," as though there were a tomorrow or a yesterday or a last week in any but a physiological sense. And the instincts of humanity were catered to by having the activities of Eternity tailored to an arbitrary twenty-four "physiohour" day, with a solemn assumption of day and night, today and tomorrow.

Finge said, "In the two *physioyears* since you left, a crisis has gradually gathered about the 482nd. A rather peculiar one. A delicate one. Almost unprecedented. We need accurate Observation now as we never have needed it before."

"And you want me to Observe?"

"Yes. In a way, it's a waste of talent to ask a Technician to do a job of Observation, but your previous Observations, for clarity and insight, were perfect. We need that again. Now I'll just sketch in a few details. . . ."

What those details were Harlan was not to find out just then. Finge spoke, but the door opened, and Harlan did not hear him.

He stared at the person who entered.

It was not that Harlan had never seen a girl in Eternity before. Never was too strong a word. Rarely, yes, but not never.

But a girl such as *this!* And in *Eternity!*

Harlan had seen many women in his passages through Time, but in Time they were only objects to him, like walls and balls, barrows and harrows, kittens and mittens. They were facts to be Observed.

In Eternity a girl was a different matter. And one like *this!*

She was dressed in the style of the upper classes of the 482nd, which meant transparent sheathing and not very much else above the waist, and flimsy, knee-length trousers below. The latter, while opaque enough, hinted delicately at gluteal curves.

Her hair was glossily dark and shoulder length, her lips redly penciled thin above and full below in an exaggerated pout. Her upper eyelids and her ear lobes were tinted a pale rose and the rest of her youthful (almost girlish) face was a startlingly milky white. Jeweled pendants descended forward from mid-shoulder to tinkle now this side, now that of the graceful breasts to which they drew attention.

She took her seat at a desk in the corner of Finge's office, lifting her eyelashes only once to sweep her dark glance across Harlan's face.

When Harlan heard Finge's voice again, the Computer was saying, "You'll get all this in an official report and meanwhile you can have your old office and sleeping quarters."

Harlan found himself outside Finge's office without quite remembering the details of his leaving. Presumably he had walked out.

The emotion within him that was easiest to recognize was anger. *By Time,* Finge ought not to be allowed to do this. It was bad for morale. It made a mockery——

He stopped himself, unclenched his fist, unclamped his jaw. Let's see, now! His footsteps sounded sharply in his own ear as he strode firmly toward the Communications man behind the desk.

Communications looked up, without quite meeting his eye, and said cautiously, "Yes, sir."

Harlan said, "There's a woman at a desk in Computer Finge's office. Is she new here?"

He had meant to ask it casually. He had meant to make it a bored, indifferent question. It rang out, instead, like a pair of cymbals clashing.

But it roused Communications. The look in his eye became something that made all men kin. It even embraced the Technician, drew him in as a fellow. Communications said, "You mean the babe? Wow! Isn't she built like a force-field latrine, though?"

Harlan stammered a bit. "Just answer my question."

Communications stared and some of his steam evaporated. He said, "She's new. She's a Timer."

"What's her job?"

A slow smile crept over Communications' face and grew into a leer. "She's supposed to be the boss's secretary. Her name is Noÿs Lambent."

"All right." Harlan turned on his heel and left.

Harlan's first Observation trip into the 482nd came the next day, but it lasted for thirty minutes only. It was obviously only an orientation trip, intended to get him into the feel of things. He entered it for an hour and a half the next day and not at all on the third.

He occupied his time in working his way through his original reports, relearning his own knowledge, brushing up on the language system of the time, accustoming himself to the local costumes again.

One Reality Change had hit the 482nd, but it was very minor. A political clique that had been In was now Out, but there seemed no change in the society otherwise.

Without quite realizing it he slipped into the habit of searching his old reports for information on the aristocracy. Surely he had made Observations.

He had, but they were impersonal, from a distance. His data concerned them as a class, not as individuals.

Of course his spatio-temporal charts had never demanded or even permitted him to observe the aristocracy from within. What the reasons for that might have been was beyond the purview of an Observer. He was impatient with himself at feeling curiosity concerning that now.

During those three days he had caught glimpses of the girl, Noÿs Lambent, four times. At first he had been aware only of her clothes and her ornaments. Now he noticed that she was five feet six in height, half a head shorter than himself, yet slim enough and with a carriage erect and graceful enough to give an impression of height. She was older than she first seemed, approaching thirty perhaps, certainly over twenty-five.

She was quiet and reserved, smiled at him once when he passed her in the corridor, then lowered her eyes. Harlan drew aside to avoid touching her, then walked on feeling angry.

By the close of the third day Harlan was beginning to feel that his duty as an Eternal left him only one course of action. Doubtless her position was a comfortable one for herself. Doubtless Finge was within the letter of the law. Yet Finge's indiscretion in the matter, his carelessness certainly went against the spirit of the law, and something should be done about it.

Harlan decided that, after all, there wasn't a man in Eternity he disliked quite as much as Finge. The excuses he had found for the man only a few days before vanished.

On the morning of the fourth day Harlan asked for and received permission to see Finge privately. He walked in with a determined step and, to his own surprise, made his point instantly. "Computer Finge, I suggest that Miss Lambent be returned to Time."

Finge's eyes narrowed. He nodded toward a chair, placed clasped hands under his soft, round chin, and showed some of his teeth. "Well, sit down. Sit down. You find Miss Lambent incompetent? Unsuitable?"

"As to her incompetence and unsuitability, Computer, I cannot say. It depends on the uses to which she is put, and I have put her to none. But you must realize that she is bad for the morale of this Section."

Finge stared at him distantly as though his Computer's mind were weighing abstractions beyond the reach of an ordinary Eternal. "In what way is she hurting morale, Technician?"

"There's no real necessity for you to ask," said Harlan, his anger deepening. "Her costume is exhibitionistic. Her——"

"Wait, wait. Now wait awhile, Harlan. You've been an Observer in this era. You know her clothes are standard costume for the 482nd."

"In her own surroundings, in her own cultural milieu, I would have no fault to find, though I'll say right now that her costume is extreme even for the 482nd. You'll allow me to be the judge of that. Here in Eternity, a person such as she is certainly out of place."

Finge nodded his head slowly. He actually seemed to be enjoying himself. Harlan stiffened.

Finge said, "She is here for a deliberate purpose. She is performing an essential function. It is only temporary. Try to endure her meanwhile."

Harlan's jaw quivered. He had protested and was being fobbed off. To hell with caution. He would speak his mind. He said, "I can imagine what the woman's 'essential function' is. To keep her so openly will not be allowed to pass."

He turned stiffly, walked to the door. Finge's voice stopped him.

"Technician," Finge said, "your relationship with Twissell may have given you a distorted notion about your own importance. Correct that! And meanwhile tell me, Technician, have you ever had a" (he hesitated, seeming to pick among words) "girl friend?"

With painstaking and insulting accuracy, back still turned, Harlan quoted: "In the interest of avoiding emotional entanglements with Time, an Eternal may not marry. In the interest of avoiding emotional entanglements with family, an Eternal may not have children."

The Computer said gravely, "I didn't ask about marriage or children."

Harlan quoted further: "Temporary liaisons may be made with Timers only after application with the Central Charting Board of the Allwhen Council for an appropriate Life-Plot of the Timer concerned. Liaisons may be conducted thereafter only according to the requirements of specific spatio-temporal charting."

"Quite true. Have you ever applied for temporary liaison, Technician?"

"No, Computer."

"Do you intend to?"

"No, Computer."

"Perhaps you ought to. It would give you a greater breadth of view. You would become less concerned about the details of a woman's costume, less disturbed about her possible personal relations with other Eternals."

Harlan left, speechless with rage.

He found it almost impossible to perform his near-daily trek into the 482nd (the longest continuous period remaining something under two hours).

He was upset, and he knew why. Finge! Finge, and his coarse advice concerning liaisons with Timers.

Liaisons existed. Everyone knew that. Eternity had always been aware of the necessity for compromising with human appetites (to Harlan the phrase carried a quivery repulsion), but the restrictions involved in choosing mistresses made the compromise anything but lax, anything but generous. And those who were lucky enough to qualify for such an arrangement were expected to be most discreet about it, out of common decency and consideration for the majority.

Among the lower classes of Eternals, particularly among Maintenance, there were always the rumors (half hopeful, half resentful) of women imported on a more or less permanent basis for the obvious reasons. Always rumor pointed to the Computers and Life-Plotters as the benefiting groups. They and only they could decide which women could be abstracted from Time without danger of significant Reality Change.

Less sensational (and therefore less tongue-worthy) were the stories concerning the Timer employees that every Section engaged temporarily (when spatio-temporal analysis permitted) to perform the tedious tasks of cooking, cleaning, and heavy labor.

But a Timer, and *such* a Timer, employed as "secretary," could only mean that Finge was thumbing a nose at the ideals that made Eternity what it was.

Regardless of the facts of life to which the practical men of Eternity made a perfunctory obeisance it remained true that the ideal Eternal was a dedicated man living for the mission he had to perform, for the betterment of Reality and the improvement of the sum of human happiness. Harlan liked to think that Eternity was like the monasteries of Primitive times.

He dreamed that night that he spoke to Twissell about the matter, and that Twissell, the ideal Eternal, shared his horror. He dreamed of a broken Finge, stripped of rank. He dreamed of himself with the yellow Computer's insigne, instituting a new regime in the 482nd, ordering Finge grandly to a new position in Maintenance. Twissell sat next to him, smiling with admiration, as he drew up a new organizational chart, neat, orderly, consistent, and asked Noÿs Lambent to distribute copies.

But Noÿs Lambent was nude, and Harlan woke up, trembling and ashamed.

He met the girl in a corridor one day and stood aside, eyes averted, to let her pass.

But she remained standing, looking at him, until he had to look up and meet her eyes. She was all color and life and Harlan was conscious of a faint perfume about her.

She said, "You're Technician Harlan, aren't you?"

His impulse was to snub her, to force his way past, but, after all, he told himself, all this wasn't her fault. Besides, to move past her now would mean touching her.

So he nodded briefly. "Yes."

"I'm told you're quite an expert on our Time."

"I have been in it."

"I would love to talk to you about it someday."

"I am busy. I wouldn't have time."

"But Mr. Harlan, surely you could *find* time someday."

She smiled at him.

Harlan said in a desperate whisper, "Will you pass, please? Or will you stand aside to let me pass? Please!"

She moved by with a slow swing of her hips that brought blood tingling to his embarrassed cheeks.

He was angry at her for embarrassing him, angry at himself for being embarrassed, and angry, most of all, for some obscure reason, at Finge.

Finge called him in at the end of two weeks. On his desk was a sheet of perforated flimsy the length and intricacy of which told Harlan at once that this concerned no half-hour excursion into Time.

Finge said, "Would you sit down, Harlan, and scan this thing right now? No, not by eye. Use the machine."

Harlan lifted indifferent eyebrows, and inserted the sheet carefully between the lips of the scanner on Finge's desk. Slowly it passed into the intestines of the machine and, as it did so, the perforation pattern was translated into words that appeared on the cloudy-white rectangle that was the visual attachment.

Somewhere about midpoint, Harlan's hand shot out and disconnected the scanner. He yanked the flimsy out with a force that tore its tough cellulite structure.

Finge said calmly, "I have another copy."

But Harlan was holding the remnants between thumb and forefinger as though it might explode. "Computer Finge, there is some mistake. Surely I am not to be expected to use the home of this woman as base for a near-week stay in Time."

The Computer pursed his lips. "Why not, if the spatio-temporal requirements are such. If there is a personal problem involved between yourself and Miss Lam——"

"No personal problem at all," interposed Harlan hotly.

"Some kind of problem, certainly. In the circumstances, I will go as far as to explain certain aspects of the Observational problem. This is not to be taken as a precedent, of course."

Harlan sat motionless. He was thinking hard and fast. Ordinarily professional pride would have forced Harlan to disdain explanation. An Observer, or Technician, for that matter, did his job without question. And ordinarily a Computer would never dream of offering explanation.

Here, however, was something unusual. Harlan had complained concerning the girl, the so-called secretary. Finge was afraid the complaint might go further. ("The guilty fleeth when no man pursueth," thought Harlan with grim satisfaction and tried to remember where he had read that phrase.)

Finge's strategy was obvious, therefore. By stationing Harlan in the woman's dwelling place he would be ready to make counteraccusations if matters went far enough. Harlan's value as a witness against him would be destroyed.

And, of course, he would have to have some specious explanation for placing Harlan in such a place, and this would be it. Harlan listened with barely hidden contempt.

Finge said, "As you know, the various Centuries are aware of the existence of Eternity. They know that we supervise intertemporal trade. They consider that to be our chief function, which is good.

They have a dim knowledge that we are also here to prevent catastrophe from striking mankind. That is more a superstition than anything else, but it is more or less correct, and good, too. We supply the generations with a mass father image and a certain feeling of security. You see all that, don't you?"

Harlan thought: Does the man think I'm still a Cub?

But he nodded briefly.

Finge went on. "There are some things, however, they must not know. Prime among them, of course, is the manner in which we alter Reality when necessary. The insecurity such knowledge would arouse would be most harmful. It is always necessary to breed out of Reality any factors that might lead to such knowledge and we have never been troubled with it.

"However, there are always other undesirable beliefs about Eternity which spring up from time to time in one Century or another. Usually, the dangerous beliefs are those which concentrate particularly in the ruling classes of an era; the classes that have most contact with us and, at the same time, carry the important weight of what is called public opinion."

Finge paused as though he expected Harlan to offer some comment or ask some question. Harlan did neither.

Finge continued. "Ever since the Reality Change 433–486, Serial Number F-2, which took place about a year—a physioyear ago—there has been evidence of the bringing into Reality of such an undesirable belief. I have come to certain conclusions about the nature of that belief and have presented them to the Allwhen Council. The Council is reluctant to accept them since they depend upon the realization of an alternate in the Computing Pattern of an extremely low probability.

"Before acting on my recommendation, they insist on confirmation by direct Observation. It's a most delicate job, which is why I recalled you, and why Computer Twissell allowed you to be recalled. Another thing I did was to locate a member of the current aristocracy, who thought it would be thrilling or exciting to work in Eternity. I placed her in this office and kept her under close observation to see if she were suitable for our purpose——"

Harlan thought: Close observation! Yes!

Again his anger focused itself on Finge rather than upon the woman.

Finge was still speaking. "By all standards, she is suitable. We will now return her to her Time. Using her dwelling as a base, you will be able to study the social life of her circle. Do you understand now the reason I had the girl here and the reason I want you in her house?"

Harlan said with an almost open irony, "I understand quite well, I assure you."

"Then you will accept this mission."

Harlan left with the fire of battle burning inside his chest. Finge was *not* going to outsmart him. He was *not* going to make a fool of him.

Surely it was that fire of battle, the determination to outwit Finge, that caused him to experience an eagerness, almost an exhilaration, at the thought of this next excursion into the 482nd.

Surely it was nothing else.

Five: TIMER

Noÿs Lambent's estate was fairly isolated, yet within easy reach of one of the larger cities of the Century. Harlan knew that city well; he knew it better than any of its inhabitants could. In his exploratory Observations into this Reality he had visited every quarter of the city and every decade within the purview of the Section.

He knew the city both in Space and Time. He could piece it together, view it as an organism, living and growing, with its catastrophes and recoveries, its gaieties and troubles. Now he was in a given week of Time in that city, in a moment of suspended animation of its slow life of steel and concrete.

More than that, his preliminary explorations had centered themselves more and more closely about the "perioeci," the inhabitants who were the most important of the city, yet who lived outside the city, in room and relative isolation.

The 482nd was one of the many Centuries in which wealth was unevenly distributed. The Sociologists had an equation for the phenomenon (which Harlan had seen in print, but which he understood only vaguely). It worked itself out for any given Century to three relationships, and for the 482nd those relationships stood near the limits of what could be permitted. Sociologists shook their heads over it and Harlan had heard one say at one time that any further deterioration with new Reality Changes would require "the closest Observation."

Yet there was this to be said for unfavorable relationships in the wealth-distribution equation. It meant the existence of a leisure class and the development of an attractive way of life which, at its best, encouraged culture and grace. As long as the other end of the scale was not too badly off, as long as the leisure classes did not entirely forget their responsibilities while enjoying their privileges, as long as their culture took no obviously unhealthy turn, there was always the tendency in Eternity to forgive the departure from the ideal wealth-distribution pattern and to search for other, less attractive maladjustments.

Against his will Harlan began to understand this. Ordinarily his overnight stays in Time involved hotels in the poorer sections, where a man might easily stay anonymous, where strangers were ignored, where one presence more or less was nothing and therefore did not cause the fabric of Reality to do more than tremble. When even that was unsafe, when there was a good chance that the trembling might pass the critical point and bring down a significant part of the card house of Reality, it was not unusual to have to sleep under a particular hedge in the countryside.

And it was usual to survey various hedges to see which would be least disturbed by farmers, tramps, even stray dogs, during the night.

But now Harlan, at the other end of the scale, slept in a bed with a surface of field-permeated matter, a peculiar welding of matter and energy that entered only the highest economic levels of this society. Throughout Time it was less common than pure matter but more common than pure energy. In any case it molded itself to his body as he lay down, firm when he lay still, yielding when he moved or turned.

Reluctantly he confessed the attraction of such things, and he accepted the wisdom which caused each Section of Eternity to live on the *median* scale of its Century rather than at its most comfortable level. In that way it could maintain contact with the problems and "feel" of the Century, without succumbing to too close an identification with a sociological extreme.

It is easy, thought Harlan, that first evening, to live with aristocrats.

And just before he fell asleep, he thought of Noÿs.

He dreamed he was on the Allwhen Council, fingers clasped austerely before him. He was looking down on a small, a very small, Finge, listening in terror to the sentence that was casting him out of Eternity to perpetual Observation of one of the unknown Centuries of the far, far upwhen. The somber words of exile were coming from

Harlan's own mouth, and immediately to his right sat Noÿs Lambent.

He hadn't noticed her at first, but his eyes kept sliding to his right, and his words faltered.

Did no one else see her? The rest of the members of the Council looked steadily forward, except for Twissell. He turned to smile at Harlan, looking through the girl as though she weren't there.

Harlan wanted to order her away, but words were no longer coming out of his mouth. He tried to beat at the girl, but his arm moved sluggishly and she did not move. Her flesh was cold.

Finge was laughing—louder—louder——

—and it was Noÿs Lambent laughing.

Harlan opened his eyes to bright sunlight and stared at the girl in horror for a moment before he remembered where she was and where he was.

She said, "You were moaning and beating the pillow. Were you having a bad dream?"

Harlan did not answer.

She said, "Your bath is ready. So are your clothes. I've arranged to have you join the gathering tonight. It felt queer to step back into my ordinary life after being in Eternity so long."

Harlan felt acutely disturbed at her easy flow of words. He said, "You didn't tell them who I was, I hope."

"Of *course* not."

Of *course* not! Finge would have taken care of that little matter by having her lightly psychoed under narcosis, if he felt that necessary. He might not have thought it necessary, however. After all, he had given her "close observation."

The thought annoyed him. He said, "I'd prefer to be left to myself as much as possible."

She looked at him uncertainly a moment or two and left.

Harlan went through the morning ritual of washing and dressing glumly. He had no great hopes of an exciting evening. He would have to say as little as possible, do as little as possible, be a part of the wall as much as possible. His true function was that of a pair of ears and a pair of eyes. Connecting those senses with the final report was his mind, which, ideally, had no other function.

Ordinarily it did not disturb him that, as an Observer, he did not know what he was looking for. An Observer, he had been taught as a Cub, must not have preconceived notions as to what data is desired or what conclusions are expected. The knowledge, it was said, would automatically distort his view, however conscientious he tried to be.

But under the circumstances ignorance was irritating. Harlan suspected strongly that there was nothing to look for, that he was playing Finge's game in some way. Between that and Noÿs . . .

He stared savagely at the image of himself cast in three-dimensional accuracy two feet in front of him by the Reflector. The clinging garments of the 482nd, seamless and bright in coloring, made him, he thought, look ridiculous.

Noÿs Lambent came running to him just after he had finished a solitary breakfast brought to him by a Mekkano.

She said breathlessly, "It's June, Technician Harlan."

He said harshly, "Do not use the title here. What if it is June?"

"But it was February when I joined"—she paused doubtfully—"*that* place, and that was only a month ago."

Harlan frowned. "What year is it now?"

"Oh, it's the right year."

"Are you sure?"

"I'm quite positive. Has there been a mistake?" She had a disturbing habit of standing quite close to him as they talked and her slight lisp (a trait of the Century rather than of herself personally) gave her the sound of a young and rather helpless child. Harlan was not fooled by that. He drew away.

"No mistake. You've been put here because it's more suitable. Actually, in Time, you have been here all along."

"But how could I?" She looked more frightened still. "I don't remember anything about it. Are there two me's?"

Harlan was far more irritated than the cause warranted. How could he explain to her the existence of micro-changes induced by every interference with Time which could alter individual lives without appreciable effect on the Century as a whole. Even Eternals sometimes forgot the difference between micro-changes (small "c") and Changes (large "C") which significantly altered Reality.

He said, "Eternity knows what it's doing. Don't ask questions." He said it proudly, as though he, himself, were a Senior Computer and had personally decided that June was the proper moment in time and that the micro-change induced by skipping three months could not develop into a Change.

She said, "But then I've lost three months of my life."

He sighed. "Your movements through Time have nothing to do with your physiological age."

"Well, have I or haven't I?"

"Have or haven't what?"

"Lost three months."

"By Time, woman, I'm telling you as plainly as I can. You haven't lost any time out of your life. You can't lose any."

She stepped backward at his shout and then, suddenly, giggled. She said, "You have the funniest accent. Especially when you get angry."

He frowned at her retreating back. What accent? He spoke fifty-millennial as well as anyone in the Section. Better probably.

Stupid girl!

He found himself back at the Reflector staring at his image, which stared back at him, vertical furrows deep between its eyes.

He smoothed them out and thought: I'm not handsome. My eyes are too small and my ears stick out and my chin is too big.

He had never particularly thought about the matter before, but now it occurred to him, quite suddenly, that it would be pleasant to be handsome.

Late at night Harlan added his notes to the conversations he had gathered, while it was all fresh in his mind.

As always in such cases he made use of a molecular recorder of 55th Century manufacture. In shape it was a featureless thin cylinder about four inches long by half an inch in diameter. It was colored a deep but noncommittal brown. It could be easily held in cuff, pocket, or lining, depending on the style of clothing, or, for that matter, suspended from belt, button, or wristband.

However held, wherever kept, it had the capacity of recording some twenty million words on each of three molecular energy levels. With one end of the cylinder connected to a transliterator, resonating efficiently with Harlan's earpiece, and the other end connected field-wise to the small mike at his lips, Harlan could listen and speak simultaneously.

Every sound made during the hours of the "gathering" repeated itself now in his ear, and as he listened, he spoke words that recorded themselves on a second level, co-ordinate with but different from the primary level on which the gathering had been recorded. On this second level he described his own impressions, he ascribed significance, pointed out correlations. Eventually, when he made use of the molecular recorder to write a report, he would have, not simply a sound-for-sound recording, but an annotated reconstruction.

Noÿs Lambent entered. She did *not* signal her entrance in any way.

Annoyed, Harlan removed lip-piece and earpiece, clipped them to the molecular recorder, placed the whole into its kit, and clasped that shut.

"Why do you act so angry with me?" asked Noÿs. Her arms and shoulders were bare and her long legs shimmered in faintly luminescent foamite.

He said, "I am not angry. I have no feeling for you at all." At the moment he felt the statement to be rigidly true.

She said, "Are you still working? Surely, you must be tired."

"I can't work if you're here," he replied peevishly.

"You *are* angry with me. You did not say a word to me all evening."

"I said as little as I could to anybody. I wasn't there to speak." He waited for her to leave.

But she said, "I brought you another drink. You seemed to enjoy one at the gathering and one isn't enough. Especially if you're going to be working."

He noticed the small Mekkano behind her, gliding in on a smooth force-field.

He had eaten sparingly that evening, picking lightly at dishes concerning which he had reported in full in past Observations but which (except for fact-searching nibbles) he had thus far refrained from eating. Against his will, he had liked them. Against his will, he had enjoyed the foaming, light green, peppermint-flavored drink (not quite alcoholic, something else, rather) that was currently fashionable. It had not existed in the Century two physioyears earlier, prior to the latest Reality Change.

He took the second drink from the Mekkano with an austere nod of thanks to Noÿs.

Now why had a Reality Change which had had virtually no physical effect on the Century brought a new drink into existence? Well, he wasn't a Computer, so there was no use asking himself that question. Besides, even the most detailed possible Computations could never eliminate all uncertainty, all random effects. If that weren't so, there would be no need for Observers.

They were alone together in the house, Noÿs and himself. Mekkanos were at the height of their popularity these two decades past and would remain so for nearly a decade more in this Reality, so there were no human servants about.

Of course, with the female of the species as economically independent as the male, and able to attain motherhood, if she so wished, without the necessities of physical childbearing, there could be nothing "improper" in their being together alone in the eyes of the 482nd, at least.

Yet Harlan felt compromised.

The girl was stretched out on her elbow on a sofa opposite. Its patterned covering sank beneath her as though avid to embrace her. She had kicked off the transparent shoes she had been wearing and her toes curled and uncurled within the flexible foamite, like the soft paws of a luxuriant cat.

She shook her head and whatever it was that had kept her hair arranged upward away from her ears in intricate intertwinings was suddenly loosened. The hair tumbled about her neck and her bare shoulders became more creamily lovely at the contrast with the black of the hair.

She murmured, "How old are you?"

That he certainly should not have answered. It was a personal question and the answer was none of her business. What he should have said at that point with polite firmness was: May I be left to my work? Instead what he heard himself saying was, "Thirty-two years." He meant physioyears, of course.

She said, "I'm younger than you. I'm twenty-seven. But I suppose I won't always look younger than you. I suppose you'll be like this when I'm an old woman. What made you decide to be thirty-two? Can you change if you wish? Wouldn't you want to be younger?"

"What are you talking about?" Harlan rubbed his forehead to clear his mind.

She said softly, "You live forever. You're an Eternal."

Was it a question or a statement?

He said, "You're mad. We grow old and die like anyone else."

She said, "You can tell me." Her voice was low and cajoling. The fifty-millennial language, which he had always thought harsh and unpleasant, seemed euphonious after all. Or was it merely that a full stomach and the scented air had dulled his ears?

She said, "You can see all Times, visit all places. I so wanted to work in Eternity. I waited the longest time for them to let me. I thought maybe they'd make me an Eternal, and then I found there were only men there. Some of them wouldn't even talk to me because I was a woman. *You* wouldn't talk to me."

"We're all busy," mumbled Harlan, fighting to keep off something that could only be described as a numb content. "I was very busy."

"But why aren't there more women Eternals?"

Harlan couldn't trust himself to speak. What could he say? That members of Eternity were chosen with infinite care since two conditions had to be met. First, they must be equipped for the job; second, their withdrawal from Time must have no deleterious effect upon Reality.

Reality! That was the word he must not mention under any circumstances. He felt the spinning sensation in his head grow stronger and he closed his eyes for a moment to stop it.

How many excellent prospects had been left untouched in Time because their removal into Eternity would have meant the non-birth of children, the non-death of women and men, non-marriage, non-happenings, non-circumstance that would have twisted Reality in directions the Allwhen Council could not permit.

Could he tell her any of this? Of course not. Could he tell her that women almost never qualified for Eternity because, for some reason he did not understand (Computers might, but he himself certainly did not), their abstraction from Time was from ten to a hundred times as likely to distort Reality as was the abstraction of a man.

(All the thoughts jumbled together in his head, lost and whirling, joined to one another in a free association that produced odd, almost grotesque, but not entirely unpleasant, results. Noÿs was closer to him now, smiling.)

He heard her voice like a drifting wind. "Oh, you Eternals. You are so secretive. You won't share at all. Make me an Eternal."

Her voice was a sound now that didn't coalesce into separate words, just a delicately modulated sound that insinuated itself into his mind.

He wanted, he longed to tell her: There's no fun in Eternity, lady. We work! We work to plot out all the details of everywhen from the beginning of Eternity to where Earth is empty, and we try to plot out all the infinite possibilities of all the might-have-beens and pick out a might-have-been that is better than what is and decide where in Time we can make a tiny little change to twist the is to the might-be and we have a new is and look for a new might-be, forever, and forever, and that is how it has been since Vikkor Mallansohn discovered the Temporal Field in the 24th, way back in the Primitive 24th and then it was possible to start Eternity in the 27th, the mysterious Mallansohn whom no man knows and who started Eternity, really, and the new might-be, forever and forever and forever and . . .

He shook his head, but the whirligig of thought went on and on in stranger and more jagged breaks and leaps until it jumped into a sudden flash of illumination that persisted for a brilliant second, then died.

That moment steadied him. He grasped for it, but it was gone.

The peppermint drink?

Noÿs was still closer, her face not quite clear in his gaze. He could feel her hair against his cheek, the warm, light pressure of her breath. He ought to draw away, but—strangely, strangely—he found he did not want to.

"If I were made an Eternal . . ." she breathed, almost in his ear, though the words were scarcely heard above the beating of his heart. Her lips were moist and parted. "Wouldn't you like to?"

He did not know what she meant, but suddenly he didn't care. He seemed in flames. He put out his arms clumsily, gropingly. She did not resist, but melted and coalesced with him.

It all happened dreamily, as though it were happening to someone else.

It wasn't nearly as repulsive as he had always imagined it must be. It came as a shock to him, a revelation, that it wasn't repulsive at all.

Even afterward, when she leaned against him with her eyes all soft and smiling a little, he found he had to reach out and stroke her damp hair with slow and trembling delight.

She was entirely different in his eyes now. She was not a woman, not an individual at all. She was suddenly an aspect of himself. She was, in a strange and unexpected way, a part of himself.

The spatio-temporal chart said nothing of this, yet Harlan felt no guilt. It was only the thought of Finge that aroused strong emotion in Harlan's breast. And that wasn't guilt. Not at all.

It was satisfaction, even triumph!

In bed Harlan could not sleep. The lightheadedness had worn off now, but there was still the unusual fact that for the first time in his adult life a grown woman shared his bed.

He could hear her soft breathing and in the ultra-dim glow to which the internal light of the walls and ceiling had been reduced he could see her body as the merest shadow next to his.

He had only to move his hand to feel the warmth and softness of her flesh, and he dared not do that, lest he wake her out of whatever dreaming she might have. It was as though she were dreaming for the two of them, dreaming herself and himself and all that had happened, and as though her waking would drive it all from existence.

It was a thought that seemed a piece of those other queer, unusual thoughts he had experienced just before . . .

Those had been strange thoughts, coming to him at a moment between sense and nonsense. He tried to recapture them and could not. Yet suddenly it was very important that he recapture them. For although he could not remember the details, he could remember that, for just an instant, he had understood something.

He was not certain what that something was, but there had been the unearthly clarity of the half-asleep, when more than mortal eye and mind seems suddenly to come to life.

His anxiety grew. Why couldn't he remember? So much had been in his grasp.

For the moment even the sleeping girl beside him receded into the hinterland of his thoughts.

He thought: If I follow the thread . . . I was thinking of Reality and Eternity . . . yes, and Mallansohn and the Cub!

He stopped there. Why the Cub? Why Cooper? He *hadn't* thought of him.

But if he hadn't, then why should he think of Brinsley Sheridan Cooper now?

He frowned! What was the truth that connected all this? What was it he was trying to find? What made him so sure there *was* something to find?

Harlan felt chilled, for with these questions a distant glow of that earlier illumination seemed to break upon the horizons of his mind and he almost knew.

He held his breath, did not press for it. Let it come.

Let it come.

And in the quiet of that night, a night already so uniquely significant in his life, an explanation and interpretation of events came to him that at any saner, more normal time he would not have entertained for a moment.

He let the thought bud and flower, let it grow until he could see it explain a hundred odd points that otherwise simply remained—odd.

He would have to investigate this, check this, back in Eternity, but in his heart he was already convinced that he knew a terrible secret he was not meant to know.

A secret that embraced all Eternity!

Six: LIFE-PLOTTER

A month of physiotime had passed since that night in the 482nd, when he grew acquainted with many things. Now, if one calculated by ordinary time, he was nearly 2000 Centuries in Noÿs Lambent's future, attempting by a mixture of bribery and cajolery to learn what lay in store for her in a new Reality.

It was worse than unethical, but he was past caring. In the physiomonth just gone he had, in his own eyes, become a criminal. There was no way of glossing over that fact. He would be no more a criminal by compounding his crime and he had a great deal to gain by doing so.

Now, as part of his felonious maneuvering (he made no effort to choose a milder phrase) he stood at the barrier before the 2456th. Entry into Time was much more complicated than mere passage between Eternity and the kettle shafts. In order to enter Time the coordinates fixing the desired region on Earth's surface had painstakingly to be adjusted and the desired moment of Time pin-pointed within the Century. Yet despite inner tension Harlan handled the controls with the ease and quick confidence of a man with much experience and a great talent.

Harlan found himself in the engine room he had seen first on the viewing screen within Eternity. At this physiomoment Sociologist Voy would be sitting safely before that screen watching for the Technician's Touch that was to come.

Harlan felt no hurry. The room would remain empty for the next 156 minutes. To be sure, the spatio-temporal chart allowed him only 110 minutes, leaving the remaining 46 as the customary 40 per cent "margin." Margin was there in case of necessity, but a Technician was not expected to have to use it. A "margin-eater" did not remain a Specialist long.

Harlan, however, expected to use no more than 2 minutes of the 110. Wearing his wrist-borne field generator so that he was surrounded by an aura of physiotime (an effluvium, so to speak, of Eternity) and therefore protected from any of the effects of Reality Change, he took one step toward the wall, lifted a small container from its position on a shelf, and placed it in a carefully adjusted spot on the shelf below.

Having done that, he re-entered Eternity in a way that seemed as prosaic to himself as passage through any door might be. Had there been a Timer watching, it would have seemed to him that Harlan had simply disappeared.

The small container stayed where he put it. It played no immediate role in world history. A man's hand, hours later, reached for it but did not find it. A search revealed it half an hour later still, but in the interim a force-field had blanked out and a man's temper had been lost. A decision which would have remained unmade in the previous Reality was now made in anger. A meeting did not take place; a man who would have died lived a year longer, under other circumstances; another who would have lived died somewhat sooner.

The ripples spread wider, reaching their maximum in the 2481st, which was twenty-five Centuries upwhen from the Touch. The intensity of the Reality Change declined thereafter. Theorists pointed out that nowhere to the infinite upwhen could the Change ever become zero, but by fifty Centuries upwhen from the Touch the Change had become too small to detect by the finest Computing, and that was the practical limit.

Of course no human being in Time could ever possibly be aware of any Reality Change having taken place. Mind changed as well as matter and only Eternals could stand outside it all and see the change.

Sociologist Voy was staring at the bluish scene in the 2481st, where earlier there had been all the activity of a busy space-port. He barely looked up when Harlan entered. He barely mumbled something that might have been a greeting.

A change had indeed blasted the space-port. Its shininess was gone; what buildings there stood were not the grand creations they had been. A space-ship rusted. There were no people. There was no motion.

Harlan allowed himself a small smile that flickered for a moment, then vanished. It was M.D.R. all right. Maximum Desired Response. And it had happened at once. The Change did not necessarily take place at the precise moment of the Technician's Touch. If the calculations that went into the Touch were sloppy, hours or days might elapse before the Change actually took place (counting, of course, by physiotime). It was only when all degrees of freedom vanished that the Change took place. While there was even a mathematical chance for alternate actions, the Change did *not* take place.

It was Harlan's pride that when *he* calculated an M.N.C., when it was *his* hand that contrived the Touch, the degrees of freedom vanished at once, and the Change took place instantly.

Voy said softly, "It had been very beautiful."

The phrase grated Harlan's ears, seeming to detract from the beauty of his own performance. "I wouldn't regret," he said, "having space-travel bred out of Reality altogether."

"No?" said Voy.

"What good is it? It never lasts more than a millennium or two. People get tired. They come back home and the colonies die out. Then after another four or five millennia, or forty or fifty, they try again and it fails again. It is a waste of human ingenuity and effort."

Voy said dryly, "You're quite a philosopher."

Harlan flushed. He thought: What's the use in talking to any of them? He said, angrily, with a sharp change of subject, "What about the Life-Plotter?"

"What about him?"

"Would you check with the man? He ought to have made some progress by now."

The Sociologist let a look of disapproval drift across his face, as though to say: You're the impatient one, aren't you? Aloud he said, "Come with me and let's see."

The name plate on the office door said Neron Feruque, which struck Harlan's eye and mind because of its faint similarity to a pair of rulers in the Mediterranean area during Primitive times. (His weekly discourses with Cooper had sharpened his own preoccupation with the Primitive almost feverishly.)

The man, however, resembled neither ruler, as Harlan recalled it. He was almost cadaverously lean, with skin stretched tightly over a high-bridged nose. His fingers were long and his wrists knobby. As he caressed his small Summator, he looked like Death weighing a soul in the balance.

Harlan found himself staring at the Summator hungrily. It was the heart and blood of Life-Plotting, the skin and bones, sinew, muscle and all else. Feed into it the required data of a personal history, and the equations of the Reality Change; do that and it would chuckle away in obscene merriment for any length of time from a minute to a day, and then spit out the possible companion lives for the person involved (under the new Reality), each neatly ticketed with a probability value.

Sociologist Voy introduced Harlan. Feruque, having stared in open annoyance at the Technician's insigne, nodded his head and let the matter go.

Harlan said, "Is the young lady's Life-Plot complete yet?"

"It is not. I'll let you know when it is." He was one of those who carried contempt for the Technician to the point of open rudeness.

Voy said, "Take it easy, Life-Plotter."

Feruque had eyebrows which were light almost to invisibility. It heightened the resemblance of his face to a skull. His eyes rolled in what should have been empty sockets as he said, "Killed the spaceships?"

Voy nodded. "Cut it down a Century."

Feruque's lips twisted softly and formed a word.

Harlan folded his arms and stared at the Life-Plotter, who looked away in eventual discomfiture.

Harlan thought: He *knows* it's his guilt too.

Feruque said to Voy, "Listen, as long as you're here, what in Time am I going to do about the anti-cancer serum requests? We're not the only Century with anti-cancer. Why do we get all the applications?"

"All the other Centuries are just as crowded. You know that."

"Then they've got to stop sending in applications altogether."

"How do we go about making them?"

"Easy. Let the Allwhen Council stop receiving them."

"I have no pull with the Allwhen Council."

"You have pull with the old man."

Harlan listened to the conversation dully, without real interest. At least it served to keep his mind on inconsequentials and away from the chuckling Summator. The "old man," he knew, would be the Computer in charge of the Section.

"I've talked to the old man," said the Sociologist, "and he's talked to the Council."

"Nuts. He's just sent through a routine tape-strip. He has to fight for this. It's a matter of basic policy."

"The Allwhen Council isn't in the mood these days to consider changes in basic policy. You know the rumors going round."

"Oh, sure. They're busy on a big deal. Whenever there's dodging to do, the word gets round that Council's busy on some big deal."

(If Harlan could have found the heart for it, he would have smiled at that point.)

Feruque brooded a few moments, and then burst out, "What most people don't understand is that anti-cancer serum isn't a matter of tree seedlings or field motors. I know that every sprig of spruce has to be watched for adverse effects on Reality, but anti-cancer always involves a human life and that's a hundred times as complicated.

"Consider! Think how many people a year die of cancer in each Century that doesn't have anti-cancer serums of one sort or another.

You can imagine how many of the patients want to die. So the Timer governments in every Century are forever forwarding applications to Eternity to 'please, pretty please ship them seventy-five thousand ampules of serum on behalf of the men critically stricken who are absolutely vital to the cultures, enclosed see biographical data.' "

Voy nodded rapidly, "I know. I know."

But Feruque was not to be denied his bitterness. "So you read the biographical data and it's every man a hero. Every man an insupportable loss to his world. So you work it through. You see what would happen to Reality if each man lived, and for Time's sake, if different *combinations* of men lived.

"In the last month, I've done 572 cancer requests. Seventeen, count them, seventeen Life-Plots came out to involve no undesirable Reality Changes. Mind you, there wasn't one case of a possible *desirable* Reality Change, but the Council says neutral cases get the serum. Humanity, you know. So exactly seventeen people in assorted Centuries get cured this month.

"And what happens? Are the Centuries happy? Not on your life. One man gets cured and a dozen, same country, same Time, don't. Everyone says, Why *that* one? Maybe the guys we didn't treat are better characters, maybe they're rosy-cheeked philanthropists beloved by all, while the one man we cure kicks his aged mother all around the block whenever he can spare the time from beating his kids. They don't know about Reality Changes and we can't tell them.

"We're just making trouble for ourselves, Voy, unless the Allwhen Council decides to screen all applications and approve only those which result in a desirable Reality Change. That's all. Either curing them does some good for humanity, or else it's out. Never mind this business of saying: 'Well, it does no harm.' "

The Sociologist had been listening with a look of mild pain on his face, and now he said, "If it were *you* with cancer . . ."

"That's a stupid remark, Voy. Is that what we base decisions on? In that case there'd never be a Reality Change. Some poor sucker always gets it in the neck, doesn't he? Suppose you were that sucker, hey?

"And another thing. Just remember that every time we make a Reality Change it's harder to find a good next one. Every physioyear, the chance that a random Change is likely to be for the worse increases. That means the proportion of guys we can cure gets smaller anyway. It's always going to get smaller. Someday, we'll be able to cure only one guy a physioyear, even counting the neutral cases. Remember that."

Harlan lost even the faintest interest. This was the type of griping that went with the business. The Psychologists and Sociologists, in their rare introvertive studies of Eternity, called it identification. Men identified themselves with the Century with which they were associated professionally. Its battles, all too often, became their own battles.

Eternity fought the devil of identification as best it could. No man could be assigned to any Section within two Centuries of his homewhen, to make identification harder. Preference was given to Centuries with cultures markedly different from that of their homewhen. (Harlan thought of Finge and the 482nd.) What was more, their assignments were shifted as often as their reactions grew suspect. (Harlan wouldn't give a 50th Century grafenpiece for Feruque's chances of retaining this assignment longer than another physioyear at the outside.)

And still men identified out of a silly yearning for a home in Time (the Time-wish; everyone knew about it). For some reason this was particularly true in Centuries with space-travel. It was something that should be investigated and would be but for Eternity's chronic reluctance to turn its eyes inward.

A month earlier Harlan might have despised Feruque as a blustering sentimentalist, a petulant oaf who eased the pain of watching the electro-gravitics lose intensity in a new Reality by railing against those of other Centuries who wanted anti-cancer serum.

He might have reported him. It would have been his duty to do so. The man's reactions obviously could no longer be trusted.

He could not do so, now. He even found sympathy for the man. His own crime was so much greater.

How easy it was to slip back to thoughts of Noÿs.

Eventually he had fallen asleep that night, and he awoke in daylight, with brightness shining through translucent walls all about until it was as though he had awakened on a cloud in a misty morning sky.

Noÿs was laughing down at him. "*Goodness*, it was hard to wake you."

Harlan's first reflexive action was a scrabble for bedclothes that weren't there. Then memory arrived and he stared at her hollowly, his face burning red. How should he feel about this?

But then something else occurred to him and he shot to a sitting position. "It isn't past one, is it? Father Time!"

"It's only eleven. You've got breakfast waiting and lots of time."

"Thanks," he mumbled.

"The shower controls are all set and your clothes are all ready."

What could he say? "Thanks," he mumbled.

He avoided her eyes during the meal. She sat opposite him, not eating, her chin buried in the palm of one hand, her dark hair combed thickly to one side and her eyelashes preternaturally long.

She followed every gesture he made while he kept his eyes lowered and searched for the bitter shame he knew he ought to feel.

She said, "Where will you be going at one?"

"Aeroball game," he muttered, "I have the ticket."

"That's the rubber game. And I missed the whole season because of just skipping the time, you know. Who'll win the game, Andrew?"

He felt oddly weak at the sound of his first name. He shook his head curtly and tried to look austere. (It used to have been so easy.)

"But surely you know. You've inspected this whole period, haven't you?"

Properly speaking, he ought to maintain a flat and cold negative, but weakly he explained, "There was a lot of Space and Time to cover. I wouldn't know little precise things like game scores."

"Oh, you just don't want to tell me."

Harlan said nothing to that. He inserted the pene-prong into the small, juicy fruit and lifted it, whole, to his lips.

After a moment Noÿs said, "Did you see what happened in this neighborhood before you came?"

"No details, N—noÿs." (He forced her name past his lips.)

The girl said softly, "Didn't you see us? Didn't you know all along that——"

Harlan stammered, "No, no, I couldn't see myself. I'm not in Rea—— I'm not here till I come. I can't explain." He was doubly flustered. First, that she should speak of it. Second, that he had almost been trapped into saying, "Reality," of all the words the most forbidden in conversation with Timers.

She lifted her eyebrows and her eyes grew round and a little amazed. "Are you ashamed?"

"What we did was not proper."

"Why not?" And in the 482nd her question was perfectly innocent. "Aren't Eternals allowed to?" There was almost a joking cast to that question as though she were asking if Eternals weren't allowed to eat.

"Don't use the word," said Harlan. "As a matter of fact, we're not, in a way."

"Well, then, don't tell them. I won't."

And she walked about the table and sat down on his lap, pushing the small table out of the way with a smooth and flowing motion of her hip.

Momentarily he stiffened, lifted his hands in a gesture that might have been intended to hold her off. It didn't succeed.

She bent and kissed him on his lips, and nothing seemed shameful any more. Nothing that involved Noÿs and himself.

He wasn't sure when first he began to do something that an Observer, ethically, had no right to do. That is, he began to speculate on the nature of the problem involving the current Reality and of the Reality Change that would be planned.

It was not the loose morals of the Century, not ectogenesis, not matriarchy, that disturbed Eternity. All of that was as it was in the previous Reality and the Allwhen Council had viewed it with equanimity then. Finge had said it was something very subtle.

The Change then would have to be very subtle and it would have to involve the group he was Observing. So much seemed obvious.

It would involve the aristocracy, the well-to-do, the upper classes, the beneficiaries of the system.

What bothered him was that it would most certainly involve Noÿs.

He got through the remaining three days called for in his chart in a gathering cloud that dampened even his joy in Noÿs's company.

She said to him, "What happened? For a while, you seemed all different from the way you were in Eter—in that place. You weren't stiff at all. Now, you seem concerned. Is it because you have to go back?"

Harlan said, "Partly."

"Do you have to?"

"I have to."

"Well, who would care if you were late?"

Harlan almost smiled at that. "They wouldn't like me to be late," he said, yet thought longingly just the same of the two-day margin allowed for in his chart.

She adjusted the controls of a musical instrument that played soft and complicated strains out of its own creative bowels by striking notes and chords in a random manner; the randomness weighted in favor of pleasant combinations by intricate mathematical formulae.

The music could no more repeat itself than could snowflakes, and could no more fail of beauty.

Through the hypnosis of sound Harlan gazed at Noÿs and his thoughts wound tightly about her. What would she be in the new dispensation? A fishwife, a factory girl, the mother of six, fat, ugly, diseased? Whatever she was, she would not remember Harlan. He would have been no part of her life in a new Reality. And whatever she would be then, she would not be Noÿs.

He did not simply love a *girl.* (Strangely, he used the word "love" in his own thoughts for the first time and did not even pause long enough to stare at the strange thing and wonder at it.) He loved a complex of factors; her choice of clothes, her walk, her manner of speech, her tricks of expression. A quarter century of life and experience in a given Reality had gone into the manufacture of all that. She had not been his Noÿs in the previous Reality of a physioyear earlier. She would not be his Noÿs in the next Reality.

The new Noÿs might, conceivably, be better in some ways, but he knew one thing very definitely. He wanted this Noÿs here, the one he saw at this moment, the one of this Reality. If she had faults, he wanted those faults, too.

What could he do?

Several things occurred to him, all illegal. One of them was to learn the nature of the Change and find out definitely how it would affect Noÿs. One could not, after all, be certain that . . .

A dead silence wrenched Harlan out of his reverie. He was in the Life-Plotter's office once more. Sociologist Voy was watching him out of the corner of his eye. Feruque's death's-head was lowering at him.

And the silence was piercing.

It took a moment for the significance to penetrate. Just a moment. The Summator had ceased its inner clucking.

Harlan jumped up. "You have the answer, Life-Plotter."

Feruque looked down at the flimsies in his hand. "Yeah. Sure. Sort of funny."

"May I have it?" Harlan held out his hand. It was trembling visibly.

"There's nothing to see. That's what's funny."

"What do you mean—nothing?" Harlan stared at Feruque with eyes that suddenly smarted till there was only a tall, thin blur where Feruque stood.

The Life-Plotter's matter-of-fact voice sounded thin. "The dame doesn't exist in the new Reality. No personality shift. She's just out, that's all. Gone. I ran the alternatives down to Probability 0.0001. She doesn't make it anywhere. In fact"—and he reached up to rub his cheek with long, spare fingers—"with the combination of factors you handed me I don't quite see how she fit in the old Reality."

Harlan hardly heard. "But—but the Change was such a small one."

"I know. A funny combination of factors. Here, you want the flimsies?"

Harlan's hand closed over them, unfeeling. Noÿs gone? Noÿs nonexistent? How could that be?

He felt a hand on his shoulder and Voy's voice clashed on his ear. "Are you ill, Technician?" The hand drew away as though it already regretted its careless contact with a Technician's body.

Harlan swallowed and with an effort composed his features. "I'm quite well. Would you take me to the kettle?"

He *must not* show his feelings. He must act as though this were what he represented it to be, a mere academic investigation. He must disguise the fact that with Noÿs's nonexistence in the new Reality he was almost physically overwhelmed by a flood of pure elation, unbearable joy.

Seven: PRELUDE TO CRIME

Harlan stepped into the kettle at the 2456th and looked backward to make certain that the barrier that separated the shaft from Eternity was truly flawless; that Sociologist Voy was not watching. In these last weeks it had grown to be a habit with him, an automatic twitch, there was always the quick backward glance across the shoulder to make sure no one was behind him in the kettle shafts.

And then, though already in the 2456th, it was for *up*when that Harlan set the kettle controls. He watched the numbers on the temporometer rise. Though they moved with blurry quickness, there would be considerable time for thought.

How the Life-Plotter's finding changed matters! How the very nature of his crime had changed!

And it had all hinged on Finge. The phrase caught at him with its ridiculous rhyme and its heavy beat circled dizzyingly inside his skull: It hinged on Finge. It hinged on Finge. . . .

Harlan had avoided any personal contact with Finge on his return to Eternity after those days with Noÿs in the 482nd. As Eternity closed in about him, so did guilt. A broken oath of office, which seemed nothing in the 482nd, was enormous in Eternity.

He had sent in his report by impersonal air-chute and took himself off to personal quarters. He needed to think this out, gain time to consider and grow accustomed to the new orientation within himself.

Finge did not permit it. He was in communication with Harlan less than an hour after the report had been coded for proper direction and inserted into the chute.

The Computer's image stared out of the vision plate. His voice said, "I expected you to be in your office."

Harlan said, "I delivered the report, sir. It doesn't matter where I wait for a new assignment."

"Yes?" Finge scanned the roll of foil he held in his hands, holding it up, squint-eyed, and peering at its perforation pattern.

"It is scarcely complete," he went on. "May I visit your rooms?"

Harlan hesitated a moment. The man was his superior and to refuse the self-invitation at this moment would have a flavor of insubordination. It would advertise his guilt, it seemed, and his raw, painful conscience dared not permit that.

"You will be welcome, Computer," he said stiffly.

Finge's sleek softness introduced a jarring element of epicureanism into Harlan's angular quarters. The 95th, Harlan's homewhen, tended toward the Spartan in house furnishings and Harlan had never completely lost his taste for the style. The tubular metal chairs had been surfaced with a dull veneer that had been artificially grained into the appearance of wood (though not very successfully). In one corner of the room was a small piece of furniture that represented an even wider departure from the customs of the times.

It caught Finge's eye almost at once.

The Computer put a pudgy finger on it, as though to test its texture. "What is this material?"

"Wood, sir," said Harlan.

"The real thing? Actual wood? Amazing! You use wood in your homewhen, I believe?"

"We do."

"I see. There's nothing in the rules against this, Technician"—he dusted the finger with which he had touched the object against the side seam of his trouser leg—"but I don't know that it's advisable to allow the culture of the homewhen to affect one. The true Eternal adopts whatever culture he is surrounded by. I doubt, for instance, if I have eaten out of an energic utensil more than twice in five years." He sighed. "And yet to allow food to touch matter has always seemed unclean. But I don't give in. I don't give in."

His eyes returned to the wooden object, but now he held both hands behind his back, and said, "What is it? What is its purpose?"

"It's a bookcase," said Harlan. He had the impulse to ask Finge how he felt now that his hands rested firmly upon the small of his back. Would he not consider it cleaner to have his clothes and his own body constructed of pure and undefiled energy fields?

Finge's eyebrows lifted. "A bookcase. Then those objects resting upon the shelves are books. Is that right?"

"Yes, sir."

"Authentic specimens?"

"Entirely, Computer. I picked them up in the 24th. The few I have here date from the 20th. If—if you intend to look at them, I wish you'd be careful. The pages have been restored and impregnated, but they're not foil. They take careful handling."

"I won't touch them. I have no intention of touching them. Original 20th Century dust is on them, I imagine. Actual books!" He laughed. "Pages of cellulose, too? You implied that."

Harlan nodded. "Cellulose modified by the impregnation treatment for longer life. Yes." He opened his mouth for a deep breath, forcing himself to remain calm. It was ridiculous to identify himself with these books, to feel a slur upon them to be a slur upon himself.

"I dare say," said Finge, still on the subject, "that the whole content of those books could be placed on two meters of film and stored in a finger's end. What do the books contain?"

Harlan said, "They are bound volumes of a news magazine of the 20th."

"You read that?"

Harlan said proudly, "These are a few volumes of the complete collection I have. No library in Eternity can duplicate it."

"Yes, your hobby. I remember now you once told me about your interest in the Primitive. I'm amazed your Educator ever allowed you to grow interested in such a thing. A complete waste of energy."

Harlan's lips thinned. The man, he decided, was deliberately trying to irritate him out of possession of calm reasoning faculties. If so, he must not be allowed to succeed.

Harlan said flatly, "I think you've come to see me about my report."

"Yes, I have." The Computer looked about, selected a chair, and sat down gingerly. "It is not complete, as I said over the communicator."

"In what way, sir?" (Calm! Calm!)

Finge broke into a nervous twitch of a smile. "What happened that you didn't mention, Harlan?"

"Nothing, sir." And though he said it firmly, he stood there, hangdog.

"Come, Technician. You spent several periods of time in the society of the young lady. Or you did if you followed the spatio-temporal chart. You did follow it, I suppose?"

Harlan's guilt riddled him to the point where he could not even rise to the bait of this open assault upon his professional competence.

He could only say, "I followed it."

"And what happened? You include nothing of the private interludes with the woman."

"Nothing of importance happened," said Harlan, dry-lipped.

"That is ridiculous. At your time of life and with your experience, I don't have to tell you that it is not for an Observer to judge what is important and what is not."

Finge's eyes were keenly upon Harlan. They were harder and more eager than quite befitted his soft line of questioning.

Harlan noted that well and was not fooled by Finge's gentle voice, yet the habit of duty tugged at him. An Observer must report *everything*. An Observer was merely a sense-perceptive pseudopod thrust out by Eternity into Time. It tested its surroundings and was drawn back. In the fulfillment of his function an Observer had no individuality of his own; he was not really a man.

Almost automatically Harlan began his narration of the events he had left out of his report. He did it with the trained memory of the Observer, reciting the conversations with word-for-word accuracy, reconstructing the tone of voice and cast of countenance. He did it lovingly, for in the telling he lived it again, and almost forgot, in the process, that a combination of Finge's probing and his own healing sense of duty was driving him into an admission of guilt.

It was only as he approached the end result of that first long conversation that he faltered and the shell of his Observer's objectivity showed cracks.

He was saved from further details by the hand that Finge suddenly raised and by the Computer's sharp, edgy voice. "Thank you.

It is enough. You were about to say that you made love to the woman."

Harlan grew angry. What Finge said was the literal truth, but Finge's tone of voice made it sound lewd, coarse, and, worse than that, commonplace. Whatever else it was, or might be, it was not commonplace.

Harlan had an explanation for Finge's attitude, for his anxious cross-examination, for his breaking off the verbal report at the moment he did. Finge was jealous! That much Harlan would have sworn was obvious. Harlan had succeeded in taking away a girl that Finge had meant to have.

Harlan felt the triumph in that and found it sweet. For the first time in his life he knew an aim that meant more to him than the frigid fulfillment of Eternity. He was going to keep Finge jealous, because Noÿs Lambent was to be permanently his.

In this mood of sudden exaltation he plunged into the request that originally he had planned to present only after a wait of a discreet four or five days.

He said, "It is my intention to apply for permission to form a liaison with a Timed individual."

Finge seemed to snap out of a reverie. "With Noÿs Lambent, I presume."

"Yes, sir. As Computer in charge of the Section, it will have to go through you. . . ."

Harlan wanted it to go through Finge. Make him suffer. If he wanted the girl himself, let him say so and Harlan could insist on allowing Noÿs to make her choice. He almost smiled at that. He hoped it would come to that. It would be the final triumph.

Ordinarily, of course, a Technician could not hope to push through such a matter in the face of a Computer's desires, but Harlan was sure he could count on Twissell's backing, and Finge had a long way to go before he could buck Twissell.

Finge, however, seemed tranquil. "It would seem," he said, "that you have already taken illegal possession of the girl."

Harlan flushed and was moved to a feeble defense. "The spatiotemporal chart insisted on our remaining alone together. Since nothing of what happened was specifically forbidden, I feel no guilt."

Which was a lie, and from Finge's half-amused expression one could feel that he knew it to be a lie.

He said, "There will be a Reality Change."

Harlan said, "If so, I will amend my application to request liaison with Miss Lambent in the new Reality."

"I don't think that would be wise. How can you be sure in advance? In the new Reality, she may be married, she may be deformed. In fact I can tell you this. In the new Reality, she will not want you. She will *not* want you."

Harlan quivered. "You know nothing about it."

"Oh? You think this great love of yours is a matter of soul-to-soul contact? That it will survive all external changes? Have you been reading novels out of Time?"

Harlan was goaded into indiscretion. "For one thing, I don't believe you."

Finge said coldly, "I beg pardon."

"You're lying." Harlan didn't care what he said now. "You're jealous. It's all it amounts to. You're jealous. You had your own plans for Noÿs but she chose me."

Finge said, "Do you realize——"

"I realize a great deal. I'm no fool. I may not be a Computer, but neither am I an ignoramus. You say she won't want me in the new Reality. How do you know? You don't even know yet what the new Reality will be. You don't know if there must be a new Reality at all. You just received my report. It must be analyzed before a Reality Change can be computed, let alone submitted for approval. So when you affect to know the nature of the Change, you are lying."

There were a number of ways in which Finge might have made response. Harlan's heated mind was aware of many. He did not try to choose among them. Finge might stalk out in affected dudgeon; he might call in a member of Security and have Harlan taken into custody for insubordination; he might shout back, yelling as angrily as Harlan; he might put in an immediate call to Twissell, lodging a formal complaint; he might—he might . . .

Finge did none of this.

He said gently, "Sit down, Harlan. Let's talk about this."

And because that response was completely unexpected, Harlan's jaw sagged and he sat down in confusion. His resolution faltered. What was this?

"You remember, of course," said Finge, "that I told you that our problem with the 482nd involved an undesirable attitude on the part of the Timers of the current Reality toward Eternity. You do remember that, don't you?" He spoke with the mild urging of a schoolmaster toward a somewhat backward student, yet Harlan thought he could detect a kind of hard glitter in his eye.

Harlan said, "Of course."

"You remember, too, that I told you that the Allwhen Council was reluctant to accept my analysis of the situation without specific confirming Observations. Doesn't that imply to you that I had already Computed the necessary Reality Change?"

"But my own Observations represent the confirmation, don't they?"

"They do."

"And it would take time to analyze them properly."

"Nonsense. Your report means nothing. The confirmation lay in what you told me orally moments ago."

"I don't understand you."

"Look, Harlan, let me tell you what is wrong with the 482nd. Among the upper classes of this Century, particularly among the women, there has grown up the notion that Eternals are really Eternal, literally so; that they live forever. . . . Great Time, man, Noÿs Lambent told you as much. You repeated her statements to me not twenty minutes ago."

Harlan stared blankly at Finge. He was remembering Noÿs's soft, caressing voice as she leaned toward him and caught at his eyes with her own lovely, dark glance: *You live forever. You're an Eternal.*

Finge went on, "Now a belief like that is bad, but, in itself, not too bad. It can lead to inconveniences, increase difficulties for the Section, but Computation would show that only in a minority of cases would Change be necessary. Still, if a Change *is* desirable, isn't it obvious to you that the inhabitants of the Century who must, above all, change maximally with the Change, be those who are subject to the superstition. In other words, the female aristocracy. Noÿs."

"It may be, but I'll take my chance," said Harlan.

"You have no chance at all. Do you think your fascinations and charm persuaded the soft aristocrat to fall into the arms of an unimportant Technician? Come, Harlan, be realistic about this."

Harlan's lips grew stubborn. He said nothing.

Finge said, "Can't you guess the additional superstition which these people have added to their belief in the actual eternal life of the Eternals? Great Time, Harlan! Most of the women believe that intimacy with an Eternal will enable a mortal woman (as they think of themselves) to live forever!"

Harlan swayed. He could hear Noÿs's voice again so clearly: *If I were made an Eternal . . .*

And then her kisses.

Finge went on. "The existence of such a superstition was hard to believe, Harlan. It was unprecedented. It lay within the region of random error so that a search through the Computations for the previous Change yielded no information respecting it one way or the other. The Allwhen Council wanted firm evidence, direct substantiation. I chose Miss Lambent as a good example of her class. I chose you as the other subject——"

Harlan struggled to his feet. "You chose *me?* As a *subject?*"

"I'm sorry," said Finge stiffly, "but it was necessary. You made a very good subject."

Harlan stared at him.

Finge had the grace to squirm a bit under that wordless stare. He said, "Don't you see? No, you still don't. Look, Harlan, you're a cold-fish product of Eternity. You won't look at a woman. You consider women and all that concerns them unethical. No, there's a better word. You consider them *sinful.* That attitude shows all over you, and to any woman you'd have all the sex appeal of a month-dead mackerel. Yet here we have a woman, a beautiful pampered product of a hedonistic culture, who ardently seduces you on your first evening together, virtually begging for your embrace. Don't you understand that that is ridiculous, impossible, unless—well, unless it is the confirmation we were looking for."

Harlan struggled for words. "You say she sold herself——"

"Why that expression? There is no shame attached to sex in this Century. The only strange thing is that she chose you as partner, and *that* she did for the sake of eternal life. It's plain."

And Harlan, arms raised, hands claw-bent, with no rational thought in his mind, or any irrational one other than to choke and throttle Finge, sprang forward.

Finge stepped back hastily. He brought out a blaster with a quick, trembling gesture. "Don't touch me! Back!"

Harlan had just enough sanity to halt his rush. His hair was matted. His shirt was stained with perspiration. His breath whistled through pinched white nostrils.

Finge said shakily, "I know you very well, you see, and I thought your reaction might be violent. Now I'll shoot if I have to."

Harlan said, "Get out."

"I will. But first you'll listen. For attacking a Computer, you can be declassified, but we'll let that go. You will understand, however, that I did not lie. The Noÿs Lambent of the new Reality, whatever else may be or not be, will lack this superstition. The whole purpose of the Change will be to wipe out the superstition. And without it, Harlan"—his voice was almost a snarl—"how could a woman like Noÿs want a man like you?"

The pudgy Computer backed toward the door of Harlan's personal quarters, blaster still leveled.

He paused to say, with a sort of grim gaiety, "Of course, if you had her now, Harlan, if you had her now, you could enjoy her. You could keep your liaison and make it formal. That is, if you had her now. But the Change will come soon, Harlan, and after that, you will not have her. What a pity, the now does not last, even in Eternity, eh, Harlan?"

Harlan no longer looked at him. Finge had won after all and was leaving in clear and leering possession of the field. Harlan stared unseeingly at his own toes, and when he looked up Finge was gone—whether five seconds earlier or fifteen minutes Harlan could not have said.

Hours had passed nightmarishly and Harlan felt trapped in the prison of his mind. All that Finge had said was so true, so transparently true. Harlan's Observer mind could look back upon the relationship of himself and Noÿs, that short, unusual relationship, and it took on a different texture.

It wasn't a case of instant infatuation. How could he have believed it was? Infatuation for a man like himself?

Of course not. Tears stung his eyes and he felt ashamed. How obvious it was that the affair was a case of cool calculation. The girl had certain undeniable physical assets and no ethical principles to keep her from using them. So she used them and that had nothing to do with Andrew Harlan as a person. He simply represented her distorted view of Eternity and what it meant.

Automatically Harlan's long fingers caressed the volumes in his small bookshelf. He took one out and, unseeingly, opened it.

The print blurred. The faded colors of the illustrations were ugly, meaningless blotches.

Why had Finge troubled to tell him all this? In the strictest sense he ought not to have. An Observer, or anyone acting as Observer, ought never to know the ends attained by his Observation. It removed him by so much from the ideal position of the objective nonhuman tool.

It was to crush him, of course; to take a mean and jealous revenge!

Harlan fingered the open page of the magazine. He found himself staring at a duplication, in startling red, of a ground vehicle, similar to vehicles characteristic of the 45th, 182nd, 590th, and 984th Centuries, as well as of late Primitive times. It was a very common sort of affair with an internal-combustion motor. In the Primitive era natural petroleum fractions were the source of power and natural rubber cushioned the wheels. That was true of none of the later Centuries, of course.

Harlan had pointed that out to Cooper. He had made quite a point of it, and now his mind, as though longing to turn away from the unhappy present, drifted back to that moment. Sharp, irrelevant images filled the ache within Harlan.

"These advertisements," he had said, "tell us more of Primitive times than the so-called news articles in the same magazine. The news articles assume a basic knowledge of the world it deals with. It uses terms it feels no necessity of explaining. What is a 'golf ball,' for instance?"

Cooper had professed his ignorance readily.

Harlan went on in the didactic tone he could scarcely avoid on occasions such as this. "We could deduce that it was a small pellet of some sort from the nature of the casual mentions it receives. We know that it is used in a game, if only because it is mentioned in an item under the heading 'Sport.' We can even make further deductions that it is hit by a long rod of some sort and that the object of the game is to drive the ball into a hole in the ground. But why bother with deduction and reasoning? Observe this advertisement! The object of it is only to induce readers to buy the ball, but in so doing we are presented with an excellent close-range portrait of one, with a section cut into it to show its construction."

Cooper, coming from an era in which advertisement was not as wildly proliferative as it was in the later Centuries of Primitive times, found all this difficult to appreciate. He said, "Isn't it rather disgusting the way these people blow their own horn? Who would be fool enough to believe a person's boastings about his own products? Would he admit defects? Is he likely to stop at any exaggeration?"

Harlan, whose homewhen was middling fruitful in advertisement, raised tolerant eyebrows and merely said, "You'll have to accept that. It's their way and we never quarrel with the ways of any culture as long as it does not seriously harm mankind as a whole."

But now Harlan's mind snapped back to his present situation and he was back in the present, staring at the loudmouthed, brassy advertisements in the news magazine. He asked himself in sudden excitement: Were the thoughts he had just experienced really irrelevant? Or was he tortuously finding a way out of the blackness and back to Noÿs?

Advertisement! A device for forcing the unwilling into line. Did it matter to a ground-vehicle manufacturer whether a given individual felt an original or spontaneous desire for his product? If the prospect (that was the word) could be artificially persuaded or cajoled into feeling that desire and acting upon it, would that not be just as well?

Then what did it matter if Noÿs loved him out of passion or out of calculation? Let them but be together long enough and she would grow to love him. He would *make* her love him and, in the end, love and not its motivation was what counted. He wished now he had read some of the novels out of Time that Finge had mentioned scornfully.

Harlan's fists clenched at a sudden thought. If Noÿs had come to *him*, to *Harlan*, for immortality, it could only mean that she had not yet fulfilled the requirement for that gift. She could have made love to no Eternal previously. That meant that her relationship to Finge had been nothing more than that of secretary and employer. Otherwise what need would she have had for Harlan?

Yet Finge surely must have tried—must have attempted . . . (Harlan could not complete the thought even in the secrecy of his own mind.) Finge could have proved the superstition's existence on his own person. Surely he could not have missed the thought with Noÿs an ever-present temptation. Then she must have refused him.

He had had to use Harlan and Harlan had succeeded. It was for that reason that Finge had been driven into the jealous revenge of torturing Harlan with the knowledge that Noÿs's motivation had been a practical one, and that he could never have her.

Yet Noÿs had refused Finge even with eternal life at stake and *had* accepted Harlan. She had that much of a choice and she had made it in Harlan's favor. So it wasn't calculation entirely. Emotion played a part.

Harlan's thoughts were wild and jumbled, and grew more heated with every moment.

He *must* have her, and *now*. Before any Reality Change. What was it Finge had said to him, jeering: *The now does not last, even in Eternity.*

Doesn't it, though? Doesn't it?

Harlan had known exactly what he must do. Finge's angry taunting had goaded him into a frame of mind where he was ready for crime and Finge's final sneer had, at least, inspired him with the nature of the deed he must commit.

He had not wasted a moment after that. It was with excitement and even joy that he left his quarters, at all but a run, to commit a major crime against Eternity.

Eight: CRIME

No one had questioned him. No one had stopped him. There was that advantage, anyway, in the social isolation of a Technician. He went via the kettle channels to a door to Time and set its controls. There was the chance, of course, that someone would happen along on a legitimate errand and wonder why the door was in use. He hesitated, and then decided to stamp his seal on the marker. A sealed door would draw little attention. An unsealed door in active use would be a nine-day wonder.

Of course, it might be Finge who stumbled upon the door. He would have to chance that.

Noÿs was still standing as he had left her. Wretched hours (physiohours) had passed since Harlan had left the 482nd for a lonely Eternity, but he returned now to the same Time, within a matter of seconds, that he had left. Not a hair on Noÿs's head had stirred.

She looked startled. "Did you forget something, Andrew?"

Harlan stared at her hungrily, but made no move to touch her. He remembered Finge's words, and he dared not risk a repulse. He said stiffly, "You've got to do as I say."

She said, "But is something wrong, then? You just left. You just this minute left."

"Don't worry," said Harlan. It was all he could do to keep from taking her hand, from trying to soothe her. Instead he spoke harshly. It was as though some demon were forcing him to do all the wrong things. Why had he come back at the first available moment? He was only disturbing her by his almost instantaneous return after leaving.

(He knew the answer to that, really. He had a two-day margin of grace allowed by the spatio-temporal chart. The earlier portions of that period of grace were safer and yielded least chance of discovery. It was a natural tendency to crowd it as far downwhen as he could. A foolish risk, too, though. He might easily have miscalculated and entered Time before he had left it physiohours earlier. What then? It was one of the first rules he had learned as an Observer: One person occupying two points in the same Time of the same Reality runs a risk of meeting himself.

Somehow that was something to be avoided. Why? Harlan knew he didn't want to meet himself. He didn't want to be staring into the eyes of another and earlier [or later] Harlan. Beyond that it would be a paradox, and what was it Twissell was fond of saying? "There are no paradoxes in Time, but only because Time deliberately avoids paradoxes.")

All the time Harlan thought dizzily of all this Noÿs stared at him with large, luminous eyes.

Then she came to him and put cool hands on either burning cheek and said softly, "You're in trouble."

To Harlan her glance seemed kindly, loving. Yet how could that be? She had what she wanted. What else was there? He seized her wrists and said huskily, "Will you come with me? Now? Without asking any questions? Doing exactly as I say?"

"Must I?" she asked.

"You must, Noÿs. It's very important."

"Then I'll come." She said it matter-of-factly, as though such a request came to her each day and was always accepted.

At the lip of the kettle Noÿs hesitated a moment, then stepped in.

Harlan said, "We're going upwhen, Noÿs."

"That means the future, doesn't it?"

The kettle was already faintly humming as she entered it and she was scarcely seated when Harlan unobtrusively moved the contact at his elbow.

She showed no signs of nausea at the beginnings of that indescribable sensation of "motion" through Time. He was afraid she might.

She sat there quietly, so beautiful and so at ease that he ached, looking at her, and gave not the particle of a damn that, by bringing a Timer, unauthorized, into Eternity, he had committed a felony.

She said, "Does that dial show the numbers of the years, Andrew?"

"The Centuries."

"You mean we're a thousand years in the future? Already?"

"That's right."

"It doesn't feel like it."

"I know."

She looked about. "But how are we moving?"

"I don't know, Noÿs."

"You *don't?*"

"There are many things about Eternity that are hard to understand."

The numbers on the temporometer *marched*. Faster and faster they moved till they were a blur. With his elbow Harlan had nudged the speed stick to high. The power drain might cause some surprise in the power plants, but he doubted it. No one had been waiting for him in Eternity when he returned with Noÿs, and that was nine tenths the battle. Now it was only necessary to get her to a safe place.

Again Harlan looked at her. "Eternals don't know everything."

"And I'm not an Eternal," she murmured. "I know so little."

Harlan's pulse quickened. *Still* not an Eternal? But Finge said . . .

Leave it at that, he pleaded with himself. Leave it at that. She's coming with you. She smiles at you. What more do you want?

But he spoke anyway. He said, "You think an Eternal lives forever, don't you?"

"Well, they call them Eternals, you know, and everyone says they do." She smiled at him brightly. "But they don't, do they?"

"You don't think so, then?"

"After I was in Eternity a while, I didn't. People didn't talk as though they lived forever, and there were old men there."

"Yet you told me I lived forever—that night."

She moved closer to him along the seat, still smiling. "I thought: who knows?"

He said, without being quite able to keep the strain out of his voice, "How does a Timer go about becoming an Eternal?"

Her smile vanished and was it his imagination or was there a trace of heightened color in her cheek. She said, "Why do you ask that?"

"To find out."

"It's silly," she said. "I'd rather not talk about it." She stared down at her graceful fingers, edged with nails that glittered colorlessly in the muted light of the kettle shaft. Harlan thought abstractedly and quite apropos of nothing that at an evening gathering, with a touch of mild ultraviolet in the wall illumination, those nails would glow a soft apple-green or a brooding crimson, depending on the angle she held her hands. A clever girl, one like Noÿs, could produce half a dozen shades out of them, and make it seem as though the colors were reflecting her moods. Blue for innocence, bright yellow for laughter, violet for sorrow, and scarlet for passion.

He said, "Why did you make love to me?"

She shook her hair back and looked at him out of a pale, grave face. She said, "If you must know, part of the reason was the theory that a girl can become an Eternal that way. I wouldn't mind living forever."

"I thought you said you didn't believe that."

"I didn't, but it couldn't hurt a girl to take the chance. Especially——"

He was staring at her sternly, finding refuge from hurt and disappointment in a frozen look of disapproval from the heights of the morality of his homewhen. "Well?"

"Especially since I wanted to, anyway."

"Wanted to make love to me?"

"Yes."

"Why me?"

"Because I liked you. Because I thought you were funny."

"*Funny!*"

"Well, odd, if you like that better. You always worked so hard not to look at me, but you always looked at me anyway. You tried to hate me and I could see you wanted me. I was sorry for you a little, I think."

"What were you sorry about?" He felt his cheeks burning.

"That you should have such trouble about wanting me. It's such a simple thing. You just ask a girl. It's so easy to be friendly. Why suffer?"

Harlan nodded. The morality of the 482nd! "Just ask a girl," he muttered. "So simple. Nothing more necessary."

"The girl has to be willing, of course. Mostly she is, if she's not otherwise engaged. Why not? It's simple enough."

It was Harlan's turn to drop his eyes. Of course, it was simple enough. And nothing wrong with it, either. Not in the 482nd. Who in Eternity should know this better? He would be a fool, an utter and unspeakable fool, to ask her now about earlier affairs. He might as well ask a girl of his own homewhen if she had ever eaten in the presence of a man and how dared she?

Instead he said humbly, "And what do you think of me now?"

"That you are very nice," she said softly, "and that if you ever relaxed—— Won't you smile?"

"There's nothing to smile about, Noÿs."

"*Please.* I want to see if your cheeks can crease right. Let's see." She put her fingers to the corners of his mouth and pressed them backward. He jerked his head back in surprise and couldn't avoid smiling.

"See. Your cheeks didn't even crack. You're almost handsome. With enough practice–standing in front of a mirror and smiling and getting a twinkle in your eye–I'll bet you could be really handsome."

But the smile, fragile enough to begin with, vanished.

Noÿs said, "We *are* in trouble, aren't we?"

"Yes, we are, Noÿs. Great trouble."

"Because of what we did? You and I? That evening?"

"Not really."

"That was my fault, you know. I'll tell them so, if you wish."

"Never," said Harlan with energy. "Don't take on any fault in this. You've done nothing, *nothing,* to be guilty for. It's something else."

Noÿs looked uneasily at the temporometer. "Where are we? I can't even see the numbers."

"*When* are we?" Harlan corrected her automatically. He slowed the velocity and the Centuries came into view.

Her beautiful eyes widened and the lashes stood out against the whiteness of her skin. "Is that *right?*"

Harlan looked at the indicator casually. It was in the 72,000's. "I'm sure it is."

"But where are we going?"

"To *when* are we going. To the far upwhen," he said, grimly. "Good and far. Where they won't find you."

And in silence they watched the numbers mount. In silence Harlan told himself over and over that the girl was innocent of Finge's charge. She had owned up frankly to its partial truth and she had admitted, just as frankly, the presence of a more personal attraction.

He looked up, then, as Noÿs shifted position. She had moved to his side of the kettle and, with a resolute gesture, brought the kettle to a halt at a most uncomfortable temporal deceleration.

Harlan gulped and closed his eyes to let the nausea pass. He said, "What's the matter?"

She looked ashen and for a moment made no reply. Then she said, "I don't want to go any further. The numbers are so high."

The temporometer read: 111,394.

He said, "Far enough."

Then he held out his hand gravely, "Come, Noÿs. This will be your home for a while."

They wandered through the corridors like children, hand in hand. The lights along the mainways were on, and the darkened rooms blazed at the touch of a contact. The air was fresh and had a liveliness about it which, without sensible draft, yet indicated the presence of ventilation.

Noÿs whispered, "Is there no one here?"

"No one," said Harlan. He tried to say it firmly and loudly. He wanted to break the spell of being in a "Hidden Century," but he said it in only a whisper after all.

He did not even know how to refer to anything so far upwhen. To call it the one-one-one-three-ninety-fourth was ridiculous. One would have to say simply and indefinitely, "The hundred thousands."

It was a foolish problem to be concerned with, but now that the exaltation of actual flight was done with, he found himself alone in a region of Eternity where no human footsteps had wandered and he did not like it. He was ashamed, doubly ashamed since Noÿs was witness, at the fact that the faint chill within him was the faint chill of a faint fear.

Noÿs said, "It's so clean. There's no dust."

"Self-cleaning," said Harlan. With an effort that seemed to tear at his vocal cords he raised his voice to near-normal level. "But no one's here, upwhen or downwhen for thousands and thousands of Centuries."

Noÿs seemed to accept that. "And everything is fixed up so? We passed food stores and a viewing-film library. Did you see that?"

"I saw that. Oh, it's fully equipped. They're all fully equipped. Every Section."

"But why, if no one ever comes here?"

"It's logical," said Harlan. Talking about it took away some of the eeriness. Saying out loud what he already knew in the abstract would pin-point the matter, bring it down to the level of the prosaic. He said, "Early in the history of Eternity, one of the Centuries in the 300's came up with a mass duplicator. Do you know what I mean? By setting up a resonating field, energy could be converted to matter with subatomic particles taking up precisely the same pattern of positions, within the uncertainty requirements, as those in the model being used. The result is an exact copy.

"We in Eternity commandeered the instrument for our own purposes. At that time, there were only about six or seven hundred Sections built up. We had plans for expansion, of course. 'Ten new Sections a physioyear' was one of the slogans of the time. The mass duplicator made that all unnecessary. We built one new Section complete with food, power supply, water supply, all the best automatic features; set up the machine and duplicated the Section once each Century all along Eternity. I don't know how long they kept it going—millions of Centuries, probably."

"All like this, Andrew?"

"All exactly like this. And as Eternity expands, we just fill in, adapting the construction to whatever fashion turns out to be current in the Century. The only troubles come when we hit an energy-centered Century. We—we haven't reached this Section yet." (No use telling her that the Eternals couldn't penetrate into Time here in the Hidden Centuries. What difference did that make?)

He glanced at her and she seemed troubled. He said hastily, "There's no waste involved in building the Sections. It took energy, nothing more, and with the nova to draw on——"

She interrupted. "No. I just don't remember."

"Remember what?"

"You said the duplicator was invented in the 300's. We don't have it in the 482nd. I don't remember viewing anything about it in history."

Harlan grew thoughtful. Although she was within two inches of being as tall as himself, he suddenly felt giant-size by comparison. She was a child, an infant, and he was a demigod of Eternity who must teach her and lead her carefully to the truth.

He said, "Noÿs, dear, let's find a place to sit down and—and I'll have to explain something."

The concept of a variable Reality, a Reality that was not fixed and eternal and immutable was not one that could be faced casually by anyone.

In the dead of the sleep period, sometimes, Harlan would remember the early days of his Cubhood and recall the wrenching attempts to divorce himself from his Century and from Time.

It took six months for the average Cub to learn all the truth, to discover that he could never go home again in a very literal way. It wasn't Eternity's law, alone, that stopped him, but the frigid fact that home as he knew it might very well no longer exist, might, in a sense, never have existed.

It affected Cubs differently. Harlan remembered Bonky Latourette's face turning white and gaunt the day Instructor Yarrow had finally made it unmistakably clear about Reality.

None of the Cubs ate that night. They huddled together in search of a kind of psychic warmth, all except Latourette, who had disappeared. There was a lot of false laughter and miserably poor joking.

Someone said with a voice that was tremulous and uncertain, "I suppose I never had a mother. If I go back into the 95th, they'd say: 'Who are you? We don't know you. We don't have any records of you. You don't exist.'"

They smiled weakly and nodded their heads, lonely boys with nothing left but Eternity.

They found Latourette at bedtime, sleeping deeply and breathing shallowly. There was the slight reddening of a spray injection in the hollow of his left elbow and fortunately that was noted too.

Yarrow was called and for a while it looked as though one Cub would be out of the course, but he was brought around eventually. A week later he was back in his seat. Yet the mark of that evil night was on his personality for as long as Harlan knew him thereafter.

And now Harlan had to explain Reality to Noÿs Lambent, a girl not much older than those Cubs, and explain it at once and in full. He had to. There was no choice about that. She must learn exactly what faced them and exactly what she would have to do.

He told her. They ate canned meats, chilled fruits, and milk at a long conference table designed to hold twelve, and there he told her.

He did it as gently as possible, but he scarcely found need for gentleness. She snapped quickly at every concept and before he was half through it was borne in upon him, to his great amazement, that she wasn't reacting badly. She wasn't afraid. She showed no sense of loss. She only seemed angry.

The anger reached her face and turned it a glowing pink while her dark eyes seemed somehow the darker for it.

"But that's criminal," she said. "Who are the Eternals to do this?"

"It's done for humanity's good," said Harlan. Of course, she couldn't really understand that. He felt sorry for the Time-bound thinking of a Timer.

"Is it? I suppose that's how the mass duplicator was wiped out."

"We have copies still. Don't worry about that. We've preserved it."

"*You*'ve preserved it. But what about us? We of the 482nd might have had it." She gestured with little movements of two clenched fists.

"It wouldn't have done you good. Look, don't be excited, dear, and listen." With an almost convulsive gesture (he would have to learn how to touch her naturally, without making the movement seem a sheepish invitation to a repulse) he took her hands in his and held them tightly.

For a moment she tried to free them, and then she relaxed. She even laughed a bit. "Oh, go ahead, silly, and don't look so solemn. I'm not blaming you."

"You mustn't blame anyone. There is no blame necessary. We do what must be done. That mass duplicator is a classic case. I studied it in school. When you duplicate mass, you can duplicate persons, too. The problems that arise are very complicated."

"Isn't it up to the society to solve its own problems?"

"It is, but we studied that society throughout Time and it doesn't solve the problem satisfactorily. Remember that its failure to do so affects not only itself but all its descendant societies. In fact, there is no satisfactory solution to the mass-duplicator problem. It's one of those things like atomic wars and dreamies that just can't be allowed. Developments are never satisfactory."

"What makes you so sure?"

"We have our Computing machines, Noÿs; Computaplexes far more accurate than any ever developed in any single Reality. These Compute the possible Realities and grade the desirabilities of each over a summation of thousands and thousands of variables."

"Machines!" She said it with scorn.

Harlan frowned, then relented hastily. "Now don't be like that. Naturally, you resent learning that life is not as solid as you thought. You and the world you lived in might have been only a probability shadow a year ago, but what's the difference? You have all your memories, whether they're of probability shadows or not, haven't you? You remember your childhood and your parents, don't you?"

"Of course."

"Then it's just as if you lived it, isn't it? Isn't it? I mean, whether you did or not?"

"I don't know. I'll have to think about it. What if tomorrow it's a dream world again, or a shadow, or whatever you call it?"

"Then there would be a new Reality and a new you with new memories. It would be just as though nothing had happened, except that the sum of human happiness would have been increased again."

"I don't find that satisfying, somehow."

"Besides," said Harlan hastily, "nothing will happen to you now. There *will* be a new Reality but you're in Eternity. You won't be changed."

"But you say it makes no difference," said Noÿs gloomily. "Why go to all the trouble?"

With sudden ardor Harlan said, "Because I want you as you are. Exactly as you are. I don't want you changed. Not in any way."

He came within a hair of blurting out the truth, that without the advantage of the superstition about Eternals and eternal life she would never have inclined toward him.

She said, looking about with a slight frown, "Will I have to stay here forever, then? It would be—lonely."

"No, no. Don't think it," he said wildly, gripping her hands so tight that she winced. "I'll find out what you will be in the new Reality of the 482nd, and you'll go back in disguise, so to speak. I'll take care of you. I'll apply for permission for formal liaison and see to it that you remain safely through future Changes. I'm a Technician and a good one and I know about Changes." He added grimly, "And I know a few other things as well," and stopped there.

Noÿs said, "Is all this allowed? I mean, can you take people into Eternity and keep them from changing? It doesn't sound right, somehow, from the things you've told me."

For a moment Harlan felt shrunken and cold in the large emptiness of the thousands of Centuries that surrounded him upwhen and down. For a moment he felt cut off even from the Eternity that was his only home and only faith, doubly cast out from Time and Eternity; and only the woman for whom he had forsaken it all left at his side.

He said, and he meant it deeply, "No, it is a crime. It is a very great crime, and I am bitterly ashamed. But I would do it again, if I had to, and any number of times, if I had to."

"For me, Andrew? For me?"

He did not raise his eyes to hers. "No, Noÿs, for myself. I could not bear to lose you."

She said, "And if we are caught . . . ?"

Harlan knew the answer to that. He knew the answer since that moment of insight in bed in the 482nd, with Noÿs sleeping at his side. But, even yet, he dared not think of the wild truth.

He said, "I am not afraid of anyone. I have ways of protecting myself. They don't imagine how much I know."

Nine: *INTERLUDE*

It was, looking back at it, an idyllic period that followed. A hundred things took place in those physioweeks, and all confused itself inextricably in Harlan's memory, later, making the period seem to have lasted much longer than it did. The one idyllic thing about it was, of course, the hours he could spend with Noÿs, and that cast a glow over everything else.

Item One: At the 482nd he slowly packed his personal effects; his clothing and films, most of all his beloved and tenderly handled news-magazine volumes out of the Primitive. Anxiously he supervised their return to his permanent station in the 575th.

Finge was at his elbow as the last of it was lifted into the freight kettle by Maintenance men.

Finge said, choosing his words with unerring triteness, "Leaving us, I see." His smile was broad, but his lips were carefully held together so that only the barest trace of teeth showed. He kept his hands clasped behind his back and his pudgy body teetered forward on the balls of his feet.

Harlan did not look at his superior. He muttered a monotoned "Yes, sir."

Finge said, "I will report to Senior Computer Twissell concerning the entirely satisfactory manner in which you performed your Observational duties in the 482nd."

Harlan could not bring himself to utter even a sullen word of thanks. He remained silent.

Finge went on, in a suddenly much lower voice, "I will not report, for the present, your recent attempt at violence against me." And although his smile remained and his glance remained mild, there was a relish of cruel satisfaction about him.

Harlan looked up sharply and said, "As you wish, Computer."

Item Two: He re-established himself at the 575th.

He met Twissell almost at once. He found himself happy to see that little body, topped by that lined and gnomelike face. He was even happy to see the white cylinder nestling smokily between two stained fingers and being lifted rapidly toward Twissell's lips.

Harlan said, "Computer."

Twissell, emerging from his office, looked for a moment unseeingly and unrecognizingly at Harlan. His face was haggard and his eyes squinted with weariness.

He said, "Ah, Technician Harlan. You are done with your work in the 482nd?"

"Yes, sir."

Twissell's comment was strange. He looked at his watch, which, like any watch in Eternity, was geared to physiotime, giving the day number as well as the time of day, and said, "On the nose, my boy, on the nose. Wonderful. Wonderful."

Harlan felt his heart give a small bound. When he had last seen Twissell he would not have been able to make sense of that remark. Now he thought he did. Twissell was tired, or he would not have spoken so close to the core of things, perhaps. Or the Computer might have felt the remark to be so cryptic as to feel safe despite its closeness to the core.

Harlan said, speaking as casually as he could to avoid letting it seem that his remark had any connection at all with what Twissell had just said, "How's my Cub?"

"Fine, fine," said Twissell, with only half his mind, apparently, on his words. He took a quick puff at the shortening tube of tobacco, indulged in a quick nod of dismissal, and hurried off.

Item Three: the Cub.

He seemed older. There seemed to be a greater feeling of maturity to him as he held out his hand and said, "Glad to see you back, Harlan."

Or was it merely that, where earlier Harlan had been conscious of Cooper only as a pupil, he now seemed more than a Cub. He now seemed a gigantic instrument in the hands of the Eternals. Naturally he could not help but attain a new stature in Harlan's eyes.

Harlan tried not to show that. They were in Harlan's own quarters, and the Technician basked in the creamy porcelain surfaces about him, glad to be out of the ornate splash of the 482nd. Try as he might to associate the wild baroque of the 482nd with Noÿs, he only succeeded in associating it with Finge. With Noÿs he associated a pink, satiny twilight and, strangely, the bare austerity of the Sections of the Hidden Centuries.

He spoke hastily, almost as though he were anxious to hide his dangerous thoughts. "Well, Cooper, what have they been doing with you while I was away?"

Cooper laughed, brushed his drooping mustache self-consciously with one finger and said, "More math. Always math."

"Yes? Pretty advanced stuff by now, I guess."

"Pretty advanced."

"How's it coming?"

"So far it's bearable. It comes pretty easy, you know. I like it. But now they're really loading it on."

Harlan nodded and felt a certain satisfaction. He said, "Temporal Field matrices and all that?"

But Cooper, his color a little high, turned toward the stacked volumes in the bookshelves, and said, "Let's get back to the Primitives. I've got some questions."

"About what?"

"City life in the 23rd. Los Angeles, especially."

"Why Los Angeles?"

"It's an interesting city. Don't you think so?"

"It is, but let's hit it in the 21st, then. It was at its peak in the 21st."

"Oh, let's try the 23rd."

Harlan said, "Well, why not?"

His face was impassive, but if the impassiveness could have been peeled off, there would have been a grimness about him. His grand, intuitional guess was more than a guess. Everything was checking neatly.

Item Four: research. Twofold research.

For himself, first. Each day, with ferreting eyes, he went through the reports on Twissell's desk. The reports concerned the various Reality Changes being scheduled or suggested. Copies went to Twissell routinely since he was a member of the Allwhen Council, and Harlan knew he would not miss one. He looked first for the coming Change in the 482nd. Secondly he looked for other Changes, any other Changes, that might have a flaw, an imperfection, some deviation from maximum excellence that might be visible to his own trained and talented Technician's eyes.

In the strictest sense of the word the reports were not for his study, but Twissell was rarely in his office these days, and no one else saw fit to interfere with Twissell's personal Technician.

That was one part of his research. The other took place in the 575th Section branch of the library.

For the first time he ventured out of those portions of the library which, ordinarily, monopolized his attention. In the past he had haunted the section on Primitive history (very poor indeed, so that most of his references and source materials had to be derived from the far downwhen of the 3rd millennium, as was only natural, of course). To an even greater extent he had ransacked the shelves devoted to Reality Change, its theory, technique, and history; an excellent collection (best in Eternity outside the Central branch itself, thanks to Twissell) of which he had made himself full master.

Now he wandered curiously among the other film-racks. For the first time he Observed (in the capital-O sense) the racks devoted to the 575th itself; its geographies, which varied little from Reality to Reality, its histories, which varied more, and its sociologies, which varied still more. These were not the books or reports written about the Century by Observing and Computing Eternals (with those he was familiar), but by the Timers themselves.

There were the works of literature of the 575th and these stirred memories of tremendous arguments he had heard of concerning the values of alternate Changes. Would this masterpiece be altered or not? If so, how? How did past Changes affect works of art?

For that matter, could there ever be general agreement about art? Could it ever be reduced to quantitative terms amenable to mechanical evaluation by the Computing machines?

A Computer named August Sennor was Twissell's chief opponent in these matters. Harlan, stirred by Twissell's feverish denunciations of the man and his views, had read some of Sennor's papers and found them startling.

Sennor asked publicly and, to Harlan, disconcertingly, whether a new Reality might not contain a personality within itself analogous to that of a man who had been withdrawn into Eternity in a previous Reality. He analyzed then the possibility of an Eternal meeting his analogue in Time, either with or without knowing it, and speculated on the results in each case. (That came fairly close to one of Eternity's most potent fears, and Harlan shivered and hastened uneasily through the discussion.) And, of course, he discussed at length the fate of literature and art in various types and classifications of Reality Changes.

But Twissell would have none of the last. "If the values of art can't be computed," he would shout at Harlan, "then what's the use of arguing about it?"

And Twissell's views, Harlan knew, were shared by the large majority of the Allwhen Council.

Yet now Harlan stood at the shelves devoted to the novels of Eric Linkollew, usually described as the outstanding writer of the 575th, and wondered. He counted fifteen different "Complete Works" collections, each, undoubtedly, taken out of a different Reality. Each was somewhat different, he was sure. One set was noticeably smaller than all the others, for instance. A hundred Sociologists, he imagined, must have written analyses of the differences between the sets in terms of the sociological background of each Reality, and earned status thereby.

Harlan passed on to the wing of the library which was devoted to the devices and instrumentation of the various 575th's. Many of these last, Harlan knew, had been eliminated in Time and remained intact, as a product of human ingenuity, only in Eternity. Man had to be protected from his own too flourishing technical mind. That more than anything else. Not a physioyear passed but that somewhere in Time nuclear technology veered too close to the dangerous and had to be steered away.

He returned to the library proper and to the shelves on mathematics and mathematical histories. His fingers skimmed across individual titles, and after some thought he took half a dozen from the shelves and signed them out.

Item Five: Noÿs.

That was the really important part of the interlude, and all the idyllic part.

In his off-hours, when Cooper was gone, when he might ordinarily have been eating in solitude, reading in solitude, sleeping in solitude, waiting in solitude for the next day—he took to the kettles.

With all his heart he was grateful for the Technician's position in society. He was thankful, as he had never dreamed he could be, for the manner in which he was avoided.

No one questioned his right to be in a kettle, nor cared whether he aimed it upwhen or down. No curious eyes followed him, no willing hands offered to help him, no chattering mouths discussed it with him.

He could go where and when he pleased.

Noÿs said, "You've changed, Andrew. Heavens, you've changed."

He looked at her and smiled. "In what way, Noÿs?"

"You're smiling, aren't you? That's one of the ways. Don't you ever look in a mirror and see yourself smiling?"

"I'm afraid to. I'd say: 'I can't be that happy. I'm sick. I'm delirious. I'm confined in an asylum, living in daydreams, and unaware of it.' "

Noÿs leaned close to pinch him. "Feel anything?"

He drew her head toward him, felt bathed in her soft, black hair.

When they separated, she said breathlessly, "You've changed there, too. You've become very good at it."

"I've got a good teacher," began Harlan, and stopped abruptly, fearing that would imply displeasure at the thought of the many who might have had the making of such a good teacher.

But her laugh seemed untroubled by such a thought. They had eaten and she looked silky-smooth and warmly soft in the clothing he had brought her.

She followed his eyes and fingered the skirt gently, lifting it loose from its soft embrace of her thigh. She said, "I wish you wouldn't, Andrew. I really wish you wouldn't."

"There's no danger," he said carelessly.

"There *is* danger. Now don't be foolish. I can get along with what's here, until—until you make arrangements."

"Why shouldn't you have your own clothes and doodads?"

"Because they're not worth your going to my house in Time and being caught. And what if they make the Change while you're there?"

He evaded that uneasily. "It won't catch me." Then, brightening, "Besides my wrist generator keeps me in physiotime so that a Change can't affect me, you see."

Noÿs sighed. "I don't see. I don't think I'll ever understand it all."

"There's nothing to it." And Harlan explained and explained with great animation and Noÿs listened with sparkling eyes that never quite revealed whether she was entirely interested, or amused, or, perhaps, a little of both.

It was a great addition to Harlan's life. There was someone to talk to, someone with whom to discuss his life, his deeds, and thoughts. It was as though she were a portion of himself, but a portion sufficiently separate to require speech in communication rather than thought. She was a portion sufficiently separate to be able to answer unpredictably out of independent thought processes. Strange, Harlan thought, how one might Observe a social phenomenon such as matrimony and yet miss so vital a truth about it. Could he have predicted in advance, for instance, that it would be the passionate interludes that he would later least often associate with the idyl?

She snuggled into the crook of his arm and said, "How is your mathematics coming along?"

Harlan said, "Want to look at a piece of it?"

"Don't tell me you carry it around with you?"

"Why not? The kettle trip takes time. No use wasting it, you know."

He disengaged himself, took a small viewer from his pocket, inserted the film, and smiled fondly as she put it to her eyes.

She returned the viewer to him with a shake of her head. "I never saw so many squiggles. I wish I could read your Standard Intertemporal."

"Actually," said Harlan, "most of the squiggles you mention aren't Intertemporal really, just mathematical notation."

"You understand it, though, don't you?"

Harlan hated to do anything to disillusion the frank admiration in her eyes, but he was forced to say, "Not as much as I'd like to. Still, I have been picking up enough math to get what I want. I don't have to understand everything to be able to see a hole in a wall big enough to push a freight kettle through."

He tossed the viewer into the air, caught it with a flick of his hand, and put it on a small end-table.

Noÿs's eyes followed it hungrily and sudden insight flashed on Harlan.

He said, "Father Time! You can't read Intertemporal, at that."

"No. Of course not."

"Then the Section library here is useless to you. I never thought of that. You ought to have your own films from the 482nd."

She said quickly, "No. I don't want any."

He said, "You'll have them."

"Honestly, I don't want them. It's silly to risk——"

"You'll have them!" he said.

For the last time he stood at the immaterial boundary separating Eternity from Noÿs's house in the 482nd. He had intended the time before to be the last time. The Change was nearly upon them now, a fact he had not told Noÿs out of the decent respect he would have had for anyone's feelings, let alone those of his love.

Yet it wasn't a difficult decision to make, this one additional trip. Partly it was bravado, to shine before Noÿs, bring her the book-films from out of the lion's mouth; partly it was a hot desire (what was the Primitive phrase?) "to singe the beard of the King of Spain," if he might refer to the smooth-cheeked Finge so.

Then, too, he would have the chance once again of savoring the weirdly attractive atmosphere about a doomed house.

He had felt it before, when entering it carefully during the period of grace allowed by the spatio-temporal charts. He had felt it as he wandered through its rooms, collecting clothing, small *objets d'art*, strange containers, and instruments from Noÿs's vanity table.

There was the somber silence of a doomed Reality that was past merely the physical absence of noise. There was no way for Harlan to predict its analogue in a new Reality. It might be a small suburban cottage or a tenement in a city street. It might be zero with untamed scrubland replacing the parklike terrain on which it now stood. It might, conceivably, be almost unchanged. And (Harlan touched on this thought gingerly) it might be inhabited by the analogue of Noÿs or, of course, it might not.

To Harlan the house was already a ghost, a premature specter that had begun its hauntings before it had actually died. And because the house, as it was, meant a great deal to him, he found he resented its passing and mourned it.

Once, only, in five trips had there been any sound to break the stillness during his prowlings. He was in the pantry, then, thankful that the technology of that Reality and Century had made servants unfashionable and removed a problem. He had, he recalled, chosen among the cans of prepared foods, and was just deciding that he had enough for one trip, and that Noÿs would be pleased indeed to intersperse the hearty but uncolorful basic diet provided in the empty Section with some of her own dietary. He even laughed aloud to think that not long before he had thought her diet decadent.

It was in the middle of the laugh that he heard a distinct clapping noise. He froze!

The sound had come from somewhere behind him, and in the startled moment during which he had not moved the lesser danger that it was a housebreaker occurred to him first and the greater danger of its being an investigating Eternal occurred second.

It *couldn't* be a housebreaker. The entire period of the spatio-temporal chart, grace period and all, had been painstakingly cleared and chosen out of other similar periods of Time because of the lack of complicating factors. On the other hand, he had introduced a micro-Change (perhaps not so micro at that) by abstracting Noÿs.

Heart pounding, he forced himself to turn. It seemed to him that the door behind him had just closed, moving the last millimeter required to bring it flush with the wall.

He repressed the impulse to open that door, to search the house. With Noÿs's delicacies in tow he returned to Eternity and waited two full days for repercussions before venturing into the far upwhen. There were none and eventually he forgot the incident.

But now, as he adjusted the controls to enter Time this one last time, he thought of it again. Or perhaps it was the thought of the Change, nearly upon him now, that preyed on him. Looking back on the moment later, he felt that it was one or the other that caused him to misadjust the controls. He could think of no other excuse.

The misadjustment was not immediately apparent. It pin-pointed the proper room and Harlan stepped directly into Noÿs's library.

He had become enough of a decadent himself, now, to be not altogether repelled by the workmanship that went into the design of the film-cases. The lettering of the titles blended in with the intricate filigree until they were attractive but nearly unreadable. It was a triumph of aesthetics over utility.

Harlan took a few from the shelves at random and was surprised. The title of one was *Social and Economic History of our Times.*

Somehow it was a side of Noÿs to which he had given little thought. She was certainly not stupid and yet it never occurred to him that she might be interested in weighty things. He had the impulse to scan a bit of the *Social and Economic History,* but fought it down. He would find it in the Section library of the 482nd, if he ever wanted it. Finge had undoubtedly rifled the libraries of this Reality for Eternity's records months earlier.

He put that film to one side, ran through the rest, selected the fiction and some of what seemed light non-fiction. Those and two pocket viewers. He stowed them carefully into a knapsack.

It was at that point that, once more, he heard a sound in the house. There was no mistake this time. It was not a short sound of indeterminate origin. It was a laugh, a man's laugh. He was *not* alone in the house.

He was unaware that he had dropped the knapsack. For one dizzy second he could think only that he was trapped!

Ten: *TRAPPED!*

All at once it had seemed inevitable. It was the rawest dramatic irony. He had entered Time one last time, tweaked Finge's nose one last time, brought the pitcher to the well one last time. It had to be then that he was caught.

Was it Finge who laughed?

Who else would track him down, lie in wait, stay a room away, and burst into mirth?

Well, then, was all lost? And because in that sickening moment he was sure all was lost it did not occur to him to run again or to attempt flight into Eternity once more. He would face Finge.

He would kill him, if necessary.

Harlan stepped to the door from behind which the laugh had sounded, stepped to it with the soft, firm step of the premeditated murderer. He flicked loose the automatic door signal and opened it by hand. Two inches. Three. It moved without sound.

The man in the next room had his back turned. The figure seemed too tall to be Finge and that fact penetrated Harlan's simmering mind and kept him from advancing further.

Then, as though the paralysis that seemed to hold both men in rigor was slowly lifting, the other turned, inch by inch.

Harlan never witnessed the completion of that turn. The other's profile had not yet come into view when Harlan, holding back a sudden gust of terror with a last fragment of moral strength, flung himself back out the door. Its mechanism, not Harlan, closed it soundlessly.

Harlan fell back blindly. He could breathe only by struggling violently with the atmosphere, fighting air in and pushing it out, while his heart beat madly as though in an effort to escape his body.

Finge, Twissell, all the Council together could not have disconcerted him so much. It was the fear of nothing physical that had unmanned him. Rather it was an almost instinctive loathing for the nature of the accident that had befallen him.

He gathered the stack of book-films to himself in a formless lump and managed, after two futile tries, to re-establish the door to Eternity. He stepped through, his legs operating mechanically. Somehow he made his way to the 575th, and then to personal quarters. His Technicianhood, newly valued, newly appreciated, saved him once again. The few Eternals he met turned automatically to one side and looked steadfastly over his head as they did so.

That was fortunate, for he lacked any ability to smooth his face out of the death's-head grimace he felt he was wearing, or any power to put the blood back into it. But they didn't look, and he thanked Time and Eternity and whatever blind thing wove Destiny for that.

He had not truly recognized the other man in Noÿs's house by his appearance, yet he knew his identity with a dreadful certainty.

The first time Harlan had heard a noise in the house he, Harlan, had been laughing and the sound that interrupted his laugh was of something weighty dropping in the next room. The second time someone had laughed in the next room and he, Harlan, had dropped a knapsack of book-films. The first time he, Harlan, had turned and caught sight of a door closing. The second time he, Harlan, closed a door as a stranger turned.

He had met himself!

In the same Time and nearly in the same place he and his earlier self by several physiodays had nearly stood face to face. He had misadjusted the controls, set it for an instant in Time which he had already used and he, Harlan, had seen him, Harlan.

He had gone about his work with the shadow of horror upon him for days thereafter. He cursed himself for a coward, but that did not help.

Indeed from that moment matters took a downward trend. He could put his finger on the Great Divide. The key moment was the instant in which he had adjusted the door controls for his entry into the 482nd for one last time and somehow had adjusted it wrongly. Since then things went badly, badly.

The Reality Change in the 482nd went through during that period of despondency and accentuated it. In the past two weeks he had picked up three proposed Reality Changes which contained minor flaws, and now he chose among them, yet could do nothing to move himself to action.

He chose Reality Change 2456–2781, V-5 for a number of reasons. Of the three, it was farthest upwhen, the most distant. The error was minute, but was significant in terms of human life. It needed, then, only a quick trip to the 2456th to find out the nature of Noÿs's analogue in the new Reality, by use of a little blackmailing pressure.

But the unmanning of his recent experience betrayed him. It seemed to him no longer a simple thing, this gentle application of threatened exposure. And once he found the nature of Noÿs's analogue, what then? Put Noÿs in her place as charwoman, seamstress, laborer, or whatever. Certainly. But what, then, was to be done with the analogue herself? With any husband the analogue might have? Family? Children?

He had thought of none of this earlier. He had avoided the thought. "Sufficient unto the day . . ."

But now he could think of nothing else.

So he lay skulking in his room, hating himself, when Twissell called him, his tired voice questioning and a little puzzled.

"Harlan, are you ill? Cooper tells me you've skipped several discussion periods."

Harlan tried to smooth the trouble out of his face. "No, Computer Twissell. I'm a little tired."

"Well, that's forgivable, at any rate, boy." And then the smile on his face came about as close as it ever did to vanishing entirely. "Have you heard that the 482nd has been Changed?"

"Yes," said Harlan shortly.

"Finge called me," said Twissell, "and asked that you be told that the Change was entirely successful."

Harlan shrugged, then grew aware of Twissell's eyes staring out of the Communiplate and hard upon him. He grew uneasy and said, "Yes, Computer?"

"Nothing," said Twissell, and perhaps it was the cloak of age weighing down upon his shoulders, but his voice was unaccountably sad. "I thought you were about to speak."

"No," said Harlan. "I had nothing to say."

"Well, then, I'll see you tomorrow at opening in the Computing Room, boy. I have a great deal to say."

"Yes, sir," said Harlan. He stared for long minutes at the plate after it went dark.

That had almost sounded like a threat. Finge had called Twissell, had he? What had he said that Twissell did not report.

But an outside threat was what he needed. Battling a sickness of the spirit was like standing in a quicksand and beating it with a stick. Battling Finge was another thing altogether. Harlan had remembered the weapon at his disposal and for the first time in days felt a fraction of self-confidence return.

It was as though a door had closed and another had opened. Harlan grew as feverishly active as previously he had been catatonic. He traveled to the 2456th and bludgeoned Sociologist Voy to his own exact will.

He did it perfectly. He got the information he sought.

And more than he sought. Much more.

Confidence is rewarded, apparently. There was a homewhen proverb that went: "Grip the nettle firmly and it will become a stick with which to beat your enemy."

In short, Noÿs had no analogue in the new Reality. No analogue at all. She could take her position in the new society in the most inconspicuous and convenient manner possible, or she could stay in Eternity. There could be no reason to deny him liaison except for the highly theoretical fact that he had broken the law—and he knew very well how to counter that argument.

So he went racing upwhen to tell Noÿs the great news, to bathe in undreamed-of success after a few days horrible with apparent failure.

And at this moment the kettle came to a halt.

It did not slow; it simply halted. If the motion had been one along any of the three dimensions of space, a halt that sudden would have smashed the kettle, brought its metal to a dull red heat, turned Harlan into a thing of broken bone and wet, crushed flesh.

As it was, it merely doubled him with nausea and cracked him with inner pain.

When he could see, he fumbled to the temporometer and stared at it with fuzzy vision. It read 100,000.

Somehow that frightened him. It was too round a number.

He turned feverishly to the controls. What had gone wrong?

That frightened him too, for he could see nothing wrong. Nothing had tripped the drive-lever. It remained firmly geared into the upwhen drive. There was no short circuit. All the indicator dials were in the black safety range. There was no power failure. The tiny needle that marked the steady consumption of meg-megcoulombs of power calmly insisted that power was being consumed at the usual rate.

What, then, had stopped the kettle?

Slowly, and with considerable reluctance, Harlan touched the drive-lever, curled his hand about it. He pushed it to neutral, and the needle on the power gauge declined to zero.

He twisted the drive-lever back in the other direction. Up went the power gauge again, and this time the temporometer flicked downwhen along the line of Centuries.

Downwhen—downwhen—99,983—99,972—99,959—

Again Harlan shifted the lever. Upwhen again. Slowly. Very slowly.

Then 99,985—99,993—99,997—99,998—99,999—100,000—

Smash! Nothing past 100,000. The power of Nova Sol was silently being consumed, at an incredible rate, to no purpose.

He went downwhen again, farther. He roared upwhen. Smash!

His teeth were clenched, his lips drawn back, his breath rasping. He felt like a prisoner hurling himself bloodily against the bars of a prison.

When he stopped, a dozen smashes later, the kettle rested firmly at 100,000. Thus far, and no farther.

He would change kettles! (But there was not much hope in that thought.)

In the empty silence of the 100,000th Century, Andrew Harlan stepped out of one kettle and chose another kettle shaft at random.

A minute later, with the drive-lever in his hand, he stared at the marking of 100,000 and knew that here, too, he could not pass.

He raged! Now! At this time! When things so unexpectedly had broken in his favor, to come to so sudden a disaster. The curse of that moment of misjudgment in entering the 482nd was still on him.

Savagely he spun the lever downwhen, pressing it hard at maximum and keeping it there. At least in one way he was free now, free to do anything he wanted. With Noÿs cut off behind a barrier and out of his reach, what more could they do to him? What more had he to fear?

He carried himself to the 575th and sprang from the kettle with a reckless disregard for his surroundings that he had never felt before. He made his way to the Section library, speaking to no one, regarding no one. He took what he wanted without glancing about to see if he were observed. What did he care?

Back to the kettle and downwhen again. He knew exactly what he would do. He looked at the large clock as he passed, measuring off

Standard Physiotime, numbering the days and marking off the three coequal work shifts of the physioday. Finge would be at his private quarters now, and that was so much the better.

Harlan felt as though he were running a temperature when he arrived at the 482nd. His mouth was dry and cottony. His chest hurt. But he felt the hard shape of the weapon under his shirt as he held it firmly against his side with one elbow and that was the only sensation that counted.

Assistant Computer Hobbe Finge looked up at Harlan, and the surprise in his eyes slowly gave way to concern.

Harlan watched him silently for a while, letting the concern grow and waiting for it to change to fear. He circled slowly, getting between Finge and the Communiplate.

Finge was partly undressed, bare to the waist. His chest was sparsely haired, his breasts puffy and almost womanish. His tubby abdomen lapped over his waistband.

He looks undignified, thought Harlan with satisfaction, undignified and unsavory. So much the better.

He put his right hand inside his shirt and closed it firmly on the grip of his weapon.

Harlan said, "No one saw me, Finge, so don't look toward the door. No one's coming here. You've got to realize, Finge, that you're dealing with a Technician. Do you know what that means?"

His voice was hollow. He felt angry that fear wasn't entering Finge's eyes, only concern. Finge even reached for his shirt and, without a word, began to put it on.

Harlan went on, "Do you know the privilege of being a Technician, Finge? You've never been one, so you can't appreciate it. It means no one watches where you go or what you do. They all look the other way and work so hard at not seeing you that they really succeed at it. I could, for instance, go to the Section library, Finge, and help myself to any curious thing while the librarian busily concerns himself with his records and sees nothing. I can walk down the residential corridors of the 482nd and anyone passing turns out of my way and will swear later on he saw no one. It's that automatic. So you see, I can do what I want to do, go where I want to go. I can walk into the private apartments of the Assistant Computer of a Section and force him to tell the truth at weapon point and there'll be no one to stop me."

Finge spoke for the first time. "What are you holding?"

"A weapon," said Harlan, and brought it out. "Do you recognize it?" Its muzzle flared slightly and ended in a smooth metallic bulge.

"If you kill me . . ." began Finge.

"I won't kill you," said Harlan. "At a recent meeting you had a blaster. This is not a blaster. It is an invention of one of the past Realities of the 575th. Perhaps you are not acquainted with it. It was bred out of Reality. Too nasty. It can kill, but at low power it activates the pain centers of the nerve system and paralyzes as well. It is called, or was called, a neuronic whip. It works. This one is fully charged. I tested it on a finger." He held up his left hand with its stiffened little finger. "It was very unpleasant."

Finge stirred restlessly. "What is all this about, for Time's sake?"

"There is some sort of a block across the kettle shafts at the 100,000th. I want it removed."

"A block across the shafts?"

"Let's not work away at being surprised. Yesterday you spoke to Twissell. Today there is the block. I want to know what you said to Twissell. I want to know what's been done and what will be done. By Time, Computer, if you don't tell me, I'll use the whip. Try me, if you doubt my word."

"Now listen"—Finge's words slurred a bit and the first edge of fear made its appearance, and also a kind of desperate anger—"if you want the truth, it's this. We know about you and Noÿs."

Harlan's eyes flickered. "What about myself and Noÿs?"

Finge said, "Did you think you were getting away with anything?" The Computer kept his eyes fixed on the neuronic whip and his forehead was beginning to glisten. "By Time, with the emotion you showed after your period of Observation, with what you did during the period of Observation, did you think we wouldn't observe *you?* I would deserve to be broken as Computer if I had missed that. We know you brought Noÿs into Eternity. We knew it from the first. You wanted the truth. There it is."

At that moment Harlan despised his own stupidity. "You knew?"

"Yes. We knew you had brought her to the Hidden Centuries. We knew every time you entered the 482nd to supply her with appropriate luxuries; playing the fool, with your Eternal's Oath completely forgotten."

"Then why didn't you stop me?" Harlan was tasting the very dregs of his own humiliation.

"Do you still want the truth?" Finge flashed back, and seemed to gain courage in proportion as Harlan sank into frustration.

"Go on."

"Then let me tell you that I didn't consider you a proper Eternal from the start. A flashy Observer, perhaps, and a Technician who went through the motions. But no Eternal. When I brought you here on this last job, it was to prove as much to Twissell, who values you for some obscure reason. I wasn't just testing the society in the person of the girl, Noÿs. I was testing you, too, and you failed as I thought you would fail. Now put away that weapon, that whip, whatever it is, and get out of here."

"And you came to my personal quarters once," said Harlan breathlessly, working hard to keep his dignity and feeling it slip from him as though his mind and spirit were as stiff and unfeeling as the whiplashed little finger on his left hand, "to goad me into doing what I did."

"Yes, of course. If you want the phrase exactly, I tempted you. I told you the exact truth, that you could keep Noÿs only in the then-present Reality. You chose to act, not as an Eternal, but as a sniveler. I expected you to."

"I would do it again now," said Harlan gruffly, "and since it's all known, you can see I have nothing to lose." He thrust his whip outward toward Finge's plump waistline and spoke through pale lips and clenched teeth. "What has happened to Noÿs?"

"I have no idea."

"Don't tell me that. What has happened to Noÿs?"

"I tell you I don't know."

Harlan's fist tightened on the whip; his voice was low. "Your leg first. This will hurt."

"For Time's sake, listen. Wait!"

"All right. What has happened to her?"

"No, listen. So far it's just a breach of discipline. Reality wasn't affected. I made checks on that. Loss of rating is all you'll get. If you kill me, though, or hurt me with intent to kill, you've attacked a superior. There's the death penalty for that."

Harlan smiled at the futility of the threat. In the face of what had already happened death would offer a way out that in finality and simplicity had no equal.

Finge obviously misunderstood the reasons for the smile. He said hurriedly, "Don't think there's no death penalty in Eternity because you've never come across one. We know of them; we Computers. What's more, executions have taken place, too. It's simple. In any Reality, there are numbers of fatal accidents in which bodies are not recovered. Rockets explode in mid-air, aeroliners sink in mid-ocean or crash to powder in mountains. A murderer can be put on one of those vessels minutes, or seconds, before the fatal results. Is this worth that to you?"

Harlan stirred and said, "If you're stalling for rescue, it won't work. Let me tell you this: I'm not afraid of punishment. Furthermore, I intend to have Noÿs. I want her now. She does not exist in the current Reality. She has no analogue. There is no reason why we cannot establish formal liaison."

"It is against regulations for a Technician——"

"We will let the Allwhen Council decide," said Harlan, and his pride broke through at last. "I am not afraid of an adverse decision, either, any more than I am afraid of killing you. I am no ordinary Technician."

"Because you are Twissell's Technician?" and there was a strange look on Finge's round, sweating face that might have been hatred or triumph or part of each.

Harlan said, "For reasons much more important than that. And now . . ."

With grim determination he touched finger to the weapon's activator.

Finge screamed, "Then go to the Council. The Allwhen Council; *they* know. If you are that important——" He ended, gasping.

For a moment Harlan's finger hovered irresolutely. "What?"

"Do you think I would take unilateral action in a case like this? I reported this whole incident to the Council, timing it with the Reality Change. Here! Here are the duplicates."

"Hold on, don't move."

But Finge disregarded that order. With a speed as from the spur of a possessing fiend Finge was at his files. The finger of one hand located the code combination of the record he wanted, the fingers of the other punched it into the file. A silvery tongue of tape slithered out of the desk, its pattern of dots just visible to the naked eye.

"Do you want it sounded?" asked Finge, and without waiting threaded it into the sounder.

Harlan listened, frozen. It was clear enough. Finge had reported in full. He had detailed every motion of Harlan's in the kettle shafts. He hadn't missed one that Harlan could remember up to the point of making the report.

Finge shouted when the report was done, "Now, then, go to the Council. I've put no block in Time. I wouldn't know how. And don't think they're unconcerned about the matter. You said I spoke to Twissell yesterday. You're right. But I didn't call him; he called me. So go; ask Twissell. Tell them what an important Technician you are. And if you want to shoot me first; shoot and to Time with you."

Harlan could not miss the actual exultation in the Computer's voice. At that moment he obviously felt enough the victor to believe that even a neuronic whipping would leave him on the profit side of the ledger.

Why? Was the breaking of Harlan so dear to his heart? Was his jealousy over Noÿs so all-consuming a passion?

Harlan did scarcely more than formulate the questions in his mind, and then the whole matter, Finge and all, seemed suddenly meaningless to him.

He pocketed his weapon, whirled out the door, and toward the nearest kettle shaft.

It was the Council, then, or Twissell, at the very least. He was afraid of none of them, nor of all put together.

With each passing day of the last unbelievable month he had grown more convinced of his own indispensability. The Council, even the Allwhen Council itself, would have no choice but to come to terms when it was a choice of bartering one girl for the existence of all of Eternity.

Eleven: *FULL CIRCLE*

It was with a dull surprise that Technician Andrew Harlan, on bursting into the 575th, found himself in the night shift. The passing of the physiohours had gone unnoticed during his wild streaks along the kettle shafts. He stared hollowly at the dimmed corridors, the occasional evidence of the thinned-out night force at work.

But in the continued grip of his rage Harlan did not pause long to watch uselessly. He turned toward personal quarters. He would find Twissell's room on Computer Level as he had found Finge's and he had as little fear of being noticed or stopped.

The neuronic whip was still hard against his elbow as he stopped before Twissell's door (the name plate upon it advertising the fact in clear, inlaid lettering).

Harlan activated the door signal brashly on the buzzer level. He shorted the contact with a damp palm and let the sound become continuous. He could hear it dimly.

A step sounded lightly behind him and he ignored it in the sure knowledge that the man, whoever he was, would ignore him. (Oh, rose-red Technician's patch!)

But the sound of steps halted and a voice said, "Technician Harlan?"

Harlan whirled. It was a Junior Computer, relatively new to the Section. Harlan raged inwardly. This was not quite the 482nd. Here he was not merely a Technician, he was Twissell's Technician, and the younger Computers, in their anxiety to ingratiate themselves with the great Twissell, would extend a minimum civility to his Technician.

The Computer said, "Do you wish to see Senior Computer Twissell?"

Harlan fidgeted and said, "Yes, sir." (The fool! What did he think anyone would be standing signaling at a man's door for? To catch a kettle?)

"I'm afraid you can't," said the Computer.

"This is important enough to wake him," said Harlan.

"Maybe so," said the other, "but he's outwhen. He's not in the 575th."

"Exactly when is he, then?" asked Harlan impatiently.

The Computer's glance became a supercilious stare. "I wouldn't know."

Harlan said, "But I have an important appointment first thing in the morning."

"*You* have," said the Computer, and Harlan was at a loss to account for his obvious amusement at the thought.

The Computer went on, even smiling now, "You're a little early, aren't you?"

"But I must see him."

"I'm sure he'll be here in the morning." The smile broadened.

"But——"

The Computer passed by Harlan, carefully avoiding any contact, even of garments.

Harlan's fists clenched and unclenched. He stared helplessly after the Computer and then, simply because there was nothing else to do, he walked slowly, and without full consciousness of his surroundings, back to his own room.

Harlan slept fitfully. He told himself he needed sleep. He tried to relax by main force, and, of course, failed. His sleep period was a succession of futile thought.

First of all, there was Noÿs.

They would not dare harm her, he thought feverishly. They could not send her back to Time without first calculating the effect on Reality and that would take days, probably weeks. As an alternative, they might do to her what Finge had threatened for him; place her in the path of an untraceable accident.

He did not take that into serious consideration. There was no necessity for drastic action such as that. They would not risk Harlan's displeasure by doing it. (In the quiet of a darkened sleeping room, and in that phase of half sleep where things often grew queerly disproportionate in thought, Harlan found nothing grotesque in his sure opinion that the Allwhen Council would not dare risk a Technician's displeasure.)

Of course, there were uses to which a woman in captivity might be put. A beautiful woman from a hedonistic Reality . . .

Resolutely Harlan put the thought away as often as it returned. It was at once more likely and more unthinkable than death, and he would have none of it.

He thought of Twissell.

The old man was out of the 575th. Where was he during hours when he should have been asleep? An old man needs his sleep. Harlan was sure of the answer. There were Council consultations going on. About Harlan. About Noÿs. About what to do with an indispensable Technician one dared not touch.

Harlan's lips drew back. If Finge reported Harlan's assault of that evening, it would not affect their considerations in the least. His crimes could scarcely be worsened by it. His indispensability would certainly not be lessened.

And Harlan was by no means certain that Finge *would* report him. To admit having been forced to cringe before a Technician would put an Assistant Computer in a ridiculous light, and Finge might not choose to do so.

Harlan thought of Technicians as a group, which, of late, he had done rarely. His own somewhat anomalous position as Twissell's man and as half an Educator had kept him too far apart from other Technicians. But Technicians lacked solidarity anyway. Why should that be?

Did he have to go through the 575th and the 482nd rarely seeing or speaking to another Technician? Did they have to avoid even one another? Did they have to act as though they accepted the status into which the superstition of others forced them?

In his mind he had already forced the capitulation of the Council as far as Noÿs was concerned, and now he was making further demands. The Technicians were to be allowed an organization of their own, regular meetings—more friendship—better treatment from the others.

His final thought of himself was as a heroic social revolutionary, with Noÿs at his side, when he sank finally into a dreamless sleep. . . .

The door signal awoke him. It whispered at him with hoarse impatience. He collected his thoughts to the point of being able to look at the small clock beside his bed and groaned inwardly.

Father Time! After all that he had overslept.

He managed to reach the proper button from bed and the view-square high on the door grew transparent. He did not recognize the face, but it carried authority whoever it was.

He opened the door and the man, wearing the orange patch of Administration, stepped in.

"Technician Andrew Harlan?"

"Yes, Administrator? You have business with me?"

The Administrator seemed in no wise discommoded at the sharp belligerence of the question. He said, "You have an appointment with Senior Computer Twissell?"

"Well?"

"I am here to inform you that you are late."

Harlan stared at him. "What's this all about? You're not from the 575th, are you?"

"The 222nd is my station," said the other frigidly. "Assistant Administrator Arbut Lemm. I'm in charge of the arrangements and I'm trying to avoid undue excitement by by-passing official notification over the Communiplate."

"What arrangements? What excitement? What's it all about? Listen, I've had conferences with Twissell before. He's my superior. There's no excitement involved."

A look of surprise passed momentarily over the studious lack of expression the Administrator had so far kept on his face. "You haven't been informed?"

"About what?"

"Why, that a subcommittee of the Allwhen Council is holding session here at the 575th. This place, I am told, has been alive with the news for hours."

"And they want to see me?" As soon as he asked that, Harlan thought: Of course they want to see me. What else could the session be about but me?

And he understood the amusement of the Junior Computer last night outside Twissell's room. The Computer knew of the projected committee meeting and it amused him to think that a Technician could possibly expect to see Twissell at a time like that. Very amusing, thought Harlan bitterly.

The Administrator said, "I have my orders. I know nothing more." Then, still surprised, "You've heard nothing of this?"

"Technicians," said Harlan sarcastically, "lead sheltered lives."

Five besides Twissell! Senior Computers all, none less than thirty-five years an Eternal.

Six weeks earlier Harlan would have been overwhelmed by the honor of sitting at lunch with such a group, tongue-tied by the combination of responsibility and power they represented. They would have seemed twice life-size to him.

But now they were antagonists of his, worse still, judges. He had no time to be impressed. He had to plan his strategy.

They might not know that he was aware they had Noÿs. They could not know unless Finge told them of his last meeting with Harlan. In the clear light of day, however, he was more than ever convinced that Finge was not the man to broadcast publicly the fact that he had been browbeaten and insulted by a Technician.

It seemed advisable, then, for Harlan to nurse this possible advantage for the time being, to let *them* make the first move, say the first sentence that would join actual combat.

They seemed in no hurry. They stared at him placidly over an abstemious lunch as though he were an interesting specimen spread-eagled against a plane of force by mild repulsors. In desperation Harlan stared back.

He knew all of them by reputation and by trimensional reproduction in the physiomonthly orientation films. The films co-ordinated developments throughout the various Sections of Eternity and were required viewing for all Eternals with rating from Observer up.

August Sennor, the bald one (not even eyebrows or eyelashes), of course attracted Harlan most. First, because the odd appearance of those dark, staring eyes against bare eyelids and forehead was remarkably greater in person than it had ever seemed in trimension. Second, because of his knowledge of past collisions of view between Sennor and Twissell. Finally, because Sennor did not confine himself to watching Harlan. He shot questions at him in a sharp voice.

For the most part his questions were unanswerable, such as:

"How did you first come to be interested in Primitive times, young man?" "Do you find the study rewarding, young man?"

Finally, he seemed to settle himself in his seat. He pushed his plate casually onto the disposal chute and clasped his thick fingers lightly before him. (There was no hair on the back of the hands, Harlan noticed.)

Sennor said, "There is something I have always wanted to know. Perhaps you can help me."

Harlan thought: All right, now, this is it.

Aloud he said, "If I can, sir."

"Some of us here in Eternity—I won't say all, or even enough" (and he cast a quick glance at Twissell's tired face, while the others drew closer to listen) "but some, at any rate—are interested in the philosophy of Time. Perhaps you know what I mean."

"The paradoxes of Time-travel, sir?"

"Well, if you want to put it melodramatically, yes. But that's not all, of course. There is the question of the true nature of Reality, the question of the conservation of mass-energy during Reality Change and so on. Now we in Eternity are influenced in our consideration of such things by knowing the facts of Time-travel. Your creatures of the Primitive era, however, knew nothing of Time-travel. What were *their* views on the matter?"

Twissell's whisper carried the length of the table. "Cobwebs!"

But Sennor ignored that. He said, "Would you answer my question, Technician?"

Harlan said, "The Primitives gave virtually no thought to Time-travel, Computer."

"Did not consider it possible, eh?"

"I believe that's right."

"Did not even speculate?"

"Well, as to that," said Harlan uncertainly, "I believe there were speculations of sorts in some types of escape literature. I am not well acquainted with these, but I believe a recurrent theme was that of the man who returned in Time to kill his own grandfather as a child."

Sennor seemed delighted. "Wonderful! Wonderful! After all, that is at least an expression of the basic paradox of Time-travel, if we assume an indeviant Reality, eh? Now your Primitives, I'll venture to state, never assumed anything *but* an indeviant Reality. Am I right?"

Harlan waited to answer. He did not see where the conversation was aiming or what Sennor's deeper purposes were, and it unnerved him. He said, "I don't know enough to answer you with certainty, sir. I believe there may have been speculations as to alternate paths of time or planes of existence. I don't know."

Sennor thrust out a lower lip. "I'm sure you're wrong. You may have been misled by reading your own knowledge into various ambiguities you may have come across. No, without actual experience of Time-travel, the philosophic intricacies of Reality would be quite beyond the human mind. For instance, why does Reality possess inertia? We all know that it does. Any alteration in its flow must reach a certain magnitude before a Change, a true Change, is effected. Even then, Reality has a tendency to flow back to its original position.

"For instance, suppose a Change here in the 575th. Reality will change with increasing effects to perhaps the 600th. It will change, but with continually lesser effects to perhaps the 650th. Thereafter, Reality will be unchanged. We all know this is so, but do any of us know why it is so? Intuitive reasoning would suggest that any Reality Change would increase its effects without limit as the Centuries pass, yet that is not so.

"Take another point. Technician Harlan, I'm told, is excellent at selecting the exact Minimum Change Required for any situation. I'll wager he cannot explain how he arrives at his own choice.

"Consider how helpless the Primitives must be. They worry about a man killing his own grandfather because they do not understand the truth about Reality. Take a more likely and a more easily analyzed case and let's consider the man who in his travels through time meets himself——"

Harlan said sharply, "What about a man who meets himself?"

The fact that Harlan interrupted a Computer was a breach of manners in itself. His tone of voice worsened the breach to a scandalous extent, and all eyes turned reproachfully on the Technician.

Sennor harumphed, but spoke in the strained tone of one determined to be polite despite nearly insuperable difficulties. He said, continuing his broken sentence and thus avoiding the appearance of answering directly the unmannerly question addressed to him, "And the four subdivisions into which such an act can fall. Call the man earlier in physiotime, A, and the one later, B. Subdivision one, A and B may not see one another, or do anything that will significantly affect one another. In that case, they have not really met and we may dismiss this case as trivial.

"Or B, the later individual, may see A while A does not see B. Here, too, no serious consequences need be expected. B, seeing A, sees him in a position and engaged in activity of which he already has knowledge. Nothing new is involved.

"The third and fourth possibilities are that A sees B, while B does not see A, and that A and B see one another. In each possibility, the serious point is that A has seen B; the man at an earlier stage in his physiological existence sees himself at a later stage. Observe that he has learned he will be alive at the apparent age of B. He knows he will live long enough to perform the action he has witnessed. Now a man in knowing his own future in even the slightest detail can act on that knowledge and therefore changes his future. It follows that Reality must be changed to the extent of not allowing A and B to meet or, at the very least, of preventing A from seeing B. Then, since nothing in a Reality made un-Real can be detected, A never has met B. Similarly, in every apparent paradox of Time-travel, Reality always changes to avoid the paradox and we come to the conclusion that there are no paradoxes in Time-travel and that there can be none."

Sennor looked well pleased with himself and his exposition, but Twissell rose to his feet.

Twissell said, "I believe, gentlemen, that time presses."

Far more suddenly than Harlan would have thought the lunch was over. Five of the subcommittee members filed out, nodding at him, with the air of those whose curiosity, mild at best, had been assuaged. Only Sennor held out a hand and added a gruff "Good day, young man" to the nod.

With mixed feelings Harlan watched them go. What had been the purpose of the luncheon? Most of all, why the reference to men meeting themselves? They had made no mention of Noÿs. Were they there, then, only to study him? Survey him from top to bottom and leave him to Twissell's judging?

Twissell returned to the table, empty now of food and cutlery. He was alone with Harlan now, and almost as though to symbolize that he wielded a new cigarette between his fingers.

He said, "And now to work, Harlan. We have a great deal to do."

But Harlan would not, could not, wait longer. He said flatly, "Before we do anything, I have something to say."

Twissell looked surprised. The skin of his face puckered up about his faded eyes, and he tamped at the ash end of his cigarette thoughtfully.

He said, "By all means, speak if you wish, but first, sit down, sit down, boy."

Technician Andrew Harlan did not sit down. He strode up and

back the length of the table, biting off his sentences hard to keep them from boiling and bubbling into incoherence. Senior Computer Laban Twissell's age-yellowed pippin of a head turned back and forth as he followed the other's nervous stride.

Harlan said, "For weeks now I've been going through films on the history of mathematics. Books from several Realities of the 575th. The Realities don't matter much. Mathematics doesn't change. The order of its development doesn't change either. No matter how else the Realities shifted, mathematical history stayed about the same. The mathematicians changed; different ones switched discoveries, but the end results—— Anyway, I pounded a lot of it into my head. How does that strike you?"

Twissell frowned and said, "A queer occupation for a Technician?"

"But I'm not just a Technician," said Harlan. "You know that."

"Go on," said Twissell and he looked at the timepiece he wore. The fingers that held his cigarette played with it with unwonted nervousness.

Harlan said, "There was a man named Vikkor Mallansohn who lived in the 24th Century. That was part of the Primitive era, you know. The thing he is known best for is the fact that he first successfully built a Temporal Field. That means, of course, that he invented Eternity, since Eternity is only one tremendous Temporal Field short-circuiting ordinary Time and free of the limitations of ordinary Time."

"You were taught this as a Cub, boy."

"But I was not taught that Vikkor Mallansohn could not possibly have invented the Temporal Field in the 24th Century. Nor could anyone have. The mathematical basis for it didn't exist. The fundamental Lefebvre equations did not exist; nor could they exist until the researches of Jan Verdeer in the 27th Century."

If there was one sign by which Senior Computer Twissell could indicate complete astonishment, it was that of dropping his cigarette. He dropped it now. Even his smile was gone.

He said, "Were you taught the Lefebvre equations, boy?"

"No. And I don't say I understand them. But they're necessary for the Temporal Field. I've learned that. And they weren't discovered till the 27th. I know that, too."

Twissell bent to pick up his cigarette and regarded it dubiously. "What if Mallansohn had stumbled on the Temporal Field without being aware of the mathematical justification? What if it were simply an empirical discovery? There have been many such."

"I've thought of that. But after the Field was invented, it took three centuries to work out its implications and at the end of that time there was no one way in which Mallansohn's Field could be improved on. That could not be coincidence. In a hundred ways, Mallansohn's design showed that he must have used the Lefebvre equations. If he knew them or had developed them without Verdeer's work, which is impossible, why didn't he say so?"

Twissell said, "You insist on talking like a mathematician. Who told you all this?"

"I've been viewing films."

"No more?"

"And thinking."

"Without advanced mathematical training? I've watched you closely for years, boy, and would not have guessed that particular talent of yours. Go on."

"Eternity could never have been established without Mallansohn's discovery of the Temporal Field. Mallansohn could never have accomplished this without a knowledge of mathematics that existed only in his future. That's number one. Meanwhile, here in Eternity at this moment, there is a Cub who was selected as an Eternal against all the rules, since he was overage and married, to boot. You are educating him in mathematics and in Primitive sociology. That's number two."

"Well?"

"I say that it is your intention to send him back into Time somehow, back past the downwhen terminus of Eternity, back to the 24th. It is your intention to have the Cub, Cooper, teach the Lefebvre equations to Mallansohn. You see, then," Harlan added with tense passion, "that my own position as expert in the Primitive and my knowledge of that position entitles me to special treatment. *Very* special treatment."

"Father Time!" muttered Twissell.

"It's true, isn't it? We come full circle, *with my help*. Without it . . ." He let the sentence hang.

"You come so close to the truth," said Twissell. "Yet I could swear there was nothing to indicate——" He fell into a study in which neither Harlan nor the outside world seemed to play a part.

Harlan said quickly, "Only close to the truth? It *is* the truth." He could not tell why he was so certain of the essentials of what he said, even quite apart from the fact that he so desperately wanted it to be so.

Twissell said, "No, no, not the exact truth. The Cub, Cooper, is not going back to the 24th to teach Mallansohn anything."

"I don't believe you."

"But you must. You must see the importance of this. I want your co-operation through what is left of the project. You see, Harlan, the situation is more full circle than you imagine. Much more so, boy. Cub Brinsley Sheridan Cooper *is* Vikkor Mallansohn!"

Twelve: THE BEGINNING OF ETERNITY

Harlan would not have thought that Twissell could have said anything at that moment that could have surprised him. He was wrong.

He said, "Mallansohn. He——"

Twissell, having smoked his cigarette to a stub, produced another and said, "Yes, Mallansohn. Do you want a quick summary of Mallansohn's life? Here it is. He was born in the 78th, spent some time in Eternity, and died in the 24th."

Twissell's small hand placed itself lightly on Harlan's elbow and his gnomish face broke into a wrinkled extension of his usual smile. "But come, boy, physiotime passes even for us and we are not completely masters of ourselves this day. Won't you come with me to my office?"

He led the way and Harlan followed, not entirely aware of the opening doors and the moving ramps.

He was relating the new information to his own problem and plan of action. With the passing of the first moment of disorientation his resolution returned. After all, how did this change things except to make his own importance to Eternity still more crucial, his value higher, his demands more sure to be met, Noÿs more certain to be bartered back to him.

Noÿs!

Father Time, they must not harm her! She seemed the only real part of his life. All Eternity beside was only a filmy fantasy, and not a worth-while one, either.

When he found himself in Computer Twissell's office, he could not clearly recall how it had come about that he had passed from the dining area here. Though he looked about and tried to make the office grow real by sheer force of the mass of its contents, it still seemed but another part of a dream that had outlived its usefulness.

Twissell's office was a clean, long room of porcelain asepsis. One wall of the office was crowded from floor to ceiling and wall to distant wall with the computing micro-units which, together, made up the largest privately operated Computaplex in Eternity and, indeed, one of the largest altogether. The opposite wall was crammed with reference films. Between the two what was left of the room was scarcely more than a corridor, broken by a desk, two chairs, recording and projecting equipment, and an unusual object the like of which Harlan was not familiar with and which did not reveal its use until Twissell flicked the remnants of a cigarette into it.

It flashed noiselessly and Twissell, in his usual prestidigitational fashion, held another in his hands.

Harlan thought: To the point, now.

He began, a trifle too loudly, a bit too truculently, "There is a girl in the 482nd——"

Twissell frowned, waved one hand quickly as though brushing an unpleasant matter hastily to one side. "I know, I know. She will not be disturbed, nor you. All will be well. I will see to it."

"Do you mean——"

"I tell you I know the story. If the matter has troubled you, it need trouble you no more."

Harlan stared at the old man, stupefied. Was this all? Though he had thought intently of the immensity of his power, he had not expected so clear a demonstration.

But Twissell was talking again.

"Let me tell you a story," he began, with almost the tone he would have used in addressing a newly inducted Cub. "I had not thought this would be necessary, and perhaps it still isn't, but your own researches and insight deserve it."

He stared at Harlan quizzically and said, "You know, I still can't quite believe that you worked this out on your own," then went on: "The man most of Eternity knows as Vikkor Mallansohn left the record of his life behind him after he died. It was not quite a diary, not quite a biography. It was more of a guide, bequeathed to the Eternals he knew would someday exist. It was enclosed in a volume of Time-stasis which could be opened only by the Computers of Eternity, and which therefore remained untouched for three Centuries after his death, until Eternity was established and Senior Computer Henry Wadsman, the first of the great Eternals, opened it. The document has been passed along in strictest security since, along a line of Senior Computers ending with myself. It is referred to as the Mallansohn memoir.

"The memoir tells the story of a man named Brinsley Sheridan

Cooper, born in the 78th, inducted as a Cub into Eternity at the age of twenty-three, having been married for a little over a year, but having been, as yet, childless.

"Having entered Eternity, Cooper was trained in mathematics by a Computer named Laban Twissell and in Primitive sociology by a Technician named Andrew Harlan. After a thorough grounding in both disciplines, and in such matters as temporal engineering as well, he was sent back to the 24th to teach certain necessary techniques to a Primitive scientist named Vikkor Mallansohn.

"Once having reached the 24th, he embarked first on a slow process of adjusting himself to the society. In this he benefited a great deal from the training of Technician Harlan and the detailed advice of Computer Twissell, who seemed to have an uncanny insight into some of the problems he was to face.

"After the passage of two years, Cooper located one Vikkor Mallansohn, an eccentric recluse in the California backwoods, relationless and friendless but gifted with a daring and unconventional mind. Cooper made friends slowly, acclimated the man to the thought of having met a traveler from the future still more slowly, and set about teaching the man the mathematics he must know.

"With the passage of time, Cooper adopted the other's habits, learned to shift for himself with the help of a clumsy Diesel-oil electric generator and with wired electrical appliances which freed them of dependence on power beams.

"But progress was slow and Cooper found himself something less than a marvelous teacher. Mallansohn grew morose and unco-operative and then one day died, quite suddenly, in a fall down a canyon of the wild, mountainous country in which they lived. Cooper, after weeks of despair, with the ruin of his lifework and, presumably, of all Eternity, staring him in the eye, decided on a desperate expedient. He did not report Mallansohn's death. Instead, he slowly took to building, out of the materials at hand, a Temporal Field.

"The details do not matter. He succeeded after mountains of drudgery and improvisation and took the generator to the California Institute of Technology, just as years before he had expected the real Mallansohn to do.

"You know the story from your own studies. You know of the disbelief and rebuffs he first met, his period under observation, his escape and the near-loss of his generator, the help he received from the man at the lunch counter whose name he never learned, but who is now one of Eternity's heroes, and of the final demonstration for Professor Zimbalist, in which a white mouse moved backward and forward in Time. I won't bore you with any of that.

"Cooper used the name of Vikkor Mallansohn in all this because it gave him a background and made him an authentic product of the 24th. The body of the real Mallansohn was never recovered.

"In the remainder of his life, he cherished his generator and cooperated with the Institute scientists in duplicating it. He dared do no more than that. He could not teach them the Lefebvre equations without outlining three Centuries of mathematical development that was to come. He could not, dared not hint at his true origin. He dared not do more than the real Vikkor Mallansohn had, to his knowledge, done.

"The men who worked with him were frustrated to find a man who could perform so brilliantly and yet was unable to explain the whys of his performance. And he himself was frustrated too, because he foresaw, without in any way being able to quicken, the work that would lead, step by step, to the classic experiments of Jan Verdeer, and how from that the great Antoine Lefebvre would construct the basic equations of Reality. And how, after that, Eternity would be constructed.

"It was only toward the end of his long life that Cooper, staring into a Pacific sunset (he describes the scene in some detail in his memoir) came to the great realization that he was Vikkor Mallansohn; he was not a substitute but the man himself. The name might not be his, but the man history called Mallansohn was really Brinsley Sheridan Cooper.

"Fired with that thought, and with all that implied, anxious that the process of establishing Eternity be somehow quickened, improved, and made more secure, he wrote his memoir and placed it in a cube of Time-stasis in the living room of his house.

"And so the circle was closed. Cooper-Mallansohn's intentions in writing the memoir were, of course, disregarded. Cooper must go through his life exactly as he had gone through it. Primitive Reality allows for no changes. At this moment in physiotime, the Cooper you know is unaware of what lies ahead of him. He believes he is only to instruct Mallansohn and to return. He will continue to believe so until the years teach him differently and he sits down to write his memoir.

"The intention of the circle in Time is to establish the knowledge of Time-travel and of the nature of Reality, to build Eternity, ahead of its natural Time. Left to itself, mankind would not have learned the truth about Time before their technological advances in other directions had made racial suicide inevitable."

Harlan listened intently, caught up in the vision of a mighty circle in Time, closed upon itself, and traversing Eternity in part of its course. He came as close to forgetting Noÿs, for the moment, as he ever could.

He asked, "Then you knew all along everything you were to do, everything I was to do, everything I *have* done."

Twissell, who seemed lost in his own telling of the tale, his eyes peering through a haze of bluish tobacco smoke, came slowly to life. His old, wise eyes fixed themselves on Harlan and he said reproachfully, "No, of course not. There was a lapse of decades of physiotime between Cooper's stay in Eternity and the moment when he wrote his memoir. He could remember only so much, and only what he himself had witnessed. You should realize that."

Twissell sighed and he drew a gnarled finger through a line of updrafting smoke, breaking it into little turbulent swirls. "It worked itself out. First, I was found and brought to Eternity. When, in the fullness of physiotime, I became a Senior Computer, I was given the memoir and placed in charge. I had been described as in charge, so I was placed in charge. Again in the fullness of physiotime, you appeared in the changing of a Reality (we had watched your earlier analogues carefully), and then Cooper.

"I filled in the details by using my common sense and the services of the Computaplex. How carefully, for instance, we instructed Educator Yarrow in his part while betraying none of the significant truth. How carefully, in his turn, he stimulated your interest in the Primitive.

"How carefully we had had to keep Cooper from learning anything he did not prove he had learned by reference in the memoir." Twissell smiled sadly. "Sennor amuses himself with matters such as this. He calls it the reversal of cause and effect. Knowing the effect, one adjusts the cause. Fortunately, I am not the cobweb spinner Sennor is.

"I was pleased, boy, to find you so excellent an Observer and Technician. The memoir had not mentioned that since Cooper had no opportunity to observe your work or evaluate it. This suited me. I could use you in a more ordinary task that would make your essential one less noticeable. Even your recent stay with Computer Finge fitted in. Cooper mentioned a period of your absence during which his mathematical studies were so sharpened that he longed for your return. Once, though, you frightened me."

Harlan said, at once, "You mean the time I took Cooper along the kettleways."

"How do you come to guess that?" demanded Twissell.

"It was the one time you were really angry with me. I suppose now it went against something in the Mallansohn memoir."

"Not quite. It was just that the memoir did not speak of the kettles. It seemed to me that to avoid mention of such an outstanding aspect of Eternity meant he had little experience with it. It was my intention therefore to keep him away from the kettles as much as possible. The fact that you had taken him upwhen in one disturbed me greatly, but nothing happened afterward. Things continued as they should, so all is well."

The old Computer rubbed one hand slowly over the other, staring at the young Technician with a look compounded of surprise and curiosity. "And all along you've been guessing this. It simply astonishes me. I would have sworn that even a fully trained Computer could not have made the proper deductions, given only the information you had. For a Technician to do it is uncanny." He leaned forward, tapped Harlan's knee lightly. "The Mallansohn memoir says nothing about your life after Cooper's leaving, of course."

"I understand, sir," said Harlan.

"We will be free then, in a manner of speaking, to do as we please with it. You show a surprising talent that must not be wasted. I think you are meant for something more than a Technician. I promise nothing now, but I presume that you realize that Computership is a distinct possibility."

It was easy for Harlan to keep his dark face expressionless. He had had years of practice for that.

He thought: An additional bribe.

But nothing must be left to conjecture. His guesses, wild and unsupported at the start, arrived at by a freak of insight in the course of a very unusual and stimulating night, had become reasonable as the result of directed library research. They had become certainties now that Twissell had told him the story. Yet in one way at least there had been a deviation. Cooper was Mallansohn.

That had simply improved his position, but, wrong in one respect, he might be wrong in another. He must leave nothing to chance, then. Have it out! Make certain!

He said levelly, almost casually, "The responsibility is great for me, also, now that I know the truth."

"Yes, indeed?"

"How fragile is the situation? Suppose something unexpected were to happen and I were to miss a day when I ought to have been teaching Cooper something vital."

"I don't understand you."

(Was it Harlan's imagination, or had a spark of alarm sprung to life in those old, tired eyes?)

"I mean, can the circle break? Let me put it this way. If an unexpected blow on the head puts me out of action at a time when the memoir distinctly states I am well and active, is the whole scheme disrupted? Or suppose, for some reason, I deliberately choose not to follow the memoir. What then?"

"But what puts all this in your mind?"

"It seems a logical thought. It seems to me that by a careless or willful action, I could break the circle, and well, what? Destroy Eternity? It seems so. If it *is* so," Harlan added composedly, "I ought to be told so that I may be careful to do nothing unfitting. Though I imagine it would take a rather unusual circumstance to drive me to such a thing."

Twissell laughed, but the laughter rang false and empty in Harlan's ear. "This is all purely academic, my boy. Nothing of this will happen since it hasn't happened. The full circle will not break."

"It might," said Harlan. "The girl of the 482nd——"

"Is safe," said Twissell. He rose impatiently. "There's no end to this kind of talk and I have quite enough of logic-chopping from the rest of the subcommittee in charge of the project. Meanwhile, I have yet to tell *you* what I originally called you here to hear and physiotime is still passing. Will you come with me?"

Harlan was satisfied. The situation was clear and his power unmistakable. Twissell knew that Harlan could say, at will: "I will no longer have anything to do with Cooper." Twissell knew Harlan could at any moment destroy Eternity by giving Cooper significant information concerning the memoir.

Harlan had known enough to do this yesterday. Twissell had thought to overwhelm him with the knowledge of the importance of his task, but if the Computer had thought to force Harlan into line in that way, he was mistaken.

Harlan had made his threat very clear with respect to Noÿs's safety, and Twissell's expression as he had barked, "Is safe," showed he realized the nature of the threat.

Harlan rose and followed Twissell.

Harlan had never been in the room they now entered. It was large and looked as though walls had been knocked down for its sake. It had been entered through a narrow corridor which had been blocked off by a force-screen that did not go down until after a pause sufficient for Twissell's face to be scanned thoroughly by automatic machinery.

The largest part of the room was filled by a sphere that reached nearly to the ceiling. A door was open, showing four small steps leading to a well-lit platform within.

Voices sounded from inside and even as Harlan watched, legs appeared in the opening and descended the steps. A man emerged and another pair of legs appeared behind him. It was Sennor of the Allwhen Council and behind him was another of the group at the breakfast table.

Twissell did not look pleased at this. His voice, however, was restrained. "Is the subcommittee still here?"

"Only we two," said Sennor casually, "Rice and myself. A beautiful instrument we have here. It has the level of complexity of a spaceship."

Rice was a paunchy man with the perplexed look of one who is accustomed to being right yet finds himself unaccountably on the losing side of an argument. He rubbed his bulbous nose and said, "Sennor's mind is running on space-travel lately."

Sennor's bald head glistened in the light. "It's a neat point, Twissell," he said. "I put it to you. Is space-travel a positive factor or a negative factor in the calculus of Reality?"

"The question is meaningless," said Twissell impatiently. "What type of space-travel in what society under what circumstances?"

"Oh, come. Surely there's something to be said concerning space-travel in the abstract."

"Only that it is self-limiting, that it exhausts itself and dies out."

"Then it is useless," said Sennor with satisfaction, "and therefore it is a negative factor. My view entirely."

"If you please," said Twissell, "Cooper will be here soon. We will need the floor clear."

"By all means." Sennor hooked an arm under that of Rice and led him away. His voice declaimed clearly as they departed. "Periodically, my dear Rice, all the mental effort of mankind is concentrated on space-travel, which is doomed to a frustrated end by the nature of things. I would set up the matrices except that I am certain this is obvious to you. With minds concentrated on space, there is neglect of the proper development of things earthly. I am preparing a thesis now for submission to the Council recommending that Realities be changed to eliminate all space-travel eras as a matter of course."

Rice's treble sounded. "But you can't be that drastic. Space-travel is a valuable safety-valve in some civilizations. Take Reality 54 of the 290th, which I happen to recall offhand. Now there——"

The voices cut off and Twissell said, "A strange man, Sennor. Intellectually, he's worth two of any of the rest of us, but his worth is lost in leapfrog enthusiasms."

Harlan said, "Do you suppose he can be right? About space-travel, I mean."

"I doubt it. We'd have a better chance of judging if Sennor would actually submit the thesis he mentioned. But he won't. He'll have a new enthusiasm before he's finished and drop the old. But never mind——" He brought the flat of his hand against the sphere so that it rang resoundingly, then brought his hand back so that he could remove a cigarette from his lip. He said, "Can you guess what this is, Technician?"

Harlan said, "It looks like an outsize kettle with a top."

"Exactly. You're right. You've got it. Come on inside."

Harlan followed Twissell into the sphere. It was large enough to hold four or five men, but the interior was absolutely featureless. The floor was smooth, the curved wall was broken by two windows. That was all.

"No controls?" asked Harlan.

"Remote controls," said Twissell. He ran his hand over the smoothness of the wall and said, "Double walls. The entire interwall volume is given over to a self-contained Temporal Field. This instrument is a kettle that is not restricted to the kettle shafts but can pass beyond the downwhen terminus of Eternity. Its design and construction were made possible by valuable hints in the Mallansohn memoir. Come with me."

The control room was a cut-off corner of the large room. Harlan stepped in and stared somberly at immense bus bars.

Twissell said, "Can you hear me, boy?"

Harlan started and looked about. He had not been aware that Twissell had not followed him inside. He stepped automatically to the window and Twissell waved to him. Harlan said, "I can hear you, sir. Do you want me outside?"

"Not at all. You are locked in."

Harlan sprang to the door and his stomach turned into a series of cold, wet knots. Twissell was correct and what in Time was going on?

Twissell said, "You will be relieved to know, boy, that your responsibility is over. You were worried about that responsibility; you asked searching questions about it; and I think I know what you meant. This should not be your responsibility. It is mine alone. Unfortunately, we must have you in the control room, since it is stated that you were there and handled the controls. It is stated in the Mallansohn memoir. Cooper will see you through the window and that will take care of that.

"Furthermore, I will ask you to make the final contact according to instructions I will give you. If you feel that that, too, is too great a responsibility, you may relax. Another contact in parallel with yours is in charge of another man. If, for any reason, you are unable to operate the contact, he will do so. Furthermore, I will cut off radio transmission from within the control room. You will be able to hear us but not to speak to us. You need not fear, therefore, that some involuntary exclamation from you will break the circle."

Harlan stared helplessly out the window.

Twissell went on, "Cooper will be here in moments and his trip to the Primitive will take place within two physiohours. After that, boy, the project will be over and you and I will be free."

Harlan was plunging chokingly through the vortex of a waking nightmare. Had Twissell tricked him? Had everything he had done been designed only to get Harlan quietly into a locked control room? Having learned that Harlan knew his own importance, had he improvised with diabolical cleverness, keeping him engaged in conversation, drugging his emotions with words, leading him here, leading him there, until the time was ripe for locking him in?

That quick and easy surrender over Noÿs. She won't be hurt, Twissell had said. All will be well.

How could he have believed that! If they were not going to harm her, or touch her, why the temporal barrier across the kettleways at the 100,000th? That alone should have given Twissell completely away.

But because he (fool!) wanted to believe, he allowed himself to be led through those last physiohours blindly, placed inside a locked room where he was no longer needed, even to close the final contact.

In one stroke he had been robbed of his essentiality. The trumps in his hand had been neatly maneuvered into deuces and Noÿs was out of his reach forever. What punishment might lie in wait for him did not concern him. Noÿs was out of his reach forever.

It had never occurred to him that the project would be so close to its end. That, of course, was what had really made his defeat possible.

Twissell's voice sounded dimly. "You'll be cut off now, boy."

Harlan was alone, helpless, useless. . . .

Thirteen: BEYOND THE DOWNWHEN TERMINUS

Brinsley Cooper entered. Excitement flushed his thin face and made it almost youthful, despite the heavy Mallansohn mustache that draped its upper lip.

(Harlan could see him through the window, hear him clearly over the room's radio. He thought bitterly: A Mallansohn mustache! Of course!)

Cooper strode toward Twissell. "They wouldn't let me in till now, Computer."

"Very right," said Twissell. "They had their instructions."

"Now's the time, though? I'll be heading out?"

"Almost the time."

"And I'll be coming back? I'll be seeing Eternity again?" Despite the straightness Cooper gave his back, there was an edge of uncertainty in his voice.

(Within the control room Harlan brought his clenched hands bitterly to the reinforced glass of the window, longing to break through somehow, to shout: "Stop it! Meet my terms, or I'll—" What was the use?)

Cooper looked about the room, apparently unaware that Twissell had refrained from answering his question. His glance fell on Harlan at the control-room window.

He waved his hand excitedly. "Technician Harlan! Come on out. I want to shake your hand before I go."

Twissell interposed. "Not now, boy, not now. He's at the controls."

Cooper said, "Oh? You know, he doesn't look well."

Twissell said, "I've been telling him the true nature of the project. I'm afraid that's enough to make anyone nervous."

Cooper said, "Great Time, yes! I've known about it for weeks now and I'm not used to it yet." There was a trace of near-hysteria in his laugh. "I still haven't got it through my thick head that it is really my show. I—I'm a little scared."

"I scarcely blame you for that."

"It's my stomach, mostly, you know. It's the least happy part of me."

Twissell said, "Well, it's very natural and it will pass. Meanwhile, your time of departure on Standard Intertemporal has been set and there is still a certain amount of orientation to be gone through. For instance, you haven't actually seen the kettle you will use."

In the two hours that passed Harlan heard it all, whether they were in sight or not. Twissell lectured Cooper in an oddly stilted manner, and Harlan knew the reason. Cooper was being informed of just those things that he was to mention in Mallansohn's memoir.

(Full circle. Full circle. And no way for Harlan to break that circle in one, last defiant Samson-smash of the temple. —round and round the circle goes; round and round it goes.)

"Ordinary kettles," he heard Twissell say, "are both pushed and pulled, if we can use such terms in the case of Intertemporal forces. In traveling from Century X to Century Y within Eternity there is a fully powered initial point and a fully powered final point.

"What we have here is a kettle with a powered initial point but an unpowered destination point. It can only be pushed, not pulled. For that reason, it must utilize energies at a level whole orders of magnitude higher than those used by ordinary kettles. Special power-transfer units have had to be laid down along the kettleways to siphon in sufficient concentrations of energy from Nova Sol.

"This special kettle, its controls and power supply, are a composite structure. For physiodecades, the passing Realities have been combed for special alloys and special techniques. The 13th Reality of the 222nd was the key. It developed the Temporal Pressor and without that, this kettle could not have been built. The 13th Reality of the 222nd."

He pronounced that with elaborate distinctness.

(Harlan thought: Remember that, Cooper! Remember the 13th Reality of the 222nd so you can put it into the Mallansohn memoir so that the Eternals will know where to look so they will know what to tell you so you can put it. . . . Round and round the circle goes. . . .)

Twissell said, "The kettle has not been tested past the downwhen terminus, of course, but it has taken numerous trips within Eternity. We are convinced there will be no bad effects."

"There can't be, can there?" said Cooper. "I mean I did get there or Mallansohn could not have succeeded in building the field and he *did* succeed."

Twissell said, "Exactly. You will find yourself in a protected and isolated spot in the sparsely populated southwestern area of the United States of Amellika——"

"America," corrected Cooper.

"America, then. The Century will be the 24th; or, to put it to nearest hundredth, the 23.17th. I suppose we can even call it the year 2317, if we wish. The kettle, as you saw, is large, much larger than necessary for you. It is being filled now with food, water, and the means of shelter and defense. You will have detailed instructions that will, of course, be meaningless to anyone but you. I must impress upon you now that your first task will be to make certain that none of the indigenous inhabitants discovers you before you are ready for them. You will have force-diggers with which you will be able to burrow well into a mountain to form a cache. You will have to remove the contents of the kettle rapidly. They will be stacked so as to facilitate that."

(Harlan thought: Repeat! Repeat! He must have been told all this before, but repeat what must go into the memoir. Round and round . . .)

Twissell said, "You will have to unload in fifteen minutes. After that, the kettle will return automatically to starting point, carrying with it all tools that are too advanced for the Century. You will have a list of those. After the kettle returns, you will be on your own."

Cooper said, "Must the kettle return so quickly?"

Twissell said, "A quick return increases the probabilities of success."

(Harlan thought: The kettle *must* return in fifteen minutes because it *did* return in fifteen minutes. Round and . . .)

Twissell hurried on. "We cannot attempt to counterfeit their medium of exchange of any of their negotiable scrip. You will have gold in the form of small nuggets. You will be able to explain its possession according to your detailed instructions. You will have native clothing to wear or at least clothing that will pass for native."

"Right," said Cooper.

"Now, remember. Move slowly. Take weeks, if necessary. Work your way into the era, spiritually. Technician Harlan's instructions are a good basis but they are not enough. You will have a wireless receiver built on the principles of the 24th which will enable you to come abreast of the current events and, more important, learn the proper pronunciation and intonation of the language of the times. Do that thoroughly. I'm sure that Harlan's knowledge of English is excellent, but nothing can substitute for native pronunciation on the spot."

Cooper said, "What if I don't end up in the right spot? I mean, not in the 23.17?"

"Check on that very carefully, of course. But it will be right. It will be right."

(Harlan thought: It will be right because it was right. Round . . .)

Cooper must have looked unconvinced, though, for Twissell said, "The accuracy of focus was carefully worked out. I intended to explain our methods and now is a good time. For one thing, it will help Harlan understand the controls."

(Suddenly Harlan turned away from the windows and fixed his gaze on the controls. A corner of the curtain of despair lifted. What if—)

Twissell still lectured Cooper with the anxious overprecise tone of the schoolteacher, and with part of his mind Harlan still listened.

Twissell said, "Obviously a serious problem was that of determining how far into the Primitive an object is sent after the application of a given energy thrust. The most direct method would have been to send a man into the downwhen via this kettle using carefully graduated thrust levels. To do that, however, would have meant a certain lapse of time in each case while the man determined the Century to its nearest hundredth through astronomical observation or by obtaining appropriate information over the wireless. That would be slow and also dangerous since the man might well be discovered by the native inhabitants with probably catastrophic effects on our project.

"What we did then instead was this: We sent back a known mass of the radioactive isotope, niobium-94, which decays by beta-particle emission to the stable isotope, molybdenum-94. The process has a half-life of almost exactly 500 Centuries. The original radiation intensity of the mass was known. That intensity decreases with time according to the simple relationship involved in first-order kinetics, and, of course, the intensity can be measured with great precision.

"When the kettle reaches its destination in Primitive times, the ampule containing the isotope is discharged into the mountainside and the kettle then returns to Eternity. At the moment in physiotime that the ampule is discharged, it simultaneously appears at all future Times growing progressively older. At the place of discharge in the 575th (in actual Time and not in Eternity) a Technician detects the ampule by its radiation and retrieves it.

"The radiation intensity is measured, the time it has remained in the mountainside is then known, the Century to which the kettle traveled is also known to two decimal places. Dozens of ampules were thus sent back at various thrust levels and a calibration curve set up. The curve was a check against ampules sent not all the way into the Primitive but into the early Centuries of Eternity where direct observations could also be made.

"Naturally, there were failures. The first few ampules were lost until we learned to allow for the not too major geological changes between the late Primitive and the 575th. Then, three of the ampules later on never showed up in the 575th. Presumably, something went wrong with the discharge mechanism and they were buried too deeply in the mountain for detection. We stopped our experiments when the level of radiation grew so high that we feared that some of the Primitive inhabitants might detect and wonder what radioactive artifacts might be doing in the region. But we had enough for our purposes and we are certain we can send back a man to any hundredth of a Century of the Primitive that is desired.

"You follow all this, Cooper, don't you?"

Cooper said, "Perfectly, Computer Twissell. I have seen the calibration curve without understanding the purpose at the time. It is quite clear now."

But Harlan was exceedingly interested now. He stared at the measured arc marked off in centuries. The shining arc was porcelain on metal and the fine lines divided it into Centuries, Decicenturies and Centicenturies. Silvery metal gleamed thinly through the porcelain-penetrating lines, marking them clearly. The figures were as finely done and, bending close, Harlan could make out the Centuries from 17 to 27. The hairline was fixed at the 23.17th Century mark.

He had seen similar time-gauges and almost automatically he reached to the pressure-control lever. It did not respond to his grasp. The hairline remained in place.

He nearly jumped when Twissell's voice suddenly addressed him. "Technician Harlan!"

He cried, "Yes, Computer," then remembered that he could not be heard. He stepped to the window and nodded.

Twissell said, almost as though chiming in with Harlan's thoughts, "The time-gauge is set for a thrust back to the 23.17th. That requires no adjustment. Your only task is to pour energy through at the proper moment in physiotime. There is a chronometer to the right of the gauge. Nod if you see it."

Harlan nodded.

"It will reach zero-point backward. At the minus-fifteen-second point, align the contact points. It's simple. You see how?"

Harlan nodded again.

Twissell went on, "Synchronization is not vital. You can do it at minus fourteen or thirteen or even minus five seconds, but please make every effort to stay this side of minus ten for safety's sake. Once you've closed contact, a synchronized force-gear will do the rest and make certain that the final energy thrust will occur precisely at time zero. Understood?"

Harlan nodded still again. He understood more than Twissell said. If he himself did not align the points by minus ten, it would be taken care of from without.

Harlan thought grimly: There'll be no need for outsiders.

Twissell said, "We have thirty physiominutes left. Cooper and I will leave to check on the supplies."

They left. The door closed behind them, and Harlan was left alone with the thrust control, the time (already moving slowly backward toward zero)—and a resolute knowledge of what must be done.

Harlan turned away from the window. He put his hand inside his pocket and half withdrew the neuronic whip it still contained. Through all this he had kept the whip. His hand shook a little.

An earlier thought recurred: a Samson-smash of the temple!

A corner of his mind wondered sickly: How many Eternals have ever heard of Samson? How many know how he died?

There were only twenty-five minutes left. He was not certain how long the operation would take. He was not really certain it would work at all.

But what choice had he? His damp fingers almost dropped the weapon before he succeeded in unhinging the butt.

He worked rapidly and in complete absorption. Of all the aspects of what he planned, the possibility of his own passage into non-existence occupied his mind the least and bothered him not at all.

At minus one minute Harlan was standing at the controls.

Detachedly he thought: The last minute of life?

Nothing in the room was visible to him but the backward sweep of the red hairline that marked the passing seconds.

Minus thirty seconds.

He thought: It will not hurt. It is not death.

He tried to think only of Noÿs.

Minus fifteen seconds.

Noÿs!

Harlan's left hand moved a switch down toward contact. Not hastily!

Minus twelve seconds.

Contact!

The force-gear would take over now. Thrust would come at zero time. And that left Harlan one last manipulation. The Samson-smash!

His right hand moved. He did not look at his right hand.

Minus five seconds.

Noÿs!

His right hand mo—ZERO—ved again, spasmodically. He did not look at it.

Was this nonexistence?

Not yet. Nonexistence not yet.

Harlan stared out the window. He did not move. Time passed and he was unaware of its passage.

The room was empty. Where the giant, enclosed kettle had been was nothing. Metal blocks that had served as its base sat emptily, lifting their huge strength against air.

Twissell, strangely small and dwarfed in the room that had become a waiting cavern, was the only thing that moved as he tramped edgily this way and that.

Harlan's eyes followed him for a moment and then left him.

Then, without any sound or stir, the kettle was back in the spot it had left. Its passage across the hairline from time past to time present did not as much as disturb a molecule of air.

Twissell was hidden from Harlan's eyes by the bulk of the kettle, but then he rounded it, came into view. He was running.

A flick of his hand was enough to activate the mechanism that opened the door of the control room. He hurtled inside, shouting with an almost lyrical excitement. "It's done. It's done. We've closed the circle." He had breath to say no more.

Harlan made no answer.

Twissell stared out the window, his hands flat against the glass. Harlan noted the blotches of age upon them and the way in which they trembled. It was as though his mind no longer had the ability or the strength to filter the important from the inconsequential, but were selecting observational material in a purely random manner.

Wearily he thought: What does it matter? What does anything matter now?

Twissell said (Harlan heard him dimly), "I'll tell you now that I've been more anxious than I cared to admit. Sennor used to say once that this whole thing was impossible. He insisted something must happen to stop it—— What's the matter?"

He had turned at Harlan's odd grunt.

Harlan shook his head, managed a choked "Nothing."

Twissell left it at that and turned away. It was doubtful whether he spoke to Harlan or to the air. It was as though he were allowing years of pent-up anxieties to escape in words.

"Sennor," he said, "was the doubter. We reasoned with him and argued. We used mathematics and presented the results of generations of research that had preceded us in the physiotime of Eternity. He put it all to one side and presented his case by quoting the man-meets-himself paradox. You heard him talk about it. It's his favorite.

"We knew our own future, Sennor said. I, Twissell, knew, for instance, that I would survive, despite the fact that I would be quite old, until Cooper made his trip past the downwhen terminus. I knew other details of my future, the things I would do.

"Impossible, he would say. Reality must change to correct your knowledge, even if it meant the circle would never close and Eternity never established.

"Why he argued so, I don't know. Perhaps he honestly believed it, perhaps it was an intellectual game with him, perhaps it was just the desire to shock the rest of us with an unpopular viewpoint. In any case, the project proceeded and some of the memoir began to be fulfilled. We located Cooper, for instance, in the Century and Reality that the memoir gave us. Sennor's case was exploded by that alone, but it didn't bother him. By that time, he had grown interested in something else.

"And yet, and yet"—he laughed gently, with more than a trace of embarrassment, and let his cigarette, unnoticed, burn down nearly to his fingers—"you know I was never quite easy in my mind. Something *might* happen. The Reality in which Eternity was established *might* change in some way in order to prevent what Sennor called a paradox. It would have to change to one in which Eternity would not exist. Sometimes, in the dark of a sleeping period, when I couldn't sleep, I could almost persuade myself that that was indeed so.—and now it's all over and I laugh at myself as a senile fool."

Harlan said in a low voice, "Computer Sennor was right."

Twissell whirled. "What?"

"The project failed." Harlan's mind was coming out of the shadows (why, and into what, he was not sure). "The circle is not complete."

"What are you talking about?" Twissell's old hands fell on Harlan's shoulders with surprising strength. "You're ill, boy. The strain."

"Not ill. Sick of everything. You. Me. Not ill. The gauge. See for yourself."

"The gauge?" The hairline on the gauge stood at the 27th Century, hard against the right-hand extreme. "What happened?" The joy was gone from his face. Horror replaced it.

Harlan grew matter-of-fact. "I melted the locking mechanism, freed the thrust control."

"How could you——"

"I had a neuronic whip. I broke it open and used its micro-pile energy source in one flash, like a torch. There's what's left of it." He kicked at a small heap of metal fragments in one corner.

Twissell wasn't taking it in. "In the 27th? You mean Cooper's in the 27th——"

"I don't know where he is," said Harlan dully. "I shifted the thrust control downwhen, further down than the 24th. I don't know where. I didn't look. Then I brought it back. I still didn't look."

Twissell stared at him, his face a pale, unhealthy yellowish color, his lower lip trembling.

"I don't know where he is now," said Harlan. "He's lost in the Primitive. The circle is broken. I thought everything would end when I made the stroke. At zero time. That's silly. We've got to wait. There'll be a moment in physiotime when Cooper will realize he's in the wrong century, when he'll do something against the memoir, when he——" He broke off, then broke into a forced and creaky laughter. "What's the difference? It's only a delay till Cooper makes the final break in the circle. There's no way of stopping it. Minutes, hours, days. What's the difference? When the delay is done, there will be no more Eternity. Do you hear me? It will be the end of Eternity."

Fourteen: THE EARLIER CRIME

"Why? Why?"

Twissell looked helplessly from the gauge to the Technician, his eyes mirroring the puzzled frustration in his voice.

Harlan lifted his head. He had only one word to say. "Noÿs!"

Twissell said, "The woman you took into Eternity?"

Harlan smiled bitterly, said nothing.

Twissell said, "What has she to do with this? Great Time, I don't understand, boy."

"What is there to understand?" Harlan burned with sorrow. "Why do you pretend ignorance? I had a woman. I was happy and so was she. We harmed no one. She did not exist in the new Reality. What difference would it have made to anyone?"

Twissell tried vainly to interrupt.

Harlan shouted. "But there are rules in Eternity, aren't there? I know them all. Liaisons require permission; liaisons require computations; liaisons require status; liaisons are tricky things. What were you planning for Noÿs when all this was over? A seat in a crashing rocket? Or a more comfortable position as community mistress for worthy Computers? You won't make any plans *now*, I think."

He ended in a kind of despair and Twissell moved quickly to the Communiplate. Its function as a transmitter had obviously been restored.

The Computer shouted into it till he aroused an answer. Then he said, "This is Twissell. No one is to be allowed in here. No one. No one. Do you understand? . . . Then see to it. It goes for members of the Allwhen Council. It goes for them particularly."

He turned back to Harlan, saying abstractedly, "They'll do it because I'm old and senior member of the Council and because they think I'm cranky and queer. They give in to me because I'm cranky and queer." For a moment he fell into a ruminative silence. Then he said, "Do you think I'm queer?" and his face turned swiftly up to Harlan's like that of a seamed monkey.

Harlan thought: Great Time, the man's mad. The shock has driven him mad.

He took a step backward, automatically aghast at being trapped with a madman. Then he steadied. The man, be he ever so mad, was feeble, and even madness would end soon.

Soon? Why not at once? What delayed the end of Eternity?

Twissell said (he had no cigarette in his fingers; his hand made no move to take one) in a quiet insinuating voice, "You haven't answered me. *Do* you think I'm queer? I suppose you do. Too queer to talk to. If you had thought of me as a friend instead of as a crotchety old man, whimsical and unpredictable, you would have spoken openly to me of your doubts. You would have taken no such action as you did."

Harlan frowned. The man thought *Harlan* was mad. That was it!

He said angrily, "My action was the right one. I'm quite sane."

Twissell said, "I told you the girl was in no danger, you know."

"I was a fool to believe that even for a while. I was a fool to believe the Council would be just to a Technician."

"Who told you the Council knew of any of this?"

"Finge knew of it and sent in a report concerning it to the Council."

"And how do you know that?"

"I got it out of Finge at the point of a neuronic whip. The business end of a whip abolishes comparative status."

"The same whip that did this?" Twissell pointed to the gauge with its blob of molten metal perched wryly above the face of the dial.

"Yes."

"A busy whip." Then, sharply, "Do you know why Finge took it to the Council instead of handling the matter himself?"

"Because he hated me and wanted to make certain I lost all status. He wanted Noÿs."

Twissell said, "You're naïve! If he had wanted the girl, he could easily have arranged liaison. A Technician would not have been in the way. The man hated *me*, boy." (Still no cigarette. He looked odd without one and the stained finger he lay on his chest as he spoke the last pronoun looked almost indecently bare.)

"You?"

"There's such a thing, boy, as Council politics. Not every Computer is appointed to the Council. Finge wanted an appointment. Finge is ambitious and wanted it badly. I blocked it because I thought him emotionally unstable. Time, I never fully appreciated how right I was. . . . Look, boy. He knew you were a protégé of mine. He had seen me take you out of a job as an Observer and make you a master Technician. He saw you working for me steadily. How better could he get back at me and destroy my influence? If he could prove my pet Technician guilty of a terrible crime against Eternity, it would reflect on me. It might force my resignation from the Allwhen Council, and who do you suppose would then be a logical successor?"

His empty hands moved to his lips and when nothing happened, he looked at the space between finger and thumb blankly.

Harlan thought: He's not as calm as he's trying to sound. He can't be. But why does he talk all this nonsense *now?* With Eternity ending?

Then in agony: But why doesn't it *end* then? Now!

Twissell said, "When I allowed you to go to Finge just recently, I more than half suspected danger. But Mallansohn's memoir *said* you were away the last month and no other natural reason for your absence offered itself. Fortunately, Finge underplayed his hand."

"In what way?" asked Harlan wearily. He didn't really care, but Twissell talked and talked and it was easier to take part than to try to shut the sound out of his ears.

Twissell said, "Finge labeled his report: '*In re* unprofessional conduct of Technician Andrew Harlan.' He was being the faithful Eternal, you see, being cool, impartial, unexcited. He was leaving it to the Council to rage and throw itself at me. Unfortunately for himself, he did not know of your real importance. He did not realize that any report concerning you would be instantly referred to me, unless its supreme importance were made perfectly clear on the very face of things."

"You never spoke to me of this?"

"How could I? I was afraid to do anything that would disturb you with the crisis of the project at hand. I gave you every opportunity to bring your problem to me."

Every opportunity? Harlan's mouth twisted in disbelief, but then he thought of Twissell's weary face on the Communiplate asking him if he had nothing to say to him. That was yesterday. Only yesterday.

Harlan shook his head, but turned his face away now.

Twissell said softly, "I realized at once that he had deliberately goaded you into your—rash action."

Harlan looked up. "You know that?"

"Does that surprise you? I knew Finge was after my neck. I've known it for a long time. I am an old man, boy. I know these things. But there are ways in which doubtful Computers can be checked upon. There are some protective devices, culled out of Time, that are not placed in the museums. There are some that are known to the Council alone."

Harlan thought bitterly of the time-block at the 100,000th.

"From the report and from what I knew independently, it was easy to deduce what must have happened."

Harlan asked suddenly, "I suppose Finge suspected you of spying?"

"He might have. I wouldn't be surprised."

Harlan thought back to his first days with Finge when Twissell first showed his abnormal interest in the young Observer. Finge had known nothing of the Mallansohn project, and he had been interested in Twissell's interference. "Have you ever met Senior Computer Twissell?" he had once asked and, thinking back, Harlan could recall the exact tone of sharp uneasiness in the man's voice. As early as that Finge must have suspected Harlan of being Twissell's finger-man. His enmity and hate must have begun that early.

Twissell was speaking, "So if you had come to me——"

"Come to *you?*" cried Harlan. "What of the Council?"

"Of the entire Council, only I know."

"You never told them?" Harlan tried to be mocking.

"I never did."

Harlan felt feverish. His clothes were choking him. Was this nightmare to go on forever. Foolish, irrelevant chatter! *For what? Why?*

Why didn't Eternity end? Why didn't the clean peace of non-Reality reach out for them? *Great Time, what was wrong?*

Twissell said, "Don't you believe me?"

Harlan shouted, "Why should I? They came to look at me, didn't they? At that breakfast? Why should they have done that if they didn't know of the report? They came to look at the queer phenomenon who had broken the laws of Eternity but who couldn't be touched for one more day. One more day and then the project would be over. They came to gloat for the tomorrow they were expecting."

"My boy, there was nothing of that. They wanted to see you only because they were human. Councilmen are human too. They could not witness the final kettle drive because the Mallansohn memoir did not place them at the scene. They could not interview Cooper since the memoir made no mention of that either. Yet they wanted something. Father Time, boy, don't you see they would want something? You were as close as they could get, so they brought you close and stared at you."

"I don't believe you."

"It's the truth."

Harlan said, "Is it? And while we ate, Councilman Sennor talked of a man meeting himself. He obviously knew about my illegal trips into the 482nd and my nearly meeting myself. It was his way of poking at me, enjoying himself cutely at my expense."

Twissell said, "Sennor? You worried about Sennor? Do you know the pathetic figure he is? His homewhen is the 803rd, one of the few cultures in which the human body is deliberately disfigured to meet the aesthetic requirements of the time. It is rendered hairless at adolescence.

"Do you know what that means in the continuity of man? Surely you do. A disfigurement sets men apart from their ancestors and descendants. Men of the 803rd are poor risks as Eternals; they are too different from the rest of us. Few are chosen. Sennor is the only one of his Century ever to sit on the Council.

"Don't you see how that affects him? Surely you understand what insecurity means. Did it ever occur to you that a Councilman could be insecure? Sennor has to listen to discussions involving the eradication of his Reality for the very characteristic that makes him so conspicuous among us. And eradicating it would leave him one of a very few in all the generation to be disfigured as he is. Someday it will happen.

"He finds refuge in philosophy. He overcompensates by taking the lead in conversation, by deliberately airing unpopular or unaccepted viewpoints. His man-meeting-himself paradox is a case in point. I told you that he used it to predict disaster for the project and it was we, the Councilmen, that he was attempting to annoy, not you. It had nothing to do with you. Nothing!"

Twissell had grown heated. In the long emotion of his words he seemed to forget where he was and the crisis that faced them, for he slipped back into the quick-gestured, uneasily motioned gnome that Harlan knew so well. He even slipped a cigarette from his sleeve pouch and had all but frictioned it into combustion.

But then he stopped, wheeled, and looked at Harlan again, reaching back through all his own words to what Harlan had last said, as though until that moment, he had not heart them properly.

He said, "What do you mean, you almost met yourself?"

Harlan told him briefly and went on, "You didn't know that?"

"No."

There were a few moments of silence that were as welcome to the feverish Harlan as water would have been.

Twissell said, "Is that it? What if you *had* met yourself?"

"I didn't."

Twissell ignored that. "There is always room for random variation. With an infinite number of Realities there can be no such thing as determinism. Suppose that in the Mallansohn Reality, in the previous turn of the cycle——"

"The circle goes on forever?" asked Harlan with what wonder he could still find in himself.

"Do you think only twice? Do you think two is a magic number? It's a matter of infinite turns of the circle in finite physiotime. Just as you can draw a pencil round and round the circumference of a circle infinitely yet enclose a finite area. In previous turns of the cycle, you had not met yourself. This one time, the statistical uncertainty of things made it possible for you to meet yourself. Reality had to change to prevent the meeting and in the new Reality, you did not send Cooper back to the 24th but——"

Harlan cried, "What's all this talk about? What are you getting at? It's all done. Everything. Let me alone now! *Let me alone!*"

"I want you to know you've done wrong. I want you to realize you did the wrong thing."

"I didn't. And even if I did, *it's done.*"

"But it is *not* done. Listen just a little while longer." Twissell was wheedling, almost crooning with an agonized gentleness. "You will have your girl. I promised that. I still promise it. She will not be harmed. You will not be harmed. I promise you this. It is my personal guarantee."

Harlan stared at him wide-eyed. "But it's too late. What's the use?"

"It is *not* too late. Things are *not* irreparable. With your help, we can succeed yet. I must have your help. You must realize that you did wrong. I am trying to explain this to you. You must want to undo what you have done."

Harlan licked his dry lips with a dry tongue and thought: He *is* mad. His mind can't accept the truth. —or, does the Council know more?

Did it? Did it? Could it reverse the verdict of the Changes? Could they halt Time or reverse it?

He said, "You locked me in the control room, kept me helpless, you thought, till it was all over."

"You said you were afraid something might go wrong with you; that you might not be able to carry on with your part."

"That was meant to be a threat."

"I took it literally. Forgive me. I must have your help."

It came to that. Harlan's help must be had. Was he mad? Was Harlan mad? Did madness have meaning? Or anything at all, for that matter?

The Council needed his help. For that help they would promise him anything. Noÿs. Computership. What would they not promise him? And when his help was done with, what would he get? He would not be fooled a second time.

"No!" he said.

"You'll have Noÿs."

"You mean the Council will be willing to break the laws of Eternity once the danger is safely gone? I don't believe it." How could the danger safely be passed, a sane scrap of his mind demanded. What was this all about?

"The Council will never know."

"Would *you* be willing to break the laws? You're the ideal Eternal. With the danger gone, you would obey the law. You couldn't act otherwise."

Twissell reddened blotchily, high on each cheekbone. From the old face all shrewdness and strength drained away. There was left only a strange sorrow.

"I will keep my word to you and break the law," said Twissell, "for a reason you don't imagine. I don't know how much time is left us before Eternity disappears. It could be hours; it could be months. But I have spent so much time in the hope of bringing you to reason that I will spend a little more. Will you listen to me? Please?"

Harlan hesitated. Then, out of a conviction of the uselessness of all things as much as out of anything else said wearily, "Go on."

I have heard (began Twissell) that I was born old, that I cut my teeth on a Micro-Computaplex, that I keep my hand computer in a special pocket of my pajamas when I sleep, that my brain is made up of little force-relays in endless parallel hookups and that each corpuscle of my blood is a microscopic spatio-temporal chart floating in computer oil.

All these stories come to me eventually, and I think I must be a little proud of them. Maybe I go around believing them a bit. It's a foolish thing for an old man to do, but it makes life a little easier.

Does that surprise you? That I must find a way to make life easier? I, Senior Computer Twissell, senior member of the Allwhen Council?

Maybe that's why I smoke. Ever think of that? I have to have a reason, you know. Eternity is essentially an unsmoking society, and most of Time is, too. I've thought of that often. I sometimes think it's a rebellion against Eternity. Something to take the place of a greater rebellion that failed . . .

No, it's all right. A tear or two won't hurt me, and it isn't pretense, believe me. It's just that I haven't thought about this for a long time. It isn't pleasant.

It involved a woman, of course, as your affair did. That's not coincidence. It's almost inevitable, if you stop to think of it. An Eternal, who must sell the normal satisfactions of family life for a handful of perforations on foil, is ripe for infection. That's one of the reasons Eternity must take the precautions it does. And, apparently, that's also why Eternals are so ingenious in evading the precautions once in a while.

I remember my woman. It's foolish of me to do so, perhaps. I can't remember anything else about that physiotime. My old colleagues are only names in the record books; the Changes I supervised —all but one—are only items in the Computaplex memory pools. I remember her, though, very well. Perhaps you can understand that.

I had had a long-standing request for liaison in the books; and after I achieved status as a Junior Computer, she was assigned to me. She was a girl of this very Century, the 575th. I didn't see her until after the assignment, of course. She was intelligent and kind. Not beautiful or even pretty, but then, even when young (yes, I was young, never mind the myths) I was not noted for my own looks. We were well suited to one another by temperament, she and I, and if I were a Timed man, I would have been proud to have her as my wife. I told her that many times. I believe it pleased her. I know it was the truth. Not all Eternals, who must take their women as and how Computing permits, are that fortunate.

In that particular Reality, she was to die young, of course, and none of her analogues was available for liaison. At first, I took that philosophically. After all, it was her short lifetime which made it possible for her to live with me without deleteriously affecting Reality.

I am ashamed of that now, of the fact that I was glad she had a short time to live. Just at first, that is. Just at first.

I visited her as often as spatio-temporal charting allowed. I squeezed every minute out of it, giving up meals and sleep when necessary, shifting my labor load shamelessly whenever I could. Her amiability passed the heights of my expectations, and I was in love. I put it bluntly. My experience of love is very small, and understanding it through Observation in Time is a shaky matter. As far as my understanding went, however, I was in love.

What began as the satisfaction of an emotional and physical need became a great deal more. Her imminent death stopped being a convenience and became a calamity. I Life-Plotted her. I didn't go to the Life-Plotting departments, either. I did it myself. That surprises you, I imagine. It was a misdemeanor, but it was nothing compared to the crimes I committed later.

Yes, I, Laban Twissell. Senior Computer Twissell.

Three separate times, a point in physiotime came and passed, during which some simple action of my own might have altered her personal Reality. Naturally, I knew that no such personally motivated Change could possibly be authorized by the Council. Still, I began to feel personally responsible for her death. That was part of my motivation later on, you see.

She became pregnant. I took no action, though I should have. I had worked her Life-Plot, modified to include her relationship with me, and I knew pregnancy to be a high-probability consequence. As you may or may not know, Timed women are occasionally made pregnant by Eternals despite precautions. It is not unheard of. Still, since no Eternal may have a child, such pregnancies as do occur are ended painlessly and safely. There are many methods.

My Life-Plotting had indicated she would die before delivery, so I took no precautions. She was happy in her pregnancy and I wanted her to remain so. So I only watched and tried to smile when she told me she could feel life stirring within her.

But then something happened. She gave birth prematurely——

I don't wonder you look that way. I had a child. A real child of my own. You'll find no other Eternal, perhaps, who can say that. That was more than a misdemeanor. That was a serious felony, but it was still nothing.

I hadn't expected it. Birth and its problems were an aspect of life with which I had had little experience.

I went back to the Life-Plot in panic and found the living child, in an alternate solution to a low-probability forklet I had overlooked. A professional Life-Plotter would not have overlooked it and I had done wrong to trust my own abilities that far.

But what could I do now?

I couldn't kill the child. The mother had two weeks to live. Let the child live with her till then, I thought. Two weeks of happiness is not an exorbitant gift to ask.

The mother died, as foreseen, and in the manner foreseen. I sat in her room, for all the time permitted by the spatio-temporal chart, aching with a sorrow all the keener for my having waited for death, in full knowledge, for over a year. In my arms, I held my son and hers.

—Yes, I let it live. Why do you cry out so? Are *you* going to condemn me?

You cannot know what it means to hold a little atom of your own life in your arms. I may have a Computaplex for nerves and spatio-temporal charts for a bloodstream, but I do know.

I let it live. I committed that crime, too. I put it in the charge of an appropriate organization and returned when I could (in strict temporal sequence, held even with physiotime) to make necessary payments and to watch the boy grow.

Two years went by that way. Periodically, I checked the boy's Life-Plot (I was used to breaking that particular rule, by now) and was pleased to find that there were no signs of deleterious effects on the then-current Reality at probability levels over 0.0001. The boy learned to walk and mispronounced a few words. He was not taught to call me "daddy." Whatever speculations the Timed people of the child-care institution might have made concerning me I don't know. They took their money and said nothing.

Then, when the two years had passed, the necessities of a Change that included the 575th at one wing was brought up before the All-when Council. I, having been lately promoted to Assistant Computer, was placed in charge. It was the first Change ever left to my sole supervision.

I was proud, of course, but also apprehensive. My son was an intruder in the Reality. He could scarcely be expected to have analogues. Thought of his passage into nonexistence saddened me.

I worked at the Change and I flatter myself even yet that I did a flawless job. My first one. But I succumbed to a temptation. I succumbed to it all the more easily because it was becoming an old story now for me. I was a hardened criminal, a habitué of crime. I worked out a new Life-Plot for my son under the new Reality, certain of what I would find.

But then for twenty-four hours, without eating or sleeping, I sat in my office, striving with the completed Life-Plot, tearing at it in a despairing effort to find an error.

There was no error.

The next day, holding back my solution to the Change, I worked out a spatio-temporal chart, using rough methods of approximation (after all, the Reality was not to last long) and entered Time at a point more than thirty years upwhen from the birth of my child.

He was thirty-four years old, as old as I myself. I introduced myself as a distant relation, making use of my knowledge of his mother's family, to do so. He had no knowledge of his father, no memory of my visits to him in his infancy.

He was an aeronautical engineer. The 575th was expert in half a dozen varieties of air travel (as it still is in the current Reality), and my son was a happy and successful member of his society. He was married to an ardently enamored girl, but would have no children. Nor would the girl have married at all in the Reality in which my son had not existed. I had known that from the beginning. I had known there would be no deleterious effect on Reality. Otherwise, I might not have found it in my heart to let the boy live. I am not *completely* abandoned.

I spent the day with my son. I spoke to him formally, smiled politely, took my leave coolly when the spatio-temporal chart dictated.

But underneath all that, I watched and absorbed every action, filling myself with him, and trying to live one day at least out of a Reality that the next day (by physiotime) would no longer have existed.

How I longed to visit my wife one last time, too, during that portion of Time in which she lived, but I had used every second that had been available to me. I dared not even enter Time to see her, unseen.

I returned to Eternity and spent one last horrible night wrestling futilely against what must be. The next morning I handed in my computations together with my recommendations for Change.

Twissell's voice had lowered to a whisper and now it stopped. He sat there with his shoulders bent, his eyes fixed on the floor between his knees, and his fingers twisting slowly into and out of a knotted clasp.

Harlan, waiting vainly for another sentence out of the old man, cleared his throat. He found himself pitying the man, pitying him despite the many crimes he had committed. He said, "And that's all?"

Twissell whispered, "No, the worst—the worst—— An analogue of my son did exist. In the new Reality, he existed—as a paraplegic from the age of four. Forty-two years in bed, under circumstances that barred me from arranging to have the nerve-regenerating techniques of the 900's applied to his case, or even for arranging to have his life ended painlessly.

"That new Reality still exists. My son is still out there in the appropriate portion of the Century. *I* did that to him. It was my mind and my Computaplex that discovered this new life for him, and my word that ordered the Change. I had committed a number of crimes for his sake and for his mother's, but that one last deed, though strictly in accordance with my oath as an Eternal, has always seemed to me to be my great crime, *the* crime."

There was nothing to say, and Harlan said nothing.

Twissell said, "But you see now why I understand your case, why I will be willing to let you have your girl. It would not harm Eternity and, in a way, it would be expiation for my crime."

And Harlan believed. All in one change of mind, he believed!

Harlan sank to his knees and lifted his clenched fists to his temples. He bent his head and rocked slowly as savage despair beat through him.

He had thrown Eternity away, and lost Noÿs—when, except for his Samson-smash, he might have saved one and kept the other.

Fifteen: SEARCH THROUGH THE PRIMITIVE

Twissell was shaking Harlan's shoulders. The old man's voice urgently called his name.

"Harlan! Harlan! For Time's sake, man."

Harlan emerged only slowly from the slough. "What are we to do?"

"Certainly not *this*. Not despair. To begin with, listen to me. Forget your Technician's view of Eternity and look at it through a Computer's eyes. The view is more sophisticated. When you alter something in Time and create a Reality Change, the Change may take place at once. Why should that be?"

Harlan said shakily, "Because your alteration has made the Change inevitable?"

"Has it? You could go back and reverse your alteration, couldn't you?"

"I suppose so. I never did, though. Or anyone that I heard of."

"Right. There is no intention of reversing an alteration, so it goes through as planned. But here we have something else. An unintentional alteration. You sent Cooper into the wrong Century and now I firmly intend to reverse that alteration and bring Cooper back here."

"For Time's sake, how?"

"I'm not sure yet, but there *must* be a way. If there were no way, the alteration would be irreversible; Change would come at once. But Change has not come. We are still in the Reality of the Mallansohn memoir. That means the alteration is reversible and *will* be reversed."

"What?" Harlan's nightmare was expanding and swirling, growing murkier and more engulfing.

"There must be some way of knitting the circle in Time together again and our ability to find the way to do it must be a high-probability affair. As long as our Reality exists, we can be certain that the solution remains high-probability. If at any moment, you or I make the wrong decision, if the probability of healing the circle falls below some crucial magnitude, Eternity disappears. Do you understand?"

Harlan was not sure that he did. He wasn't trying very hard. Slowly he got to his feet and stumbled his way into a chair. "You mean we can get Cooper back——"

"And send him to the right place, yes. Catch him at the moment he leaves the kettle and he may end up in his proper place in the 24th no more than a few physiohours older; physiodays, at the most. It would be an alteration, of course, but undoubtedly not enough of one. Reality would be rocked, boy, but not upset."

"But how do we get him?"

"We know there's a way, or Eternity wouldn't be existing this moment. As to what that way is, that is why I need you, why I've fought to get you back on my side. You're the expert on the Primitive. Tell me."

"I can't," groaned Harlan.

"You can," insisted Twissell.

There was suddenly no trace of age or weariness in the old man's voice. His eyes were ablaze with the light of combat and he wielded his cigarette like a lance. Even to Harlan's regret-drugged senses the man seemed to be enjoying himself, actually enjoying himself, now that battle had been joined.

"We can reconstruct the event," said Twissell. "Here is the thrust control. You're standing at it, waiting for the signal. It comes. You make contact and at the same time squeeze the power thrust in the downwhen direction. How far?"

"I don't know, I tell you. I don't know."

"*You* don't know, but your muscles do. Stand there and take the control in your hand. Get hold of yourself. Take them, boy. You're waiting for the signal. You're hating me. You're hating the Council. You're hating Eternity. You're wearying your heart out for Noÿs. Put yourself back at that moment. Feel what you felt then. Now I'll set the clock in motion again. I'll give you one minute, boy, to remember your emotions and force them back into your thalamus. Then, at the approach of zero, let your right hand jerk the control as it had done before. Then take your hand away! Don't move it back again. Are you ready?"

"I don't think I can do it."

"You don't think—— Father Time, you have no choice. Is there another way you can get back your girl?"

There wasn't. Harlan forced himself back to the controls, and as he did so emotion flooded back. He did not have to call on it. Repeating the physical movements brought them back. The red hairline on the clock started moving.

Detachedly he thought: The last minute of life?

Minus thirty seconds.

He thought: It will not hurt. It is not death.

He tried to think only of Noÿs.

Minus fifteen seconds.

Noÿs!

Harlan's left hand moved a switch down toward contact.

Minus twelve seconds.

Contact!

His right hand moved.

Minus five seconds.

Noÿs!

His right hand mo—ZERO—ved spasmodically.

He jumped away, panting.

Twissell came forward, peering at the dial. "Twentieth Century," he said. "Nineteen point three eight, to be exact."

Harlan choked out, "I don't know. I tried to feel the same, but it was different. I knew what I was doing and that made it different."

Twissell said, "I know, I know. Maybe it's all wrong. Call it a first approximation." He paused a moment in mental calculation, took a pocket computer half out of its container and thrust it back without consulting it. "To Time with the decimal points. Say the probability is 0.99 that you sent him back to the second quarter of the 20th. Somewhere between 19.25 and 19.50. All right?"

"I don't know."

"Well, now, look. If I make a firm decision to concentrate on that part of the Primitive to the exclusion of all else and if I am wrong, the chances are that I will have lost my chance to keep the circle in time closed and Eternity will disappear. The decision itself will be the crucial point, the Minimum Necessary Change, the M.N.C., to bring about the Change. I now make the decision. I decide, definitely——"

Harlan looked about cautiously, as though Reality had grown so fragile that a sudden head movement might shatter it.

Harlan said, "I'm thoroughly conscious of Eternity." (Twissell's normality had infected him to the point where his voice sounded firm in his own ears.)

"Then Eternity still exists," said Twissell in a blunt, matter-of-fact manner, "and we have made the right decision. Now there's nothing more to do here for the while. Let's get to my office and we can let the subcommittee of the Council swarm over this place, if that will make them any happier. As far as they are concerned, the project has ended successfully. If it doesn't, they'll never know. Nor we."

Twissell studied his cigarette and said, "The question that now confronts us is this: What will Cooper do when he finds himself in the wrong Century?"

"I don't know."

"One thing is obvious. He's a bright lad, intelligent, imaginative, wouldn't you say?"

"Well, he's Mallansohn."

"Exactly. And he wondered if he would end up wrong. One of his last questions was: What if I don't end up in the right spot? Do you remember?"

"Well?" Harlan had no idea where this was leading.

"So he is mentally prepared for being displaced in Time. He will do something. Try to reach us. Try to leave traces for us. Remember, for part of his life he was an Eternal. That's an important thing." Twissell blew a smoke ring, hooked it with a finger, and watched it curl about and break up. "He's used to the notion of communication across Time. He is not likely to surrender to the thought of being marooned in Time. He'll know that we're looking for him."

Harlan said, "Without kettles and with no Eternity in the 20th, how would he go about communicating with us?"

"With *you*, Technician, with *you*. Use the singular. You're our expert on the Primitive. You taught Cooper about the Primitive. You're the one he would expect to be capable of finding his traces."

"*What* traces, Computer?"

Twissell's shrewd old face stared up at Harlan, its lines crinkling. "It was intended to leave Cooper in the Primitive. He is without the protection of an enclosing shield of physiotime. His entire life is woven into the fabric of Time and will remain so until you and I reverse the alteration. Likewise woven into the fabric of Time is any artifact, sign, or message he may have left for us. Surely there must be particular sources you used in studying the 20th Century. Documents, archives, films, artifacts, reference works. I mean primary sources, dating from the Time itself."

"Yes."

"And he studied them with you?"

"Yes."

"And is there any particular reference that was your favorite, one that he knew you were intimately acquainted with, so that you would recognize in it some reference to himself?"

"I see what you're driving at, of course," said Harlan. He grew thoughtful.

"Well?" asked Twissell with an edge of impatience.

Harlan said, "My news magazines, almost surely. News magazines were a phenomenon of the early 20's. The one of which I have nearly a complete set dates from early in the 20th and continues well into the 22nd."

"Good. Now is there any way, do you suppose, in which Cooper could make use of that news magazine to carry a message? Remember, he'd know you'd be reading the periodical, that you'd be acquainted with it, that you'd know your way about in it."

"I don't know." Harlan shook his head. "The magazine affected an artificial style. It was selective rather than inclusive and quite unpredictable. It would be difficult or even impossible to rely on its printing something you would plan to have it print. Cooper couldn't very well create news and be sure of its appearance. Even if Cooper managed to get a position on its editorial staff, which is very unlikely, he couldn't be certain that his exact wording would pass the various editors. I don't see it, Computer."

Twissell said, "For Time's sake, think! Concentrate on that news magazine. You're in the 20th and you're Cooper with his education and background. You taught the boy, Harlan. You molded his thinking. Now what would he do? How would he go about placing something in the magazine; something with the exact wording he wants?"

Harlan's eyes widened. "An advertisement!"

"What?"

"An advertisement. A paid notice which they would be compelled to print exactly as requested. Cooper and I discussed them occasionally."

"Ah, yes. They have that sort of thing in the 186th," said Twissell.

"Not like the 20th. The 20th is peak in that respect. The cultural milieu——"

"Considering the advertisement now," interposed Twissell hastily, "what kind would it be?"

"I wish I knew."

Twissell stared at the lighted end of his cigarette as though seeking inspiration. "He can't say anything directly. He can't say: 'Cooper of the 78th, stranded in the 20th and calling Eternity——' "

"How can you be sure?"

"Impossible! To give the 20th information we know they did not have would be as damaging to the Mallansohn circle as would wrong action on our part. We're still here, so in his whole lifetime in the current Reality of the Primitive he's done no harm of that sort."

"Besides which," said Harlan, retreating from the contemplation of the circular reasoning which seemed to bother Twissell so little, "the news magazine is not likely to agree to publish anything which seems mad to it or which it cannot understand. It would suspect fraud or some form of illegality and would not wish to be implicated. So Cooper couldn't use Standard Intertemporal for his message."

"It would have to be something subtle," said Twissell. "He would have to use indirection. He would have to place an advertisement that would seem perfectly normal to the men of the Primitive. Perfectly normal! And yet something that is obvious to us, once we knew what we were searching for. Very obvious. Obvious at a glance because it would have to be found among uncounted individual items. How big do you suppose it would be, Harlan? Are those advertisements expensive?"

"Quite expensive, I believe."

"And Cooper would have to hoard his money. Besides which, to avoid the wrong kind of attention, it would have to be small, anyway. Guess, Harlan. How large?"

Harlan spread his hands. "Half a column?"

"Column?"

"They were printed magazines, you know. On paper. With print arranged in columns."

"Oh yes. I can't seem to separate literature and film somehow. . . . Well, we have a first approximation of another sort now. We must look for a half-column advertisement which will, practically at a glance, give evidence that the man who placed it came from another Century (in the upwhen direction, of course) and yet which is so normal an advertisement that no man of that Century would see anything suspicious in it."

Harlan said, "What if I don't find it?"

"You will. Eternity exists, doesn't it. As long as it does, we're on the right track. Tell me, can you recall such an advertisement in your work with Cooper? Anything which struck you, even momentarily, as odd, queer, unusual, subtly wrong."

"No."

"I don't want an answer so quickly. Take five minutes and think."

"No point. At the time I was going over the news magazines with Cooper, he hadn't been in the 20th."

"Please, boy. Use your head. Sending Cooper to the 20th has introduced an alteration. There's no Change; it isn't an irreversible alteration. But there have been some changes with a small 'c,' or micro-changes, as it is usually referred to in Computation. At the instant Cooper was sent to the 20th, the advertisement appeared in the appropriate issue of the magazine. Your own Reality has micro-changed in the sense that you may have looked at the page with that advertisement on it rather than one without that advertisement as you did in the previous Reality. Do you understand?"

Harlan was again bewildered, almost as much at the ease with which Twissell picked his way through the jungle of temporal logic, as at the "paradoxes" of Time. He shook his head, "I remember nothing of the sort."

"Well, then, where do you keep the files of that periodical?"

"I had a special library built on Level Two, using the Cooper priority."

"Good enough," said Twissell. "Let's go there. *Now!*"

Harlan watched Twissell stare curiously at the old, bound volumes in the library and then take one down. They were so old that the fragile paper had to be preserved by special methods and they creaked under Twissell's insufficiently gentle handling.

Harlan winced. In better times he would have ordered Twissell away from the books, Senior Computer though he was.

The old man peered through the crinkling pages and silently mouthed the archaic words. "This is the English the linguists are always talking about, isn't it?" he asked, tapping a page.

"Yes. English," muttered Harlan.

Twissell put the volume back. "Heavy and clumsy."

Harlan shrugged. To be sure, most of the Centuries of Eternity were film eras. A respectable minority were molecular-recording eras. Still, print and paper were not unheard of.

He said, "Books don't require the investment in technology that films do."

Twissell rubbed his chin. "Quite. Shall we get started?"

He took another volume down from the shelf, opening it at random and staring at the page with odd intentness.

Harlan thought: Does the man think he's going to hit the solution by a lucky stab?

The thought might have been correct, for Twissell, meeting Harlan's appraising eyes, reddened and put the book back.

Harlan took the first volume of the 19.25th Centicentury and began turning the pages regularly. Only his right hand and his eyes moved. The rest of his body remained at rigid attention.

At what seemed aeonic intervals to himself Harlan rose, grunting, for a new volume. On those occasions there would be the coffee break or the sandwich break or the other breaks.

Harlan said heavily, "It's useless your staying."

Twissell said, "Do I bother you?"

"No."

"Then I'll stay," muttered Twissell. Throughout he wandered occasionally to the bookshelves, staring helplessly at the bindings. The sparks of his furious cigarettes burned his finger ends at times, but he disregarded them.

A physioday ended.

Sleep was poor and sparse. Midmorning, between two volumes, Twissell lingered over his last sip of coffee and said, "I wonder sometimes why I didn't throw up my Computership after the matter of my—— You know."

Harlan nodded.

"I felt like it," the old man went on. "I felt like it. For physiomonths, I hoped desperately that no Changes would come my way. I got morbid about it. I began to wonder if Changes were right. Funny, the tricks emotions will play on you.

"*You* know Primitive history, Harlan. You know what it was like. Its Reality flowed blindly along the line of maximum probability. If that maximum probability involved a pandemic, or ten Centuries of slave economy, a breakdown of technology, or even a—a—let's see, what's really bad—even an atomic war if one had been possible then, why, by Time, it *happened*. There was nothing to stop it.

"But where Eternity exists, that's been stopped. Upwhen from the 28th, things like that don't happen. Father Time, we've lifted our Reality to a level of well-being far beyond anything Primitive times could imagine; to a level which, but for the interference of Eternity, would have been very low probability indeed."

Harlan thought in shame: What's he trying to do? Get me to work harder? I'm doing my best.

Twissell said, "If we miss our chance now, Eternity disappears, probably through all of physiotime. And in one vast Change all Reality reverts to maximum probability with, I am positive, atomic warfare and the end of man."

Harlan said, "I'd better get on to the next volume."

At the next break Twissell said helplessly, "There's so much to do. Isn't there a faster way?"

Harlan said, "Name it. To me it seems that I must look at every single page. And look at every part of it, too. How can I do it faster?"

Methodically he turned the pages.

"Eventually," said Harlan, "the print starts blurring and that means it's time for sleep."

A second physioday ended.

At 10:22 A.M., Standard Physiotime, of the third physioday of the search Harlan stared at a page in quiet wonder and said, "This is it!"

Twissell didn't absorb the statement. He said, "What?"

Harlan looked up, his face twisted with astonishment. "You know, I didn't believe it. By Time, I never really believed it, even while you were working out all that rigmarole about news magazines and advertisements."

Twissell had absorbed it now. *"You've found it!"*

He leaped at the volume Harlan was holding, clutching at it with shaking fingers.

Harlan held it out of reach and slammed the volume shut. "Just a moment. *You* won't find it, even if I showed you the page."

"What are you doing?" shrieked Twissell. "You've lost it."

"It's not lost. I know where it is. But first——"

"First what?"

Harlan said, "There's one point remaining, Computer Twissell. You say I can have Noÿs. Bring her to me, then. Let me see her."

Twissell stared at Harlan, his thin white hair in disarray. "Are you joking?"

"No," said Harlan sharply, "I'm not joking. You assured me that you would make arrangements—— Are *you* joking? Noÿs and I would be together. You promised that."

"Yes, I did. That part's settled."

"Then produce her alive, well, and untouched."

"But I don't understand you. I don't have her. No one has. She's still in the far upwhen, where Finge reported her to be. No one has touched her. Great Time, I told you she was safe."

Harlan stared at the old man and grew tense. He said, chokingly, "You're playing with words. All right, she's in the far upwhen, but what good is that to me? Take down the barrier at the 100,000th—"

"The what?"

"The barrier. The kettle won't pass it."

"You never said anything of this," said Twissell wildly.

"I haven't?" said Harlan with sharp surprise. Hadn't he? He had thought of it often enough. Had he never said a word about it? He couldn't recall, at that. But then he hardened.

He said, "All right. I tell you *now*. Take it down."

"But the thing is impossible. A barrier against the kettle? A temporal barrier?"

"Are you telling me you didn't put one up?"

"I didn't. By Time, I swear it."

"Then—then——" Harlan felt himself grow pale. "Then the Council did it. They know of all this and they've taken action independently of you and—and by all of Time and Reality, they can whistle for their ad and for Cooper, for Mallansohn and all of Eternity. They'll have none of it. None of it."

"Wait. Wait." Twissell yanked despairingly at Harlan's elbow. "Keep hold of yourself. Think, boy, think. The Council put up no barrier."

"It's there."

"But they can't have put up such a barrier. No one could have. It's theoretically impossible."

"You don't know it all. It's there."

"I know more than anyone else on the Council and such a thing is impossible."

"But it's there."

"But if it is——"

And Harlan grew sufficiently aware of his surroundings to realize that there was a kind of abject fear in Twissell's eyes; a fear that had not been there even when he first learned of Cooper's misdirection and of the impending end of Eternity.

Sixteen: THE HIDDEN CENTURIES

Andrew Harlan watched the men at work with abstracted eyes. They ignored him politely because he was a Technician. Ordinarily he would have ignored them somewhat less politely because they were Maintenance men. But now he watched them and, in his misery, he even caught himself envying them.

They were service personnel from the Department of Intertemporal Transportation, in dun-gray uniforms with shoulder patches showing a red, double-headed arrow against a black background. They used intricate force-field equipment to test the kettle motors and the degrees of hyper-freedom along the kettleways. They had, Harlan imagined, little theoretical knowledge of temporal engineering, but it was obvious that they had a vast practical knowledge of the subject.

Harlan had not learned much concerning Maintenance when he was a Cub. Or, to put it more accurately, he had not really wished to learn. Cubs who did not make the grade were put into Maintenance. The "unspecialized profession" (as the euphemism had it) was the Hallmark of failure and the average Cub automatically avoided the subject.

Yet now, as he watched the Maintenance men at work, they seemed to Harlan to be quietly, tensionlessly efficient, reasonably happy.

Why not? They outnumbered the Specialists, the "true Eternals," ten to one. They had a society of their own, residential levels devoted to them, pleasures of their own. Their labor was fixed at so many hours per physioday and there was no social pressure in their case to make them relate their spare-time activity to their profession. They had time, as specialists did not, to devote to the literature and film dramatizations culled out of the various Realities.

It was they, after all, who probably had the better-rounded personalities. It was the Specialist's life which was harried and affected, artificial in comparison with the sweet and simple life in Maintenance.

Maintenance was the foundation of Eternity. Strange that such an obvious fact had not struck him earlier. They supervised the importation of food and water from Time, the disposal of waste, the functioning of the power plants. They kept all the machinery of Eternity running smoothly. If every Specialist were to die of a stroke on the spot, Maintenance could keep Eternity going indefinitely. Yet were Maintenance to disappear, the Specialists would have to abandon Eternity in days or die miserably.

Did Maintenance men resent the loss of their homewhens, or their womanless, childless lives? Was security from poverty, disease, and Reality Change sufficient compensation? Were their views ever consulted on any matter of importance? Harlan felt some of the fire of the social reformer within him.

Senior Computer Twissell broke Harlan's train of thought by bustling in at a half run, looking even more haunted than he had an hour before, when he had left, with Maintenance already at work.

Harlan thought: How does he keep it up? He's an old man.

Twissell glanced about him with birdlike brightness as the men automatically straightened up to respectful attention.

He said, "What about the kettleways?"

One of the men responded, "Nothing wrong, sir. The ways are clear, the fields mesh."

"You've checked everything?"

"Yes, sir. As far upwhen as the Department's stations go."

Twissell said, "Then go."

There was no mistaking the brusque insistence of his dismissal. They bowed respectfully, turned, and hastened out briskly.

Twissell and Harlan were alone in the kettleways.

Twissell turned to him. "You'll stay here. Please."

Harlan shook his head. "I must go."

Twissell said, "Surely you understand. If anything happens to me, you still know how to find Cooper. If anything happens to you, what can I or any Eternal or any combination of Eternals do alone?"

Harlan shook his head again.

Twissell put a cigarette between his lips. He said, "Sennor is suspicious. He's called me several times in the last two physiodays. Why am I in seclusion, he wants to know. When he finds out I've ordered a complete overhaul of the kettleway machinery . . . I must go now, Harlan. I can't delay."

"I don't want delay. I'm ready."

"You insist on going?"

"If there's no barrier, there'll be no danger. Even if there is, I've been there already and come back. What are you afraid of, Computer?"

"I don't want to risk anything I don't have to."

"Then use your logic, Computer. Make the decision that I'm to go with you. If Eternity still exists after that, then it means that the circle can still be closed. It means we'll survive. If it's a wrong decision, then Eternity will pass into nonexistence, but it will anyway if I don't go, because without Noÿs, I'll make no move to get Cooper. I swear it."

Twissell said, "I'll bring her back to you."

"If it is so simple and safe, there will be no harm if I come along."

Twissell was in an obvious torture of hesitation. He said gruffly, "Well, then, come!"

And Eternity survived.

Twissell's haunted look did not disappear once they were within the kettle. He stared at the skimming figures of the temporometer. Even the scaler gauge, which measured in units of Kilocenturies, and which the men had adjusted for this particular purpose, was clicking at minute intervals.

He said, "You should not have come."

Harlan shrugged. "Why not?"

"It disturbs me. No sensible reason. Call it a long-standing superstition of mine. It makes me restless." He clasped his hands together, holding them tightly.

Harlan said, "I don't understand you."

Twissell seemed eager to talk, as though to exorcise some mental demon. He said, "Maybe you'll appreciate this, at that. You're the expert on the Primitive. How long did man exist in the Primitive?"

Harlan said, "Ten thousand Centuries. Fifteen thousand, maybe."

"Yes. Beginning as a kind of primitive apelike creature and ending as Homo sapiens. Right?"

"It's common knowledge. Yes."

"Then it must be common knowledge that evolution proceeds at a fairly rapid pace. Fifteen thousand Centuries from ape to Homo sapiens."

"Well?"

"Well, I'm from a Century in the 30,000's——"

(Harlan could not help starting. He had never known Twissell's homewhen or known of anyone who did.)

"I'm from a Century in the 30,000's," Twissell said again, "and you're from the 95th. The time between our homewhens is twice the total length of time of man's existence in the Primitive, yet what change is there between us? I was born with four fewer teeth than you, and without an appendix. The physiological differences about end with that. Our metabolism is almost the same. The major difference is that your body can synthesize the steroid nucleus and my body can't, so that I require cholesterol in my diet and you don't. I was able to breed with a woman of the 575th. That's how undifferentiated with time the species is."

Harlan was unimpressed. He had never questioned the basic identity of man throughout the Centuries. It was one of those things you lived with and took for granted. He said, "There have been cases of species living unchanged through millions of Centuries."

"Not many, though. And it remains a fact that the cessation of human evolution seems to coincide with the development of Eternity. Just coincidence? It's not a question which is considered, except by a few here and there like Sennor, and I've never been a Sennor. I didn't believe speculation was proper. If something couldn't be checked by a Computaplex, it had no business taking up the time of a Computer. And yet, in my younger days, I sometimes thought——"

"Of what?" Harlan thought: Well, it's something to listen to, anyway.

"I sometimes thought about Eternity as it was when it was first established. It stretched over just a few Centuries in the 30's and 40's, and its function was mostly trade. It interested itself in the reforestation of denuded areas, shipping topsoil back and forth, fresh water, fine chemicals. Those were simple days.

"But then we discovered Reality Changes. Senior Computer Henry Wadsman, in the dramatic manner with which we are all acquainted, prevented a war by removing the safety brake of a Congressman's ground vehicle. After that, more and more, Eternity shifted its center of gravity from trade to Reality Change. Why?"

Harlan said, "The obvious reason. Betterment of humanity."

"Yes. Yes. In normal times, I think so too. But I'm talking of my nightmare. What if there were another reason, an unexpressed one, an unconscious one. A man who can travel into the indefinite future may meet men as far advanced over himself as he himself is over an ape. Why not?"

"Maybe. But men are men——"

"—even in the 70,000th. Yes, I know. And have our Reality Changes had something to do with it? We bred out the unusual. Even Sennor's homewhen with its hairless creatures is under continual question and that's harmless enough. Perhaps in all honesty, in all sincerity, we've prevented human evolution because we don't *want* to meet the supermen."

Still no spark was struck. Harlan said, "Then it's done. What does it matter?"

"But what if the superman exists just the same, further upwhen than we can reach? We control only to the 70,000th. Beyond that are the Hidden Centuries! Why are they hidden? Because evolved man does not want to deal with us and bars us from his time? Why do we allow them to remain hidden? Because we don't want to deal with them and, having failed to enter in our first attempt, we refuse even to make additional attempts? I don't say it's our conscious reason, but conscious or unconscious, it's a reason."

"Grant everything," said Harlan sullenly. "They're out of our reach and we're out of theirs. Live and let live."

Twissell seemed struck by the phrase. "Live and let live. But we don't. We make Changes. The Changes extend only through a few Centuries before temporal inertia causes its effects to die out. You remember Sennor brought that up as one of the unanswered problems of Time at our breakfast. What he might have said was that it's all a matter of statistics. Some Changes affect more Centuries than others. Theoretically, any number of Centuries can be affected by the proper Change; a hundred Centuries, a thousand, a hundred thousand. Evolved man of the Hidden Centuries may know that. Suppose he is disturbed by the possibility that someday a Change may reach him clear to the 200,000th."

"It's useless to worry about such things," said Harlan with the air of a man who had much greater worries.

"But suppose," went on Twissell in a whisper, "they were calm enough as long as we left the Sections of the Hidden Centuries empty. It meant we weren't aggressing. Suppose this truce, or whatever you wish to call it, were broken, and someone appeared to have established permanent residence upwhen from the 70,000th. Suppose they thought it might mean the first of a serious invasion? They can bar us from their Time, so their science is that far advanced beyond ours. Suppose they may further do what seems impossible to us and throw a barrier across the kettleways, cutting us off——"

And now Harlan was on his feet, in full horror, "*They* have Noÿs?"

"I don't know. It's speculation. Maybe there is no barrier. Maybe there was something wrong with your ket——"

"There was a barrier!" yelled Harlan. "What other explanation is there? Why didn't you tell me this before."

"I didn't believe it," groaned Twissell. "I still don't. I shouldn't have said a word of this foolish dreaming. My own fears—the question of Cooper—everything—— But wait, just a few minutes."

He pointed at the temporometer. The scaler indicated them to be between the 95,000th and 96,000th Centuries.

Twissell's hand on the controls slowed the kettle. The 99,000th was passed. The scaler's motions stopped. The individual Centuries could be read.

99,726—99,727—99,728—

"What will we do?" muttered Harlan.

Twissell shook his head in a gesture that spoke eloquently of patience and hope, but perhaps also of helplessness.

99,851—99,852—99,853—

Harlan steeled himself for the shock of the barrier and thought desperately: Would preserving Eternity be the only means of finding time to fight back at the creatures of the Hidden Centuries? How else recover Noÿs? Dash back, back to the 575th and work like fury to—

99,938—99,939—99,940—

Harlan held his breath. Twissell slowed the kettle further, let it creep. It responded perfectly to the controls.

99,984—99,985—99,986—

"Now, now, now," said Harlan in a whisper, unaware that he had made any sound at all.

99,998—99,999—100,000—100,001—100,002—

The numbers mounted and the two men watched them continue to mount in paralytic silence.

Then Twissell cried, "There *is* no barrier."

And Harlan answered, "There was! There was!" Then, in agony, "Maybe they've got her, and need a barrier no longer."

111,394th!

Harlan leaped from the kettle, and raised his voice. "Noÿs! Noÿs!"

The echoes bounced off the walls of the empty Section in hollow syncopation.

Twissell, climbing out more sedately, called after the younger man, "Wait, Harlan——"

That was useless. Harlan, at a run, was hurtling along the corridors toward that portion of the Section they had made a kind of home.

He thought vaguely of the possibility of meeting one of Twissell's "evolved men" and momentarily his skin prickled, but then that was drowned in his urgent need to find Noÿs.

"Noÿs!"

And all at once, so quickly that she was in his arms before he was sure he had seen her at all, she was there with him, and her arms were around him and clutching him and her cheek was against his shoulder and her dark hair was soft against his chin.

"Andrew?" she said, her voice muffled by the pressure of his body. "Where were you? It's been days and I was getting frightened."

Harlan held her out at arm's length, staring at her with a kind of hungry solemnity. "Are you all right?"

"*I'm* all right. I thought something might have happened to you. I thought——" She broke off, terror springing into her eyes and gasped, "Andrew!"

Harlan whirled.

It was only Twissell, panting.

Noÿs must have gained confidence from Harlan's expression. She said more quietly, "Do you know him, Andrew? Is it all right?"

Harlan said, "It's all right. This is my superior, Senior Computer Laban Twissell. He knows of you."

"A Senior Computer?" Noÿs shrank away.

Twissell advanced slowly. "I will help you, my child. I will help you both. The Technician has my promise, if he would only believe it."

"My apologies, Computer," said Harlan stiffly, and not yet entirely repentant.

"Forgiven," said Twissell. He held out his hand, took the girl's reluctant one. "Tell me, girl, has it been well with you here?"

"I've been worried."

"There's been no one here, since Harlan last left you."

"N—no, sir."

"No one at all? Nothing?"

She shook her head. Her dark eyes sought Harlan's. "Why do you ask?"

"Nothing, girl. A foolish nightmare. Come, we will take you back to the 575th."

On the kettle back Andrew Harlan sank, by degrees, into a troubled and deepening silence. He did not look up when the 100,000th was passed in the downwhen direction and Twissell had snorted an obvious sigh of relief as though he had half expected to be trapped on the upwhen side.

He scarcely moved when Noÿs's hand stole into his, and the manner in which he returned the pressure of her fingers was almost mechanical.

Noÿs slept in another room and now Twissell's restlessness reached a peak of devouring intensity.

"The advertisement, boy! You have your woman. My part of the agreement is done."

Silently, still abstracted, Harlan turned the pages of the volume on the desk. He found his page.

"It's simple enough," he said, "but it's in English. I'll read it to you and then translate it."

It was a small advertisement in the upper left-hand corner of a page numbered 30. Against an irregular line drawing as background were the unadorned words, in block letters:

ALL THE
TALK
OF THE
MARKET

Underneath, in smaller letters, it said; "Investments News-Letter, P. O. Box 14, Denver, Colorado."

Twissell listened painstakingly to Harlan's translation and was obviously disappointed. He said, "What is the market? What do they mean by that?"

"The stock market," said Harlan impatiently. "A system by which private capital was invested in business. But that's not the point at all. Don't you see the line drawing against which the advertisement is set?"

"Yes. The mushroom cloud of an A-bomb blast. An attention getter. What about it?"

Harlan exploded. "Great Time, Computer, what's wrong with you? Look at the date of the magazine issue."

He pointed to the top heading, just to the left of the page number. It read March 28, 1932.

Harlan said, "That scarcely needs translation. The numbers are about those of Standard Intertemporal and you see it's the 19.32nd Century. Don't you know that at that time no human being who had ever lived had seen the mushroom cloud? No one could possibly reproduce it so accurately, except——"

"Now, wait. It's just a line pattern," said Twissell, trying to retain his equilibrium. "It might resemble the mushroom cloud only coincidentally."

"Might it? Will you look at the wording again?" Harlan's fingers punched out the short lines: "All the—Talk—Of the—Market. The initials spell out ATOM, which is English for atom. Is that coincidence, too? Not a chance.

"Don't you see, Computer, how this advertisement fits the conditions you yourself set up? It caught my eye instantly. Cooper knew it would out of sheer anachronism. At the same time, it has no meaning other than its face value, no meaning at all, for any man of the 19.32nd.

"So it must be Cooper. That's his message. We have the date to the nearest week of a Centicentury. We have his mailing address. It is only necessary to go after him and I'm the only one with enough knowledge of the Primitive to manage that."

"And you'll go?" Twissell's face was ablaze with relief and happiness.

"I'll go—on one condition."

Twissell frowned in a sudden reversal of emotion. "Again conditions?"

"The same condition. I'm not adding new ones. Noÿs must be safe. She must come with me. I will not leave her behind."

"You *still* don't trust me? In what way have I failed you? What can there be that still disturbs you?"

"One thing, Computer," said Harlan solemnly. "One thing still. There *was* a barrier across the 100,000th. Why? That is what still disturbs me."

Seventeen: THE CLOSING CIRCLE

It did not stop disturbing him. It was a matter that grew in his mind as the days of preparation sped by. It interposed itself between him and Twissell; then between him and Noÿs. When the day of departure came, he was only distantly aware of the fact.

It was all he could do to rouse a shadow of interest when Twissell returned from a session with the Council subcommittee. He said, "How did it go?"

Twissell said wearily, "It wasn't exactly the most pleasant conversation I've ever had."

Harlan was almost willing to let it go at that, but he broke his moment's silence with a muttered "I suppose you said nothing about——"

"No, no," was the testy response. "I said nothing about the girl or about your part in the misdirection of Cooper. It was an unfortunate error, a mechanical failure. I took full responsibility."

Harlan's conscience, burdened as it was, could find room for a twinge. He said, "That won't affect you well."

"What can they do? They must wait for the correction to be made before they can touch me. If we fail, we're all beyond help or harm. If we succeed, success itself will probably protect me. And if it doesn't——" The old man shrugged. "I plan to retire from active participation in Eternity's affairs thereafter anyway." But he fumbled his cigarette and disposed of it before it was half burned away.

He sighed. "I would rather not have brought them into this at all, but there would have been no way, otherwise, of using the special kettle for further trips past the downwhen terminus."

Harlan turned away. His thoughts moved around and about the same channels that had been occupied to the increasing exclusion of all else for days. He heard Twissell's further remark dimly, but it was only at its repetition that he said with a start, "Pardon me?"

"I say, is your woman ready, boy? Does she understand what she's to do?"

"She's ready. I've told her everything."

"How did she take it?"

"What? . . . Oh, yes, uh, as I expected her to. She's not afraid."

"It's less than three physiohours now."

"I know."

That was all for the moment, and Harlan was left alone with his thoughts and a sickening realization of what he must do.

With the kettle loading done and the controls adjusted Harlan and Noÿs appeared in a final change of costume, approximating that of an unurbanized area of the early 20th.

Noÿs had modified Harlan's suggestion for her wardrobe, according to some instinctive feeling she claimed women had when it came to matters of clothing and aesthetics. She chose thoughtfully from pictures in the advertisements of the appropriated volumes of the news magazine and had minutely scrutinized items imported from a dozen different Centuries.

Occasionally she would say to Harlan, "What do you think?"

He would shrug. "If it's instinctive knowledge, I'll leave it to you."

"That's a bad sign, Andrew," she said, with a lightness that did not quite ring true. "You're too pliable. What's the matter, anyway? You're just not yourself. You haven't been for days."

"I'm all right," Harlan said in a monotone.

Twissell's first sight of them in the role of natives of the 20th elicited a feeble attempt at jocularity. "Father Time," he said, "what ugly costumes in the Primitive, and yet how it fails to hide your beauty, my—my dear."

Noÿs smiled warmly at him, and Harlan, standing there impassively silent, was forced to admit that Twissell's rust-choked vein of gallantry had something of truth in it. Noÿs's clothing encompassed her without accentuating her as clothing should. Her make-up was confined to unimaginative dabs of color on lips and cheeks and an ugly rearrangement of the eyebrow line. Her lovely hair (this had been the worst of it) had been cut ruthlessly. Yet she was beautiful.

Harlan himself was already growing accustomed to his own uncomfortable belt, the tightness of fit under armpits and in the crotch and the mousy lack of color about his rough-textured clothing. Wearing strange costumes to suit a Century was an old story to him.

Twissell was saying, "Now what I really wanted to do was to install hand controls inside the kettle, as we discussed, but there isn't any way, apparently. The engineers simply must have a source of power large enough to handle temporal displacement and that isn't available outside Eternity. Temporal tension while occupying the Primitive is all that can be managed. However, we have a return lever."

He led them into the kettle, picking his way among the piled supplies, and pointed out the obtruding finger of metal that now marred the smooth inner wall of the kettle.

"It amounts to the installation of a simple switch," he said. "Instead of returning automatically to Eternity, the kettle will remain in the Primitive indefinitely. Once the lever is plunged home, however, you will return. There will then be the matter of the second and, I hope, final trip——"

"A second trip?" asked Noÿs at once.

Harlan said, "I haven't explained that. Look, this first trip is intended merely to fix the time of Cooper's arrival precisely. We don't know how long a Time-lapse exists between his arrival and the placing of the advertisement. We'll reach him by the post-office box, and learn, if possible, the exact minute of his arrival, or as close as we can, anyway. We can then return to that moment plus fifteen minutes to allow for the kettle to have left Cooper——"

Twissell interposed, "Couldn't have the kettle in the same place at the same time in two different physiotimes, you know," and tried to smile.

Noÿs seemed to absorb it. "I see," she said, not too definitely.

Twissell said to Noÿs, "Picking up Cooper at the time of his arrival will reverse all micro-changes. The A-bomb advertisement will disappear again and Cooper will know only that the kettle, having disappeared as we told him it would, had unexpectedly appeared again. He will not know that he was in the wrong Century and he will not be told. We will tell him that there was some vital instruction we had forgotten to give him (we'll have to manufacture some) and we can only hope that he will regard the matter as so unimportant that he won't mention being sent back twice when he writes his memoir."

Noÿs lifted her plucked eyebrows. "It's very complicated."

"Yes. Unfortunately." He rubbed his hands together and looked at the others as though nursing an inner doubt. Then he straightened, produced a fresh cigarette, and even managed a certain jauntiness as he said, "And now, boy, good luck." Twissell touched hands briefly with Harlan, nodded to Noÿs, and stepped out of the kettle.

"Are we leaving now?" asked Noÿs of Harlan when they were alone.

"In a few minutes," said Harlan.

He glanced sideways at Noÿs. She was looking up at him, smiling, unfrightened. Momentarily his own spirits responded to that. But that was emotion, not reason, he counseled himself, instinct, not thought. He looked away.

The trip was nothing, or almost nothing; no different from an ordinary kettle ride. Midway there was a kind of internal jar that might have been the downwhen terminus and might have been purely psychosomatic. It was barely noticeable.

And then they were in the Primitive and they stepped into a craggy, lonely world brightened by the splendor of an afternoon sun. There was a soft wind with a chilly edge to it and, most of all, silence.

The bare rocks were tumbled and mighty, colored into dull rainbows by compounds of iron, copper, and chromium. The grandeur of the manless and all but lifeless surroundings dwarfed and shriveled Harlan. Eternity, which did not belong to the world of matter, had no sun and none but imported air. His memories of his own homewhen were dim. His Observations in the various Centuries had dealt with men and their cities. He had never experienced *this*.

Noÿs touched his elbow.

"Andrew! I'm cold."

He turned to her with a start.

She said, "Hadn't we better set up the Radiant?"

He said, "Yes. In Cooper's cavern."

"Do you know where it is?"

"It's right here," he said shortly.

He had no doubt of that. The memoir had located it and first Cooper, now he, had been pin-pointed back to it.

He had not doubted precision pin-pointing in Time-travel since his Cubhood days. He remembered himself then, facing Educator Yarrow seriously, saying, "But Earth moves about the Sun, and the Sun moves about the Galactic Center and the Galaxy moves too. If you start from some point on Earth, and move downwhen a hundred years, you'll be in empty space, because it will take a hundred years for Earth to reach that point." (Those were the days when he still referred to a Century as a "hundred years.")

And Educator Yarrow had snapped back, "You don't separate Time from space. Moving through Time, you share Earth's motions.

Or do you believe that a bird flying through the air whiffs out into space because the Earth is hurrying around the Sun at eighteen miles a second and vanishes from under the creature?"

Arguing from analogy is risky, but Harlan obtained more rigorous proof in later days and, now, after a scarcely precedented trip into the Primitive, he could turn confidently and feel no surprise at finding the opening precisely where he had been told it would be.

He moved the camouflage of loose rubble and rock to one side and entered.

He probed the darkness within, using the white beam of his flash almost like a scalpel. He scoured the walls, ceiling, floor, every inch.

Noÿs, remaining close behind him, whispered, "What are you looking for?"

He said, "Something. Anything."

He found his something, anything, at the very rear of the cave in the shape of a flattish stone covering greenish sheets like a paperweight.

Harlan threw the stone aside and flipped the sheets past one thumb.

"What are they?" asked Noÿs.

"Bank notes. Medium of exchange. Money."

"Did you know they were there?"

"I knew nothing. I just hoped."

It was only a matter of using Twissell's reverse logic, of calculating cause from effect. Eternity existed, so Cooper must be making correct decisions too. In assuming the advertisement would pull Harlan into the correct Time, the cave was an obvious additional means of communication.

Yet this was almost better than he had dared hope. More than once during the preparations for his trip into the Primitive, Harlan had thought that making his way into a town with nothing but bullion in his possession would result in suspicion and delay.

Cooper had managed, to be sure, but Cooper had had time. Harlan hefted the sheaf of bills. And he must have used time to accumulate this much. He had done well, the youngster, marvelously well.

And the circle was closing!

The supplies had been moved into the cave, in the increasingly ruddy glow of the westering sun. The kettle had been covered by a diffuse reflecting film which would hide it from any but the closest of prying eyes, and Harlan had a blaster to take care of those, if need be. The Radiant was set up in the cave and the flash was wedged into a crevice, so that they had heat and light.

Outside it was a chill March night.

Noÿs stared thoughtfully into the smooth paraboloid interior of the Radiant as it slowly rotated. She said, "Andrew, what are your plans?"

"Tomorrow morning," he said, "I'll leave for the nearest town. I know where it is—or should be." (He changed it back to "is" in his mind. There would be no trouble. Twissell's logic again.)

"I'll come with you, won't I?"

He shook his head. "You can't speak the language, for one thing, and the trip will be difficult enough for one to negotiate."

Noÿs looked strangely archaic in her short hair and the sudden anger in her eyes made Harlan look away uneasily.

She said, "I'm no fool, Andrew. You scarcely speak to me. You don't look at me. What is it? Is your homewhen morality taking hold? Do you feel you have betrayed Eternity and are you blaming me for that? Do you feel I have corrupted you? What is it?"

He said, "You don't know what I feel."

She said, "Then describe it. You might as well. You'll never have a chance as good as this one. Do you feel love? For me? You couldn't or you wouldn't be using me as a scapegoat. Why did you bring me here? Tell me. Why not have left me in Eternity since you have no use for me here and since it seems you can hardly bear the sight of me?"

Harlan muttered, "There's danger."

"Oh, come now."

"It's more than danger. It's a nightmare. Computer Twissell's nightmare," said Harlan. "It was during our last panicky flash upwhen into the Hidden Centuries that he told me of thoughts he had had concerning those Centuries. He speculated on the possibility of evolved varieties of man, new species, supermen perhaps, hiding in the far upwhen, cutting themselves off from our interference, plotting to end our tamperings with Reality. He thought it was they who built the barrier across the 100,000th. Then we found you, and Computer Twissell abandoned his nightmare. He decided there had never been a barrier. He returned to the more immediate problem of salvaging Eternity.

"But I, you see, had been infected by his nightmare. I had experienced the barrier, so I knew it existed. No Eternal had built it, for Twissell said such a thing was theoretically impossible. Maybe Eternity's theories didn't go far enough. The barrier was there. Someone had built it. Or something.

"Of course," he went on thoughtfully, "Twissell was wrong in some ways. He felt that man *must* evolve, but that's not so. Paleontology is not one of the sciences that interest Eternals, but it interested the late Primitives, so I picked up a bit of it myself. I know this much: species evolve only to meet the pressures of new environments. In a stable environment, a species may remain unchanged for millions of Centuries. Primitive man evolved rapidly because his environment was a harsh and changing one. Once, however, mankind learned to create his own environment, he created a pleasant and stable one, so he just naturally stopped evolving."

"I don't know what you're talking about," said Noÿs, sounding not the least mollified, "and you're not saying anything about us, which is what I want to talk about."

Harlan managed to remain outwardly unmoved. He said, "Now why the barrier at the 100,000th? What purpose did it serve? You weren't harmed. What other meaning could it have? I asked myself: What happened because of its presence that would not have happened had it been absent?"

He paused, looking at his clumsy and heavy boots of natural leather. It occurred to him that he could add to his comfort by removing them for the night, but not now, not now . . .

He said, "There was only one answer to that question. The existence of that barrier sent me raving back downwhen to get a neuronic whip, to assault Finge. It fired me to the thought of risking Eternity to get you back and smashing Eternity when I thought I had failed. Do you see?"

Noÿs stared at him with a mixture of horror and disbelief. "Do you mean the people in the upwhen wanted you to do all that? They planned it?"

"*Yes.* Don't look at me like that. *Yes!* And don't you see how it makes everything different? As long as I acted on my own, for reasons of my own, I'll take all the consequences, material and spiritual. But to be *fooled* into it, to be *tricked* into it, by people handling and manipulating my emotions as though I were a Computaplex on which it was only necessary to insert the properly perforated foils——"

Harlan realized suddenly that he was shouting and stopped abruptly. He let a few moments pass, then said, "That is impossible to take. I've got to undo what I was marionetted into doing. And when I undo it, I will be able to rest again."

And he would—perhaps. He could feel the coming of an impersonal triumph, dissociated from the personal tragedy which lay behind and ahead. The circle was closing!

Noÿs's hand reached out uncertainly as though to take his own rigid, unyielding one.

Harlan drew away, avoided her sympathy. He said, "It had all been arranged. My meeting with you. Everything. My emotional make-up had been analyzed. Obviously. Action and response. Push this button and the man will do that. Push that button and he will do this."

Harlan was speaking with difficulty, out of the depths of shame. He shook his head, trying to shake the horror of it away as a dog would water, then went on. "One thing I didn't understand at first. How did I come to guess that Cooper was to be sent back into the Primitive? It was a most unlikely thing to guess. I had no basis. Twissell didn't understand it. More than once he wondered how I could have done it with so little understanding of mathematics.

"Yet I had. The first time was that—that night. You were asleep, but I wasn't. I had the feeling then that there was something I must remember; some remark, some thought, *something* that I had caught sight of in the excitement and exhilaration of the evening. When I thought long, the whole significance of Cooper sprang into my mind, and along with it the thought entered my mind that I was in a position to destroy Eternity. Later I checked through histories of mathematics, but it was unnecessary really. I already knew. I was certain of it. How? How?"

Noÿs stared at him intently. She didn't try to touch him now. "Do you mean the men of the Hidden Centuries arranged that, too? They put it all in your mind, then maneuvered you properly?"

"Yes. Yes. Nor are they done. There is still work for them to do. The circle may be closing, but it is not yet closed."

"How can they do anything now? They're not here with us."

"No?" He said the word in so hollow a voice that Noÿs paled.

"Invisible superthings?" she whispered.

"Not superthings. Not invisible. I told you man would not evolve while he controlled his own environment. The people of the Hidden Centuries are Homo sapiens. Ordinary people."

"Then they're certainly not here."

Harlan said sadly, "You're here, Noÿs."

"Yes. And you. And no one else."

"You and I," agreed Harlan. "No one else. A woman of the Hidden Centuries and I . . . Don't act any more, Noÿs. Please."

She stared at him with horror. "What are you saying, Andrew?"

"What I must say. What were *you* saying that evening, when you gave me the peppermint drink? You were talking to me. Your soft voice—soft words . . . I heard nothing, not consciously, but I remember your delicate voice whispering. About what? The downwhen journey of Cooper; the Samson-smash of Eternity. Am I right?"

Noÿs said, "I don't even know what Samson-smash means."

"You can guess very accurately, Noÿs. Tell me, when did you enter the 482nd? Whom did you replace? Or did you just—squeeze in. I had your Life-Plot worked out by an expert in the 2456th. In the new Reality, you had no existence at all. No analogue. Strange for such a small Change, but not impossible. And then the Life-Plotter said one thing which I heard with my ears but not with my mind. Strange that I should remember it. Perhaps even then, something clanged in my mind, but I was too full of—you to listen. He said: '*with the combination of factors you handed me, I don't quite see how she fit in the old Reality.*'

"He was right. You didn't fit in. You were an invader from the far upwhen, manipulating me and Finge, too, to suit yourself."

Noÿs said urgently, "Andrew——"

"It all fit in, if I had the eyes to look. A book-film in your house entitled *Social and Economic History*. It surprised me when first I saw it. You needed it, didn't you, to teach you how best to be a woman of the Century. Another item. Our first trip into the Hidden Centuries, remember? *You* stopped the kettle at the 111,394th. You stopped it with finesse, without fumbling. Where did you learn to control a kettle? If you were what you seemed to be, that would have been your first trip in a kettle. Why the 111, 394th, anyway? Was it your homewhen?"

She said softly, "Why did you bring me to the Primitive, Andrew?"

He shouted suddenly, "To protect Eternity. I could not tell what damage you might do there. Here, you are helpless, because I know you. Admit that all I say is true! Admit it!"

He rose in a paroxysm of wrath, arm upraised. She did not flinch. She was utterly calm. She might have been modeled out of warm, beautiful wax. Harlan did not complete his motion.

He said, "Admit it!"

She said, "Are you so uncertain, after all your deductions? What will it matter to you whether I admit it or not."

Harlan felt the wildness mount. "Admit it, anyway, so that I need feel no pain at all. None at all."

"Pain?"

"Because I have a blaster, Noÿs, and it is my intention to kill you."

Eighteen: THE BEGINNING OF INFINITY

There was a crawling uncertainty inside Harlan, an irresolution that was consuming him. He had the blaster in his hand. It was aimed at Noÿs.

But why did she say nothing? Why did she persist in this impassive attitude?

How could he kill her?

How could he not kill her?

He said hoarsely, "Well?"

She moved, but it was only to clasp her hands loosely in her lap, to look more relaxed, more aloof. When she spoke her voice seemed scarcely that of a human being. Facing the muzzle of a blaster, it yet gained assurance and took on an almost mystic quality of impersonal strength.

She said, "You cannot wish to kill me only in order to protect Eternity. If that were your desire, you could stun me, tie me firmly, pin me within this cave and then take to your travels in the dawn. Or you might have asked Computer Twissell to keep me in solitary confinement during your absence in the Primitive. Or you might take me with you at dawn, lose me in the wastes. If it is only killing that will satisfy you, it is only because you think that I have betrayed you, that I have tricked you into love first in order that I might trick you into treason later. This is murder out of wounded pride and not at all the just retribution you tell yourself it is."

Harlan squirmed. "Are you from the Hidden Centuries? Tell me."

Noÿs said, "I am. Will you now blast?"

Harlan's finger trembled on the blaster's contact point. Yet he hesitated. Something irrational within him could still plead her case and point up the remnants of his own futile love and longing. Was she desperate at his rejection of her? Was she deliberately courting death by lying? Was she indulging in foolish heroics born of despair at his doubts of her?

No!

The book-films of the sickly-sweet literary traditions of the 289th might have it so, but not a girl like Noÿs. She was not one to meet her death at the hands of a false lover with the joyful masochism of a broken, bleeding lily.

Then was she scornfully denying his ability to kill her for any reason whatever? Was she confidently relying on the attraction she knew she had for him even now, certain that it would immobilize him, freeze him in weakness and shame.

That hit too closely. His finger clamped a bit harder on the contact.

Noÿs spoke again. "You're waiting. Does that mean you expect me to enter a brief for the defense?"

"What defense?" Harlan tried to make that scornful, yet he welcomed the diversion. It could postpone the moment when he must look down upon her blasted body, upon whatever remnants of bloody flesh might remain, and know that what had been done to his beautiful Noÿs had been done by his own hand.

He found excuses for his delay. He thought feverishly: Let her talk. Let her tell what she can about the Hidden Centuries. So much better protection for Eternity.

It put a front of firm policy on his action and for the moment he could look at her with as calm a face, almost, as she looked at him.

Noÿs might have read his mind. She said, "Do you want to know about the Hidden Centuries? If that will be a defense, it is easily done. Would you like to know, for instance, why Earth is empty of mankind after the 150,000th? Would you be interested?"

Harlan wasn't going to plead for knowledge, nor was he going to buy knowledge. He had the blaster. He was very intent on no show of weakness.

He said, "Talk!" and flushed at the little smile which was her first response to his exclamation.

She said, "At a moment in physiotime before Eternity had reached very far upwhen, before it had reached even the 10,000th, we of our Century—and you're right, it was the 111,394th—learned of Eternity's existence. We, too, had Time-travel, you see, but it was based on a completely different set of postulates than yours, and we preferred to view Time, rather than shifting mass. Furthermore, we dealt with our past only, our downwhen.

"We discovered Eternity indirectly. First, we developed the calculus of Realities and tested our own Reality through it. We were amazed to find we lived in a Reality of rather low probability. It was a serious question. Why such an improbable Reality? . . . You seem abstracted, Andrew! Are you interested at all?"

Harlan heard her say his name with all the intimate tenderness she had used in weeks past. It should grate on him now, anger him with its cynical faithlessness. And yet it didn't.

He said desperately, "Go on and get it over with, woman."

He tried to balance the warmth of her "Andrew" with the chill anger of his "woman" and yet she only smiled again, pallidly.

She said, "We searched back through time and came across the growing Eternity. It seemed obvious to us almost at once that there had been at one point in physiotime (a conception we have also, but under another name) another Reality. The other Reality, the one of maximum probability we call the Basic State. The Basic State had encompassed us once, or had encompassed our analogues, at least. At the time we could not say what the nature of the Basic State was. We could not possibly know.

"We did know, however, that some Change initiated by Eternity in the far downwhen had managed, through the workings of statistical chance, to alter the Basic State all the way up to our Century and beyond. We set about determining the nature of the Basic State, intending to undo the evil, if evil it was. First we set up the quarantined area you call the Hidden Centuries, isolating the Eternals on the downwhen side of the 70,000th. This armor of isolation would affect us from all but a vanishingly small percentage of the Changes being made. It wasn't absolute security but it gave us time.

"We next did something our culture and ethics did not ordinarily allow us to do. We investigated our own future, our upwhen. We learned the destiny of man in the Reality that actually existed in order that we might compare it eventually with Basic State. Somewhere past the 125,000th, mankind solved the secret of the interstellar drive. They learned how to manage the Jump through hyperspace. Finally, mankind could reach the stars."

Harlan was listening in growing absorption to her measured words. How much truth was there in all this? How much was a calculated attempt to deceive him? He tried to break the spell by speaking, by breaking the smooth flow of her sentences. He said:

"And once they could reach the stars, they did so and left the Earth. Some of us have guessed that."

"Then some of you have guessed wrong. Man *tried* to leave Earth. Unfortunately, however, we are not alone in the Galaxy. There are other stars with other planets, you know. There are even other intelligences. None, in this Galaxy at least, are as ancient as mankind, but in the 125,000 Centuries man remained on Earth, younger minds caught up and passed us, developed the interstellar drive, and colonized the Galaxy.

"When we moved out into space, the signs were up. *Occupied! No Trespassing! Clear Out!* Mankind drew back its exploratory feelers, remained at home. But now he knew Earth for what it was: a prison surrounded by an infinity of freedom . . . And mankind died out!"

Harlan said, "Just died out. Nonsense."

"They didn't *just* die out. It took thousands of Centuries. There were ups and downs but, on the whole, there was a loss of purpose, a sense of futility, a feeling of hopelessness that could not be overcome. Eventually there was one last decline of the birth rate and finally, extinction. Your Eternity did that."

Harlan could defend Eternity now, the more intensely and extravagantly for having so shortly before attacked it so keenly. He said, "Let us at the Hidden Centuries and we will correct that. We have not failed yet to achieve the greatest good in those Centuries we could reach."

"The greatest good?" asked Noÿs in a detached tone that seemed to make a mockery of the phrase. "What is that? Your machines tell you. Your Computaplexes. But who adjusts the machines and tells them what to weigh in the balance? The machines do not solve problems with greater insight than men do, only faster. Only faster! Then what is it the Eternals consider good? I'll tell you. Safety and security. Moderation. Nothing in excess. No risks without overwhelming certainty of an adequate return."

Harlan swallowed. With sudden force he remembered Twissell's words in the kettle while talking about the evolved men of the Hidden Centuries. He said: "*We bred out the unusual.*"

And wasn't it so?

"Well," said Noÿs, "you seem to be thinking. Think of this, then. In the Reality that now exists, why is it that man is continually attempting space-travel and continually failing? Surely each space-travel era must know of previous failures. Why try again, then?"

Harlan said, "I haven't studied the matter." But he thought uneasily of the colonies on Mars, established again and again, always failing. He thought of the odd attraction that space-flight always had, even for Eternals. He could hear Sociologist Kantor Voy of the 2456th, sighing at the loss of electro-gravitic space-flight in one Century, and saying longingly: "*It had been very beautiful.*" And Life-Plotter Neron Feruque, who had sworn bitterly at its passing and had launched into a fit of railing at Eternity's handling of anti-cancer serums to ease his spirit.

Was there such a thing as an instinctive yearning on the part of intelligent beings to expand outward, to reach the stars, to leave the prison of gravity behind? Was it that which forced man to develop interplanetary travel dozens of times, forced him to travel over and over again to the dead worlds of a solar system in which only Earth was livable? Was it the eventual failure, the knowledge that one must return to the home prison, that brought about the maladjustments that Eternity was forever fighting. Harlan thought of the drug addiction in those same futile Centuries of the electro-gravitics.

Noÿs said, "In ironing out the disasters of Reality, Eternity rules out the triumphs as well. It is in meeting the great tests that mankind can most successfully rise to great heights. Out of danger and restless insecurity comes the force that pushes mankind to newer and loftier conquests. Can you understand that? Can you understand that in averting the pitfalls and miseries that beset man, Eternity prevents men from finding their own bitter and better solutions, the real solutions that come from conquering difficulty, not avoiding it."

Harlan began woodenly, "The greatest good of the greatest number——"

Noÿs cut in. "Suppose Eternity had never been established?"

"Well?"

"I'll tell you what would have happened. The energies that went into temporal engineering would have gone into nucleonics instead. Eternity would not have come but the interstellar drive would. Man would have reached the stars more than a hundred thousand Centuries before he did in this current Reality. The stars would then have been untenanted and mankind would have established itself throughout the Galaxy. *We* would have been first."

"And what would have been gained?" asked Harlan doggedly. "Would we be happier?"

"Whom do you mean by 'we'? Man would not be a world but a million worlds, a billion worlds. We would have the infinite in our grasp. Each world would have its own stretch of the Centuries, each its own values, a chance to seek happiness after ways of its own in an environment of its own. There are many happinesses, many goods, infinite variety. . . . *That* is the Basic State of mankind."

"You're guessing," said Harlan, and he was angry at himself for feeling attraction for the picture she had conjured. "How can you tell what would have happened?"

Noÿs said, "You smile at the ignorance of the Timers who know only one Reality. We smile at the ignorance of the Eternals who think there are many Realities but that only one exists at a time."

"What does that gibberish mean?"

"We don't calculate alternate Realities. We view them. We see them in their state of non-Reality."

"A kind of ghostly never-never land where the might-have-beens play with the ifs."

"Without the sarcasm, yes."

"And how do you do that?"

Noÿs paused, then said, "How can I explain that, Andrew? I have been educated to know certain things without really understanding all about them, just as you have. Can you explain the workings of a Computaplex? Yet you know it exists and works."

Harlan flushed. "Well, then?"

Noÿs said, "We learned to view Realities and we found Basic State to be as I have described. We found, too, the Change that had destroyed Basic State. It was not any Change that Eternity had initiated; it was the establishment of Eternity itself—the mere fact of its existence. Any system like Eternity, which allows men to choose their own future, will end by choosing safety and mediocrity, and in such a Reality the stars are out of reach. The mere existence of Eternity at once wiped out the Galactic Empire. To restore it, Eternity must be done away with.

"The number of Realities is infinite. The number of any subclass of Realities is also infinite. For instance, the number of Realities containing Eternity is infinite; the number in which Eternity does not exist is infinite; the number in which Eternity does exist but is abolished is also infinite. But my people chose from among the infinite a group that involved me.

"I had nothing to do with that. They educated me for my job as Twissell and yourself educated Cooper for his job. But the number of Realities in which I was the agent in destroying Eternity was also infinite. I was offered a choice among five Realities that seemed least complex. I chose this one, the one involving you, the only Reality system involving you."

Harlan said, "Why did you choose it?"

Noÿs looked away. "Because I loved you, you see. I loved you long before I met you."

Harlan was shaken. She said it with such depths of sincerity. He thought, sickly: She's an actress——

He said, "That's rather ridiculous."

"Is it? I studied the Realities at my disposal. I studied the Reality in which I went back to the 482nd, met first Finge, then you. The one in which you came to me and loved me, in which you took me into Eternity and the far upwhen of my own Century, in which you misdirected Cooper, and in which you and I, together, returned to the Primitive. We lived in the Primitive for the rest of our days. I saw our lives together and they were happy and I loved you. So it's not ridiculous at all. I chose this alternative so that our love might be true."

Harlan said, "All this is false. It's false. How can you expect me to believe you?"

He stopped, then said suddenly, "Wait! You say you knew all this in advance? All that would happen?"

"Yes."

"Then you're obviously lying. You would have known that I would have you here at blaster point. You would have known you would fail. What is your answer to that?"

She sighed lightly, "I told you there are an infinite number of any subclass of Realities. No matter how finely we focus on a given Reality it always represents an infinite number of very similar Realities. There are fuzzy spots. The finer we focus, the less fuzzy, but perfect sharpness cannot be obtained. The less fuzzy, the lower the probability of chance variation spoiling the result, but the probability is never absolutely zero. One fuzzy spot spoiled things."

"Which?"

"You were to have come back to the far upwhen after the barrier at the 100,000th had been lowered and you did. But you were to have come back alone. It is for that reason that I was momentarily so startled at seeing Computer Twissell with you."

Again Harlan was troubled. How she made things fit in!

Noÿs said, "I would have been even more startled, had I realized the significance of that alteration in full. Had you come alone, you would have brought me back to the Primitive as you did. Then, for love of humanity, for love of me, you would have left Cooper untouched. Your circle would have been broken, Eternity ended, our life together here safe.

"But you came with Twissell, a chance variation. While coming, he talked to you of his thoughts about the Hidden Centuries and started you on a train of deductions that ended with your doubting *my* good faith. It ended with a blaster between us. . . . And now, Andrew, that's the story. You may blast me. There is nothing to stop you."

Harlan's hand ached from its spastic grasp on the blaster. He shifted it dizzily to the other hand. Was there no flaw in her story? Where was the resolution he was to have gained from knowing certainly that she was a creature of the Hidden Centuries. He was more than ever tearing at himself in conflict and dawn was approaching.

He said, "Why two efforts to end Eternity? Why couldn't Eternity have ended once and for all when I sent Cooper back to the 20th? Things would have ended then and there would not have been this agony of uncertainty."

"Because," said Noÿs, "ending this Eternity is not enough. We must reduce the probability of establishing any form of Eternity to as near zero as we can manage. So there is one thing we must do here in the Primitive. A small Change, a little thing. You know what a Minimum Necessary Change is like. It is only a letter to a peninsula called Italy here in the 20th. It is now the 19.32nd. In a few Centicenturies, provided I send the letter, a man of Italy will begin experimenting with the neutronic bombardment of uranium."

Harlan found himself horrified. "You will alter Primitive history?"

"Yes. It is our intention. In the new Reality, the final Reality, the first nuclear explosion will take place not in the 30th Century but in the 19.45th."

"But do you know the danger? Can you possibly estimate the danger?"

"We know the danger. We have viewed the sheaf of resulting Realities. There is a probability, not a certainty, of course, that Earth will end with a largely radioactive crust, but before that——"

"You mean there can be compensation for that?"

"A Galactic Empire. An actual intensification of the Basic State."

"Yet you accuse the Eternals of interfering——"

"We accuse them of interfering many times to keep mankind safely at home and in prison. We interfere once, *once*, to turn him prematurely to nucleonics so that he might never, *never*, establish an Eternity."

"No," said Harlan desperately. "There must be an Eternity."

"If you choose. It is yours to choose. If you wish to have psychopaths dictate the future of man——"

"*Psychopaths!*" exploded Harlan.

"Aren't they? You know them. Think!"

Harlan stared at her in outraged horror, yet he could not help thinking. He thought of Cubs learning the truth about Reality and Cub Latourette trying to kill himself as a result. Latourette had survived to become an Eternal, with what scars on his personality none could say, yet helping to decide on alternate Realities.

He thought of the caste system in Eternity, of the abnormal life that turned guilt feelings into anger and hatred against Technicians. He thought of Computers, struggling against themselves, of Finge intriguing against Twissell and Twissell spying on Finge. He thought of Sennor, fighting his bald head by fighting all the Eternals.

He thought of himself.

Then he thought of Twissell, the great Twissell, also breaking the laws of Eternity.

It was as though he had always known Eternity to be all this. Why else should he have been so willing to destroy it? Yet he had never admitted it to himself fully; he had never looked it clearly in the face, until, suddenly, now.

And he saw Eternity with great clarity as a sink of deepening psychoses, a writhing pit of abnormal motivation, a mass of desperate lives torn brutally out of context.

He looked blankly at Noÿs.

She said softly, "Do you see? Come to the mouth of the cave with me, Andrew?"

He followed her, hypnotized, appalled at the completeness with which he had gained a new viewpoint. His blaster fell away from the line connecting it and Noÿs's heart for the first time.

The pale streakings of dawn grayed the sky, and the bulking kettle just outside the cave was an oppressive shadow against the pallor. Its outlines were dulled and blurred by the film thrown over it.

Noÿs said, "This is Earth. Not the eternal and only home of mankind, but only a starting point of an infinite adventure. All you need do is make the decision. It is yours to make. You and I and the contents of this cave will be protected by a physiotime field against the Change. Cooper will disappear along with his advertisement; Eternity will go and the Reality of my Century, but *we* will remain to have children and grandchildren, and mankind will remain to reach the stars."

He turned to look at her, and she was smiling at him. It was Noÿs as she had been, and his own heart beating as it had used to.

He wasn't even aware that he had made his decision until the grayness suddenly invaded all the sky as the hulk of the kettle disappeared from against it.

With that disappearance, he knew, even as Noÿs moved slowly into his arms, came the end, the final end of Eternity.

—And the beginning of Infinity.